DARK DESCENT

ANCIENT ORIGINS BOOK 2

ROBERT STOREY

Darkness resides in us all; but when it surrounds us, closes in on us, it's the only time when we truly know the power of our light.

– Robert Storey

FACT:

On the 8th January 2011 an asteroid with the potential to impact Earth in 2040 was discovered by the Mount Lemmon Survey. This near-Earth object was given the designation, 2011 AG5.

The governments of the world's most powerful nations have secret contingencies for global disasters. These plans are kept from the public for a reason.

There are still many life forms on Earth that are yet to be discovered by science. Many of these mysterious microbes, insects, plants and animals populate our deepest oceans and darkest caves.

YEAR

2041 A.D.

PROLOGUE

Some people say the cosmos is a mere reflection of life on Earth, a mirror with which one can gaze into the depths of everything that life was, is, and will be. Others hold to the belief that God created the night sky in a matter of days, or that what we are actually seeing is merely a projection, a trick or sleight of hand on an epic scale. Scientists tell us with an unyielding certainty that the light from the stars is millions, even billions, of years old and that as we gaze into the night sky we are looking back through time and witnessing the past; a past before any one of us first drew a mortal breath or long before our species had even evolved.

Whatever theories of the universe you hold to, one thing is clear; it brims with glorious beauty in all shapes and forms. Pinpricks of flickering light populate the heavens while dazzling magnificent rotating discs, so bright and vast that they can only be appreciated from afar, punctuate an expanse beyond measure. But without the darkness there would only be light. And without contrast there is no beauty, no good, no evil, no life. If there is one, there must be the other; as with all things, equilibrium must always resolve itself.

On the fringes of space, framed against this backdrop of blissful cosmic serenity, a small craft orbited the once majestic vista that was planet Earth. Where before beautiful clear skies, glistening deep blue oceans and lush green forests could be seen, now only an all-encompassing thick, dark cloud remained. Far from featureless, the predominantly brown and black veil remained in a constant state of flux. Hurricane-force winds created huge vortices which revealed fleeting glimpses of the surface below; such momentary insights into what lay beneath were quickly swallowed up, snuffed out of existence like a small candle within a great and volatile tempest. Enormous thunderstorms coalesced over half a continent, sending lightning flashing and flickering across the upper atmosphere, with the occasional super plume reaching out into space itself.

Drifting through the celestial sphere, untouched by the maelstrom far below, the tiny vessel continued its balletic odyssey; and on the side of this distant wayfarer's white hull, large, black letters read:

U.S.S.S. ORBITER ONE

Underneath this, the evocative flag of the United States of America, the star-spangled banner, glinted majestically as the light of the sun streamed across its cold, pristine surface. Rotating through the icy vacuum of space, Orbiter One turned in slow motion, small white lights blinking on and off in leisurely regularity along its silken, metallic length. Inside, through this thin alloy skin, past bulkheads and cocooned within a mass of electrical and finely tuned mechanical equipment, a small yet comfortable area provided room to live and work for two resident NASA astronauts.

Tyler Magnusson and his colleague, Ivan Sikorsky, currently on long term assignment, sat at the observation and control deck. The large, transparent, domed window provided the two men with a clear view of their target, an imposing disc-shaped structure that approached from their port side. Concave and smooth, the massive ship's topside was crammed full of high-yield solar panels while the underbelly sprouted an intricate latticework of intersecting walkways and modules of various shapes and sizes. The United States Space Station, also known as the U.S.S.S. Archimedes, moved within final docking range.

'Orbiter One, this is Archimedes on final approach,' a strong female voice said over the internal speaker system. 'Prepare clamps and adjust position as per the navigation graphics showing on your screen projection.'

'Copy that, Archimedes,' Tyler replied before dialling into the computer the new parameters for the craft's trajectory. 'Action pitch and yaw adjustments on my count,' he told Ivan. 'Three – two – one – manoeuvre.'

Small puffs of air vented into space as Orbiter One lined up with one of the space station's external entry ports.

'Synchronising,' Ivan intoned, carrying out the final docking procedures.

'Reduce thrust by fifteen per cent aft,' Tyler said.

Ivan rotated a small joystick, its white rubber surround stretching as it inched back, notch by minute notch. 'Reducing thrust by fifteen per cent aft,' he confirmed.

The two space vehicles came together and Tyler felt a soft but perceptible jolt pass through the orbital vehicle. A clunk of dense metal on metal, and a muffled hiss of hydraulics, indicated the sophisticated dampers, locks and clamps activated flawlessly to secure Orbiter One in place.

'Welcome home, gentlemen,' the female flight controller said. 'Once you have acclimatised from micro gravity to the partial gravity environment here on Archimedes we can proceed with a full mission debrief at zero four hundred hours.'

'Copy that, Flight,' Tyler said. 'We'll look forward to some hot chocolate and cookies, which I'm sure the captain will have waiting for us when we get there.'

'I'll be sure to let him know of the request,' the woman replied with no hint of humour. 'Archimedes out.'

Ivan flicked off some switches overhead. 'She's a barrel of laughs.'

Tyler shrugged. 'She must be new.' He powered down Orbiter One's systems, putting the ship they'd spent many months aboard into hibernation. 'All I know is, it's good to be back.'

♦

A mere three hundred and sixty minutes later, at four hours past midnight, Central Standard Time, Tyler and Ivan found themselves loosely strapped into chairs in front of a large, oblong, transparent table in a circular conference room. Each held an Orbiter One mission folder. Across from them the captain of the Archimedes, Bo Heidfield, sat on a similar seat, flanked by various members of NASA, the U.S. military and the GMRC, the Global Meteor Response Council.

It had always irked Tyler that the GMRC had such control over NASA and the U.S. space programme in general. Well, perhaps *control* wasn't the right word, *influence* may have been more appropriate. The GMRC would recommend, request and suggest with increasing frequency until the powers that be relinquished or came up with alternatives to satisfy the GMRC bigwigs. Of course, it wasn't just the U.S. that had to submit to this kind of intervention; the Europeans, Chinese and International space programmes also had to toe the GMRC line. Unilateral cooperation was paramount to the survival of the human race, or that's what he was told, anyway; what all select NASA employees were told when they were given the real truth.

In order to ensure an efficient and effective planetary response to the asteroid threat the GMRC would lead the way and every nation on the planet had signed up to abide by its guidance. While this sounded fair and just, it was far from democratic, as the world's entire civilian population had no vote on the issue, or any idea what was to come. As far as Tyler understood it, and gossip was rife within the segregated space station fraternity, over ninety-five per cent of each country's politicians also had no idea of the scale of the threat to humanity and planet Earth itself.

Everyone, of course, was aware of the first meteorite, 2011 AG5, which had struck in 2040 – over six months ago – off the South African coastline. 2011 AG5's existence and predicted repercussions had been disclosed to the public in 2022. However, what the rest of the populace was blissfully unaware of was that six more asteroids were on their way and that life on the surface of Earth was nearly at an end. It was a stark and terrifying thought that life as we knew it was to cease in 2045 when the last of the asteroids arrived. Thankfully, for Tyler and his family, his job had ensured their continued survival. They were guaranteed precious harbour in one of the United States' underground facilities. Even Tyler and his small circle of colleagues in the know were left in the dark as to the location or scale of the base they were destined to live out their days in. He only knew its name, United States Subterranean Base Steadfast, or USSB Steadfast for short.

Tyler glanced up as movement caught his eye through the large transparent ceiling above. A streamlined Sabre space-aircraft had just arrived from Earth and was coming to rest at a refuelling arm. Tentacle-like hoses snaked out from Archimedes to lock onto it, like a giant squid with its prey. Yet this squid was supplying life, not taking it, as the craft's exhausted tanks were replenished with vital oxygen and fuel.

The NASA captain cleared his throat, bringing Tyler back to the present.

'Gentlemen,' Bo Heidfield said, addressing the two Orbiter One astronauts in a formal, business-like tone. 'First I'd like to congratulate you both on the completion of your mission. You have been in micro gravity for one year, so I hope your transition to life on Archimedes has not been too taxing. As you will have been informed, we are joined by GMRC representatives who are here to ensure all information transfer conforms with their strict protocols.'

'My apologies for interrupting, Captain,' said a woman sitting immediately to Bo Heidfield's left, 'but we are more than mere observers and administrators. We are here to report directly to the GMRC's senior Directorate and to advise them on the information gathered here today.'

Tyler noticed Bo's eyebrow twitch and a clear expression of anger appeared on his face at the woman's comment, an indicator that he was far from his usual impassive self. Tyler knew Bo well enough to realise tensions were running high between the factions in the room; looking around at the faces assembled he wondered how he'd missed it before. What the GMRC were up to now to cause such feelings he was sure to find out later. Now, though, he was here to report on Orbiter One's mission.

Ivan began their presentation on the weather patterns of the all-pervasive dust cloud caused by the fallout of the asteroid, 2011 AG5.

'As you can see,' Ivan said, while everyone in the room turned to the current page of his report, the paper documents rustling in unison, 'the dust cloud has reached a stable density in Earth's upper atmosphere. The Coriolis effect produced by the Earth's rotation and axial tilt has reasserted its force and the cloud now conforms to a new, but predictable, weather pattern. The circulation cells are now clearly visible due to the cloud's particulates providing a visual reference of their direction and path.

'From observations made on Orbiter One, over hundreds of tracks at varying compass points, we were able to extrapolate a lot of useful data on the intense weather currently being experienced on the surface. The unusual and powerful lightning strikes which have caused disruption to the GMRC's Subterranean Programme across the Americas and Eurasian continent are symptomatic of the negatively charged particulates and the enormous super cells that have been forming on a regular basis over the last few months.

'Utilising large data groups,' Ivan continued, 'we have been able to accurately predict the occasional breaks in the global cloud cover. This will obviously be useful in scheduling Sabre flights to and from the surface, and to position and launch rockets into orbit for various purposes.'

Ivan went into further detail about forecast weather patterns and areas of specific scientific interest, and then Tyler took over the report.

'If you turn to the next section,' Tyler told them, flipping over a couple of pages from his own folder. 'You will note the thermal images we have taken over the last six months. Underneath each image are corresponding charts and tables outlining temperature drops in comparison to the previous month and to the location's normal rolling ten-year average temperature, prior to the asteroid AG5's strike.

'Figure five point three dash A is an enhanced image taken of the Sahara Desert two weeks after Impact Day—'

The GMRC observer who had irritated Bo Heidfield, interrupted Tyler's flow. 'Pilot Commander Magnusson,' the woman said, addressing Tyler by his formal title and with a supercilious air. 'Can you tell me why there appear to be no images here for the two weeks after Impact Day? Surely this was the most important time to collect such information?'

Bo looked like he was about to intervene, but Tyler was prepared for the question. 'Due to the unforeseen speed of the dust cloud kicked up by the primary strike we were unable to record said data as scheduled. As I'm sure you are aware the cloud was meant to take six to twelve months to cover the entire planet and yet in actuality this event took only days to unfold. Orbiter One operates on a strict prearranged course to maximise fuel and operational efficiency. We were unable to react to the cloud's speed at such short notice without significantly compromising future mission parameters. Two weeks was the time it took to reposition.'

Tyler waited for a response, but the woman merely nodded and motioned for him to continue.

'As I was saying,' he said, 'figure five point three dash A is a thermal image of the Sahara Desert two weeks after Impact Day. It clearly shows a dramatic temperature drop compared to the previous month and to previously observed averages. The following images for this particular location show further temperature drops over the next three months, not of the same magnitude as the initial fall, but significant nonetheless. After this the figures become steadier and in line with averages, albeit at a much colder level. Across the surface of the planet we have witnessed a drop in temperature equivalent to eight degrees Celsius or fourteen point four Fahrenheit. Africa has experienced a higher than average fall of ten degrees Celsius or eighteen degrees Fahrenheit; this is mainly due to the thicker cloud cover over the region due to the extensive wildfires instigated by the initial strike. Impact winter is very much upon us, although it is not as severe as some models predicted.'

Tyler carried out the remainder of his report in greater detail before closing the Orbiter One report folder. He then pulled a secure case onto his lap, the exertion required to lift it a tenth that of normal due to the partial gravity experienced on Archimedes. He activated the security locks using a combination of biometrics and codes, a process Ivan had to repeat before handing it back to him. Tyler opened the case and withdrew a bundle of reports, each wrapped within bright red film. Tyler passed one to Ivan, took one for himself and handed the rest to Bo, who distributed them to those sitting either side of him.

Once everyone had a copy, Tyler took his file and tore away the top edge using the supplied metal strip manufactured into the film. Everyone else followed suit, the tearing noises briefly filling the room. Removing the red sheath revealed the black folder inside. On the front of this a white panel had been placed containing the following bold, red text:

CLASSIFIED DOCUMENTS

GMRC Clearance Level: 10 Alpha
Special Access Personnel Only

NASA Clearance Level: AMBER 1
SEGREGATED PERSONNEL

EYES ONLY

Inside the front cover the NASA insignia was printed on white paper, its familiar blue disc and white lettered logo standing out against the background. Below this a heading read:

D.S.D.A.
Deep Space Detection Array
& PROJECT ARES

Collated Report
February, 2041

Tyler began detailing the information to the room. He noted the main attributes of each of the six approaching asteroids, including the latest composition, spectral light and deviation analysis. Potential fracturing events had also been assessed and predicted and proffered up graphically for the various scenarios. Everyone in the room knew that any splitting of the asteroids prior to impact would result in vastly different outcomes and subsequent fallout. This collective foresight was due in the main to one such occurrence having already happened when 2011 AG5 had gravitational forces exerted on it as it passed the Moon. A smaller chunk had broken free and ended up wiping out a large city in northern India. Nothing could alter the final outcome, of course, but there would be some form of human activity on the surface of Earth until 2045, and the GMRC wanted to avoid any hindrance to its subterranean programme prior to its final protocols reaching fruition.

Finally Tyler reached the most anticipated part of the report, the plain white page he'd turned to displaying an elegant silver logo in its centre:

PROJECT
ARES

While on their analytical, fact-finding mission aboard Orbiter One, the two astronauts had also been tasked with testing a new piece of technology devised by the U.S. military and the highly secretive GMRC R&D Division. Strangely, the substantial piece of equipment in question was missing a large, critical component. Ivan had pointed out as much when the two astronauts had first been prepped for the operational procedures prior to their deployment. They had been told they were to test the system's functionality in the rigours of space. They were not there to test its full capability or to even understand what it was they were actually testing. This was perhaps the strangest part of the whole operation. The ambiguity and secrecy of what it was they had on board and were tasked to carry out a multitude of diagnostics on, was more than a little disturbing especially considering the military's involvement.

As Tyler went through the results from Project Ares, which encompassed an assortment of observational data, computer readout analysis, error codes and system parameters during partial operation, he was asked the occasional question by a couple of the GMRC personnel who were lead scientists on the programme. As he completed the debrief the questions increased.

'Did you experience any undue fatigue when the device was activated for longer than thirty minutes?' one of the scientists said, peering intently at the two astronauts over the rim of his glasses.

'We both felt a little tired,' Tyler looked at Ivan for confirmation, 'but that may have been due to the intensity of the daily schedule we were adhering to.'

The scientist nodded and jotted something down on his notepad.

Before Tyler could continue, the second scientist asked, 'Did either of you witness any unusual visual activity during the final testing period?'

Tyler didn't really understand the question. 'Such as?'

'Any hallucinations or disturbances around the module when it was deployed outside of Orbiter One?'

Again Tyler glanced at Ivan who shook his head. 'Not that we noticed.'

The other scientist once more scribbled something down on his notepad. Tyler was beginning to get an uneasy feeling about the direction the line of questioning was taking and looked to his captain for reassurance. Grim-faced, Bo avoided his gaze.

'And did either of you encounter any difficulties sleeping or breathing during or after the operation of the machine?' asked another man at the opposite end of the table, a U.S. military officer who had, until now, remained silent.

Tyler looked around the room. 'Is there some danger attached to using this device?' Like Bo, some of them – mainly the NASA employees – avoided eye contact with him, while others looked on impassively. He suddenly understood how a rat might feel when being experimented on by men in white coats, an array of disturbing apparatus close to hand; it was not a pleasant feeling.

'Of course not, Commander,' the GMRC woman said. 'We are just being thorough. We can check through your bio readouts and visual records for the mission at our leisure rather than bore you with any further questions.'

After some final statements everyone handed back the mission reports, which Tyler resealed in the case before handing it to Captain Heidfield, who in turn handed it to the military man who had been the last to question them. As everyone filed out from the room, aided by semi-magnetic footwear for ease of movement, Bo indicated to

Tyler that he wanted to speak with him; he moved to one side and waited until they were left alone.

The captain approached him. 'Follow me, Commander,' he said and moved off down a deserted corridor, his shoes echoing metallically on the grid flooring. With Tyler at his heels, Bo Heidfield passed through a more populated section of the vessel and then down another confined walkway, its small windows filled with the view of the blighted Earth, its long, curved surface stark against the blackness of space. The next intersection they came across had eight diverging passageways. Two of these offshoots were guarded by four heavily built GMRC security operatives, who moved to bar any entry to the areas beyond. Such restricted access on Archimedes was unheard of and clearly this constraint also seemed to include the captain himself, who neither slowed nor looked in the guards' direction as he passed.

Tyler, however, found himself gawping at the spectacle and he craned his neck to watch as the eyes of the GMRC men followed his every move until he'd disappeared from view. While projectile weapons aboard a spacecraft were strictly prohibited, for obvious reasons, Tyler had been quick to recognise the advanced Taser and stun gun devices each guard had holstered at their waist. The reason for the animosity towards the GMRC personnel the Archimedes captain had displayed during the debrief suddenly became clear. Not only had the GMRC brought with them armed soldiers, but they had also cordoned off parts of the ship, which even the captain was apparently prevented from accessing.

It wasn't long until Bo halted his march at a white, nondescript, reinforced hatch. Looking up and down the passage to ensure no one was around, Tyler's commanding officer tapped in a six digit passcode and swung the door open. Entering, he motioned Tyler to follow. Once they were both inside he shut the door, turning the large wheel attached to its inner skin and locking it in place; the circular handle reached the end of its rotation with a dull thud, the noise echoing in the small room in which they now found themselves ensconced.

Without saying anything further the captain turned on a computer station and fired up a large screen located on one of the walls.

'Sir, what's going on?' Tyler asked. The captain was now accessing some part of the ship's internal computer system. 'Why is that section of the ship off limits? Have you seen what they are guarding? And they have weapons too, that's against one of NASA's fundamental directives.'

The captain stopped what he was doing while a small dialogue box on the screen read *accessing data feed* in bold green letters. He looked at Tyler with haunted eyes. 'The GMRC and U.S. military have deemed it in the global and national interest to utilise the USSS Archimedes as a base of operations for some kind of bastardised scientific research programme.'

'What kind of programme?'

'The kind that NASA would never sanction unless it was forced upon them. The kind that seals off whole parts of the damn ship and prevents even her captain from knowing what's been brought on board.'

The computer beeped and an error message popped up on screen. The captain swore and started typing on the keyboard once more. The previous message reappeared: *accessing data feed.*

'Ten days ago,' Bo continued, 'I was contacted by Mission Command at Houston. On a conference call I was informed that the military and GMRC would be requisitioning Archimedes for something we are all too familiar with, Project Ares. Amidst high security a cargo was flown from the surface and placed within the main laboratory modules and access has been limited ever since, with guards like you just saw posted around the clock. Whatever they are doing on this ship one thing is for certain, the safety of every one of my crew has been compromised as a result.

'Since they arrived, five of our team have experienced vivid nightmares and two have exhibited breathing difficulties. One of our youngest pilots also experienced extreme psychological events and he had to be sedated and, with the rest, sent back to the surface. As far as I was able to ascertain through the official and unofficial channels all of them are under quarantine, pending further tests. A team of doctors has been on board to carry out exams on the rest of us; so far we all seem to be in the clear of whatever it is that's causing these symptoms.'

'Jesus,' Tyler said as he tried to take in what he'd just been told. 'So what are we doing here?'

Bo glanced at the screen, which still displayed the same message. He looked back to Tyler. 'Before they took control up here I was informed that the lab was to be cleared and all cameras and recording equipment were to be extracted, barring life support and critical systems sensors. Having to adhere to their request, I cleared the area under GMRC supervision. However, the safety of my crew is my priority, first and foremost, and so in order to find out what they were bringing with them I managed to install a small remote camera with the help of Sandy Turner.'

'The spacewalk specialist?' Tyler said.

Bo nodded. 'When Sandy was on her way out for some routine maintenance I slipped her the device and she positioned it on a limb which has line of sight to the laboratory's window cluster. Initially I was unable to get a look at whatever they had in there, but my luck changed yesterday when it was repositioned.'

Tyler's curiosity was peaking, but not in a good way. Whatever was occurring on this space station was tied directly to the machine he and Ivan had been extensively testing on Orbiter One, a piece of equipment intrinsically linked to a project that had already compromised some of the crew's health, both physically and mentally.

'Here we go,' the captain told him as the screen dissolved into a four picture live stream of the outside of the Archimedes main laboratory complex.

Tyler scanned the images for anything unusual. 'What am I looking for?'

'There.' Bo pointed at the bottom right feed. He tapped a couple of buttons and expanded it so it filled the whole screen.

At first Tyler could only see the movement of technicians, all of whom wore white hazmat suits and breathing apparatus. 'I can't see—'

'Wait,' Bo said, cutting him off and pointing to one particular window.

Tyler watched and then one of the people moved out of the way and he could see part of – something. 'What is that?' he said in a hushed tone as he stood transfixed, staring at the screen.

'I have no idea. It's like nothing I've ever seen before.'

'It looks—'

'Alive.'

Tyler couldn't take his eyes off it. 'Yes.'

'If you look at the technicians,' the captain told him, 'you can see they are documenting their work on a computer terminal on the right-hand side of the room. I know ten years back you were tasked with the simulations for all of Archimedes' internal sensors.'

'That's right,' Tyler said with a small nod of his head, still intently watching the oddity.

'Are you able to access them and get us some audio to go with this picture?'

Tyler thought for a moment, recalling memories he thought he would never use again. *Yes, I can do that*, he concluded. It was relatively easy for someone who had spent eighteen months fault finding to the nth degree. Taking over the console, he executed a few commands and altered a subroutine and then rerouted the sensor's signal.

'That should do it,' Tyler informed his captain.

Bo turned up the volume on the display.

A strange oscillating noise came through the audio system. At first Tyler thought he had made a mistake, but as he watched the screen once more he realised he had utilised a sensor in the room where the object was located. He also noted that the technicians were wearing some kind of hearing protection underneath their suits; he presumed the noise must have been a lot louder in the room itself.

At that point the sound changed; its pitch made the hairs stand up on the back of his neck and sent an odd tingling sensation running down his spine. A movement in the room dragged his eyes away from the strange vision that had so mesmerised him. The captain, hyperventilating, his breath coming in ragged gasps, had dropped to one knee.

'Sir, what's wrong?' Tyler asked, gripping the man's shoulders in an attempt to stop him shaking. The audio coming through the room's speakers changed again and Bo convulsed, froth seeping from his mouth.

'Sir!' Tyler shouted in alarm, but he was helpless to do anything as his superior's legs beat wildly on the floor. Realising the feed from the lab had sparked the fit he slammed the audio off, almost breaking the touchscreen as he did so. Turning back, he saw that Bo now lay unmoving; his eyes open in a fixed stare. Tyler felt for his pulse; there wasn't one. In a panic-induced state, he made sure the man's airway was clear, repositioned the body and began CPR. After what seemed like mere moments, but must have been many minutes, he stopped to regain his breath; his arms ached and his head throbbed. He looked down in despair at his long-term colleague. Getting unsteadily to his feet, he reached out and hit the emergency response alarm, sending lights flashing and sirens wailing throughout the ship. The captain was dead.

CHAPTER ONE

New York City, USA. Year: 2041.

Sirens wailed and chirruped, drifting on the wind while red and blue lights pulsed and flickered over the buildings of Manhattan Island as emergency vehicles sped through its troubled and turbulent streets. In the foreboding black skies above, police and civilian helicopters fought a battle of cat and mouse, one seeking to impose a no-fly zone on the other. Ominous storm clouds gathered on the horizon, warning those in its path of the rain to come by bellowing out deep, far reaching claps of thunder and thrusting down dazzling bolts of lightning.

In the centre of this maelstrom of activity a seemingly endless line of large, jet-black, twin propeller helicopters approached from the Hudson River to the east. Emblazoned on their sides was a familiar white logo.

One by one they fell into a holding position around a large circular skyscraper, carrying out an intricate aerial dance while other pilots sought to unload their passengers as quickly as possible while avoiding the next wave coming in to land on the tiered helipads adorning the building's roof.

Far below, at street level, tens of thousands of protestors had gathered outside the edifice and right in the heart of the chaos, a small, handsome woman stood facing a cameraman. She wore a bright red, fur-lined, three-quarter length hooded trench coat and thick, blue, thermal mittens, her long, dark hair falling in immaculate waves across her shoulders. In one hand she held a clipboard and in the other a microphone. Behind her, an imposing blockade had been erected from metal fencing, steel bollards and – for good measure – heavy-duty plastic and wooden barriers, replete with red and white stripes, each pillar topped with a flashing orange beacon. Behind these obstructions, a vast array of NYPD officers had assembled. Further back, in the shadows, heavily armed U.S. soldiers lurked, assault rifles locked and most certainly loaded, ready and willing to repel any unwanted visitors to the gathering unfolding inside.

A bitter wind whistled down Ninth Avenue. Paper bags and other detritus swirled around the feet of the protestors, who shouted their fury at the untouchable dignitaries being ferried in high above. For what seemed like the hundredth time, the woman swept back her hair with one hand, placing it to one side in order to keep it from covering her face. A few strands caught in her mouth; she pulled them away as she looked around her to make sure she had the required space to work.

The camera and light operator held up five fingers, then four, three – the woman's face changed from a look of concentration to one of serious intent as she shook her hair back and squared up to the camera's lens – two, and finally his index finger pointed straight out to indicate she was on air.

'This is Jessica Klein reporting live from New York City for the BBC's Worldwide News Service,' the woman said in a flawless English accent, her voice raised to be heard over the cacophony of noise filling the air around her. 'In the skies above me, as I speak, the world's leaders, greatest scientific and military minds are being flown in from this iconic city's surrounding airports for the Global Meteor Response Council's annual summit. As ever, this vital meeting is being held behind closed doors, with the tightest of security and the minimum of disclosure. What will be discussed in the GMRC's imposing HQ behind me is a matter of great debate and of increasing national and international concern.

'It has been six months since the meteorite impact and in that time the world has experienced devastating climate change, plunging the northern hemisphere into sub-zero temperatures. The all-pervasive dust cloud transformed our days into twenty-four hour long nights, resulting in catastrophic failure of ecosystems on an unprecedented scale. The GMRC has long prepared us all for these events, but the reality of them has been far more traumatic and chaotic than anyone could have imagined.

'The initial panic and terror caused by the unexpected speed of the meteorite's fallout, specifically the dust cloud itself, threatened to bring humanity to its knees. Swift action taken by governments around the world acting on GMRC protocols did well to prevent a global collapse of law and order. The methods utilised to accomplish this task, however, are still being questioned. As ever, the GMRC has covered up the true cost every nation has paid. The countless deaths of civilians only equalled in ignominy by the far greater number of those injured as National Guards ruthlessly quelled widespread rioting and violent disorder. The blood of the innocent, many say, is on the GMRC's hands.

'Since those horrific times, now referred to as the Days of Blood and Dust, civilisation has teetered on the brink of disintegration in the majority of the world's nations. Those countries that were already fragile, where stability had already been sporadic, have disintegrated into wastelands of social anarchy and economic collapse.

'While civil wars rage across South America, China – emboldened by its heinous missile assault on Japan and South Korea – has expanded into other neighbouring sovereign nations to harvest their natural resources and exploit their labour force. Strangely the GMRC, United Nations and the U.S., and its allies, have only instigated token sanctions against the Chinese, followed by empty threats of military action. The reasoning behind this weak resolve is to avoid a world war at a time when humanity needs to be uniting rather than tearing itself apart. While this is a sensible standpoint, it begs the question whether China will ever be punished for its crimes.

'On the other side of the coin, the Chinese argue they were merely responding to an assault on its people in a prior engagement of hostilities that, it says, were instigated by the Koreans and Japanese. As the BBC understands it, at this time there is little evidence to support these claims; however, some inside sources at the GMRC indicate there may be some truth to China's version of events. A special programme entitled *China's War,* tackling this and other issues, will be aired on this channel and via our other media streams at the local time now displayed on screen.

'In Europe and the USA food and water rationing is taking its toll and protests, like the one surrounding me now, are testament to the ill will and anger currently aimed at the politicians in their ivory towers. Unfortunately our elected officials seem to be in a position of impotence as the GMRC gathers more and more powers to itself in the name of *humanity's best interests.* As the world's economies crumble and stock markets plummet to record lows, plant and animal life continues to die off at alarming rates while the contingencies installed by the GMRC to ensure food stocks last until the dust cloud breaks up, in five to ten years' time, seem disturbingly inadequate.

'Despite the best efforts of the GMRC and the world's leading nations to ensure the global economy continues to operate effectively, it is clear this goal was optimistic, to say the least. In the USA, the western world's leading manufacturing powerhouse, inflation is skyrocketing, unemployment is at a one hundred year high and consumer confidence is at an all-time low.'

Jessica paused for breath and steeled herself as the unusual sensation of nervousness rippled through her body. Her lips became dry and she fought down the urge to run her tongue over them while live on air. *This is it*, she thought to herself, *why wait? Just go for it.*

'So is there any good news on the horizon?' she continued. 'Perhaps; independent studies have proposed the dust cloud may break up more quickly than the GMRC has predicted. If this is the case, the impact winter may lose some of its teeth within the next twenty-four months. As ever, the GMRC has played down such reports and dismissed these findings as specious and ill-informed. Coming from the GMRC, however, such a statement smacks of double standards bordering on outright hypocrisy.'

At this point in Jessica Klein's report her cameraman, James, looked out from behind his equipment and shook his head at her. She resisted the temptation to flick her eyes towards the movement. Jessica's producer, Martin, located hundreds of miles away back in an office in London and connected to her via an earpiece, also chose to add his twopenn'orth.

'Jessica,' Martin said, 'be careful what you say. We only have one shot at this.'

Jessica computed this dialogue on the fly and as ever showed no sign to the camera that she was receiving any remote communication.

'Switch to Keira's feed we have on the roof,' Martin continued, 'and we can take a break and discuss this one last time.'

As she heard this Jessica shifted her stance, adjusted her hand on the microphone and altered tack from what she had been about to say. 'We're now going to hear from Keira Jones, our latest dedicated GMRC correspondent, who is on the roof high above us. Keira, over to you.'

Jessica paused.

'And ... we're out,' James the cameraman said.

Jessica slumped into a more comfortable posture and pulled her hood up to warm her head. The crowd around them was chanting as loud as ever. Many held placards with slogans like *NO MORE RATION CARDS* and *DOWN WITH WATER CREDITS*. Others displayed the usual anti-GMRC rhetoric, or the simplistic yet effective GMRC logo itself surrounded by a red circle with a line through it.

The street was well-lit due to the substantial increase in lighting introduced by many major cities to distinguish between daytime and night-time hours. The simulation effect even ran in conjunction with the cycle of the sun; the extra lights dimmed at dusk and turned off at night, leaving just the normal street lighting in place.

James took the microphone from Jessica and handed her a flask of hot tea. Sticking one of her mitts in her mouth, she gripped it with her teeth and pulled her hand out. Unscrewing the lid, the steam escaped its container and she took a satisfying sip and wetted her parched lips.

'I thought you were going to wait,' James said as they huddled together while the mob around them kept up its relentless verbal barrage against its caged enemy.

Jessica shrugged. 'I thought it was the perfect time to transition into it.'

'Hmmm.' James sounded sceptical. 'Are you sure you want to go through with this?'

Jessica frowned at him in answer.

He held up his hands. 'Okay, you know what you're doing and Martin is backing you, but if I were you I'd leave it alone.'

Jessica ignored him and took another drink of the tea, feeling its heat warm her from within. She didn't care what he thought. He'd voiced his concerns before, she'd given them due consideration and dismissed them. She'd already had such discussions, and much more in-depth, with her husband, Evan, and it was his advice she valued above any other.

'At the end of the day,' he'd told her one evening when they sat up in bed discussing it, as they usually did when work matters were a problem, 'the decision is up to you, but from what you've told me it seems like the right thing to do regardless of the consequences. It's not like we need the money, if the worst happened.'

'That might not be the worst that could happen,' Jessica had said.

'No. But even they wouldn't be able to cover up that. It would be too obvious. You're too high profile.'

As usual, he was right. Well, Jessica hoped he was right, anyway; otherwise her life could change dramatically and quite quickly. Pushing the thought from her mind she felt her phone vibrate in her pocket. She gave the flask back to James, withdrew the device, saw it was her producer and moved away for more privacy before answering it.

'What the fuck, Jessica?' Martin's voice blared in her ear. 'We agreed what we were going to do and you nearly fucked it all up. I've already had the editor on the phone giving me all kinds of grief after your little tirade. It was touch and go for him to keep the GMRC bastards off our backs. If we're going to do this we've got to stick to the plan. We won't get a second chance at it.'

'I know, I'm sorry.' Jessica walked across to the far side of the road to get away from some of the noise. 'I thought I might as well get it over with. The intro was perfect and as I spoke it unfolded so I could just flow into it. I didn't think you'd mind.'

'You mean you just didn't think.'

Jessica bristled at his tone. 'Look, it isn't just your neck on the line here. And you came to me, remember? I'm the idiot who everyone will be watching, not you, so ease off, will you?'

A momentary silence ensued as Martin computed Jessica's point of view. 'Fine,' he said, 'but just stick to what we agreed, that's all I ask. We owe it to them to get it right and get it said. They can't get away with it any longer. Something has to be done.'

She suddenly remembered why this meant so much to him. 'I know. We'll find out what happened to him and the others too. It's what we do. We find the truth and we tell the world.'

'I hope so,' he said with feeling, and yet Jessica could hear the defeat in his voice. Like her, he knew what they were up against.

'It's time,' he told her.

'Okay. You're sure you can stop them from cutting the broadcast?'

'For a while, but by then the damage will be done.'

'Right.' She didn't know what else to say.

'Good luck,' Martin said and hung up.

Jessica put the phone back in her pocket. 'You too,' she murmured before walking back towards James, who still stood amidst the screaming masses. Squeezing past some protestors, she caught the eye of a woman, the rage in her face a vivid and powerful image that spurred Jessica onwards and strengthened a resolve which had begun to falter as she contemplated the words to come. Pulling her glove back on, she accepted the microphone from James.

'You ready for this?' he asked.

Jessica nodded despite her stomach suddenly feeling like it was barrel rolling within her. 'You?'

'Fucking A!' he said, noticing the tremor in her voice and trying to induce some courage. 'Let's give it to the fuckers, both barrels. I wanna see Jessica Klein at her bitchin' best. No prisoners.'

She knew what he was doing, but it worked all the same. Years of hardened debate on numerous television shows flashed back through her mind. She was Jessica Klein – *I am Jessica Klein, and yes, I take no prisoners.*

'Let's do this.' She positioned herself back in front of the camera, double checked her earpiece and put on her game face.

It wasn't long until she heard Martin's voice. 'Keira is cutting back to you in ten, Jessica,' he said, as if it was just another day at the office. She was then patched into Keira's feed and she could hear her colleague's voice as she wound up her set.

'—final one has landed. This has been Keira Jones reporting on—'

Jessica steadied herself, going through in her mind one last time what she was about to say. James' hand came up as a fist which turned into five fingers, four. *This is it*, she thought, *no turning back now*. Three – two – one. She was live on air – and she froze. Her perception of time faded into a treacle-like pace, the protestors' movements slowed and the noise around her became muffled and distorted. The microphone felt heavy in her hand and the smell of the fires set by the crowd to keep warm tasted strong and pungent, like incense on her tongue.

James popped his head up from behind the camera as her silence continued, his eyes asking a question.

'Jessica, you're on.' Martin's voice echoed in her ear. 'Snap out of it!'

Everything came back into focus coupled with a roar of noise. She blinked a couple of times and then started to speak. 'Thank you, Keira,' she said woodenly. 'It's good to have you on the case up there.'

Jessica hesitated again before finding a stronger voice. The moment was upon her and she must deliver.

♦

Martin West, Jessica's producer, sat back in his chair in his state-of-the-art broadcasting control suite. In the room with him his usual production crew of ten, including audio-visual technicians responsible for producing and transmitting all live output content for the BBC's Worldwide News Service, across all media platforms. In front of him a sweeping curved screen dominated the wall, the flickering images of multiple video feeds within laid out like a living patchwork quilt. Those to the left showed footage of other channels being aired on the BBC, while those to the right spun up local, national and overseas news networks. The core area consisted of a large grid which displayed the previous, back-up, current and future feeds, the current live transmission taking centre stage. Of course, this had a slight delay on it in order to prevent any technical issues or unwanted content escaping the confines of the studio.

Using his personal control terminal Martin tapped a few keys and brought up a secure login screen to which he entered his username and password. Accessing a little used command programme which looked like a simple black box containing a flashing white cursor, he entered the following code:

Live_channel > worldnews_1

Override_external_source_control > Y

Override_internal_shutdown_control > Y

Broadcast_multiple_feed > UHF > ALL

Sound_carrier_frequencies > LINKED

Terrestrial_MHz_Band > 400.00–900.25

International_Bands > ALL

Live_feed_delay > ZERO

SAVE > Y

Martin hit the Enter key and a message popped up followed by the same cursor, the small, hypnotic, blinking line sucking in his attention like a whirlpool, demanding he make a decision.

Disable live feed delay? Y/N _

Martin hesitated before entering the letter Y and pressing the Return key. The main screen on the wall flashed once and a message in red text briefly appeared:

ADJUSTING TRANSMISSION

'Martin, did you see that?' his assistant producer asked, noticing the interruption to the stream.

'Yes, it's just a scheduled update to the system, nothing to worry about.'

The assistant nodded, apparently satisfied with his answer.

Martin got up from his seat and ambled over to the only door into the office and quietly locked it before slipping the key into his trouser pocket. Returning to his chair, he settled in to watch Jessica's report.

♦

'As you may know I have been one of the BBC's main news anchors for the last five years,' Jessica began, addressing the camera and now easing back into her usual professional style. 'In that time I have been privileged to report to you, our viewers, the headline stories as they have broken around the world. Unfortunately in many instances, regarding the most important matters, I have not been given or allowed the freedom to report on the issues that I believe you have a right to hear.

'I, like many in my profession, hold dear the simple principle of the freedom of the press. A principle which a free and fair society must cherish and protect, lest those in power become above reproach, and injustice and corruption rots civilisation from the top down and from the inside out. Without a free press governments may act with impunity and commit atrocities in our name for the benefit of the few belonging to organisations and companies without borders; the few in power who publicly preach patriotism and yet privately practice treason, treason against their nation and against humanity itself. The greatest threat to humanity's future is not the dust cloud or the nuclear bomb, but the hidden sociopath in a position of power. How can the human race function with compassion if we are ruled by those without any?

'But I digress. In what will probably be my last broadcast for the BBC, I want to bring you the alarming truth about a global cover-up perpetrated by the world's leading nations. A cover-up planned and directed by the GMRC itself. What is this secret that we are not being told? I do not know. What I do know is that there is a cover-up and they will go to any lengths to make sure it stays hidden from view.

'How can I prove this bold claim? As ever, direct proof is hard to come by. The GMRC has seen to that. What I can prove is the surrounding evidence. A wise man once said you don't need to see something directly to know that it is there. Anything with substance, physical or otherwise, leaves telltale ripples which reveal its presence. The fact is, for over fifty years governments, powerful companies and organisations have been manipulating these ripples to cover their tracks. How do they do this so effectively? The utilisation of the media is key to their plans.

'I am reporting to you now for the first time operating under true freedom of the press. What you have been told is a lie. Whatever the GMRC is hiding, they are willing to suppress, silence and murder those seeking the truth to keep it hidden. So what is my proof? I can reveal the ripples surrounding the lie. Within the BBC alone over fifty journalists and researchers have disappeared or died in supposed accidents in the last ten years, over half this number within the last three years alone. Coincidence? No. Many of these people have been linked with, and reprimanded over, anti-government and anti-GMRC reports. What's more, my contacts have revealed a disturbing trend within the entire media industry, across seemingly every nation. I personally know broadcasters from CNN and Fox News in the USA, and CTV News in Canada, who tell me there is a deep unease and fear within the networks about reporting any overly negative views against their government and even more so with regard to the GMRC itself. As with the BBC, these organisations have experienced similar disappearances and *accidents* to their workforce.

'This high labour turnover in the journalistic profession is also replicated across Europe, Australia, India, China, Brazil and anywhere that has a high quality, so-called independent, press. I myself have been told on numerous occasions to avoid anti-GMRC viewpoints and not to report my findings on my missing colleagues. I have witnessed first-hand the seizure and destruction of BBC News computers by government and GMRC officials on no fewer than three occasions. Reporters have also been arrested while others have just disappeared without trace.

'The question is not whether the media is being suppressed, but why. What is the GMRC hiding from the people of the world that it will go to such lengths to cover it up? I hope this report will go some way towards exposing the truth and to galvanising and fostering public support for an end to unilateral GMRC control. It's time our politicians said "no more" to GMRC protocols and sanctions and stood up for the rights of the people they were elected to protect.'

'Jessica.' Martin's voice came through her earpiece. 'They've blocked the signal internationally; it's only a matter of time before the terrestrial feed goes too.'

Jessica gave an imperceptible nod. 'Even now,' she continued, 'the GMRC seeks to halt this broadcast. They don't want anyone to know the truth. What are they hiding from us? What are they hiding from you, from everyone? What are they planning for our future, for our children's futures and for the generations to come? Why is it that—'

'Jessica, we're off air,' Martin told her, 'it's over.'

'How did I do?'

'Brilliantly,' he replied with real warmth, 'you did us proud, did us all proud. I—'

Martin's voice cut off. 'Martin?' Jessica said, her concern audible. 'Martin!?'

There was no reply.

♦

In London, Martin West relaxed in his chair as his phone rang for the umpteenth time. His ten colleagues looked at him with nervous eyes; the banging on the door to the broadcasting suite continued unabated as the people outside shouted their demands for entry.

Casually, Martin picked up the phone. 'Yes?'

'Martin, open the door.' It was his editor's voice, fraught with emotion. 'The GMRC are on their way. Don't make this harder than it already is.'

'I told you to do something,' Martin told his boss. 'My brother went missing and you did nothing. No investigation. No reports to even suggest there might have been foul play by the Government or by the GMRC. What did you expect, for me to forget the whole thing, forget my brother even existed?'

'I couldn't do anything; I'd have lost my job!'

Martin snorted in derision and slammed down the phone just as the door to the room burst open with a bang. Wooden splinters flew across the floor as grey garbed GMRC soldiers stormed inside. The other workers screamed and cried out in fear, some putting their hands in the air while others fell submissively to the floor. Pulled from his chair, Martin was thrust against a wall, handcuffed and marched from the room.

♦

Back in New York, James had come round to the front of the camera to give Jessica an uncharacteristic hug. The noise of the crowd increased and Jessica turned to see the barriers had opened up at the front of the building. The NYPD brutally held back the protestors as a team of GMRC operatives swarmed out of the entrance and headed straight towards the BBC news crew.

James swore and turned to run, but he was brought up short by the sight behind them; U.S. troops had cut off their escape.

'Relax.' Jessica laid a reassuring hand on his shoulder as the grim-faced men bore down on them. 'This was inevitable. Just stay strong and we'll get through this together.'

Before James could reply they were forced to the ground by angry, shouting, armed men. As Jessica's face was held down hard against the freezing cold tarmac, all she could see were feet shod in heavy, black, military boots with the occasional glimpse of a terrified looking James, a few feet away, trying to maintain eye contact with her. Jessica gave him what she hoped was a reassuring smile and at the same time wondered if she'd ever see her children and husband again.

CHAPTER TWO

MALCOLM JOINER, director of the powerful and feared GMRC Intelligence Division, stepped out of his plush helicopter and onto the roof of the GMRC's western hemisphere headquarters. No sooner had the director and his entourage disembarked than the twin-rotored aircraft's wheels lifted back into the air. The helicopter angled up and away, creating a tremendous downdraft. A deafening, reverberating, whump, whump, whump of the massive blades accompanied its departure as they cut through the dark, turbulent skies above. Reaching a set altitude, the dazzling landing lights turned off and when the ponderous bulk of that vehicle had shrunk into the distance, another soon took its place, the relentless procession continuing without pause.

One hundred storeys high, the building punched its way heavenward, but it was by no means the tallest tower in the Manhattan skyline. What it lacked in height, however, it made up for in sheer volume – above and below the surface. The chrome and glass clad, purpose-built, circular structure had an impressive diameter and dominated its block on uptown Ninth Avenue; it had to, as it housed thousands of staff in key hub offices for the various departments of the GMRC.

The whistling ice-cold wind had initially sought to snatch Joiner's breath away and turn his skin to stone as his ridiculously expensive shoes had touched down onto the helipad's hard, painted surface. The intelligence director fought back the urge to shiver as he strode across the vast rooftop towards one of the four main entrances to the building. In front of him other arrivals garbed in dense layers of fur-lined clothing made their way past high levels of security, the first of many such interventions before they reached their final destination.

For the sake of appearances, Joiner refused to dress like a cocooned Eskimo and cover his body from head to toe in thick thermal attire, like many of the dignitaries now filtering towards the warm interior. Instead he wore his usual close-fitting suit, which accentuated his considerable height, although, as ever, he wore a classic pair of soft Italian leather gloves, a thin yet warm knee-length handmade overcoat, and a pair of narrow, rectangular glasses, to which he had attached flip down sunshades. It wasn't that the sun was ever an issue these days, it was that he liked his appearance to be in keeping with his role and, since he was also head of U.S. Intelligence, it was almost a prerequisite to exude an ominous, untouchable and superior air; nothing could state this more than a pair of dark glasses.

The fact that he was untouchable was beside the point. He wanted to make sure others knew he was untouchable and that to consider otherwise was a very bad idea; not just for their own health but for the health of everyone else they held dear. Joiner had spent many years cultivating his aura of invincibility and power, and he wasn't prepared to let it falter by wearing the wrong kind of clothing. As every politician and civil servant knew, appearance was everything.

Like those before him, Joiner subjected himself to the preliminary security station. A GMRC guard in arctic weather gear waved him forward.

'Keep your arms inside the scanner at all times!' the man told Joiner, raising his voice to be heard above the roaring winds and heavy air traffic above.

Without any acknowledgment he'd heard the guard's instruction, Joiner stepped onto a shoulder-width, round, rubberised mat; a red circle at its rim and the representation of a person in the centre. The automated scanner hummed into life. White light illuminated Joiner from above, the beam emanating from an integrated fitting sunk into an overhang from the building's entrance. Joiner and the mat he stood on were situated within an inconspicuous two inch wide square metal border that had been set into the floor and which now rose up to reveal itself. The scanner produced a high-pitched drawn-out whine as the metal structure swished up, down and around Joiner's body in short, sharp motions, intense, ice-blue lasers sending short arcs of light over his whole frame.

After ten seconds the security device sank back into the floor. Joiner stepped forwards, passing beneath a strong, continuous jet of hot air and into a warm, brightly lit foyer. When the rest of Joiner's team had been similarly swept they boarded a short escalator which whisked them to a row of gold doors, each embossed with the GMRC logo. At the edges of the room six well-armed soldiers stood to fixed attention, their grey-clad forms virtually invisible to the flow of VIPs passing by them on a regular basis.

A pair of the plush doors opened and Joiner's group entered the lift's glass interior. After descending a number of floors, Joiner emerged into a massive, open atrium. Bustling with orderly activity, the large, internal expanse consisted of a grand airport-style check-in system, the one hundred foot oval desk at its centre manned by a veritable army of administrative staff and encircled by row upon row of seating.

Joiner's primary aide and his assistant collected up the party's overcoats and deposited them at the counter. Further clerical security checks were actioned and passes handed out, with the appropriate clearance levels assigned to the embedded digital architecture. They were then ushered through a gate built into the desk itself and accompanied by an administrator down another escalator, two more lift shafts, two more security check points and, at last, into the joint largest council chamber in the world, the twin of which was located in the GMRC's near identical sister HQ building in Shanghai.

The huge, domed room's functional design consisted of circular rows of polished mahogany desks and comfortable blue and grey upholstered seating. The simplicity of the décor was not to be misconstrued for cost saving, however, as the area bristled with conferencing technology on a mind-boggling scale. Hundreds of active holographic computer displays and a multitude of interface devices adorned each table. Large OLED screens hung from the ceiling at regular intervals, while even bigger displays encircled the central hub of the summit chamber, this focal point acting as the main stage of interaction between council members and their guests.

Proceedings adhered to a strict schedule and a specially produced handbook and guide to the summit was duly handed out to every person of every delegation that attended. Joiner had been to such summits on many occasions over the years, but since the arrival of AG5 in 2040 the world was now a very different place. The buzz in the air from the ever-growing number of people congregating in the chamber was noticeable to Joiner as he made his way through the throng. He shook hands and spoke to world leaders and other influential dignitaries, whilst all the while extracting and storing information for future use. He was always on the job, a master of manipulation and deception; it was what he did, what he excelled at, amongst other considerable talents.

Finally Joiner made his way to a segregated area raised above all other seating except that of the Council's Chief Chair, who sat at a similar level in the central hub. Joiner enjoyed sitting in his elevated position amongst the elite GMRC Directorate. It was a public display of his global power and influence for the benefit of those that were not previously aware. Joiner settled into his seat, his retinue close behind although at a lower level. He picked up a crystal glass and poured some iced spring water into it from a plain glass jug that had sat off to one side. As he sipped his drink the screens above spooled up information on the schedule of the soon-to-commence summit.

Joiner used the brief lapse before the endless talk began to take in his immediate surroundings and the people populating it. The Global Meteor Response Council consisted of many departments, some vastly more powerful and influential than others, but all operating, to varying degrees, under the following criteria:

PUBLIC: Activities disclosed to society
COVERT: Activities not disclosed to society
CLASSIFIED: Existence not disclosed to society

The departmental powerhouses, the main players that drove the GMRC's policies and actions the world over, were as follows:

- Subterranean Programme: *Covert & Classified*
- Space Programme: *Public & Covert*
- *R&D Division: Covert & Classified*
- Intelligence Division: *Covert*
- Population Education: *Public & Covert*
- Population Control: *Covert & Classified*
- Economic Control: *Public & Covert*
- Conservation: *Public & Covert*
- Resource Control: *Public & Covert*
- Operations & Military: *Public & Covert*
- U.N. Integration: *Public*
- GMRC Oversight: *Public & Covert*

At the head of each one of these departments was an elected director, each of whom took their rightful place on the most powerful body of them all, the pre-eminent GMRC Directorate. People not in the know wrongly assumed that the highly classified Subterranean Programme wielded the most clout within the GMRC. This had been the case for the last two decades, but since the underground bases around the world were all but completed the balance had shifted slightly, and Joiner had been quick to exert his authority over the power vacuum that had resulted during this transitionary time. Through his dark lenses he looked over at the chair which held the Subterranean Programme's Acting Director General, Shen Zhǔ Rèn, the now controversial Chinese replacement for Professor

Steiner, who had been taken ill while on assignment at USSB Steadfast.

Professor Steiner's illness was, of course, a fabrication of Joiner's own making and a deception he had sold to the rest of the GMRC Directorate in a perfectly choreographed display of misinformation, and video and audio manipulation. It was amazing what one could do with video editing software and the political power to push it through. There were mutterings about Steiner's sudden disappearance in certain circles, but that was inevitable and one imperfection of his plan to get rid of the insufferable professor he could live with. The fact the Subterranean Director General's stress-induced illness just happened to coincide with USSB Steadfast going into lockdown procedure for the impact of the asteroid AG5 and an inopportune breakdown in the underground base's communication system was perhaps more difficult to explain away; and yet as the intelligence director he could manoeuvre and subvert those who complained the loudest regardless of their position in the GMRC or otherwise. Joiner not only had an extensive reach, he had allies around the world whose cunning, power and resolve all but matched his own.

Now that Steiner was out of the picture and the Chinese had caused political and military headaches for the West by attacking Japan and South Korea, Joiner was able to better pursue his more secretive agendas, agendas outside of his GMRC remit and in some cases directly opposed to what the GMRC was trying to achieve. Flicking up his sunshades to reveal the clear lenses beneath, he caught the eye of the R&D director and gave him an almost imperceptible nod of acknowledgment. The R&D director, Dagmar Sørenson, a sallow, grim-faced individual always seemingly on the edge of a life threatening illness, lifted his hand in reply. Dagmar had proved a key ally to Joiner over the years and represented an asset he could ill afford to lose at this point in time. *If the evil bastard were to drop dead now*, he thought, *it could prove a significant annoyance.*

As the summit got underway, Joiner took another sip of his water and tuned in to proceedings. When each person spoke they utilised a sophisticated translation algorithm to ensure everyone present received the most accurate information in real-time; each team had back-up translators in order to make sure no errors were made, but it enabled a flowing interaction between all speakers, regardless of their mother tongue; a true technical marvel of the modern age.

'As you can see,' a climate and ecosystem expert from France was saying, 'ice sheets have advanced significantly in the last six months, making most of Scandinavia and Canada virtually uninhabitable. North American States and northern European countries are now experiencing extreme weather conditions ranging from tumultuous rainfall one week to sustained hail and snow the next. Temperature drops and zero sunlight across the world are wreaking havoc with our ecosystems and the extinction of plant and animal life on land has begun. Tipping points will be reached in the next six months, ensuring the inevitable irreversible decline. Earth's aquatic life is also experiencing mass upheaval; however, full extinction of life in our oceans will only be reached in 2045 when the last two asteroids strike.'

The speakers came and went, each outlining various unfolding scenarios that for many years everyone in the room had been well prepared for, resigned in their expectations of the inevitable. These events consisted of chaotic and sudden breakdowns in law and order in a quarter of the world's nations, with civil unrest in the remaining seventy-five per cent. It was all the GMRC and leading governments of the world could do to keep up the appearance that things would get better, when in fact they were fighting a losing battle that would ultimately result in the death of ninety-nine point nine per cent of the world's population. The remaining lucky few would be evacuated to the forty-five massive underground bases constructed around the globe in order to continue humanity's way of life and very existence on Earth.

A scheduled break brought with it light relief for the assembled masses. Joiner stood up and surreptitiously stretched out his back and arms, which had begun to ache after the long hours of inactivity. His aide informed him that the rest of the day's presentations regarded administration and government integration concerns, something he had decided weeks before he did not need to attend. Taking his leave, he retired to his allocated suite in the accommodation wing of the building.

Later that evening, Joiner reclined on a soft leather chair with matching footstool as he read through the week's upcoming summit schedule. The final two days would prove to be the most interesting as they were open only to the highest clearance holders, which naturally included him. In particular a slot led by Dagmar Sørensen regarding something called Project Ares caught his eye. As intelligence director, Joiner had prior knowledge of the array of black projects conducted by the GMRC's R&D Division; however, this one did not ring any bells. He was impressed; not much got past Joiner these days, but when something did he was quick to sit up and take note. He would make sure to get a team of his top intelligence agents on it and work up a profile by the end of the week. He didn't like surprises. In fact, he employed others to make sure they didn't arise. His mood darkened and he pressed the intercom button to summon his aide.

Moments later the man Joiner referred to as Debden appeared. 'Yes, sir?'

Joiner continued reading the schedule. 'What is your job title?'

Debden squared his shoulders. 'Primary Aide to the GMRC Intelligence Director.'

'And as primary aide it is your duty to inform me about important developments within the GMRC, those that may have escaped my attention.'

'Yes, sir,' Debden said, an edge of uncertainty creeping into his voice.

'Then why is it,' Joiner continued as he swung his chair round twenty degrees so he could fix Debden with his steely gaze, 'that the R&D Division is presenting to the Directorate a project I know nothing about?'

'Specific schedule details were only released and disseminated upon commencement of the summit, sir. We would—'

'We work in the damn Intelligence Division!' Joiner's eyes flashed fierce. 'We should've had a copy of the schedule a day before it was written and a dossier on the project should have been on my desk the day it was conceived!'

Debden looked shaken by his director's anger at this apparent oversight and stood locked in Joiner's unrelenting stare, unable to formulate an appropriate response – most likely because there wasn't one.

Joiner watched and waited, maintaining silence in order to intensify Debden's discomfort and to instil in him the knowledge that failing in his duties was not an option. More agonising seconds ticked by ... then he swivelled his chair back round.

'Project Ares,' Joiner said, as he once more perused the schedule, his glasses perched at the end of his pointed nose. 'Get a team on it, full work up. I want to know everything there is to know.'

'Very good, sir.' Debden departed, leaving Joiner to ponder on what Project Ares might be. As his irritation mounted due to his lack of information on the subject his phone, which rested on a glass table to his left, emitted a small beep which progressed into a drawn out repeating singular note.

Joiner drew the phone to his ear. 'Yes?'

'Director Joiner, my apologies for this intrusion at such a late hour. My name is Duncan Sanderfield. I'm a senior on-site Population Control manager. Earlier today a major public relations situation transpired and my superiors suggested you may want some input into how we go about clearing up the mess.'

'How major?'

'A Code Two media breach, national and international exposure by a prominent and credible source.'

'Duration?'

'A few minutes.'

'Has it got legs?'

'We've prevented further broadcasting of the coverage and hunted down and destroyed any copies stored on public and private mobile and static devices. There were some files we were unable to access straight away, but our computer coders ensure us it will only be a matter of time before we have them all.'

Joiner considered the implications of such a Code Two event. 'How prominent is prominent?'

'Does the name Jessica Klein ring any bells?'

Joiner swore.

'Quite,' Sanderfield said. 'They don't come much bigger, do they?'

'Where is she being held?'

'Here, in this very building.'

Joiner sat up straighter. 'Convenient. Where are you located?'

'Sub-basement Green, Sector twelve. Use the east side elevator shafts. Interrogation Suite One.'

'I'll be with you shortly.' Joiner hung up the phone. Clearly Population Control was finding this potato too hot to handle. As was often the case the Intelligence Division was at hand to mop up the messes others could not. Any issue of a smaller scale and Joiner would not have even been considered as a point of contact, but in this instance his experience was invaluable and it was well known he relished dealing with such cases. *Who wouldn't,* he mused; a chance to throw one's weight around was always something to savour.

Ten minutes later, after taking a couple of travelators and a lift, Joiner walked into a sizable conference room to be greeted by Sanderfield and various other personnel from the Population Control Division of the GMRC. As ever Joiner's aide, Debden, and a few other intelligence agents had accompanied him.

Sanderfield led Joiner through the events that had taken place and showed him the footage that had been broadcast around the world.

'This has been very damaging to the GMRC's reputation,' Sanderfield concluded.

Clearly the man's talents lay in stating the blindingly obvious, Joiner noted. He gave Sanderfield a withering look before walking over to watch the BBC news crew on a video wall. Secured in separate holding cells, the team of two awaited their fate. The cameraman had his head in his hands while the woman of the hour, Jessica Klein, paced around her small room like a caged animal, occasionally staring up at the camera that filmed her movements.

Joiner knew the broadcaster was well liked by her many viewers and even within the upper reaches of the UK establishment. People believed what she said. The British Prime Minister had even referred to her as a 'national treasure' on a couple of occasions. This support had evidently given the news anchor a false sense of security and emboldened her to take such an ill-advised step against the GMRC.

However, a five minute speech by one woman could only do so much damage. The problem now was how to react and how to quell any further rants that might spout from her mouth. Joiner knew they were nearly at the stage when such concerns would no longer be a problem. In a few years' time they could even have just let it go altogether, but as it was they needed to deal with it, with her.

'Options?' Joiner asked one of his agents, testing his subordinate's acumen.

'Profile the target,' the agent replied after a moment's pause. 'Determine past indiscretions. Work up possible scenarios to discredit them.'

Joiner nodded. 'What about elimination?'

'A last resort.'

'Is it?'

The agent looked at Joiner, unsure if his director was testing him again or proposing a serious solution.

'You can't just kill her,' Sanderfield spoke up, visibly shocked at the suggestion.

Joiner turned to look at the man as one might look at a bug on one's shoe.

'Can't?' Joiner said, his voice cold and flat and yet loaded with a threatening challenge.

Sanderfield, suddenly realising who he was talking to, swallowed nervously.

Joiner looked meaningfully to his aide, Debden, who acted as required.

'Take your people and vacate this room immediately,' Debden

told the Population Control manager as he ushered him away. 'Your services are no longer needed.'

Sanderfield and his team scuttled from the interrogation suite, leaving the intelligence agents alone with their director.

'Sir,' another agent said, 'surely killing them will cause more problems than it solves; the damage has already been done, has it not?'

'Of course it has.' Joiner removed his glasses and polished the lenses with a cloth. 'No their deaths would not alter anything. But we need to make sure they – or more specifically, *she* – cannot cause the GMRC any more bad publicity.'

'We could permanently relocate her to one of the subterranean bases,' Debden suggested as he rejoined the group.

Joiner shook his head. 'No, she would be too much of a liability to have running around inside the system. We will keep her under twenty-four hour surveillance and discredit her with a subtle finesse. We will need to get creative on this one. Laying it on too thick with multiple infractions will appear too convenient, but infidelity or sexual deviance will be too weak or implausible. Dig up what you can on her family and her past. There will be something we can use. If not, run an audio-visual study on her and we can then make sure there is. A basic profile work up won't be necessary as we already have every top employee within the media fully documented. Everything we need is at our fingertips. Make it happen.'

'Yes, sir,' his men replied in unison, then went their separate ways to carry out his orders.

As Joiner watched the two prisoners once more he took out his phone and spoke in a command. 'Call UK Prime Minister.'

'Downing Street,' a man answered almost immediately, 'how may I direct your call?'

'Put me through to the Prime Minister.'

'I'm sorry; he's in a cabinet meeting for the rest of the day. Please call back tomorrow.'

'Not good enough,' Joiner told the civil servant. 'Can you not see from your display who this is?'

A pause left Joiner waiting on his phone.

'I'm sorry, Director Joiner, forgive me. I will ask him if he is able to speak with you. I take it this is a matter of some urgency?'

'It is.'

The phone went silent once more and it was some time before another voice came on, a deeper and more powerful one. 'Director Joiner, how goes the GMRC's annual summit?'

'Prime Minister,' Joiner said respectfully. 'It goes very well, thank you; your presence has been greatly missed.'

'You're too kind, Director; how might I be of help to you today?'

'You have no doubt been made aware of the incident that occurred earlier with one of your BBC newsreaders?'

'I have.' The PM sounded grave. 'We have collaborated with your GMRC office here in London to ensure the fallout has been minimal.'

'May I ask what alterations have been made to the BBC's managerial structure?'

'A full review of the computer systems responsible for all television and media broadcasts has been instigated,' the PM said. 'Any flaws will be found and corrected. Rest assured, Director, lessons have been learnt.'

'With all due respect, Prime Minister, that is not what I asked.'

'Yes, of course. I have reprimanded Lord Eaton, who is the Chairman of the BBC Trust, and he has assured me that no such event will occur again under his watch.'

Joiner introduced a firmness to his voice. 'I'm afraid that is not good enough, Prime Minister. The GMRC will require a clean sweep of the BBC's hierarchy, including the replacement of Lord Eaton, who is clearly as incompetent as his staff for allowing this to happen in the first place.'

'A clean sweep,' the PM repeated. 'You can't be serious?'

'Responsibility begins at the top,' Joiner said, enjoying himself as he dictated terms to one of the world's foremost leaders. 'Please don't force me to take this to the GMRC Directorate, as it will only end in your capitulation and subsequent humiliating concession. I want the

BBC's management replaced with more malleable counterparts within the day; do I make myself clear, Prime Minister?'

As Joiner waited for a reply he could almost visualise the Englishman's blood boiling as he computed what he'd just heard.

'I'll see what I can do,' the PM said with barely concealed fury and hung up the phone.

'And a good day to you, Prime Minister.' Joiner put his own phone down with a satisfied smile tugging at his lips.

Once more Joiner's eyes were drawn to the images of the two captives displayed on the video wall. He knew it would be so much easier and significantly more satisfying to torture and then kill these puerile fools for their crimes, but even he had to abide by the rules on occasion. The rat-a-tat of his finger tapping the table brought him out of his reverie. He clenched his fist to quell the outward display of frustration.

'Release these two idiots to the NYPD for processing,' Joiner told one of his agents. 'They can then be deported with immediate effect to the United Kingdom.'

The agent bobbed his head in response. 'Yes, sir.'

'And get the UK Government to revoke their passports when they get back. Their days of travelling are over. In fact,' Joiner said, 'confiscate their passports and then put them on a plane to somewhere inhospitable, like Siberia.'

'That will stick them in limbo when they get there,' the agent informed him. 'They won't be able to get back to the UK for some time.'

'That's the idea,' Joiner said, as he walked from the room. 'That is most definitely the idea.'

CHAPTER THREE

SMALL, dimmed, oblong lights ran in rows along the walkways in the main cabin of the Airbus A380 super jumbo airliner, their faint illumination highlighting the slumbering passengers as they flew across European airspace towards London. The plane's massive engines droned away in the background. Internal fixtures and fittings squeaked and rattled, responding to the repetitive rise and fall of the fuselage, held aloft by vast, swept wings that sliced through tumultuous, interconnecting weather systems.

Jessica Klein shifted in her economy class window seat, trying to regain some semblance of comfort after being awoken by a hostess wheeling a rattling trolley cart along the nearby aisle. Her eyelids rested shut, but she could feel the tension within them preventing her from drifting back to sleep. Keeping her eyes closed, she willed her mind to slow, to relax into a state of calm, while attempting to block out the noise of the aircraft and its many inhabitants. A person coughed in the seat behind her, a child cried out for its mother off to one side and the mutterings of two people a couple of rows in front was enough to make her blink and stir fully awake.

She wasn't getting back to sleep anytime soon and now, she realised, she needed to relieve herself. Oh, how she hated flying like this, cramped and uncomfortable and hemmed in on all sides. It was a far cry from the roomy and opulent surroundings of business class, which she had grown accustomed to over the years, one of the many privileges of being amongst the BBC's highest paid television presenters; privileges she now had to learn to live without.

James, the cameraman who had been Jessica's constant companion since they were ejected from the United States, was no longer with her. He had taken an earlier flight destined for Birmingham, England's second largest city, and James' home town.

She was on her own now, returning from the ice-laden municipality of Novosibirsk, Russia's third most populous city. Since the arrival of the asteroid AG5, the drop in temperature had hit parts of Siberia the hardest and now, even in its warmest months, temperatures of minus forty centigrade were commonplace. It had taken many trips by British embassy staff to the main terminal building in the Tolmachevo Airport, on the outskirts of the Russian city, to secure them passage back to England. The confiscation of their passports by the U.S. Customs and Border Protection officers, prior to their departure from JFK International, had caused them no end of headaches and stranded them for a month in a part of Russia that was in total disarray. Jessica had almost been glad they hadn't been allowed out of the arrivals lounge into the city proper as law and order was at breaking point. It was all the police and local government departments could do to keep critical services operational. Poorer parts of the city had turned into complete no go areas, even for the military.

Unable to put it off any longer, Jessica stood up awkwardly. The backs of her knees rested against the seat and she had to hold the headrest with one hand to stop herself from falling back down again. The man sitting next to her was fast asleep, but he was reasonably slim, enabling her to squeeze past without disturbing him. Unfortunately the next chair was occupied by a rather large lady whose ample legs barred Jessica's much needed escape. As she debated whether she should wake the immovable blockade a hostess, seeing her movement, came over to offer assistance. Taking the proffered hand, Jessica stretched out a leg and managed to hop out into the relative freedom of the aisle.

Sharing a quick smile with her saviour, Jessica thanked her and then walked on unsteady legs towards the rear of the plane and into a cramped toilet. Pulling the narrow door shut behind her, she engaged the small lock and then looked down at the toilet seat with trepidation. Apparently some economy class fliers had decided hygiene and cleaning up after themselves was not on their 'to do' list. Gagging slightly, she exited and selected a cleaner abode to enter. After she'd cleaned this new seat with copious amounts of toilet paper and gone about her business, she was greeted with an up close and personal view of her countenance in a mirror.

Washing her hands vigorously, she placed her ever present handbag onto the sink and opened it up. She looked at her reflection once more. The face that peered back was supposedly attractive. According to some UK magazines she was deemed as *top posh totty* and had claimed the embarrassing title of *Sexiest Female Newsreader* on three separate occasions. Such accolades made her uncomfortable and sometimes they even brought a blush to her cheeks. Normally she shrugged off such comments with an easy indifference and modesty, but deeper down she felt a guilty rush of girlish pleasure at the unsolicited flattery.

At the moment, however, all she saw were heavy bags underneath overly large, deep brown eyes. High cheek bones gave way to a squarish jaw, a gift from her father, which ensured her looks favoured handsome rather than the conventional pretty that most men seemed to favour.

Her hair, usually perfectly arranged, looked like a pterodactyl had decided to nest in it while dancing a Scottish jig. Also, according to her husband, she tended to sleep with her mouth open and this always resulted in dry, cracked lips. Taking out a tiny tub of Vaseline she unscrewed the lid and popped a small amount onto the tip of her little finger. Expertly she then applied it to her bottom, and then upper, lip. Smacking them and rubbing them against each other she worked the balm well into the skin. Happy with the result, she took out her comb and went to work on the fantastically arranged bird's nest located on her head. After ten minutes she'd regained some semblance of humanity, and rather than a weary forty-something, a passable thirty-something woman looked back at her; at least that's what she hoped, anyway.

Emerging from the tiny room she bumped into a large youth who towered over her. 'Watch it!' she said, her foot crushed beneath his size twelve.

He mumbled an apology and disappeared into the filthy lavatory she'd had the misfortune of entering earlier. Jessica's stature was diminutive but she had never paid it much heed or let it hold her back in any way. She had a fearsome reputation if riled and would not let anyone take advantage of her, regardless of their size or position.

Back in her seat and a few monotonous hours later, the plane touched down at Heathrow airport and Jessica collected her luggage and made her way through customs without incident. Despite her general inner self-assurance and sometimes hard demeanour, Jessica found herself welling up as she caught sight of her family waiting for her at Arrivals. Her two daughters – Victoria, five, and Daniela, seven – ducked underneath the railing, unable to contain their excitement at seeing their mother for the first time in many weeks. Detaching herself from the main cavalcade of passengers, Jessica veered towards her two girls, dropped her luggage and knelt to embrace them. Evan, her husband, soon joined them and she found herself wrapped in his strong arms and sharing a long, lingering kiss.

'It's good to be home,' she murmured in his ear.

He held her tighter. 'It's good to have you home, we've missed you. *I've* missed you.'

Jessica leant back from him and looked deep into his eyes before the girls drew her attention back to them.

The journey home was a pleasant one as she caught up on the trivia of family life while their black cab wove them through the congested traffic of West London and on into Kensington. Exhausted after her trip, she slept well and with a fresh vigour upon waking, she instigated lovemaking with Evan as they renewed their physical bond after their enforced separation. While the passion Evan returned towards her matched that of her own, she sensed his tension throughout and after they had uncoupled he left the room without a word to go into the en-suite. Normally they settled into a fulfilled cuddle after sex so she was acutely aware of his unusual behaviour. Sliding out of bed she padded naked and bare of foot into the bathroom after him. He stood, head bowed, in front of the sink unit.

She approached from behind and wrapped her arms around his waist. 'What's the matter?'

'I lost my job last week,' he said without turning round, his voice taut with stress.

Her eyes widened in disbelief. 'What? How? You've worked there for years; you're a damn partner in the company for god's sake. They can't just sack you!'

He turned round and her grip on him fell away. 'They didn't, the firm folded, our business dried up overnight. One minute we had corporate clients lining up out the door and the next, nothing, apart from the odd small case.

'Do you know why?' she asked, already knowing the answer.

'Why do you think? The GMRC apparently don't take kindly to public airing of their business and they like to spread the pain to anyone involved, or just involved by association.'

'Why didn't you tell me before?' Jessica's mind was reeling in despair as she enclosed his clasped hands within her own.

He grunted something unintelligible. She drew him to her and he encircled her with his arms. Leaning his head on her small shoulder, he heaved a deep sigh. 'I suppose we should have seen this coming.'

Jessica didn't reply as her guilt had already set in for ruining his career. Now they were likely to both be out of work by the end of the week. Her disciplinary hearing with her bosses at the BBC was scheduled for two days' time and, all things considered, its final outcome was almost a forgone conclusion.

Her hand stroked his hair. 'I'll make this right,' she told him but her words, while said with heartfelt conviction, rang hollow in her ears.

♦

Jessica, in a crisp blue suit, made her way into work as she always did. Catching the London Underground from West Kensington, she changed at Green Park onto the Victoria line and got off after one stop at Oxford Circus. Making her way through the station and past the ticket gates, the usual press of bodies accompanying the commute, she emerged out into the street. Overhead floodlights installed for daytime simulation glared down as she made her way along the crowded pavement towards her destination, passing cars creating miniature tsunamis as their tyres cut through the pooling rain. Saving her from a drenching, newly erected awnings lined the roads of London town, protecting commuters and shoppers alike from the ferocious weather that had been battering Europe for the last few months. Mirroring the sunless brooding sky above, grim-faced armed police officers stalked the roads, adding a sinister air to the UK's capital city.

Jessica crossed a narrow road and walked past a stationary armoured military patrol vehicle, then on into the familiar building of BBC Broadcasting House, leaving the noisy bustle of the city behind. Usually she would have taken another entrance, but as an enquiry into her actions on air was pending, she had to report to the main desk. Leaning atop the counter, with its illuminated white signage bearing the famous BBC logo, Jessica waited for one of the receptionists to finish helping someone else. The man was soon with her and handing her a temporary security pass. He gave her an understanding smile before she turned and left to enter the building proper.

As she strode along the functional carpeted corridors, her anger at her treatment and at Evan's forced redundancy, which had been simmering for the last two days, rose to the surface. Jessica's presence moved before her like a wave and people parted at her passing like the red sea preceding Moses. People called out greetings to her, some even clapped while others merely nodded to her in grim recognition of her personal sacrifice for their lost colleagues. Jessica's face was set and steely when she banged open the doors to the executive offices. Following her arrival at the room designated for the hearing, she didn't have long to wait before being told to go in.

Jessica stood up and prepared herself for what was to come.

A woman from Human Resources gave her an encouraging smile. 'Good luck, Jessica.'

Jessica nodded to her, opened the door and went inside. A lot had changed since she had last been at work. It seemed the senior management team had undergone a rapid transformation of personnel. She only knew one of the four people present and none of them showed the support she had witnessed on the way up. This was likely due to the fact that one of the four, and the only one she did recognise, was not a BBC employee at all but an MP from the Prime Minister's Cabinet Office.

'Ms Klein,' the Member of Parliament said, after Jessica had taken a seat opposite the disciplinary panel, 'thank you for coming here today. You understand the gravity of your situation. Shall we begin?'

♦

The Human Resources receptionist leaned forwards, perched on the very edge of her chair, straining to hear what was being said in Jessica Klein's hearing, which had sounded heated from the outset. The occasional swear word and raised voice was easily discerned as emanating from the well-known newsreader as she fought her corner with an expected vigour.

When the duration of the meeting neared the one hour mark, a sudden barrage of swearing and shouting erupted from the room. This time it wasn't just Jessica's voice to be heard. The receptionist, however, still couldn't make out the gist of the exchange and in her eagerness to find out what was going on she rolled her chair closer. At which point the door to the room flew open, making her jump in surprise.

Jessica Klein stood bristling with fury in the doorway and looked back into the office. '—well you know what you can do with your job!' Jessica bellowed at her tormentors. 'You can stick it up your fucking arses, you pathetic, snivelling wretches. I hope you and the GMRC are happy with this cover-up. The blood of all those journalists is on your hands now as you are all a party to this shit!' Jessica's finger, which pointed accusingly at the people in the room, shook with enraged tension, an emotion mirrored in its owner's face.

The receptionist, who had stood up, gawped at the scene unfolding before her. The former renowned BBC presenter heaved the door closed with an almighty effort. The heavy fireproof door smashed into its frame with a loud bang, sending it rattling in its hinges and near tearing it from the wall. Jessica Klein, dishevelled yet defiant, all but flew out of the office leaving a deathly silence in her wake. The receptionist watched for some time to see if anything else was about to happen, but all was quiet once more in BBC Broadcasting House. The show was over and yet another BBC icon had made their last bow.

♦

'I'm surprised you didn't punch him,' her husband said as Jessica relived her experience with him.

'Believe me, I felt like it.' Jessica poured herself another glass of wine and took a long draught. 'That smug piglet-eyed MP's face really got my fucking dander up. The piece of shit is totally a GMRC puppet and the bloody idiots now in charge of the BBC might as well have *cunt* written on their foreheads.'

Evan nearly choked on his drink at his wife's unexpected use of the C word. Jessica rarely used profanity and when she did it was only 'shit' or 'bugger'. To hear her curse like that was a queer experience for him.

A melodic undulating ring tone drew Jessica's attention to her bag, which sat perched on the central worktop in the kitchen. Taking out her phone she saw she'd received a text message from Martin, her old producer, who'd himself been sacked from the BBC for gross misconduct two weeks earlier. It read:

need 2 TLK 2nite. Come aloN.
hav som important news.
Meet @ Colton Arms @ 8

Strange, Jessica thought; she hadn't seen hide nor hair of Martin since a brief video call she'd made when she was stuck out in Russia. If he was all the way over in West London in person it must be important.

Taking her leave of Evan a few hours later, Jessica sat alone, as requested, in the Colton Arms pub, located a few streets away from her home. Nursing her second glass of wine, she looked at her watch: nine o'clock. *Where the hell is he?*

Her mind wandered and she found herself studying a rather nice wooden cabinet positioned next to where she sat. One particular carving portrayed lions pulling a chariot. Above this, winged angels blessed the vehicle's occupants while all around other strange images of semi-naked men and women cavorted and leapt.

A hand touched Jessica's arm, making her jump. Martin sat down in a seat next to her. He looked out of breath. Droplets of sweat beaded on his brow and ran down his temples. Wiping them away with the back of his sleeve, he picked up Jessica's glass and downed the contents in two swift gulps. The Colton Arms was quite a small place and a couple of the locals eyed Martin with interest before turning back to chat with the barman.

Jessica looked at her empty glass, feeling a little aggrieved. 'What happened to eight?'

'Had a tail, had to shake him,' Martin said, and then asked the barman to bring over two more drinks.

'Tail?'

'GMRC spook, probably.' Martin removed his coat and placed it on the back of his chair as the drinks were brought over. He took a big sip of his lager and rested it down on the table with a sigh of satisfaction.

Jessica was confused. 'Why would they be bothering to follow you round now? You were sacked, like I was today. We don't have the means to give them anymore trouble.'

Martin took another sip, eyeing her over the top of his glass before lowering it back down again. 'That's where you're wrong. You really think I was going to give this up? My brother is still missing, and many others too, some dead.'

'I know, but our hands are tied. Evan's lost his job, I've just lost mine. I did what I could and it doesn't seem to have made much of a difference, apart from ruining my family's prospects.'

'You're not listening to me.' Martin lowered his voice and leaned in towards her. 'I have a lead, a good one. It could deal the GMRC a big blow if we could get it into the public domain, but I need your help to do it.'

'Why me? What can I do that you can't?'

'Speak German, for one.'

It was true Jessica could speak German fluently. Her father had insisted she take lessons as a child to please her grandparents who were both born and bred in the Fatherland. She hadn't used it for years, however, and didn't know Martin even knew about it.

'What kind of lead?' she asked. 'What sort of blow? Do you have proof they targeted journalists?'

He looked around to make sure they weren't being overheard. 'Better, I think we can find out what they're covering up. Why the media is being gagged in the first place.'

'And how do you propose to do that when so many have failed before?'

'Because my lead is a hacker and he says he can get us what we want.' Martin grabbed Jessica's hand, his eyes intense. 'We can still break this story, you and me – together.'

Jessica couldn't help but be drawn in by Martin's fervour, but due to what had already transpired she knew the risks of taking this further were great.

'I don't know—' she said, her heart telling her to go for it while her brain warned her to let it go.

Martin didn't seem to acknowledge her reticence and slid a grubby piece of paper across the table to her. She picked it up. Scribbled across its centre, a German address and a set of numbers:

'This person wants us to go here,' she said, 'to Berlin? You do remember I have no passport; getting out of the country is going to be a bit of a problem, especially since the GMRC locked down every nation's borders.'

Without a word Martin placed a brown padded envelope on the table and pushed that across to her, too. Jessica glanced at the bar, suddenly feeling her actions were very conspicuous. Picking up the packet, she looked inside to see a set of documents. She looked up at Martin, who returned her gaze expectantly and flicked his eyes to the envelope indicating he wanted her to extract its contents. She did so and found herself holding a folded piece of paper and a British Passport. Opening the paper out first, she saw that it was a GMRC border pass, a blank one at that, ready to accept whoever wanted to use it. All she needed to do was fill in her details. Wondering how her old producer had got his hands on such a thing she opened the passport, expecting it to be his, but the image inside made her catch her breath. It was a photo of her ... well, a photo that had been doctored to give her short, bright red hair, glasses and a large dose of make-up she wouldn't want to be seen dead in.

'How?' she asked.

'I have my sources. All you need to do is make yourself look like that,' he indicated her new passport photo, 'and you're good to go. Your new pseudonym is Eliza Sterling. I think the name fits the new you, don't you think?'

Jessica stared at the passport photo again. 'What about yours?' She knew that the UK Government had confiscated his travel documents, as the U.S. authorities had hers.

Martin withdrew some more paperwork and waggled it in front of her. 'I have a flight and train booked in our new names. Your Eurostar ticket is in that envelope. You leave next week and I fly out to Berlin tomorrow.'

Jessica didn't know what to say. She knew he wouldn't rest until he'd found out what happened to his brother, but she had other priorities to think about.

'I'm going with or without you,' Martin told her as he finally realised her zeal for the plan didn't match his own.

'Martin,' Jessica said, her voice heavy with a mixture of emotions, 'I want the GMRC to answer for their crimes as much as you, but I just can't leave my family, not now.'

'I thought you of all people would want to take this further.' His smile was bitter. 'Obviously I was wrong.' Martin got up, reclaimed the piece of paper with the address on it and made to leave.

Jessica grabbed his arm. 'Martin, wait!'

He looked down at her. 'For what?'

Again, Jessica couldn't find the words, an anguished expression her only answer.

Martin shrugged off her arm. 'Goodbye, Jessica,' he said and stalked away, leaving her alone in the pub once more.

CHAPTER FOUR

THE REST of that week Jessica fretted about not helping Martin track down his lead, but she knew she'd been right to turn him down. His motivations dwarfed her own and right now she needed to take stock of recent events and to nurse her mental wounds rather than make any rash decisions. It hadn't made her feel any less guilty, though; to let down a friend in need weighed heavily upon her, not to mention the frustration of passing up on the chance to expose the GMRC for what they were and to get some payback both for her and her colleagues. *Ex-colleagues now*, Jessica thought sadly as she made her way down the stairs of her London home.

It was Saturday evening and she'd just spent time reading a storybook to Victoria and Daniela. She'd then sung the prerequisite Purple Ducky song she'd made up especially for them. The two girls had giggled in sheer delight when Jessica had carried out the accompanying dance moves. Kissing them both goodnight, she'd switched off the light in the large shared room and then decided to rejoin Evan, who rested downstairs in the living room, watching the TV.

'Did they get you to do the dance?' Evan asked her as she settled down onto the sofa next to him.

She smiled fondly. 'They did.'

'I'll have to record you doing that someday, for posterity.'

'You'd better not.' She dug him in the ribs.

Evan looked across at her, perhaps gauging her mood. Leaping up, he grabbed her and pinned her down, an impish grin lighting up his eyes as he looked down from above.

'No!' she said. 'Don't, or I'll scream and wake the kids.'

His smile broadened. 'Ha ha, that old excuse won't wash with the tickle master!'

As usual she descended into a screeching, laughing mad thing, fending him off as he tickled her under the arms. Just as she felt like she couldn't take any more, she caught sight of the television in the melee of arms and legs.

'Evan stop!' she said trying to regain her breath as the shock of seeing her picture on TV subdued her laughter.

'No chance, I've started so I'll finish!'

In no mood for him to continue she pinched him hard until he let out a yelp of pain.

He rubbed his arm. 'What was that for?'

She pointed at the television. 'Shut up and look.'

The BBC news was on and in a slot sometimes presented by Jessica herself, a story about her was running. Picking up the remote control Jessica rewound the stream to watch it from the beginning.

'—a late breaking news story,' the presenter read from the autocue. Jessica knew the woman well, new blood from a rival channel and with the morals of an overripe dead frog. 'Controversy rocks the reputation of one of the BBC's recently departed presenters, Jessica Klein, tonight, as revelations about the disgraced news anchor, sacked this week for gross misconduct, hits the front pages of tomorrow's newspapers. Video footage of Ms Klein, forty-two, from London, has surfaced today appearing to show the mother of two receiving bundles of cash on three separate occasions from members of a right-wing, extremist group with a well-known anti GMRC agenda and ties to terrorist factions in the Middle East. A spokesperson for the group, known as Humanity 1, has denied ever having any contact with Ms Klein, who herself has refused to comment on the allegations at this time. The footage, however, which we are about to show you, seems to be a damning indictment in itself.'

Jessica watched, dumbfounded, as the promised video ran on screen. She watched herself, filmed from a concealed camera, taking possession of a plastic carrier bag from a well-known Humanity I activist. In the video Jessica then unfurled and withdrew wads of used notes tied together with elastic bands. She appeared to go through the process of counting the money. Two more similar videos were shown, filmed at the same location, this time with audio. Jessica could easily be heard conversing with the same activist, discussing how she would hijack the news channel. The last footage showed her receiving a typed piece of paper, some of which she read aloud. It was word for word what she had said on that fateful day outside the GMRC headquarters back in New York.

The screen switched back to the presenter. 'The BBC asked the GMRC if they would like to comment on this shocking turn of events and in the last few minutes they have released the following statement.'

The broadcast greyed out before a white rectangle appeared containing a short paragraph of text, which read:

"It is not GMRC policy to comment on unsubstantiated evidence. The video footage and supporting documentation we have received from a third party has been passed to our legal department. If it is deemed that there is a case to answer, we will pursue our interests vigorously through the courts."

— GMRC Public Relations Department

'If this wasn't bad enough,' the newsreader continued, reappearing, 'another leaked film, this time from within the BBC itself, has shed further light on the volatility of Jessica Klein's darker side. Viewers are advised the following content contains bad language unsuitable for younger viewers.'

Jessica, still in shock, now saw herself on television once more. This time she stood in a doorway, the footage shot from inside the room where she had her disciplinary hearing earlier that week.

'—well you know what you can do with your job!' Jessica shouted at the panel. 'You can stick it up your fucking arses you pathetic, snivelling wretches. I hope you and the GMRC are happy with this—'

Jessica sank down onto the sofa as more footage of her swearing and ranting during the meeting was played on screen. She suddenly realised that the hearing had been designed to goad her into losing her cool for the specific purpose of using it against her later – and she'd fallen for it, hook, line and most definitely sinker.

Evan looked to Jessica when the news story finished 'How did they film you taking that money?'

'They must have fabricated it somehow,' she said, massaging her tired eyes. 'I didn't realise they had the capability to create something that realistic. It looked perfect, totally authentic; if I didn't know I hadn't done it, I'd believe it myself.'

'I take it that stuff in the office was real, though?'

She nodded. 'It seems the GMRC wasn't content with making us lose our jobs, they're out to destroy me.'

The next day soon arrived and so did a mass of news crews and camera vans outside Jessica and Evan's home. Their telephones rang off the hook as journalists hunted for the elusive headline quote from the former BBC employee now in the eye of a media feeding frenzy. Setting foot outside their Kensington home with this circus of vultures parked on their doorstep was ill-advised and Jessica and Evan decided to keep the girls out of school until everything had calmed down.

This latest development in the fallout from Jessica's verbal assault on the GMRC had infuriated Evan. Understandably he was angry at the loss of their jobs, but he had resolved not to let it affect them detrimentally, holding onto the fact that everything would blow over and they could get new work somewhere else. Now, however, they were attacking his wife in ways he could not protect her from. It also impacted on the children, and this was something that he just couldn't handle. When yet another opportunistic photographer sneaked into the back garden, he found Daniela on her way to feed the rabbits and, unsurprisingly, the little girl had screamed when she'd come face-to-face with the unexpected intruder. Evan had stormed outside and a physical altercation had ensued, resulting in one smashed camera and an aggravated scuffle that only made matters worse when the police were called by one of the neighbours.

The final straw came the following day when a letter arrived from the bank, which advised them that they would be foreclosing on the house due to missed mortgage payments. Jessica had been quick to ring them as they had already paid a substantial amount off over the years and only missed two recent repayments. Trying to reason with them, though, was akin to talking to a brick wall as her, and then Evan, were taken round and round in dizzying circles by various bank employees without resolving the situation. Evan had exploded when it became clear that the house was lost and there was nothing either of them could do about it. Jessica had argued with her husband before, but nothing on this scale and intensity.

The situation was compounded as Victoria and Daniela, unable to understand why their parents were at each other's throats, both sat crying their eyes out in their bedroom.

'This can't go on,' Evan told Jessica after they had calmed the children down. 'I'm going to take the girls to my parent's house. They can't be exposed to this toxic cauldron any longer. You can follow us when they're settled in and everything has calmed down again.'

'What? You're just going to up and leave me here, to deal with all this on my own?'

'I don't want to, but it's what's best for the kids that matters. If you came with us then the hounds outside our front door would soon follow.'

Jessica could see his logic and she didn't want the girls traumatised any more than he did, so she had relented and let them go. The separation had been difficult, considering the circumstances, and Victoria, being the youngest, had clung to Jessica, unwilling to let her mother go. Finally they had departed and Jessica was left alone in the big, depressingly quiet house.

Unsure what to do next, she wandered into the office after hearing an alarm sound on the computer. She logged onto her email account, more out of habit than any real need to see what was contained within. Two hundred and eighteen unread messages had filled the inbox in just two days of neglect. Deleting the obvious junk files and opportunistic messages from several amoral journalists, she whittled it down to fifty and then went through them one by one. Some were from friends offering their support while many were sent by old colleagues trying to get her to comment on her situation for an inside scoop. Some people had little shame in her profession, but to experience it like this gave her a different perspective on an industry that had previously been so good to her.

Disgusted by these underhand tactics, she shook her head in disbelief before hitting the delete button again. Carrying on through the inbox, three messages didn't appear to be related to current events; two of these were from Internet shopping firms providing information about her accounts and one was from her mobile network provider. She deleted the first two but the third kept displaying the following message:

Error: Unable to delete message.
Attached linked file contains active connection.

Frustrated, she accessed the email once again to see if she could delete it when it was open. This also failed; however, instead of getting an error message a separate white pane flashed up on the monitor. After a couple of seconds this window filled with black text resembling some kind of computer code. The text scrolled endlessly down the page until it stopped. A second window appeared, this time with a luminous green background and a white flashing cursor in the top left corner. Jessica stared at it before attempting a hard shutdown of the computer, which strangely failed to work. As she contemplated pulling out the power cord, worried she'd infected the computer with a virus, the cursor moved across the screen leaving behind it three words which made Jessica sit back down in her chair.

Are you alone? _

Wondering what to do, she watched the cursor move once more.

Jessica Klein.

I have bad news for you _

Without her touching anything, a photo materialised onto the screen. Jessica's hand went to her mouth and she let out a sound of despair and loss when she realised what she was seeing. The image showed a pavement next to a tarmac road, in the gutter lay the body of a man. His limbs rested at distorted angles and a trail of blood seeped out from underneath the torso to flow into a large pool. The dead man's eyes stared up to the sky, his face a mask of fear and pain. Jessica couldn't look away from the horrific photo of Martin, but she didn't have to as it soon disappeared. The cursor moved again.

You are in danger _

Jessica typed in a reply with shaky hands and hit return. *Who is this?*

. . .

I can give you answers Jessica Klein _

What answers?

Who killed your friend. Why they killed your friend _

Tell me now, she wrote. The cursor blinked on and off, unmoving for some moments, before the reply came.

GMRC Intelligence. To hide a secret _

What secret? Tell me now! she typed, as she lost patience with this mysterious digital intruder.

Take your train tomorrow. Meet @:
Philological Library
Freie Universität Berlin
Habelschwerdter Allee 45
14195 Berlin, Deutschland
3.14 _

As the message appeared her printer hummed to life and spewed out a piece of paper with the same address on it. Another message displayed soon after, a message that chilled Jessica to the bone.

. . .

You have been classified as a credible suicide risk, Jessica Klein. Easy to kill. Easy to explain. Get out of your house. NOW! _

The last message was too much for her to take and Jessica sprang out of her chair and yanked the computer's plug from the mains supply, sending the screen black, its threat nullified. Angry at herself for believing every word this anonymous person had fed her, she took to the kitchen for a glass of red to calm her nerves.

That night she slept fitfully, her mind struggling to deal with the day's events. Rising at three a.m., she went downstairs in her nightwear to get some cereal to eat, a routine she usually reverted to whenever she couldn't sleep.

Was the photo of Martin's dead body real? she asked herself for the umpteenth time. If the GMRC could recreate her in a video, a photograph would be relatively simple by comparison. Although why would the GMRC bother to infiltrate her computer when they had already discredited and all but destroyed her? She was metaphorically on her knees, no further threat, yet a multitude of nagging doubts remained. The hacker had provided the same address as she'd seen on the piece of paper Martin had shown her in the pub. And the fact that they *were* a hacker, matching the profession of Martin's contact in Germany, also spoke volumes as to their credibility.

Crunching down her cereal, the noise sounding loud in the surrounding quiet, Jessica eyed the train ticket Martin had bought for her. It lay conspicuously on the kitchen work surface, next to the printout produced by the hacker. *What if the hacker was right and the GMRC have deemed me a suicide risk, perfect for elimination? They could be coming for me right now ... surely not*, part of her scoffed at the idea. *With all those reporters outside, one of them would see someone breaking into the house – wouldn't they?* She glanced around the dark kitchen, and the hallway, which led to the staircase and front rooms.

Getting up, she turned on the light switch and went back upstairs and on up to the second floor of the town house. Jessica may have been petite and physically weak compared to most people, but she had never allowed it to make her feel vulnerable, not like she did right now. Retrieving a stick, she hooked open the attic door and hauled down the ladder. Climbing up, the aluminium rungs squeaked and rattled until she took her weight from them and onto the bare wooden floorboards of the third floor. Bending down, she felt in the dark for the light switch she knew was concealed off to one side. Locating it, she clicked it on and headed towards the far end, navigating through many years of dusty accumulated clutter.

Unearthing a large oak chest from beneath some old clothing, Jessica heaved up the creaking lid. A lingering smell of old leather and musty books settled in the air around her. Moving aside some dusty volumes, she located a heavy metallic box. Shifting her body to the right, in order to remove the cast of her shadow, she spun the numbered dial located on the top of the small safe back and forth to enter a six digit combination. The latch sprang up with an audible click and she opened the lid to reveal a soft, partially oiled, light-brown cloth. Moving it to one side exposed a present her father had bought her for her twenty-first birthday; a stainless steel Smith and Wesson Model 60LS.

Taking it out of its moulded insert, she flicked open the cylinder to make sure it wasn't loaded. Placing the gun back down, she took a key out of the gun safe and then opened another box, which had been well concealed behind a hidden compartment in the trunk. Inside rested a cardboard box stamped with *.357 Magnum High Velocity Ammunition*. Jessica opened it and slid out the bullets, the shiny metal casings held vertically in a plastic tray. Picking the gun back up by its wooden grip she loaded the rounds into each of the five chambers and then double checked the safety was on.

Her father had been in the British military all his working life and he'd taken a young Jessica with him when he went to the shooting range, which he did every weekend when he was stationed at home. She'd become quite proficient with the weapon and at this point in time appreciated feeling its snug weight in her grasp once more.

Sleep came surprisingly quickly now that she felt safer, although she had left the lights on throughout the house to make any would-be assailants less sure of themselves if, heaven forbid, they did come-a-knocking.

In the morning Jessica woke with the heavy loaded gun resting underneath the palm of her right hand. She sighed and rolled her eyes heavenward. Is this what it had come to? If her father had taught her anything, it was not to let anyone push her around, regardless of their position. This advice had stood her in good stead for the previous forty-two years of her life, so why had she stopped paying heed to it now? So the GMRC were the biggest and most powerful organisation anyone could come up against. *So what?* she could hear her father say. *The bigger they come—*

Martin had gone to Germany and ended up dead, but she could well end up the same way if she stayed here. She was damned if she did and damned if she didn't. She had to wrest control of her life back, *and that is exactly what I'm going to do*, she decided, *starting right now*.

Five hours later Jessica had packed a case, left a letter for Evan, collected the train ticket, Berlin address, and passport papers, and left the house, the front door swinging shut behind her with purposeful finality. Fighting her way through the assembled massed ranks of the media, still camped on her doorstep, she reached the street and her parked silver Mercedes. Shouts and cries from the paparazzi wanting a comment fell on deaf ears, the flashing of cameras dazzling her as she struggled into the confines of her car. Glad she'd put on her dark glasses, she was amazed the cameras hadn't sparked some kind of epileptic fit as there were so many going off. *I don't know how these big celebrities deal with this on a regular basis*, she thought, securing her documents in the glove compartment and starting the car.

Revving the engine on her diesel driven classic, she edged her way past the people and roared off down the street, the twin turbos whining as they kicked into gear. As Jessica raced through the West London streets she felt free and empowered and back in control. Next stop Berlin.

CHAPTER FIVE

THE HEAT from the big yellow sun felt hot on her skin, pleasant and comforting. Springing up from the dry, cracked earth, bright orange flowers with tall, green, luscious shoots swayed in the soft breeze. They were nearly as tall as her! She bent and sniffed inside the cup of petals; a wondrous smell flooded through her senses. Leaning back up, she jumped in surprise, letting out a small yelp when a huge, bright red and orange butterfly flitted past her face. It moved funny, jerky like a puppet on a string, but coupled with an effortless ease. Leaping high, she attempted to catch it in her small hands, but on inspection only her empty palms were revealed. It had been too quick for her.

Searching around, she spotted her quarry once more, skimming over the surface of the lawn. Chasing it across the dry, mown grass, she couldn't help but giggle as every time she closed in on her prey it escaped her clutches. With the butterfly always just out of reach, she danced and hopped along behind the flying beauty until her foot caught on something and she fell onto a hard, flat surface. Pain exploded within her and she couldn't help but cry.

'Sarah, come here, little one,' her mother's voice called out, the sound seeking to make itself heard through the agony of the fall.

Sarah clambered to her feet, her hands pressed onto her left leg as tears streamed down her face and racking sobs escaped her mouth. Each step made the pain seem worse, but at last she made the long walk down the garden to be embraced in her mum's arms.

'Have you hurt your knee?'

Sarah nodded mutely, the shock lessening.

'You have? Oh no,' her mother said in deep concern. 'Do you want me to kiss it better for you?'

Sarah very much wanted it better so she nodded again as she wiped the tears away from her chubby cheeks. The kiss helped and then she was lifted into the air and she found herself sitting on her mum's lap. Cuddling into her warm body, Sarah felt safe and enclosed, away from the sharp, hard world she had just experienced. The sound of her mother's slow, rhythmic heartbeat became louder to her ears, the gentle thump, thump, thump morphing into an all-encompassing, hypnotic embrace.

Sarah felt herself drifting off to sleep and the heat of the sun increased on her skin, hotter and hotter it got, accompanied by a roaring noise that exuded a thick, dense smoke. Shouting and other noises sought to overwhelm her senses as she felt her lungs choke with the pervasive black gases that sprang from the fire that now blazed around her. A piercing scream punctuated the night sky, an awful sound entwined with pain and terror. Sarah looked on as her mother's hair caught alight and her skin blistered and burned. Screaming out as loud as she could, Sarah sat bolt upright in her bed, feeling traumatised and confused, her breathing shallow.

Sarah Morgan placed her hands over her face, which felt cold and sweaty. Her mind cleared, but the emotions evoked by the horrific dream lingered. She sank back onto her bedroll as the cruel reality of her situation re-asserted itself in her now fully conscious psyche. A single powerful, bright LED lamp hung suspended high above the bed, shedding its crisp light over the confined space. The small area, spartan, cold and unwelcoming, smelled of bleach, and a musty neglect, which hung in the stale air. Rough linen clung to the small bed on which Sarah lay and harsh grey tiles lined the floor and walls. A formidable steel door dominated the room, a small slit in its centre the only means of access to the outside world.

Sitting back up on the cot, Sarah pulled her knees up to her body to keep warm. The ill-fitting bright orange jumpsuit she'd been forced to endure itched and scratched at her skin as she moved. She felt tired, exhausted, but couldn't sleep now, not after that dream. The dazzling light on the ceiling also didn't assist her condition. She'd been imprisoned for weeks, perhaps months now, living on rationed food and water. She must have lost quite a few pounds during her captivity and her stomach had definitely shrunk in size during that time.

Her body clock told her it was nearly time again – time for more questions – time for the same answers. She wondered when they would stop these endless interrogations and mental mind games. She had told them everything she knew – well, almost everything. She wasn't prepared to let them have it all their own way; it was one of the only things left that was hers to control and she wouldn't give it up lightly.

Sarah's head came up when a muffled bell sounded outside of her cell. Footsteps followed and a key was inserted into the lock and turned, the clank and click of metal on metal echoing in the enclosed space. The door slid to one side in one fluid motion, accompanied by a grinding noise and a heavy boom as it hit the end of its rails.

'Morgan. Let's go!'

Sarah glared at her guard, a burly, shaven-headed U.S. marine dressed in loose-fitting combats and black, steel toecapped boots.

She didn't move.

'Don't make me come in there again, Morgan,' he said in warning.

Sarah sighed, swept her unkempt blonde hair back, unfurled her long legs and dropped to the floor, her thin plimsolls squeaking on the shiny surface. Once she'd emerged the guard slammed the door shut and relocked it. Stowing the bunch of keys on his belt, he moved past her, leading the way down a passage and up a flight of stairs she knew only too well. A left and right followed by another left and they were entering a large room, empty except for a plain table and two functional chairs.

Sarah pulled out one of the seats and sat down on it while the guard left to stand outside the door. It wasn't long until her tormentor, one Sergeant Major Collins, appeared and sat down opposite her. He had with him the same red folder he always had and opened it the same way he always did, arranging it just so on the desk and then placing a white plastic pen alongside.

'So,' he said in his sharp cutting voice, which accentuated his American accent, 'how did you access this facility?'

'By magic,' Sarah replied almost smiling at her own insolence.

Collins slammed his hand down on the table with a loud BANG, making Sarah jump. 'Do not fuck with me, girl,' he said, eyeballing her, 'or things will go badly for you. You think what you've experienced so far has been hard, then think again. I can make your life unbearable in so many ways you wouldn't believe. I'd have you begging for me to end your miserable existence in less than twenty-four hours if I wanted to, so stop fucking me about and start talking!'

Sarah looked at the man and his flat, dead eyes told her he wasn't messing about. She dreaded to think what he was referring to and as she didn't want to find out, she played along, as usual. 'We found this place, this *facility*, through tunnels and an entrance we located on the surface,' she said, her tone sullen.

'Where on the surface?'

'Tancama.'

The sergeant major noted something down in his red folder. 'And where exactly is that?'

'In the mountains in Mexico.'

Collins looked up and his eyes flashed a warning.

'East of a small town called Jalpan de Serra,' Sarah said, knowing full well he knew the answer.

'And this Tancama, it's an old ruin?'

'Yes, it's an archaeological site built over a thousand years ago.'

'You're English, why were you in Mexico?'

Sarah really wanted to say *on holiday* but knew she shouldn't push the man; he wasn't right in the head. She also wanted to point out to him he was an American and ask him why he was in Mexico, or should that be beneath Mexico; sadly, though, she decided on a non-antagonistic answer. 'We were exploring the site; we're archaeologists, that's what we do.'

'This entrance,' he said, going back to her first answer, 'how did you find it?'

'From a map.'

He took an A4 photo from the folder and put it in front of her. It was a picture of a rectangular metallic artefact with Mayan hieroglyphs on it, a single line intersecting them.

'This map?'

'Yes.'

'And where did you find it?'

'As I've told you before, we dug it up in the Mayan ruins of Copán in Honduras.'

'How did you know it was there?'

'Using a scanner, I found it buried in one of the stone stelae.'

'Stelae?'

She sighed. 'Sculpted stone monuments, or statues, you could call them.'

It was quite true; the metallic map had been a wonderful find, although Sarah had to deface a priceless Mayan statue to extract it. On a sanctioned dig, breaching the integrity of the site in such a way would have been a big no-no, but as it was they were there without authorisation and Sarah had certain motivating factors which had driven her into desecrating the world heritage site.

Collins stood up and picked up the folder, turning over the pages as he read through it. 'Have you found other ancient artefacts in the past?'

'Many,' she said.

He considered her for a moment. 'Have you ever discovered bones and artefacts which you thought were much older than human civilisation?' he said, rephrasing the question.

'Yes.'

'How many?'

'A handful.'

'Where?'

'In Turkey, near Mount Ararat.'

'And where are those now?'

'They were stolen from us.'

'By whom?'

'I don't know who.'

'But you suspect someone, an organisation?

'The Catholic Church, but now you lot are on the scene I'm beginning to wonder.'

Collins ignored her quip. 'Have you found anything anywhere else?'

'A few locations,' she said evasively.

'Recently?' he added, his face growing angry again.

'South Africa.'

'What did you find there?'

'More bones and a canister.'

'Were these bones human?'

'No.'

'What were they?'

'I think they're from a human ancestor or cousin who evolved on the planet over half a million years ago.'

'And you refer to these human ancestors as—' Collins said, pausing as he looked in the folder once more, 'Homo gigantis, correct?'

Sarah nodded. It was the most appropriate scientific Latin name and one generally agreed upon by those who believed in its existence. She liked it; it rolled off the tongue and fitted in well with the names of humanity's other close relatives, Homo erectus, Homo floresiensis and Homo neanderthalensis.

'And what was in the canister?' the U.S. soldier asked her.

'A parchment.'

He glared at her.

'A map on a parchment,' she conceded.

He took out a piece of light brownish paper and laid it in front of her.

She picked it up, feeling its odd texture and noting the small circle indented into it at the top. It was also completely blank.

Collins' eyes narrowed. 'And where is that map now?'

'I don't know. It was on here,' she told him, knowing full well that you had to access the images on it using her pentagonal pendant; something else they had confiscated from her.

The pendant in question was similar to another one Sarah had found over a year ago, buried deep in the ground amongst bone fragments and what turned out to be hair. Carbon dating had revealed the bone and hair to be five hundred thousand years old, raising the tantalising question that the pendant had been forged in the same era. Since humans, as they are known today, hadn't even evolved at that point in time, it posed the question, who made it? The answer soon became apparent: Homo gigantis, a large ancient human ancestor who may have been as advanced, if not more advanced, as modern humans themselves.

The second pendant, which activated the map, Sarah had found in a curious canister she'd dug up on the Turkish plains during a quest that had ultimately led to her current location. Amazingly, this small artefact had also enabled Sarah to operate some kind of lift transportation device that had brought her deep underground. Of course she wasn't about to disclose any of these facts to Collins and it was the one thing she'd been holding onto. She knew if the U.S. military found out about the pendant and its amazing properties she would definitely never see it again and she couldn't allow that to happen for anything. She had made the discovery and she was damn well going to keep it. At least that was the plan.

'I think it runs on some kind of battery,' Sarah continued by way of explaining the oddity of the disappearing map. 'It's like digital paper and the power source has run dry.'

'That's what your friends keep telling me.' Collins looked frustrated at receiving corroborating information which was of no use to him.

The friends he referred to, who'd accompanied her on her journey of discovery, included her best friend Trish from London, whom she'd known since university, and Jason, another archaeologist she'd met on a dig site and whom she'd also grown close to over the years. After their capture in this – for want of a better word, underground city – and prior to their separation, the three friends had benefited from some precious moments alone. Sarah had told them both not to disclose anything about the pendant and its secrets and how they'd managed to activate the ancient device that had brought them there. They'd also devised a basic cover story to cover their tracks.

Apparently Jason and Trish had stuck out as stubbornly as she had, apart from a few slip ups like letting Collins know the parchment was capable of displaying moving images. However, this new knowledge about her friends, to know they were still nearby and on her side, helped to strengthen her flagging resolve. Collins was slipping, it seemed; this was the first titbit of information he'd relinquished in all the many hours she'd had the misfortune of spending with him.

Collins sat down again and pondered his precious red folder. 'These tunnels that brought you from the surface,' he began, 'how far from this facility did they bring you out?'

And there it was – the question that caused Sarah the most problems. Since she had used the ancient device to descend into the depths of the Earth, there weren't any actual tunnels to speak of. Therefore the exit, by simple deduction, was also non-existent. The issue came when Collins and his military colleagues wanted to know where, *exactly*, Sarah and her two companions had been able to infiltrate this most secret of compounds.

'A few miles away from here,' Sarah said.

'Elaborate,' Collins demanded, his eyes searching her face, perhaps for the telltale signs that she might be lying to him.

'When we emerged from the tunnels we found ourselves on a narrow path next to a high cliff with a deep drop on the other side.'

'And where did you go from there?'

'We scaled a few rock faces, travelled underneath a couple of massive carved archways and then passed through what appeared to be a long dead forest. Which is weird, as we're deep underground, so how did that happen?'

'And then what?' he said, ignoring her question.

'And we saw a light. I saw a light, and we followed it to here. That's when your men chucked a stun grenade at us, arrested us and stuck us in here.'

Collins' brow furrowed further as he frowned down at his folder. He rubbed his temples with his hands. In something resembling agitation, he flicked through the pages until he stopped, and then amazingly closed it altogether. 'I want to know exactly where these tunnels came out, do you hear me? Exactly!'

'I don't know exactly, it was pitch-black and we only had small torches with us.'

'Try harder,' he said, an odd desperation to his tone accompanied by a curious twitch in his right eye.

'I can't tell you what I don't know,' Sarah replied, her tone placating, her hands held open and an apologetic half-smile playing across her lips.

The sergeant major banged the metal table once more. 'UNACCEPTABLE!'

Before Sarah knew what was happening he'd risen up, hurled the desk to one side and grabbed her by the throat. Sarah may have been nearly six foot tall and athletic, but Collins, although slightly shorter, was powerfully built and she found herself up against the wall while he slowly crushed her windpipe. Fighting for breath, she felt herself blacking out as she fought to prise his vice-like grip from her throat. With her vision fading to a blur, she caught sight of the guard sprinting into the room. Grabbing Collins around his neck, he grappled him to the floor as two more soldiers came running in from the corridor to subdue the out of control interrogator.

Sarah dropped to her knees coughing and gasping for air. Her lungs and face burned with heat and it took some time to get her breath back. By then the sergeant major had vacated the room, whether by force or of his own volition Sarah hadn't seen. As long as he was no longer around, that was good enough for her.

Instead of receiving any kind of medical attention or even just an apology, Sarah was left on her own in the room for another hour. As she sat on her chair facing the now empty seat across from her, the utilitarian clock on the wall ticking away time, a noise from behind made her turn round. A man stood in the doorway. This person was new to her and he also wasn't a soldier; at least he wore a suit and not military issue. He also had a red folder; in fact it was the same one Collins so cherished. The new arrival, however, didn't seem to hold the brightly coloured file in the same reverence as, walking round to stand in front of her, he plonked it down in the middle of the table.

'Look,' Sarah said, rubbing her bruised throat protectively, 'I've answered your questions for today; just put me back in my cell and leave me be.'

The man, who had also brought with him a cup of gloriously sweet-smelling tea, placed the steaming mug in front of her. Sarah looked at him questioningly.

'Go ahead,' he told her with a smile. 'It's fresh.'

A smile, what a simple thing, you didn't realise how much emotion such a simple gesture could provide when you had been starved of it for so long. Sarah didn't need to be told twice; compared to endless water and cold food, tea was a treat not to be passed up. Burning her lips, she sipped the drink, relishing its taste.

'So it says here—' the man said as he idly perused the folder on the desk while standing up, 'you're an archaeological anthropologist.'

Sarah nodded at the man, not sure how to take this new softly-softly approach.

'You're a published academic,' he continued, 'and have a lot of hours in the field from dig sites all around the world, although your career seems to have stalled after some outlandish claims regarding an extinct human relative you call Homo gigantis.'

'That's right,' she said, her expression noncommittal.

'And you've circulated on the outskirts of your chosen field's community ever since?'

Sarah nodded again.

'I see,' the man said. 'So, what with the discovery of your most recent artefacts and the revelation of this subterranean facility, it appears your theories have actually – in fact – been proved correct.'

Sarah had been looking down while picking at one of her fingernails, but on hearing this, her head shot up. 'They are? I mean you acknowledge that they are?'

He smiled. 'Of course.'

Sarah looked at him in stunned amazement. 'Are you willing to testify to that fact?'

The man chuckled. 'They told me you were a live one,' he said, then his expression grew serious; 'but I'm afraid my answer is no. However, it appears that my military colleagues have decided you're not to be classed as a direct threat to this base or its objectives – their words, not mine – and as such you are to be discharged from this detention centre with immediate effect.'

Sarah's hopes soared. 'I'm free to go?'

'I wouldn't go as far to say "free".' He put a small object on the table in front of her.

'What's that?' she said, her eyes wary.

'*That* is a transmitter which will monitor and track your movements within this base for the duration of your stay, which I'm afraid is going to be quite a long time.'

Her hopes turned painfully inward. 'How long?'

'There's no easy way to say this,' he told her with an apologetic smile, 'for the rest of your life.'

'What?! You can't do this, I have rights!'

'Unfortunately, you actually don't. This is a secure operation and you have breached its security, and as such you are now trespassing on United States territory, making you an illegal alien. You have no rights, I'm afraid.'

Sarah's heart was pumping. She got up and strode about the room, her tea long forgotten. She stopped pacing and looked at the man across from her. 'And if I refuse?'

'Unadvisable. You've already experienced the pleasures of the only alternative and I can imagine they're not nice or particularly spacious.'

Sarah gave a hopeless sigh and slumped down into her chair once more.

'Look, it's not as bad as you think,' he told her with annoying optimism. 'There are many benefits to living down here. Zero crime – well, nearly zero. No dust cloud from the meteorite strike, we still have sunlight down here, albeit artificial. There's even a simulation for the moon and its lunar cycle. There's always good food and intelligent conversation, depending on your sector, and you're protected from all manner of nasties down here. If it makes you feel any better, the twenty million or so people in this subterranean base are all here for life, we signed over our freedom to participate in this project.'

Sarah didn't care what this man had done, or anyone else for that matter, she couldn't remain a prisoner underground for the rest of her life.

The man put a comforting hand on her shoulder. 'Look,' he continued in a conciliatory tone, 'the majority of people here are civilians. Wait until you're cleaned up and well fed, and have had a good night's sleep; things will seem better in the morning, trust me.'

The man slipped the tracking bracelet onto Sarah's wrist; she didn't resist. She then let herself be led out the door and down into a long corridor she didn't recognise. They passed through some security gates – the military guards waving them past – and finally emerged from a large, low-slung building. Above, a dazzling blue sky extended into the distance and an indistinct sun sent down its rays to warm her upturned face. Sarah savoured the simulated scene created by the dome the man had alluded to and she herself had glimpsed on entering the base they called ... USSB Sanctuary.

CHAPTER SIX

THE NEXT DAY Sarah woke late, her soft new bed a glorious luxury compared to her previous digs. Arching her back and then scrunching up her body again, she snuggled back down under the duvet cover and – then she felt it, the tracking device attached to her wrist. The previous day's memories came flooding back to her and she groaned and turned over, splaying out like a star on the bed. Realising you're trapped in some government-run science project for the rest of your life is something to sober up anyone's morning. Sighing, she flung off the cover, sat up and rubbed her face to life. Dropping her feet to the floor, she got out of bed, enjoying the warmth of the room and the feel of the carpet on the soles of her feet as the fibres pushed up between her toes.

After being released from custody Sarah had been allocated an apartment; apparently homelessness in Sanctuary was non-existent. The civilian man, Andrew – who had rescued her from the prison – had chattered away as he'd led her through various administrative departments, going through the process of enrolling her into the relevant databases and systems of the military controlled base. Eventually she had been escorted to her new home and, by then exhausted, she'd had little time or inclination to take in her new surroundings.

Now that she was feeling refreshed, however, she was keen to look around, locate Trish and Jason, and then plan their escape.

Getting up, she found new clothes laid out regimentally in a chest of drawers nestled in the corner of the room. Taking out some white underwear from the top drawer, she chose a crisp, yet tight-fitting short-sleeved white T-shirt and a pair of grey jogging bottoms from the middle drawer. As she sat on the edge of her bed putting on her clothes, she glanced around. The décor was well done yet a little gaudy for her taste. Red swirling patterns intersected with silver grids crisscrossed the walls and flooring, blending perpendiculars in a simple yet pleasing way. Curious to see the view from the building Sarah, still half clothed, crossed to the window and touched a green button sunk into a panel on the glass. The blinds outside rolled up into the ceiling, the mechanism producing a deep whirring noise, to reveal an elevated pathway with lots of people walking along it, some of whom were now staring at her and smiling. Looking down Sarah realised her top half was still bare! Wrapping her arms around herself she whacked the red button with her elbow to bring the blind back down again.

'Bloody Ada,' she cursed, 'who puts a bedroom next to a busy public footpath?' Going back to the bed she put on her bra and top. Now moving into the kitchen-cum-diner, she poured herself a glass of orange juice and swigged it down, letting out a satisfying gasp once she'd drained it. After refilling the glass she drank more slowly, savouring the taste. In a cupboard she found an unwrapped fresh loaf of crusty bread and a new block of cheese. Cutting and buttering four slices and breaking off a hunk of Cheddar, she munched down on the veritable feast with a voracious vigour, washing it all down with some more juice. Wiping the back of her arm across her mouth, she stretched her arms up high, her fingertips brushing the opaque ceiling. It felt good to have a full stomach for once, especially one off the back of a good night's sleep.

Looking around as she further inspected her new abode Sarah noticed some shrink-wrapped training shoes sitting by the front door. Cutting them loose, she slipped them on and did the customary new shoe dance as she tested them out, although she forewent checking the position of the big toe, she wasn't buying the damn things after all. Satisfied at their soft cushiony feel, she noticed a white envelope stuck to the door, just above the handle. On the front in faint pencil and in capital letters, her first name had been scrawled. Plucking it off, she prised open the unstuck flap which had been tucked inside and with a rustle of paper she extracted a folded sheet. Opening it up, it read:

Sarah

I trust your new accommodation is to your liking. It's not the largest of spaces but it should be better than you've been used to of late. I can only apologise for the way you have been treated during your stay at Sanctuary so far; however, I can assure you the civilian contingent at this base will prove a lot more welcoming.

You have by now seen your multifunction card. This is your life; make sure you look after it as it will ensure you can pay for essentials and negotiate the city and the various sectors available to your clearance level, which sadly is very low. Due to your qualifications I have managed to secure you a position as an archivist at the Smithsonian Institution. While this position will be a waste of your talents, it was the best one I could get for you that the military were happy to sign off on. You'll notice your photograph has not been engraved onto the card; this will have to be done when you turn up for your first day of work, which will be tomorrow. Make sure you're not late – you start at eight a.m. sharp. A map of how to get there can be found on the wallscreen in your living room.

Pausing in the middle of the letter, Sarah looked in the envelope again to see a credit card sized shape nestling at the bottom. Taking it out, she noted it felt metallic, appeared very durable, and was quite dense and heavy for its size. On one side it had an emblem embossed into the surface and the other contained her details.

She continued reading the letter:

Before you start to explore your new surroundings you will need to watch the induction video that all new residents to USSB Sanctuary are required to sit through. To access the presentation simply swipe your card over the data induction panel at the side of the wallscreen in your quarters and you will be shown a simple menu enabling you to access it. All screens are equipped with built in face recognition cameras so the software can ascertain if you have watched the full film. If it decides you haven't watched the presentation properly, your multifunction card will not have its basic restrictions lifted. This will prevent you from accessing even the most fundamental functions on the card, such as acquiring food, using public transport and accessing the designated sector areas covered by your Level 1 Beta clearance.

As I told you yesterday, the military don't want you to know the whereabouts of your two friends, who were relocated into other parts of the city a few days ago. To me this seems rather pointless, as you will be able to look them up easily enough once you have unlocked the Resident Database on your wallscreen after watching the Induction Video. Oops, did I just say that? Silly me.

Once again, welcome to Sanctuary, and I wish you well with your future endeavours here. If you have any problems let me know and I'll be more than happy to help. Good luck!

Sincerely

Andrew Melanie

Civilian Affairs Officer

Well, that makes life easier, she thought with some relief; finding Trish and Jason was going to be the first thing on her to do list and that had now become a lot easier. Sarah looked at the card again and then walked over to the wallscreen which made up one side of a small living area. Noting the panel Andrew had described in the letter, she ran the multifunction card over it. The eight foot high video wall sprang to life, accompanied by a simple yet elegant introductory music sample which faded to silence. In the centre of the screen a three dimensional rendering of the USSB Sanctuary logo rotated, glinting and reflecting an unseen light source from its glossy surface. On the right hand side a segregated touchscreen option list was revealed. Each selection appeared as an individual, glossy blue button with accompanying silver text. The list of options available was as follows:

INDUCTION VIDEO >

CIVILIAN RESOURCES >

INFORMATION >

EMERGENCY >

Sarah tapped *Induction Video* and the button expanded and transposed onto the main screen. Taking this as her cue to take a seat, she moved over to a comfortable, yet small, pale blue sofa and settled in for the show. A swirling chrome graphic swooped across a bright, white background and then dissolved into a large GMRC logo, which in turn faded away, disappearing to leave behind the following text in bold black letters:

This induction video was produced by USSB Sanctuary's Public

Relations Department in conjunction with the GMRC Directorate's Office and on behalf of the United States Subterranean Program.

The text disappeared to be replaced by an image of a slim, congenial woman dressed in a simple, grey uniform. 'Hello and welcome,' she said. 'This induction video will introduce to you United States Subterranean Base Sanctuary, also referred to as USSB Sanctuary. This large scale project was instigated, designed and constructed by divisions within the GMRC and United States Subterranean Programmes.

'As a previous resident of one of the GMRC's other United States Subterranean Bases, you will be aware of the classified nature of facilities such as this. However, while the existence of these other bases is undisclosed to the general populace, and even to the majority of the U.S. Government, Sanctuary operates at an even higher level of secrecy. Little about this base is known even to some of the most high-ranking GMRC officials, and the handful that are aware of what goes on here are, first and foremost, United States citizens and are beholden to the Espionage Act of 1917.

'Unlike the other underground facilities operated by the GMRC throughout the world, Sanctuary, while retaining some minor GMRC civilian oversight, is purely a U.S. military run installation. All residents within this base, military and civilian alike, will have previously been stationed in one of the other nine United States Subterranean Bases. As you may have already noticed when you made your way into the base, Sanctuary is rather unusual in many ways when compared to its siblings.

'In order to provide you, our new residents, with a greater understanding of Sanctuary, who better to explain than the lead designer of USSB Sanctuary and Director General of the GMRC Subterranean Programme himself, the esteemed Professor Steiner.'

The screen switched scenes to a small silver-haired man with a neat, bushy beard, glasses, an open face and sharp, intelligent eyes. He stood, with his hands loosely clasped together, in a well-lit studio with a large wall display on his left hand side. Like the woman before him he wore a simple, grey uniform, but his cuffs and epaulettes were adorned with a golden weave similar to dress uniforms worn by many military leaders the world over.

'Firstly, I bid you a warm welcome to USSB Sanctuary,' the man said, his voice powerful and his American accent soft. 'This facility, the jewel in the crown of the United States Subterranean Programme, has been many years in the making and still has many years ahead of it for expansion.

'The predicted arrival of the asteroid 2011 AG5 may have precipitated the worldwide effort to create sustainable liveable habitats below ground, but Sanctuary's scope goes much further than being just a bolthole. It is a long-term project utilising humanity's finest technologies, brightest minds and most valuable resources to produce something truly remarkable – a virtual guarantee of continued human existence on Earth, regardless of any catastrophic events that may occur on the surface.

'It may seem strange to some that a member of the GMRC Directorate such as myself is privy to and supportive of a highly clandestine U.S. facility and quite assuredly the largest *black project* in our great nation's history. Conflicts of interest are unfortunately something I have had to address on occasion, but it has been possible to ensure my role in the GMRC has never been compromised as a result.

'So what makes this base so special? Let me show you,' he said, with a twinkle in his eye and a boyish grin tugging at the corners of his mouth. Facing the screen next to him he brought up a complex blue and green, three dimensional diagram. With a flick of his hand, this image moved from the screen and into the air next to him by means of a holographic projector.

'This is a detailed schematic of USSB Sanctuary,' the professor said, indicating the image with a small gesture of one hand. 'Like all our underground bases, this USSB operates on multiple levels. However, Sanctuary stands apart from the rest due to its sheer scale. Currently the USSB in which you now stand is home to twenty million people and a capacity for half as many again will be reached by 2055.

'Sanctuary also contains the world's largest man-made PSSBO, or partial self-sustaining biological organism, boasting forests, fields, rivers, lakes and even weather systems. The main dome which you can see in this projection encloses the top level of the base, and is crucial to maintaining the PSSBO. The dome is by far the largest suspended structure in existence and spans an incredible twenty miles in diameter. Not only can the dome produce weather events such as rainfall and wind, it also replicates the sun using sunlight wave technology similar to that found in some other bases.'

Sarah, transfixed by the video, shifted in her seat to make herself more comfortable.

'Now,' the professor continued on the screen, sounding quite excited, 'here comes the good bit.' With a flick of his hand he shrank down the image next to him and then using an expansion gesture he introduced an irregular-shaped transparent red graphic around the now much smaller depiction of the USSB. 'This—' he said, opening his arms wide in an expansive attempt to indicate the larger holographic area, 'is what is known as Sanctuary Proper. You see,' he continued as he looked back into the camera, 'USSB Sanctuary is actually contained within a much larger structure, Sanctuary Proper, or – confusingly – simply Sanctuary, from which the USSB takes its name.

'This massive structure, and it is indeed massive, runs for more than two hundred miles in length, one hundred miles in width and twenty miles in depth, although latest surveys are beginning to reveal that the depth may in fact be closer to thirty miles in most places. To give you a true idea of its size, the USSB can fit into Sanctuary Proper over one hundred and eighty-eight times. Or, to put it another way, it is estimated the surface area of Sanctuary Proper, due to its many, many levels, is anywhere from ten to thirty million square miles, or roughly as much as half the surface area of all the land mass on Earth.' Professor Steiner paused at this point to let that amazing information sink into his audience.

'So – I hear you ask – how did we construct something so vast, so quickly? The simple answer?'

'You didn't,' Sarah whispered.

'We didn't.' His expression turned mischievous. 'Whoa! Calm down now everyone,' he said to his invisible viewers. 'I know, I know. It poses the most tantalising of questions, does it not? If we didn't build it, then who did? Well,' he said, obviously enjoying his role of storyteller, 'let's go back in time a little – or a lot, depending on your point of view.'

Turning around he did away with the image of Sanctuary and with an upward lifting motion of his right hand he drew up a new graphic, seemingly from the floor. This one was a plain two dimensional affair with a single axis at the bottom entitled *Millions of years before present-day*.

The main heading of the simple graph read *Hominid Evolutionary Timeline*. Above the axis were multi-coloured blocks placed at different levels and intervals. Each block had the same height, but varying lengths, and each had its own unique text identifier next to it. 'So,' the professor continued as he looked at the graph and then back to the camera once more, 'here we have a Hominid evolutionary graph. For those of you who don't know what a Hominid is, take a quick look in the mirror. Humans,' he said, pointing to the last block on the far right, which expanded forwards from the image at his mere reference to its name, 'are the only living member of the Hominidae family. As you can see there are many extinct relatives of Homo sapiens, dating back almost seven million years. One of these extinct human cousins is well known, of course; the Neanderthal, also referred to as Homo neanderthalensis. Two more *celebrity* species, if you will, include Homo erectus and Homo floresiensis, nicknamed the Hobbit. Some, or maybe all, of you will be asking where I'm going with this,' the professor said with a small smile. 'Well, the graph you see before you is in fact incomplete. There is one member missing.'

Sarah watched, her heartbeat quickening, as, turning back to the image, the professor pointed to the hologram and another block materialised from the ether.

'Behold, Homo giganthropsis,' he said dramatically. 'Humanity's long-lost relative and one, as the name suggests, substantially larger than ourselves.'

The graph faded from view and a revolving anatomical image appeared, portraying a large man alongside a much smaller one. Sarah instantly recognised that the bigger figure was, in fact, what she knew as Homo gigantis, its facial structure matching the skull she and her team had unearthed on the Turkish plains. Next to this the smaller image was of a human, almost two thirds the height of its giant kin.

'Current projections,' the professor said, 'estimate giganthropsis lived between one point three million and as recently as twenty thousand years ago. Why they died out is still a mystery, as is much of their history. However, they left behind a legacy like no other, Sanctuary; built over nine hundred thousand years ago and left deserted for countless centuries, this immense structure was rediscovered by a special team formed by the sixth President of the United States, John Quincy Adams, in 1826.

'So, unlike our other long-dead ancestors, Homo giganthropsis was able to evolve into a species capable of advanced thought, a species with creativity and a thirst for knowledge that rivals our own. In many ways sapiens and giganthropsis are very alike. We both learned to shape our environment around us, we both created tools and technology, but perhaps most significantly, we both created civilisations. The fact that their civilisations lasted for hundreds of thousands of years is also why some of their technology and capabilities far exceeded that of our own. How they managed to build such a large and deep underground expanse containing chambers of phenomenal dimensions is still something we are yet to answer.

'So,' Professor Steiner said in an amused conversational tone, 'hands up those of you who thought aliens must have built Sanctuary. Don't worry,' he said as if he could see people putting their hands up, 'a surprising number of people jump to that conclusion. Unfortunately the answer is much more terrestrial, but I think you'll agree the reality is still out of this world.'

He paused and looked down as if gathering his thoughts. When his head came back up, his expression grew serious. 'That these two monumental discoveries, Sanctuary and giganthropsis, have been kept hidden from the rest of the world is highly controversial. Needless to say, the U.S. Government deemed the existence of Sanctuary to be of significant national importance, despite it being located beneath Mexican soil.'

Sarah listened as the professor went on to explain how Sanctuary was claimed by the United States. Apparently the U.S. purchased the site from the Mexican Government in the latter stages of the twentieth century for the purposes of building a subterranean base. The Mexicans, believing it to be just a large naturally occurring cave system, were willing to let the Americans build their base there under certain conditions; and to this day were none the wiser as to what lay beneath their feet.

The director general of the GMRC Subterranean Programme also explained how the existence of Homo giganthropsis was known to various factions in Europe perhaps as early as the eleventh century; although it was mainly the Vatican that erased any evidence of their existence in order to preserve the doctrine of the day.

'I knew it!' Sarah said out loud, unable to contain herself as her own theories were confirmed. This all but guaranteed that the Catholic Church had been behind the seizure of her gigantis finds back in Turkey and stolen artefacts in Oxford. It also meant that her theory on the circumstances of her mother's death became distressingly more concrete. A set of ancient maps Sarah had found many years earlier in Iran's Zagros Mountains had been destroyed in the same fire that ended her mum's life and Sarah knew in her heart that the fire had been deliberately started by those also responsible for taking her other evidence which exposed the existence of Homo gigantis; it fitted too perfectly to be coincidence. Those people would stop at nothing to protect their faith and if that included murder, so be it. History was testament to this disturbing reality and Sarah was, first and foremost, a student of the past.

As her hate for the Vatican churned within her mind like a dark, simmering volcano, the professor continued. 'The main reason gigan-thropsis left relatively little trace of their habitation on Earth was that they lived mostly underground. Their reasons for this have been speculated on for many years, but basically they are just that, specu-lative, and we may never know the real reason they chose to exist as they did.

'One thing is a certainty, however; due to Sanctuary's web of inter-locking levels, chambers, near infinite tunnel system and various areas of structural instability, the majority – currently ninety-eight per cent – of the construct is still uncharted. The fantasists among you, and I count myself as one, will wonder what fabulous treasures may rest tantalisingly close to hand. But before you pick up a shovel and head for the nearest tunnel in a gold rush-like fervour, be aware that exploring outside the USSB's boundaries is strictly forbidden. This is not only for your own safety, but also to preserve the fragility and integrity of virgin archaeological ground which is of significant scientific importance.

'So there it is,' Steiner said, pacing across the studio floor, each hand thought provokingly poised against the other like a priest in a ceremonial procession, while behind him the previously shown holo-grams in his presentation flowed past. 'The truth, one you didn't even know existed, is now yours to digest, reflect on and discuss to your heart's content. As you will be well aware, when you severed all ties to the surface, signed the relevant documents and committed to living out the rest of your days here in Sanctuary, the knowledge you now hold cannot be disclosed to anyone outside of this facility for national security reasons. In time, the communication isolation for residents will be lifted in a carefully staged progression when it is seen fit to reveal to the world Sanctuary's existence and true nature. Perhaps in the far future, passage into and out of Sanctuary will be granted to other USSBs, and then beyond. Until that time your sacri-fice and commitment to this long-term programme is appreciated beyond measure. Without you, Sanctuary could not succeed in its purpose to create a fully functioning self-sustaining subterranean ecosystem and civilisation; completely independent from the surface above.

'Your dedication to the cause will not go unrewarded, however,' Steiner said, as the lights in the studio brightened with natural light and the screens behind him lifted up into the ceiling. 'All residents are provided with accommodation, a career, and perhaps most crucially, a privileged purpose – to ensure the long term existence of our species.'

The professor was now walking alongside the camera as he headed to a large open balcony filled with clear blue skies and punctuated by small wisps of cloud. 'You are now living in what is effectively the 51st, and largest, state of the U.S. of A.' As he emerged from the building, the camera moved past him revealing a dazzling, beautiful city laid out below like a paradise on Earth, the edges of the great dome barely visible against the power of the artificial sunlight it generated above. Professor Steiner came back into shot. 'Welcome,' he said with a broad smile and a sweep of his arm, 'to Sanctuary. You are now, and forever will be, a Sancturian.'

CHAPTER SEVEN

SARAH'S HEAD swam with all the information that had just been rammed into it, along with the many implications it held; getting out of this place and back to the surface was going to be far harder than she'd imagined. Uncurling her tall frame from the cramped sofa, she paused the induction video and refreshed herself with a cup of coffee and a sumptuous chocolate-coated biscuit; the kitchen had been well stocked for her arrival, as the Civilian Affairs officer had promised her the day before.

Sitting back down, the packet of biscuits in tow, she hoped the wallscreen had voice command as she couldn't be bothered getting up again. 'Play,' she said. The pause icon disappeared and the film resumed. Feeling pleased with herself, she took out another Hobnob delight, enjoying its oaty taste while the woman who had begun the presentation came back on screen.

'Thank you, Professor Steiner,' she said with genuine warmth as she looked off to one side before turning back to the camera to continue the induction. 'For much more information about Sanctuary and Homo giganthropsis please visit the Smithsonian Institution's Museum of Sanctuary located on the Dome level in the New

Park district. A USSB Sanctuary rules, regulations and information handbook can be found in your residency, all of which is also available on the USSB's cloud system, accessible via your wallscreen's navigation panel.'

An image resembling Sarah's wallscreen displayed next to the woman. 'Now that you are up to speed on the main aspects of Sanctuary I can introduce you to the main areas of the base and advise you as to how to make the most of your experience here. This menu,' she said, indicating a navigation panel identical to one Sarah had used on her own wallscreen, 'will be key to you navigating the base, contacting friends, relatives and colleagues, and pretty much everything else you may want to do in your life as a Sancturian.'

Sarah watched the presenter outline the options on the screen one by one. Some of those she listed were only available to military personnel and the video skipped these sections automatically due to Sarah's clearance level and civilian status. From what Sarah could gather, Sancturians earned United States Credits by working, in her case, at the Smithsonian Institution. Each USC was equivalent to one U.S. dollar, which was simple enough to remember. Not that she had any plans to stick around long enough to bother with it all, but if she wanted to escape she first needed to know what was what.

The credits, as Andrew had indicated in his letter, would be held on her multifunction card, which would also be used to access public transport systems and confirm her identity to military personnel and civilian authorities throughout the base. The card could also be used to purchase goods and services. It all seemed a very comprehensive system and Sarah couldn't help but be impressed by the magnitude of it all, despite the surreality of her situation seeking to blur her perception like a hallucinatory drug.

The film eventually came to a close and a final message appeared on screen, accompanied by a female computer generated voice, which said: 'Multifunction card: restrictions lifted. USSB cloud access now fully activated.'

'Thanks,' Sarah said to it and moved to swipe her card across the induction panel, instantly bringing up a new extended navigation menu, as per the video. The available options were:

MAP SIMULATOR >
RESIDENT DATABASE >
SOCIAL DATABASE >
APPLICATIONS >
TV >
RETAIL >
SERVICES >
INFORMATION >
EMERGENCY >

Selecting *Resident Database* she typed in her friend's name, Trish Brook, and pressed enter. 'Trish Brook,' the computer confirmed, 'Sector eighteen residential district, level twenty-five, chamber five, route twenty, domicile one hundred and ninety two.'

Trish's photograph appeared on the main screen and Sarah felt tears welling at seeing her friend's face again. A code displayed below her image, *S18 L25 C5 R20 D192*, and then both shrank to the left hand side and a large three dimensional graphic of the base displayed with a red pulsating dot on it. Assuming this must be Trish's location, Sarah tapped the dot on the big screen and the view zoomed in, rotating in an anti-clockwise spiral as it did so. Sector eighteen appeared, highlighted in orange against the surrounding USSB, which was now greyed out. Another box sprang up next to the red dot detailing a suggested route to Trish's apartment from Sarah's own, but a warning message at the bottom of the information flashed on and off:

WARNING!

Travel to this sector is only available at weekends. To unlock restrictions a higher clearance level is required.

To view your restrictions please visit the INFORMATION portal.

Sarah cursed under her breath and looked at the navigation screen to see the bold letters *MONDAY* written large; five days to wait until she could travel to Trish's sector. A telephone icon also rested within the graphical box. She pressed it. This time an error message appeared:

ERROR!
No suitable credits available.

Letting out a growl of frustration, Sarah flicked through to the information section. After a few minutes she'd worked out she had credits for necessities only; once she'd been to work she'd have what they called *Active Credits*. The information portal also revealed a whole raft of restrictions on her movements: too many to remember, so many, in fact, that the list of what she could do would have been more helpful – *and a lot shorter, too*, she guessed. Knowing the outcome already, Sarah entered Jason's details. The same problems arose, although thankfully Jason's home looked to be only one sector over from Trish's.

Giving up on seeing or speaking to her friends that day, she decided to get outside and explore as far as she was able. A cleverly concealed wardrobe in her bedroom contained a smart grey uniform, like those worn by the two people in the induction video. Deciding this must be for special occasions, she plumped for the only other available garment, a black hooded sweater. Dragging it on, she arranged her long tresses inside it and then collected her multifunction card.

With some trepidation she opened the front door and stepped outside. She found herself at the top of a short flight of stairs, one she briefly remembered having climbed up the evening before in near darkness. Looking up she expected to see the great tower and a bright blue sky, but she recalled she was on a lower level of the base, having descended a massive lift system with Andrew and then been transported by a car to this apartment. Instead of the dome the chamber's smooth, dense, rock ceiling lurked some hundred feet above, lined with row upon row of powerful floodlights which tailed off into the distance in all directions. Buildings, some nearly reaching the lights themselves, surrounded the area, all seemingly residential, much like the apartment she'd just been given.

To her left the street ended abruptly in a large transparent wall. Through it she could see an amazing sight. A vast thoroughfare cut through the chamber, and not just on that level; as she approached the wall she could make out at least ten levels extending up towards the dome and ten more down towards the lower reaches of the base. Great lift systems, interconnected with a mass of complex road layouts, teemed with moving traffic, the muted roar and whine of fast moving machines penetrating the chamber where she stood looking out. Close to either side of the gigantic swathe, hewn out of the rock, wide walkways bustled with human activity as people went about their daily lives; as she'd learned to her cost earlier, the rear of Sarah's apartment backed onto one of them.

Looking left, and then right, she could make out a large, white, rectangular beam that hugged the rock walls. As she watched, on the far side and along such a beam, a blue and white train flew past at high speed. Below it another came in the other direction, but this one slowed, coming to rest in a futuristic glass-clad station, passengers exiting and boarding like on any major city network the world over. This place was something else.

Looking back at her front door, she made a note of the numbers, *S5 L15 C8 R12 D274*. How could she be expected to remember that? She recalled the card in her zipped trouser pocket; Andrew had shown her this last night. *Wake up Sarah!* she told herself. Swiping the MF Card over the entry pad caused a red light to replace the green that had been glowing through the transparent plastic. Now the door was locked, her address code, *S5 L15 C8 R12 D274*, lit up in a muted white light on the emblem side of the card and then slowly disappeared. According to Andrew, the card was able to read her fingerprints and pulse rate, providing a unique identifier so only she could utilise it. Anytime she wanted to see the address all she had to do was hold the card for a few seconds and it would appear again. *Simple*, she thought, *as long as I don't lose it, that is.*

The inner streets of the chamber were quiet as Sarah made her way along them, her new shoes helping her to bounce along in comfort. Turning a corner, she found herself on a wide, sloping walkway that took her down to the transport channel she had just been looking at. A noisy cacophony of traffic came thrusting along the path towards her as she drew closer.

Approaching the bottom, her nerves came to the fore when she saw two armed U.S. soldiers standing watch over a multi-arched gate system. As people moved through each barrier, they held up their card to something on the inside of the arch and then a blue laser flashed over their body in the blink of an eye. Most people walked through almost without slowing, but Sarah halted in front of one, apprehensive.

One of the soldiers ambled over to her. 'Are you OK, ma'am?'

'Err, yes,' she said, cursing her reluctance to just walk through as if she belonged. 'Do I just swipe my card and walk on past? I won't get zapped or anything, will I?'

The soldier chuckled as his partner came over to join them, increasing her tension further. 'No ma'am, no zapping. It just scans you – see.' He pointed to a man as he passed beneath an arch unscathed. 'It makes sure you have no unauthorised weapons, explosives, liquids and the like on you.'

'Standard protocol,' the other soldier told her gruffly.

She gave a nervous smile. 'That's a relief; I didn't fancy getting incinerated today.'

'I like your accent,' the first soldier said, 'what is it, Australian?'

Sarah laughed as she relaxed a little. 'Australian! It's English, East London. Land of Hope and Glory 'n' all that.'

He brightened. 'Ah, like the Royal family, yeah, I know. I really like your King and Queen, cool couple.'

The other guard eyed her with suspicion. 'We don't get many foreigners in Sanctuary.'

'Don't mind him,' the first man said, 'he was born to get out of the wrong side of the bed.'

Sarah looked at him. 'You couldn't tell me how to get to the Smithsonian Institution, could you?'

'Sure.' He held out his hand for Sarah's MF Card.

Taking the card from her he walked over to a robust looking wallscreen and swiped her card into the system. Up came all her details and her location on the map of the base.

'So,' the soldier said, as his colleague wandered off, disinterested, 'you're here and the Smithsonian is—' he tapped and rotated the screen with practised ease, 'here. Basically, you can get the monotube straight through without needing to change; you're lucky.'

'That makes a change.'

'Bad day?'

She made a face. 'Bad few months.'

'Well, things are looking up. You're very lucky to get a job at the museum. It's smack in the middle of the nicest part of the base. Most people need a high clearance level to be able to go there as much as you can.'

'As much as I can?'

He grinned at her naivety. 'You really are new, aren't you. Basically, as you work there, you could go seven days a week if you wanted, but most people would need a clearance level of six or above to go there that much. I have level three clearance, so I can only go to the New Park district on my days off.'

Sarah was confused. 'But you're military; I thought you could go anywhere you liked?'

'I wish,' he said with feeling. 'Military or not, we all have clearance levels and we all have restrictions; it's how the base works. You haven't got it all your own way, though; since you're a level one, you won't be able to get off at any other stop or sector along the way – during the days you work, anyway. Weekends or days off, some of your restrictions will be lifted to the main areas of recreation and commerce.'

Sarah's brow furrowed as she looked at the screen; she felt more disorientated now than she had before, and it must have shown.

'Don't worry,' the soldier said, 'you'll get used to it. It always takes a while to adjust to Sanctuary; it's so much bigger than the other bases.'

'I haven't been to the other bases,' Sarah mumbled to herself.

He leaned forward. 'What was that?'

'Eh? Oh, nothing. So I just catch this monotube thing straight to New Park Central?'

'That's right; you'll need to cross over to the other side to catch it, though, or you'll end up in the industrial sector.'

The soldier gave Sarah directions to the station on the other side of the road and rail system, and it didn't take her long to cross over using a few travelators and an elevator. The monotube took a while to arrive, but at last the futuristic machine cruised into the station and came to rest with the venting of some kind of gas, which rolled across the surface of the platform, covering the shoes of the waiting travellers, including Sarah; some kind of discharge from the braking system, she presumed. The bright blue and white exterior of the train was adorned at specific intervals with the transport system's logo:

MONOTUBE

When the doors opened, the barriers that prevented station users from plummeting to their deaths sank into the platform surface with a pneumatic hiss.

Sarah boarded, deciding to sit at a window seat which provided some interesting views as the train sped through different sectors, levels and chambers of the base. After a particularly long section of interconnecting enclosed tunnels, the monorail burst out of the darkness and onto the top surface of Sanctuary. Sarah couldn't help but peer out from her vantage point in awe as the train took an elevated section of track towards its destination. The tower she had only glimpsed once before, located in the very centre of the base, cut a sleek profile high above, disappearing from view as it sliced through the realistic-looking blue sky of the great dome itself.

The spectacle of the rest of the dome level of the city was also beautiful to behold. Trees and plants dominated swathes of the landscape, interspersed with ornate buildings utilising the most modern and aesthetically pleasing designs. A few miles away she could also make out an impressive huddle of manmade skyscrapers, *or should that be domescrapers*, she wondered. And off to the right the flat landscape was punctuated by a group of high hills, bordering on small mountains, and at their feet what looked like a sparkling chain of lakes.

After a couple more stops, the train slowed again and a simulated voice announced the destination she wanted. 'New Park Central station. Please enjoy your visit.'

Sarah departed the monotube and passed through the cleanest and most minimalistic station she had ever been in, the footfalls of the other passengers echoing between the glass confines and tiled flooring as they made their way out. Sarah took note that many of the people in this district wore casual and expensive looking clothing, compared to the more functional work attire of those she had been around at the start of her journey. As before, armed soldiers patrolled the area; however, these guardians wore a grey uniform instead of standard issue, the smart attire befitting their surroundings.

The gate system at this station matched the one she had previously used and Sarah flashed her card at the arch. Having been scanned, she moved off out into a pleasant sun-drenched plaza bordered by various exits and well-tended flowerbeds, the sweet scents drifting on a light breeze to prickle her senses.

Digital scrolling signposts guided her to the museum. Unfortunately, once she got there, she was unable to enter as she hadn't the credits. More than a little disappointed, she spent the rest of the day wandering the area and looking for ways someone might escape. From a high vantage point, atop an observation platform, she couldn't see any lift mechanisms, not one, throughout the twenty mile wide expanse, that led to the surface, which meant only one thing; they were located outside of the dome and the USSB itself, a fact that would prove to be a major obstacle to her plans.

That night, after returning to her new quarters, she slept well, tired after the day's exploration and a lot of walking, which she was unused to after her long confinement. Like a finely woven silk sheet, the night slipped past and Sarah woke, the prospect of her new job the first thought to penetrate her mind. Deciding it prudent to dress in the grey uniform rather than go baggy casual, Sarah was careful not to open the blind of her window prematurely having given everyone an eyeful the day before.

After a quick breakfast of cereal and toast, she left the apartment for the museum once more; this time, however, it was seven in the morning. Outside the air was surprisingly crisp and fresh, almost as if she was on the surface rather than in the bowels of the Earth.

Normally starting a new job would bring with it a certain anxiety and thrill, but as she had no intention of staying there, or making a good impression, she just felt alert, and wary of the people she might meet. All she wanted was to earn some credits and then meet up with Trish and Jason at the earliest opportunity.

This time when she reached the impressive building of the Smithsonian Institution she was able to gain admittance via the workers' entrance she had scoped out the day before. Reception guided her through some open-plan offices and up a flight of stairs to the archives department, where her enforced labour was to begin. Greeted by a tiny elderly woman whom Sarah towered over, her photo was engraved onto her new MF Card and she was then presented with a company computer phone. The phone had a direct link to the USSB's cloud system, but also had a few credits on, perhaps enough to enable her to call Trish and Jason. Her spirits rising, the rest of the day flashed by as she bumbled along, forgetting most of what she was being taught, which was very little and all utterly tedious.

Rather than waste all the phone credits on a voice call, she sent a text message to both Trish and Jason and was overjoyed when she received replies from each of them. The following three days began and finished much the same way, although Sarah made sure to take photos and videos of the base whenever she was able; people needed to know about this place, she knew it was far too important to be kept hidden away like it was.

When the end of the week arrived Sarah's desire to see her friends grew with each passing hour. They had arranged to meet at the museum on Saturday morning and Sarah found it difficult to sleep the night before; her excitement spilled over into the next day as she took her now usual route into work. As she'd been informed by her supervisor in the office, her credits for that week would enter her account at midnight on Friday and, thankfully, they were as good as their word.

Jason and Trish were both waiting for Sarah when she disembarked the first train of the day from her sector to arrive at New Park Central station. Approaching the gates, she drank in the sight of them as they stood impatiently at the main exit. Trish, her best friend, looked thinner than she remembered her, but then that was to be expected if she had been fed the same way Sarah had while in the military jail. Her hairstyle had also changed from being tied back to being let loose into a big frizzy explosion, like she'd worn it back in her uni days. Trish's dark brown locks framed a harsh but attractive face, her light brown skin and full lips a giveaway to her mixed ancestry. Jason, the Welsh moron as Trish occasionally referred to him, sometimes to his face, didn't seem to have lost much weight, but his tanned skin had definitely lost some of its colour, much like her own. Jason's face, as ever, looked mildly comical to Sarah's eyes, but then he did tend to play the fool which may have had something to do with her perception of him, besides the fact that a giant cheeky grin was never far away from hijacking his features.

After Sarah passed through one of the scanners, the three friends could contain themselves no longer; running forwards they embraced one another.

'Why are you hugging me, too?' Trish asked Jason, looking at Sarah over his shoulder and rolling her eyes in amused exasperation.

'Just getting in the spirit,' he said in his Celtic lilt.

'You're such an idiot.' Trish laid a hand on his shoulder with a fond familiarity.

Sarah noted the inflection in her friend's voice and realised for the first time that there might be something between her two pals, something more than friendship alone. She looked to Jason who winked at her. Sarah tried to hide her smile. Trish may have her hands full if he got his way. She'd always known Jason wasn't as stupid as he made out and this only served to confirm her suspicions.

As the three of them chattered away excitedly they ambled towards the Smithsonian.

'Can you believe this place?' Jason said to Sarah, looking up at the dome and marvelling at the simulated sky. 'It's friggin' awesome.'

Sarah gazed upwards too. 'I don't think I could ever get used to it, even if I lived out the rest of my days here.'

Trish made a disgruntled sound. 'That may well end up being the case for us all. How are we ever going to get out of here?'

'Get out?' Jason said in genuine surprise. 'Do you know what some people would pay to be in a place like this, to just know that it exists, even? *Hollow Earth* nuts would literally pass out in *I told you so* overload if they knew all this was down here.'

Trish gaped at him as if he'd just sprouted a tree out of his head and a long trunk from his nose. 'Are you kidding me? You want to stay here, a prisoner for the rest of your life, no chance of going back to the surface – ever?'

Jason gave the question careful consideration. 'Well, not the whole of my life, but a few years down here – imagine what you could learn. Don't you think, Saz?'

'I don't plan on staying here any longer than I absolutely have to,' Sarah said as they approached the entrance to the museum. 'Although I think we are about to find out all we need to know right now.' She indicated the large turnstile gates ahead.

The front of the museum consisted of a single convex pane of frosted acrylic nano-sheet, two hundred foot wide, with the name of the building in large, bold, chrome lettering arcing across its surface:

SMITHSONIAN
MUSEUM OF SANCTUARY

Offering their multifunction cards at one of the booths, they were each provided with a free information booklet and guide before proceeding inside. The front foyer was typically a large open area full of signposts, milling people and even the prerequisite souvenir shop off to one side. All three, however, were too busy reading through their respective pamphlets to take much notice of anything else.

'Oh my God,' Jason said, as he read through it, 'are you two seeing this?'

Sarah was indeed seeing it all. Exhibits covering a mind-boggling array of everything and anything to do with Homo giganthropsis. From the earliest remains and artefacts to detailed models of huge unearthed complexes which, according to the text, dwarfed anything seen in Egypt, Mesoamerica or anywhere else found on the surface.

'To process all this would take a lifetime,' Trish murmured.

Trish was right; the Smithsonian had amassed a staggering amount of objects and this enormous multi-level museum only contained a fraction of what was still being found on an almost daily basis. Sanctuary was, for all intents and purposes, an archaeologist's dream come true. Not just any old dream, but the mother of all dreams, a dream pumped up and engorged on a plethora of narcotics fit for a thousand drug-addicted rock stars ten times over.

Sarah withdrew her phone and checked the battery, which was at ninety-three per cent capacity. 'We should split up,' she told them in a business-like manner. 'Take your phones and take as many photos and videos as you can. Document *everything* you can, down to the smallest relic, and then meet back here when you're done. When we get out this footage will be invaluable in proving what we've found down here and exposing the truth about Homo gigantis, and this base, too, for that matter.'

Jason looked at her with a sulky expression and Sarah raised a questioning eyebrow.

'I was looking forward to enjoying this,' he explained to her. 'Now I'm going to have to rush around taking sodding photos like some demented tourist.'

Trish pouted her bottom lip out like a small child. 'Ah, diddums.'

Jason gave her the finger and Trish retaliated by sticking out her tongue. Sarah was pleased to see her friends hadn't let their recent experiences dull their natural ability to bicker with each other; strangely, this lifted her spirits as much as anything else.

'Look,' Sarah said to Jason, 'I wouldn't mind spending a few weeks looking round this place, but our priority should be to get out of here ... and besides, it costs a bomb to get in and we'd have to work for months to afford to go round this whole place thoroughly; since I don't plan on staying here longer than a week we better get cracking.'

Jason acknowledged her point with a grunt.

Agreeing to meet back at the cafeteria at noon, the three newly reunited friends split up once more to go their separate ways. As Sarah left Trish and Jason she felt a pang of loss to be leaving them again so soon. *Stop being a baby*, she chided herself; *you'll be back with them again in a few hours.*

Sarah had opted to take the lower levels of the Museum while Trish took the middle ones and Jason the top. As she descended in a large glass lift, she had already stopped a few times to take pictures of some primitive giganthropsis wall art, extracted from one of the natural caves dating back even before Sanctuary itself, over a million years past. The designs were of human-like figures, plus animals and plants. By themselves they would have been the discovery of a lifetime, but within this museum they were merely a very small appetiser and she'd had to tear herself away for what treasures lay ahead. The lift reached the bottom floor and Sarah was already hypnotised by the sight of what lay in the large high-ceilinged room she walked out into. In front of her, standing in row upon magnificent row, were statues – giant statues.

Walking between them she examined the tourist information

plaque that stood in front of one of the towering sculptures. According to this, they measured over forty feet high and had been some of the first major discoveries made by a team of explorers back in the eighteen hundreds. The scale of the statues wasn't their only remarkable feature; each one had been carved from dense granite and in exquisite detail. The strange forms and shapes of the ancient peoples they depicted also captured Sarah's attention. Realising she had been staring at one particular piece for a few minutes she grabbed her phone and took some video. This was one of the hardest things she had ever done, to walk through this place quickly was an impossibility as her thirst for knowledge and her love of archaeology exerted its powerful forces upon her, slowing her to a crawl.

Finally leaving the first hall behind, Sarah found herself in a much more regular sized exhibition full of large architectural models, each enclosed within a square glass case. The brochure told her these were scale representations of the major structures found so far within Sanctuary. As Sarah read on, she kept noticing the word 'Anakim' replacing 'giganthropsis'. It seemed this was how this race of giants was referred to, like the word 'human' was to 'sapiens', or perhaps 'Asian' or 'Hispanic' was to sapiens. Sarah needed to get hold of some books to get up to speed on the subject. It didn't escape her attention, though, that the name 'Anakim' was used in the Judeo-Christian Bible when it spoke of giant men. Clearly giganthropsis had been extinct for millennia at that point in human history, so it was most likely deemed an appropriate name to bestow on the builders of Sanctuary by latter-day explorers. Sarah liked it, despite its religious overtones. An – a – kim. Anakim. It had a good ring to it.

The buildings that had been excavated or found abandoned but intact were wide-ranging in their size, design and function. Palaces and temples were the most prevalent sites, but other, more intriguing, structures had also been discovered, their purposes as yet only speculated upon. Sarah found it more than a little strange to think that some of the ancient discoveries in this museum may have been more advanced technologically than humans were today. As she took more photos the distant sound of raucous laughter caught her attention.

Looking around she saw she was the only one in the area, probably due to it being so early in the day.

The clamour from an approaching group of people grew louder, their footfalls and voices echoing through the all but deserted halls of the museum's lower level. Finally nine people strode past, twenty feet from where Sarah stood holding her computer phone. Dressed in dusty, mud-splattered, military-style red and blue uniforms, each of these individuals also sported a robust utility jacket and carried in one hand an expensive-looking high-tech helmet. They walked like they owned the place and with an arrogance born of a superior self-confidence that was replicated in their tone of voice and general demeanour.

A couple of them turned to look at Sarah as they passed and one man made lingering eye contact with her before turning back to join in with his comrades once more, cajoling and joking. As they moved away and just before they disappeared from view around a corner, their footfalls receding on the hard flooring, Sarah glimpsed a sign on the backs of their jackets. In bold white lettering it read:

DEEP REACH
SURVEY TEAM
ALPHA SIX

Her curiosity piqued, Sarah decided to follow this close-knit crew of men and women to see where they were headed. Ensuring she stayed at a comfortable distance to avoid detection, and after a few twists and turns, Sarah lost track of her quarry, the sounds of their passage no longer in earshot. Scampering along, she found a door swinging shut on an emergency exit stairwell, the echoes of activity drifting up from below. Pursuing them inside and down the flight of steps, Sarah found herself emerging into a darkened corridor with illuminated exit signs directing her to the right. The noise of the survey team, however, could be heard coming from the left. Hurrying to catch up, Sarah found another door closing in front of her. Grabbing it just before it shut, she saw it bore a restricted access sign and the words *Authorised Personnel Only*; to one side of this entrance, on the wall, was a swipe card reader and at its top a small light glowed a bright, neon green. With only a moment's hesitation Sarah ducked inside, the door shutting behind her with an audible click. A duplicate card reader sat on the other side of the entrance and – unseen by Sarah, who now traversed along a narrow corridor – its green light switched to red.

CHAPTER EIGHT

SARAH MOVED through the deserted area, her senses heightened, like an athlete waiting for the starter's gun. The low-lit echoing hallways extended into a rabbit warren of little-used office space and storage rooms full of unopened crates and curiosities large and small, many bound in copious amounts of bubble wrap.

Not wanting to get left behind in unfamiliar surroundings, her bearings already shot to hell, Sarah made sure to keep pace with the team of people walking ahead of her. Turning a corner, she had to duck back out of sight as the team had halted outside a large black opening fronted by bright red and yellow safety barriers. Peeking around to see what they were up to, she realised they were waiting for some kind of industrial-sized lift. Soon enough, a whirring screech of metal cables, travelling at high speed, announced the arrival of the roofless platform which the mysterious survey team boarded and then activated, disappearing into the depths below.

Sarah, now completely alone, darted out from her hiding place, her footsteps pitter-pattering over the vinyl flooring. Craning her neck to see over one of the barriers, she could just make out the service lights of the elevator as it continued its rapid journey down, ever deeper, the muted sound of its descent now barely audible. Now that she had come this far she felt almost desperate to find out where these people were leading her. The chase and her commitment to it were too far advanced to give up now. There was a problem, however; the lift didn't seem to have any controls to call it back up. It must operate on a remote switch, she concluded, wirelessly called by whoever needs it.

Sarah brushed back some long strands of hair behind one ear, as she stared into space. An idea popped into her head. Taking out her phone, she directed its light into the shaft, illuminating its steel clad, girdered interior. The beams were placed at such angles and intervals to make climbing down them a real possibility. *I can do that*, she reasoned, as she attempted to mount one of the waist-high safety gates to enter the void. Holding onto one of the side walls, she balanced both feet on top of one of the narrow barriers, wobbling precariously as she did so. As she hung out a long leg to traverse to the nearest girder, her standing leg slipped from under her, sending her flailing into nothingness.

Sarah's shriek sang out into the abandoned expanse. She flung out her arms and somehow latched onto the floor. Clinging on for dear life, her hands slid an inch on the vinyl surface, almost sending her plummeting to certain death. Her heart thumping and her breath ragged, Sarah dared not move her legs or body in case her fingers, which had now begun to perspire, might slip from their tenuous hold. Her brain frantically sought a solution to her problem, but as the milliseconds flashed by she knew with a gut-wrenching, fear-inducing certainty that she wasn't going to be able to prevent herself from falling. Millimetre by excruciating millimetre edged her closer and closer to oblivion. A strange noise, flashing lights and the image of her mother's beautiful smile were Sarah's final thoughts as she slipped from the ledge.

Air rushed past and then she hit a flat surface – hard, twisting a leg painfully, the air knocked from her lungs. She'd never been so pleased to hurt so much in her life as she lay on the cold steel floor of the lift which had been returning from below. As the elevator halted Sarah groaned and sat upright. With a tender touch she probed her left kneecap, checking to see the extent of the damage. It was a bad twist, but not as bad as it could have been. Standing, she put pressure on it, wincing at the pain which lanced up her leg. Testing it further, she managed to walk a few hesitant steps. Bending to massage it, she bit down on her lip against the agony before she deemed it fit for purpose.

Thanking her lucky stars that the lift had returned of its own accord, but cursing her own reckless stupidity, Sarah considered her options. The platform consisted of a checker plate floor and a thick handrail that ran around three sides; attached to this thick tube was a rugged control panel comprising large, well-worn, coloured plastic buttons. Moving to the panel, she eyed it while deliberating as to what to do next. *Should I carry on or go back*, she asked herself, *or just stand here like a lemon?* Her hand hovered over the big green button with the down arrow on it. *Sod it!* she thought, depressing the button to send the platform whizzing back from whence it came.

As the lift continued down, Sarah questioned the sanity of her actions. Her inhibitions in risk-taking over the last twelve months had slowly been eroded and her reasoning to continue had suppressed an intuitive warning for caution. Was this the real her, a risk-taker, a chancer? Or had she just become too used to such situations, her mind learning to adapt to them ... or worse, was she seeking out danger? She didn't think she was as she attempted to look inside her own mind with an objective eye. While mentally wrestling with herself, the whine of the elevator decreased as it slowed before coming to a shuddering stop, the sensation bringing her back to the present.

Exiting the lift and still slightly favouring her injured knee, Sarah found herself in a large brick tunnel, a stark contrast to the museum's interior. A row of bright strip lighting ran off into the distance and out of sight, as the dazzling panels traced a bend in the wide passageway's ceiling ahead. To her mind, judging by the bricks used and the construction, it was similar to something built in the Victorian era rather than a part of the super modern clandestine project located above and around it. She presumed it was one of the first things built by the U.S. President's team back in the eighteen hundreds, still surviving as a tribute to those that first discovered Sanctuary all those years ago.

Moving on, it took only a few minutes to reach the end of the wide passageway, which consisted of an old rusty iron door located in a brick surround. With no obvious locking mechanism, Sarah lifted the latch and pushed open the heavy metal obstruction. A cacophony of noise rushed in through the ever-increasing gap. She dived inside in one fluid movement, sealing the opening behind her with a dull clang. With her back to a wall, Sarah peered out over a large crate and into the inside of an enormous steel and glass clad building. A high, expansive atrium with a circular design encompassed the entire circumference of a curiously shaped inner structure full of floors and rooms with transparent walls, and staircases made of crosshatched metal grating. The whole building had a sparse military feel to it, aided in no small part by the presence of camouflaged, gun-toting soldiers, who bustled about inside alongside their civilian counterparts. Where the tunnel had been old-tech, this place was the polar opposite, with cutting edge technology bristling from seemingly every surface.

Whatever was going on here, it was a large scale operation and one Sarah felt sure she shouldn't be privy to. Sensing no one would notice her presence and feeling oddly emboldened by her previous brush with death, she stood up from her hiding place and walked into the building as though she belonged. Walking amongst the people Sarah didn't exactly blend in, but she didn't stand out like a sore thumb either. The continuous activity inside consisted of individuals wearing a whole range of clothing, from grim-faced, armoured, Special Forces personnel to bumbling lab technicians in their stereotypical white coats.

Having read her fair share of spy novels Sarah believed she knew the basics of blending in to somewhere you didn't belong. Passing an empty desk she snatched up a paper-laden ring binder, opened it out and pretended to refer to it as she wandered in towards the centre of the busy place of operations.

'Out of the way!' a woman called out as she approached Sarah at speed along a tight corridor. She pushed a flatbed trolley loaded with what looked like an overabundance of climbing equipment.

Sarah, initially thinking she'd been rumbled, pressed herself flat against a wall.

'Thank you!' The woman rattled on past.

Intrigued and more than a little relieved her cover remained intact, Sarah trailed along behind. Passing a doorway she saw an unattended lab coat hanging on a hook. Filching that, too, she shrugged it on and hurried to keep pace with the fast moving trolley and its owner as they barrelled along at breakneck speed. The hallway soon opened out into some kind of warehouse, or staging area, where men and women checked and donned various pieces of equipment and outerwear. The woman and trolley disappeared into the melee of activity, but Sarah's attention was drawn to the people at the far end and some kind of command centre. Above this, a large, impressive emblem hung, cast in thick, pockmarked, burnished steel:

S.E.D.

SANCTUARY

EXPLORATION DIVISION

FOUNDED
IN 1826

Nearby, the elusive red and blue clad survey team had gathered, mingling with other similarly garbed men and women. This must be an assembly room for teams going outside of the USSB, Sarah realised. Edging forwards she glimpsed many other team designations on the backs of the ever-growing number of people that now streamed into the vicinity. As far as she could tell there were five types of team, including Mapping, Structural, Archaeological, Scientific and Deep Reach, the latter the only type with the oddly shaped high-tech head gear. The helmets in question drew Sarah forwards, closer to the original team she had followed from the museum. Surreptitiously she took out her phone and began to record what she was seeing; *this is good footage*, she thought while easing past a couple of trolleys, *I can definitely utilise this when exposing Sanctuary back on the surface.*

'Quiet down now, people!' A man's voice rang out over a speaker system into the large oval chamber. The assembled masses, which Sarah estimated now numbered a few thousand strong, settled into a respectful silence. Sarah looked expectantly, along with everyone else around her, towards some kind of command centre, where a broad-shouldered man stood on a large platform. He wore a simple white shirt, blue tie and plain black trousers. His silver-grey hair and demeanour intimated seniority, while his voice left it in no doubt that he expected, nay, demanded, your attention.

'Now listen up,' he said, 'as ever it's my pleasure to provide some words of wisdom to all of you taking a trip out into our fair Sanctuary. Many of you will have heard them before, but equally there are many of you still green around the gills who will need reminding of the dangers you are about to face outside of this base. You all have the potential to come up against situations which even the most experienced among you will never have encountered. Safety is paramount, people; if you discover something that looks dangerous, it probably is. We have no idea what you will stumble upon out there and if the human race is anything to go by, our older and larger cousins may have left behind some pretty nasty stuff.

'Ensure all personal gauges and detectors are checked regularly. Seismometers and structural stability maps for all teams except Deep Reach are to be adhered to at all times. No exceptions. Always keep in radio contact with your teammates; due to the rock composition many parts of Sanctuary Proper will limit long range transmissions. If you get in trouble don't be afraid to call for help; egos will get you dead down there very quickly.

'Make sure you double check your kit before you disembark; most of you will be gone for a few weeks and you may need your emergency supplies when you least expect it, so no trying to lighten your pack by taking out things you *think* are non-essential. As ever, as far as our signal relays will permit, rescue and decontamination teams will be on standby in the field to respond to any distress beacons.'

The man looked at his watch. 'It's eleven hundred hours. We are a go for deployment at thirteen hundred. Make ready and good luck!'

The crowd began breaking apart and Sarah found herself standing on her own in the middle of the room. She turned to walk away, but as she did so a hand grasped her left wrist. Looking to see who had accosted her, Sarah peered up into the dark brown eyes of the Deep Reach team member who had held her gaze back in the museum.

'Hi there,' he said with a smile, but still holding firmly to her arm. 'Are you lost?'

Sarah, feeling like a wild animal trapped in a cage, managed to produce a confident sounding laugh at the suggestion. 'No, not at all.' She brandished her folder. 'Just taking some notes.'

'Really?' He looked amused and proffered a hand. 'Do you mind if I take a look?'

'Of course,' she said, while inwardly cursing her stupidity for thinking she could walk in and out of such a facility without getting caught.

Releasing his grip he plucked the folder from her hands and opened it up to peruse. Sarah, now free to make a dash for it, stood frozen to the spot. As she waited with bated breath her tormentor continued to read the folder.

'So,' he said at last looking up at her, his annoying smile still plastered across his handsome features. 'I can't see any notes in here about the final debrief before the off, just some computations on thermodynamics.'

Sarah had no idea what was actually in the file apart from some odd diagrams and meaningless numbers; thankfully he'd slipped up and revealed to her its contents – *what an idiot.*

She tapped her temple. 'It's all up here. I was just about to write it all down before you interrupted me.'

'Ah, how silly of me.' He passed the folder back to her. 'I'll let you get back to your physics.'

'Thank you,' she said with what she hoped was a conciliatory tone, 'those computations won't get done on their own.'

Sarah turned and walked away, while her mind screamed at her to run. As she reached an exit – thanking her lucky stars she'd managed to blag her way out of such a tight spot – his voice called out to her from behind.

'Just one more thing.'

Sarah paused and looked back round.

He walked towards her, closing the gap between them. 'It's strange,' he gestured to the ring binder in her hand, 'that file contains the food supply logistics for the mapping teams. There's nothing in it on thermodynamics.'

Sarah's anxiety resurfaced and she stood looking at him, desperately trying to think of a plausible defence. 'I must have picked up the wrong folder,' she said, the lie sounding lame even to her own ears.

'Ah, is that the reason.' He moved closer to invade her personal space. 'Didn't I just see you back in the museum?'

'I think you must have me confused with someone else.'

'I don't think so. Can I see you MF card, please?'

Reluctantly Sarah removed the card from her pocket and gave it to him.

'Ah, so you work in the Smithsonian,' he said, looking at the card before handing it back. 'It seems, however, you have but a lowly level one clearance, and since this outfit requires seven or above, you most definitely don't belong.'

Sarah didn't know what to say, so she decided to say nothing at all as she tried to avoid his penetrating gaze.

'Do you know the punishment for being down here without clearance?' he asked, more serious now. 'No?' he continued when she still didn't respond. 'I'll tell you what; instead of calling in the military to arrest you right now, I'll give you a three minute head start on them. Sound fair?'

Sarah gawked at him, unsure if he was being serious or not.

'Clock's ticking, Sarah Morgan.' He tapped a watch on his wrist. 'Two minutes fifty-five – fifty-four – fifty-three—'

Sarah, realising he was giving her chance to get away, bolted down a corridor while throwing away the incriminating folder. Flying up some stairs, she dodged in and out of people, startling many of them as she flew past. Within a minute she'd flung open the old iron door and ran down the brick tunnel. Already she could hear signs of pursuit; it seemed the three minute head start had been rescinded. Too bent on escape, she had little time to curse the man who'd blown her cover. Instead she tapped furiously at the up button in the lift she'd just boarded. Shouting could be heard now and as the lift moved upwards Sarah caught sight of armed men swarming down the tunnel towards her.

Sinking to her knees to catch her breath, Sarah tried to remember the winding route back to the museum for when she exited the lift. Unable to recall it, she prepared to run again, massaging her injured knee, which throbbed painfully. The platform jolted to a stop and the barriers rose up. Sarah was out and running, her long legs propelling her round a corner to collide with a soldier approaching from the opposite direction. As they tumbled to the ground, the soldier let out a shout of alarm. Sarah, quicker to her feet, scrambled away, but another soldier appeared in front of her.

'Halt!' he shouted, bringing his assault rifle to bear.

Skidding to a stop, her hands gaining purchase on the floor, Sarah turned to go back, but as she did so she glimpsed the other man, she'd just sent flying, behind her. The raised butt of his gun snapped down in a jarring jab to her temple. Lights flashed before her eyes and she crumpled to the floor, a deep blackness engulfing her with its inescapable smothering embrace.

CHAPTER NINE

London's St Pancras International railway station, conceived in 1863 and completed by 1868, had at the time boasted the largest enclosed space in the world. Now fronted by the St Pancras Renaissance Hotel, a Victorian gothic architectural masterpiece, the station acted as the city's land-based gateway into Europe and due to this, as ever, it pulsated with vibrant activity. Businessmen and women strode with purpose and an assured air of self-importance as they sought their destination with a determined focus. Students and school children, while mirroring their elders' self-involved demeanour, seemed more haphazard in their progress through the station, more relaxed and less stressed, taking time to cavort with their companions or to pause and ensure their favourite tune played over their headphones.

Tourists, still ready and willing to travel despite the strict GMRC protocols, stood in small, excited and bewildered groups like clusters of pebbles surrounded by a continuous flowing stream of water. Like all other areas of the city a military presence made itself known as armed soldiers stalked the platforms and guarded entrances and exits, ensuring civil unrest would be met with a swift and fierce resistance if it dared to rear its ugly head.

Amongst the hither and thither of the station's patrons, a petite woman gazed up at the departures board. She wore a short, black, heavy weave plaid skirt, thick white thigh length socks and a pair of chunky black leather ankle boots. On her back perched a turquoise rucksack which resembled some kind of furry animal with huge eyes and a surprised expression on its face, beneath which a tight transparent padded jacket had been secured. A shock of bright red hair topped off the woman's ensemble, along with a pair of thick, black, horn-rimmed glasses.

Jessica Klein pursed her lips, the skin feeling tight as she did so. She'd almost forgone the makeup, as once she had kitted herself out in her ridiculous outfit she hadn't recognised herself in the mirror. However, the passport photo Martin had mocked up for her required the addition, so she had plastered it on. She'd needed quite a bit of foundation anyway – passing off middle-age as early twenties was always an ask – but she was quite pleased with the results. A slim frame helped with the impression of youth, of course, and Jessica had always been slight.

She didn't have long to wait for the train to Berlin. According to the timetable, which scrolled across the departure screen, the Eurostar was on schedule. Taking out the train ticket, Jessica hobbled to the gate entrance for the appropriate platform. *These shoes are killing me*, she thought. *Why I decided platforms were a good idea, heaven only knows. They add to my wanna-be-Japanese appearance, though, so I can live with it for now, but as soon as I get settled for the journey they're coming off – quick smart!*

There was one thing about her costume that Jessica did like, the anonymity it gave her; normally in public she would draw the classic double take as people recognised her from the television; some would even spark up a conversation with her out of the blue or ask for an autograph or picture. While she didn't mind now and then, it could begin to grate when it continued throughout a whole day. Now, however, she could walk around incognito; it felt quite liberating in a peculiar kind of way.

Standing in a short queue as she waited for the ticket to be checked, she couldn't help but follow the movements of the soldiers as they patrolled the area beyond. She was acutely aware she was travelling A, illegally, and B, armed. Her cherished and loaded revolver even now nestled in the bag perched on her back, its dense weight, along with that of the extra ammo, noticeable as it pulled against the straps of the bag on her shoulders. The closer she came to the turnstile the clammier her hands became, her nerves taut and her fear of discovery growing.

She double-checked the GMRC border pass, which also acted as a travel order, and which she'd had stamped upon entry to the station. The pass allowed her to circumvent usual security checks, fast-tracking her through the otherwise tiresome boarding procedure; it had also enabled her to bring the gun with her, a risk she had to take considering her circumstances. She just prayed a spot bag check wasn't instigated when she passed through.

Her new name, Eliza Sterling, had been scrawled across the top of the border pass in what she hoped was an adequate disguise of her normal handwriting. Not that she should need to hide this aspect of her real identity, but with her producer's untimely death and the warning from the hacker that the GMRC might try to kill her off, her paranoia was sky-high.

As she stepped forward, the queue growing shorter, she felt a hand brush against her bottom. Turning round, she saw the man standing directly behind her looking off to one side. Frowning at him, she turned back only to once more feel a hand on her behind, this time lingering longer and accompanied by a slight squeeze.

Jessica whirled round. 'What do you think you're playing at?!'

The man, dressed in a suit and in his mid-forties, looked at her, innocent-eyed.

She pointed at him. 'Touch me again and I'll report you for sexual assault.'

'I didn't touch you,' he protested.

She took a step closer and stared up at him with baleful eyes. 'Don't take me for some naïve little girl.'

Unfortunately her confrontational approach didn't have the desired effect and the man, instead of backing off, had the audacity to reach out again sliding his hand up the outside of her exposed thigh. Jessica smacked it away but it was too late as the quarrel had attracted the attention of a soldier.

'What seems to be the problem here?' the armed guard asked.

Jessica cursed inwardly and prayed no one would recognise her. 'This man is harassing me,' she said loudly making people look round in their direction, 'touching me inappropriately.'

'I didn't touch her,' the groper repeated.

'We can soon find out.' The soldier indicated the CCTV dome which protruded from the high ceiling above. 'Do you want to take this further, miss?'

As much as she would have liked to, she didn't have the time or the inclination to bring more eyes upon them, especially considering her predicament. 'No,' she said, her tone reluctant. 'I have a train to catch.'

The guard nodded and sauntered off, leaving her in the queue with the man who now smiled at her with sickening smugness.

'Just because I didn't report you doesn't mean I want you to keep touching me,' she told him in no uncertain terms, keeping her distance from his wandering hands.

The man winked at her and then ran his eyes over her body, mentally undressing her and making her feel distinctly uncomfortable in the process. Thankfully, she was able to ignore him as it was her turn to have her ticket punched and passport papers checked. The Eurostar employee, apparently satisfied everything was in order, handed the documents back to her and she carried on through the gate and onto the platform. Boarding at the centre of the train, Jessica found her seat and removed her footwear with a great sigh of relief.

An hour later, the train sped through the dark Kent countryside on its way towards the Channel Tunnel and France beyond. The carriage had near half its seats occupied and Jessica's paranoia had increased even further since she'd boarded. A few seats along from her own, in an empty section, a woman sat facing her. Jessica felt she had seen her before, but couldn't place her, which made her uneasy. Able to adjust the lenses on her glasses to make them darker and lighter at will, Jessica altered them to their darkest setting, enabling her to keep an eye on the woman without fear of discovery. Every so often the passenger flicked her gaze at Jessica, far too frequently to be mere curiosity.

Jessica put her shoes back on, sat back down and then pretended to fall asleep, letting her head loll to one side, but all the time keeping the woman in sight. The train was now underneath the English Channel and some of the lights around her flickered and went out, sending areas of the compartment into dark shadows and yet leaving her own seat in bright light. Jessica, straining to see what the woman was doing, glimpsed movement in the half-light. Unable to see directly, Jessica switched her gaze to the reflection in the glass which produced a better angle. The woman, leaning down, fiddled with something in her hands. As she sat up Jessica realised with horror the woman now held a gun, a silencer screwed to its barrel. Instantly alert, Jessica grabbed her bag and rolled smoothly from her seat to hurry down the aisle and into the next coach. Reaching the end of the carriage she turned to see the woman had followed her. Sliding past a sleeping passenger, Jessica cowered down beside them to tear at her bag, desperately hunting for her own weapon without success. The woman, much taller than Jessica, strolled past. She didn't have a gun at all but a hair brush and she disappeared into one of the lavatories further along towards the locomotive.

Heaving a sigh of relief, Jessica was about to apologise to the person who she'd squeezed in next to but the words caught in her throat. She looked into the face of the man she'd had the altercation with in the queue. He grinned at her and twisted in his seat, eager hands reaching out to touch her. *Crap!* Feeling like a fly trapped in a spider's web, Jessica jabbed out her right palm, impacting the man's nose with a sickening crunch. As he let out a yelp of pain Jessica made her escape. She almost felt sorry for him – almost. He must have thought it was his lucky day, except that Jessica had always enjoyed going to courses over the years, bettering herself, and she had excelled at self-defence classes; making use of her small stature had always appealed to her and it was nice to be able to put it into action in real life.

Sliding back into her seat, she indulged in a small smile. *Oh – that felt good*, she thought, her composure regained and a semblance of self reinstated. Outside the window she saw they had exited the tunnel and were now in France, the lights of distant buildings apparent in the darkness. She smoothed down her short skirt, trying without success to close the gap between it and her long socks in an attempt to hide the flesh on display. Part of her regretted opting for the sexy schoolgirl look, although it had done its job as, even when she had solicited the attention at the station, no one had twigged it was her, and she hadn't even tried to alter her voice. Now that she was out of the country, however, she would make a point of putting on some jeans, not only to heighten her dignity but to increase her warmth as, according to weather reports, Berlin was in the midst of a snow storm. *Wonderful*, she thought, dreading the prospect while the train continued on.

Five hours later and Jessica, now feeling snug in her trousers, having changed an hour earlier, left the high-speed train behind and walked into the confines of Berlin Hauptbahnhof; the German capital city's main railway station. Once more, Jessica passed through passport control without incident and she headed outside into the cold night air, her breath easy to see as she looked around to gain her bearings. The snow had stopped falling, but the roads were clogged with drifts, and ploughs were out in force clearing the streets. Unlike the armed forces back in London, the German military kept their heavy machinery in plain sight. Two large grey tanks dominated the area outside the station and a gun emplacement had been positioned on the other side of the road. Jessica skirted past a huddle of soldiers and on towards a taxi rank. She stopped next to the first car and the driver wound down his window.

'*Kannst du mich an diese Adresse nehmen bitte*?' Jessica asked the nearest cab driver handing him the address the hacker had printed out for her.

The man looked at it and nodded. '*Ja, das ist kein Problem.*'

Jessica entered the back, settling in for the ride. '*Wie lange wird es dauern*?' she asked him, wondering how long it would take to get to the library

'Bei diesem Wetter? Zwei Stunden,' he replied.

Two hours in the snow, not as bad as it could have been, she reflected, staring again at the printout.

Philological Library
Freie Universität Berlin
Habelschwerdter Allee 45
14195 Berlin, Deutschland

CHAPTER TEN

The five numbers were clearly the postcode; but on the scrap of paper that Martin had shown her she'd thought they looked like some kind of cypher, requiring decryption. The only numbers left were 3.14, which could have been a time, but if it was she had missed the meet by quite a margin. *No,* she decided, *the hacker would have known I wouldn't have been able to make it, so it must pertain to something else ... but what?* Unable to think of another meaning for it she abandoned her ponderings to soak up the snow-draped, floodlit sights of Berlin as the taxi crept along the icy roads.

The time soon drifted by, the driver bringing them to a careful stop outside the Freie Universität Berlin. Having left her computer phone at home, for fear of it being tracked, she had to pay with cold, hard cash, which she had procured back in a bureau de change in London. Stepping out of the cosy taxi and into the freezing street, Jessica pulled the zip on her coat up to its highest point to keep the sub-zero temperatures at bay.

Now glad of her thick-soled shoes, Jessica crunched through some virgin snow and onto a path treated with brown grit, which had helped melt the tiny ice crystals into a thick slush. Slip-sliding her way along, she found firmer footing when she entered a municipal building. A sign to the library guided her along a wide, carpeted corridor and then back outside into the cold once more. In front of her stood the Philological Library of the university, its black and white chequerboard dome exterior framed by the dark skies behind it. Hurrying along, she was soon inside and knocking off excess snow from her shoes on a thick fuzzy brown doormat.

Not having been to the library before, Jessica was surprised to see the interior layout. A third of the space in the dome was empty while in front of her two, three storey open-tiered floors dominated the rest; almost resembling a giant staircase, it was beautifully designed. Each level had a thick white surround supported by white cylindrical pillars. The stepped floors were also exposed to the dome's interior and consequently, if you were so inclined, you could quite easily climb unimpeded onto a desk and drop down twenty foot to the wider tier below.

Moving forwards, Jessica passed over a large university emblem woven into the carpet itself and made her way into the right of the two mirror image structures. As she expected, the library was deathly quiet apart from the odd low mutterings and occasional rustle of paper emanating from its patrons. Up on the first floor a few students lined the continuous desk which ran around the outside of the level. Old-fashioned computer terminals interspersed the workspace, while the interior of the floor was lined with what one usually found in a library: books.

Feeling like she blended in well with her bug-eyed animal rucksack, horn-rimmed glasses, bright red hair and copious amounts of makeup, Jessica sauntered across the staircase and up onto the next tier. All the time she kept her eyes peeled for the meaning of the three digits, 3.14; but it soon became apparent that they didn't fit in with the library's classification system or the desk numbers either. Her frustration mounting at her lack of progress, she finished her round trip of the third and final floor and then traipsed over to the staircase joining the two tiers and on down into the second structure. Unable to see anything on this side either, Jessica slumped down into a vacant chair and stared out in defeat at the inside of the dome. The desk at which she sat had a computer so, flicking on the screen, she entered the term '3.14' within the library's in-house system and hit the search button. *Ergebnisse: Null* displayed on screen, Results: Zero. *Wonderful*, she thought, *I've come all this way literally for nothing*. Just as she considered her next options and a depressing trip back home, she noticed a small section of underlined text at the top right of the screen, which read, *Systeminformationen*. Moving the cursor up to the link using the quaint, touchpad interface, she clicked on it. A small drop down box on the screen appeared detailing the computer's software, processor and hardware specifications. The thing that caught Jessica's attention, however, was the single line at the bottom, *Terminal-Nummer*. Next to this were the digits *2.19*. Second floor, terminal nineteen! Jumping to her feet and garnering curious stares from some of the students, Jessica trotted back upstairs and went from computer to computer until she had located terminal 3.15. The next station along had to be 3.14 but there was a problem, it was occupied.

'*Entschuldigung*,' Jessica apologised to the slim young man sitting at the desk. '*Kann ich diesen Computer benutzen*?' she asked him.

'Use another one,' he said in German without looking up. 'There are plenty free.'

'I have to use that one.'

'Tough,' he said, continuing his work.

Not in the mood to take insolence from some obnoxious man-child Jessica leaned over his shoulder and switched off the system's power supply, sending the screen blank.

'Oi, what do you think you're doing!' he said, finally looking round at her.

Jessica put one foot on the front edge of his swivel chair between his legs and leaned down to look him in the eye. 'I'm taking this computer,' she said with a smile and then bracing her right hand on the desk, shoved out with her leg, propelling the surprised student two desks along. Picking up his books and satchel, she strode over to him and dumped them down on his new desk.

'*Danke*.' She gave him a condescending pat on the head. The young man stared at her open-mouthed as she returned to the terminal she had just claimed, dragging another chair behind her to sit on.

Feeling a little too pleased with her acquisition, she turned the terminal back on and waited for it to boot back up. Now that she was on it, she realised there was little difference between it and any of the other computers lining the surrounding desks. Sitting there, she stared at it, unsure of what she should do to attract the attention of the hacker, if indeed this is where she needed to be. She typed her own name in the system and hit search. Nothing. She tried Martin's name. Again, nothing happened. After entering combinations of her name, profession and Martin's particulars, she gave up, letting out a loud noise of discontent which earned her a shushing from a librarian who had appeared to put some books back on one of the shelves behind Jessica's desk. It was at this instant that her luck changed. The computer beeped. A small chat window appeared at the bottom of the screen and text crept across it.

Ms Klein. It's nice to finally meet you. _

Jessica typed in response: I wouldn't call this meeting. Where are you?

Close by. I'm sorry about your friend, Martin. He was a good man.

_

Yes he was. The best. We must make sure he didn't die for nothing. We must meet and you need to give me the answers you promised.

Answers? There are only more questions. But I will do my best. I have noticed disturbing trends in the data I work with. Trends I have been following for some years. A mutual friend put Martin in touch with me so that I could attempt to get my findings into the public domain. _

Why didn't you use someone in Germany?

Too risky, the German Government is stricter than most when it comes to censorship. I had to go outside of the country. I had hoped the BBC would have been strong enough to withstand outside influence. I was wrong. _

You were. Did you see my broadcast?

I did not. There were rumours about it on Deepnet but actual recordings were quickly hunted out by GMRC Hounds and deleted or corrupted. _

What is Deepnet? She waited for the response onscreen.

Deepnet is what people call the hidden web. It has a number of other names Deep Web, Undernet, Invisible Web, Darknet. It is the name given to digital content and traffic that is hidden from mainstream indexers and regular commercial web constructs. Over the years it has evolved into a whole plethora of forms, consisting of many layers, each harder to infiltrate than the one above. _

But the GMRC are able to control Deepnet?

They like to think they can and to an extent they can delve very deep indeed. Anything that enters from the Surface Web is trackable for a time and with the vast resources the GMRC has at its disposal it can send in armies of operators and intelligent spyware, what we hackers call Hounds, to comb the digital verse. Only the very gifted can evade their reach. _

And you are one of these?

No. I only operate in the upper levels of Deepnet. I skim the data and messages left by those who dare to resist the GMRC and global governments; and yet if you know how, and I do, this is enough to find out information otherwise completely hidden from the general populace. The system we are on now is totally independent of the web; nevertheless it is still patrolled by subversive GMRC spyware programmes, three in fact. Fortunately I have been able to trick them into leaving me alone. _

So what are these trends you have noticed? Jessica typed, unhappy that this hacker seemed to be backing out of their promise to enlighten her with the truth of why journalists were being targeted and murdered.

Movement of resources. Not just your run of the mill government logistics, but relocation on an industrial scale of epic proportions. Foodstuffs, water reserves, oil, gas, you name it, it is being taken from stockpiles allocated for the general populace. The same stockpiles that are needed to see out the after effects from the impact of the asteroid AG5. _

Taken where?

I don't know, that is the problem. It simply disappears from the records, records that have been very carefully monitored and suppressed. The only reason I noticed it is that I plugged masses of data into a sophisticated programme that hunts out different types of numerical patterns. If I'd looked on a local, or even a national scale, I wouldn't have seen anything out of the ordinary, but I was looking on a global scale and the patterns are there and they are as stark as the daytime sky is dark. There is no mistake; the world's resources are being siphoned off at an exponential rate. Within six months half of the stockpiles will be empty; within the next two years, if the speed of the removal continues, they will be completely barren. _

What does that mean?

It means before the world starves to death, it will die of dehydration first. _

'Dear God,' Jessica murmured out loud. *But why would the GMRC do such a thing?* she typed, hitting the Enter key with trepidation.

I'm not sure, that is what terrifies me the most, that and the fact that at least some of the largest governments are in on it. They have to be. WAIT! _

Jessica looked at the last word, her tension increasing. For over a minute no further message appeared and she looked around, feeling more than a little disconcerted by this lapse in the conversation. *What's wrong?* she asked the hacker. No reply was forthcoming for another minute and then the screen came to life once more.

I was afraid this might happen. Ms. Klein, you must trust me now. You will find a small transmitter taped to the underside of the desk. Pull it off and place it on your ear. _

Jessica felt underneath the table and found a small object held to the surface with a piece of tape. Peeling it away, she withdrew a small earpiece which she eyed warily before brushing it off and placing it in her right ear.

'Ms. Klein,' said a man's voice in perfect English but with a heavy German accent, 'my name is Eric. The system we were just conversing on has been compromised. You will need to leave right away. The GMRC will have despatched a team.'

Her voice wavered. 'A team?'

'A team of operatives. You must leave now, hurry!'

Jessica sprang up and ran to the staircase. Clattering down the steps, she shouldered her bag, its large googly eyes swaying on her back.

'I thought the system was secure!' she said as she rushed out the front of the library.

'Take a left though the University complex,' Eric told her. 'The earpiece has a tracker so I can guide your movements.'

Jessica veered to one side, following his instructions.

'Apparently there was a fourth GMRC programme embedded within one of the components,' he continued. 'Like a sleeper agent, it activated once a set number of key words were strung together. Very clever, it was held within a component I assumed was redundant, but the GMRC must have introduced it to the manufacturer at least fifteen years ago when these computers were manufactured. They have great foresight.'

Jessica jogged down a long corridor, her breathing stretched. 'You sound like you respect them.'

'Of course, a healthy admiration of an adversary avoids complacency and aids in identifying their weaknesses and strengths.'

'Where now?' she asked, finding herself emerging from the far wing of the main building and out into the night.

'Cross the road ahead of you and then head diagonally right across the park.'

Jessica angled in the direction he wanted.

'It would be a good idea to run faster,' he said.

Not for the first time, Jessica cursed her shoes as she turned a trot into an awkward running lope through the thick snow that blanketed the pitch-black park.

A deep pulsating hum approached from the air off to her right. 'I think I can hear a helicopter!'

'That will be the GMRC response team. Don't worry, you're almost there.'

'Almost where?!' she said, the blackness still all-encompassing in front of her. As she uttered the words, lights blazed out ahead, highlighting the edge of the snow covered park she had just traversed. A door slid open in the side of a beaten up old van and Jessica saw that a young man stood inside it, holding out a hand for her to take. Grabbing it, she was hauled inside before the door closed behind her with a swish and a bang, which vibrated through the floor pan. The youth, for he was barely an adult, jumped into the driver's seat. Starting the old petrol engine, he shifted the vehicle into gear and floored the accelerator, sending the rear wheels spinning in the snow. The tyres gained traction and they shot forwards, forcing Jessica to brace herself as they did so.

After they reached a steady speed, Jessica squeezed through into the front passenger seat, falling down into it with a great exhalation of breath. The adolescent looked over at her, a broad grin on his young features.

'Nice run,' he said, his voice higher pitched and less manly than the one she had been speaking to over the communication device.

She frowned. 'That was you I was just speaking to?'

'Yes, I disguised my voice just in case. You can never be too careful when you're dealing with the GMRC.'

'You're just a kid.' She felt foolish to have been led up the garden path by a person only just out of diapers.

'I'm nineteen,' he said, without any hint of taking offence at her comment. 'We were lucky,' he continued as he drove past the slow moving traffic which had ventured out in the treacherous conditions. 'Any longer and they would have caught your heat trail. As it is, they will only find your physical passage and we'll have been long gone by then. *Dummkopfs*!' He gave a whoop of joy.

Jessica blinked in disbelief at his lack of fear at their situation. 'You do realise we would have been in serious trouble had we been caught?'

Seeing that she was less than impressed by his attitude, Eric became subdued in a belated attempt at mature gravitas. 'Of course,' he said, glancing over to her, 'but I had it under control. I always have redundancies in place. I'm not called *das Gespenst* for nothing, you know.'

'The Ghost. Who calls you that?'

'Well – I do,' he admitted, 'but if people knew who I was they would know me as *das Gespenst*.' He sat up higher in his chair at the mere mention of the handle he had bestowed upon himself.

Seeing that he set great store by it and deciding not to comment further, Jessica took in his appearance. He wore an old, worn-out, leather biker jacket, black jeans, grubby white trainers that had seen better days and a T-shirt with some obscure words and images adorning it. His short blonde hair stuck up at odd angles and an almost effeminate profile matched his less than masculine voice. *Dear God*, she thought, *what am I doing here? This kid is young enough to be my son, how can he possibly help me against the might of the GMRC?*

'So, where are we heading, Eric?'

He shot her another broad smile. '*Hauptsitz*.'

Headquarters. She groaned inwardly, praying it wasn't located in his mother's basement. This definitely wasn't going as she'd hoped, although what she'd been expecting she wasn't quite sure. But not this, that was for certain, not a thrill-seeking youth.

'I like your hair,' he said, trying to start a conversation as she sat looking out of the window wondering what her next move should be. 'You look very different from how you do on the television.'

'It's a disguise.'

'Ah.' He tapped his nose and nodded. 'It is a good one, Jessica; may I call you Jessica?'

Jessica nodded and an uncomfortable silence ensued with Jessica lost in thought until they eventually slowed and came to a stop outside an old warehouse complex. Eric hit a button on his dashboard and a rickety metal shutter wound up from the ground and disappeared above. The van edged inside and came to a halt. Eric whacked on the handbrake, cut the engine and hit the button once more on the dash. Exiting the vehicle, he led Jessica through a cold, empty garage as the external door sank back down behind them. A dim, flickering fluorescent light hung on a wall above an old door that was filled with dents and covered in flaking green paint to reveal a rotting, blackened wood surface beneath. The whole place smelled of damp timber and engine oil. So far Eric's head office left a lot to be desired.

Taking out a set of jangling keys, the young hacker opened the door and stepped through, with Jessica close behind. Inside, a small elevator took them up three storeys to the top floor. As they emerged from the lift, Jessica was taken aback by the room in front of her. Having expected some filthy damp pit, the spacious, clean open-plan apartment that Eric moved into was a welcome relief. The subdued lighting highlighted a pristine white kitchen off to one side, which was complemented by a luxurious living-cum-dining area in the centre. Over to the right of the high ceilinged room, a ladder led up to a second level, which looked like a bedroom. Underneath, gathering little dust, was a bank of computers and screens, and a mass of cabling and wires which led off in all directions. Setting off the whole scene, a sweeping glass wall provided a spectacular view of the Berlin skyline.

Jessica walked over to take in the vista and their surroundings outside. As she looked, Eric came to stand beside her.

'It's a beautiful sight, isn't it?' he said.

'It is, very beautiful.' The image of the brightly lit city hunkering beneath its snowy blanket looked picture-perfect in all respects.

'The glass is covered in one way film so the outside looks like part of the metal façade,' Eric told her, as if she had inquired about it. 'This whole place was left to me by a friend; well, dead relative, to be more precise. My uncle was in the car manufacturing business, made specialist parts for some of the top companies until he went bust. Luckily before he died he left all of this to me in his will. I say "luckily" as he wasn't really my uncle, he and his wife used to look after me when I was little and not having children of their own they decided to leave everything to me.'

'You don't have any other family?'

'No, I'm an orphan.'

'I'm sorry,' she said, suddenly feeling for this young man.

Eric looked out across the city for a moment without saying anything. 'Don't be. I'm doing pretty well for an orphan, don't you think?' He waved a hand around his impressive home, lightening the mood.

'You are, this is a lovely place; but aren't you worried about being discovered by the GMRC or German authorities?'

'Why?' he said with genuine surprise. 'I haven't done anything wrong and I operate below the radar. I am *das Gespenst*, they don't even know I exist.'

'Until today,' Jessica pointed out.

Eric made a face to show his doubt about that observation. 'They won't find any trace of me.'

'Not of you, but what about me? We both know the manpower the GMRC has behind it. It won't be long until they pin me down, or at least to someone matching my description. And I will lead them to you.'

'Then we will have to change your appearance again,' he told her. 'Not a problem. Look – relax – we are safe here, I guarantee it.'

And there it is, Jessica thought to herself, *the folly of youth ... or is it arrogance?* Either way Eric didn't instil her with the confidence he obviously felt in abundance.

She pointed to his grotto of high-tech equipment. 'So, is this how you hacked into my computer at my home?'

Eric gave her an odd look, a look of incomprehension.

'When you showed me the photo of Martin's body on-screen and then told me to get out of the house,' she said.

He looked bewildered. 'I don't know what you mean.'

Jessica, getting concerned now, struggled with her wallet and pulled out the sheet of paper with the library's address on it; she handed it to him. 'You printed this out for me, that's why I'm here. You told me to come here twenty-four hours ago!'

'I'm sorry, Jessica, I did not contact you at your home. Yes, I did expect your arrival, but only from speaking to Martin. Whoever hacked your home computer, it was not me.'

Jessica's head spun at the implication. 'Someone else knows I am here. Someone else knows about you, Martin, everything!'

'That's impossible. No one else knows.'

'Then who hacked my computer and printed out that? Who sent the image of Martin? Who told me I was a credible suicide risk and that I had to get out of the house?!'

Eric finally looked worried. 'A credible suicide risk?'

'This could be some kind of elaborate trap to draw you out, or to implicate me further.' Jessica put down her bag and hunted through it. At last she found what she was looking for and withdrew her gun.

'*Heilige Scheiße.*' Eric swore at the sight of the pistol.

Out of habit Jessica checked to see if the gun was still loaded – it was. 'We need to get out of here – fast!' she said.

Eric backed away, his eyes wide and transfixed on the weapon, before he switched them back to Jessica as though she were a live cobra, ready to strike.

An alarm sounded within Eric's computer room and Jessica whirled in its direction, gun pointed, ready to shoot.

'*Sich beruhigen*! Relax!' Eric told her, before moving over to one of his computers to tap at some keys.

Jessica joined him to see what was happening.

'*Verdammt*! This isn't good.' Eric's fingers danced with dizzying speed across his keyboard.

'What's wrong?'

'Someone has breached my system. This is not possible!' He began yanking out power cords left, right and centre.

As he did so, Jessica looked at his main monitor in shock. 'Stop!' she shouted at him and then hauled him away from his electrical demolition when he didn't respond.

'Look!' she said, pointing.

He turned round. On the screen, within a luminous green window, were three lines of white text followed by a flashing cursor. It read:

Eric. Forgive my intrusion.

Jessica Klein. We need to talk.

DMI _

'*Mutter, hab Erbarmen,*' Eric said in awe.

Jessica glanced at him, confused by his sudden reverence. 'What is it?'

'DMI,' he said as if that explained everything.

'DMI?'

'Da Muss Ich.'

'Because I Must,' she translated. 'What does that mean?'

'It means we're speaking to the greatest hacker in the world. The greatest hacker of a generation. He is a legend. A true ghost. A God amongst men. '

Jessica felt tense. 'What does he want with us?'

'With *you*,' he said. 'I don't know. Shall we find out?'

CHAPTER ELEVEN

Jessica looked at the flashing cursor as if it were an unexploded landmine, armed and incredibly dangerous. This was the person who had hacked her home computer, not young Eric who stood with her now.

'What else do you know about him?' Jessica asked, as at Eric's gentle insistence she sat down in front of his keyboard.

'He is one of the most wanted men on the planet,' Eric said. 'Most people outside of underground circles will not have heard of him, although he does go by many other names. The GMRC have been after him for a decade, with little success. He is the only one who has been able to repel the Hounds. Well, that isn't totally true; there have been many who have been able to fight back at the GMRC operators and intelligent code clusters, but out of them all he is the only one left standing. Or so it is whispered on the Deepnet. Many say he is from South America or Japan, but I think *Da Muss Ich* is German.'

'What are his other names?' Jessica said, still reluctant to begin a conversation with such an intangible and nefarious individual.

'Deforcement Insidious. D'Force. Bic. Because I Can. Elusive D. There are many others, it depends which country you come from. The Japanese simply refer to him as *Oyakata*, or Master.'

'Hang on.' She recognised one of the names. 'You don't mean B.I.C. the cyber terrorist do you?'

'That is what I said. Bic. Because I Can. Although that is what he is called in America.'

'Oh my God, I think I have heard of him. A hacker called B.I.C. stole millions of dollars from multiple banks about eight years ago, but the U.S. government said they'd caught him. They exposed him, his photo, background, everything.'

Eric gave her a knowing smile. 'That is what they wanted everyone to believe. They couldn't let the public think there was someone running around stealing that much money and getting away with it. It would give other people ideas. He also devised a combined attack on the Chinese government three years later, stealing secret documents and codes. There are many other successful hacks he is credited with, plus the greatest infiltration ever – a hack into the GMRC archives themselves. That particular incident resulted in a massive virtual flooding of the system four years ago. Whatever he found must have been big, as the kick back was unprecedented; Deepnet hasn't been the same since and proactive hackers are a dying breed.'

'How do you know so much?' she asked. 'You're so young.'

'I started getting into hacking when I was twelve and haven't looked back since. It's my life. I'm not the greatest; I just dip into Deepnet and back out again. I did do some local hacking and even some national stuff when I was younger but, as I said, Deepnet and the Surface Web is different now; more dangerous for people like me to operate.'

Jessica, still staring at the monitor, digested what Eric had just told her. An international terrorist, that's who she was relying on to help her, to give her the truth she was now closer to than ever before. Eric's disturbing news on the world's resources could well be what the GMRC was trying to hide, but it still begged the question why. Why were they transferring critical food and water supplies away from the populace and, just as importantly, where was it going to?

'Are you going to answer him?' Eric said. 'He's still waiting.'

Jessica rested her fingers on the keys and began to type.

Who are you? Eric says you are Da Muss Ich but I think you're an international terrorist, a wanted criminal. Jessica hit Enter and waited for a response.

You are both correct _

Then why should I trust you?

The reasons are many. Your options are few _

'Of course we can trust him,' Eric said, reading over her shoulder, his excitement plain to hear. 'Ask him what he wants to talk about.'

Why do you want to talk to me?

'That's not what I meant,' Eric said, sounding exasperated.

'Look, neither of us really knows who we're speaking to,' she told him. 'He could be the GMRC for all we know. Let's just be careful, okay?'

Eric muttered something in German that she didn't quite catch.

You are well known, Jessica Klein. You have a following. People listen to you when you talk. You are the conduit to the people _

. . .

Why do you need a conduit, and why me? There are plenty of other newsreaders out there.

I saw your broadcast, Jessica Klein. You have power, a presence, motivation and are known the world over. You are the perfect one, the only one to bring truth to the people _

What truth?

I cannot tell you the truth. You need to see it. Document and record it _

And then what happens when I have seen this truth?

I will release The Playground _

'What the hell is The Playground?' she said in frustration. 'This cryptic cloak and dagger charade is getting old fast.'

'The Playground is supposedly a part of Deepnet that is free from all other digital influences,' Eric explained. 'It operates like a single bubble in a sea of liquid. Nothing can get in and nothing can get out. This bubble, however, can disintegrate and reappear anywhere at any time, which is why it is impossible to track, hack or intercept. Whoever controls The Playground is able to produce massive amounts of pristine code, unaffected by hidden programmes or operators.'

'Supposedly?' Jessica felt way out of her depth.

'I thought it was just a myth.'

'Obviously not.'

Eric nodded and looked as though he was in shock.

'So what happens if it was released, this Playground?' she asked.

'Its effects, if it was released into Deepnet and beyond into the Surface Web, would depend upon what it contained inside. That's its main weapon; no one knows what would happen. It would be a law unto itself.'

She typed another message. You mean to expose the GMRC and whatever it is they are hiding from us?

Yes _

And you will use whatever I record and witness to be part of the exposure, to give credence to your message?

Yes _

She hesitated. Where do you want me to go?

Stuttgart to meet a GMRC insider _

And he will take me to see for myself what the GMRC is hiding from us?

Yes. He works on a classified programme _

Will this be dangerous?

. . .

Yes _

I have a family to think about, what makes you think I will do as you ask?

You know as well as I that your family and the rest of the world's population will be starved to death within two years. Eric's observations are correct. The world's resources are secretly being eroded. To ensure your family's survival you must do anything I ask. Besides, either way you will both be leaving soon anyway _

Why would we be doing that?

The GMRC are coming _

What!? How? When?!

I have access to local GMRC transmissions. They have scoured the library. They know who you are. They know someone is helping you. They are interrogating the programmes within the library system. It will only be a matter of time before they query the German government's big data servers, they will track you down within the hour. Tell Eric to plug his printer back in, I have some instructions for you both. It is time to move _

Eric didn't need telling twice; he was already reattaching various plugs to their respective sockets. The printer hummed to life and spewed forth a sheet of paper. Eric snatched it up.

'What does it say?' Jessica said.

'Instructions to get to a safe house, and information on how to keep in constant communication with him during our journey.'

'What about this place?' She indicated his plush home.

He shrugged his shoulders. 'Easy come, easy go. This is way more important than a nice house. We could be changing the world, saving lives. This is bigger than big. It's as big as it gets.'

Eric handed the paper to her and then rushed off to start gathering supplies together. Jessica read the sheet and then typed one more line into the computer and hit Enter.

I'm trusting you, Bic. Do not let me down.

The truth shall set you free, Jessica Klein _

A few seconds after the last message displayed, the screen went blank and shut down. One thing was for sure; she had more reasons to trust Bic than the GMRC or the authorities. Jessica knew the risks involved, but this is what she did. This is what she was born to do. If she couldn't accept this challenge as a reporter then she might as well give up now. Whatever it was the GMRC were hiding, it was big, massive. If what Eric had told her about the resources was true, and she believed it was, then her family was as good as dead if she didn't do something about it. In fact, the whole world's population was as good as dead if she didn't do anything about it. She had to find out what was going on and help this DMI, Bic or whatever his name was to expose the truth, whatever it might be. If Bic wanted to play games, then she would just have to follow the rules until she had what she really needed; the information to protect her family. After that, she would concentrate on exposing the GMRC itself, with or without Bic's help, perhaps changing the game in her favour in the process.

♦

In less than thirty minutes Eric had disassembled all the equipment he deemed too valuable to leave behind and loaded up his van with that, and other cardboard boxes full of clothing, food and drink. Following the instructions Bic had provided, Eric connected up some odd looking pieces of electrical equipment and positioned a small touchscreen in the middle of the van's dashboard. He tapped a few keys on his computer, the screen glowed into life, and Bic was once more in direct contact with them.

Time to go Eric _ the screen read.

Eric started the engine, activated the garage door and drove out into the freezing night.

♦

Jessica slept for the first few hours of the journey as they travelled south-west down the E51, a route within the European international road network. She woke to the sound of Eric singing along to a German pop song.

Frowning at the noise, she stretched out her back, which had cramped up during her sleep. 'Where are we?' she asked, her voice groggy.

'Approaching Nuremberg.' Eric looked over to her. 'Have a nice sleep?'

'Has our mysterious friend been back in touch?' she said, ignoring his question.

'On and off. I've opened up a voice command our end so we can just speak and he will hear what we say. Just press this button,' he pointed to one side of the touchscreen, 'when you want him to hear us.'

'What did he have to say for himself? Anything interesting?'

'Some, yes.'

'And?' Jessica said, when Eric failed to elaborate.

'Oh, yes, sorry. Well, he says he has been following both our movements and helping to hide our tracks from prying eyes. He's been aware of my activities within Deepnet for a couple of years. Fancy that, *Da Muss Ich* taking an interest in *das Gespenst*!'

Jessica could see Eric was ecstatic that his hero had been keeping tabs on him. She, however, felt more than a little violated that someone had been monitoring her every move, regardless of their intentions. It creeped her out and stripped away the façade of privacy even further, on top of that already stolen from her by the GMRC itself.

After a few more miles, they pulled into a lay-by and Jessica took over the driving, enabling Eric to catch up on some sleep. The information that she had been tracked was playing on Jessica's mind. Now that the GMRC knew she was in Germany, she'd decided her appearance needed to be altered, although there was little she could do at that point in time. She settled for wearing a baseball cap loaned to her by Eric, which covered up her red hair. It was an hour into her stint that Bic decided to get back in touch via the screen, a small bleep announcing the arrival of a message.

Our secret is out. The van has been identified. Increase your speed and take the next exit. GMRC aerial drones are en route _

Jessica swore and stepped on the gas. The racket from the van's old engine increased in volume as it strained to obey the mechanical command of its driver. Jessica watched the speed on the main dial edge upwards towards one hundred and fifty kilometres per hour. The van, now in the fast lane, flew past slower traffic on the inside. A blue road sign, alerting her to the next exit, appeared out of the darkness ahead, lit up by the van's headlights. Jessica aimed the vehicle down the off ramp, hitting the brakes hard to slow down their rapid transition onto a tight bend. The van's suspension rolled to one side, the tyres screeching on the road surface as they flew round and onto a smaller single lane back road. Jessica slowed the pace, checking her mirrors for any sign of pursuit; they might have drones in the air, but the feeling of being chased was a powerful one and her senses were all on edge.

Keep your speed up and pull off into the town of Aalen. Follow the map I am about to put on this screen _

Jessica increased her speed again, overtaking a couple of slower vehicles in the process, but wary of the smaller road which appeared to have less salt on it to keep the snow and ice at bay. Following the coloured map on the screen, she soon found herself pulling into a small field. The van bumped and bounced across the uneven surface, which roused Eric from his deep sleep.

'What's going on? Why have we left the main road?' he asked in concern.

'We're being followed. They're looking for the van. Bic guided us here; we're on the outskirts of a town called Aalen.'

'What does he want us to do, hide?'

'No.' She pointed to the screen, which had changed back to text. 'He wants us to do that.'

Take what you can carry from the van and then run it into the lake in front of you. Hurry – the drones are in the area and are scanning for you _

. . .

Eric spoke into the screen. 'What about all my things? There's too much to carry!'

There is no time to argue Eric. Just do as I say or you will get caught _

Jessica stopped the van near the edge of the body of water, which looked to have a thin covering of ice over it, and clambered into the back to join Eric, who was throwing things around in a blind panic.

'Calm down!' Jessica said. 'Think. Just take the bare essentials.'

It wasn't long until the two stood outside on the hard snow, their breath sending dissipating puffs of hot air twisting into the starless night sky. Each carried a cardboard box crammed with Eric's most cherished computer equipment, a few items of clothing, and some packs of food. Jessica put her box down, got back into the van, turned the engine on and backed it up twenty feet. Leaving the handbrake on, she put it into first gear and then wedged down the accelerator with one of Eric's discarded box of tricks. Opening the driver's door, Jessica dropped the handbrake and jumped clear. The van gained some speed and then crunched down into the ice at the edge of the lake, its momentum sending it further in as water rushed in around it. Eric looked downcast as the top of the vehicle disappeared from view, consumed by the black depths of the lake it to which had just been sacrificed.

Jessica glanced down at the screen perched in the top of the open box she now cradled in her arms. 'Come on,' she told him. 'Bic says to follow this map.'

The two fugitives trudged out of the field and onto the road. Five minutes on and they'd reached a residential housing estate, Bic's messages guiding them to an empty house wired into a high-tech security system. Regrettably for the absent owners, the system hadn't accounted for coming into contact with a world class hacker and Bic had soon disabled it, providing them with entry through the back door. Taking the opportunity to create new disguises to aid with any future evasion of the GMRC and police, the two searched the bedrooms for clothing. The women's clothing Jessica found in one of the wardrobes was way too large for her small frame, but Eric had found the house was also home to two teenage boys; perfect for him and adequate for her. Gathering up some sports jackets, trousers, trainers and sweatshirts, the two went into separate rooms to change. Jessica, alone in a stranger's house and putting on boy's attire while on the run from the GMRC, felt a strange kind of detachment from reality as she struggled into a tight T-shirt. Managing to wrestle it over her head, she saw that Eric stood in the doorway watching her.

She let out a small scream. 'Get out!' she shouted, acutely aware she was only in her knickers below the waist.

Eric ducked back out of the room. 'Sorry!' he said, from the other side of the door.

Jessica emerged a few minutes later and gave him a stern look. 'You should knock if a lady is changing.'

Eric blushed and nodded in mute recognition of his inadequate etiquette. Now ready to move again, they worked their way through into the attached double garage which contained a brand new electric sports car.

Eric whistled in appreciation. '*Schön*. I get to drive it first.'

Eric took the lead this time and used one of his gizmos to unlock the doors and start up the electric motor. Stowing their dwindling gear into the tiny boot, Jessica opened the large up and over door and then returned to sit in the passenger seat next to an eager Eric.

'Be careful,' she said, 'it's still icy out there.'

Eric heeded her warning and they only picked up speed once they'd returned to the autobahn. As they kept to the limit, to avoid drawing attention, a high pitched whistling noise passed overhead. Peering out of the windscreen they caught sight of a small fast moving object in the sky above.

Jessica's eyes narrowed. 'GMRC drone.'

'Except they're looking for an old beat-up van, not a state-of-the-art sports car,' Eric said, a mischievous grin spreading across his boyish face.

He was right to be pleased, too, as they arrived at Stuttgart without further incident. Again following Bic's directions, the two found themselves driving the car into what looked like an old monastery, the cobbles beneath making it feel like the car was being shaken to pieces as it travelled over the uneven surface. From out of a small building within a courtyard, a man dressed in plain brown ecclesiastical garb directed them into a small carport. Exiting the stolen vehicle, the doors shutting with two soft thuds, the companions retrieved their possessions and followed the man into a nearby building without a word being exchanged between them. Eric entered first with Jessica close behind. Shutting the door, she turned around to see Eric standing with his hands in the air.

'*Hände hoch*!' the man said. He held a large double-barrelled shotgun and it was pointed at her chest.

Jessica put down her box and rucksack and raised her hands in the air.

The man motioned at the floor with his gun. '*Hinlegen, legen Sie Ihre Hände hinter dem Rücken*!'

Eric and Jessica did as they were bid, lying face down on the floor and putting their hands behind their backs. As she lay on the cold, hard stone, her face going numb, Jessica remembered her experience back in New York and felt an unpleasant sense of déjà vu. The man, who dressed like a monk but acted like a soldier, grabbed her wrists. A plastic cable tie was pulled tight around them, the sound of its small ratchet teeth loud to her ears as it bit deep into her flesh.

'I don't know who you two are,' the man said in English, his accent Middle Eastern, 'but you have made a big mistake coming here.'

Jessica closed her eyes and sighed. They had been betrayed.

CHAPTER TWELVE

SARAH AWOKE WITH A START, another nightmare lingering on the edges of memory, the same images of maps, fire and smoke haunting her dreams like a vengeful spirit reluctant to depart. She could almost taste the ash in her mouth and feel the heat on her skin, so vivid and powerful were the departing visions; she put her hands to her face as her emotions sought to release tears she was determined not to let fall. Sweat had beaded on her brow and the rest of her skin felt cold and clammy. Curling into a ball, she attempted to preserve some body heat and opened her eyes to take in her stark surroundings. The familiar cramped cell was an unwelcome sight, so she pulled her small blanket up over her head to block it from view.

This was the fifth day of her second stint in the military prison. Mercifully, so far at least, she hadn't had to endure the company of Sergeant Major Collins; *although*, she mused, *the way my luck is going – give it time.*

Why did I venture into that restricted area so soon after my reunion with Trish and Jason? she asked herself. *I'd barely had time to speak to them and now I could be locked up for God knows how long.* She inwardly cursed her own stupidity, but another part of her mind, a quieter, more sensible part, advised her that hindsight was a wonderful thing.

Given the high level of security clearance required to enter the Sanctuary Exploration Division – level seven, according to the man who had blown her cover – her stay could well be a long one. Military justice was not often associated with a fair trial; *in fact, I'll be lucky to get a trial at all*, she decided.

Strangely her guard seemed almost happy to see her return to the prison. She assumed he must get lonely down there and be only too pleased to have someone to feed and water on a regular basis. It made the atmosphere of confinement marginally better than her previous experience, but when he'd given her a small rubber ball to while away her time she'd felt like a caged pet that had just been gifted with a new toy. While being a kind gesture, it was still humiliating, and she'd refused to play with it as a matter of principle and pride.

Hours came and went and Sarah shifted round the cell in varying positions as her boredom mounted. When she found herself lying upside down on the bed with her head hanging towards the floor, she could resist it no longer. The small orange ball which she had been trying to ignore all but shouted *'play with me, Sarah!'* from its position in the corner of the room. Jumping up, she grabbed it and squeezed it in the palm of her hand; the sensation felt oddly comforting. She bounced it a few times on the floor, each impact echoing around the enclosed space. Positioning herself on the bed she bounced the ball from floor to wall and back over to the bed, where she caught it deftly. Repeating the process she zoned out, enjoying the basic pastime with a mindless enthusiasm. The fact that the activity resembled an old movie she'd once seen was not lost on her, the rhythm of the ball hitting the hard surfaces becoming almost hypnotic in its regularity.

Sarah was unsure how much time had passed when the sound of her cell door being unlocked roused her from her game. She was almost annoyed at the intrusion as she'd been varying the ball's speed and trajectory, making it harder and harder to catch; it was actually quite entertaining.

The guard pulled back the heavy sliding door. 'I see you like the ball.'

Sarah shrugged and made an odd noise of indifference. She didn't want to show her appreciation too soon; perhaps he would try harder and bring her something even better next time.

As he led her down the all too familiar corridor a feeling of dread descended upon her. 'You're not taking me to see Collins are you?'

'No. The Sergeant Major has been suspended from duty since – well, you know why.'

Thank God for that, she thought to herself, sitting down in the interrogation room.

'Someone will be with you shortly,' the guard told her and then left her alone once more. From the sound of it he wasn't even sticking around to prevent her from escaping; his footfalls receded down the corridor until they were out of earshot.

Once more the time dragged inexorably by and Sarah fiddled with her fingers. As more time passed, the clock on the wall ticking away the seconds, she found herself chewing at her fingernails. Biting one off, she leant to her left and spat it onto the floor. As she looked back, Sarah near jumped out of her skin as someone sat down in front of her.

'Jesus!' she said in shock. 'Creep much, why don't you?'

The man looked amused. 'Lost your nail clippers, have you?'

'You!' she said, her eyes narrowing in recognition.

The man smiled. 'Yes, me.'

'What happened to the three minutes' head start you promised me?' she said, as various emotions vied for control within her.

'I don't remember promising anything, I offered you three minutes and then you shot off like a cheetah with its tail on fire and I had to revaluate my position. I'm Riley Orton, by the way.' He held out a hand.

Sarah looked at the proffered digits with disdain, refusing to take them.

Riley didn't take offence and instead pointed to her face. 'How's the bruise?'

Sarah's hand went to the right side of her face before she snatched it back down, her expression fierce. 'What do you care?'

'It looks painful. Butt of a gun, I heard?'

Sarah looked at the floor, not caring to speak any further to the man who'd been pivotal to her current incarceration.

'Look,' he said as he put a hand out towards her to try and regain her attention. 'I didn't know you had form. I thought you would just get a rap on the knuckles; no harm, no foul. How was I to know you'd already been in here for months? Everyone who lives and works in Sanctuary is selected on merit, no one is ever down here unless they're allowed to be down here; which, by the way, is very impressive – you gaining access to a top secret facility over two miles underground – you'll have to tell me the story sometime.'

Sarah glared at him.

'Or not,' he said quickly. 'Anyway, when I heard of your indefinite term in the prison I thought I'd better act, seeing as I was the one who landed you here.'

He paused; waiting for a reaction but Sarah still sat stony faced, refusing to interact with him. Whatever he wanted she wasn't going to make it easy.

'I used to work in the military,' he told her as if she cared, 'so I called in some markers and I've got you released.'

Sarah's distrust switched to disbelieving hope as she looked at Riley in a new light.

'So you'll be free to go as soon as the paperwork is completed,' he said.

'What's the catch?' She feared some kind of 'but...' coming on.

'No catch. Well, that's not strictly true. I will need you to commit to something for me.'

Sarah heaved a sigh; she knew it was too good to last. 'Something?'

'Yes. I want you to come and work at the SED.'

'What? You want me, a level one interloper, to work in Sanctuary's Exploration Division? Why and how!?'

Riley smiled at her. 'The how is easy. I lead one of the elite Deep Reach teams for the SED, so I operate with a certain amount of autonomy and I also wield some clout with SED Command. As to the why, I want you on my team. It's as simple as that.'

Her mistrust returned. 'Nothing is that simple.'

'Well, no, you're right,' he conceded. 'There are many reasons why I, and the SED, want you working for us. First, you've already seen our hub of operations, which we would like to keep out of the public sphere. If you worked for us we wouldn't have to worry about exposure. Most of our work is highly classified and if word got out that teams of people were regularly going outside the USSB and deep into Sanctuary Proper, then unrest could spread through the rank and file.

'Secondly, according to your file, you are an accomplished climber with extensive field experience in a variety of challenging terrains. Such skills make you a perfect candidate for a Deep reach survey team. Thirdly, you are a qualified anthropological archaeologist who has not only managed to uncover ancient artefacts and remains belonging to a race that has been hidden away for generations, but someone who has managed to locate and penetrate the most secretive and secure facility on the planet. Sarah, if anyone was born to work in Sanctuary's Exploration Division, it's you.

'If you want further reasons, you have helped highlight significant flaws in the SED's security procedures, and last, but by no means least, your deployment to the SED will alleviate my guilt for getting you into this mess. Also, on an entirely more selfish note, your addition to my team will give me the edge over the competition.

'So, what do you think?' he asked her. 'Fancy becoming a member of one of the most exciting, dangerous and important professions in the world?'

Sarah couldn't help but chuckle and shake her head in disbelief at the sudden turnaround in her fortunes. Riley certainly put up a good case for why she should take him up on the offer. What he didn't know was she had an even better reason for joining; it would gain her precious access outside of the USSB and much greater freedom to document, and then to potentially escape, Sanctuary itself.

Sarah gestured to his red and blue uniform. 'Do I get to wear the helmet that goes with that suit?'

Riley grinned at her and the effect was contagious.

♦

Riley was as good as his word and later that day Sarah was released from military custody back into the general populace of the United States Subterranean Base. Amazingly, Riley had already managed to secure her a new apartment, located within a chamber reserved for SED personnel. Upon leaving the military enclave she had also had her MF Card upgraded to a clearance level of Seven Delta, a far cry from the level One Beta she had initially been allocated.

Riley himself had shown her round her new home, which was a two storey affair with over four times the space of the old apartment; although, as before, half the rooms, including her bedroom, backed onto a transport route, pedestrian walkways passing right next to her windows. Nothing was ever perfect, it seemed.

Once Riley had departed, Sarah, readjusting to her new reality, was overwhelmed to see her MF Card now contained a sizeable number of credits. An advance on future earnings, she assumed, or perhaps another bribe from Riley; either way she was pleased to have it, as it enabled her to call Trish and Jason and to arrange a meet up in the New Park district.

An hour later, the three friends sat next to a burbling stream in a picturesque café in one of the parks that surrounded the museum complex. This was the first time they'd had the luxury of an in depth discussion since they'd been in the USSB, Sarah's latest arrest having thrown a spanner in the works of any meaningful conversation when they'd visited the museum almost a week earlier.

She filled them in on her new job at the SED and how Riley had ended up saving her bacon, a big turnaround from initially being the villain of the piece. Of course, she wasn't supposed to disclose such sensitive information, but quite frankly she didn't give a damn.

'You're a jammy bastard,' Jason said with envy. 'I'm stuck with refuse collection and poor old Trish is working in some kind of sweatshop.'

'Oh, it's not that bad,' Trish told Sarah, giving Jason a withering look. 'I work in a factory; we produce machine parts for the construction industry, which is expanding the base. It's quite important, really.'

'Well, none of our jobs matter anyway,' Sarah said. 'Now that I'm going to get access outside the base we can begin to plan our escape. In the meantime we can all keep documenting Sanctuary, the museum – everything.'

'We wondered what had happened to you,' Jason said as they sipped their drinks and nibbled on a rich selection of iced cakes Sarah had ordered for them. 'It was only when some guy came to see us a few days later that we found out you'd been arrested by the military again.'

'What guy? Riley?'

Jason looked thoughtful. 'Yeah, I think that was his name. Tall chap, yeah? Seemed nice enough. Same bloke that gave you your job, I suppose.'

Sarah looked to Trish. 'You met him too?'

'Yes, I was with Jason when he came round. He's rather nice, isn't he?'

Sarah gave a shrug. 'He's okay, I suppose.'

'Oh, come on, Sarah, he's more than okay. He's gorgeous; tall, handsome, in control and definitely charming.'

'He looked like a bit of a twat to me,' Jason said.

Trish frowned. 'You just said he seemed nice.'

'I was being kind; it's not nice to put someone down when they're not around.'

'But you'd do it to their face, then, would you?' Trish said, unconvinced.

'I might do, if I wanted to. Anyway he was a bit of a letch, he probably only gave Sarah that job to get into her knickers.'

Sarah crossed her arms. 'Oh, thanks.'

'No offence,' Jason added, with little deference.

'Some taken.'

'Well, it's obvious, isn't it,' Jason continued, unabashed.

'What is?' Trish asked, her tone hardening.

'Single guy. It would have been his main driving force. I'm a man—'

'That's debatable,' Trish said.

'I'm a man,' he repeated, 'and if I was in a position of power—'

Trish snorted at the prospect.

'—I'd employ young single women, not some old frump who was over the hill. It's the way of the world. Sarah could have been some boss-eyed goon, but if she had a nice bum and a good pair of legs then she'd have got the job.'

Trish picked up a piece of cake and chucked it at him in disgust. Jason looked down at the offending projectile, picked it off his shirt and popped it in his mouth. 'Thanks,' he said with an insolent grin.

'You disgust me,' Trish said.

Jason appeared smug. 'Just telling it how it is, way of the world 'n' all that.'

'So let me get this straight,' Sarah said. 'The reason Riley gave me the job had nothing to do with my hard-earned qualifications or skills in the field, but because I've got a nice bum and a good pair of legs?'

Jason put a finger to his nose and pointed to Sarah with his other hand as he munched down another cake. 'Correct!' he said with his mouth full. 'And to be honest, your legs and bum don't even need to be that nice, as long as you're youngish and firm you'd have got in, no probs.'

This time a whole cream cake flew into Jason's face; he squawked in protest. 'Oi!'

'Nice shot.' Trish held out her hand to Sarah, who slapped it with a resounding smack of solidarity.

'Some people just can't take the truth,' Jason muttered to himself, as the two women looked at him with a mixture of amused disapproval and superior contempt.

While Jason cleaned himself up, Sarah told Trish more about her new position at the SED and how they might use it to their advantage.

'Perhaps you could get us on the team, too?' Jason suggested, butting into the conversation as he rid himself of the last remnants of Sarah's cake attack.

'It had crossed my mind.' Sarah glanced at Jason and then turned to face Trish again. 'If all three of us had passes out of the base, then it would make things a lot easier.'

'You could put in a good word for us,' Jason said. 'We've got good field experience and we're good archaeologists, too.'

'There's one problem with that,' Trish told him. 'Your legs and bum are hideous and hairy and as for your face – well. I suppose we could shave you and put you in a dress, but we want to get a job in the SED, not in a cabaret club for the blind.'

Sarah couldn't help but laugh as Trish turned the tables on Jason's previous outdated rhetoric.

He held up his hands. 'Okay, perhaps I deserved that, but—' He got to his feet and turned round to stick his bum out. 'This is one fine piece of Welsh rump. I reckon it'd get me in, what do you think?' He wiggled his bottom round and round and then jiggled it up and down energetically.

Trish looked mortified as other patrons of the café peered in their direction. 'Oh my God, stop it!'

Sarah, not wanting to encourage him, turned away and put her hand over her mouth to stifle her laughter as her shoulders shook with mirth.

Jason sat back down again with a big beaming grin on his face, his attempt at reconciling their differences by self-humiliation a resounding success.

'You're an idiot,' Trish told him.

He gave her a wink. 'And proud of it.'

As time went on, their fleeting altercation forgotten and Jason's misogyny forgiven, talk inevitably turned to Sanctuary, the museum and Homo gigantis.

'Can you believe there are forty-five underground bases around the world?' Jason said. 'They kept that quiet, didn't they? You'd have thought word would have got out that these places were being built.'

'They won't all be as big as this one,' Trish replied, 'but yes, you'd think there would have been rumours or leaks at some point.'

Sarah sat up straighter. 'They must have been building them for a long time. The cost must have been monumental; so much for the governments not having much money to spend.'

'Well, that's probably true,' Jason said, 'because they've spent it on all these bases. Oh, and what about the induction video?' he added, his eyes alight with excitement.

'What about it?' Trish asked.

'The bit where that professor guy said put your hands up if you thought aliens built Sanctuary. I put my hand up, I said it was aliens, didn't I?

'Yes, you did.' She looked at Sarah and rolled her eyes.

'Even though I thought it probably was Homo gigantis, I said aliens, as it's—'

'Always aliens,' Trish and Sarah said in unison, stealing his punchline and laughing at his perplexed expression.

A waiter came over to the table. 'Excuse me, sir,' he said, addressing Jason, 'one of our female customers asked me to bring you this drink.' He placed a lavish cocktail down on the table.

'Excellent!' Jason picked it up and saluted his admirer a few tables away.

The waiter coughed. 'Yes, sir. She also asked me to give you a message.'

'Which was?'

'The lady said, "You can wiggle your booty for her anytime".'

'No way!' Trish said, looking at the woman in question. 'Is she blind?'

The waiter leaned forward. 'Excuse me, sir.' He extended a hand

and plucked a cake peanut from Jason's hair and placed it on his plate.

'Thanks.' Jason picked up the offending item and popped it in his mouth.

'All part of the service, sir.' The waiter moved away.

If Jason's smile gets any bigger it's going to swallow his head, Sarah thought.

'Am I dreaming?' Trish asked.

Sarah laughed. 'No, 'fraid not.'

While Jason basked in his glory and savoured his free drink, Sarah continued the conversation with Trish. 'I'm gutted we haven't made the find of the century. I thought we'd found ground-breaking evidence of Homo gigantis, but with this place sitting down here it pales into insignificance.'

Trish shook her head. 'You don't know that. What about the pendant? You figured that out and from what Jason and I saw in the museum they haven't figured out how to operate any of the ancient technology they've found. They haven't even been able to decode any of the languages yet, as far as I can see.'

Jason sipped his drink. 'There was also no sign of any pendants like yours in the display cases.'

'That's something, I suppose.' Sarah felt a bit more upbeat. 'That's what we need to do as well; recover our artefacts and gear, mainly the artefacts.'

'Your higher clearance might make that easier,' Trish told her, 'although the military might still have it all under lock and key.'

Sarah pursed her lips. 'Riley said he used to be in the military. I'll try and broach the subject at some point and see what he thinks. You never know, the Smithsonian might have it by now; they are after all Anakim related.'

'I wonder what happened to our camp on the surface?' Jason said. 'The canister and bones might still be up there, sitting out in the open for anyone to get their thieving hands on.'

Trish leant forwards. 'I've been thinking about that too. They're either still where we left them or the locals or Vatican have nabbed them, or maybe the military from this base sent out a communication to have everything picked up and brought back down here.'

'Sadly, we may never find out,' Sarah said. 'I try not to think about it. We have enough to worry about down here. We can think on that when we get to the surface.'

'If we don't find any trace of our stuff down here that is,' Jason added.

Sarah nodded in agreement. 'I have to admit, though, the knowledge that this place exists and actually being in it comes a very close second to having discovered Sanctuary ourselves, don't you think?'

'Most definitely,' Trish said.

'Bloody hell, yes,' Jason agreed. 'This place is unbelievable.'

Sarah looked around, making sure they remained out of earshot of any eavesdroppers. 'It shouldn't be a secret, though. To keep something like this hidden is a crime against humanity. Also, some of these people may seem nice, but I don't trust any of them; we are basically prisoners down here for all intents and purposes. We must never forget that.'

'I suppose you're right,' Trish said.

Sarah looked up at the sun, or at least the simulation of sunlight, from the dome above. She thought it strange to be underground and basking in this light, whereas on the surface everyone else was consigned to living beneath a blackened sky. It was perhaps this abstract image, in a roundabout way, that made her realise she needed to unburden herself. 'There's something I need to tell you both.'

Trish and Jason looked at her expectantly as she struggled with how to begin. 'After my artefacts were stolen in Oxford, I realised my previous discoveries hadn't been taken from me in freak occurrences. The stolen femur and burnt maps must have been the work of the same people who broke into the vault in Oxford. The confrontation with Carl and the Italian in Turkey reinforce my certainty that my theory is actually fact and that the Vatican was behind all four incidents.'

Sarah halted and fiddled with her fingers as she sought more words to say while Trish and Jason exchanged looks, unsure where this was leading.

'As the maps were taken from me on purpose,' Sarah continued, 'that also means the fire was started deliberately and in turn my mother's subsequent death was no accident. The inconclusive report on how the fire started also lends itself to arson. Since they targeted my maps and I put the maps in my mum's house for safekeeping, it's down to me that she died before her time.'

'Sarah, no!' Trish's voice was full of concern. 'You can't possibly blame yourself for that, you didn't start that fire and even if someone did do it to destroy your evidence of gigantis, then they are to blame, not you!'

Sarah knew her friend was right, she didn't start the fire and couldn't have prevented her mother's death, but it didn't stop her from feeling a deep sense of guilt, shame and despair about her indirect contribution to it. 'They may have started the fire, but it was my actions that led to her death and there's nothing you can say to convince me otherwise. It's a fact.'

Trish looked at Jason for some support, but he seemed reluctant to say anything. Trish frowned at him and with a subtle head movement indicated she wanted him to say something supportive.

'It might not have been deliberate – the fire,' Jason said at Trish's instigation. 'It could have been just an accident, a coincidence.'

Sarah gave him a weak smile and knew he meant well, but she could tell he believed that as much as she did. 'I want to bring the people responsible for her death to justice,' Sarah told them, her voice flat and cold as she fought to keep her emotions in check.

'How will you do that?' Trish asked, choosing her words with care. 'The police didn't find anything at the scene, if I remember rightly.'

Sarah shifted in her seat 'I don't know, but I won't stop until I find out who killed my mother, or at the very least expose the cover-up of gigantis, which will strike a blow at the Vatican and the people that work for them.'

'Is that why you were so intent on extracting that Mayan plaque from the monument in the Copán ruins?' Trish said, finally able to understand her friend's motivations.

'And why you were so keen to go to South Africa, despite the danger involved?' Jason added.

Sarah nodded.

No one spoke for a moment as they digested Sarah's revelations.

'Have you considered the GMRC or U.S. Government might have started the fire that destroyed the maps?' Trish asked, her tone tentative.

'The thought crossed my mind,' Sarah admitted, 'but my online group always fingered the Catholic Church for the cover-ups, especially in Europe. Plus our run in with the Italian all but seals it for me. There were other fires that destroyed gigantis evidence in the past, according to my group, and from records found dating back to the middle ages the Vatican even admitted they set fires to purge heresies from being spread; specific cases even hint that the objects targeted for destruction may have been of gigantis origin.'

'That the Vatican set fires to maintain their doctrine isn't new, Sarah,' Trish said, 'and your group can come up with some pretty outlandish claims in their quest to prove gigantis exists.'

'I don't think the U.S. or GMRC had anything to do with the fire or the theft of the other artefacts,' Jason said to Sarah. 'There was mention of the Catholic Church's activities in Sanctuary's museum; I saw it on the day you got rearrested. It goes into some detail about the lengths that the Catholic Church went to in covering up the existence of gigantis in Europe and South America. The U.S. Government had altercations with agents of the Church back in the eighteen hundreds and even as recently as the late twentieth century. The major difference between the two factions – the Vatican and the U.S. Government – is that one wants to destroy the existence of gigantis, while the other just wants to keep it hidden. The museum we visited should be testament to that fact on its own.'

Trish looked at Jason with some surprise, clearly impressed by his serious and well thought out argument.

Sarah wasn't taken aback by Jason's new information, but it did confirm beyond a shadow of a doubt who was to blame for the fire that had robbed her of much more than evidence of the historical existence of giants.

Jason leaned forward and lowered his voice. 'The references in the museum also indicate that there is still friction between the Smithsonian Institution and the Vatican to this day. It didn't go into details, but that's what it implied. There was also one interesting passage of text about another organisation that has links to the Roman Catholic Church and one that may have knowledge of the Anakim.'

'What are they called?' Sarah knew every scrap of information could help her in her quest for justice.

'The Apocryphon. It doesn't say anything else about them. I thought you might be interested so I looked up the term on the USSB's library database and there's no further reference to it anywhere.'

Sarah listened as Jason described other interesting titbits of information he'd unearthed at the museum and Trish also joined in, relaying details of her own discoveries. Sarah, happy to let talk divert away from the painful subject she had finally had the courage to share with her two friends, sat back, only joining in to ask the odd question. Some time later she took her leave and made her way back to her new digs, the emotional drain from bringing up the subject of her mother making her seek out her own company.

♦

Trish, now alone with Jason, had time to discuss Sarah and the concerns she had for her friend.

'I'm just worried about her,' she said, as they walked around a small lake in the park.

Jason made a dismissive gesture. 'She'll be fine. She's just got a lot on her mind, is all.'

Trish's brows remained furrowed. 'I know she wants to blame someone for her mum's death, but if she thinks she can bring the Vatican, or individuals working for them, to book for their crimes she'll only meet with failure and the only one left to blame, according to her, will be Sarah herself.'

Jason plucked a flower from a nearby bush and began detaching the petals from it one by one. 'What do you propose we do about it? She's made up her mind. You know Sarah; when she gets a mind to do something, she doesn't stop until she achieves it.'

'You're right, but I can't help thinking she's seeking revenge rather than justice; and revenge is unhealthy, it will eat away at her from the inside.'

'You don't know she's out for revenge,' Jason said, 'and besides, revenge is a form of justice in itself. An eye for an eye 'n' all that; although considering it's the Church who she's up against, that phrase is perhaps a little inappropriate, but you know what I mean.'

Trish did know what he meant, he wasn't the subtlest of people, but she couldn't help but fear for Sarah. Jason was right about one thing, though; once Sarah had made her mind up there was little chance of changing it. They would just have to be there to help her when she needed it, or pick up the pieces if things went badly.

Trish glanced up at the dome's simulated sunset, which announced its presence above them with a sumptuous display of colour. Deep reds, blues and greens intermingled in a vision that amazingly managed to outstrip the real thing. 'Keep an eye on her for me, will you?' she asked Jason as they made their way back to the monotube station.

'Of course.' He gave her shoulder a reassuring squeeze. 'She'll be fine, though, you'll see. You worry too much.'

'I hope so,' she said, her vexation undiminished. 'I do hope so.'

CHAPTER THIRTEEN

LOUD, drawn out grinding noises punctuated the air, accompanied by a deep rumbling that sent powerful vibrations through the SED Command Centre and its surrounding building. These mysterious sounds petered away to nothing before starting again minutes later, indicating to Sarah that giant mechanisms were at work behind the scenes somewhere in the complex – somewhere close.

Nearby, a bewildering array of staff manned a multi-tiered office kitted out with state-of-the-art work stations, computers and communication systems – a control centre set-up resembling something utilised by NASA or the CNSA, China's national space agency. Huge transparent wallscreens dominated the rear of a raised platform which backed onto a large area Sarah recognised as the room in which Riley had become aware of her infiltration.

Now in Sanctuary's Exploration Division legitimately, Sarah could relax and take in her surroundings at leisure. She had yet to see Riley, but so far her first day had consisted of boring and yet necessary administrative procedures to enrol her in the programme as an SED employee. She didn't expect to understand the full workings of the extensive outfit on her first attempt, but from what she'd seen so far, and from her initial illegal foray, it would take many months to get up to speed on what went on here, if not longer. One thing was for sure, however, the SED beat the pants off the archivist position she'd previously been given in Sanctuary's Smithsonian Institution.

Currently, from her location in a reception room on the third floor of the Command Centre, Sarah watched a number of survey teams performing a rigorous set of training exercises. The instructor looked military and shouted out various commands in order to get his graduates to switch positions or to improve their energy or technique. One man fell to the floor in utter exhaustion, but rather than offer any kind of assistance, the drill sergeant moved to stand over him and scream out obscenities until his victim forced himself back to his feet to continue the punishing session, only to fall back down again moments later. Sarah's chest tightened in sympathy before a movement glanced out of the corner of her eye made her turn her head.

Riley had appeared at a doorway in front of her and waved her inside. 'Sarah, come in, he'll see you now.'

Sarah, dressed in her plain grey USSB uniform, stood up and brushed her hair back with a nervous hand before walking past Riley, who gave her a brief smile of support.

'Sit down, Miss Morgan,' a man seated behind a desk said, his voice rich with authority. Riley, remaining with her, closed the door behind them.

Sarah instantly recognised the man who had addressed the SED teams during her impromptu visit. Close up, he seemed a little less imposing and a tad older. His silvery hair, cropped in a military style, accentuated his powerful shoulders and strong jaw. Unlike before, he wore a white and red uniform, similar to the red and blue one Riley sported; the Deep Reach team leader in question took an informal seat on top of a desk off to her right.

'My name is Dresden Locke,' the man behind the desk began, his hands clasped in front of him on the table as Sarah settled into a chair opposite. 'I am the Sanctuary Exploration Division's commanding officer. While the SED operates with military oversight, we are primarily a civilian outfit and as such we have our own strict codes of conduct which we expect all our personnel to adhere to at all times. Riley, here,' he said, indicating his subordinate, 'tells me you will prove a valuable asset to the SED and has requested you be assigned to his survey team, Alpha Six.'

Sarah glanced at Riley who gave her a wink.

'You will be aware that your clearance level has already been upgraded,' Locke continued, 'but before I can sign off your deployment, you will need to pass the necessary tests and exams, both mental and physical. Everyone at the SED who goes outside the base is required to achieve a certain proficiency, but members of our Deep Reach teams are in privileged positions and only the best have what it takes to make the grade.

'Since your introduction to Sanctuary has been less than regular and your standing with the military is blotchy at best, Riley will be overseeing your training. He is also your guarantor and will be responsible for your actions. Any transgressions on your part will not only land you back in military custody, but will also have significant consequences for Riley himself. Needless to say, you are now representing the SED and I expect you to uphold our reputation with an exemplary and sustained commitment. If any of your actions are to the detriment of the SED I will personally drag you back to your cell and throw away the key. Do I make myself clear?'

Sarah nodded.

'The proper response is *yes, sir*,' Riley told her.

Sarah bobbed her head. 'Yes, sir.'

'Since Riley is to begin an important assignment in six weeks' time,' Locke continued, 'your training has been compressed to suit. Usually it takes four months to prepare for the assessments, so you are being thrown in at the deep end and will have to hit the ground running if you want to succeed. Fail the tests and you will be moved to admin, your clearance downgraded. Pass the tests but fail to meet the levels required for Deep Reach and you will be put on an archaeological team. Given the circumstances, an archaeological position is the most likely outcome, but it should not be seen as an easy ride.

The work of all our teams outside of Deep Reach is still highly demanding, although it is not as dangerous and you will only be working on sites already found by other teams.'

Dresden Locke appraised her for a moment before continuing. 'Personally I don't care if you succeed or not,' he told her. 'If you do, however, you will have joined an elite group undertaking perhaps the most important work on the planet. Surveying Sanctuary Proper will be extremely challenging, exciting and immensely rewarding, as you uncover lost civilisations, discover ancient artefacts, and potentially document new materials, species of plants, insects and even small animals.

'You should also be aware that the SED has a long and illustrious history, dating back to the year 1826 when Sanctuary was first discovered.' Locke indicated a black and white photograph mounted on the wall behind him, portraying a group of bearded men wearing nineteenth century clothing and kitted out with similarly antiquated climbing equipment. 'Our founder, John Quincy Adams, the sixth and, in my opinion, greatest ever President of the United States, wanted to create a legacy for those that followed in his footsteps. In various guises, and over many generations, the SED has functioned as the first and foremost agency in the exploration of this vast subterranean world. We were here long before the USSB was built, and long before the military even knew it existed and the GMRC was ever conceived. Our purpose, and now your purpose, is to uphold the SED's traditions and values for our brothers and sisters that will follow us in the future. I want you to think long and hard about your motivations to be here and what you want to get out of an opportunity many others have strived for their whole careers, only to fall short. To tarnish our long history by underperforming is to demean the hard work of those around you, those that have gone before and those that will surely come after. I employ the best, so I expect the best. Any questions?'

She shook her head.

'No? Good. Take her away, Riley,' he told him and shooed the two of them out of his room with a motion of his hands, the one sided conversation at an end.

Outside the office Riley slapped her on the shoulder. 'Welcome aboard, and don't worry about Locke, he's a pussycat really; he just hasn't got much time for new recruits. If you pass the tests he'll have more respect for you and will give you the time of day; it may be a short time but you'll get it nonetheless.'

'You're my guarantor; are you crazy?' she said as Locke's words sank in. 'You do know my track record here, don't you? I have a tendency to break the rules.'

'You're an explorer, that's what you do; I get it, it's my job too. You just happened to discover somewhere that's protected.'

'Twice,' Sarah pointed out, following him down a corridor.

'And that's exactly the sort of tenacity I look for in my team.'

Sarah smiled at his smooth answer. 'You failed to mention the exams and tests when you offered me the position.'

'Don't worry about it, you'll breeze it, especially with me as your trainer.'

'Confident aren't you?'

He opened a door to a room marked *GYMNASIUM*. 'I back my abilities and I trust my judgement. In my line of work you have to be able to make snap decisions, there's no room for uncertainty or the unskilled. We're the best at what we do; it's as simple as that.'

Sarah liked his attitude; it was one she'd like to replicate; to have that much faith in yourself must be a great feeling. She'd felt she could reach a peak at certain times, but she had always found it hard to keep herself there. *Although*, she reasoned, *if someone had a job on an SED team, then motivation would be unlikely to be a problem.* The energy and buzz of the place was infectious and she found herself being sucked in by it as Riley took her on a tour of the facilities on offer. A group of multifaceted and extensive climbing courses took up a huge segment on one side of the building and around the grand atrium that surrounded it. Every type of climb imaginable could be replicated, with some reaching up hundreds of feet.

Other areas included various departments, ranging from Decontamination Simulation to Subterranean Survey Equipment and Training, and from Archaeology to Structural Engineering. The scientific departments even had their own dedicated building located to one side of the main SED complex. Sarah was amazed at the resources they had available to them, but it wasn't until Riley took her down a couple of floors that she was truly bowled over.

'This is the inner workings of the transport system all the teams use when they are launched into Sanctuary Proper,' Riley said.

Sarah took in the scene before her, not quite sure what she was looking at. Dominating the area ahead a massive gaping hole disappeared into the ground, its interior brightly lit by an array of strip lighting. Spanning two hundred feet across, the giant oval shaft had eight evenly distributed vertical tracks attached to its inner surface. At its pinnacle, each twin-railed track twisted one hundred and eighty degrees and then curved at right angles to the vertical drop, bringing them onto a horizontal plane and up onto the ceiling of the level on which Sarah and Riley now stood. One of these tracks, its shiny metal rails glinting above her, ran past and into some kind of garage with grey frosted shutters blocking out whatever mysterious machine lay beyond.

'They're the docking stations for the air-shuttles,' Riley said when he saw her looking.

'Air-shuttles?'

'The vehicles we use to travel outside the USSB and into various areas of Sanctuary Proper.'

'Each track goes to a different place?'

'Pretty much. Mostly they head out west, but one takes a southern route while another heads due north.'

'None go east?'

'No, the density of the rock in that direction is unusually hard to penetrate and the huge chamber that contains the USSB's dome has collapsed to the East. We think there might be a significant chamber behind it, but our equipment has been ineffective in penetrating it so far. That section also suffers from a higher frequency of quakes and has been deemed too high-risk for exploration. Personally I think they're being over cautious, as there are plenty of structural and geological disturbances elsewhere, although a whole survey team was lost many years back on one of the first eastern surveys, which had a big bearing on the decision made by SED Command.'

'Can we take a look at one of the shuttles?'

'Not right now, everything has been locked down. Don't worry,' Riley said, noticing Sarah's disappointment, 'you'll get to see one soon enough when you go on your first mission, although your enthusiasm may be short-lived once you've ridden one.'

'Rough ride?' Sarah took one last glance behind as they made their way back upstairs.

'Some think so, its nickname is the Rollercoaster.'

'Sounds fun.'

Riley just grinned and moved off to show her yet another part of the SED's operation.

◆

The next few weeks flew past in a blur as Riley pushed Sarah to her limits and beyond. The mental side of the training taxed her, but at times the gruelling, physical workouts she found almost impossible.

'No more!' Sarah said on one such occasion, collapsing to the floor in a heap, her energy reserves spent.

Riley squatted down next to her, also breathing hard from his own exertions. 'Circuit training is perfect for your situation. We don't have much time to get you ready and CT condenses a lot of exercise into a shorter time period. You'll gain muscle mass on your scrawny limbs, which will help with climbing, and it'll improve your cardio-vascular endurance, which is currently pathetic.'

Sarah usually retorted with a well-aimed quip when he directed one of his playful jibes her way; now, however, she just resorted to giving him the finger.

'Having trouble with your new recruit, Riley?' a woman's voice said from nearby.

Sarah rolled her head sideways to see a group of people entering the gym; at their head was the person who'd made the comment, a tall muscular woman with short, spiky, jet-black hair, hawk-like features and a web of colourful tattoos covering her upper arms and shoulders.

'Shouldn't you be competing, Cora?' Riley replied as he held out a hand, which Sarah took to be pulled to her feet, her sweat-soaked vest clinging to her skin.

Cora stopped to talk further while her colleagues walked on past, acknowledging Riley and giving Sarah interested looks of appraisal.

'I've already won my heats,' Cora said, looking Sarah up and down as if she were a prize sow in a farmer's fair.

'You think you'll be beating Richardson again this year?' Riley asked. 'Some say he's faster than ever.'

Cora shifted her gaze back to him. 'I don't care what some people say. I am the best and I'll win.'

'I see your modesty is in check, as ever,' Riley said with a wry smile. 'This is Sarah, by the way; she'll be taking her assessments at the end of the week.'

'Ah, the girl who supposedly broke into Sanctuary.' Cora held out a hand. 'I was expecting someone less—'

'Less what?' Sarah frowned as she took the woman's powerful grip, not appreciating being referred to as *girl*.

'Fragile.' Cora squeezed Sarah's hand harder before releasing it.

'I'm stronger than I look,' Sarah said, cursing her defensive stance when Cora smiled at her pathetic attempt to save face in front of Riley.

Cora grabbed one of Sarah's wrists, wrenching it up and out. Sarah, taken by surprise and unable to stop herself, stumbled forwards into Cora, who held her gaze with an intensity that took Sarah off guard. The hold on her arm was hurting, so she went to release it with her free hand, but as she did Cora snaked out her other meat hook, locking that arm in place too. The woman was freakishly strong and Sarah was held fast like an insect caught in liquid amber.

'You'd better build up some muscle, girl.' Cora held her gaze while Sarah's forearms shook from the tension as she resisted the woman's strength. 'Sanctuary is a dangerous place. You wouldn't want to lose your hold in the darkness, it could prove – fatal.' At the word *fatal* Cora released her grip and nodded to Riley before departing after her fellows.

Sarah watched Cora stalk away. 'What the fuck was that all about?'

'Don't worry about her, she's all talk; well, sometimes she is. Cora's always a little—'

'Mental?'

'Competitive. She's threatened by you.'

'By me? Why?'

'Word's out, you're the woman who broke into Sanctuary. You must have expected it sooner or later.'

'I hadn't even thought about it,' Sarah said. And it was true; she hadn't given her previous exploits a second thought; well, not in that sense anyway.

Riley chuckled. 'You'd better get used to the attention. You're infamous within the SED already. You have a lot to live up to, so you better do me proud and make it into my team, or I'll look like a right fool.'

Sarah didn't reply. *Infamous*, she thought, *that's all I need*. She wanted to keep a low profile and stay under the radar in order to escape. If everyone knew who she was, that would make it that much harder to sneak around. She needed help and so she broached the subject she'd been plaguing Riley with once more.

'Have you thought any more about Trish and Jason?'

Riley sighed. 'Again? As I've said a thousand times already, it was a problem getting you in. Locke would chew me a new one if I pushed him.'

'Can't you just ask? He might be okay with it.'

'I'll tell you what, just to shut you up, if you meet the Deep Reach requirements in your tests then I'll ask him about your friends working here at the SED.'

Sarah brightened. 'Promise?'

Riley swore. 'Yes, I promise; now get your butt back round this course. You've got three more circuits to complete.'

CHAPTER FOURTEEN

THE FINAL WEEKS of Sarah's SED training came and went as quickly as the previous ones. During this time Riley had cranked up the intensity even further until Sarah ate, drank and slept Deep Reach. When yet another new day dawned Sarah rose early, an anxious excitement ensuring her night's sleep had been spent in restless anticipation. A few days before she'd received word that she'd qualified for a position on Riley's Deep Reach Survey Team. Riley, keeping his promise, had posed the question to the commander about Trish and Jason also being enrolled into the Exploration Division. Sadly, the answer had been a firm 'no'. Riley suggested Locke might change his mind at a later date, especially if Sarah proved herself in the field, and today was the day she was about to be given that chance as her first deployment outside the USSB had arrived.

As she walked through the main entrance to the SED, Sarah twisted the small tracking bracelet encircling her left wrist. She'd got used to the device now, but she knew the hindrance it presented to her cause. Now that she was a fully fledged member of Alpha Six many of the restrictions had been lifted from her MF Card, enabling her to move freely around the complex. The band, however, ensured her location was known at all times to the military and their surveillance systems. Apparently her presence unnerved the non-civilian, oversight committee and to ensure she didn't wander where she shouldn't they had requested she keep wearing the device at all times. She had wanted to point out that the tracking system obviously hadn't worked when she'd sneaked into the SED, but she'd decided there was no point rocking the boat any further and to alert them to a possible flaw in its design would be downright stupid. Riley had said it was unheard of for an SED member to be so mistrusted, but it was something she had to accept if she was to be allowed off-site. No go areas included the scientific departments and the U.S. military's laboratory complex, located in a highly restricted sector close by the SED itself. These laboratories were off limits to all SED personnel anyway, but Sarah had attracted special attention due to her past record.

The last ten days had flown by as, even after her assessments, Riley, confident she would pass the tests, had then submitted her to an intensive course on the numerous protocols every Deep Reach officer had to be familiar with before they could venture outside the USSB. Now that all the preparations had been completed her excitement mounted at the prospect of exploring parts of Sanctuary untouched by humans. Of course she had already been outside the base and even operated Anakim devices, but this was different. She was now venturing out with state-of-the-art kit and backed up by a highly qualified and experienced team, who would take her into areas believed to be of great scientific and archaeological importance. If she was honest with herself, she couldn't wait.

An hour later, now dressed in her red and blue coveralls, Sarah looked at herself in the mirror of the women's changing room. Turning round she peered over her shoulder and pulled her long blonde hair to one side to catch sight of the sign on her back:

DEEP REACH
SURVEY TEAM
ALPHA SIX

She then moved to look at the patch on her uniform's shoulder:

Steadying herself, she left the room with her head held high and strode along a couple of interconnecting hallways and into the main ready-room where the rest of her team were busy gearing up. She had already been introduced to many of the people in Alpha Six, but she saw a couple of new faces.

A bald heavyset man, sporting a thick black beard, approached her. 'Welcome aboard, I'm Jefferson.' He held out a hand.

'Sarah,' Sarah said, introducing herself.

'Looking forward to your first outing?'

'Yes, very much.'

'Glad to hear it. I'm the archaeological lead so I hope I can rely on your support when needed.'

She smiled. 'Of course.'

Jefferson looked pleased and returned to what he'd been doing.

The only other person she didn't recognise nodded in her direction when she caught his eye. He had a cropped haircut and athletic build, and seemed much more withdrawn than the other people around him, keeping to himself and refraining from verbal interaction.

Sarah became alert as Riley walked in, flanked by Cora, the woman she'd had the brief displeasure of meeting previously. Riley made a beeline for Sarah while Cora moved boisterously amongst the team, slapping people on the arm, hugging some and high fiving others. Sarah suspected Cora might be doing it to intimidate her; if she was it was working.

'Let me help you on with your kit,' Riley said as Sarah struggled with her multipurpose harness.

She turned round so he could pull it up over her shoulders. 'Thanks, I still can't get the hang of this thing.'

'You'll get used it; it'll feel like your second skin after a while.'

'What's she doing here?' she whispered indicating Cora with a nod of her head.

'Cora? She's my number two, Deputy Team leader. Didn't I mention that?'

'No.' Sarah felt like her parade had been well and truly rained on.

'She may have given you a hard time, but out there you'll want her at your back; besides, I'm in charge so I'll keep her in check if she gets funny with you.'

'I don't need babysitting.' Sarah's expression turned angry. 'I can handle the tattooed freak.'

Riley laughed. 'Of that I have no doubt.'

Turning from her, now that she'd shouldered her heavy back-pack, Riley addressed the twenty-two people gathered in the room. 'Okay, quieten down!'

'Listen up, Team Leader on deck!' Cora shouted out at the top of her voice to help shut up those who had kept talking.

Riley made a wry smile. 'Thank you, Cora.'

Cora gave him a mocking bow in response.

'Right, we're on an open-ended deployment commencing at twelve hundred hours,' Riley told them. 'All the other teams have already shipped out so we're the last to go.'

Sarah had thought she'd felt intermittent vibrations travelling through the room, it must have been the air-shuttles travelling down into the Earth.

'Unusually our target zone will already be occupied by the time we arrive,' Riley continued. 'An SFSD unit was sent there three weeks ago, along with some military scientists. And before you ask,' Riley said as many of them had begun to protest at the prospect, 'I don't know why they're there. SED Command is not in the loop on this one so we'll all have to tread carefully.'

Jefferson looked over at the quiet loner. 'Perhaps the lieutenant can shed some light on it for us?'

'I'm not at liberty to say,' the man said.

'Fucking bullshit!' Cora fumed. 'What's the point of having army on the team,' she gestured at the lieutenant, 'if he can't contribute?'

'You know why he's here,' Riley said to her as everyone else looked on, 'deal with it. Now saddle up; we've got a shuttle to catch.'

Everyone filed out of the room and as Cora passed by the lieutenant she said, 'Fucking waste of space.'

The lieutenant glanced up, appearing impervious to the hostility and hard stares of his team-mates as they walked by. *He must be used to it*, Sarah assumed, following Riley out of the door.

As they approached the *departure lounge* – as some liked to call it – each person collected their helmet from a large wall rack, a sign above it reading *Alpha Six*, their team's designation. The plethora of other racks surrounding it were empty, indicating they were the last to depart, as Riley had informed them. Sarah had been fitted for the sophisticated headgear a few days previous; she'd also trained on a simulator to get used to all the commands that were available on the inbuilt computer and its optical and audio systems. Riley had told her she wouldn't need most of the functions the helmet provided, which was a relief, as even the basic communication procedures had been difficult to master.

Each helmet had seen its fair share of use, with nicks and scrapes adorning the black protective outer shell. As Sarah knew, though, they were each tailor-made for the individual members of the Deep Reach team and as such they each had identifying marks. The person's first initial followed by a full stop and then their surname adorned the right hand side in white block lettering, while on the front, above the visor, an individual's call sign was placed. Sarah had been offered a huge array of fonts, colours and formats for her own call sign, which she'd also been able to choose herself. She hadn't yet seen the finished article, so when she saw her helmet hanging on its hook a thrill of delight and pride ran through her.

Riley chuckled. 'Morgan,' he said, noting her call sign, 'not very original.'

Sarah felt embarrassed by her lack of imagination. 'I couldn't think of anything that didn't sound stupid and self-serving.'

'What like mine?' He pointed at his own name plastered across the front of his helmet.

'Ace,' she read, 'not bad, and I like your picture of the Ace of Spades on the side.'

He peered over at the other side of her helmet. 'And your picture is?'

'A white pentagon.' She angled the helmet so he could see it.

'Interesting choice, does it have any significance?'

'No, I just like the shape,' she said, feeling lame and cursing herself for even considering putting it on there in the first place. She wanted to be unobtrusive so God only knew what she was thinking when she told the designer to put an image mirroring the shape of her Anakim pendant on the side. In truth, she hadn't been thinking and the five sided image had just presented itself at the time. She'd been more interested in the helmet's shape. Two raised strips ran over the top, like two large, flattened ears and it was these elongated nodules which contained the lights, sensors and cameras, the controls of which fed back into the head-up-display, or HUD, on the visor, operated by the wearer's eye movements and a cluster of command buttons on the outside.

With her helmet in place, Riley led Sarah and the team out into the massive oval-shaped shuttle bay, overlooked by a large swathe of the Command Centre; its panoramic angled glass windows giving operators a perfect view of the launch platform below. The centre of the floor consisted of a large, thick, oval metal plate which Sarah assumed covered the huge similarly shaped hole beneath. Around the edge eight, fifty foot long, metallic platforms protruded from the flat concrete outer surround.

Walking on a metal walkway around the edge, their many feet rattling the surface as they went, Team Alpha Six approached one of the platforms. On an unheard command, flashing red and yellow beacons spun into life and sirens wailed out an unpleasant tune as immense machinery ground into action. Before Sarah's eyes the central metal floor separated out into a star-like pattern, each point sliding back from an ever widening hole in the middle of the room. Eventually, with a resounding boom, the process finished. The floor, now fully retracted, revealed the deep, wide shaft below, its smooth rock sides displaying the eight tracks that bore the air-shuttles down and out into Sanctuary Proper.

After everyone had assembled atop the raised platform, Sarah watched as more mechanisms whined into action, presenting to the waiting passengers an air-shuttle from beneath. This was the first time Sarah had seen one of the machines and it wasn't at all like she'd expected. Instead of an enclosed vehicle like a train or even a car, the air-shuttle consisted of a sharp contoured nose cone attached to an open compartment, which housed the seating. Around the chairs a silver skeletal sub-frame held everything together.

'You're up front with me,' Riley told Sarah, waving a hand for her to move up to the craft's first row of seating.

Four abreast, the chairs ran in rows ten deep. At the rear, two substantial, remote-operated, all-terrain vehicles had been loaded, on top of which durable looking black and chrome crates had been lashed down, carrying essential supplies for their mission. These low-slung, snake-like, multi-wheeled robotic machines, encased in bright yellow metal panels that had seen their fair share of knocks and scrapes, were each fifteen feet long and would be their lifeline out in the dangerous environments that awaited them.

After stowing their backpacks in an allotted rear compartment they moved to the front of the craft. Declining Riley's offered hand,

Sarah climbed into the air-shuttle, sliding into a snug winged seat. As she rested her head back onto the headrest, an audible click could be heard. Her head was now locked back, allowing only minimal movement up and down and left and right. A small beep emitted in her left ear and the inside of the helmet lit up like the proverbial Christmas tree, ice-blue digital dials and displays buzzing to life as the visor slid down over her face to lock in place.

An efficient-sounding voice came through her headgear's internal speakers. 'This is SED Command. We are a go for shuttle launch in T minus ninety seconds.'

Sarah's nerves came to the fore as their imminent departure loomed, an anxiety deep in the pit of her stomach matched only by the rising excitement within her mind at the prospect of her first air-shuttle ride out of the USSB.

'Keep your arms down,' Riley's voice said next to her when an odd shaped metal frame swung up from between her legs and wedged against her shoulders and chest, securing her in place.

She moved her forearms and hands, getting used to the odd sensation of being unable to move the rest of her torso. 'I can see why they call it the rollercoaster,' she said, her voice a little shaky.

Riley gave her a pat on the knee. 'You haven't seen anything yet. Just relax – try and enjoy the ride. The front seats provide the best view, but I know many people shut their eyes during their first trip.'

I don't like the sound of that, Sarah thought, as the air-shuttle shuddered to sink down through the floor's thick concrete and into the area she'd seen once before during Riley's tour. A loud clanking noise filled the air and the shuttle slid to the left before latching onto the twin rails above. In front of her, the track twisted out into the abyss and then sharply down and out of sight.

A transparent screen raised out of the nearest part of the nosecone, providing a windshield for the journey ahead. Either side of the vehicle, technicians and ground crew went along the rows checking each person was secured in place. The man who checked Sarah's security bar yanked it backwards and forwards a few times increasing Sarah's anxiety further.

'Is it supposed to do that?' Sarah asked the man in concern as the bar moved a couple of inches from her and then back again.

He grinned. 'First time?'

'Does it show?'

'Just make sure you don't bite off your tongue when the rocket fires.' He tapped her helmet twice and raised his hand above his head. 'Clear!' he shouted to a colleague and moved away.

Sarah felt sick. 'Rocket? I thought this was an air-shuttle?'

'It's a series of long drops, climbs and straights,' Riley said. 'Some sections need extra speed to navigate the twists and turns. A warning message on your visor will tell you when the boosters are about to be fired. Hold tight—' He sounded excited as the air-shuttle crept forwards. 'Here we go!'

'T minus fifteen seconds to launch,' SED Command informed them through their helmets.

Sarah's visor, tinted around the edges where all the computer displays were located, threw up a red countdown timer in the central clear section where the field of vision was unimpeded.

The air-shuttle had reached the twist in the track and Sarah's view spun one hundred and eighty degrees upside down. Her body sagged against the restraints. She hung there, sucked forwards by gravity as they settled into a holding position. Suspended by powerful brakes, the immense sheer drop below now engulfed Sarah's eye line, the light around the massive oval shaft fading away into a pitch-black hole a hundred yards beneath them.

The countdown timer sank under ten seconds and SED Command spoke again. 'T minus seven seconds ... five, four, three, two, one – launch.'

CHAPTER FIFTEEN

A SENSE of weightlessness stole over Sarah's body as the brakes released, sending the air-shuttle plummeting into the bowels of the Earth. Despite the front screen, wind ripped at the passengers' clothing while a speedometer on Sarah's visor shot up to one hundred and twenty miles an hour in the blink of an eye. Down and down they fell. Small lights flickered on along the shuttle's interior surfaces and powerful main beams stuttered to life on the nosecone, illuminating the track and tunnel ahead.

Sarah wondered when the drop would end; the answer soon came as the air-shuttle gained traction on the rails above, the tunnel curving upwards – or was that downwards? Her sense of time and space was fried as they flew onwards. When the tunnel levelled out they slowed, but Sarah could see a disturbing sight ahead; the track twisted out of view as all seven tracks around them diverged. They were soon plunging downwards once more, regaining momentum in freefall, but this time within a much smaller tunnel, increasing the sense of speed tenfold. The rock walls sped by at a dizzying rate. Her head slewed to one side when the tunnel bent left, the turn followed by a series of stomach-churning, three hundred and sixty degree spirals, sending her helmet rattling against its support as they continued to fall.

Finally they slowed, but as the tunnel regained a horizontal aspect a disturbing message appeared on her visor:

WARNING!
Rocket Propulsion Imminent
(Burn duration: 10 seconds)
Stage 1 Ignition in
T minus 3 seconds

'Stage one!?' Sarah said, the wind whipping her voice away.

The countdown timer reached one and the message disappeared. A thunderous detonation catapulted the shuttle forwards, forcing Sarah further into her seat, her arms pinned to her sides. Sarah watched in despair as the speedometer's digits flashed by until it reached two hundred miles an hour. Feeling like she was being shaken to pieces, the tunnel system disappeared and they were flying along the suspended track through a vast impenetrable blackness, untouched by the lighting of the vehicle. The track veered upwards and Sarah felt nauseous when they slowed once more. Another message appeared on her visor's head-up-display:

WARNING!
Rocket Propulsion Imminent
(Burn duration: 30 seconds)
Stage 2 Ignition in
T minus 3 seconds

Sarah looked in horror at the duration displayed for the second burn. *Thirty seconds? This isn't a rollercoaster, it's a tethered space rocket!* The shuttle sent another explosion thundering through the air around them, thrusting her back into the seat again. Sarah shut her eyes as they entered a narrow tunnel, the vibrations of the track above rattling her teeth as they flew like an arrow through the interior of Sanctuary Proper at three and then four hundred miles an hour.

When the second burn ended and with her eyes open again she saw the shuttle slow to three, and then two, hundred mph. As they ploughed onwards yet another message appeared on her visor:

WARNING!
Track Transition Imminent
Disengaging in
T minus 3 seconds

Wondering what this message meant, Sarah watched as around them the air-shuttle became encased in a transparent skin, an outer shell spreading out from the individual sections of the sub frame enclosing the fuselage within. Ahead the track ended and it looked a certainty they would be dashed on the rock wall. With her heart in her mouth, Sarah prepared to close her eyes against the inevitable impact, but before she could the shuttle detached from the rails above with a mechanical clunk and entered a tight see-through tunnel made of what looked like the same material that now sheathed the vehicle itself.

With a sharp downwards turn, the air shuttle glided through its custom built tube. Sarah finally understood why the machine she rode was called what it was. The craft was flying along wrapped in a cushion of air, propelled forwards like a cork out of a bottle. Now able to enjoy the ride, Sarah glimpsed below them, in a brightly lit chamber, a huge lift system cutting upwards into the rock above. Around it were armoured tanks and a detachment of soldiers, some of whom looked up as the shuttle shot past. Sarah had assumed the worst of the journey was over; she was mistaken, as section after section of tight, painful turns flung her around in her seat until at last they slowed, the top of the transparent skin retracting to act as an air brake, cutting their speed even further.

Unseen brakes engaged and they cruised to a stop within a large rectangular building which contained more ground crew dressed in the same outfits as those they'd just left behind back at SED headquarters. Sarah's helmet clicked and detached from the headrest, while the metal bar jerked back and then collapsed down into the floor from whence it had come. Sarah sat there trying to decide whether to throw up or pass out.

Riley touched her arm. 'Sarah, time to get out. Are you okay?'

She stood up on wobbly legs and grabbed onto Riley's arm for support.

'The trip messes with your inner ear,' he said, 'it'll pass.'

He was right; already feeling more balanced she followed everyone else out of the shuttle and onto a waiting platform. The floor felt spongy, her body light, as if she was walking on air. Another after-effect she knew; she'd felt something similar when she'd visited a theme park as a child. The difference was funfair coasters travelled up to one hundred miles an hour; they'd just been touching four hundred.

Sarah chuckled, trying to sound nonchalant. 'I don't know how I didn't pass out.'

'The security bar connects with your vest and coveralls to create a temporary G-suit.'

'Clever,' she said and then a thought struck her. 'How do we get back?'

'Same way, but with a few more rockets.'

Sarah cursed and Riley laughed. 'Come on,' he said, 'we've got a site to explore.'

A smaller command post, housing a handful of air-shuttles and the personnel that ran it, also acted as base camp for any team that had the pleasure of using its facilities. After an hour of further prep work the Deep Reach Survey Team moved out, guided by a set of waypoints plotted by previous expeditions; behind, the two multi-wheeled, remote supply vehicles trundled along in their wake, hugging the ground like the many-legged insect to which they owed their nickname, the Centipede.

As they walked, Riley told Sarah the shuttle had taken them twenty-five miles in six minutes and they were now fifteen miles outside of the USSB. He also explained the shuttles were the quickest and sometimes the only way to travel across long distances and across multiple levels within Sanctuary Proper; the eight long twin-railed tracks having been laid down by specially designed robots many years before. Looking at the current landscape, Sarah began to see why such a transport system took precedence; building roads out here would be nigh on impossible. Unlike the wide open areas Sarah had experienced on her way into Sanctuary many months before, this section of the ancient underground complex was surprisingly confined. The chambers and tunnels they walked through still commanded a certain respect, but their scale was visible as their twin helmet lights adequately illuminated their passage.

It wasn't long before intriguing, crumbling structures surrounded the red and blue clad explorers; affording a tantalising glimpse into the distant past of the master builders, the Anakim. Sarah pressed a button on her helmet to activate the personal camera and took some stills and video. The helmets recorded everything they did anyway, but specific points of interest could be documented as a team member saw fit.

As they moved further from base camp and deeper into Sanctuary, the terrain became increasingly difficult. Four of the team, whose job it was to look after and manoeuvre the supply vehicles, broke out a large hover drone to ferry essentials to their final destination. Each of the four would operate the machine at various intervals along the extensive route, passing over control of the drone like a baton in a relay race. Multiple trips with the aerial machine would need to be made to transfer everything required for the work ahead. Once their job had been completed the supply crew would then switch to mapping new areas of Sanctuary, using the drone along with some of its smaller siblings. Out in the unknown everyone had to pull their weight and multi-tasking was a must.

Two days came and went surprisingly fast as Alpha Six tackled a series of enormous fissures that had opened up over thousands of years, driving a near impenetrable barrier through the centre of an equally large cavern. A tough ascent followed by a kilometre descent taxed Sarah's newfound endurance to the limit as they all utilised the state-of-the-art climbing equipment stored in their backpacks.

On the third day Sarah finished yet another strength-sapping climb and Riley was there, as ever, to lend a helping hand when she reached the summit. Grabbing his calloused hand with her own, she was hauled up onto a loose surface, the dirt underfoot giving way slightly when her weight settled onto it. Shifting to a less precarious position – her climbing gear clinking and rattling as the shackles, hooks and clips knocked against one another – she took in her new surroundings. Half a mile away, across a flat rolling expanse, ten floodlights positioned in a sweeping semi-circle illuminated a massive excavation site. Huge piles of displaced earth squatted together on the fringes of the dig like little hills produced by a giant mole. Across from the mounds, an extensive temporary compound of tents had sprung up. Even from this distance Sarah could see the hustle and bustle of activity as small vehicles darted in and out of the earthworks and cunningly constructed modular cranes distributed their loads. Moving amongst the machines, the small figures of people wove in and out of the shadows, carrying out their respective duties with a measured yet purposeful efficiency.

'How did they get all that machinery up here?' Sarah asked Riley.

'Piece by excruciating piece,' Jefferson answered, the bearded, bald-headed man coming to stand by his two team mates, 'and then reconstructed on site. Riley, you'll need to make communication with them; you know how they are if we drop in unannounced.'

Riley grimaced; taking off his helmet he withdrew a military type walkie-talkie and moved away from Sarah and Jefferson.

Sarah wiped the sweat from her brow. 'Who are they? The army?'

Jefferson hawked and then spat on the ground. 'Yeah.' He scratched his bear-like chest with coarse fingers. 'Damn SFSD.'

'SFSD?'

'Special Forces Subterranean Detachment,' Cora said joining them, her helmet with her Vixen call sign on the front hanging from a hook on her belt.

'A bunch of green beret wearing yahoos with above average IQs and a penchant for killing people,' Jefferson elaborated. 'They call themselves Terra Force.'

'They sound intimidating,' Sarah said, feeling uncomfortable due to Cora's close proximity.

Cora snorted. 'They're nothing of the sort, just a bunch of maggots with guns and long knives who think they can climb.'

Sarah frowned. 'What are they looking for?'

'Something to weaponise, most likely.' Jefferson pulled out a small silver hip flask, flipped off the lid and took a sip.

Cora held out a hand and Jefferson passed the drink to her. Taking a long swig Cora then offered it to Sarah who hesitated.

'Don't you English drink?' Cora asked, her tone mocking.

For England, Sarah thought, accepting the small canteen and knocking back a shot. The fiery liquid left behind a distinct caramel flavour and set the back of her throat aflame. Stifling a cough she passed it back to Jefferson who stowed it back in a compartment on his harness.

'We good to go, Ace?' Jefferson asked Riley when he returned to them.

Riley nodded and gave the command for Alpha Six to move out.

The Deep Reach Survey Team were soon setting up their own camp on the opposite side of the site to that of the U.S. Army personnel. Sarah, keen to see what the military were excavating, forwent eating her evening meal to take a look. Walking past one of the large floodlights mounted atop a telescopic tripod, the sound of the bulbs buzzing in her ears, she looked out at a large, oblong structure that had been unearthed. Amazingly they'd revealed three storeys of the building, its crumbling façade displaying what looked like windows of some description. Strange angular depressions on the roof hinted that at some point in the far distant past other structures may have protruded towards the glistening rocky ceiling of the chamber, some three hundred feet above.

'Fancy a closer look?' a familiar voice said from behind.

'Won't that piss them off?' she asked Riley who, like Sarah, had shed most of his climbing gear. In one hand he held his helmet and in the other, hers.

Riley shrugged and handed her headgear to her. 'Probably, but I want to find out what they're up to and the best way to do that is to nose about; come on.' He moved past her and down a steep slope, kicking up dust and dirt as his feet clove into the dry soil. Following him down, she caught him up, her long strides keeping pace with his.

'How is there dirt down here?' Sarah said as they neared the Anakim edifice. 'I also saw what looked like fossilised trees when I first entered Sanctuary, how is that possible?'

'The Anakim were extremely advanced. They found a way to produce, as far as we can tell, a fully functioning self-sustaining ecosystem within Sanctuary, or should I say throughout Sanctuary.'

'Throughout?'

'Yes.' He slowed to a stop and looked up. 'Have you noticed how the ceilings of the chambers sparkle when the light catches them?'

She craned her neck to look at the phenomenon. 'I suppose so, yes.'

'It's not a result of the geological composition of the rock, but because across virtually every chamber ceiling, tunnel and cave roof a translucent material has been applied.'

'What sort of material?'

'The scientists aren't sure what it is, only what it does, or did.'

'And what's that?'

'Produce light; in fact they think it functioned much like our dome back at base, but instead of being localised, like the dome, it provided light for the whole of Sanctuary.

'What, on every level?'

'Yep, every level. Well, every level we've surveyed so far has the same feature, so it's assumed it goes everywhere.'

'That's incredible. So gigantis had the ability to create huge swathes of plant life underground along with simulated sunlight too.'

Riley gave her a strange look. 'Gigantis?'

'Sorry – yes – that's what I, and many others who theorised and promoted the existence of the Anakim named them, Homo gigantis. And yes, I know, everyone down here calls them giganthropsis or Anakim.'

'Gigantis,' he said, trying out the word again. 'I like it, rolls off the tongue better than giganthropsis.'

'I know, doesn't it?' she enthused, pleased he agreed with her own viewpoint.

'It wasn't just plant life, though,' Riley continued, 'many small animal fossils have been found down here, too, and there are still many insects and different types of algae clinging onto life in certain places we've surveyed.'

'Amazing,' Sarah said, excited at the prospect.

'Some people are even holding out for larger animal remains to be found. The Anakim had to eat something, after all, and a diet consisting solely of vegetation seems unlikely considering they were omnivores much like us.'

'You know that for certain?'

Riley nodded. 'Oh yes, from the remains we've found so far their internal organs and bone structure are virtually identical to ours in every respect, the only significant difference being their size.'

'Remains, internal organs, you've found individuals that well preserved?'

He grinned at her. 'The museum doesn't have everything on show. Some discoveries are deemed too sensitive for public viewing, as is the case with most of the more advanced technological objects we find; which, to be honest, are few and far between and always snapped up by the military quicker than you can say *theft*. A lot of the remains of the Anakim themselves are not on display due to the fact that they are still being analysed and documented, plus the Smithsonian powers-that-be want to create a special exhibit dedicated to what they have ferreted away. Supposedly they're having funding issues for a new building they want to erect for it. I'll have to give you a tour of the vaults sometime; I guarantee you'll absolutely love the Boneyard.'

'Boneyard?'

'It's what we call the vault that contains the most important and impressive Anakim remains found so far. Like their technology, there've been curiously few specimens detected by our scanning equipment, although this might be down to the composition of the strata throughout Sanctuary; whatever they used to build this place plays havoc with a lot of our kit.'

The idea of such treasures sent her imagination into overdrive. 'I'll hold you to that tour.'

'It's a date then,' he said with a sly wink, before walking off towards the monument once more.

Sarah, momentarily disarmed by the implication of his wording, regained her senses and trotted to catch up.

Handily, due to the time it had taken them to set up their base of operations, the activity around the site had tailed off, allowing the two of them to walk unchallenged through a smallish opening in the rear of the impressive structure. Riley and Sarah, already having donned their headgear, switched on their lights, dropped down their visors and deployed their breathing filters by depressing the appropriate buttons on the side of their helmets. Sarah angled the twin beams of light around the dark interior with her head. Reaching out, she ran her hand along one of the walls; it felt unusual. On closer inspection the dark brown rock was riddled with perforations and pockmarks, its rough texture reminiscent of a hard dried sponge or piece of dead coral.

Curved ramps within guided them up a level, dust falling from the ceiling and swirling around their feet as their passage disturbed the still air around them. Various warning signs on the inside of Sarah's visor indicated the impurity of the atmosphere within.

'It's pretty toxic in here,' she said to Riley through the helmet's onboard communication system, her voice sounding muffled due to the breathing apparatus across her mouth and nose.

'So would you be if you'd sat around for nine hundred thousand years.'

'Is that how old this place is?'

'According to the mission brief, this is one of the oldest structures we've found so far, almost as old as Sanctuary itself.'

'Is that why the military are so interested in it?'

'That's why *everyone* is interested in it.'

'There doesn't appear to be much in here,' she said as they passed through yet another curiously shaped, yet empty, room.

'Switch to ultra violet on your visor.'

Doing as he suggested, Sarah was amazed to see the walls, ceiling and floor; seemingly every surface had been covered in intricate patterns, pictures, text and even maps.

'Oh my God.' She shook her head in reverence.

'It's pretty special,' Riley agreed while studying a spectacular scene of two Anakim warriors stalking what looked, for all the world, like a sabre-toothed tiger.

Sarah's attention was drawn elsewhere, however, as across from a large ragged crack in the floor another wall had an image of an Anakim woman wearing a pentagonal pendant, a pendant just like the one she'd used to activate the two ancient devices at the surface. Tracing the outline of the distinctive shape with her fingers, she wondered about the significance of the picture and its context amongst the writings that surrounded it. The clothing of the female owner almost looked regal. *Perhaps she was some kind of priestess*, Sarah considered. Her stance – arms heavenward, hands turned upwards as if in offering, and head bowed – pointed towards an important ritualistic rite. Without a translation of the text the answer was tantalisingly close and yet quite possibly, at the same time, infinitely far away.

She hoped the key to solving the riddle of the Anakim's language would be found, but unlike relatively modern human texts, such as the Egyptian hieroglyphs, it was doubtful that a Rosetta Stone would present itself. Human civilisation and that of the Anakim were separated by tens of thousands of years. Maybe the tablets found beneath the Pyramid of the Sun would provide the answers, if the Church hadn't already destroyed them, a possibility Sarah knew was highly probable.

Via her helmet's internal speakers, Riley's voice interrupted her musings. 'Sarah, stop dallying; we need to cover as much ground as possible before someone spots us skulking around.'

Sarah turned to see she was on her own. On the far side of the room she glimpsed Riley's light fading away into the darkness, disappearing down yet another passageway. Hurrying to catch him up once more, she kept watch of her step to avoid the many pitfalls that countless years had opened up in the ground as they worked their way deeper into the warren of tunnels. Glancing at a small map on her visor she was pleased to see their route was plotted in real-time, ensuring getting lost was unlikely.

'What are they looking for do you think?' Sarah asked.

'It's difficult to say.' Riley investigated a dark and intriguing alcove. 'When they go to this much trouble it's usually for some piece of Anakim tech. The Deep Reach team that originally found this place probably recorded an unusual signal from a ground scan. The military scientists are always first to analyse any data we bring back, so they would have flagged it and prioritised the area for one of their own units to investigate further.'

'Doesn't it annoy you, that the military are corrupting important historical sites?'

Riley glanced at her. 'Of course it does, but we're all here on the say-so of the top brass; we can't do anything about it, we just pick up the pieces as best we can.'

'Or snoop around when we're not supposed to?'

'Exactly, you're catching on to how things work down here; perhaps you're not as stupid as I thought.'

Sarah punched him on the shoulder and he chuckled in response. They walked on a little further before he stopped dead in his tracks, held his hand up and extended one finger to his breathing mask, indicating for her to keep quiet. Edging forwards, they rounded a corner and stepped into a large room lined with elaborate balconies, ascending two floors up and three down. Emerging onto the gallery's third level, Sarah could see people in the centre of the bottom floor below, powerful lighting illuminating the area and sending shadows dancing across the walls. They wore helmets similar to their own, only in white, along with matching coveralls and steel grey boots. Four of the scientists worked around a single object on the surface of the floor, taking readings with various pieces of equipment.

Riley touched some buttons on his helmet. 'There's a residual power signature coming from whatever's buried in the floor,' he whispered.

'That's incredible.' Sarah took some still images of the scene. 'This must be what they've been searching for.'

'This is the first time I've seen, or even heard of, any Anakim device emitting any kind of energy.' Riley sounded in awe of the ramifications of such a find. 'This is a major discovery.'

Sarah dearly wanted to tell him that she had actually seen and activated an ancient device in the past, but knew she mustn't. They may have grown close during her training over the past couple of months, but disclosing that kind of information would ensure she would never see the pendant again, or worse – the military might cart her off for some kind of experimentation; she wouldn't put anything past them.

Below, a team of armed men marched into view, each clad in green and brown armour topped off by a wicked looking helmet that gave them the appearance of having glowing green eyes. Slits further down the mask-like headwear indicated they, too, utilised an integrated air filtration system. The lead man, his jet-black visor reflecting the lights around him, spoke to one of the scientists. Turning back to his men, his purposeful and urgent hand signals sent his team fanning out in all directions.

'They know we're here,' Sarah said, panic rising within her. 'You know what will happen to me if I get in trouble with the military again. Fuck, I'm such an idiot!'

Riley, ducking back down, drew Sarah out of sight of the people below and looked her in the eye. 'Nothing will happen to you as long as you're with me. I'm a Deep Reach team leader, it gives me some clout. Besides,' he added, 'they haven't caught us yet.'

Retracing their footsteps using their visor maps, they made good progress until a light could be seen approaching from ahead, and then another from behind. They were trapped! Riley, without hesitating, dragged her forwards, decreasing the gap between them and their hunters.

'Are you mad?' Sarah saw the light ahead growing ever brighter.

'Turn off your helmet torches,' Riley said as his dimmed and flickered out.

Sarah did so, leaving the two of them without light. That wouldn't matter for long, though, as the soldier was almost upon them, the glow of his torch already enough to see by. Behind, the other beam of light closed in fast. At the last instant when Sarah had resigned herself to being discovered, Riley dragged her to one side.

Light blazed next to them in the passage as a member of the Special Forces, his gun raised, came into view. Sarah held her breath while Riley held her close inside the recessed alcove he'd investigated on their way in. The light crept towards them, its pervasive reach seeking to unveil their hiding place.

'There's no one in this quadrant,' the soldier said, his transmission audible as he walked past. 'Repositioning to next level.'

Once his light had faded from view, Riley and Sarah made their escape, leaving the building and making their way unseen back to the camp.

Not long after that Riley received a visit from the Terra Force commanding officer. Now sitting amongst the rest of the Deep Reach outfit, Riley and Sarah ate a meal cooked up by a couple of the mapping crew. Everyone looked up, the talk stuttering to silence as the armoured officer marched into the large tent, his rifle attached to his back-plate and helmet held under his right arm.

'Orton,' he said to Riley. 'Two of your people were inside a restricted site. After you've completed your survey of the surrounding area all of your team will submit their data recordings to my command post for download, no exceptions.'

Riley stood up from his seat. 'Protocol states we only need to submit our findings back at SED Command, not before.'

The officer strode forwards to front up to the Deep Reach team leader. 'I don't give a rat's ass about protocol. Out here what I say goes, you're lucky I don't have all your kit confiscated right now.'

Riley held the soldier's gaze. 'I'd like to see you try.'

Jefferson and Cora stood up behind Riley and Sarah did likewise from across the table.

'You think you could take me, Orton?' the officer said to Riley, more as a statement than a question, a smile playing across his lips. 'You may have been in the corp but I'm out of your league. I think you know that too, don't you? No, you're going on the false assumption that your father can protect you if you break the rules.' He took a step closer, getting right up into Riley's face. 'Don't bet on it; Ellwood is lucky to still have a job.'

Taking a look around at the rest of the Deep Reach team the officer caught sight of Sarah. 'And you,' he said, pointing at her, 'I've got my eye on you.' Giving Riley one last threatening stare he strode back out of the tent.

'Fucking hell, Riley, what have you been up to this time?' Jefferson said.

Riley glanced at the outcast of Alpha Six. The army lieutenant met his gaze, perhaps waiting for him to disclose his actions.

'Not now,' Riley told Jefferson.

The bearded archaeologist looked at the lieutenant and understood his leader's reticence to speak his mind.

Later, after everyone had gone off to fulfil other duties, Sarah found Riley sitting alone outside his tent.

'Room for one more?' She gestured at the floor next to him.

He nodded and she settled down as Riley stayed silent, lost in contemplation.

After a while, when it appeared he wasn't about to instigate a conversation anytime soon, she asked, 'Is your father someone important?'

'He's a Brigadier General here at Sanctuary.'

'The Special Forces guy called him "Ellwood".' Sarah was confused as Riley's surname was Orton.

'Orton is my mother's name; I took it when I entered the army, I didn't want any special treatment as my father was a well-known colonel at the base.'

Sarah nodded. 'Has your father done something wrong?'

'I'm not sure.' He sounded troubled. 'If he has, he hasn't spoken of it to me. I suppose you think I'm a fraud, now, getting to where I am because of my father; taking risks as I know a safety net awaits my fall?'

Sarah placed a hand on his. 'Of course not, you're great at your job. The others respect you, I respect you. You said it yourself, you trust in your own abilities and judgement, not anyone else's. You've got to where you are because *you* made it happen, not your father.'

Riley put his other hand on top of Sarah's and smiled at her in gratitude. As his eyes held hers his expression grew serious; leaning forwards, giving her time to withdraw if she wanted, he kissed her on the lips. Sarah's heartbeat fluttered as she kissed him back. His right arm encircled her shoulder as they enjoyed a lingering embrace. After a few more hedonistic moments he pulled away, leaving Sarah feeling elated and yet, for some reason, equally troubled. Getting to her feet she walked away without a word, leaving Riley looking confused and alone.

He called out after her. 'Sarah, I'm sorry.' But it was too late, she'd gone.

CHAPTER SIXTEEN

THE REST of Sarah's first Deep Reach mission passed off without significant incident. After the first day they avoided treading on the toes of the military and relocated to uncharted territory; scouting out new points of interest, mapping and taking structural readings. They had been allowed to return to the building and document the interior, although she'd noticed they were kept away from the room where they'd seen the scientists. It had also been obvious that whatever had been displaying some kind of power output had been extracted from the site, as a large squarish hole had been cut into the roof and a tripod hoist erected over it.

After she'd embarrassed herself with Riley, Sarah had kept her distance from him, making excuses to be elsewhere when he did find her alone. She still questioned her reasons for retreating from him that day. It had felt right, the kiss, but she'd been through the wringer before, with Mark, amongst others. She was sure this did seem different somehow, she felt safe and happy when she was with him; *so why am I so worried about it then?* she wondered for the umpteenth time. Perhaps because she knew deep down she wanted to escape Sanctuary and expose it; she couldn't afford to get tied down, not now.

Spending much of her remaining time with Jefferson, carrying out preliminary archaeological surveys, Sarah had taken the opportunity to quiz him about the lift systems to the surface. Apparently the giant elevator they'd passed by on the air-shuttle was the furthest one from the USSB, acting as an emergency back-up if any of the others failed. Access to it could only be achieved by taking a roundabout route on foot, and it took many days to reach from another air-shuttle termination point located elsewhere in Sanctuary. The worrying aspect was that the heavy protection allocated to each lift shaft wasn't just limited to the one she'd seen. Jefferson told her security had been intensified around the time she'd entered the base. Sarah found it hard to believe she could have caused such a large scale reaction from the military commanders, but it made sense as to why she'd been held for so long in their custody; they feared further breaches of the base.

The news that the elevators also required various access codes to operate further put paid to the three friends utilising them to get out of Sanctuary; another plan had to be devised. Realising she needed to swing things back in their favour, Sarah had taken the bold choice of ridding herself of the tracking bracelet that had been imposed upon her on release from military custody the first time around. The strap on the device hadn't been difficult to cut through, a pair of small shears in her climbing kit making light work of the task. Ensuring no one observed her, she'd chucked the bracelet into a deep crevasse, the small object falling end over end until it had vanished from sight. The device, she knew, didn't work outside the USSB. With this in mind, she reasoned, if the army detected it had been removed when she returned to the USSB, she'd say it had fallen off somewhere, which wouldn't be a lie as it had fallen off – just with a bit of help. If, on the other hand, they didn't pull her up on it then she'd have dealt with one obstacle to their escape. It was a gamble, but considering the information she'd gleaned from Jefferson regarding the lift system, it was one she had to take.

The return journey to the USSB had been as, if not more, frightening than the outward trip, the cylindrical machine threatening to shake her very bones to pieces as it propelled the Deep Reach crew back from whence they'd come. Exiting the shuttle, once more with unsteady legs, Sarah had stowed her kit and then proceeded to write up her first preliminary report; she'd then endured the mission debrief and departed for some much needed R&R at her apartment. Appreciating the soft duvet covered bed, Sarah awoke the next day, fresh and ready to meet up with Trish and Jason as they'd planned before she'd left the USSB three weeks before.

Once more the three friends met up in the New Park district, this time opting for an opulent outdoor restaurant; all three deciding that Sarah's new salary might as well be enjoyed rather than saved for what would hopefully be a short stay in Sanctuary. Savouring a delicious first course of battered mushrooms with an accompanying sour cream sauce, Trish broke a silence that had begun to feel uncomfortable after Sarah had finished regaling them with tales of her SED trip outside the base.

'The mission went well then?' Trish said.

Sarah nodded. 'Yes, but we have a big problem; the elevators that lead out of this place are so locked down, it's unbelievable. We'd have a better chance of getting into Fort Knox with a toothpick.'

Jason grunted. 'So we need to find another way out.'

'It looks that way.'

'You don't seem that concerned,' Trish said.

Sarah grew cross. 'Of course I'm concerned, why wouldn't I be?'

'We haven't seen much of you lately,' Jason said.

'Err, hello? I've been on a Deep Reach mission.'

Jason waved away her comment. 'Before that, you've been spending a hell of a lot of time with Riley.'

'What do you expect me to do?' Sarah looked at Jason and Trish in turn. 'I had to get on that team, we all agreed, didn't we, or am I missing something?'

'You've just seemed more interested in the SED than you have in us, that's all,' Trish said.

Sarah couldn't believe what she was hearing. 'Don't be stupid.'

'Oh, so we're stupid, are we?' Jason said, getting angry in return.

'You're gallivanting around, having a whale of a time, by the sound of it, and we're stuck here like lemons.'

'Okay, so I enjoyed the mission, so what? You two would have, too, if you'd gone on it. It was an amazing experience; but while I was there I got rid of my tracking device, which, by the way, seems to have gone unnoticed—'

'For now,' Jason grumbled.

'I've ascertained we can't use the lift system,' Sarah continued, ignoring him, 'and that the army has an inside man on every team that goes out of the base, keeping tabs on everything that goes on; making it impossible to sneak off without being noticed within a matter of hours.'

Despite her obvious successes, something still aggravated her two friends. Trish appeared to be apologetically annoyed with Sarah, while Jason simmered about some perceived slight.

'What gives, guys? Something else is bothering you.'

Silence.

'I'm not a bloody mind reader, for God's sake somebody tell me!'

'We want to know why you couldn't get us on the team,' Jason said at last, 'or at the very least into the SED.'

'Is that what this is all about, you think I didn't get you on the team on purpose, is that it?'

'Jason suggested you might want to have Riley all to yourself,' Trish told her.

Jason's eyes widened. 'What!? Don't just blame it on me, you agreed with me!'

Sarah sighed. 'You really think I'd do that to you both, screw you over for some guy I've only just met?'

Trish couldn't look Sarah in the eye and even Jason looked a little sheepish.

Thankfully she'd not informed them about the kiss she'd shared with Riley or their noses might have been even further out of joint. 'I tried my best to get you both into the SED, you know that. So I might like Riley a bit, but it isn't going anywhere, is it? We have to get out of here, so we need to stop bickering amongst ourselves and start putting our heads together.'

'I may have found a way out,' Jason told them.

'You have?' Trish said, amazed but dubious.

Sarah gestured for him to continue. 'Spill then.'

'Well, like we decided a few weeks back, me and Trish would carry on documenting the museum and the USSB while you were—'

'Gallivanting?' Sarah arched a brow.

'Err, yeah,' he said, aware she was having a dig at him for his previous comment. 'So when we were ferreting about I took lots of video and stills and I found this—' He rummaged in his trouser pocket and pulled out a crumpled photograph, which he handed to Trish.

'What am I looking at here?' Trish said as Sarah leaned over to take a look. It was an image of Jason taking a selfie in front of a reconstruction of an Anakim warrior; Jason had on an idiotic grin as he pulled a stupid face to the camera.

'All I can see are two dummies,' Sarah said, unable to help herself and making Trish giggle.

'What? Give me that.' He swiped the photo back. 'Wrong one,' he said, embarrassed. Taking out another photo, he checked it and passed it back to the two women.

Trish studied it. 'Is that what I think it is?'

'You bet your life it is,' he said.

Sarah was amazed. 'It's an Anakim transportation device.'

'With a circle to activate it,' he told her, sounding proud.

Sarah stared at the photo. It depicted an oblong metal plinth sitting next to a stone monolith, upon which sat a small, square metallic plaque with an indented circle within its borders. 'Why does it look – odd?' she asked.

'It's a print of a small section of a larger photo,' he said. 'It looks weird as what you're looking at isn't real, it's part of a scale model of a particular monument uncovered a few years ago by one of the museum's tethered search robots. Although knowing what we do, it was probably your Exploration Division that found it. According to the museum guide, the structure it's contained within is massive and located at one of the deepest points ever surveyed. The site designation, Temple #887, is in a really hot location. Apparently temperatures soar to fifty degrees plus, the further down you get; they theorise there's a breach in Sanctuary Proper's lower levels and magma from the Earth's core has leaked inside.'

'This could be our way out,' Sarah said, 'excellent spot.'

Jason beamed at the praise, but he didn't stop there, whipping out yet another photograph – this time on an A4 sheet. He unfolded it and pushed it across the table for them both to look at. 'This is the same shot, but zoomed out.'

This image showed not one, but five, Anakim transportation platforms, four surrounding one in the centre.

Sarah couldn't believe her eyes. 'Five devices, this is incredible!'

Trish looked at him anew. 'I have to say I'm impressed, but why didn't you tell me you'd found this before?'

'Don't get angry,' he said sensing Trish's mood had darkened, 'I only found it yesterday—'

Trish glared at him.

'Well – last week,' he admitted, under further unwavering scrutiny, 'but I wanted to tell you both together.'

'Why?' Trish said, still annoyed by his secrecy.

'Because it's more dramatic that way, and besides, I couldn't be bothered repeating myself, telling you and then telling Sarah all over again.'

Trish sighed, looking exasperated.

'There are two big problems with it,' Sarah said to them both. 'One, we don't know where they might take us if we got them to work and two, we don't have the pendant to power them up.'

Trish passed the image back to Jason. 'And three, how do we find them?'

'And four, how do we get to them when we find out where they are?' Jason said.

They each sat in contemplative silence before Sarah spoke again. 'Short of trying to blast our way out of here, and as difficult as this option sounds, I fear it might be our only choice if we ever want to see the surface again.'

'Where it goes might not be an issue,' Trish said. 'If we could power one up we could send a locator beacon through it and then track where it came out.'

'Didn't you say the composition of Sanctuary prevents signals passing through its walls?' Jason asked Sarah.

'Yeah, in places, but I'm pretty sure that's only communication and data transfer. The SED use small beacons to act as critical waypoints for teams out in the field. They act as a sort of internal navigation system for Sanctuary Proper; it's not great, but it does the job. I think if we could get our hands on one it may work. How did you think of that?' she asked Trish.

'Something I read in the museum, probably,' Trish said, pleased with her contribution.

Jason examined the photo again. 'So how do we find where this place is – exactly?'

'If it was found by a survey team,' Sarah said, 'then there will be a map to it, with associated waypoints.'

'Wouldn't that mean we'd have to take an air-shuttle to get there?' Trish asked in concern.

Jason's face lit up. 'Hell, yeah, I gotta try one of those babies out, they sound awesome!'

'We'd have to steal one,' Sarah said, thinking hard, 'and I can get my hands on the Deep Reach maps.'

Trish looked sceptical. 'Stealing an air-shuttle sounds ambitious.'

'The whole bloody plan is ambitious,' Sarah said, 'we just need to break it down into parts and solve it step by step. It's definitely doable, I'm sure of it.'

Trish chuckled. 'I'm glad you are.'

'What if we sent a beacon—' Jason said, leaning back in his chair as their empty plates were collected from the table and their main courses put down in their place. '—located it near the surface,' he continued, when the waiters had departed, 'went there and found we were trapped inside a sealed cave?'

Sarah thought for a moment. 'Explosives.'

'What if it was a really small cave?' Jason said.

Sarah looked at him in annoyance.

'Hey, just trying to be prepared,' he told her, holding his hands up, 'it could happen.'

'Shaped charges, then. The SED will have them – somewhere.'

'So say we get all that done,' Trish said, 'we still need the pendant.'

'We need to find out where that bastard Collins stashed all our gear.' Jason's expression turned innocent as he looked to Sarah. 'Perhaps your boyfriend will know?'

'He's not my sodding boyfriend.'

'Methinks she protests too much,' Jason said to Trish, who smiled as Sarah sent a rude gesture Jason's way.

His grin broadened. 'Charming.'

'He might be able to help,' Trish said to Sarah, 'if you surreptitiously pump him for information.'

Jason sniggered. 'I think he'd prefer to be pumped more overtly.'

Trish laughed and then covered her mouth, looking shocked at herself as Sarah gave her a stern look.

Sadly, Trish and Jason were probably right, as much as it pained her to admit it as the two amused themselves at her expense; Riley would be a good person to ask where their possessions were being stored. He might even be able to help her get them back, if she was really lucky.

Sarah looked back at Jason, who now acted out a romantic encounter between herself and Riley with two vegetables; apparently she was a carrot and he a stick of celery.

'Oh, Riley, you're so strong and manly,' Jason said in a hideous attempt at a female voice, wiggling the carrot in one hand.

'Of course I am,' Jason answered himself in a deep voice, revelling in his role while Trish failed to keep a grin from her face, 'I am prime beefcake sent from the stars to save you.'

Sarah watched, her eyebrow raised and her face aloof. 'Keep that up,' she said to Jason as his charade went on, 'and you'll find those vegetables shoved up somewhere the sun definitely don't shine.'

Jason looked at Sarah and nonchalantly put down his puppets. 'You're going to get me back for this, aren't you?'

Sarah smiled at him sweetly. 'You'll have to wait and see.'

Her answer added a hint of worry to Jason's semi-remorseful expression.

Trish sipped her wine. 'So then, all we need to do is get some explosives and a locator beacon, find and retrieve the pendant—'

'Steal some Deep Reach maps,' Jason continued, 'and an air-shuttle—'

'Locate the ancient transport device,' Sarah said, 'and pray to God it works and takes us to the surface.'

Trish laughed uneasily. 'Simple.'

'Sounds easy if you say it quick,' Jason said with a wry smile.

Sarah took a long draught from her own wine glass and then held it up in the air. 'To the plan then.'

Jason and Trish raised their glasses to hers. 'The plan,' they all said in unison, the chinking of their glasses sealing their respective fates.

CHAPTER SEVENTEEN

THE CORRIDORS inside Sanctuary's Exploration Division, the SED, echoed with the sounds of the hurly-burly of yet another day in the life of the clandestine facility. Along one such passageway, full of people buzzing from place to place, this way and that, strode Sarah Morgan, dressed in her red and blue uniform. It wasn't lost on her that the majority of their audacious escape plan, hatched and expanded upon over the previous days, was down to her to action. Of course Jason had been quick to point out – when Sarah had raised the issue – that if he and Trish had been in the SED, the burden could have been shared. Unfortunately Sarah had been unable to dispute this fact, but it was a moot point; getting her friends in was beyond her control. She had to concentrate on what was in her control and that included today's objectives; source a waypoint beacon, explosives and an air-shuttle user handbook. All three items would be difficult to acquire, but not impossible; or so she hoped.

Moving through the building, Sarah noticed an inordinate amount of military activity going on. Small units of armed and unarmed soldiers marched among the usual civilian ranks of the SED. Something was going on, and whatever it was it wasn't going to make her acquisitions any easier. Her hand strayed to her wrist where the tracking bracelet had been attached as she passed by a small squad of military engineers. A simmering urgency to getting the plan underway as soon as possible had been eating away at Sarah ever since they'd decided on their course of action. Surely it was only a matter of time until someone realised she'd shed the device, and when that time came any future plan of escape went out the window with it.

When yet another squad of camo-clad men and women stomped by, the metal grate flooring resounding to their combined footsteps, Sarah wondered if whatever was going on here might have actually helped distract the military when she'd dropped off the grid. If that was the case then it might not be long until usual service resumed and her secret came to light; she increased her pace, her footfalls increasing in volume, the noise echoing her internal need for speed.

Entering an office dedicated to Deep Reach personnel, Sarah spied Riley in the distance chatting to the SED Commander, Dresden Locke. Darting to her right, behind a partition, she took a seat at a computer terminal next to a man she didn't recognise from another team. Flashing him a quick smile in acknowledgment, she got down to work. Attaching a control circlet to a finger, she navigated through the system, attempting to locate the route to the temple Jason had found. After some searching she located the required maps and downloaded them onto her computer phone, before moving on to the equipment database. Typing the word *explosives* in the search box she hit the Return key and scanned the results as they appeared on screen. Five departments had entries, more than she was expecting; perhaps her luck was in. By the time she'd exhausted four of the five, this initial thought had disappeared. The last remaining department to search, the Excavation Team, however, reignited her optimism. Listed halfway down its inventory was just what she was after, shaped charges. And even better, some of the devices, according to the description, were designed to punch holes through obstructing walls and rock. Noting down on her computer phone the storeroom location within the building, she took off the interface circlet from her hand and stood up, just in time to come face-to-face with Riley.

'Long time, no see,' he said, his expression difficult to read. 'I thought I saw you scurry in down here.'

'Err, yeah.' Sarah felt trapped and uncomfortable under his gaze. 'Look, Riley, I have to go. Speak to you later?'

'Sure, how about some lunch?'

'Tomorrow?' she said, backing away from him.

'Okay, great.'

She flashed him a smile as she walked out of the office, nearly colliding with someone on their way in.

'I'll hold you to that!' His voice called out after her.

Winding her way down into the lower levels towards the store-room, Sarah's thoughts had become distracted following her encounter with Riley. She'd missed his company after she'd with-drawn from him during the Deep Reach mission outside of the base. Despite the critical nature of her current situation, her mind lingered on his handsome features, his muscular arms and his sensual lips—

'Watch out!' a man shouted.

Sarah ducked as a razor sharp cutting disc sliced through the air above her.

Another workman pointed to the flashing warning signs Sarah had just skirted around. 'Are you fucking blind?!'

'Sorry!' she said, continuing through and then out of the cordoned off maintenance zone.

'You will be when you get your damn head chopped off!' the workman yelled.

Bloody hell, get a grip Sarah, she told herself. You're acting like some doe eyed teenager, get your head in the game!

A few minutes later, she'd scanned her card into the appropriate locked room and ran her eyes over an inventory list on a small wallscreen inside. Trish and Jason had agreed two charges should be enough to cope with anything they might run into, if and when they managed to get to the surface.

Selecting the appropriate metal case, she extracted it from its snug position on the shelf and shifted it onto a workbench, its dense weight producing a resounding thud as it dropped onto the surface.

Careful, these are explosives, she cautioned herself. *More haste, less speed; if I'm not careful, I'll end up plastered all over the walls like tomato sodding soup*. Unhooking the chrome clasps, she flicked up the catches to reveal four black, circular objects, each the size of a small plate. Rather than being flat, each had an identical concave depression; this was the characteristic – or shape – that would focus the energy released by the explosive itself. Sarah reached out a hand to one of the devices, its smooth surface felt cold to the touch. Gripping its metal edges, she carefully extracted it from its soft foam surround; it was heavier than she'd expected.

The lid of the case held four transportation containers, fabricated out of smart nano materials, which – according to the information sheet provided – also acted as wireless detonators. Placing the charge in its smaller home, she snapped together its lock and then repeated the process with a second unit. Closing the case, she placed it back on the shelf, but behind two others; should someone find two charges were missing, it hopefully wouldn't be for a long time.

Cradling the weighty objects in the crook of her left arm, she opened the door to the room with her right. Retreating back out into the corridor, her jutting elbow caught someone passing by, sending one of the circular cases dropping to the floor with a clatter. The offending person happened to be an armoured Special Forces commando who turned, bent down and retrieved the explosive for her.

He handed the small canister back to Sarah. 'Ma'am, you might want to be more careful where you're walking. This ordnance could take out a whole floor.'

'Noted; thank you, Lieutenant,' she said, catching sight of his name tag which identified his rank, a nervous apologetic smile working its way onto her face.

The soldier gave her a stern nod and continued on his way. Sarah's smile fell from her face after he'd departed, the expression changing to a fearful grimace. Looking down at the two charges, she swallowed, trying to introduce some saliva into her mouth, which had gone quite dry during the incident. Blowing herself sky high was most definitely not part of the plan. Her mother had always joked that Sarah had inherited her clumsiness from her; Sarah had never felt she was particularly cack-handed, but she had to admit, even to herself, that she did have a tendency to bang into things on occasion, perhaps more than most. It wasn't a trait she relished, especially when carrying around munitions.

'Okay,' she said to herself, 'one down – two to go.'

The explosives had proved far easier to obtain than she could have hoped and she was soon depositing them in a sturdy rucksack pilfered from the Alpha Six kit room, alongside some Deep Reach uniforms she'd nabbed for Trish and Jason. The waypoint beacon, strangely, took far more effort to source than the explosives. The only place to get them was from the mapping teams, who religiously documented everything that went in and out of their manned supply station. Sarah had to fill out paperwork and make up a cock and bull story as to why she needed three beacons, deciding one would seem suspicious and the extra two might, in fact, prove beneficial when they were outside the USSB.

As she loaded the three cylindrical objects into the bag, a familiar voice spoke from behind her. 'Morgan, a word if I may?'

Sarah froze and then turned round to look into the face of Commander Locke, behind him Cora hovered like a vulture, waiting for its prey to be incapacitated.

'Sir?' Sarah said, glancing at Cora and wondering if she'd been rumbled.

Locke stared at her with penetrating eyes. 'Riley tells me you've performed well in the field and that you've been an asset to the team.'

'But?' Sarah said, fearing the inevitable.

'There's no but. Just keep up the good work and ensure that inquisitive nose of yours stays out of trouble.'

'Yes, sir, thank you, sir.' She noticed that the flap of the bag, which rested at her feet, stood partially open, revealing its contents for all to see. Shifting position, Sarah hooked the rucksack with one foot and slid it under the bench behind her in a single movement.

'Ladies,' Locke said to Sarah and Cora, and then walked away without another word.

Once Locke was out of earshot Cora turned on her. 'You think you've got Riley twisted round your little finger, don't you?'

'What?' Sarah asked, distracted by the Commander's praise. Looking back at Cora she homed in on what she'd just said. 'No, of course not, we just get on well, that's all.'

Cora's expression grew vicious. 'I can see past that pretty little face, even if he can't. There's something not right about you and I'll find out what it is, mark my words.'

'You go do that,' Sarah said, remembering she'd not be around for much longer and that she needn't take, or be threatened by, this mad woman any longer. 'Knock yourself out.'

Cora looked stunned for a moment and then stormed off. *That was enjoyable*, Sarah thought, although in hindsight angering Cora was perhaps as good as pulling a tiger's tail and then poking it in the eye for good measure; not the wisest move, especially if the plan got waylaid for any reason. Still, it was too late to worry about that now, and she still had an air-shuttle manual to get her hands on.

A few hours later Sarah sat down, defeated, outside the SED Command Centre. She'd been hanging around inside, making excuses for her presence and failing to get anywhere near the manuals, which were held in a cabinet in front of the main Control Station, which itself was permanently manned. Realising her efforts would continue to prove fruitless, Sarah had retired to reconsider her options.

The only time the Control Station was left unattended was during the nightshift, when air-shuttles underwent scheduled maintenance or were all off-site, not to return within a minimum of twelve hours. Even then, a side room off the Command Centre housed resting personnel for any emergency situations that arose. There was only one thing for it; she would have to come back much later when all was quiet and pray she wouldn't be seen.

A distant rumbling signalled the imminent arrival of an air-shuttle into the central shuttle bay. Sarah sighed, swung the now heavy rucksack onto her back and headed for home; she figured she might as well dump her current load and come back unimpeded.

Reaching the outer edges of the building, the main entrance sliding into view as she descended one of the short escalators, people began rushing past her in the opposite direction.

'What's happening?' Sarah said to a man running towards the interior.

'They've found something big!' he replied without stopping.

'Big?'

Taking the stairs two at time, he looked back over his shoulder. 'Artefacts, amazing artefacts!'

Other people, chattering in excitement, scurried past while the area around her rapidly emptied. Torn between completing part of her mission or seeing whatever had been brought back from outside the base, Sarah stood for a few seconds and then ran back the way she'd come. She had to see this, it sounded too good to miss. By the time she'd reached the centre of the building again, the corridors heaved with personnel from all over the SED, everyone flocking to witness whatever had been unearthed out in Sanctuary Proper.

'Do you know what's going on?' Sarah asked a woman next to her as they moved slowly forwards, people trying to find any vantage point they could to watch the shuttle bay.

'An archaeological team just returned, they've found a hoard, biggest yet by the sound of it.'

'A hoard?'

The woman smiled, her eyes alight. 'Treasure – artefacts – who knows?! Whatever it is, I haven't seen this level of excitement for at least five years so it will be worth a look, for sure.'

Up ahead the doorway became jammed, the press of human bodies creating a bottleneck. The woman grabbed Sarah's hand. 'Follow me,' she told her and began working her way back down the corridor against the flow of people.

Hot on her heels, Sarah followed the woman through an emergency door.

'Short cut,' the woman said and then ran up some stairs.

Keeping up with her new found friend, Sarah was led through a rabbit warren of corridors in a section of the building she'd never seen before. Eventually they emerged out onto a narrow metal walkway, directly above the shuttle bay which was packed to the rafters with people, the sea of noise from the crowds bubbling up around them. Forty feet below, an air-shuttle had been surrounded by this mass of humanity while a green clad team unloaded from it three huge, composite crates, each twenty feet long, twenty wide and fifteen feet deep. These black, bespoke containers, Sarah knew, were used by teams to transport fragile objects back to the USSB, protecting them against the extensive rigours experienced during an air-shuttle's journey.

A bulky forklift truck deposited the crates onto the ground, the archaeological team fighting for room as they struggled against the press of bodies around them. Watching the commotion below, Sarah found her attention diverted by a speaker system crackling to life throughout the shuttle bay.

'This is Commander Locke; everyone calm down and give your colleagues some space to work. You are professionals, start acting like it!'

Reprimanded by their leader, people shuffled back as best they could, but it took a contingent of the army to regain some level of order. Soldiers formed a ring around the archaeologists, forcing the onlookers back.

The first crate lid swung open, the compressed gases inside hissing out into the air and enveloping the crew around it in a misty vapour. With the gas dissipating, the precious cargo within, still covered by a transparent film and held down by heavy strapping, came into focus. Sarah had a prime view of what lay beneath, situated as she was on the high gantry. Everyone else below craned their necks to see what lay inside. Rather than a selection of items, Sarah could see just a single jet-black, oblong object, measuring approximately fifteen feet long, ten in width and perhaps the same in height.

The archaeologists, belonging to team Delta Twelve, according to the text on the reverse of their coveralls, hooked the retaining straps onto the forklift and hoisted the precious discovery up into the air and then down onto the steel clad floor. The glossy artefact, now fully exposed, had an intriguing hexagonal profile. The flat surface was so without flaw Sarah could see the reflection of the surrounding people and shuttle bay within it. The straps were released and the protective film discarded, enabling lines of silver to be seen running down its length, accompanied by a fine flowing script and curious symbols.

'Do you think it's a coffin?' the woman said to Sarah, breaking the spell that had settled upon her as she watched the scene unfold below.

'Perhaps,' Sarah said, still engrossed, as the other two transportation cases were unloaded to reveal two more near identical hexagonal shapes. Unlike the first artefact, these two had dirty, cracked and pockmarked brown surfaces, appearing as ancient as they probably were. As the last one neared the ground, the forklift operator misjudged the depth and lowered it too fast sending a heavy boom reverberating around the inside of the building, indicating to all present the immense weight of the objects on show.

'Be careful, you idiot!' one the archaeologists screamed at the forklift operator, the impact sending a small chunk of the strange monolith crumbling onto the floor.

The woman next to Sarah gasped and put a hand to her mouth in shock at seeing the object's fragility and the mistake that had resulted in its further degeneration. Sarah knew how she felt; they had to be more careful.

'Is this why the army are here in numbers today?' Sarah asked the woman next to her, putting two and two together. 'I'm Sarah, by the way.'

'Anne-Marie.' The woman gave Sarah a warm smile and held out a hand, which Sarah shook. 'No, I don't think so,' she told her, as they both looked back down once more, transfixed. 'Word is the military has something coming in later. This team came back unexpectedly.'

Now unloaded, the green clad team, enlisting the help of a few of the soldiers, grappled with the topside of each of the objects. Sarah realised they were trying to remove the lids. Inch by tantalising inch, the top of each artefact slid away, the movement accompanied by grinding noises much like the discord of heavy stone on stone. The emotive sound drifted to silence. The massive covers, now fully retracted, hung suspended off to one side, somehow still attached along one edge; perhaps by an unseen mechanism contained within.

Sarah attempted to absorb everything at once, but to do so was an impossibility and so, succumbing to the unconsidered, she let her eyes be seduced by the nearest of the now open chests. The thick sidewalls, made of the same material as its exterior – a dusty looking brown rock – surrounded not a hollow core, but a single long, rectangular, oxidised metal insert. Sunken into this thick, pitted metal were three distinct shapes; an ellipse, a semicircle with a pinched peak, and a long, slim rectangle, ending in a point at one end and a small circle at the other.

Two of the three cut-outs sat empty, the thick metallic walls reaching down a hand's width to a flat dark surface. Resting within the ellipse, however, lay something that held the attention. Sarah gazed at the strange object, its colour seeming to change and shimmer as the shuttle bay's interior lighting reflected from its intricate facets.

'It looks like a shield, don't you think?' Anne-Marie said, captivated by the same artefact.

'Hmm,' Sarah murmured in agreement. It did have the look of defensive hand-held armour. The shield, if that's what it was, consisted of a dark blue and purple material, inlaid with sparkling red gemstones and chrome-like diamonds in beautiful spiralling patterns. Just in from its outside edge, a wide band of gold enclosed the detailed centre.

Anne-Marie took a photo with her computer phone. 'It must be about seven feet in length, most likely ceremonial.'

Sarah's gaze shifted to the other two opened caskets. The second rock-hewn block held the bones of a skeleton, or at least the remnants of one. The segments of a huge Anakim skull, broken into six parts, had been positioned to give the impression of a complete piece. Each fragment had its own small compartment, sunk into a corroded metal surround, much like the shield in the other container. Along with this, around twenty other bones of various sizes had been placed in anatomically correct locations within the aging metal surface. Whoever this individual had been, they must have been important indeed; this find was a true relic in every sense of the word.

The final hexagonal container, black as night inside, as it was out, had been filled with three rows of twenty small circular holes sunk into the black onyx-like surface. Within each, apart from nine which were empty, nestled a small, round ball; around each hole were words in the same silver script, perhaps denoting some aspect of what rested within. Looking closer, Sarah realised the spherical objects weren't round at all, but multi-faceted, which gave them their orb-like appearance. Each varied in colour and, although it was difficult to tell for certain at a distance, in texture and material too.

Sarah disconnected her computer phone from her wrist and recorded some video footage, much like everyone else below. The archaeologists weren't finished, however, and one of them activated some kind of mechanism within the black vessel. The top surface containing the spheres sprang upwards a few inches and then parted, to reveal a cavernous hole beneath. At the bottom of this secret void Sarah could just make out a flash of gold.

Anne-Marie leaned forward. 'What is that?'

Sarah wasn't sure, but whatever these artefacts represented, it had become of great interest to the U.S. Army and the rest of the military fraternity. Armed Special Forces filtered through the crowds to the artefacts, the leader recognisable as the man who had clashed with Riley back on her first SED mission.

There were angry exchanges between the factions, their raised voices drowned out by dissent within the ranks of SED workers present. Finally the archaeologists succumbed to the military's demands, finding themselves relieved of their duties before being escorted away. The Terra Force commander then gave a twirling signal with one raised hand and his men went about closing and covering the artefacts.

Jeers and catcalls rang out from the spectators and then the

Command Centre's speaker system sputtered to life once more. 'SED personnel, my name is General Stevens.'

Sarah looked up to see an SFSD contingent behind the Control Station's glass windows. A large portly man in an officer's uniform stood next to Dresden Locke.

'I have authorised the acquisition of these Anakim treasures,' the General continued, 'for immediate analysis by our science division. Any video or photographs taken will need to be submitted to our security teams immediately. Please report to your nearest security officer for compliance. To ensure no mistakes are made, everyone will have their recordings downloaded from all of their devices upon leaving this building, be that today or otherwise; if you have anything of a personal nature that you don't wish us to see, we recommend deleting it now.'

There was a ferocious vocal backlash from the SED's denizens at this sudden and unjust turn of events and the scene threatened to turn ugly in short order. Weapons were raised and objects thrown before harmony was restored by Dresden Locke and General Stevens, and the real possibility of a riot and ensuing bloodshed was averted.

'This is so much bullshit,' Anne-Marie said, after things had calmed down and a soldier motioned at them from below to vacate the area.

'Do they do this often?' Sarah asked, trudging back the way they'd come, the thrill of the discoveries still fresh in her mind.

Anne-Marie shook her head. 'Rarely at the SED. They normally stamp their size twelve boots all over our teams out in the field. They must have missed something they were interested in and decided to grab it now.'

Sarah passed her phone over to a member of General Stevens' staff for her data to be downloaded, wondering at the same time if they were going to check her bag, too. *That would be bad*, she thought. Her complacency switched to fear, then transformed into relief when he handed the phone back without so much as looking at her, his attention elsewhere as others pressed in around him and his colleague. With the excitement over, Sarah bade farewell to Anne-Marie.

Conscious she still needed the air-shuttle manual, she decided to hide in the building until the majority had left and then acquire the prize and depart for home the following day. Working her way towards the quieter storage facilities she contemplated her plan. Walk in when the Control Station is unmanned, take a manual, download it, and then walk straight back out again; simple, but hopefully effective. The manuals weren't top secret, as who else could use them? They were just problematic to copy when someone had no good reason to do so. Well, Sarah knew she did have a good reason, just not one anyone else in the SED would appreciate.

After nine hours of excruciating boredom, Sarah relinquished her hiding place and weaved her way back up to the Command Centre. Padding down the now deserted halls of the SED, her footsteps echoing horrifically, she reached her destination. Sliding through into the low-lit Control Station, her eyes flicked towards the closed door located at the back of the large room where the nightshift slept. Acutely aware of this slumbering menace, Sarah made a beeline for the shuttle manuals. Leaning over the desk, she slid open the cabinet door and plucked one of the tomes from its shelf. As she did so, a chain attached to the rear of the metal folder's spine slid along with it, clinking loudly like a miniature anchor being dropped from a ship. Sarah cursed softly and looked towards the back room, holding her breath, the fear of discovery heavy upon her. Nothing, no one stirred. The sound of the chain had seemed like a thunderclap to Sarah in her cocoon of silence, surrounded by vacated desks and hibernating computer systems.

The chain, she assumed – returning to her task – ensured the key system manual wouldn't go walkabout within the Exploration Division's complex. Placing the folder on the desk and grasping the metal tether in her other hand, to prevent it from making any more undue noise, Sarah perused the front cover to make sure it was what she needed. In the centre of the matte metal fascia an embossed SED logo had the following text beneath it:

AIR-SHUTTLE RETURN
PROCEDURES

Realising she had the wrong folder, she saw each of the six manuals had a corresponding number on the spine. The one she now held had a number two on it. Reasoning number one must be what she was after, she returned number two to the shelf and selected number one, which rested on the far right hand side. *It would help if someone put them back in order*, she complained to herself, while resisting the urge to rearrange them. Placing the new folder flat she was pleased to see the text:

AIR-SHUTTLE LAUNCH
PROCEDURES

Opening it out, she activated the digital screen inside and unclipped her phone.

She muttered a curse under her breath; the manual had no data transfer induction port, which prevented her from downloading its contents.

What to do, what to do? she asked herself. *There's only one thing I can do*, she realised, her heart sinking, *I'm going to have to film every page of the manual with my phone*. Pressing a couple of control buttons on the side of the screen, she set the manual to scroll through its contents, all six hundred pages of it, while holding her phone steady above. After ten minutes, which seemed more like two hours, her ears straining for any sign of movement both from within the back room and outside the Command Centre itself, the manual reached its last page. Putting the folder back, Sarah checked the other four files in case there was anything else relevant to their plans; fortunately there didn't seem to be.

Sarah knew she had to get rid of the recordings prior to leaving the building tomorrow; the security officers, and or soldiers, would definitely be interested to know why she had launch procedure files on her person. *So I won't keep the images on my phone*, she thought. *Stick that up your arse, General Stevens!*

Firing up a nearby printer and attempting to muffle the resulting emitted beeps, Sarah utilised the peripheral's integrated software to print out the manual from her phone's video footage. More minutes ticked by, the paper copy of the manual spewing forth page by inexorable page. As she waited, to her right, through the thirty foot high windows of the Control Station, the darkened shuttle bay brightened; its array of lights flickering to life and sending a white brilliance cascading through the glass to highlight Sarah within.

Dropping down to a crouch, Sarah's heartbeat quickened. Creeping to the front desk, she peeked over the top to see who had tripped the automatic lighting below. A team of Special Forces commandos, replete in full armour, fanned out around the shuttle bay, weapons in hand. Accompanying them was a host of military engineers and scientists, who homed in on a single docking bay; also along with them was a cigar-toting man whom she'd seen earlier that day, one General Stevens.

Sarah watched the enormous metal floor retract, the wail of sirens and flashing warning beacons unusually absent. Why were they opening the bay doors? There couldn't be an air-shuttle arriving as there was no one at the Control Station to receive it. At that thought the sound of heavy booted footfalls approached from nearby. Petrified, Sarah had no time to grab the manual, which had finally finished printing, choosing instead to dive under a desk. Curling her legs up to her chest, her hair falling over one eye, she peeked out to see her rucksack in plain view next to the printer.

It was too late to do anything now as the soldiers had arrived, their black boots treading – silently now – past Sarah's hidden location. Trying to keep her breathing quiet and her pounding heart slow, Sarah could just see from her limited vantage point the two soldiers disappear from view. Moments later she could see them at the rear of the room and they appeared to be locking the door to where the emergency crew slept. Returning in their heavy shod footwear and grey and black camos, the two men retreated from the room, one to the right and the other to the left.

When Sarah believed the coast to be clear she crawled from her hiding place and collected her manual. Still on all fours she deposited the wodge of paper into her rucksack, which she hitched onto her back once more. Getting into a low crouch, she sidled up to the nearest door to try and get a bead on one of the soldiers. Her face pressed up against the glass, she scanned the office beyond, half-lit by the shuttle bay below. There didn't appear to be anyone around until a dark shape moved mere inches from her face making her jump in fright, a yelp of surprise almost escaping her lips. The soldier was right there, on the other side of the door, guarding entry to the Control Station. With her back to the wall, her breathing shallow and her chest heaving as the adrenaline sought to increase its grip on her system, Sarah spied the second soldier through the door opposite, preventing entry to the only other point of access. She was trapped!

Crawling low past the nearest door, the rough carpet feeling dirty on her hands, Sarah hid beneath another desk out of sight of prying eyes. What's going on? she wondered, surely they shouldn't be locking the night-shift in their quarters? It could prove catastrophic if a shuttle came in and the correct safety measures weren't activated.

Twisting round in her cramped cubbyhole, Sarah could just see out into the shuttle bay, the huge shaft now exposed, the imposing rock walls lit up all around. Above one of the twin tracks, the engineers had set up a strange mechanism along with an industrial-sized winch; which already worked away, steam rising from its thick wire cable while two men used a hose to spray it with water as it spun round at high velocity. The toughened glass muffled most of the noise from below, but the distant whine of the winch still managed to penetrate through. As she watched, engrossed in this queer behaviour, some of the Terra Force commandos, utilising metal ropes and grappling hooks built into their armour, abseiled down into the deep hole and out of sight. The winch's high pitched scream dropped to a low whirr and Sarah knew whatever they were bringing up was nearing its journey's end. A rush of activity preceded the arrival of a familiar shape, the tip of an air-shuttle's nosecone. Bit by bit the subterranean craft's silver sub-frame edged into view. Either side, the soldiers who had scaled the rock face reappeared at the lip of the shaft, returning to the thick concrete that surrounded the entire bay.

Instead of allowing the machine to continue along its track, the team of men and women hauled the air-shuttle to one side using what was clearly a specially designed crane. The shuttle, resting on secure ground, had been gutted, its usual seating removed to enable it to carry a special load. Using the crane once more, the general's teams unloaded the single piece of cargo, which almost filled the entire shuttle, its bulk shrouded by a thick black plastic cover. Now standing erect, Sarah estimated it to be fifty foot high and half that in depth and breadth. The object, still attached to the crane by lifting slings, hung precariously suspended until it dropped down onto a waiting flatbed lorry which had reversed unseen through the maintenance road that led out into the USSB's lower levels. Once secured onto its transport, the lifting gear fell away and with it the cover, too.

Sarah shifted closer to the glass, her hands pressed against it, eager to lay eyes on what had so preoccupied the military. It was a piece of ancient architecture, its sides made up of dense rock similar to the Anakim structure she'd witnessed on her Deep Reach mission. In fact, she decided, it looked exactly like the stone formation at the site. The size, too, sparked off her memories of the hole the military had cut into the building's roof. Is this what had been producing the energy reading she and Riley had witnessed on their unofficial scouting mission? It must be. Obviously too big and heavy to bring back to the USSB by normal means, they had gone to great lengths to bring the load across many miles of sheer drops, vertical climbs and twisting tunnels. Such commitment meant this piece of rock must be important indeed.

Turning within the shuttle bay, which had by now been resealed, the transporter executed a one hundred and eighty degree manoeuvre, its great, deep-treaded tyres bulging from the weight of its single consignment. As it turned, Sarah saw the monument had a similar shape to the caskets she'd seen brought back by the archaeological team, only this monstrous thing had the look of a pentagonal prism. The meaning of the shape wasn't lost on her; the same form as her confiscated pendants, a five-sided polygon. It also suggested a link between it and the image of the Anakim priestess Sarah had seen on the interior walls of the nine hundred thousand year old edifice.

The eighteen-wheeler completed its about turn, bringing the opposite side of the object into view. Unlike the rest of the dark, coral-like rock, run through with seams of lighter sediment, one of the wide pentagonal sides contained a large sunken cut-out, rectangular in shape. Within the recess, a foot in from the edge and half the length of the outside structure itself, a ten foot wide glass-like enclosure rested. Around this transparent case ran a corroded metal frame. At its base, a wide, flat panel had been installed, and sunk into its centre were three distinct and identical shapes – perfectly formed circles. Sarah knew the implication of these indented discs; they meant this mysterious object could be activated by three giant individuals who wore a special pentagonal pendant, the same as the one she now had to reclaim herself.

The juggernaut edged off, the movement causing the pale material behind the glass to shift. Slow, dark swirls spun out from the deep interior, suggesting the chamber contained a heavy, viscous liquid. As Sarah watched it being driven away, General Stevens spoke to some of his men and then he, too, departed the shuttle bay, leaving those remaining to clear up the area.

Realising the opportunity to get a record of the departing artefact was disappearing, Sarah held up her phone and took a picture, but in her haste her finger clipped another command setting off a powerful flash. Horrified at her mistake Sarah looked down to see an engineer looking up in her direction. The man called out to one of his Special Forces colleagues. *Surely he hadn't seen it – had he?* The engineer, now joined by the Terra Force commando, pointed up towards the Control Station's windows, behind which Sarah knelt, concealed by a piece of frosted glass and a section of desk. The armour clad soldier dropped his raised visor down over his face and turned on his interior systems, sending a green glow emanating from the helmet's eye-like sculpturing. With the forbidding mask looking in her direction, Sarah knew the man within scrolled through various spectral ranges which could identify her heat signature; her own Deep Reach headgear having the same feature. The soldier's gloved hand moved to one side of his helmet, most likely activating a communication to the men standing yards from Sarah's position.

Knowing the game was up, Sarah threw caution to the wind and scrambled out from underneath the desk. Standing upright, terror gripped her mind like a shrieking banshee, rooting her to the spot. Where could she go? A sound to her right triggered her flight or fight response. She found herself running full pelt in the opposite direction.

'Stop right there!' a man said from behind.

This failed to break Sarah's stride as the other door opened ahead of her; instead the words, 'Sod you!' erupted unbidden from her mouth as she launched herself forwards into mid-air and oblivion.

TERMINOLOGY / MAP

USSB – United States Subterranean Base
GMRC – Global Meteor Response Council
Darklight – World's largest private security contractor
SFSD – Special Forces Subterranean Detachment (*Terra Force*)
SED – Sanctuary Exploration Division

CHAPTER EIGHTEEN

Tucked away just south of Colorado, within the state of New Mexico, sits the small town of Dulce, population three thousand, four hundred and nine. Consisting almost entirely of aboriginal Americans, the remote New Mexican reservation had acted as a home for the Jicarilla Apaches for generations. Surrounded by dry scrubland and a rocky hilly terrain, the whole area exuded an arid beauty, baked dry by the endless sunshine that had once shone down upon it.

Since the asteroid AG5 had impacted, the sun had been taken, and as some knew this was an act of the creator. The dust on the ground had now been mirrored by that in the air high above, shielding the light giver from its subjects below. What the future held was unclear, but what the present supplied was plenty.

'Where is the sky, father?' the young boy asked as he looked up to the heavens, seeking glimmers of bright blue he knew should be there.

'The sky is still there, Kuruk. It is just dark.'

Kuruk eyed the brooding skies in an inquisitive yet fearless manner. 'Like the bad spirits?'

'No, my son, not like the bad spirits. The gods are testing us. If we can survive without the sun we can survive anything.'

'Anything, father? Even death?'

'The body does not survive death, Kuruk, but our spirits will live on in the Land of Ever Summer. Hardships in life give us greater strength in death.'

Satisfied with his parent's answer, Kuruk jumped down from the large boulder he'd been sitting on and bounded away into the darkness.

'Don't go too far, Kuruk!' his father called after him as the boy disappeared into the night-like day.

'I won't, father!' Kuruk threw back, switching on a small torch to seek out his favourite places to play.

Kuruk loved to run in the dark. The challenge of remembering small paths and trip hazards kept his senses honed and his balance true. Today he felt energised and so he decided to reach the secret place, somewhere known only to him.

Half an hour later Kuruk pushed aside a low branch, the light of his torch highlighting the small leaves and grey knotted wood of the bushy tree which rustled at his passing. Lying down, he squirmed his way inside a tight gap in a craggy rock face, the dust of the earth kicked up by his movements hanging in the air around him. A metre further in and Kuruk found himself in his tiny den. At the back, against the craggy stone, a deep, narrow fissure sank into the bowels of the Earth. Hot warm air gushed through this crevice to the surface, heating the cavity against the cold air from outside. Now in the wilderness the silence surrounding Kuruk was perfect. Leaning forwards and cupping his hands to his ears, he sat still and unmoving, straining to catch the sounds from below. He didn't have long to wait, as after a few minutes, on the very edge of his hearing, a small chinking sound echoed up to him. Father said the white man built their own secret places underground. Kuruk couldn't believe that. He fancied it was the spirits of his ancestors seeking their way back to the living. *I would very much like to talk to my grandfather*, he thought, the vague but comforting memory of his father's father sending a pang of yearning through his tender heart.

'Grandfather!' Kuruk shouted into the deep, black hole. 'This way grandfather, this way!'

As usual only his echoes could be heard along with the ever present *chink chink chink* drifting up from the depths.

◆

Over a kilometre below Kuruk's feet, through layers of compacted soil and dense rock, the men and women of USSB Steadfast toiled by hand to clear debris from an emergency stairwell. The sound of picks and shovels striking the dense rubble reverberated through the surrounding area and beyond, sharp edges of hardened tools biting deep into pulverised stone and broken boulders alike. The collapsed tunnels, leading to the surface, had been compromised by strategically placed explosions. Critical excavation machinery had been either removed from the base or disabled beyond repair and the interior-to-surface lift systems lay crippled.

In the heart of the subterranean complex stood the reinforced, fifty storey high Command Centre, its grey clad bulk cleaving through three chamber levels. Running vertically down one side of the building, large three dimensional lettering spelt out the name, *U.S.S.B. STEADFAST*. In the lowest rooms of this central command structure, a select team of people awaited the arrival of the man that called the shots. He wasn't normally in charge at Steadfast, only having arrived just before the meteorite impacted in 2040, but now their director had left the base the GMRC Director General of the Subterranean Programme himself had taken direct control; which was just as well, as no one else had the experience or expertise to deal with the crisis at hand.

The large glass double doors opened with a pneumatic swish and the assembled ranks stuttered to silence as everyone stood. A man of small stature and a powerful presence, flanked as ever by his personal aides, entered the room. Wearing a simple grey GMRC uniform, the Director General's only indication of rank was the inconspicuous golden weave adorning his cuffs and epaulettes, and a badge on his right shoulder; the symbol of the powerful and influential GMRC Directorate.

GMRC
DIRECTORATE
★★★★★★★★★★★★★
IN VERITATE SCIENTIA

'Please be seated,' Professor Steiner said, adjusting his glasses and taking his seat at the head of the large conference table.

A shuffling of chairs and the muted rustle of clothing followed his command as everyone sat back down. The Steadfast personnel glanced at one another in anxious anticipation, waiting for their leader to begin.

Professor Steiner cleared his throat and spread out some paperwork before him. He then looked to the greying, clean-cut, middle-aged man to his right. 'Nathan, can you bring up a map of the base on the wallscreens, please?'

'Certainly, Professor.' Nathan got to his feet and walked to the far end of the room to access the building's internal computer system.

'Ladies,' Professor Steiner said, looking over the tops of his glasses at the women in the room, 'gentleman,' he continued, perusing the men before him. 'As you are all very much aware, USSB Steadfast is still cut off from the surface. Critical systems have been patched up as best they could be and the majority of the four hundred and seventy-five thousand souls that still call this base home have been relocated to the lowest levels for safety.

'It has been many months since this – *situation* – was thrust upon us and we are no further along in securing any kind of route to the surface, despite our best efforts. The people responsible for our entombment did well when they sabotaged Steadfast's systems. The damage caused to life support has ensured most of our efforts are directed at keeping ourselves alive rather than evacuation.

'Every attempt we do make to reach the surface has been thwarted, not just by the previous efforts of our tormentors but by those still stationed on the surface tasked with preventing our escape—'

The doors to the room opened once more, causing Steiner to pause. Five U.S. Army officers marched into the room. At their head stalked a large, powerfully built man with a self-indulgent swagger, his scalp sprouting thick, dirty blonde receding hair, which flowed down into shorter bristling stubble that covered half of the owner's grizzled face. Unlike his uniformed comrades he wore heavy green and brown body armour that had seen its fair share of engagements, its thick composite metal exterior bearing the marks of combat, shiny metal gashes and grazes standing out in stark contrast to the camouflage paint around it.

'Ah, Colonel Samson,' Steiner said, while glancing pointedly at his watch, 'so good of you to join us.'

Samson sat down at the opposite end of the table to the professor, his fellow officers taking seats either side of him. The colonel, instead of responding to Steiner's acknowledgement, merely glowered, his heavy brows hovering over a pair of pale, cold eyes.

'Okay, shall we continue?' Steiner clasped his hands before him, undeterred by the antagonism permeating from the very pores of the military leader opposite him. 'Excellent,' he said in his confident tone as some of the civilians looked nervously towards Samson and his cronies. 'I have called you all here today to outline my proposal for extricating everyone from this facility. The reasons for our abandonment by the GMRC and U.S. military on the surface is still unknown, although it is clear that Intelligence Director Joiner played a leading role in the affair. Since we have been left to our own devices, it has fallen to me, and the people in this room, to take control of all our destinies. Now that we have stabilised our environment it is time to take the next step. Nathan,' Steiner motioned with a hand at his friend and confidant, 'if you will.'

Nathan Bryant nodded and activated the wallscreens around the office, each wall displaying the same image, enabling comfortable and clear line of sight for each person regardless of their physical position.

'As you can see,' Nathan said, 'this is a detailed schematic of USSB Steadfast.'

Steiner eyed the graphical representation, noting the many intricacies of the base he helped to design.

'And here,' Nathan said, highlighting in a red hue various vertical sections as he tapped the screen with a couple of fingers, 'are the main and subsidiary exits to the surface; all of which have been blocked, disabled and, as far we have been able to tell, guarded topside.' He zoomed into the top right hand side of the base and executed a command to produce a bright green line, which reached the surface by a roundabout route. 'Here is Conduit Shaft 183B.' With a flourish Nathan flicked the image into the middle of the table, the transparent hologram rotating slowly on its axis.

A woman in a prim grey suit raised a tentative hand in the air.

Nathan pointed to her. 'Yes?'

'That shaft doesn't exist. I run the engineers in that sector and I know that particular area like the back of my hand; there's nothing there.'

'You are partially correct,' Steiner told her as he gave Nathan a small nod to indicate he would take it from there. 'There is no access to the shaft, as indicated on the plans before us; however, if I have remembered correctly when this base was constructed that shaft was built but not completed, being classed as obsolete by further advances in the overall design. If that is the case – which I believe it is – then it may be possible for a team to use 183B to reach the surface without detection by those above, as it is an unknown potential exit.'

A civilian manager spoke up. 'Wouldn't the army be guarding the whole area and not just specific points of access?'

'Yes,' Samson said, his gruff manner out of place in the office environment.

'Thank you, Colonel.' Steiner turned to address the manager who had spoken. 'Yes, they will be, but as you will note on the screen this unfinished shaft bisects the surface at the furthest extremity of the upper footprint of Steadfast. This means any military presence at that location will be much less than elsewhere, or so we can hope.' He looked to Samson and his colleagues. 'Do you agree, gentlemen?'

A collection of nods and yeses answered the professor's question.

'Excellent,' Steiner enthused. 'So, with that in mind, any excursion will have a good chance of survival if exiting at that location.'

The female engineer raised her hand again. 'But, isn't this all redundant if we can't access the shaft in the first place? We don't have any functioning equipment with which to reach it.'

'And you could only squeeze a few people through that conduit tunnel,' another man said, 'which looks to run vertically for long sections. What could so few hope to achieve if they managed to evade those on the surface?'

'All valid points.' Steiner was buoyed by the input. 'First, access to the shaft can be attained by some good ol' hard labour. Working through one of the collapsed emergency stairwells, we can use the destruction of the surrounding rock to our advantage; there will be no need for any equipment or to risk further destabilising the exterior walls of the base by using any kind of explosives. As to reaching the surface, a team of well-trained climbers can make it, and our resident Special Forces Subterranean Detachment,' Steiner extended an open hand towards Colonel Samson, 'will be perfectly suited to making the ascent and securing a pathway to safety. As to what such a small number of people can achieve, that will depend on those who will be taking the trip with them.'

Samson frowned. 'And who might that be?'

'A few select individuals,' Steiner responded, a serious intent to his tone. 'Communication experts and someone who can call on contacts within the GMRC to go against whatever orders Director Joiner has managed to put into motion.'

'Who will be able to do that?' one of the other army officers asked.

'That would be me,' Steiner said.

The room erupted into a cacophony of complaints and dissent at the suggestion.

Waiting for everyone to calm down, including Nathan, who perhaps voiced the loudest protests, Steiner held up his hands. 'I expected such a reaction,' he said, although he noted Samson had not raised any objections whatsoever, 'however, I am the only person in Steadfast who has the power to counteract Malcolm Joiner's commands.'

'You're also the person we're all relying on to keep this place functioning, Professor,' Nathan said. 'Who else could run this place with you gone? The majority who had the expertise to overcome Steadfast's ongoing system issues fled the base with Richard Goodwin; without you we'd be floundering within the week.'

'They fled on my command,' Steiner reminded his friend, 'and your assertion that you would not be able to cope without me is a false one. The people in this room, every one of you,' he said, looking around at the many faces turned towards him, 'have proved they have what it takes to fill the void of those who went before them. The nuclear-powered generators have been dealt with, the air and water systems stabilised. Yes, perhaps I could apply my expertise further if future problems arose, but right now our priority must be to change the game, and I am the only one who can readjust the music to play a tune more to our liking.'

'And when do you expect this mission to take place? Samson's voice was hostile.

Steiner interlaced his fingers. 'By the end of the week.'

'Surely it will take months to break through to the conduit shaft you mentioned,' another person said.

'Yes, approximately two months,' Steiner agreed, 'but since I put three teams to work on it round the clock seven weeks ago the route through will be available to use sooner rather than later.'

Samson snorted in derision. 'You had this planned two months ago and you've just decided to let us in on the fact?' He looked around at those present. 'And you look to this man as though he's your saviour? You people are a bunch of simpering fools. Can't you see this man is no different from the one who put us here? Everyone on the GMRC Directorate is the same, cold, calculating, cowardly and devious.'

A few of the civilians gasped in shock at Samson's words while the other military officers present appeared embarrassed by the colonel's outburst.

Professor Steiner, his face grave, held up his hand to quieten those coming to his rescue. 'Coming from you, Colonel, I find such hypocrisy obscene.'

Samson stood up, placed his hands on the table and leant towards Steiner. 'I may be cold and calculating, but I don't try and hide the fact from these simpletons you're quick to heap with false praise.'

'You forget yourself, Colonel.' Steiner rose from his own chair, his powerful voice belying his lesser physical stature. 'These men and women do not need their courage undermined by a bully such as yourself and I never – ever – praise those that don't deserve it, which is why you have never heard those words directed at yourself.'

The two men stood, eyes locked and unwilling to back down as everyone else watched the clash of wills with a fearful anxiety.

Nathan stepped forwards as if to intervene. The movement caught Steiner's attention dragging his gaze away from the colonel's detestable face.

'Sit down, Colonel,' Steiner said, returning to his own chair, his fury ebbing away, 'or leave this meeting. Your destructive input is not welcome here.'

Without a word, Samson stomped down the side of the room towards the door and paused next to the professor. 'You may not like to hear the truth of my words,' he said to Steiner in a deathly calm voice, 'but your plan will need my leadership and men for it to succeed. All of you will be relying on me,' he said to the rest of the room. 'We'll see how much my input is needed then.'

The doors opened and closed. Samson had gone, leaving behind an uncomfortable silence enveloping those who remained, which included the four other military officers.

'Why do you persist on inviting that man to our meetings?' Nathan asked Steiner, his exasperation plain to hear. 'He's unable to act in a civil manner and always seems bent on challenging your authority and disrupting an otherwise constructive debate.'

'Samson is a man of action, not talk.' One of the officers, another colonel, spoke up in defence of his colleague. 'He may not be to most people's tastes, God knows I've had my fair share of run-ins with the man, but he demands respect in our ranks, which makes him a valuable asset.

'Ever since our generals left us to die down here,' the man continued, 'he has been crucial in maintaining discipline, not only in his own men, but throughout the rest of the armed forces stationed within this base. He may be confrontational and unstable, but without him the large number of soldiers, trapped underground, fearful and nervous, may well have lost all sense of control; if that happened we would be facing a breakdown of law and order very quickly and that's something we can ill afford right now.'

Steiner nodded. 'Well said, Colonel Weybridge. We owe more to Samson than perhaps we would wish.' He looked to Nathan and those around the room. 'These are trying times and putting up with one man's outbursts is the least of our worries.'

'If Samson is so crucial to keeping Steadfast's military in check,' a senior manager from the transport department said, 'then to have him heading the expedition to the surface is counterproductive, is it not?'

'It's not ideal,' Steiner admitted, a small frown appearing on his brow as he leaned back into his chair, 'however, needs must. Others will just have to step up to the plate.' He held the gaze of Weybridge at the other end of the table; the colonel returned the look, his expression unreadable.

After a further three hours spent discussing the ins and outs of the escape plan and the utilisation of the conduit shaft, including how they would proceed with a full scale evacuation of the base once the surface had been secured, the meeting drew to a close. Steiner, making sure he was the last to leave the room, made a point of exchanging a few words with each person as they left.

'Professor,' Weybridge said as he departed, 'be aware the rest of the military in Steadfast do not share Colonel Samson's opinions about you and your leadership. We are more than willing to follow your lead.'

Steiner shook Weybridge's offered hand. 'Thank you, Colonel. Samson is right about one thing though, he is critical to our plans. When the team reaches the surface we may well be in a fight for our lives—'

'And there is no man in this base as fierce or as skilled in battle as Samson,' Weybridge said.

'Or so it is said.' Steiner found it hard to keep a note of scepticism from his voice.

'Don't be fooled by the man's short temper,' Weybridge cautioned him, 'he can turn off his emotions like a switch. It is surprising such a volatile individual can act well in the field, but I have seen the man in action and you need a calm mind to react as he does under fire.'

'That's good to know,' Steiner said, feeling grim that he had to utilise the talents of such a man. 'Let's hope he's as good as you say – for all our sakes.'

CHAPTER NINETEEN

Five days had passed since Professor Steiner had disclosed his full proposal to save Steadfast's trapped residents. In that time there had been a lot to prepare and he and Nathan hadn't had a spare moment to converse in private, one thing or another cropping up to draw their attention elsewhere. Now alone in his office, Steiner sat in his large chair, elbows on his desk, hands propping up his chin as he closed his eyes to accommodate a deep sense of tiredness that had suddenly swept over him. He expected Nathan to arrive in an hour; *time enough for a snooze,* he decided, and he took off his glasses, folded his arms on the desktop, rested his head on them and drifted off to sleep.

It seemed no sooner had Steiner shut his eyes than a persistent bleeping noise roused him from his slumber. Wiping his eyes with one hand, he searched the table for his glasses with the other, his fingers probing and then finding the familiar frame close by. Popping on his spectacles, he focused in on the intercom built into the polished mahogany desktop. 'Yes?' he said, thinking whoever had disturbed his sleep had better have a good reason for doing so.

'Sir, Nathan Bryant is here to see you,' said the disembodied voice of one of his Darklight bodyguards, the private security contractor positioned fifty feet away outside of Steiner's command suite.

'He wasn't due until ten o'clock,' Steiner replied, trying – and failing – to keep the annoyance from his tone.

'It is twenty-two hundred hours, sir.'

Where did that time go? he wondered, feeling far from refreshed after his sleep. *I must be getting old*, he decided, the boundless energy he'd enjoyed in his youth and middle age leaving him as the years ticked by. *Such demanding times have brought my physical limitations to the fore it seems*, he thought, stifling a yawn before advising the security operative to send his friend in.

Nathan soon knocked on the door and entered at Steiner's invitation.

'Professor,' Nathan greeted him, his usual broad smile a bright welcome to Steiner's weary eyes. 'You look awful,' he added, sitting down in one of four chairs opposite.

'Thank you for that kind observation.' Steiner gave a small smile of his own. Not many people spoke to Steiner that way, and fewer still that got away with it; Nathan, though, had been his friend and colleague for almost as long as Steiner's GMRC career and was the one person in Steadfast he knew he could count on, no matter what.

'I'd say to arrange to meet up another time,' Nathan said, 'but considering you're leaving in a couple of days I doubt we'll have another opportunity such as this.'

'I'm fine—' Steiner put a hand over his mouth as a full blown yawn took control of him. 'Just in need of a little sleep that's all.'

'Perhaps a drink will get you going.' Nathan got up and poured them each a small glass of cognac from the ornate decanter which sat on Steiner's desk.

Steiner accepted the offered glass and savoured the aromatic brandy as it warmed his throat on its way down.

'So,' Nathan said, looking into his own glass and swilling the golden liquid around inside it, 'two days until you place your trust and everyone's lives in the hands of a madman – confident?'

Steiner let out a small chortle. 'As confident as any man of my age would be when attempting a gruelling climb followed by a potential firefight. As to relying on Samson, I believe my trust is not misplaced.

He wants out of Steadfast as much as we do and is no friend of Joiner's. Nevertheless, once he has secured the team's safe passage from the immediate vicinity on the surface, his role will become less important. That is when I will attempt to establish communication with select people within the GMRC and U.S. Government. The sooner I can secure a solid platform of support, the sooner I can reassert my control and counter command Malcolm Joiner's orders.'

'Hmm.' Nathan sounded unconvinced. 'There's a lot that can go wrong, but as you've said before we have little choice in the matter. When the next asteroid hits in eight months' time everyone in Steadfast will either die instantly or suffocate soon after. I still don't understand how Joiner kept the altered trajectory of AG5-C a secret for so long; how can you hide that kind of information from the thousands of people working for NASA and all the other space agencies?'

'It's been done before and it will probably be done again,' Steiner said, finishing his drink and pouring another. 'If you control the flow of information, all you need to do is select a particular spot before the data cascades down, altering it almost without trace. Many teams work independently of one another and if the oversight itself was compromised, which it must have been, then such an outcome was possible; albeit an outcome that must have taken a great deal of effort and planning to accomplish. Since Joiner is the intelligence director for both the GMRC and the U.S. Government, a position one person should never have been allowed to achieve, in my opinion, it's not as crazy as it sounds to keep such a small detail hidden.'

'That small detail may end up killing half a million people,' Nathan pointed out.

'Small in mathematical terms,' Steiner said, 'not that I consider the deaths of five hundred thousand people to be inconsequential.' He sipped his cognac. 'The alteration to the data was tiny, but enough to put the impact zone of AG5-C almost directly on top of Steadfast. If Joiner hadn't shown his hand by sealing us down here, I would never have spotted it.'

'And you're positive none of the other data streams were corrupted?' Nathan said.

'How many times have you asked me this?'

Nathan shrugged. 'Twice?'

Steiner laughed. 'More like twenty times. But no, the other sets of telemetry were, as far as I could see, untouched. The other five asteroids will be impacting as predicted.'

Nathan downed the remainder of his drink. 'Unless Joiner intercepted the information flow even higher up the chain.'

Steiner made a face. 'That's something I'd rather not consider, and the likelihood is extremely remote.'

'I have to say,' Nathan said, placing his empty glass down on a leather coaster, 'I wasn't too happy you kept secret the fact that you'd be going to the surface as part of the team. You couldn't trust me enough to tell me beforehand?'

Steiner noted his friend's hurt demeanour. 'I didn't say anything because I knew you wouldn't relent until you'd talked me out of it.' Steiner gave Nathan a fond look. 'You can be quite persuasive when you want to be.'

Nathan seemed a little mollified by the comment and picked up his glass again, twizzling it round in his fingers in contemplation. 'I don't think Steadfast's new command group was convinced by your explanations for leaving them without you or Samson at the base.' Nathan looked up from his tumbler.

'That's because they don't know all the facts. Our predicament is more dire than they know.'

Nathan shifted in his seat. 'Perhaps we should tell them, then? Don't they deserve to know; doesn't everyone down here deserve to know?'

'What they deserve is of no consequence,' Steiner said, 'as much as I hate saying so. If we revealed to them we have a finite time frame to get out of this facility, what do you think would be the result? The fact is, informing them of their impending doom would only cause mass hysteria. Colonel Weybridge said it himself, only with Samson's iron hand did they keep their personnel in line during the initial uproar when everyone found out we were trapped down here. I consider our course of action sound and the only one available to us at present. Believe me when I say I have deliberated every other option to the nth degree – as well you know, I've talked most of them through with you. We have to maintain calm until no other option is left to us.' Steiner opened a drawer in his desk and withdrew a folder, which he placed in front of Nathan.

'What's this?' Nathan picked it up.

'Final contingency protocols.'

'For?' Nathan flicked through the thick wodge of paper inside.

'To help the leader of Steadfast and his team make final arrangements, if my mission fails.'

Nathan looked wary. 'What sort of arrangements?'

'Necessary ones. If I'm unable to secure freedom for all Steadfast's residents, then there will only be one alternative for your escape.'

'Fight our way out,' Nathan said, his expression grim.

'Yes, and undoubtedly such an assault against the forces on the surface will result in significant losses, perhaps as much as ninety per cent.' Steiner rubbed his beard in distraction, the coarse bristles feeling comforting against his palm. 'Joiner may have even put in place orders to detonate large devices within our lift shafts to prevent any such action.'

Nathan folded his arms across his chest. 'That's an awful thought.'

Steiner considered his friend, whose kind face and compassionate soul masked an intelligent mind full of untapped strength. 'I just wish I didn't have to leave you all down here,' he said, ending the pause in conversation. 'I feel like a captain abandoning his ship as it sinks, but I know if I don't go it increases the likelihood that everyone left in Steadfast will perish.'

'It's a difficult decision,' Nathan said. 'Not one I agreed with at first, I admit, but now that I've had time to think about it, it does appear to be the best and perhaps only option we have to save all these people.'

'I'm glad you feel that way.' Steiner braced himself for the complaints to come when his next words were spoken. 'With that in mind and in respect to the contingencies which you now hold—' He paused, looking at his friend, gauging his mood; *there's no right time for this, best get it over with,* he decided as Nathan looked at him, blissfully unaware of the responsibility he was about to inherit. 'I will be leaving you in command of Steadfast.'

Nathan's expression portrayed a myriad of emotions all at once, fear, shock and horror the most prevalent that Steiner could see.

'What? Are you out of your mind?!' Nathan got up and stared down at Steiner as if he had indeed lost his senses. 'I'm no leader, especially not one who could command half a million people!'

'Four hundred and seventy thousand,' Steiner said, the pedantic comment not even registering with his friend, who failed to deliver his customary look of reproach as he paced around the room like a caged animal seeking escape.

Nathan came back to stand in front of the desk as he rallied. 'This is wrong. There are lots of people who can run Steadfast and they are all better choices than me.'

Steiner raised an eyebrow.

'Colonel Weybridge, for one.' Nathan answered the unspoken challenge. 'A well-spoken and highly regarded officer, a born leader. He has the respect of both military and civilian personnel, which is something I can never hope to have.'

'Weybridge will have his hands full, filling the void left by Samson,' Steiner said. 'Besides, he knows nothing of running the civilian led systems which operate this base; his tenure would quickly lead to disaster. Also, while you may not realise it, you already have the respect of many of the people who currently run Steadfast.'

Nathan, ignoring Steiner's last comment, ploughed ahead. 'The Chief of Police, what's her name?'

Steiner tried to keep a smile from his face as he watched his friend begin to flounder. 'Helen Warren?'

'Yes! Helen,' Nathan said, struggling to keep his composure. 'She's worked closely with the U.S. Army in the past and she has civilian authority.'

'And knows nothing about Steadfast's multitude of systems when compared to you,' Steiner added, blowing that argument out of the water with ease.

'James Fullerton,' Nathan continued, 'Senior Data Analyst and Director of Human Resources. He also has experience in various critical systems throughout the base and has been here for over a decade.'

'The military will not accept a backroom administrator without operational knowledge and oversight,' Steiner told him. 'Nathan, I have considered all the options you are presenting and many more besides, and the only one that comes out on top is the man I'm looking at now. A man who has been involved in the GMRC since its inception, a man who has also operated within the inner circles of the GMRC Directorate and is privy to some of the most sensitive information on the planet. You have worked in multiple divisions for the GMRC and within multiple USSBs. You have excellent communication and leadership skills—'

Nathan snorted at the mention of the word leadership.

'You are also the only person who will be left in this base who knows about the asteroid. Plus, and perhaps most importantly, you are the only man I trust to lead these people to safety in my absence.'

Nathan looked distraught. 'But—'

'No buts.' Steiner grew stern and a little angry that his friend couldn't recognise the leadership qualities he so clearly possessed. 'Nathan, listen to me, you need to trust in your own abilities. Whatever doubts you have about your capacity to lead, whatever shortcomings you have convinced yourself of over the years, are most likely born of redundant situations from your youth and it is time to let them go. I have worked with you for nearly thirty years and in that time I have seen you develop into a powerful individual capable of dealing with the sort of highly charged, complex situations most people would find overwhelming. You have excelled in the jobs you have been assigned to, but you have never sought out responsibility; it has always been accepted reluctantly. This time, however, I am putting you in a position where thousands of people will rely on you for their very lives, and I would not do so if I didn't think you were up to the task. I need you to put away your fears and be ready to lead these people with confidence; can you do that for me? Can you lead these people to safety when they need you most?' Steiner looked at his friend as he struggled with his own internal demons. Steiner knew Nathan had to accept the position willingly to ensure the best possible outcome for Steadfast and its people. 'Well?' he prompted, as Nathan sat looking at the floor in silent contemplation.

'Very well.' Nathan looked up and squared his shoulders as though physically accepting the burden placed upon him. 'I will take charge of Steadfast. If you think I can do it then I must be able to,' he added with a self-deprecating smile.

Steiner, able to relax somewhat, nodded and smiled at his friend in gratitude. 'Thank you. It's a big weight off my mind knowing that I leave you in charge. You will, of course, have Sophie, my primary aide, to help you in your daily duties, along with other members of the team I've had working with me here. I will also transition your command by addressing the whole of Steadfast before I leave, outlining – where I can – what we are proposing to accomplish with the mission to the surface. You will find in the contingencies a code which, along with your biometrics, will unlock a film I have recorded for you to air to the base when the deadline has passed for my return or contact. The code will also be able to verify I am who I say I am, when – if – I get back in touch with you.'

'A film; what does it say?'

'It discloses the arrival of the next wave of asteroids, and the imminent arrival of AG5-C and its impact proximity to this base. The contingencies allow for a staggered revelation of the truth over a couple of weeks to nullify panic as much as possible. I have also formulated a full scale assault plan, with the help of the colonels, of course, against the surface emplacements; these plans will need to be enacted as directed, although once it begins it may be that events take a direction all of their own.'

Nathan looked surprised. 'Didn't the colonels wonder why you wanted such a plan?'

'I claimed belt and braces. They may not know about the asteroids, but they know we have to get out of here eventually and force may be the only route. What they're unaware of is how soon we may have to put such a plan into action and how far we may have to take it.'

'Can we use the missiles we have stored down here?' Nathan said.

'It's debatable. Joiner also disabled all our external weapons systems before he departed. If we can rig something up it will be dangerous and to be used only as a last resort. Using such high-powered weaponry could collapse whole sections of the base, killing more than it might save.'

'Let's hope it doesn't come to that, then,' Nathan said with feeling.

Steiner raised his glass. 'I'll drink to that.'

CHAPTER TWENTY

THE NEXT DAY found Steiner once more in the Command Centre at Steadfast, his office a welcome refuge from the crash course he'd had to endure in climbing equipment and its use. Over the last few days a commando from Terra Force had put Steiner through his paces with no regard for his age or position. Steiner was pleased the man had pushed him so hard as he didn't fancy falling to his death; although, on reflection, he decided that might just be delaying the inevitable as, on the surface, he might get shot or be blown up.

Thankfully Steiner knew most of the hard work on the ascent through the conduit shaft would be shouldered by those around him. He would be getting not a free ride, as such, but as near to it as was possible from what he'd been told by those within Samson's team.

While Steiner perused his itinerary for that day, prepared by his irreplaceable aide, Sophie, he was disturbed by a commotion outside his office. Raised voices could be heard coming through the thick wooden double doors that separated his room from reception.

The intercom buzzed and one of his security guards began to speak, but the sound cut off before he could form a word.

'Hello?' Steiner said into the microphone. 'Is everything okay out there?'

No answer. Standing up, Steiner walked round his desk and reached out to one of the brass door handles, but just as he did so it jerked away from his grasp. The tall, imposing figure of Colonel Samson filled his vision, as ever garbed in his combat armour.

'Colonel?' Steiner stared into Samson's deadpan eyes. 'I have a busy schedule today, can I ask you to—' Steiner's voice tailed off as he peered around Samson to see the prone bodies of his two Darklight security guards. Sophie lay sprawled across her desk, unmoving. 'What's going on here?!'

Samson shoved him back into his office without a word.

Staggering back, Steiner turned and ran to his desk to call for assistance. As his fingers reached his phone, a metal-clad hand slammed down onto his own, crushing it in place. Samson lifted Steiner's arm away from the desk and then pushed him down into a chair.

'You don't want to call for help,' Samson told him in his gravelly voice. 'You don't know what I might tell them.'

'What's the meaning of this, Colonel?!' Steiner cradled his throbbing hand. 'And what have you done to my staff?'

Samson gripped the edge of Steiner's desk and heaved it away from him, sending papers flying and everything else tumbling to the floor.

Samson glared at him. 'Your people are sleeping off a sedative.'

'You do realise you've just crossed the line, Colonel, assaulting my bodyguards and an unarmed woman. There's no going back from this.'

Samson laughed, the disturbing sound making Steiner question whether Samson was experiencing some kind of mental break. If that was the case there was no knowing what he might do next.

'*I've* crossed the line?' Samson kicked out at a wooden chair, sending it crashing into the wall and splintering into pieces. 'If I've crossed the line then you've taken the line and fucking obliterated it!'

Steiner stared at the irate Terra Force commander, whose chest heaved up and down as his face seethed with a fury that made Steiner fear for his life. He glanced over to his desk; he couldn't reach anything to call for help. *If only I'd kept my earpiece on*, he thought, ruing the fact that he declined to wear it because it made his skin sore.

'Nothing to say, Professor?'

'I don't know what you want, Colonel, but I assure you I'll be lenient when charges are brought against you.'

'Oh you will, will you? Perhaps it'll be me that is lenient toward *you*.'

Steiner floundered for something to say. *What was the man going on about?*

'My fucking God, the great Professor Steiner, Director General for the GMRC's most powerful division, lost for words. Let me show you something which might make you more talkative.' Samson removed a small device from a side pocket on his utility belt and pressed it against the room's wallscreen data pad. The flat display flickered to life and a scrambled black and white mass of pixels danced across it, accompanied by a loud hissing crackle. This same repetitive noise and picture went on for some time.

'What are we supposed to be looking at here?' Steiner said as Samson watched him like a bird of prey eyeing up its quarry.

Samson didn't respond and Steiner moved his eyes back to the screen in an attempt to avoid the Colonel's unnerving stare. Finally a picture resolved itself, a section at a time, and a garbled audio track stuttered to life. Steiner realised what Samson had brought him to watch and his heart sank, the reason for the man's actions becoming clear. The voice emanating around his office from the speaker system, now fully recognisable, was his own. He watched in shock as the imperfect footage of himself he'd recorded months before on a computer phone in this very building played out on screen.

'—about to tell you is well beyond top secret,' Steiner's slightly younger self was saying, 'and is far above your clearance level, but given the new circumstances forced upon us by Malcolm Joiner I feel full disclosure is very necessary at this point. When the asteroid 2011 AG5 was first discovered twenty-nine years ago NASA had already begun testing a new high Earth orbit deep space detection array. This system was categorised as an unacknowledged Special Access Programme, or black project as we call them, due to its unique capabilities, which included satellite disruption technology that was to be utilised against enemies of the United States as required.

'During its first year of full operation the array surveyed large swathes of space. In 2012 this new system revealed an extremely disturbing image. Following in the same trajectory as AG5 were six other asteroids. The first four of the six will be impacting Earth in 2042 the last—'

The picture distorted wildly and then went black, the sound also cutting out. Steiner found himself gawping at the wallscreen; he composed himself, his jaw tightening as he turned back to his tormentor. 'How did you come by that message?'

'You don't deny its authenticity then?' Samson said, now frighteningly measured, serene even. 'Good. As to where I got it, I'll tell you a little story.'

Wonderful, Steiner thought, his inner voice dripping with witty sarcasm, just what I always wanted, a tale from a psychotic Neanderthal.

'I've been wondering, as many people have,' Samson began, 'why the Director of Intelligence, Malcolm Joiner, buried us all down here. Why would a member of the GMRC Directorate be willing to condemn a whole base, including the Director General of its prized Subterranean Programme, to a slow and painful death?'

'If you think I know why Joiner did what he did, you are mistaken.' Steiner knew that he could only guess at Joiner's duplicitous actions.

Samson's mouth twisted into a sneer of contempt, his disbelief at Steiner's comment complete. 'A few months back,' the Colonel said, resuming his tale, 'I ran into a technician from the Signal Corps. They carry out communications development, management and—'

'I'm well aware of the function of the army's Signal Corps, Colonel,' Steiner said, in no mood to be lectured by a man who effectively held him hostage.

Samson, now in his favourite position of control, didn't become agitated by Steiner's scathing tone; in fact what passed for a smile flitted across his craggy features, a bitter and twisted smile, perhaps, but a smile nonetheless.

'The technician revealed to me,' the Colonel continued, 'he'd been trying to trace and pinpoint Joiner's transmissions prior to him ordering our forces to take out your precious Darklight mercenaries. He believed if he could retrieve the streams from the ether it may shed some light on what had transpired and the reasoning behind it. He failed, but the idea was sound. I asked him if he'd found anything else around the same time, on other frequencies or systems. Turns out it takes time to trawl through the data and track down what could constitute something of interest. I told him I wanted him to spend as much time on it as he could and if he found anything to send it directly to me without watching or listening to whatever it was himself. If there was something important, I didn't want an NCO finding out about it and blabbing it all round the base first.'

'And you're sure he did what you asked?' Steiner said, now more concerned that this information might not be just in the hands of Samson.

'I can be very persuasive,' Samson replied ominously.

Of that Steiner had no doubt, and it was perhaps just as well in this instance, he concluded. 'And there are no copies?' he said, pressing the SFSD commander.

Samson smiled at Steiner again; *most likely happy to have me just where he wants me*, Steiner presumed with bitter remorse. He'd thought the data file he'd sent to Richard Goodwin had enough encryption to be secure; he was wrong. At least only a partial section had been retrievable, the full truth still eluded the Colonel, but Steiner knew Samson wanted the whole shebang and wouldn't relent until he had it.

'I wonder what would happen if your precious followers found out that six more asteroids are headed our way?' Samson said, his calm voice belying the vicious nature of the remark. 'Would they remain loyal to you or would they string you up from the rafters?'

'Colonel, the information you hold is very dangerous; if there are any copies they need to be destroyed.'

Samson laughed at him. 'Are you pleading with me, Professor?'

Steiner wanted to curse at Samson and physically wipe that filthy smirk from his cruel, spiteful face; he knew, however, Samson could squash him like a bug and to reveal his emotions to the man would only please him further and weaken Steiner's own precarious position. *I must find out if a copy of the video has been made*, he told himself.

'If this information got out it wouldn't just be my neck on the line,' Steiner said after a momentary pause, attempting to tackle the colonel by another route. 'You think your men would believe you didn't know either? Everyone in authority would be enemy number one.'

Samson considered Steiner in return. 'What are the impact zone coordinates for the six asteroids?' he asked, his intensity and anger frothing back to the surface. He walked over to the dishevelled table to pick up a glass. Looking at Steiner, he crushed the thick tumbler to dust within his metal-shrouded hand; a crude yet effective threat of violence, which Steiner had no doubt was designed to intimidate him into submission. The sad fact was, he had no other hand to play than the truth; a physical beating would be extremely unpleasant, but one he could ill afford if he was to attempt to save the lives of all those entrusted to his care. Besides, Samson knew too much and further lies would be pointless and transparent; the colonel was no fool, despite his actions intimating otherwise.

'There's an atlas on my bookshelf,' Steiner said, pointing.

Samson strode to the shelving, his heavy, metal-clad boots thudding dully on the carpeted floor. He selected a large, leather bound volume, the cover whispering as he withdrew it from between its fellows, then stomped back and dumped the atlas into Steiner's lap, making him jump slightly at the force.

Opening the cover, Steiner flicked to an illustration of the world, located within twin, intersecting ovals and spread across two adjacent pages. Angling the book towards Samson, Steiner pointed, one by one, at the locations where each asteroid would touch down.

'Wait,' Samson said after Steiner had touched the map near the New Mexico and Colorado border. 'That's right on top of us.'

Steiner looked up at Samson and gave a solemn nod.

'When will it hit?'

'We have eight months,' Steiner told him, expecting the man to go ballistic, but instead Samson walked to the other side of the room, deep in concentration.

Facing the wall, the colonel put a hand to his mouth and flicked his head back as though taking a pill of some kind. 'The size, what size is it?' Samson asked, his voice strained.

'Half that of AG5 itself. It will decimate the continental United States; the south eastern and central states will face annihilation.'

'What of the others in 2042?' Samson said, still with his back to Steiner.

Steiner looked at the door, but decided it would be futile to try and run. He looked back to see Samson had turned around, his blue eyes fixed once more on his hostage.

'Another is a little larger and will hit in northern Africa,' Steiner said. 'The one making landfall near the Russian Mongolian border is twice the size of AG5 and the fourth, touching down in the Pacific Ocean, is five times as big.'

'The other two. When and where?'

'Both will impact in 2045. The first in the southern Atlantic, the next in the Pacific; each is much larger than AG5, and the final one may well be large enough to trigger an ignition event.'

'Which means?' Samson said.

'That the detonation from the resulting strike may set in motion a chain reaction that would destroy the Earth's atmosphere.'

'So that's why so many bases were made,' Samson muttered to himself. 'Not to protect us from AG5, but from what was to follow.'

'Now do you see why we had to keep it a secret?' Steiner said. 'If people had known the truth, the construction projects would have been severely limited and delayed by mass hysteria. Dissemination of the information we had was not an option; the future of our entire race was at stake, of all life on Earth, for that matter.'

Samson didn't appear to hear Steiner as he leaned one hand

against a wall, the information apparently too much even for the hardened colonel to take in.

'Colonel, this information must not get out. Please can you tell me if there are any copies of that recording?'

'There are no copies,' Samson told him, finally relenting, 'but this one,' he held up the small data device, 'stays with me as collateral.'

Steiner turned as the office doors burst open and armed Darklight forces swarmed inside, the black-clad security contractors shouting at Samson to kneel down and put his hands on his head.

'Are you okay, sir?' one of the Darklight officers asked Steiner, as Samson held his ground, his own weapons drawn.

'I'm fine, Captain, thank you. Tell your men to stand down.'

The Darklight man looked confused. 'Sir?'

'The colonel is no longer a threat, he's free to go.'

The captain nodded and barked out orders for his team to shoulder their weapons. As they did, Samson did likewise.

Pushing his way past the similarly armoured Darklight operatives, Samson paused in front of Steiner. 'Thank you for your cooperation, Professor,' he said, his inflection condescending, a malicious glint in his eye. 'I'll look forward to working with you on the ascent to the surface.'

Steiner's eyes narrowed in suspicion and anger at the colonel's insincerity. Samson threw an insolent salute in the direction of the Darklight captain and walked away, passing Nathan who was making his way in.

Nathan's expression was full of concern. 'What's been going on? Are you okay, Professor?'

'Do you know how that famous saying goes regarding Houston?'

Nathan appeared uncertain. 'The Apollo thirteen reference?'

'Yes, that one.'

'Why, do we have a problem?'

'Oh yes,' Steiner said, watching through the reception's windows as Samson disappeared from view, 'a big one.'

CHAPTER TWENTY-ONE

WATER CASCADED over Professor Steiner's hands, miniature rivulets tracing the lines in his cracked and weathered skin. Many of his early years had been spent working on various engineering projects, and the materials and chemicals used to perfect pioneering developments in the field had taken their toll, affecting the ability of the skin on his hands to maintain its moisture. Steiner shook the droplets free over the sink and then looked at himself in the mirror.

'I hope you know what you're doing,' he said to himself; his reflection failed to supply a response.

Looking down he twisted a simple golden band around a finger on his left hand. Amelia, his wife, had died in a freak accident many years ago, back when he was still a fresh-faced lecturer at Stanford University. He still vividly remembered the day when a police officer had interrupted one of his classes. Steiner initially joked with his students, asking which of them had parked their car in the Dean's space again. His laughter turned to confusion and then despair when he was given the news that his wife was being flown by a Lifelight helicopter to the ICU at the university's own medical centre.

The words hadn't made sense to him at the time, the information – illogical.

'Amelia can't be in Stanford,' he assured the policeman, 'she left the county this morning. She was driving down to Bakersfield for a conference.' He looked at his watch. 'She should almost be there by now.'

'I'm sorry, sir,' the officer replied, 'as I said, there's been an accident. Your wife stopped at a convenience store outside of town; a large vehicle lost control in the street and ended up smashing into the front of the building, causing the roof to collapse. Your wife was critically injured. It took some time to cut her free. She may not have long to live; she's asking for you.'

Numb, he was led away, his trance-like state only allowing his senses to roar back to life when he caught sight of the woman he loved. Wires and machines surrounded the bed on which she lay. The emotive sound of the ventilator filled the sterile room as it helped Amelia to breathe, her chest rising and falling in time to the slow and insistent rhythmic compression of air. A heart rate monitor bleeping erratically in the background served as a relentless reminder of his wife's tenuous hold on life. Sitting beside her, Steiner reached out and gently squeezed her hand with his own. Her face was pallid and a tube led into her nose. A large graze on one side of her face brought a tear to his eye, which he brushed away when a nurse walked in to check on her patient.

'Can she hear me?' he asked.

'She drifts in and out of consciousness,' the nurse said. 'Whenever she wakes, she asks where you are.'

Steiner gently moved aside a lock of Amelia's hair, which had fallen across one eye, and as he did so her eyelids flickered open. Turning her head with painful difficulty she focused on his face.

'George,' she said, her voice barely audible.

Her hand grasped his and he leaned in closer. 'I'm here, my love,' he told her, 'I'm here.'

'I'm sorry,' she said, as ever thinking about him rather than herself.

'What have you got to be sorry for?'

'I don't want to leave you, it's too soon.'

'You will never leave me,' he said, his voice choking as his emotions overwhelmed him. 'I love you.'

Her voice grew fainter. 'Promise me, you will follow your dreams.'

'I promise I will,' he said as his tears came.

'You can do great things, George,' she whispered. 'I believe in you—'

At those words she had lost consciousness, never to regain it. They'd turned off the life support equipment a few hours later and Steiner's world had been changed forever. The first few years after his loss, his carefree demeanour had left him and bitterness had sought to consume his mind. His work had been his only motivator, fuelled by Amelia's final words. Eventually he'd learnt to enjoy life once more, although he knew he'd never be able to love another woman like he did Amelia and so shied away from emotional bonds. On the odd occasion later in life when loneliness raised its ugly head, Steiner was in no position to act upon the instinct, as he was, by then, far too deeply entrenched in directing the GMRC's Subterranean Programme.

Now, whenever Steiner needed inspiration or courage, something to light his darkest hours, the memory of Amelia, inextricably linked to the single gold band on his ring finger, gave him the strength of will he needed. Her presence, as ever, guided him in life as he knew it would in death.

The door to the washroom opened behind Steiner and a familiar face appeared to snap him out of his poignant thoughts. 'They're ready for you, Professor,' Sophie said.

'Thank you, my dear.' He mustered a smile. 'I'll be right out.'

Steiner looked at himself in the mirror one last time. His usual grey GMRC uniform had been replaced by new and alien attire. A heavy climbing harness overlaid a pair of sturdy red coveralls normally reserved for Steadfast's maintenance workers. Unlike the Special Forces commandos he was about to join, Steiner's body was small and slightly rotund, his frame unsuited to the gear worn by the SFSD. Even the clothes he wore now had been hastily adjusted to suit. His normal footwear, comfortable GMRC issue, had also been substituted by special climbing shoes, adapted for use inside the man-made confines of USSB Steadfast.

Various ropes, krabs, cams, pulleys and clamps hung from him like the small tassels on a brightly coloured piñata; he just hoped he wouldn't be broken open so others could see what lay inside. 'Right then,' he said to himself, 'let's get this show on the road.'

Pushing open the door, he walked out into a clearing surrounded by tall fir trees on one side and a sheer, light grey rock face on the other. Behind him stood the small outpost he'd just been inside, the building normally utilised by workers managing the underground ecosystem and bio-chamber complex in which he now found himself. The air here seemed fresher than elsewhere in the base, a pleasant by-product of the oxygenation process taking place within the forest of trees and plants that surrounded them. In the treetops a few birds could be heard whistling and chirruping to one another, unaware and uninterested in the events unfolding close by. A few hundred feet above, bolted to the chamber's vast ceiling, the powerful, magnificent and all-encompassing sunlight generator threw down rays of light, bathing those beneath it in a warm and pleasant glow.

'Professor,' Nathan said, moving away from a crowd of people to meet him. 'The team is assembled and ready to depart. As requested, the Darklight captain, Iwamoto, will be accompanying you along with nineteen of his men. With Samson's Terra Force unit and the three communication technicians, there'll be seventy-four of you making the ascent. Do you have everything you need? Iwamoto says he has some bulletproof clothing for you for when you reach the surface. Make sure you follow their every command. If the fighting is fierce, stay back until a safe path has been cleared.'

Steiner placed his hand on Nathan's wrist. His friend's face already looked stressed due to his new role as Acting Director of the base and his concern for Steiner's safety was evident and quite touching.

'Don't worry about me,' Steiner said. 'I'm in safe hands.'

Nathan eyed Colonel Samson as he readied his men on the outer edge of the clearing. 'That's debatable.'

'I was actually referring to Captain Iwamoto,' Steiner said, following his friend's gaze towards the man on whom so much of his plan rested.

'The fact Samson knows about the next wave of asteroids unnerves me more than I can say,' Nathan said as he looked back to Steiner, his brow creased and his voice drawn.

Steiner had been quick to tell Nathan about Samson's new insight into the events that would be unfolding on the surface over the coming years. Nathan's reaction had been that of shock and utter consternation, a feeling that Steiner well understood and shared.

'There is little we can do about it,' Steiner told him. 'It appears he's willing to keep the information to himself; we must hope he's true to his word. The repercussions in Steadfast if such knowledge got out could be devastating, but if word spread on the surface...' Steiner left his sentence hanging.

'Would be an unprecedented disaster,' Nathan finished for him. 'I don't understand why you didn't have him arrested when you had the chance.'

'Because he would have told all and sundry about the next wave of asteroids and his team wouldn't act while their leader was imprisoned. Furthermore, despite what he says to the contrary, he may have another recording of the message I sent to Richard Goodwin. I trust Samson about as far as I can throw him.'

'Perhaps he should be taken care of when he's served his purpose?'

'No,' Steiner said. 'I'm not Malcolm Joiner. Such a thought is beneath you, Nathan, I'm surprised at you.'

Nathan sighed. 'I'm sorry. I'm just worried for you, for us all. The GMRC has worked so hard to ensure humanity's continued survival. For a man such as Samson to have the slightest chance of endangering that, no matter how small that possibility may be, shouldn't we do something about it?'

'I'll keep a close eye on him, you can be assured of that. Besides, Joiner's Intelligence Division, despite its methods leaving a repugnant taste in the mouth, would be able to quash any chatter, if word did somehow begin to circulate.'

Nathan didn't look convinced and he had to admit that Samson's unpredictability left Steiner himself feeling nervous and exposed.

The information Samson was now privy to gave him power a man such as he shouldn't possess. As he looked in Samson's direction again he saw that the colonel had completed his duties and was striding across the forest floor towards them.

'This should be fun,' Nathan murmured as Samson drew nearer.

'Colonel,' Steiner said to the Terra Force commander.

'We're ready,' Samson answered the greeting, his customary lack of manners and respect seemingly unaltered.

'Are you and your men prepared to engage U.S. Army personnel on the surface, Colonel?' Steiner asked.

Samson bristled. 'Why wouldn't we be?'

'Your team is still part of the U.S. Army. You'll effectively be fighting men on your own side. Now that the time approaches I find it hard to believe your team hasn't voiced any concerns over the issue.'

'They haven't and nor will they,' Samson said matter-of-factly. 'We're Special Forces; we are trained for all eventualities. My men will follow my orders without question.'

'And you will follow the professor's,' Nathan added.

Samson paused as he looked at Nathan and then back to Steiner. 'Of course.'

'I only ask, Colonel,' Steiner continued, 'because we're in a highly unorthodox situation. Our priority is to ensure the safety of the men and women of this base, despite what Intelligence Director Joiner has planned for them.'

'How do you know the GMRC or the government aren't complicit in Joiner's action?' Samson said. 'Perhaps you have been deemed surplus to requirements, along with everyone else in Steadfast.'

Nathan's temper rose. 'Preposterous. The professor has almost single-handedly made the global Subterranean Programme the force it is today; without his innovations and designs the world's preparations would be a shadow of what they are.'

Steiner, remaining calm, touched Nathan's arm to halt his defence. 'You are quite right to question the motives of those above ground, Colonel. We are cut off and without any knowledge of what occurs in our absence. However, let me be clear that I believe Joiner is acting alone and does not have the support of the Government or GMRC Directorate. He may well be manipulating those in power to deflect his actions and explain away Steadfast's communication issues and my sudden disappearance. Make no mistake, as soon as I have regained a position of safety and a platform from which to address the Directorate, I will have Joiner removed from office and punished for his crimes, along with all those that aided him.'

'Strong words,' Samson said. 'I hope you're able to back them up when it matters.'

'It matters now.' Steiner watched Sophie, now Nathan's primary aide, approach.

'Gentlemen,' she said by way of interruption, 'the last of the engineers has pulled out of the tunnel; the way into the conduit shaft is clear.'

'Thank you, Sophie,' Steiner replied and then held out an arm to Samson, inviting him to lead the way. 'Shall we?'

Samson grunted and stalked off to his fifty strong SFSD contingent, who had now assembled close to where the entrance to the destroyed emergency stairwell had been excavated. Steiner, followed by Nathan and his retinue, walked over to the twenty strong Darklight team. Captain Iwamoto extricated himself from an animated conversation with his lieutenants to meet Steiner as he approached.

'Director General.' Iwamoto greeted him with a perfunctory bow, his Japanese accent indicative of the various nationalities that made up the private security forces of Darklight.

'Captain Iwamoto,' Steiner said, addressing the lean figure of the black-clad officer, 'ready for the off?'

'Yes, sir.' Iwamoto's voice implied otherwise.

'Is there a problem, Captain?'

'Sir, some of my team are still reluctant to work alongside the Colonel and his men.'

Steiner stifled a sigh. 'I thought this wasn't going to be an issue.'

'I didn't think it would be, sir, but now that they're alongside the SFSD it seems tensions are running high.'

'It is understandable,' Steiner said. 'I've asked a lot of the men and women within the Darklight ranks while you have been deployed here at Steadfast. Ever since you arrived circumstances have been anything but run-of-the-mill. I can well understand the difficulty of working with those who, only some months ago, were responsible for the deaths of many of your colleagues. Since I ordered your release from their custody, I have tried to keep Darklight personnel away from U.S. military forces within the base as best I could. To put your two sides together now would not have been considered were it not totally necessary.'

Steiner made sure they were out of earshot of anyone else before continuing. 'I require your protection, Captain. While I believe that the colonel will do his duty, I do not have the same faith in him as I do in Darklight. The colonel will be susceptible to being coerced into the fold of his military superiors once on the surface and, as we know, these generals are being controlled, directly or indirectly, by Malcolm Joiner. I will be relying on your men and women to ensure my safety and freedom; my capture may prove disastrous for those left behind in this base. If you can instil in your unit the importance of their involvement in this mission, it may serve to help put aside their animosity to those working beside them.'

Iwamoto, after listening intently to every word Steiner said, nodded his understanding. 'Thank you, sir. Your words are welcome and I will relay them to my team. *Aisatsu wa toki no ujigami*,' he added in Japanese.

Steiner raised an eyebrow, unsure of what had just been said.

'It means, a word of mediation at the right time is blessed,' Iwamoto said.

Steiner smiled, nodded and held out a hand, which Iwamoto shook. The Darklight captain then bowed low before retreating to re-engage his lieutenants.

Steiner watched the captain for a moment and then moved away to make his final goodbyes to those remaining behind, including Sophie, who gave him a warm embrace.

Nathan came to stand by Steiner's side as the first of Samson's men disappeared into the excavated hole in the cliff face. 'This is it then.'

'It appears so,' Steiner said, feeling a mixture of emotions as he prepared to say goodbye to his friend, quite possibly for the last time. 'I will do everything in my power to get you all out as soon as I can. If I fail you know what to do.'

Nathan nodded and held out a hand, which Steiner clasped in both of his.

'Be careful, Professor.'

'Likewise my dear friend; good luck.'

'Good luck to you too, to us all.'

Steiner gave Nathan's hand a final squeeze, released his grip and looked around at those assembled. 'Until we meet again,' he said, and with a confident smile and a farewell wave he turned and followed Samson's men into the tunnel.

CHAPTER TWENTY-TWO

THE CLIMB so far had been cramped, long and arduous, and they still had a way to go until they reached the surface. Steiner had lost count of the number of times his small safety helmet had clonked against a wall or pipe of some description. Sweat drenched his clothing as he exerted himself far beyond what he normally had to endure. Those around him took some of the strain, assisting his ascent using a pulley system laid down by those preceding them. He was grateful for all the help he could get; he was, after all, in his early sixties and by far the oldest of those making their way to the surface.

A small torch on his head lit up his immediate vicinity, a tight concrete channel three and a half feet square and currently running at a forty-five degree angle. There was barely enough room to shrug your shoulders, let alone haul up the heavy kit the soldiers had to contend with. His climbing gear clinked and rattled as he crawled forwards, his feet occasionally slipping from under him. Holding on grimly to the guide ropes, his special gloves gripping to them like a gecko's feet to glass, Steiner hauled himself onwards. The noises of those accompanying him echoed down the tight passage. Voices issued direction, while others let out a variety of curses and replies as everyone did their best to cope with the difficult conditions. Leading the way, the Terra Force unit forged ahead; next came Steiner himself, then the three communication technicians and bringing up the rear, the Darklight team.

After another hour, Steiner scrambled out into a wider area where twenty of the SFSD commandos had assembled, accompanied by their colonel. On one side of the smooth circular concrete wall, the code '183B' had been stencilled in pale blue paint, looking for all the world as if it had been put there recently rather than three decades past. Above, the small chamber narrowed once more, taking a vertical path straight up. Ropes dangled down from it, half of Samson's men having already moved on. Catching his breath, Steiner leaned against the wall for support.

Captain Iwamoto emerged from behind soon after, seemingly no worse for wear than when he'd started twelve hours before. 'Are you okay, sir?'

'Fine,' Steiner said, gasping, 'thank you, Captain.'

'This is the final section of the conduit shaft,' Iwamoto told him. 'After that we'll reach another area much like this one, where we can regroup and prepare for our exit strategy.'

Steiner nodded in understanding as he took a water bottle from his harness and gulped down some much needed fluid. The enclosed space they now occupied didn't lend itself to ventilation, the smell of warm bodies pressing in around them. Steiner sank to the floor to ease his aching back and tired limbs. He watched while Samson hooked himself onto one of the ropes and, using some sort of hand-held mechanism, with little effort pulled himself up and through the opening overhead. One by one his unit followed suit, their position in the round junction room soon replaced by the Darklight personnel still filing out from below. It was now Steiner's turn to head upwards. With the help of Iwamoto and a female Darklight lieutenant at the bottom, and an SFSD commando above, Steiner embarked on the vertical climb.

Feeling like a piece of baggage, Steiner was pulled upwards, his own feeble efforts doing little to aid those taking the strain. He'd already resigned himself to relying on the assistance of others; near the start of the climb, when he'd attempted to propel himself along using his own strength, he'd quickly tired, his exertions merely serving to delay the whole group.

Back in the present, and now passing the shaft's halfway point, Steiner became aware that those below had encountered a problem. One of the technicians had become entangled in their gear and only someone from above could rectify the issue. Since Steiner was unversed in such things it had been decided to winch him up and then send someone else back down to resolve the issue. Carrying on, Steiner now had no one following him, only a dark, ever increasing void ending in the faint light of the stuck communications technician far below.

The end of the tunnel finally approached, finishing in a deep overhang. It looked, from Steiner's perspective, like he would need to clip himself onto another rope in order to enter the area above. The men that had been helping in his ascent had forged ahead to disappear from view, almost as if they'd forgotten he was relying on their help to move. Unsure what to do he called out. A face emerged upside down from the nearby aperture, it was the colonel.

'Grab my hand.' Samson held his arm out towards him.

'I need to clip myself onto the other rope,' Steiner said, unnerved by Samson's appearance.

'Stay attached, take my hand and I'll transfer you over.'

Steiner considered Samson for a moment, his distrust for the man sending warning bells ringing in his head.

'Come on, man,' Samson said, 'we don't have all day!'

Steiner looked down and then back to Samson's outstretched hand, and decided he didn't really have any other option. Grasping Samson's hand, Steiner swung out into the middle of the shaft. Now suspended over a sheer drop, he held onto Samson's vice-like grip, the colonel's bunched muscles and sinews standing out as he held Steiner's full weight. With his free hand, Samson unclipped Steiner from the safety rope.

'Wait, transfer me first!' Steiner yelled at him but it was too late, his mistake had been made. Steiner's life now hung in the balance, only Samson preventing him from falling to his death. The Colonel's eyes bored into Steiner's own, the man's manic expression indecipherable.

'Can you get us into Sanctuary?' Samson asked, while straining against Steiner's dead weight.

Frantic, Steiner tried in vain to hitch himself back onto the safety line that ran parallel to the wall.

'Professor,' Samson said, his voice shaking with the effort required to hold Steiner aloft, 'I don't know how much longer I can hold you for. Can you get us into USSB Sanctuary if we get out of here, yes or no?'

'Yes! Now clip me on!'

'How can I be sure you're telling me the truth?'

Steiner felt his hand slip half an inch inside his glove. 'Because I helped design it and I'm a GMRC Director General.' Steiner glanced below at his flailing legs and the darkness beyond. 'I know all the access points; I helped oversee software creation for Sanctuary's security systems. You have my word, I can get us inside!'

More moments passed, Samson searching Steiner's face to see if he told the truth. Finally he reached out his other hand and hooked Steiner's harness onto the second line. With a heave, Samson pulled Steiner through and up into the section above.

Steiner now found himself in a small intersection, a low doorway leading off to one side. Samson brushed past him without another word, calling to two of his men to head back down the shaft to clear the way for the technicians and the Darklight crew, still caught up below.

Steiner felt too shaken to tackle Samson over the incident that had just transpired and the colonel had now rejoined his men, perhaps in a ploy to head off such a confrontation. Why the colonel hadn't just asked him about Sanctuary without risking his life, God only knew. The man was once more living up to his unpredictable nature.

The plan was to relocate Steadfast's residents to a variety of bases, when and if he could get them safely to the surface. The bulk of the near half a million souls that remained in Steadfast would indeed be heading to Sanctuary if Steiner had his way. Why Samson wanted to go to Sanctuary specifically made no sense; had he seen more of the message Steiner had sent to Goodwin than he was letting on? And why did he ask if Steiner could get them inside? If they were successful in their plan, Steiner would be back in command of the whole GMRC Subterranean Programme and access would be a formality.

As he pondered on these thoughts, and more, the problem with the technician's ropes was resolved and he was eventually rejoined by Captain Iwamoto and his unit. Not wanting to cause further problems between Darklight and the Terra Force commandos, Steiner refrained from informing Iwamoto about Samson's recent actions. Assuming they made it past the forces waiting for them above and he secured his position back within the GMRC, he would have Samson dealt with once and for all; *a sturdy prison cell in USSB Alaska should suit him just fine*, he thought grimly.

The climb completed, everyone assembled in the final area of the conduit shaft, a long horizontal corridor attached to another round concrete-clad structure. Two more hours passed while people shed their climbing equipment and replaced it with battle armour and weaponry. Steiner and the three technicians, huddled together, wore bulletproof vests and flexible shielding over the rest of their bodies. Around them Darklight and Terra Force soldiers alike clipped on their metal and composite plating until they were encased in suits of lightweight armour; visored helmets followed. The blue glow of the Darklight forces' internal combat displays emanated out of the eye-like holes, mirrored by the headgear worn by the SFSD, the light from their helmets a steady green.

The top of the shaft had been capped off by two thick circular steel covers, riveted into place and spot welded one above the other. These metal barriers had already been removed using special thermal cutting gear. Above, a two foot compacted layer of earth hung suspended over the open hole beneath. The accumulation of soil had been deposited over the shaft after its construction was deemed obsolete many years ago, this dry permeable substrate now the only barrier between those in the shaft and the forces that would surely be waiting for them, somewhere, out there in the darkness.

♦

Samson's helmet slid over his head, the interior fabric fitting snugly into place and feeling comfortingly familiar against his skin. With a command panel on the inside of his wrist plate, Samson tapped in a code to give him full connectivity to those around him, including the Darklight mercenaries to the rear.

'Listen up,' Samson said, noting with satisfaction that, as one, his men ceased whatever they were doing to look in his direction, their visors retracting to reveal their faces. 'That includes you too, Darklight,' Samson added when some of the black-clad soldiers failed to heed his voice.

Satisfied he now had everyone's attention, he continued. 'Any second we'll be on the surface, leaving this rabbit hole behind. A scope recon up through the ground layer has revealed very little. Sending up small aerial drones is out as any wireless signals will be detected. We will have to assume the forces above will be concentrated in and around the interior footprint of Steadfast, but we must be prepared for any eventuality.

'As we haven't had time to work as a single unit, we'll keep things simple. Terra Force will initiate a fifty yard defensive perimeter to the north. Darklight, under Captain Iwamoto, will secure the south on our six. If all goes well we'll then transition, undetected, to the designated RV before making for the Darklight enclave twenty clicks due east.

'Anyone who hasn't completed a full diagnostic on their combat system should do so now; we can't afford to have even one person out of sync with the rest. The director general and the coms techs will remain under Darklight protection unless circumstances dictate otherwise. I want all my orders actioned swiftly and precisely. If anyone fucks up out there and they don't die, they'll wish they had by the time I've finished with them. Do you get me?!'

'Ooyah!' The Terra Force commandos responded as one.

Samson nodded, pleased with the response, but noted that the Darklight troops had failed to acknowledge his demands. Opening a pouch on his utility belt, Samson extracted one of his red pills and flicked it into his mouth, swallowing it down. Pressing a button on the side of his helmet, the visor and face plate snapped into place, the two pieces interlocking to form a seamless shield. The rest of the soldiers did likewise, creating a low steady glow of green and blue within the enclosed space.

'Activate partial camouflage,' Samson ordered, watching the armour on his men and Darklight troops alike ripple and shimmer, the surfaces contorting visually until each individual composite metal plate matched the background behind the soldier wearing it.

'Major,' Samson said to his second in command, 'we're a go.'

The major, a few feet away, nodded to his superior and gave the order to collapse the compacted earth above the open top of the conduit shaft. Two commandos dug into the dry soil with their large knives, sending dust and dirt sifting down in waves around their feet. Clumps of earth dropped with dull thuds to the concrete floor, old tree roots drifting down with them. As the debris ceased to fall, the hole now fully exposed, Samson reached behind his back and unclipped his assault weapon from its snap-on clamp. Drawing the rifle down, he checked its digital display within the scope and then synced it with his visor; spooling up ammo, range and targeting data on his head-up combat display.

'Lock and load,' Samson said to his men, who similarly prepared their weapons on his order. 'Defence pattern Sigma Two. Major, take point.'

The SFSD major didn't need further encouragement. Getting a boost from two of his men, he disappeared through the opening, in one smooth, silent motion. More soldiers followed him out, until

Samson himself put his foot in the hands of one of his men to be launched upwards, his metal-encased hand digging into the shaft's dusty, dirt exterior to aid his ascent.

Rolling to one side, enabling the next man to exit from beneath as quickly as possible, Samson gained his feet and scanned the terrain with an expert eye. The optics on his gun and visor, operating on the same combined spectral fields, produced a strange multi-coloured image that picked out even the smallest of details from the darkest of landscapes. As if to hail the arrival of their small band, a distant rumble of thunder echoed in the dark skies above. It had been many months since Samson had been topside and the lack of stars and moon in the night sky was an ominous reminder that the predicted dust cloud had shrouded the planet on cue.

Acting on instinct, Samson relocated to take cover behind a nearby cluster of boulders, the position offering a healthy overview of his men as they fanned out ahead. The red, yellow and blue spectral image of the camouflaged soldiers, processed by the combat system, made them stand out against the brown and grey topography that surrounded them.

The radar, displayed on the far left of his visor, indicated that the Darklight team exited behind, heading south as ordered. The single red and three yellow dots amongst the black, indicated the position of the communication technicians and the director general. His mind processing everything at high speed, Samson noticed a small movement in the air three hundred yards from their location. A drone!

'We have a fast mover north-north-west,' Samson broadcasted. 'All units evade protocol four. Shelter and cease movement.'

Samson sank down to his haunches, remaining stock still as the small drone flew closer to their position. He trained his scope on the target, zooming in on it as it approached. The illuminated red crosshairs and green range finder, supported by the digital read outs and tracking lines that ran throughout the length of the scope, helped guide his aim. There was no mistaking the model, a typical six rotored affair used throughout the U.S. Army. Samson slowed his breathing and considered his next course of action. He knew from the radar scans they'd made of the area prior to their breach of the surface, that drones were deployed in the skies. He also knew their armour should enable them to remain hidden from view, unless the vehicles had been retrofitted, in which case they were screwed.

'Iwamoto,' Samson said to the Darklight captain while tracking the drone's path with his weapon. 'Make safe the director and the coms techs.'

'Already done, Colonel,' came the immediate response via his helmet's internal speakers.

The drone had slowed as it neared the outer boundary of the USSB's surface footprint. Now one hundred yards from Samson's position and a mere fifty from their perimeter, the circular machine spun on its axis, hovering for a few seconds before altering course. Samson swore. It was heading straight for them. Had it caught a small movement from one of his team, or did the intelligent software spy something else? Either way the drone had overstayed its welcome. Samson's finger, already resting on the trigger, tightened. The first stage of the firing mechanism's pretravel complete, Samson followed the drone, the crosshairs locked in on the tiny craft's central hub.

Deciding the machine had spent far too long in their vicinity Samson made a split second decision.

'I'm taking the shot,' Samson informed his team. Squeezing the trigger through its second stage, his rifle fired, the silencer muffling the sound as the butt of the stock kicked hard back into his shoulder. The bullet ripped through the drone, sending sparks flying and the crippled object plummeting to the ground.

'We have multiple targets inbound,' the major's voice crackled through the com. 'Prepare to engage!'

No sooner had his XO given them the heads up than a raft of drones appeared on radar. At the same time a barrage of flares soared into the skies around them, bursting into life and shedding a dull yellow light over the New Mexican landscape.

'Take out those drones,' Samson said as he himself selected one of the flying machines, fired and then cycled to the next target.

Sporadic gunfire from the left flank erupted into a continuous exchange as the SFSD defended their line. Samson's onboard graphics highlighted a worrying scene as ground troops and vehicles homed in on their location from all directions. A bullet whizzed past his head, followed by another three, one grazing an armoured panel on his shoulder. Switching to his gun's grenade launcher, Samson fired a quick succession of projectiles towards the onrushing vehicles, taking out two and disabling another.

Explosions and bullets rained down on the SFSD unit as they fought a rearguard action, driven backwards by the sheer weight of numbers now upon them. Joiner really didn't want anyone escaping Steadfast, it seemed. Samson advanced to the front, making use of various depressions and trees for cover. Dispatching two U.S. Marines who'd already circumvented his men's line, and scooping up one of their radios as an afterthought, Samson stepped over the body of a dead comrade to join his major.

'I don't think we're going to be able to hold them for much longer!' the major shouted to Samson, his voice muffled through his helmet.

Samson didn't reply as he took down four more men, two of them in one shot. His back to a craggy rock, Samson saw the shadowy semi-transparent forms of Darklight rushing to replenish his Terra Force's depleted ranks.

Flash grenades and smoke canisters shot into the air as the enemy altered tack, trying to disorientate the smaller group from Steadfast. The thump of the projectiles hitting the ground sounded all too familiar to Samson, the noise quickly followed by ear-shattering detonations. Light exploded all around them, coupled with thick, oozing clouds of acrid grey smoke. Checking his visor's display, Samson saw that Iwamoto and another Darklight operative had fled from the battle out to the agreed coordinates, escorting the red dot of Steiner along with them. A hundred yards behind this group of three, two more Darklight soldiers shepherded the three yellow dots of the communication technicians in the same direction. If Samson's men and the remaining Darklight soldiers could waylay the U.S. Army long enough, those two small groups might be able to escape undetected.

Samson knew if he was to make his move, it had to be now. 'Major, take command and hold them back for as long as you can. No surrender!'

'Yes, sir!' The Major rattled off a clip of armour piercing rounds into an approaching personnel carrier that had appeared through the misty haze.

Knowing his last order would be adhered to, Samson retreated back to the opening of the conduit shaft, dodging in and out of cover as he went. Detaching a dense hexagonal object from the armour on the outside of his left thigh, he flicked a switch to start a small green light pulsing along its length. Flinging the device down through the opening, Samson ran off into the darkness, away from the chaotic firefight behind. Securing his rifle diagonally onto its clasp in the centre of his back, the barrel poking out over one shoulder, Samson picked up speed as he hunted down the people ahead making for safety.

His well-conditioned body enabled him to catch up to the first group, heavy boots eating up the distance with each powerful stride, the ground beating to the rhythm of his footfalls as he passed by. In front, his visor picked out the first of the Darklight men protecting the three coms techs. Had Samson been without the correct frequencies the Darklight man's armour utilised, he would have found it difficult to get a bead on him; as it was he stood out like a pig in a top hat, ludicrously plump and ready to be slaughtered.

Sliding to a halt, his boots kicking up gravel and dust in the darkness, Samson unhooked his rifle again. Switching in a clip of armour piercing rounds, Samson pulled back the heavy bolt and loaded a bullet into the chamber and took aim at the Darklight operative's head. With one swift movement he squeezed off a round. Sixty yards away the Darklight man fell as he ran, his life snuffed out without warning.

The sound of a low-flying drone overhead made Samson freeze in place. Now in combat mode, the robotically controlled machine bombarded the other Darklight soldier and the communication technicians alike. Samson watched a small but deadly accurate grenade deployed by the drone deal the soldier a fatal blow, throwing his broken body into the air. The drone's controller then switched to a small machine gun turret located on its underbelly to strafe the technicians with a hail of bullets. After the massacre, Samson took aim, sending the drone spiralling to the desert floor.

Making his way to the crash site, Samson surveyed the scene. Four bodies lay motionless on the ground. Moving amongst them, Samson put a bullet in each of their heads before taking off on foot once more. His radar told him Steiner and his two Darklight bodyguards had reached and then passed the rendezvous point; they knew as well as he that the battle was lost.

Half a click later and Samson had run the three of them down.

'Colonel?' Iwamoto's voice came out of the darkness ahead as Samson slowed to a walk.

'Yes, it's me.' Samson joined the Darklight captain and his female lieutenant. Samson disliked women in the armed forces; they distracted the concentration of a good soldier. He made a point of having no females in any unit he commanded. Of course the army didn't agree with that view, but Samson ensured any woman that passed the rigorous vetting process for the SFSD had to undertake a special strength test, purposefully designed to ensure failure. He always got his way, by hook or by crook.

'Where are the technicians?' Iwamoto asked him.

'Dead, drone strike. Is Steiner unhurt?'

'The professor is fine, he's just over there.' Iwamoto pointed to where he stood.

Samson peered over his shoulder and caught sight of the small figure of the professor pacing about, twenty yards away. To Steiner, without a combat helmet, the darkness would've appeared all encompassing.

Gunfire echoed in the distance. 'Sir, we have to move,' the lieutenant said to her captain.

As Iwamoto turned towards her, Samson, now within touching

distance, slid his large knife out from its sheath and lanced the blade up underneath the back of Iwamoto's helmet, the shuddering blow severing his spinal cord. The Darklight captain's body fell towards the lieutenant, who reacted to Samson's attack by rolling to one side. Unfortunately for her Samson was quicker. Smacking the pistol from her hand, the two highly trained soldiers grappled on the dusty ground.

The lieutenant initially had the upper hand, as the move against Iwamoto had surrendered Samson's advantage; however, his superior strength and skill quickly told. On top now, Samson rained down blows upon the Darklight officer's helmet, the dull thud of metal on metal ringing out onto the night. The blue light from the woman's black helmet grew brighter and then went out as Samson smashed his fists into the face plate, the helmet caving inwards under his animalistic ferocity. The lieutenant's arms went limp and Samson paused, realising she was dead. To make doubly sure of the kills, Samson slit each of his victim's throats, noting the legs of the lieutenant still twitched as he did so. *The body is a fragile thing*, Samson thought idly as he retrieved his rifle, which had fallen off during the struggle.

Samson approached Steiner, whose back was to him, the professor unaware of his close proximity. Samson reached out a hand in the darkness but, just before he touched him, Steiner turned around and Samson dropped his arm back down to his side.

'Who's that?' Steiner said, the faint green light from Samson's visor reflecting off the professor's face in the dark. 'Colonel, is that you?'

Samson stared at the small man in front of him, thinking how easy it would be to end the old man's life here and now; a quick strike, simple and swift, over in a heartbeat.

♦

'Colonel?' the professor said, unnerved by the lack of response coming from the shadowy form of what he believed was the Terra Force commander.

Samson moved closer. 'Yes, it's me.'

'Where are Captain Iwamoto and his lieutenant? I heard a commotion, but the explosions in the distance turned me around. It's difficult to get your bearings in the dark.'

'They're both dead,' Samson replied in his usual cold manner. 'Sniper took them out, I took out the sniper.'

'Oh, dear God.' Steiner was in shock. He'd only been talking to them a few moments before. 'Are you injured, Colonel?' Steiner noticed what looked like the glint of blood on his armour.

Samson didn't respond. Instead he slid a small device from a clip on his chest plate and launched it into the air, the tiny blades whirring away into the darkness.

'There's no further pursuit,' Samson said as he assessed information being fed back to his combat system by the miniature aerial drone. 'Let's move. I need to get you to safe harbour.'

'What about the technicians, the equipment, the rest of our team? We need them to complete our mission.'

'The coms techs are gone, the equipment lost and the rest of my unit are as good as dead. Their sacrifice will help us escape. We cannot wait here any longer. They will find our tracks soon enough.' Samson nudged Steiner forwards with a forearm, lighting his way with a small dimmed torch mounted on the side of his assault rifle.

'Wait.' Steiner stopped. 'What about the conduit shaft? We can't leave it exposed or they'll send engineers down to collapse it from the bottom up. We must preserve its structure, at least in part.'

Samson turned over his wrist and opened a small panel on his armour, revealing a digital display. Extending his metal-clad index finger, he tapped away at it for a moment, finally pressing a square section that lit up in red. A massive explosion ripped through the night sky, back from whence they came. A huge fireball billowed out and up, the sound far louder than the thunder that closed in on their position.

'Problem solved,' Samson said after the blast and flames had dissipated.

Steiner stared out into the darkness as the first drops of rain pitter-pattered onto the dusty ground around them. 'That was a big blast. You probably just killed any of our men who were still left alive back there.'

'As I said, they were as good as dead.'

Steiner looked at Samson's expressionless mask, the green glow pulsing from the visor in the oppressive blackness. He felt sickened by the man's lack of compassion for the lives of the people he'd just snuffed out like a candle.

'If the blast didn't kill them, the army would have,' Samson said as if that exonerated him from the crime.

'They might have been taken prisoner.' Steiner's tone was accusatory.

'And they would have talked – eventually. They're better off dead, for our sakes and for the mission.'

Steiner stood unmoving, numb from his adrenaline filled flight from the battle and the unsettling callous nature of his lone companion.

Samson nudged Steiner again, motioning with his gun for him to carry on walking. Knowing he must go on and that he now needed Samson more than ever, Steiner put one foot in front of the other.

Drops of rain transformed into a torrent and lightning flashed through the heavens, for a split second the bright, white light high-lighting the path ahead. Thunder cracked out its deep rumbling reply, a mournful echo of Steiner's heavy heart as the two men disap-peared into the endless night.

CHAPTER TWENTY-THREE

GMRC SUBTERRANEAN BASE Director Richard Goodwin lay on his bed staring up at the white fabric roof of his tent, the intricate pattern of the stitching between the durable cloth panels keeping his subconscious mind occupied while his higher brain wandered free of visual constraint. Currently Goodwin's thoughts lingered on the same quandaries that had plagued him every day for many months; how to locate Sanctuary's USSB and how to keep up the morale of those he was duty bound to protect.

As the former director of Steadfast, Goodwin was used to leadership and, by all accounts, quite good at managing those under his care; until now, however, he'd not had to contend with such an array of adverse challenges. Having to provide people with a steady supply of food and clean water signified the magnitude of his problems, although a welcome stroke of luck had ensured this most pressing of issues had thankfully fallen down his list of priorities. With the basic necessities taken care of, getting out of their current location had taken centre stage.

Ever since their arrival in the deserted Anakim city well over two hundred days earlier, the thirty thousand people he'd brought with him from Steadfast, predominantly civilians but including five thousand Darklight contractors, had been living out their existence in the revelation that was Sanctuary. Unfortunately setting up home in this frankly unbelievable and barren ancient underground structure had not been their goal.

Professor Steiner, Goodwin's direct superior within the GMRC, had directed him to break into USSB Sanctuary; a facility Goodwin had believed to be just another underground base, built as a failsafe against the asteroid AG5 that had finally impacted off the South African coastline in 2040. The reality was the USSB, a United States Subterranean Base, was contained within a much larger structure of the same name.

Sanctuary's immensity, Goodwin's unauthorised access and an earthquake, had all conspired against the Steadfast evacuees, who'd quickly become lost and trapped within a ghostly abandoned city of – at the time – unknown origins. Only the arrival of a pre-recorded video message from Professor Steiner had enlightened Goodwin to the truth, not just about Sanctuary and those that built it, but about the continued threat from space and the six remaining asteroids destined for Earth.

Thoughts of the disclosure of the catastrophe that awaited those on the surface always brought a deep melancholy upon him, and now was no different. Goodwin still had relatives on the surface, as did many others that shared his current predicament. If only he could escape this place and warn them, bring them back underground to safety. A sardonic chuckle escaped his lips making his chest shake. Safety, pah! It was all he could do to stay alive, the thought of rescuing anyone at this point seemed deliciously ludicrous to his mind. *And even if I could warn those I held dear, would I, or more importantly should I?* Professor Steiner had entrusted the secret to him in the belief he would hold it close, not for his sake but for the sake of humanity itself. *Could I really be that cold and leave those on the surface to die without doing something to save them?* The professor had; the loathsome thought declared itself unbidden and unwelcome, driving its way to the forefront of his deliberations. Goodwin knew the professor's actions were disconnected from normal reality, but they were still cold and distant, the condemnation of billions of lives apparently accepted as an inevitability. *What else could he have done?* Goodwin wondered. The answer came quickly: *nothing. There was nothing that he could have done.*

Goodwin had decided early on to keep the momentous secret about the future between himself and one other person; for now, anyway. If he disclosed the truth to everyone, it would only serve to nullify his efforts to keep those with him calm and functioning. Knowledge such as he now possessed would send many over the brink. Despair was the one thing the Steadfast evacuees could do without right now. The one person he knew he could burden with the information was the Darklight leader, Commander Hilt. The man was the proverbial rock and had taken the news surprisingly well, accepting what Goodwin told him without question. His impassive features had altered to show a deep consternation, of course, anyone hearing that the planet, as we know it, was nearly at an end would give some kind of reaction; any sane person at least.

A noise nearby caused Goodwin to lapse back into reality and he rolled his head to one side to listen as low voices murmured on the edge of hearing; *probably a couple of soldiers preparing breakfast*, Goodwin surmised, as the sound of footfalls faded away. His thoughts turned to the professor again, his friend and mentor. He hoped he was okay. Malcolm Joiner was holding him under arrest when Goodwin left Steadfast and it had seemed the Director of Intelligence would go to any lengths to stop its evacuation. This could mean that Steiner and the rest of Steadfast's staff were still trapped in the base. That, combined with the fact that, according to the professor's message, Steadfast could be destroyed when the asteroid hit, didn't bode well for the professor or the hundreds of thousands left behind in the base. Goodwin heaved a sigh. There was very little he could do about it now if that was the case; he must live in hope that the professor had got them out somehow, and he believed if anyone could it was him. He might even be on his way to Sanctuary at that very moment, or already preparing to send out search parties for Goodwin; a pleasant thought indeed, but an unlikely one.

The sensation of the bedcovers shifting brought his mind back to his surroundings once more. More movement and the sheets were pulled away, leaving half his body exposed to the cold outside air. Smiling, he propped himself up on one elbow and leaned over to look at the small woman who shared his bed. Dark brown, shoulder-length hair lay fanned out over her well-tanned skin, the dyed blonde highlights almost completely grown out; a consequence of their stay in Sanctuary where luxuries were few and far between. Kara Vandervoort murmured in her sleep as Goodwin bent down and kissed her on her soft, freckled, upturned cheek. She was such a beauty; he was a lucky man to have such a brave, intelligent woman in his corner. He'd always seen himself as rather plain and ordinary, an unattractive proposition to such as her. At first he'd been confused by her advances, finding it hard to believe she would be interested in him. When she'd failed to lose interest he eventually built up the courage to do something about it; he was glad he had.

To the casual observer Kara appeared only to be in her early twenties and since he was a forty-four year old man the match would have seemed ill suited, to some anyway. In actuality Dr Vandervoort had thirty-three years under her belt and had been Steadfast's Ecosystem director, part of Goodwin's key management team at the base.

He'd told Kara many times that he couldn't have held everything together if she hadn't been around to lend her support and buoy him up when the stress and strain of their current situation sought to overwhelm him. Kara, as ever, had told him he'd have performed just as well without her; if only she knew how wrong she was.

Not wanting to disturb her sleep, Goodwin decided to rise and slid from the bed, the cold floor sending a shiver through his body as he did so. Taking his clothes from the crumpled heap on the floor where they lay, he pulled on his suit trousers, the belt much looser on his waist than it had been when he'd first arrived at Sanctuary.

'I'll need to make another notch,' he mumbled to himself, shrugging into his creased white shirt. Pulling on some dirty looking socks and a pair of repaired Darklight issue boots, Goodwin picked up his red body warmer, opened the tent flap and ducked outside. A gust of cold air ruffled his thick, black hair. *So strange*, he thought, *I'm miles underground and yet there is definitely wind down here*. He'd surmised it was probably a result of the size of the chamber they were currently in. At around three miles high the cavernous space was – well – words failed to do it justice, but as Kara said in her South African drawl, it was *bloody massive*. The scale of the towers within the city also boggled the mind, not that they were visible in the pitch blackness that surrounded them; they could only be seen using some high-tech Darklight visual spectrum enhancement goggles. They were there, though, just a few hundred yards away. Goodwin looked up into the black, visualising the hundreds of gigantic edifices that populated the Anakim city; the name the professor had used for the race that had built them. Knowing who'd created these monstrous buildings didn't detract from their eerie nature, in fact it enhanced it; Goodwin could almost feel their presence permeating through the air towards him. Another shiver ran down his spine, this one not induced by the low temperature.

He looked at his watch. The time was five a.m. and the rest of the camp remained quiet, or at least the section he was in did. Thirty thousand people covered a substantial amount of land. It had been decided early on that setting up residence in the city would have been too unnerving, and many of the civilians and even some of the Darklight soldiers had voiced their unease about such a plan. Goodwin had been quick to agree with them.

The supplies brought along by the Darklight forces had quickly proved inadequate, but somehow enough makeshift tents had been erected, interspersed by small, water powered generators that ensured the portable floodlights stayed on twenty-four seven; without them they'd have been totally blind. That the gennies worked with water wasn't luck, the state-of-the-art equipment brought along by the Darklight private security firm was capable of producing electricity using a variety of fuel sources, even bio matter.

What was fortuitous was the presence of a huge fresh water aquifer located two miles away from the city and their camp. They'd needed something to go in their favour, considering what had gone before, and a steady supply of drinking water and fuel for the lights hadn't been the final surprise relayed by one of Commander Hilt's reconnaissance teams.

Whether by design or otherwise, the body of water teemed with a mackerel-like fish. Alongside this animal, many other species had been extracted by improvised angling gear. Giant catfish, supposedly nearing world record size, had been landed, alongside other creatures that looked distinctly prehistoric, many of which may have been unknown to science. The forms of these aquatic wonders hauled from the depths resembled marine life usually found in the world's deepest oceans. Prehistoric, pale, white skin and transparent bodies with large black eyes and razor sharp teeth did little to whet Goodwin's appetite, but eat them he did, as did everyone else; it was either that or starve. An enforced pescatarian diet did not suit most, but proved impossible for others. Those who found the pungent fish too difficult to keep down had to make do with a variety of edible plants found around the fringes of the lake. To Goodwin the colourless vegetation appealed far less than the meat on offer and the taste had confirmed his observations.

The reason how so much life thrived underground was unclear, although the lake itself turned out to be in line with everything else around it; its enormity more akin to a Scottish loch or inland sea. From what they could tell, the expanse of water stretched for over three miles in breadth and thrice that in length. When it came to the depth, a crude plumb line had been unable to find the bottom, which shelved off sharply; the line used had run out after one and a half miles had disappeared beneath the inky black surface.

Walking through the camp, Goodwin headed for what served as the command post, a lean-to against a large outcrop of rock a few minutes away from his and Kara's tent. Hilt's recon teams had been due back late the previous night and Goodwin was eager for news of their scouting mission, which was most likely the reason he'd awoken so early. Perhaps today would yield some better results than the previous expeditions undertaken.

Hysterical laughter drifted on the soft breeze, making Goodwin pause in his passage, the light from a distant lantern barely highlighting the path ahead. A shriek and a scream made him alter his direction; jogging along, he made haste towards the source of the commotion that still echoed into the darkness. A young man came into view ahead, his height towering above a woman he now grappled with, both toppling to the floor.

Rushing forwards in the half-light, Goodwin grabbed onto the man's heavy knit sweater, doing his best to haul him off his victim. Staggering back, it was all Goodwin could do to hold onto the person as he twisted and wriggled in his grasp.

'Wait! It's okay, he's just playing,' the woman said to Goodwin, picking herself up from the floor.

Goodwin squinted at the shadowy figure. 'Rebecca, is that you?'

'Richard, yes and Joseph too,'

'Joseph?' Goodwin let go of the man who'd become limp and still at the sound of his voice.

Joseph turned around and beamed at him, his wide, innocent smile infectious, making Goodwin laugh in relief.

'Thank God.' He gave Joseph a pat on the arm. 'I thought someone was being attacked.'

A strong beam of light appeared ten yards away, making Goodwin and Rebecca cover their eyes with a forearm while Joseph pulled his jumper up over his head.

'What's going on here?' an authoritative voice demanded.

'It's fine, just a misunderstanding,' Goodwin said to the Darklight soldier who'd also been drawn to the kerfuffle.

The soldier angled the torch in his direction. 'Director Goodwin, forgive me, I didn't recognise you back there.'

'Yes, thank you. Do you mind not pointing that thing in my face?' Goodwin turned his head as he tried to maintain some of his night vision.

'Of course, sorry, sir. Perhaps you could try and keep the noise down, miss,' the Darklight man said to Rebecca once he'd dimmed the light down to an acceptable level. 'Sound travels quite far out here and we've had some complaints recently about your group.'

'I don't think that will be possible,' Goodwin said, coming to Rebecca's aid as she floundered for a response. 'And you should tell anyone who has a problem to come and see me.' Goodwin knew Rebecca had her hands full with caring for her wards; she didn't need anyone else foisting their stress onto her.

'Very good, sir.' The soldier gave him a crisp salute before going back about his business.

Joseph pulled Goodwin forwards with typical childlike exuberance. 'Winnie, play?'

'Richard can't play, Joseph,' Rebecca said, 'he's a busy man.'

A look of intense concentration stole over Joseph's face. 'Guess, Winnie.' Puckering up his mouth, he made a squawking noise, uncannily like a parrot.

'Parrot!' Goodwin said, having played the game of imitation many times before.

Joseph grinned and clapped his hands. Screwing his face up again, he let out a realistic roar.

'Lion!' Goodwin said.

Joseph beamed again and then made a noise like a chimpanzee.

'Monkey!'

Joseph giggled joyously and gave Goodwin a big hug. Goodwin couldn't help but smile at the man, as ever a bright ray of sunshine in a sunless world. The name Joseph had bestowed on him, Winnie, was sweet and endearing and made Goodwin feel quite protective of the young lad. According to Rebecca he'd been mentally handicapped from an early age, when he'd been accidentally smothered by his foster parent. The ensuing brain damage caused by the lack of oxygen had severely limited his ability to learn and understand the world around him in anything other than the capacity of a toddler. Joseph had been a full time resident at Rebecca's place of work, a care home in Albuquerque, before the dust cloud kicked up by the asteroid had encircled the world, throwing it into chaos. A series of unconnected events had led to Rebecca and those she cared for becoming embroiled in Goodwin's flight from Steadfast, all of them winding up in Sanctuary, lost and disorientated.

Goodwin still felt guilty for having led Rebecca and her vulnerable patients into the mess they were now all subjected to. Rebecca, as sweet and kind as ever, had never once placed any blame on Goodwin, accepting her lot with good grace and battling on as only she knew how. If Hilt was a rock then Rebecca was a mountain, unshakeable in her duty to protect those she cared for, regardless of her own well-being and the obstacles thrown in her path.

Goodwin helped Rebecca lead Joseph back to one of the biggest enclosures in the camp, its ample size enough to house Rebecca, Joseph, another two carers called Julie and Arianna, and ten other patients of varying ages and degrees of mental disability.

'I'm so sorry for causing a problem,' Rebecca said as they entered the large tent. 'Joseph can run wild sometimes. I used to have trouble with him in the daylight in a large park, but here—'

'I understand.' Goodwin watched Joseph bounce away to join his friends. His heart went out to this young woman who struggled to do the best she could with limited resources in an alien world. He reached out to lay an understanding hand on her shoulder but as his fingers touched her she shied away, a haunted look flickering across her face.

Folding her arms tightly across her chest, Rebecca gave Goodwin a forced smile and moved away to attend to the rest of her flock.

'She still doesn't like people touching her,' a small voice said from next to him, 'apart from Joseph, me and the other patients.'

Goodwin looked down to see Rebecca's friend and co-worker, Julie, had come to stand by his side.

'She went through a lot of trauma,' Goodwin said, inwardly cursing the sick filth who had seen fit to rape Rebecca during the civil unrest on the surface.

'I hoped she would have got better by now, but I fear this place, this darkness, hasn't helped her to let it go.' Julie's sad voice echoed

Goodwin's own thoughts and compounded his need for action to rid them of this dank existence.

'She'll improve over time,' Goodwin told her, trying to lift her mood, 'she has all of you to look after her and I'll try and get us all out of here as soon as I can. I'm just on my way to see the commander; I'm hoping he'll have some good news for us all.'

'Really?' Julie's eyes brightened.

Goodwin berated himself for his hasty words; false hope was a dangerous thing to bandy about. 'We'll have to wait and see.' He watched her expression crumble, making him feel like he'd just kicked a small kitten.

At that point Joseph came back up to Goodwin, pulling a reluctant thirty year old woman called Susan with him.

'Present!' Joseph pushed the shy woman towards him. Susan had taken a shine to Goodwin ever since he'd first visited them at their new home a week after the camp had been set up. Holding out a podgy fist, Susan dangled a heavy bracelet for him to take, the fear of rejection on her face barely outweighed by the hope of acceptance.

He smiled. 'For me?'

Susan nodded, chewing her lower lip and scuffing at the ground with one shoe.

'She's been making it all week,' Rebecca said, coming up as Julie departed without a backward glance.

'It's very nice, thank you, Susan,' Goodwin enthused, making a point of examining the crude object with interest before sliding it onto his left wrist, the small shells and stones adorning it softly jangling.

Susan put her head to his arm, cupping her hands around the bracelet. Goodwin looked at Rebecca for help, unsure what the woman was doing.

Rebecca chortled at his confusion. 'Some of the stones on it glow in the dark.'

Susan stood up and waited for Goodwin to try for himself. Pulling his thick shirt sleeve up over his new gift he shielded his eyes with his free hand to create a dark space in which to view the phenomenon.

Rebecca was quite right. Many of the stones did indeed glow and brightly, too, their iridescent blues surprising Goodwin with their intensity.

'Wow, that's great!' he said, genuinely pleased with the effect. It would look excellent in the darkness, and considering their current location's dearth of light it would be appreciated on a regular basis.

Susan grinned and pulled up a sleeve on her jumper to show off her own bracelet to him.

'Excellent.' He put his wrist next to hers. 'We're bracelet buddies.'

'Buddies,' Susan said, looking at him as if trying to figure out the meaning of his words. If images could materialise out of thin air, a small light bulb would've appeared over Susan's head as her eyes widened in understanding. Letting out a squawk of sheer happiness the young handicapped woman flung herself forwards, gripping Goodwin in a tight embrace.

Goodwin held his arms aloft caught off guard by the sudden show of affection.

'I think you've got a friend for life there,' Rebecca said as Joseph, feeling left out, gave Rebecca a similarly full-blooded bear hug.

Goodwin chuckled and put his hands on Susan's shoulders to gently prise her limpet-like grip from around his waist. He didn't want to encourage any romantic feelings in the girl, but his embarrassment at the situation was balanced out by the touching nature of the moment.

Soon after, Goodwin said his farewells to them all and took his leave; as nice as it was to be in the presence of such joyous innocence, he had important matters to attend to. He did, however, promise to return when he was able, the happy group lightening his day almost as much as it did when he found the time to be alone with his precious Kara.

Back out in the darkness, Goodwin felt his new bracelet slip down to his hand. Out here its luminous attributes were beautiful. Allowing himself a moment of contentment, he surveyed the area, the brisk air tugging at the edges of his clothing. In all directions the camp's lights sparkled and shone, holding the unrelenting blackness at bay and conjuring up the effect of a never-ending blanket of stars. It would've been a sight to behold had their circumstances been otherwise. Instead the vision merely served to depress him, bringing him back down to reality. With a sigh he moved away from the tent in search of answers that might never come.

CHAPTER TWENTY-FOUR

GOODWIN APPROACHED the centre of the camp after his pit stop with Rebecca and Joseph. The constant hum of electrical generators was louder and more incessant here than elsewhere in the sprawling and often haphazard site of Steadfast's refugees. The number of lighting rigs also increased around the central hub of the encampment, their tripod-like design dotted around the cobbled-together command centre.

Five large tents had been disassembled and rearranged to create three sides and a roof for the temporary structure, their black material rippling against the faint currents of air that circulated within the enormous subterranean chamber. To the rear, the smooth rock face of a small promontory acted as the final wall to the enclosure. On top of the makeshift shelter someone had erected a Darklight flag, proudly displaying the security firm's white logo on a black background.

DARKLIGHT

At first the Darklight Commander had posted two sentries outside the entrance to the command post, but as the days turned to weeks and then months it became clear every able body needed to be utilised for more critical tasks. Goodwin walked unchallenged into the tent, ducking his head as he entered.

Inside, portable computer hardware and communication equipment lay dormant and unmanned on top of an ingenious system of interlocking pop-up ultra-lightweight tables. More of these flimsy desks stood off to the right and there, standing alone, was the bulky figure of the Darklight leader, Commander Hilt.

Standing over six foot, six inches tall, the commander was an imposing sight. Barrel-chested, Hilt's massive arms mirrored the tree trunk like appendages he called legs. Unlike most men of his size, Hilt wasn't lacking in speed and agility, his lightning quick reflexes belying his muscle-bound frame. The man's physical prowess, coupled with his calm, controlled demeanour, exuded competency, leadership and strength. If anyone were to search for a person to epitomise the term 'warrior', then they need look no further than the Darklight officer.

As Goodwin moved around the desk, Hilt looked up, his granite like features as ever marred by a nasty scar that ran down the centre of his face, the tip of his nose partially missing; a war wound from whatever or whoever had dared to take a swipe at the man.

'Commander,' Goodwin said formally, knowing full well how Hilt liked to keep his distance from a first name, or even a surname, basis.

'Sir,' Hilt replied in his deep baritone.

'You're up early.'

'You could say that.' Hilt looked back down at the array of unfurled maps and computer screens that covered the surface on which he worked.

'You've been up all night?' Goodwin noticed on closer inspection that the Commander did indeed seem somewhat weary.

'Yes, I wanted to compile the latest data that came in yesterday evening.'

'The recon teams?'

Hilt nodded. 'We had a preliminary debrief on their findings. I've been transferring their data onto our maps ever since.'

'Anything interesting?' Goodwin said, hopeful.

'Nothing that will get us to the USSB, but I think we have a clearer picture as to the lay of the land.'

Goodwin's heart sank, his disappointment almost palpable within him. Were they ever going to get out of this place? Every search so far had ended in failure; he was beginning to lose hope that they would ever see the light of day again. *Bad choice of words*, he thought to himself when he remembered what had happened, and what was to come, on the surface miles above them.

The way they'd entered Sanctuary, through a maze of natural cave formations, had become blocked when an earthquake had struck, collapsing the ceiling behind them. At the time they'd been attempting to find a back route into the USSB to find a place to lay up, so that Goodwin could negotiate their transition into the secretive military run base.

Creating a path back through the rubble that barred their way had been the first course of action. The danger had been that the whole area had become unstable, preventing removal of the debris by hand; not that that much rock could have been moved quickly anyway, far from it. So the decision had been made to use explosives. Hilt had said it would be a risk and his fears had turned out to be well-founded. The charges had been set and detonated. The result, a huge cloud of dust which settled to reveal they'd only made things worse, much worse. A quarter mile of the twisting, naturally occurring tunnels had completely caved in, ending whatever faint hopes they'd had of escaping the same way they'd entered.

Goodwin moved round the central table when Hilt gestured for him to take a look at the screen he'd been working on. In front of him a two dimensional digital map had been drawn, depicting the chamber they now called home.

'There's a lot more information on here,' Goodwin said. 'The last time I looked at this, it was less than half the size of what you have now.'

'I've pushed my teams to the limit.' Hilt stood upright and stretched his thick neck to one side to probe a shoulder with his fingers. 'Our situation is becoming desperate,' he continued, apparently feeling the need to justify his actions. 'Our medical supplies are running low. We never envisaged we'd be spending so long away from a supply station. Not only are we having to deal with an increasing number of minor to mid-level injuries, it's only a matter of time before more serious treatment is needed. People who have chronic conditions are running dangerously low on their medication and will most likely be the first to require emergency care. If we don't get out of here soon, we could be facing our first fatalities since we arrived – and sooner rather than later.'

'You've got no argument from me.' Goodwin understood all too well the pressure Hilt was under. 'We have to do what we have to do. If any of us civilians can help, just say the word.'

'We have a limited number of torches as it is,' Hilt told him. 'More bodies scouring this place wouldn't be feasible or safe. Besides, your people need to concentrate on keeping everyone fed and watered; the fish they've been pulling from the lake keeps us all going.'

Hilt was quite right. Goodwin's twenty-five thousand strong, civilian workforce was doing a wonderful job, many working just as hard, if not harder, than the Darklight forces themselves. Everyone strove to maximise the materials at hand to produce a variety of fishing equipment. They'd even created rafts out of the ancient, long-dead tree trunks that littered the ground surrounding the ancient city, trees that lurked in the shadows, sprouting from the earth, their black crystallised forms yet another oddity that made up the complex riddle that was Sanctuary.

'So, where do we stand now?' Goodwin said.

Hilt cleared his throat and ran a hand through his short jet-black hair as he collected his thoughts. 'We've finally determined where the cavern ends on two sides. Here and here.' He pointed to two lines running down the left hand side and bottom of the map. 'This section,' he continued, tracing the line on the left, 'is five miles from our location and two miles from the edge of the city's southern border. As our remote drones don't function down here, some kind of interference I'm told, we're still to pinpoint where the chamber terminates to the north and east. My teams report the terrain further out becomes increasingly difficult to navigate, full of deep chasms and sheer cliff faces. As you can see by the scale here,' Hilt tapped the graphical tablet to switch the image to a three dimensional render, 'they've managed to penetrate almost thirty miles in both directions, with no end in sight.'

'Thirty miles? That's insane,' Goodwin said in disbelief. 'The professor said this place was big, but I never imagined an individual chamber could be this size.'

Hilt glanced at him. 'Given it touches three miles high in places, is it so hard to believe? Some of the towers in the city are two miles in height. Everything down here is on a massive scale. Who knows how far this chamber could go, fifty, a hundred, a thousand miles?'

Goodwin's mind reeled, and not for the first time, at the magnitude and reality shifting implications of this most mysterious of places. 'I still find it hard to believe the U.S. military in the USSB don't know this Anakim city is down here. We waltzed right into it, but according to the U.S. Army Decontamination Team we took prisoner on our way into Sanctuary, they never knew anything like this existed.'

'I've been thinking about that,' Hilt said. 'Do you remember we walked through a section where the floor was covered with rocks and pulverised stone?'

Goodwin thought back. 'Vaguely.'

'Well, I think that area used to be blocked off but a seismic event, which we know occur in that area, could easily have brought it down, opening up whole new sections of the cave system. If that's true, then any previous exploration would have finished at a dead end. This could well be virgin territory.'

'For humans anyway,' Goodwin said.

'Indeed.' The gravitas of Hilt's tone emphasising the seriousness with which he now viewed the notion of the Anakim, their existence and the implications therein.

'How are the USSB soldiers settling in with your men and women of Darklight?' Goodwin asked the Commander. 'They've been working with you for a few weeks now, any trouble with them following your orders?' Goodwin was keen to find out if the two factions were getting along; it was his idea to release them from Darklight's custody when it became apparent they weren't getting back to civilisation anytime soon. Initially Hilt had put restrictions on their movements, coupled with round the clock surveillance. As their situation progressed from dire to critical, it had slowly dawned on the small captured unit of U.S. military personnel that Goodwin, his Steadfast GMRC civilians and Darklight weren't the enemy they'd initially believed them to be. Obviously, when they had been sent from USSB Sanctuary to carry out decontamination procedures on Goodwin and a handful of civilian personnel, they had been expecting a routine job. What had greeted them was a small army of heavily armed and armoured Darklight mercenaries escorting in twenty-five thousand civilians. From their perspective, Goodwin and his cohorts were a huge hostile force and, after they'd been compelled to surrender, they'd reacted as their training dictated – only giving out their name, rank and service number when questioned. The irony was if they had helped Goodwin at the time they'd all be safely tucked up in the USSB; sadly, it seemed, things were never that easy.

'They're a pain,' Hilt grumbled in a rare show of emotion.

'Really?' Goodwin was surprised. 'I thought they were getting on well. There are only thirty of them, how much trouble can they make?'

'Sergeant Alvarez, their C.O., and his corporal, Walker, keep pestering me to let them have their weapons back. If it isn't that, it's Alvarez sticking his nose in; he seems to think, as he's from Sanctuary, he knows best.'

'His insight is invaluable isn't it?' Goodwin said.

'That's the problem, and he knows it too.'

'I'm sure you'll get a handle on it.'

Hilt grunted and Goodwin took the hint; the commander didn't want to discuss the subject any further.

'I was speaking to a couple of them the other day, the Decontamination Team, I mean,' Goodwin said, changing the subject slightly and looking about to make sure no one was around to overhear. 'It appears they're not aware of the next wave of asteroids either.'

Hilt shot him a look, his brows furrowing in concern.

'Don't worry, I haven't told them or anyone else,' Goodwin said. 'I just posed some searching questions, very subtly, and it's clear they only know about the first one, AG5.'

Hilt looked at him impassively, perhaps wondering what Goodwin was leading up to.

'I think,' Goodwin continued, 'that no one else in Sanctuary can know either. If the military personnel are clueless, then it goes without saying that the civilians within the USSB are also in the dark. It may be that even Sanctuary's generals have no idea what is to come.'

'Someone knows,' Hilt said with an ominous air.

He was right. There must be at least a few within Sanctuary who knew the full truth. Joiner did – that was for certain – and he could probably move in and out of Sanctuary as he pleased, too; nothing would surprise Goodwin now about the reach of the GMRC's Intelligence Director. The professor had been bound for USSB Sanctuary before he'd decided to stay at Steadfast, but surely others knew too? Everyone within the GMRC Directorate had to know, but what about the politicians? Not for the first time, Goodwin felt a headache coming on as he tried to unravel the complexities of the cover-up. *It's no good worrying about it now*, he chided himself, his mind returning to the here and now.

'They all know about these Anakim, though,' Goodwin continued, referring to the U.S. Army personnel once more. He was pleased to be able to talk freely in front of the commander. With things as they were, Hilt and Goodwin, the appointed leaders, rarely found time to converse in private and it made a change not having to watch what he said all the time for fear of revealing something he shouldn't. 'It sounds like the existence of these giants is common knowledge within the USSB, from what they say.'

'Which is still very little.' Hilt continued to add data to his map. 'There's a lot they're not telling us. As soon as you ask them about the USSB they clam up tighter than a gnat's ass.'

'I know,' Goodwin said. 'But can you blame them? We had them tied up for days and then held prisoner for weeks on end. When we finally set them free, we keep their weapons from them. How would you feel in their shoes?'

Hilt didn't respond to the question, typically keeping his thoughts to himself. Goodwin had noticed over the months they'd been together the Commander had let down his guard ever so slightly. He wasn't as stand-offish with him as he had been at the beginning. The Darklight officer was an enigma and Goodwin was sure he'd only begun to scratch the surface of the man that lay beneath. What he did know was that he could put his trust in him one hundred per cent; you got the feeling that when Hilt accepted you as a friend that was it, he'd back you all the way. And Goodwin did feel like they'd created a friendship of sorts, or if not yet that, then a definite mutual respect had been forged between them; at least that was his take on it.

'So, have there been any other developments I should know about?' Goodwin asked.

'The teams I sent back into the city have returned empty handed again. Every tower they've searched is completely devoid of anything, just large, strangely decorated, hollow shells.'

'Perhaps whoever used them, lived in them, had no need for

furniture or possessions.' Goodwin leant against the rock wall at the back of the room due to the lack of any seating. 'Who knows how they lived? Their way of life could've been totally alien to ours.'

'Whatever the case there's nothing of use to us in them,' the Darklight man said.

'And it would take years to search them all thoroughly,' Goodwin added, 'and from what you've said before, they can't access the upper levels of the towers as there are no staircases.'

'Yes, they must have used a mechanism we've been unable to locate. One of my teams did enter the first floor of one the smaller structures. The grappling gun they used just reached one of the windows. They have no glass in them; they're just open apertures into the building.'

'The same thing, empty interior?'

Hilt nodded in confirmation.

Goodwin wandered around the room, picking up and perusing random maps brought back by the reconnaissance teams. 'Where are we at, then? How the hell do we get out of this place?'

Hilt sighed and squeezed the bridge of his nose with a thumb and forefinger. 'Okay, our options are running out.' He picked up a large knife that had been doubling as a paperweight and pondered the polished blade as he turned it over in his hands. 'We can't stay here forever, but there is no obvious route out. The lake has underwater caves within its structure, according to our scanners, but we have no equipment to even attempt to explore them. Sergeant Alvarez suggested the caves might lead back to the USSB, although he refused to elaborate on why he thought this. My guess is this water source is used in the USSB, if not for drinking water, then for other utilities within the base. Such a large resource would not be ignored, if access to it was at hand. The cave system that led us here is now even more congested, unstable and impassable after our disastrous attempt at blasting our way out and the tunnels we've found beneath the city are a veritable labyrinth, the most promising of which have proved to be dead ends.'

'So far,' Goodwin said.

'Indeed.' Hilt seemed unperturbed by his director's interruption. 'Although the tunnels that keep on going all descend into the bowels of the Earth, which is the wrong direction. The areas to the south are a mass of deep crevasses, gaping wide ravines and vertical and reverse angled cliffs, all of which require a host of climbing equipment to circumvent, equipment we don't possess. According to Alvarez and his U.S. Army Decontamination Team, there's no point exploring this chamber any further east, as that leads us in the opposite direction to the USSB. So as far as I see it, we're left with three choices, all of which are shots in the dark.

'One, we send a team north as far as they can go. Behind this team we place units at specific intervals to act as a supply chain, enabling the unit on point to roam much further before having to return. Hopefully they'll find a route out.

'Two, we use the same tactic in the tunnels under the city, a roving unit backed up with a supply chain. And finally, three, we fabricate climbing gear from other bits of kit and send our best climbers south, although without any support their range will be limited and chances of success, slim.'

Goodwin didn't want to state the obvious, except he had little choice but to do so. 'None of those sound particularly promising,' he said, his mouth set in a grim line of displeasure, his frustration mounting.

'Failing those, we can go east,' Hilt replied.

'Which is in the wrong direction to the USSB!' Goodwin slammed the tabletop in anger, sending everything on it jumping an inch into the air.

Hilt stared at Goodwin, unfazed by his sudden outburst.

Goodwin calmed himself. 'I'm sorry, Commander.'

'Perfectly understandable, sir, given the circumstances.'

'I feel like I'm letting everyone down.'

'No one else thinks that.'

'No, you mean no one *says* that. They're all thinking it. I am, so they are. I brought us here, apparently out of the fire and into the damn frying pan.'

Hilt didn't deny it, opting to stay quiet. *The man never was any good at moral support*, Goodwin thought, *damn him*.

So their future prospects didn't look good. Goodwin didn't need to ask what would happen if none of these ideas panned out. Some would end up dying down here while the remainder would have to endure an increasingly bleak existence as equipment slowly failed over the years and decades. Goodwin pushed such thoughts from his mind. That way led to madness.

'I'll schedule a briefing with my officers and your management team,' Hilt said, breaking the silence. 'Everyone needs to know our objectives.'

Goodwin bobbed his head, acknowledging the comment, his mood as dark as it ever had been since they'd been in Sanctuary. Even the name of the place elicited a bitter taste in his mouth.

The two men discussed their options in more depth before Goodwin decided he needed a break. 'Get some sleep, Commander. We can resume this later.'

'Yes, sir.'

Goodwin turned to leave.

'Sir, one more thing,' Hilt said.

Goodwin looked back inquiringly.

'I forgot to say. Tell your people not to go in the water, even if it's just ankle deep, and to take extra precautions on their rafts.'

'Why's that?'

'One of my men sustained an injury when he and his unit were out surveying the lake.'

'What sort of injury?'

'Leg lacerations; they're not deep but they look to be festering.'

'What caused it, a fish?'

Hilt paused. 'Perhaps – something caught him, came out of the water. They didn't get a good look at it.'

'He was attacked then?

'The wound didn't look like any fish bite I've ever seen. Just make sure your people know.'

'Will do, Commander,' Goodwin said, leaving Hilt to it.

Walking back through the camp Goodwin decided to make a detour, heading out to the nearest section of the lake. Switching on his torch, he left the lights of the camp behind and ventured out into the black void. In the distance he could just make out the twinkling lights of his GMRC staff as they collected water and fished for food. Treading carefully, he slowed, giving himself plenty of warning in case he came upon the lake quicker than expected. You could never be too careful in this place, the lack of light was inhibiting at the best of times, but add to that a completely alien environment and the dangers went up considerably.

The dry layer of soil that covered this area of the chamber crunched under his boots as he moved forwards. Another thing about the chamber was the muffling effect it had on noise; as soon as you were any distance away from other people the silence that closed in around you was almost intense, the absence of sound complete.

A silky shimmer ahead, an effect produced by his beam of light, announced his arrival at the water's edge. Goodwin was still some way from the activities further down the shoreline. With care he negotiated some small boulders, leaning on a couple with one hand to pick his way through the uneven surface. Hopping down, his feet sank into a shingle beach, but the jarring landing made his torch flicker and go out, plunging him into darkness. Goodwin swore and rapped the torch with the palm of his hand in an attempt to restore the battery's electrical contacts. It didn't work. With his eyes rendered redundant his other senses launched into overdrive, his ears detecting the sound of the water gently lapping at the shore nearby and a faint odour specific to the lake tickling his nose and taste buds. He dialled back the torch's intensity and the light sprang back to life, albeit fainter than before. *The batteries must be low*, he reasoned, *not a good thing to happen out in the middle of nowhere*. A tiny splash out in the lake brought his attention back and he flashed his torch out in the direction it came from. Nothing could be seen, except for an ever expanding ring of ripples, the only evidence of whatever had seen fit to disturb the surface.

Goodwin wondered what sort of fish came out of the water to

attack a person. His mind returned to Hilt's words. *The wound didn't look like any fish bite I've ever seen.* Goodwin searched the water in front of him with large slow sweeps of his torch. *Who knows what lies out there in the depths,* Goodwin mused, an equal measure of curiosity and foreboding stealing over him. Gazing out beyond the reach of his light, Goodwin shuddered and turned, his need for the company of others suddenly an overwhelming compulsion.

CHAPTER TWENTY-FIVE

ANOTHER LARGE RAFT reached the shore. Its dark timber hull breached the shallows, cleaving its way through the water to grind to a halt on the gravel beach that awaited it. Ten people knelt on board its deck, five on each side. This civilian crew held a variety of crudely fashioned paddles which they'd used to propel the simple vessel through the water. In the centre of the craft, a large lamp hung at the top of a pole. Hemming in this sturdy post at all sides lay a mass of pale scaly bodies, which in turn were held in place by a bulging fabric fence.

Goodwin caught one of the lines as it was thrown to him from atop the vessel. Together, with around sixty other people, they heaved the craft up out of the water and onto dry land.

'Looks like you have another good haul,' Goodwin said to one of the crew after they'd hopped down to the ground next to him.

'One of the biggest catches yet.' The man grinned and gave Goodwin a congenial slap on the back before moving away to help his friends unload the fish from the centre of the raft.

Goodwin dusted his hands off on the side of his trousers and walked away to the top of the beach, his boots displacing the loose pebbly surface with each step. Not far away, on a rocky outcrop, Kara

Vandervoort sat waiting for him. Smiling, she gave him a little wave as he approached. 'Having fun?' she asked in her rich and vibrant South African accent.

'It makes a change from organising rotas and deliberating on finding the USSB.' Goodwin sat down next to her and kissed her in greeting.

'Physical exercise is always good to clear the mind,' Kara said with a twinkle in her eye.

Goodwin smiled and accepted the small flask she held out to him. Taking a swig of water, he savoured its refreshing taste as he quenched his thirst. He'd been working with the teams at the lake for half the day. His hands had been rubbed raw and his arms ached, as did his back, but despite all these niggles he felt reinvigorated, his fears temporarily pacified. What Kara said was true, exercise helped relieve stress and he'd needed some release after the less than inspiring news delivered by Hilt earlier that morning.

Sitting beneath one of the lighting rigs, it felt nice to be bathed in light; he could almost feel it warming his skin like the rays of the sun he often craved. As the saying went, you don't know what you have 'til it's gone – and it was true, you didn't. Goodwin often woke up these days with dreams fresh in his mind. Some faded quickly, without trace; while others lingered on, their message clear. It was one of these dreams that Goodwin could always recall with clarity throughout the day, the heat from the sun on his skin as he sunbathed on a holiday he'd never taken. The crash of waves as they broke on a beach he'd never been to, the distant sorrowful cry of gulls circling in a cloudless blue sky.

He'd been underground for many years in Steadfast, but the base that had been his home possessed a powerful artificial sunlight generator, strong enough to produce heat for those under its glare. He'd also had a special screen fitted to his USSB office in order to fight the bouts of depression he suffered due to his underground existence. *This place, on the other hand, is a whole different kettle of fish*, he thought, absently noting the inadvertent pun in the phrase. The months spent underground in the darkness tended to suck at a person's soul after a while, even for the hardiest or most sun averse; which was probably why Kara and Goodwin weren't alone where they sat. Many others had gathered to bask in the steady glow of the floodlight. In fact, whenever people took a break from their duties they congregated in the light, drawn like moths to a very bright flame. Even now as Goodwin looked along the shoreline, every pool of light had attracted its own group of workers, each taking a much deserved rest.

They watched the fish being gutted and carved up, ready to be taken back to camp. The overwhelming stench drifted up the beach in waves, making Goodwin wish he had a cold to dull his senses, which protested at the gag-inducing onslaught.

'I hear things didn't go too well,' Kara said.

'No, not the best,' he replied, distracted.

'I'm sure you and the commander will come through for us in the end.' She placed a comforting hand on his knee.

'Yes.' He put his hand on hers. 'I'm sure we will.' Whether Kara could hear the defeat in his voice, Goodwin was unsure. If she did she didn't acknowledge it.

'Have you ever wondered how the air is so breathable down here?' she asked, perhaps in an attempt to change the subject and take his mind off the worries that she had just inadvertently reignited in his mind.

'I have, although since you were in charge of the bio-chambers back in Steadfast, I'd have thought you were better qualified to answer that than me.'

'I have a few theories.'

'Are you going to enlighten me then?' he asked, when she failed to continue.

She grinned, her eyes alight with mischief; an expression he knew all too well. Kara was quite cheeky when she had a mind to be. Her buoyant mood always seemed to rub off on him and was partly why he loved her so.

He tried to keep his own smile in check and failed miserably. 'Am I going to have to beg?'

'Later,' she said with a wink, 'but seriously, though,' she continued, looking around their surroundings, 'there's nothing to suggest there should be any air down here at all; nothing to produce it in the quantities and quality that we're experiencing.'

Goodwin looked at her expectantly, waiting for her to further enlighten him.

'The algae and other plant life in the lake may produce a certain amount of oxygen,' she said, 'but not enough to keep the air fresh and perfectly balanced. The nitrogen levels, according to Darklight's high-tech sensors in those helmets of theirs, also stay at a constant seventy-eight per cent. There doesn't appear to be any kind of mechanisms down here, mechanical or otherwise, to ensure this consistency. Sanctuary's USSB, like Steadfast itself, will undoubtedly have its own integrated air generation and purification system. The USSB isn't connected to this part of Sanctuary, however, and even if it was, unless I'm missing something, it couldn't possibly churn out the volume required to fill this place.'

'So what's happening, then?' Goodwin was intrigued.

'There must be something elsewhere producing a breathable atmosphere on a Biblical scale.'

'What, a machine of some kind?'

'Either that or a big – and I mean big – ecosystem, replete with copious amounts of flora, able to sustain significant oxygen output.'

'We have a lot of water here,' Goodwin said, 'couldn't there be some kind of plankton creating it?'

'Phytoplankton, yes, but they require energy from the sun which, if you'd noticed, there isn't much of down here. And as big as the lake is, its surface area is too small.'

'Won't the lack of sunlight prevent other plant life flourishing?' he asked.

'In most instances, but we do know plant and animal life can exist in the deepest oceans; congregating around thermal vents and thriving without any sunlight at all. Since the professor told you Sanctuary reaches twenty miles down, then it's possible it operates by harnessing the heat from a magma chamber located beneath, or even within, the structure itself.'

'Inside?' Goodwin didn't like the sound of that idea.

Kara laughed and slapped his thigh, picking up on his concern. 'Don't worry; if these Anakim were as clever as they appear to have been, then it was probably built into the design plans. A permanent source of energy for something this large would have been a must, I imagine.'

'They weren't that clever or they'd still be here,' he said.

'Hmm,' Kara murmured in response.

A shout went up from the people unloading that day's catch. Kara and Goodwin stood up to get a better view, as did others around them. It seemed a large cod-like fish wasn't dead. The poor beast thrashed on the deck of the raft. Some workers got out of its way, while others moved in to subdue it. A man carrying a large block of wood finally dispatched it with one swift blow to the head, the fish flopping limp. The show over, Kara and Goodwin took it as their cue to leave. Goodwin had to get back to assist Hilt with his planning and Kara was needed to help with the logistics of distributing the food and water supplies amongst Steadfast's evacuees.

Leaving the lights and people on the shoreline behind them, they switched on their respective torches and slipped away into the darkness. In the distance a single lantern, glinting like a tiny star, had been erected at the outskirts of the encampment to act as a guide to those returning from the lake.

'One of Hilt's men got bitten then?' Kara said as they trudged along, hand in hand.

'Yes. I've relayed the message to all the team leaders that no one should venture into the water, including the shallows.'

'And you've banned all bathing and swimming, too?'

'Bathing in the water, yes, but people can still clean themselves, in fact I encourage it. We need to be careful with hygiene; we can't afford an outbreak of anything down here.'

'What's that?' she asked, holding his arm up, their hands still clasped.

'It's my new bracelet.' Goodwin stopped to let her examine the stones which had been faintly glowing before he'd turned his torch onto them. 'It's lovely isn't it? Susan gave it to me earlier.'

Kara eyes narrowed. 'Who's Susan?'

'One of Rebecca's patients, I've mentioned her before.'

'Rebecca,' Kara said, attaching a strange emphasis to the name.

'It glows really brightly in the dark,' Goodwin told her. 'Look.' He turned off his torch and reached over to click the switch on hers. Now cast into darkness, the bracelet radiated powerful shades of gleaming blues, strong enough to highlight his skin around it.

Kara ran her fingers over the stones, seemingly unable to stop herself from being interested in their vibrancy. 'I don't like you seeing that woman,' her disembodied voice said out of the dark.

'She's a friend,' Goodwin told her a tad too defensively for his own liking, 'nothing more.'

'You're always saying how resourceful she is,' Kara said. 'How she's so amazing with how she copes with everything.'

'Well she is amazing—'

'What?! You're not supposed to agree with me, you idiot!'

'I'm not actually agreeing with you,' Goodwin said, pointing out her imprecise semantics, 'just confirming my previous position.'

Kara turned her light on, gave him a filthy look and stormed away into the dark.

'Kara, wait, you're going the wrong way!'

Cursing, Goodwin flicked on his torch and jogged after her. Unfortunately the bouncing movement sent his light blinking out, just as it had earlier that day.

'Not again.' He halted his advance and whacked the side of the torch's tubular metal shroud with his hand. Glancing up, he saw Kara's silhouette striding further away, taking with it his only source of light. 'Kara wait, my torch has broken!'

Kara didn't stop, however. Hurrying to catch up, Goodwin stumbled over the uneven terrain as he tried in vain to dim the strength of the torch, to bring it back to life like he did before. This time though, it was totally dead.

After nearly sprawling flat on his face on numerous occasions, Goodwin caught up with an irate Kara, who'd stopped, presumably to enable him to rejoin her.

'Thank you,' he said as he came to stand in front of her.

Kara glared at him and then grasped his arm to hold up his wrist with the bracelet on, the homemade jewellery still glowing brightly, her torch light aimed away at the ground.

'You do realise this could be radioactive,' she said, still holding onto his arm. 'Its glow is too strong, you should take it off.'

'What, you can't be serious?'

Kara didn't respond, her expression difficult to read as over half her face was in deep shadow.

'Look, Kara, I'm sorry but—'

'What's that?' she said, before he could finish his apology, an apology he didn't think he needed to say but one he thought he'd better, just to keep the peace.

'What's what?' he asked.

She shone the light away to one side. 'That, over there.' She gestured with her torch in the direction she wanted him to look.

Goodwin couldn't see a thing.

Kara switched her light off and as they adjusted to the pitch blackness, she grabbed his upper arm, her fingernails biting into his flesh. 'There, do you see it?' She sounded excited.

'I'm not—' he began and then he did see something, barely visible, an indistinct blue-green light hanging in the air, shimmering in and out of existence. It was difficult to tell how far away it was in the dark, there being no point of reference against which to measure it.

Kara switched her torch back on and trotted off in its direction. 'Come on,' she said to him over her shoulder, their argument apparently forgotten, 'let's go and see what it is.'

'I don't think that's a good idea.' He stayed where he was in the hope she would return. 'Kara, I don't have a light, come back!'

Kara didn't stop. She just called him onwards, her voice becoming fainter as she ran away into the void ahead.

'For pity's sake,' he said and ran after her into the dark.

Up ahead, Goodwin could no longer see the ethereal light they'd both spotted, but Kara apparently still followed something as she didn't slow or stop despite his calls for her to do so. The outline of Kara's compact figure continued to shrink with every step before her light blinked out.

Goodwin swore. 'Kara, come back!' he yelled out at the top of his voice. Looking around he could no longer see any light, not from the lake, the camp or Kara. He was lost and blind, totally turned around and without direction.

'Richard, over here!' Kara called back, her voice sounding far away.

Looking in the direction of the sound, a light appeared off to his right. Kara's torch! Moving with care Goodwin closed the distance as Kara came back to meet him.

'You ran off and left me in the dark!' he said as they reunited.

'Sorry, I thought you were right behind me. I tracked the light into the city; I think it went into one of the towers. Come on.' Still buoyed by the chase, she trotted off once more.

A little out of breath, Goodwin didn't have the chance to argue and, not wanting to get left behind again, he ran to stay close to her. *Is she trying to prove a point?* he wondered, *maybe trying to compete with Rebecca somehow by hunting down some mysterious light?* He didn't dare ask. He might put his foot in it sometimes, but he wasn't that stupid; at least he hoped he wasn't.

Around them and at the very limits of the light from Kara's torch, the shadowy forms of long dead trees appeared only to slip from view back into the darkness, indicating they were indeed close to the edge of the ancient, abandoned city. Their indistinct cone of light splayed out like a fan to reveal the lay of the land ahead, eventually illuminating the side of one of the huge Anakim edifices. The purplish stone structure reared up out of the gloom like the prow of some great ship, sliding through the fog on a becalmed high sea. The corner of the building soon hove into view, its strange architectural nuances testament to the fact that human hands had not been responsible for its fabrication.

They slowed to a walk. The enormous entrance of the tower appeared on their left, its interior barely encroached upon by the light from Kara's small torch.

'Where did you say it went?' Goodwin said.

'Down here somewhere.' Kara moved her head this way and that, her eyes intent on scanning the area. 'I lost sight of it when I came back for you.'

His good sense prevailing, Goodwin didn't rise to the inference that it was his fault they'd failed to keep track of whatever it was they'd seen. He actually wanted to point out it had been Kara who'd left him high and dry in the middle of no man's land. 'We should go back,' he said instead.

'What? No way.' Kara's South African inflection strengthened along with her resolve. 'It could be someone from the USSB searching for us; we should at least have a look around.'

'I don't think it's someone from the base,' Goodwin said.

'Why?'

'Just a feeling.'

'What do you think it is then?'

'Some flying insect, perhaps.'

'Hmm, could be I suppose,' she said. 'A group of fireflies, it would account for the inconsistent light.'

His hopes rose. 'Shall we go back then?'

Just when it looked as if she was about to agree, the weird fluctuating light appeared once again, its shimmering luminescence gliding along a hundred yards ahead.

'Look! There it is again!' She darted forwards once more with Goodwin in tow.

Half a minute later, when it looked like they were gaining on it, the light vanished.

'I think it's entered a building,' Kara said as they closed in on where they'd last seen it.

Another huge tower had eased into view on their right. This one's surface appeared almost translucent, as Kara's torchlight reflected from its great bulk. The ground on which they trod was hard, uneven, compacted earth. When the doorway emerged from the shadows, their footfalls echoing in the oppressive silence, Kara paused beneath the great arch. Narrowing the beam of light with a twist of the torch's mechanism, she traced the entrance from one side to the other. Standing fifty feet across and the same high, the great opening dwarfed their tiny figures.

Kara made to go inside.

'What are you doing?' Goodwin grabbed her hand and pulled her back.

'Taking a look around. Whatever went in here can't get out again without coming back this way. According to Commander Hilt's teams, all these towers only have one way in and one way out.'

She was right; Hilt had told Goodwin the same thing. He didn't let go of her hand, however.

She looked up into his face. 'You're not scared are you?'

'No, we just—'

'Excellent, come on then.' She pulled him forwards through the cavernous aperture.

Goodwin let himself be led along while Kara shone her light around, the two of them moving deeper into the blackest of blacks. Goodwin's throat tightened, his anxiety spiking as he looked into the light ahead, fearful at what it might – at any moment – unveil.

He tugged on her hand. 'Kara, I've got a bad feeling about this, let's go back.'

At his words, Kara's torch flickered and Goodwin held his breath, praying that her light didn't fail like his had. The beam regained its power and Kara looked at him, her eyes betraying her own disquiet, the reality of being without illumination in a large unearthly structure that something else had just entered hitting home for the first time.

Goodwin's eyes widened and his grip tightened on Kara's hand. 'Did you hear that?'

'What?' Hear what?!' Kara said, her voice quavering as she swung her torch around.

'Shh.' He moved closer to her.

On the edges of his hearing, Goodwin thought he could hear something, something that sounded a lot like ... breathing.

Goodwin pressed his mouth to Kara's ear. 'I think there's something else in here with us,' he whispered. 'I can hear it breathing.'

Kara gave a small nod, her fingers clenched around his. Silently they moved back, step by step, the way they'd come. As they retreated, Kara kept the torch moving in a continuous three hundred and sixty degree sweep. Something touched Goodwin's back and he shouted out in terror, making Kara scream.

Spinning round, his heart in his mouth, Goodwin felt the cold smooth surface of a wall with his hand. 'It's just a wall! Just a wall!'

Turning back Goodwin wondered why Kara hadn't answered him. The reason soon became apparent. She stood transfixed by the ghostly light which had reappeared in what must have been the far corner of the high vaulted room, a hundred feet away. A bone-chilling screech rang out into the darkness and the light sprang forwards, heading right for them.

Pure unadulterated terror gripped Goodwin's heart like a vice, freezing his legs in place.

Kara's shrieks brought him back to life as the light bore down on them with terrifying speed. Scrambling back, hand in hand, they fled through the giant doorway, sprinting with a swiftness only those being chased can muster.

The next moments were lost to Goodwin. His breath came in great gulps as he pumped his legs for all his worth. He was just conscious of Kara to his right, her torch light flailing ahead of them as her hand rose and fell as she too pushed herself to her physical limit. They were out onto the uneven plain now, free from the city and beyond the dead trees; the bumps and dips making them both stumble. Kara was the first to trip and fall, their wild flight impossible to maintain. Goodwin slid to a stop and went back to pull her to her feet. Without a word they ran once more, hand in hand again, until Goodwin could take no more and slowed to a canter, then a jog and finally a walk; his energy depleted, lactic acid filling his muscles and his breathing coming in hoarse, drawn out gasps.

Looking fearfully behind them, back towards the city, nothing stirred. No apparition dogged their footsteps.

Kara aimed her light in all directions. 'Let's – keep – going,' she said, each enunciated word punctuated by gasps for air.

Goodwin nodded and they set off again, at a slower but consistent pace. Whatever had chased them might still be following, just no longer visible. Goodwin looked back over his shoulder yet again, searching for any sign of pursuit.

When they finally reached the camp, they both collapsed underneath a beautiful and welcome floodlight. People nearby looked over at the couple, curious as to why they were so out of breath.

It took the two of them a few minutes to regain their composure when, at Goodwin's insistence, they headed straight to the command tent. Once there Goodwin informed Hilt about their brief excursion into the city, much to the interest of some of his officers, who worked alongside him.

'And you didn't get to see whatever was holding this light?' Hilt asked them both, not for one second doubting the information they relayed to him.

'No,' Goodwin said, as he accepted a cup of steaming water prepared for him by a Darklight soldier, 'we didn't get close enough, thank God.'

Kara shook her head, taking a sip from her own hot beverage before moving to lean against the rear wall, close to Goodwin.

Hilt grunted an obscure affirmation and walked over to the communications desk, picked up a small device and put it to his left ear. 'This is Commander Hilt, broadcasting on all frequencies, Code Yellow. I repeat, Code Yellow alert. Hostile contact of unknown origin sighted two clicks north-north-west of base camp. I want weapons ready and eyes on at every location, further orders to follow, Hilt out.' The commander discarded the earpiece and called over one of his men.

'Sir?' the Darklight soldier said to his commander.

'I want roving patrols around this camp in five minutes. Make it happen.'

'Yes, sir!' The man saluted, spun on his heel and rushed off to carry out his orders.

Hilt got back on the radio, connecting to his executive officer, Major Offiah. 'Major, I need a security detail, to and from the lake, set up immediately. I also want our units at the beach doubled.'

'Copy that, sir,' the response came back over the radio.

'Thank you, Commander,' Goodwin said. 'I'm glad you and your people are here.'

'Sir, if I may speak freely?' Hilt asked.

'Of course,' Goodwin said, somewhat exasperated by the man's continued need for such formality.

'What possessed you to go into the city without an escort?'

Goodwin glanced at Kara, who looked suitably guilty.

'It was my fault, Commander.' Kara spoke up before Goodwin could say anything. 'I saw the light and decided to investigate.'

Hilt looked from Kara to Goodwin, who gave his Darklight friend an apologetic half-smile.

'You're lucky things turned out the way they did,' Hilt said, formulating his words carefully as he trod the fine line of reprimanding his director.

'I can't believe it chased us,' Kara said. 'I was so scared I nearly passed out.'

Goodwin held out a hand, which Kara took before flashing him a strained smile.

'Whatever, or whoever, it was,' Hilt said to them, 'you followed it into the city, effectively chasing it, and then cornered it. What did you expect it to do?'

There wasn't much Kara or Goodwin could say to that. The man had a point.

'So there's something down here with us,' Goodwin said after Kara had returned to her tent with an armed escort, at Goodwin's request.

Hilt looked at him across the table, his heavy features, as ever, masking his emotions. 'It looks that way.'

Goodwin sighed. 'And I thought things couldn't get any worse.'

CHAPTER TWENTY-SIX

DAZZLING LIGHT MOMENTARILY BLINDED Professor Steiner as – almost immediately – a deafening clap of thunder announced the storm's presence overhead. Rain hammered down like stair rods, the intensity soaking him to the bone. Behind, Colonel Samson lit their way with a torch attached to the side of his tactical assault rifle. Every so often Steiner felt a nudge in the small of his back, the action an attempt by Samson to encourage him to move faster across the uneven and rocky topography of the New Mexican desert.

Steiner's thoughts still lingered on those who had just perished, a harrowing guilt over their deaths gnawing deep into his heart. His orders and his alone had seen them to an early grave. Captain Iwamoto and his lieutenant, a powerful woman whose name he couldn't recall, had been taken out by some unseen assassin. The rest who'd made the arduous journey to the surface from USSB Steadfast had been cut down on Malcolm Joiner's orders and by the callous actions of Samson, whose company he now had to endure alone.

'Get down!' Samson shouted from behind.

Steiner, shoved to the ground, had the air squeezed from his lungs when the Colonel landed painfully on top of him, the man's heavy bulk pinning him to the muddy earth.

'What are you doing?!' Steiner said as Samson held him down.

'I'm shielding your body, don't move!'

A loud, penetrating roar shot by overhead, the very earth trembling at its passing.

Steiner knew that sound; it wasn't anything produced by nature, but by a high velocity, low flying aircraft. Peering out from underneath the Terra Force leader's camouflaged body, Steiner caught sight of the twin afterburners of a jet fighter as it banked steeply, vanishing up into the flickering storm clouds above.

The weight lifted from Steiner's back and a metal shrouded hand heaved him to his feet.

'This rain will wash away our tracks,' Samson said, as the two men moved forwards once more, 'but they'll keep searching the area in case they missed anyone. We need to up the pace.'

The ground sloped down, Steiner stumbled and grabbed onto a stunted, sodden tree. The branch he'd selected, too brittle to support his weight, snapped with a resounding crack. Falling to his knees, Steiner found himself looking into a small hole sunken into a shelf of bedrock. Peering back at him out of this shadowy pit was a face, its eyes wide.

Steiner barely had time to move as a small figure flashed past him, out into the rain and off into the night. Scrambling up, Steiner saw Samson had raised his gun, preparing to shoot. Without thinking Steiner threw himself at the Colonel just as a stifled shot exploded from the muzzle with a flash of flame and smoke.

'Are you out of your fucking mind?!' Samson's voice seethed from within his helmet.

'I just stopped you from murdering a small boy.'

'No, you just compromised our position!' Samson shoved his heavy rifle into Steiner's unresisting hands and loped off, his indistinct outline fading quickly from view.

Now all alone, Steiner directed the small light from the heavy weapon at the rain swept desert floor, gingerly following the path taken by Samson and the startled boy. A full quarter of an hour passed before Samson returned; the limp body of a child under one arm.

'He was a fast little bastard,' Samson said as he approached.

'You killed him?' Steiner was horrified beyond measure.

Samson didn't reply, opting instead, to dump his lifeless load at Steiner's feet.

No sooner had Samson let him go than the child sprang up, making to flee once more. Samson's arm struck out like an uncoiling viper, his cat-like reflexes snuffing out the boy's escape plan in the blink of an eye.

'Let me go!' The child struggled against Samson's unyielding grip, his limbs and body contorting wildly in an attempt to break free.

Samson placed a hand over the bedraggled boy's mouth and knelt down to his eye level. The colonel's mask-like helmet, emanating an eerie green glow, must have been a terrifying sight to behold for one so young.

'Be quiet, boy,' Samson said, pulling out a long serrated bowie knife, which he then held in front of the child's terrified eyes, 'or I'll make sure you stay silent – permanently.'

'Leave him be, Colonel,' Steiner said in his most authoritative tone, placing a hand on the boy's small shoulder and moving to stand in front of him, shielding him from Samson's monstrous form.

Samson stood up, towering over Steiner and their new companion. 'You'd risk our mission for a child?' Samson's voice was cutting. 'He'll be dead like everyone else soon enough; in fact he might even be better off dying now, considering what's to come.'

'Life is still life, Colonel, regardless of its longevity. I'll look after the boy if you're so worried about him.'

Samson stared down at Steiner, the faceless visor concealing his expression. 'Fine, but if he becomes a problem I won't hesitate to do what's necessary.'

'You'll do as I command, Colonel, and you won't touch another hair on this child's head. Do you understand me? Not a hair!'

Samson grunted and leant down, extending his shrouded face towards Steiner's own. 'If you think you're still in control, old man, you're mistaken. Keep the infant close; he's your responsibility now.'

Reclaiming his rifle, Samson stood aside and motioned for Steiner and the boy to lead on, and lead on they did. The rain had slowed now, the storm shifting its position northwest as the troop of three headed east, away from Steadfast and the U.S. military that guarded its exits. Despite the passing of the tempest, the night sky remained oppressive, its starless nature a poignant reminder as to the ever present dust cloud drifting in the upper atmosphere high above them.

'We need shelter,' Samson told Steiner after they'd walked another half mile. 'They're sending out more drones and helicopters from Fort Bliss to search the area.'

'How do you know that?' Steiner picked his way with care through a dense section of brush, the small lad close on his heels.

'A marine was kind enough to let me borrow his radio. I patched into their feed. I don't get all communications, but enough to improve our chances of evasion.'

'There is no shelter.' Steiner felt desperation rising. 'We're still miles from the Darklight compound. If we're caught out here they'll kill us all where we stand.'

'I know a place,' a timid voice spoke up.

Samson turned his torch light onto the young boy's face; he blinked against the sudden brightness, his pupils contracting while drops of rain trickled down his face.

Steiner bent down on one knee, giving the boy what he hoped was a friendly smile. 'What's your name? Mine's George.'

The child glanced at Samson looking fearful.

'Don't worry about him.' Steiner gave Samson a stern stare. 'He's just a nasty bully. Do you have any bullies at your school?'

The boy nodded mutely.

'And what have your parents told you to do when dealing with a bully?'

'My father says I must stand up to them,' the boy said, regaining confidence at the mention of his parent.

'That's right,' Steiner said encouragingly. 'A bully is a coward, we all know that, don't we, Colonel?'

Samson gave a growl. 'Don't push your luck.'

Steiner laughed, trying to show he wasn't scared by Samson's threats. 'See, he's not so scary is he?'

'Kuruk,' the boy said, 'my name's Kuruk.'

'Kuruk,' Steiner repeated, pleased he'd managed to get him to open up. 'Do you know somewhere we can hide, Kuruk, a building maybe?'

Kuruk nodded his head again. 'There's a barn not far from here, I go there to play sometimes.'

'Does it have a storm shelter?' Samson said.

Kuruk looked to Steiner, still clearly afraid of the colonel. Steiner raised his eyebrows and smiled once more, conscious that forces from Fort Bliss closed on their location.

'Yes,' Kuruk said.

Steiner brushed raindrops from his glasses. 'Can you take us there?'

'Uh-huh.' Kuruk held out his hand which Steiner took. 'This way,' he said, pulling Steiner in the opposite direction to the one in which they'd been headed.

It wasn't long before a rickety, high-sided barn inched into sight out of the darkness. Its walls had seen better days, with planks of wood hanging off in places, exposing the interior to the elements. Steiner pulled at the double doors. They were locked. Samson lashed out with a heavy boot, splintering the wood with ease and sending both doors swinging inwards.

Steiner went to walk inside but Samson had gone stock still, blocking his way with an outstretched arm.

'Colonel?' Steiner said.

Samson held up a hand for quiet. 'Someone's approaching,' he said, after a moment's pause, 'get inside.'

Steiner did as he was told, guiding Kuruk along with him. The Colonel must have picked up a signal on the radar system built into his helmet's HUD. This technology always seemed to Steiner to give its user the impression they possessed some kind of precognitive ability. *It's just as well it does, considering our current predicament*, Steiner thought.

At that moment a voice could be heard, calling out into the night.

'Kuruk! Kuruk, where are you?!'

'Father?' Kuruk pulled against Steiner's hold. 'Father!'

The boy slipped beyond Steiner's reach, turned on a torch he'd been keeping hidden and headed for the exit. Simultaneously the barn doors swung open to reveal a Native American man holding a shotgun.

'Drop it!' Samson's voice came from out of the shadows, halting Kuruk in his tracks.

The Apache Indian bent down, placed his weapon on the damp dusty floor and then stood back up, arms raised. Samson's translucent shape hovered in Kuruk's torchlight, the beam appearing to bend as the rays came into contact with the armour's individual panels.

'Who are you people?' the man said, his arms encircling his son protectively.

Samson, his assault rifle trained on the newcomer, deactivated his active camouflage and walked round to stand next to Steiner, while Kuruk hugged his father around the waist.

Steiner moved forwards. 'We mean you no harm.'

'Your friend doesn't appear to agree with you.'

'Lower your gun, Colonel,' Steiner said, 'they're not a threat.'

The imposing weapon dipped towards the floor, Samson perhaps seeing the sense in Steiner's request.

'Sir, we need your help,' Steiner said to Kuruk's father.

'I'm no sir, but you may call me Norroso.'

'Norroso, I need your help, it is a matter of extreme importance. Many lives depend on my actions and perhaps now, on yours too. People are looking for us and we need a place to hide, or better still some transport.'

The Apache considered Steiner's heartfelt request, seemingly undaunted by the situation that faced him. 'My people come to me for advice,' Norroso said, his tone conversational. 'They tell me things they have done. They ask me if the spirits of our forefathers see their deeds. I tell them if they are worried then their actions are shameful. If they are hopeful they need not be troubled. Do you know what my people are called?'

Steiner shook his head; the man's measured yet abstract words almost hypnotic in their effect.

'We go by many names,' Norroso continued his narrative. 'Jicarilla Apache, Native American, or in days past the white man called us the Red Indian. But we are to ourselves the Tinde, or Dinde, *the People*. Our brothers from the plains name us Kinya-Inde, *people who live in fixed houses*. Tan-nah-shis-en, *men of the woodland*. Keop-tagui, *mountain Apache* and many more. But we have another name, a little used name, Haisndayin, which translates as *people who came from below*. We are descended from the first peoples to leave the underworld, the ancestors of mankind. Our history is passed down from generation to generation, unaltered through song and verse.'

Fascinated, Steiner listened, all the time wondering what the man was leading up to.

After Norroso had let his words sink in he began again. 'You have led man back to the underworld in our time of darkness,' Norroso said. 'Beneath the earth is our true nature. We belong to the land as the land belongs to us.'

Is he indicating he knows we are from Steadfast? Steiner wondered. It certainly seemed that way. The GMRC were aware of certain theories about underground facilities that circulated amongst minority groups around the world; these tales of fancy had been around long before the Subterranean Programme had even existed. Was it so surprising that their secret was more transparent than they'd previously thought? After all, aboriginal peoples, still living off the land, were always more in touch with their surroundings than those living in modernity.

'We are kindred spirits, you and I,' Norroso told Steiner. 'If I can help you, I will. Come, follow me.'

The Apache turned, his long braided hair, separated into twin tassels on either side of his head, swaying across his proud chest as he moved.

'Stop!' Samson's gun surged up as the man reached out to open the doors which had swung closed.

Norroso looked back, shaking his head he moved Kuruk out of harm's way. 'If you mean to shoot me, *man of mist*,' he said, holding out his arms to provide Samson with a perfect target, 'shoot now and return me to our creator.'

'Put your weapon down, man,' Steiner said, his tone hushed. 'Don't look a gift horse in the mouth.'

Samson lowered the rifle again, but only when Steiner moved between it and the Apache, bisecting his line of sight.

Norroso and Kuruk took this as their cue to move back outside.

'Are you coming?' Steiner asked the colonel.

Samson strode forward to pick up Norroso's discarded firearm. 'Are you buying this cryptic bullshit?'

'We need this man's help,' Steiner said, keeping his voice low, 'and if he wants to help us, I don't particularly care what he says. Now let's go before he changes his mind.'

Samson didn't reply, but his silence spoke volumes as he followed Steiner out of the ramshackle building. With Norroso in the lead, the group of four moved with haste through a selection of trails that criss-crossed the hidden landscape. In less than a quarter of an hour they approached a small huddle of buildings, the windows of one brimming with a warm yellow light which flooded out onto the damp veranda that surrounded it.

Norroso mounted the steps that led up to his house.

'Stop!' Samson said.

'You wanted a means to travel, did you not?' The big Apache pointed to a row of stables across from the house. 'I need to unlock the outbuilding over yonder, and to do that I need keys.'

'You wait here, with me,' the Colonel said to Norroso. 'You,' he gestured to Steiner, 'go in with the boy.'

Steiner took Kuruk's hand in his own after Norroso nodded to the lad to indicate he should go with Steiner.

'Be quick about it,' Samson said, before Steiner and the boy disappeared inside. 'They'll be here soon.'

The door closed behind the professor, Samson's warning that the reinforcements from Fort Bliss were on their way at the forefront of his mind, the need for urgency essential.

Steiner had little time to take in the warm surroundings of Kuruk's home as the young boy rushed to the other side of the room, picked up a set of keys and returned to Steiner to deposit them in his hand.

'You won't let the demon hurt my father will you, George?' Kuruk's eyes searched Steiner's face for reassurance.

The question and Kuruk's fearful expression made Steiner feel awful. 'You have my word,' Steiner said, while praying he could keep a rein on Samson's actions.

Kuruk, only nine or ten years old, seemed to accept Steiner's words and opened the door so the team of two could return outside. Steiner handed the keys to Norroso, who then led them to the end section of the building he'd previously mentioned. Putting his shoulder against the edge of the door, Norroso pushed it to one side, the thick timber panel sliding on a set of metal rails with a great screeching groan. The air that had been trapped inside wafted out, the smell of fresh manure and hay unmistakable.

Norroso, now using his son's torch, shone a light over a thick mud splattered white sheet, which covered a bulky shape in the gloom. With a quick tug, Norroso pulled the cover free to reveal a glossy, deep red, thirty year old pick-up truck. Steiner gaped at the huge alloy wheels that sparkled in the shadows, their thick knobbly off-road tyres setting off the imposing front grille and bull bars of the AEV Dodge Ram expedition vehicle.

'Wow,' Steiner said in awe.

Norroso mustered a chuckle at Steiner's surprise. 'What did you expect, a horse?'

'I always wanted one of these.' Steiner stroked the pristine metal panelling with a gentle caress.

'Does it have fuel?' Samson asked, bypassing Steiner, opening a door and climbing into the driver's seat.

'It's a hybrid. I had it converted. The rear tray acts like a tip-up truck, too, a special mechanism I added myself, and it does have gas in, yes.'

Steiner opened the passenger door and pulled himself up into the mechanical beast. Norroso put his foot onto the door sill and leaned inside to flick down the vanity mirror, dropping a set of keys into Steiner's lap. Samson snatched them up, inserted the key into the ignition and turned her over. The engine roared into life.

'Norroso, I don't know how to thank you.' Steiner closed the door and wound down the electric window. 'People may come and ask questions; it would be a good idea if you weren't here when they do.'

'May is not will,' Norroso said, 'but if they come we know less than nothing, only that someone stole our truck. Isn't that so, Kuruk?'

Kuruk nodded at his father's behest.

Samson selected first gear from the manual gearbox and instantly stalled it, giving Steiner the opportunity to get back out of the vehicle.

'What are you doing?!' Samson restarted the truck.

Steiner took Norroso's hand in both his own. 'You have trusted me so far, God only knows why. I must return the favour. In eight months' time this whole area will be destroyed. I can't tell you why or how, but you must take your family far away from here, the eastern states if you can. Do you understand? This place is no longer safe for you.'

Norroso looked at Steiner with sad eyes. 'We can leave our home as much as our home can leave us.'

Steiner didn't think the man would just up and leave his ancestors' land on his say so; why would he? they'd only just met, after all. It hadn't stopped him trying, though, which at least gave him some small comfort. Able to stay no longer, Steiner ruffled Kuruk's bushy black hair and then, with a final despairing look at Norroso, got back into the pick-up. Samson gunned the accelerator and the vehicle lurched forwards, its wide tyres thrusting them out into the open air.

The main headlights ablaze, the truck soon breached the outer fence of the smallholding but rather than continue Samson hit the brakes, sending them into a four wheel skid. Stopped, Samson made to get out, but Steiner caught his arm.

'Where are you going?'

'They've seen us,' Samson said by way of explanation.

'So?'

'You think Joiner won't have his agents scour this whole area in case anyone escaped?'

'So help me, God, Colonel, if you kill those people, I will turn you in at my first opportunity.'

Samson hesitated, Steiner's conviction compelling him to reconsider.

Steiner's eyes blazed with an unquenchable fire. 'Do not doubt me, Colonel.'

Samson closed the door and pressed a button on the side of his helmet to retract the visor and face plate, his own gaze no less potent. 'Very well, but remember this moment; you owe me now.'

With that Samson re-engaged his visor and floored the accelerator. The tail of the truck swung out as it slid from the gravel and bounced up onto a tarmac road. Now thundering along, they quickly reached an intersection. Samson slowed down as they approached and Steiner squinted out of the windscreen at the road signs ahead.

'We need to head east to the Darklight compound,' Steiner told him. 'We might be able to pick up more equipment there and get some support from any soldiers manning it.'

Samson turned left onto the highway.

'Where are you going?' Steiner said. 'We needed to take a right; you're going the wrong way!'

'Change of plan.' Samson drove at high speed down Route 64 in the wrong direction.

'What? What do you mean, change of plan?! There is only one plan!!'

'There's something else we need to do before we help the people in Steadfast.'

'There is nothing more important than that.' Steiner swivelled around in his seat as if he could see their intended destination retreating before his eyes through the rear window.

'There is for me,' Samson said, 'and you're going to help me do it.'

'Like hell I will!'

'If you don't, the people in Steadfast are already dead. Help me and I guarantee, afterwards, I will do everything possible to get those left behind in Steadfast to safety. Besides, you owe me, unless I should go back and deal with that loose end?' Samson slowed their travel with the brake pedal.

Steiner cursed Samson to the four winds, struggling to get his intense anger and frustration back under control. 'What do you need me to do?' he said at last, aware that Samson held all the cards.

Samson increased their speed again and the heavy-duty four-by-four barrelled on into the night. 'That's for me to know and you to find out.'

CHAPTER TWENTY-SEVEN

'WHERE ARE WE GOING, COLONEL?' Steiner asked the SFSD commander in weary resignation. Samson had been driving for hours, intentionally avoiding the interstate network, citing their passage would be less conspicuous on the smaller roads.

'Are you heading for the western coast? If you want my help, you need to tell me something.'

Samson stayed silent, as he had ever since they'd begun their impromptu journey. Reaching down to his waist, without taking his eyes off the road, the colonel popped open a pouch on his belt and withdrew something small and red, placing it in his mouth.

Steiner gritted his teeth, the Colonel's obstinacy getting to him. *What is this madman up to?*

'Colonel, I will need your help to rescue those in Steadfast. On my own, the chances of success are greatly reduced. Whatever it is you need to accomplish, it is clearly important to you. If you tell me what your plans are I might be able to help you achieve them more quickly, which will, in turn, let us return our attention to our main mission.'

Samson glanced in Steiner's direction, a reaction that told him the man was at least listening to what he said.

'Give me something, damn it, man!' Steiner raged at him, unable to keep his emotions in check any longer.

Samson looked over at Steiner again, appraising him. 'There's an army outpost in the city of St. George,' he said, breaking his silence.

'And what is it you want in St. George?'

'Supplies.'

Steiner's hopes rose. 'To replace the communication systems we lost?'

'Perhaps.'

A lorry whooshed past them in the opposite direction, its cab lit up like a Christmas tree on crack.

Steiner's mind raced, seeking a way to phrase his questions that would elicit more than monosyllabic responses. 'You need me to help you, don't you? I'm a key part of whatever you're planning to do. Don't you think your chances of success will go up if you let me in on the details? You might as well make use of me now that you have me.'

Samson snorted in derision.

Steiner frowned. 'What, you don't think I can improve your chances, or I'm not necessary to achieve your goal?'

'Pick one.'

Steiner gave up; he knew Samson wasn't about to let him in on his little secret anytime soon. *I'll just have to play along until I find a way not to*, he thought. At least they'd evaded the army's forces in and around Dulce and those deployed from Fort Bliss; they were well away from that threat now. Would Joiner's forces discover two people had escaped Steadfast and the fight on the surface? Hopefully not; he just prayed Norroso had the good sense to reconsider his warnings and leave town, or better yet, the state.

Steiner was well aware this major diversion in his plan, instigated by Samson, would severely delay his efforts in rescuing Nathan and everyone else left behind in Steadfast; but he also knew it was eight months until the next meteorite hit, time aplenty to get things back on track. The problem was, the more time he dedicated to Samson's agenda, the greater the chances of being apprehended by Joiner's agents, or the army acting under his control. As various scenarios unfolded in Steiner's head the roadside scenery sped past, briefly illuminated at the extremities of the pick-up's main beams.

Another hour faded from reality, the conversation continuing its previous incarnation of non-existence. Steiner, exhausted by recent events, felt himself dozing off, his head heavy and his eyelids drooping.

♦

Professor Steiner awoke with a start, his concept of time foggy and skewed. Rather than the brightly lit road ahead, only blackness remained. The non-existent engine noise belied the sensation that the car still moved at high speed, felt by Steiner through the seat and floorpan. Looking to his left, the faint glow from the instrument panel barely registering, the outline of the armour-clad figure of Samson still sat at the wheel. Steiner, his faculties returning, deduced the colonel had switched to the vehicle's electrical power train and was using his helmet's night vision capabilities to continue driving in the dark.

Steiner sat up straighter in his seat. 'Are you expecting trouble?'

'Checkpoints,' Samson said.

Steiner assumed they must be approaching the city limits. As if on cue a signpost drifted by, a single light suspended over the lettering, which read: *Welcome to the City of St. George, Utah.*

'Won't it look suspicious if we cruise up with no lights on?' Steiner asked.

'I want to get the lay of the land before we enter,' Samson said.

Wow, a whole sentence, it must be my birthday, Steiner thought to himself, a bitter smile creeping onto his face.

In the distance a large barrier had been erected, floodlights all around, as the road they were on merged with the larger interstate converging from the right. Samson pulled the Dodge Ram over to the side of the road and onto the sparsely vegetated dry earth of the Mojave Desert, the wide off-road tyres crunching to a quiet halt. To Steiner, all was dark except for the faint light from the dashboard. In the deep shadows he could make out Samson putting his hand to his helmet, pressing a combination of buttons on its side.

A minute passed before the colonel opened the car door and got out, the vehicle's interior light switching on and a cold breeze gusting inside as he did so. 'Get out,' Samson told him.

Steiner unfastened his seat belt and stepped down from the pick-up, his movements restricted by the black body armour he still wore. Samson moved around the car to meet him and then slipped a long-bladed dagger from its sheath.

Steiner's eyes widened in fear and he took a step backwards. 'What are you doing!?'

Samson advanced and the knife flicked out towards him. Looking down, Steiner waited for the searing pain to begin and the blood to flow. Neither happened, instead his armour covering his chest and back, fell to the floor with a clunk. Steiner looked up in surprise. 'What—'

'Turn around,' Samson said, cutting off his question before it had formed.

Steiner did as he was told and the rest of the bulky gear was sliced free, until Steiner stood, wearing only the red climbing coveralls he'd started out with back in Steadfast.

Samson put the knife away. 'Drive into the city, I'll meet you inside, six blocks in. Don't park near the street lights, keep to the shadows.'

'I only have my GMRC paperwork,' Steiner said while Samson scooped up the obsolete protective clothing and deposited it in the rear passenger seat foot-well.

'Tell the checkpoint guards, you're a mechanic passing through town and you need some gas.' Samson attached his gun to his back-plate and then tapped at some buttons on the inside of his wrist armour. 'They'll give you a temporary pass and let you through. On your own you should be fine; if I was with you we'd stick out like sore thumbs and they'd note down our passage in their log book, or worse, report the entrance of an unauthorised military officer from an unheard of regiment to their superiors and then try and detain us.'

Samson activated his armour, sending tendrils of miniature lightning discharging over each panel, the camouflage system shimmering over his entire body like a stardust encrusted cloak. 'I'll see you on the other side.' The ghostly figure of the colonel jogged away into the darkness.

Steiner stood for a moment gathering his thoughts before shutting his door, walking round the vehicle and getting into the driver's seat. Adjusting it so he could reach the pedals, a thought sprang into his mind. *Why don't I just turn the car around and head back to the Darklight compound in New Mexico? Samson can run off and do what he likes and I can get on with helping those stranded in Steadfast.* The idea was very tempting, but he knew he might never make it to the Darklight base and, even if he did, there was no guarantee there would be anyone there to help him. It could even be staked out by the U.S. Army. If he approached on his own, his lack of military nous might lead him straight into the arms of those he wanted to avoid. He needed Samson, as the colonel, no doubt, still needed him.

Turning the combustion engine back on, Steiner turned a knob to activate the car's headlights and then pulled back out onto the road. In no time at all he drew to a stop in front of a slim, yellow and black chequerboard barrier.

Two men in National Guard uniforms approached from either side of the vehicle, their assault weapons held in their hands with a nonchalant ease. Steiner wound his window down.

'Good morning, sir.' The man withdrew a flashlight from his breast pocket and shone it into Steiner's face, making him squint.

'Morning.' Steiner conjured up a tired smile as the second man shone his own torch into the front and back seats of the pick-up.

'Nice truck,' the first soldier said, 'anything in the back?'

Steiner swore inwardly, he had no idea if anything was stored in the flatbed. He shook his head a fraction.

'Papers, ID.' The soldier held out a hand and took his eyes off Steiner when his colleague flipped down the tailgate and climbed up onto the tray area, sending the suspension rocking.

Steiner made a show of looking in the glove compartment. 'I'm sorry, I must have left it in my other car.'

The soldier glared at him and then the car bounced again as the other man, after finishing his inspection, jumped back down to the ground.

'Would it be possible to get a temporary pass?' Steiner asked, following Samson's instructions. 'I just need to refuel, I've got a job on in the next town along and I'm not sure if I've got enough gas to go back to—' he stuttered to a halt. *What was the name of the last town they came through? I don't know*, he thought, *I was asleep at the time!* 'Everything okay?' he said to the second man, who'd come to stand by his window, wheedling out of his faltering lie with aplomb.

'What do you do, exactly?' the second soldier asked.

'I'm a mechanic, work on cars, mostly classics like this one.' *Shut up George*, he said to himself, *the key to a good lie is in its simplicity*.

The two men looked at him with what Steiner thought must be intense suspicion. *Do I even look like a mechanic?* he wondered.

The first man got out a paper pad and started scribbling on it. He walked round to the rear of the car, came back, tore off a sheet, and handed it to Steiner, the thin paper rustling.

'That's your pass,' the man told him. 'You've got two hours before you need to exit the western boundary of the city. If you stay any longer than that you may be arrested for a violation of GMRC curfew regulations.'

Steiner thanked the men and gave them an appreciative wave when they lifted the barrier, allowing him to pass underneath. Steiner drove through the outskirts of St. George, its centre blazing with light in response to the dust cloud created by AG5. This was the first time Steiner had witnessed the daytime measures actually working, having been ensconced in Steadfast ever since the asteroid collided with the planet many months before.

Passing the fifth road on the left, Steiner brought the truck to a stop down a side road, away from the street lights. Twenty minutes later Samson had still not reappeared. *Has something happened to him? I hope not,* he thought, *otherwise I'm in serious trouble.* Contemplating his concern for Samson's welfare and the perversity therein, Steiner nearly jumped out of his skin when he looked to his left, to see two green glowing eyes peering back at him.

Samson opened the door and Steiner shuffled over to the passenger seat, letting the Terra Force commander enter. A potent smell of stagnant water and refuse wafted inside, forcing Steiner to put the back of his hand to his nose.

Samson dumped his weapon on the back seat and removed his helmet. His armour was covered in mud and dirt; coupled with the foul aroma, this suggested he'd been through an assault course, doubling as a cesspit, rather than running across an arid desert plain.

'You took your time,' Steiner said. 'Did you find the outpost?'

Samson ran a hand over his sweaty scalp, his short hair spraying out a fine mist. 'I did. Do you have a pass?'

Steiner nodded, handing over the scrap of paper.

'Good, I'll drive in and you'll stay inside the vehicle. If I can, I'll requisition some communication equipment to replace the kit we lost.'

Was Samson trying to make up for his past transgressions? If he was, he had a long, long way to go, but it was a start.

♦

Samson drove up to the small U.S. Army compound, stopping at the metal mesh gate which served as its entrance. A soldier dressed in green and brown camos appeared out of a rectangular Portakabin to greet them. Samson had prepared for such an eventuality back in Steadfast and held out his identity badge for the man to read.

The guard noted something down on his clipboard and handed the card back to Samson. 'Thank you, sir. Parking is straight down, second turning on your right.'

The soldier unlocked the gate, swinging it back and in, and then snapped into a bolt upright stance to salute Samson as he moved the pick-up inside. Samson nodded to the guard as he passed, throwing him an easy salute in return.

'Haven't you just declared our location to all and sundry?' Steiner's grating voice said, as Samson followed the empty road into the tiny base.

Samson fought down the urge to jab his elbow into the man's face. 'I handed him a doctored ID badge.' He looked left and right, searching the brightly lit area for his intended destination. 'Some of us came prepared.'

The professor made a huffing noise, perhaps in disapproval of his comment. Samson didn't much care what the professor thought; he had a job to do. *Now, where is their supply depot*, he wondered? The vehicle crawled along the primary avenue, rolling past the turn for the car park suggested by the corporal on the gate. There! Off to one side, he saw a heavily fortified building. Samson kicked the car up a gear and took it round to the rear of the structure. Reversing it up to a secured loading bay entrance, he switched the ignition off, the purr of the engine rumbling to silence.

Without a word to the professor he got out, slamming the door shut behind him. A small square metal box hung on the wall to the side of the up and over door. Pulling the front panel open, its rusty hinges screeching in protest, Samson hit the intercom button located inside.

'Yes, what do you want?' A voice crackled through the antiquated system.

'I need access to this facility,' Samson said with authority, 'crack open loading bay two.'

'There's no one scheduled for a pick up today, who is this?'

'Colonel Hemmingway,' Samson replied, quoting his pseudonym.

A lengthy pause followed. 'Can you put your service badge up to the camera please, Colonel,' the man's voice said, the tone more respectful than before.

Samson stepped back, turning his head left, right and then finally up, to see a CCTV mast protruding from the upper storey of the three floored structure. He held his card up to it and waited.

A few more moments passed. 'Thank you, sir,' the voice said.

Soon after, a deep hum vibrated through the thick metal door, an internal mechanism hoisting it up to reveal an expansive loading area. Samson returned to the car, reversed it inside and then got out once again, at no point speaking to his passenger.

Leaving his helmet and rifle behind, Samson stomped up a flight of concrete steps at the rear of the garage and into a narrow corridor, which brought him to the acquisitions desk. During his jog into the city, he'd taken the opportunity to cover his armour in filth and soil from a drainage ditch; the purpose of such action, to hide the emblems on his armour from prying eyes. He may have had the rank of Colonel in the U.S. Army, but he was also deployed in a top secret underground base and a member of a highly classified Special Forces team. Operating on the surface for the Subterranean Detachment was not unheard of, but wandering around amongst regular army staff was, and since he wanted to fly below the radar he'd decided to take the appropriate measures.

The bulk of the room in which he now stood was blocked off by a counter that ran from one side to the other. Behind this substantial piece of furniture, rows upon rows of shelving stood in alignment, jammed full of crates and brown cardboard cartons of all shapes and sizes. Interspersed throughout, a muddle of vacuum wrapped clothing and all manner of sundries and surplus. On the wall behind Samson, a large depiction of the regimental insignia for the United States Army Ordnance Corps had been painted. The flaming black bomb, combined with two crossed cannons, surrounded by a red circular belt and containing the inscription *ORDNANCE CORPS U.S.A.*, in gold lettering.

'The design was approved in 1986,' a croaky voice said from behind the desk, making Samson turn to see a haggard, balding veteran hobbling into view, dressed in plain green combats. 'Although,' he continued, pointing with a gnarled hand, 'the branch insignia, the shell and flame depicted by the flaming bomb at the top there, was commissioned in the eighteen thirties, over two hundred years ago. It's the oldest insignia in the army.'

Samson looked back at the emblem again. 'I always liked the 504th's myself.'

'Ah, don't tell me.' The ordnance officer waggled his finger in Samson's direction. 'Parachute infantry, a blue shield with a flaming yellow sword. Am I right?'

'Almost.' Samson walked over to place his armoured gloves on the desk, while he scanned the shelving for any sign of the equipment he desired. 'The sword is actually yellow with a white blade, surrounded by yellow fire.'

'Yes, yes! A white blade, you're quite right, Colonel. Now let me see, their motto is—' The aging sergeant removed his U.S. Army embossed baseball cap and rubbed his chin.

'Strike Hold,' Samson said, after giving the man ample opportunity to recollect it.

'Strike Hold, yes, of course! So, Colonel,' the soldier said putting his cap back on, 'what can I do for you this miserable day?'

Samson gauged the man before him, a Sergeant Rogers according to his name tag; was he a rule breaker? *No, but a rule bender – perhaps*, he decided. 'I need your help, Sergeant.' He leaned in and lowered his voice, despite there being no one else present. 'I'm on a covert, time critical mission and I need high end, high power ordnance to get the job done. I was told you might be the man to help me.'

The sergeant blew his cheeks out with a puff of air. 'Do you have any acquisition orders processed through the computer system?'

Samson shook his head.

Rogers sighed, his shoulders slumping. 'Then, I'm afraid I can't help you. Everything must go through the system these days. Long gone are the times when a senior officer could fill out a form on the fly.'

'Is there really nothing you can do?' Samson asked, thinking fast. 'I have men stranded down in Mexico on a black op gone bad. The top brass have disavowed our excursion into the sovereign territory of another nation. I'm on my own and my men's only chance of getting back over the border alive is down to me – down to this.'

'I thought your armour looked high-tech; elite Special Forces?' The sergeant searched Samson's grubby attire for identifying marks.

Samson nodded.

'And your boys are stuck over the border?'

Samson didn't respond, holding the sergeant's gaze in what he hoped was a look of needy desperation.

'It's not like we're in peace time, is it?' Rogers said, more to himself than to Samson, searching for a way around the problem and trying to justify such a move in his own mind. 'We're at Defcon 3 after all. Mitigating circumstances equate to special dispensation in my book. In fact—' He moved away from the counter with his awkward gait and disappeared from sight, before reappearing a minute later with a crumpled form in his hand. 'Voila!' He banged the paperwork down on the desk in front of Samson, who looked at it with a critical eye.

Rogers, a tad downcast that his efforts didn't receive the accolade he believed they deserved, flattened out the paper with two hands and then rearranged it so it was perfectly aligned for Samson to read, giving it one last twitch so it was just so. Stepping back he gave Samson a grin, raised his eyebrows and flicked his eyes at the form.

Samson held back his frustration, which had been mounting ever since their conversation had started. Pulling the pale green document towards him, he ran his eyes over the heading.

E.A.R.

Emergency Acquisition Request

FORM AJ11

'I'd forgotten about the old E.A.R. form,' Sergeant Rogers said, 'not sure how with a name like that, but there you go. Haven't used one for – well – must be going on fifteen years now. Just fill it in and I can run it through the system later. Strictly speaking the AJ form series went defunct years back, but it can be explained away as an admin error. I'll probably get a bawling out for it, but if it's gonna save some of our boys, then it's the least I can do.'

Rogers handed Samson a pen, which he used to fill in the form with his falsified information and then passed it back for the sergeant to check over.

'Excellent.' Rogers put the document to one side. 'So, Colonel, what did you have in mind?'

♦

Half an hour passed and Samson had loaded up a mound of equipment on a trolley, including some old communication gear Rogers had found tucked away. According to the sergeant the coms kit was part of a much larger cache that had found its way into the ordnance lock-up instead of the warehouse used by the Quartermaster Corps at another base. It wasn't top-of-the-range by any stretch of the imagination, but considering their circumstances the professor would have to make do.

'Anti-vehicle mines, as ordered.' Rogers banged down a heavy steel case onto the worktop. 'These suckers will take out a tank no problem.'

Samson surveyed the assembled boxes of ammo, Claymore mines and grenades. Picking up the latest case, he slipped it between a collection of miniature drones and a couple of MX4 assault rifles.

'Have you got anything – bigger?' Samson asked.

Rogers looked at him for a moment. Lifting up a hinged part of the counter, the sergeant waddled out to join Samson in the front section of the room. Samson could now see the reason for the man's abnormal movement; his left leg was a mechanical limb.

Rogers caught his look and touched his artificial device with one hand. 'Got it blown off in Argentina, back in 2023.'

'Argentina was a cunt hair away from a janfu,' Samson said, recollecting the conflict back when he was a captain in the Marine Corps. 'The whole South American war was a fucking shit storm.'

'More like a bum fuck nowhere prize clusterfuck,' Rogers said. 'Where were you deployed?'

'All over, Brazil, Chile, Panama, Argentina.'

Solemn, Rogers nodded as he too recalled long past memories of the conflict.

'What's with the leg? That thing looks like its thirty years old.'

'Government overspend, or some such bullshit,' Rogers said as he led Samson out of another door and to a flight of stairs, which he began to ascend with difficulty.

Samson followed the slow progress of the man up to the first floor. 'Sounds about right.'

Rogers glanced back. 'That's the Big Green Dick at work, my friend.'

Samson nodded in agreement; the notorious shortcomings of army administration was so entrenched in a soldier's psyche it had been coined with its own phrase.

Eventually, Samson was led to a caged section on the first floor, the faint odour of machine oil and gunpowder swimming on the edge of his perception. Rogers unlocked the area with a digital code and then, using a set of keys, opened it up so Samson could enter.

'This is where we keep anything that has a little *je ne sais quoi*,' Rogers said, while Samson looked around at the weaponry on display. 'If it's high-tech and high-powered you seek, then you'll find it here.'

Samson pulled a streamlined rifle from its brackets, turning it over in his hands and then bringing it up to his shoulder to take a look down its scope.

'Latest beam weapon,' Rogers said, 'that will cut through walls, metals, even nano armour. It has limited ammo though, and a tendency to explode if a bullet penetrates its fuel cell.'

'Explode?'

'Yeah, when one of those babies goes up you don't want to be holding it, or be within fifty yards. They go off like a small bomb.'

Samson eyed the device. 'Sounds like a liability.'

'Not really.' Rogers pointed to the underside of the stock. 'The weak spot is underneath, which minimises the soldier's exposure during combat.'

Samson considered it for a moment, before handing Rogers the weapon. 'I'll take it.'

What's this? he wondered, moving off through to another section which was empty except for a ten foot tall crate, the wooden sides branded black with a single word: *PROTOTYPE*. Samson examined a hefty padlock on the front. 'What's in here?' he asked, rattling the lock.

'No idea, came in a month back. It's due to be shipped onto Fort Bliss, destined for some classified project, no doubt.'

'You don't have the key?'

'Nope.'

Samson withdrew a heavy dagger from his utility belt.

'I don't think you'll be able to prise it open with that,' Rogers said.

Samson looked at him and then depressed a small button on the handle. A faint high pitched whine accompanied a thin orange glow that ran around the edge of the blade.

Rogers looked amazed. 'Is that what I think it is?'

Samson grinned and waited for the heat to build in the thermal knife. Once the cutting edge throbbed white hot, Samson pressed the blade against the side of the thick steel padlock. It bit deep into the metal, cutting it cleanly in two in a matter of seconds, the glowing red hot pieces falling to the ground with dull clunks. Sliding back three substantial chrome bolts, Samson prised away the front of the case and leaned it up against the wall on his right.

'Fuck me sideways,' Rogers said as Samson stood back to admire the container's contents. 'You said you wanted high end, Colonel; I think this qualifies don't you?'

Samson didn't answer. He stared at the piece of hardware inside, trying to figure out what it was. At the side of the curiously shaped object, he spied a manual. Pulling it out from its plastic folder, he scanned through the pages. 'Interesting, I'll need a forklift to move this.'

Rogers gave a nervous cough. 'I'm sorry, Colonel, I don't think I'll be able to explain this thing going AWOL.'

Samson turned to fix the sergeant with a penetrating stare, watching as his silent, passive assault wilted the man's resolve. Rogers shifted to and fro, from his good foot to his artificial one. 'I suppose I could turn a blind eye,' he said, relenting.

'Good man.' Samson turned to replace the crate's front panel for transport.

♦

It wasn't long before Samson was back down at the pick-up, putting the final items in the back of the cab, the professor still sitting patiently in the front.

A persistent beeping, accompanied by a rotating orange lamp announced the arrival of the sergeant and the prototype weapon. Emerging from an aperture at the rear of the loading bay, a forklift rolled up to the back of the truck and deposited the crate past the open tailgate. The weight was released, making the back of the vehicle's suspension dip a few inches. Rogers then withdrew the forks and returned the small loader back from whence it had come. Samson, meanwhile, had pushed past some canvas sacks piled high at the side of the garage and retrieved a tarpaulin, which he lashed down over his newly acquired cargo. Satisfied everything was in order he went back to make sure his tracks were covered.

'You want the CCTV disc?' Rogers said.

'It's for the best,' Samson told him, itching to get back on the road.

Rogers shook his head at the folly he thought Samson was bringing upon himself. 'All right, but I'll have to write it down on the incident sheet, that it went walkabout. When they send someone round to break my balls over that prototype going missing, and they will, they'll put two and two together and come up with you; I'll have put your E.A.R. form through the system by then and your name will pop up like a gopher with a hot ass.'

'Do what you have to do.' Samson knew full well his information was bogus and he'd be long gone when that time came.

Rogers handed over a disc. 'I half wish I was going with you, Colonel,' he said, a wistful look in his eye. 'I hope you're able to rescue your men, they're lucky to have a CO willing to go out on a limb for them.'

Samson nodded his thanks, shook the man's hand and turned to walk away.

'Terra Force?' Rogers said, stopping Samson in tracks. 'That's a new one. And what's USSB Steadfast when it's at home?'

Samson, looked down at his left shoulder, where the dirt he'd strategically placed over his insignias had wiped off, most likely when he'd sourced the tarp. He moved back to the counter. 'Terra Force is the codename for Special Forces Subterranean Detachment.'

'Subterranean Detachment?' Rogers leaned forwards to peer at the exposed designs on Samson's armour.

'Yes, the army operates SFSD units throughout all the USSBs . We're the future of modern warfare.'

'The future, underground?' Rogers sounded confused. 'I can't see that happening. And what's a USSB?'

'United States Subterranean Base; there are ten of them that I know of. They're large underground complexes, cities, you might say.

I was told they were built in preparation for the asteroid, AG5, but it seems they're a lot more important than that.'

'How so?' Rogers said, fascinated by the information he was receiving.

'I recently found out six more asteroids are following in the wake of AG5; they will destroy all life on this planet.'

Rogers laughed, but his mirth faded away as Samson's humourless expression remained unchanged.

'You can't be serious?'

Samson nodded, his expression grave.

'Why haven't the government told anyone?'

'Why do you think?'

Rogers stared down at the ground as he processed the information. 'It does make sense, all these stories about water and food shortages in the news, martial law, the wars in other countries, the GMRC controlling everything—' Rogers looked up at Samson in alarm. 'I have to call my sister to warn her. What can I do? Where can we go? Where's the nearest of these USSBs?'

'There's one in Dulce, New Mexico, but you don't want to go there, believe me. Besides, you needn't worry about all that now.'

'What? Why?'

Samson jabbed out a flat rigid hand into the veteran's throat. Rogers doubled over, fighting for breath. Samson walked around the counter while the sergeant slipped to his knees, wheezing against his collapsed airway.

Rogers looked up into Samson's eyes, shocked and terrified by the unprovoked attack. Samson moved behind him and encircled his neck with his arms. With a quick, sharp twist, Samson broke his cervical spine, the bone and cartilage cracking as he did so. Samson held the body for some moments and then dropped it to the floor.

'I liked you, Sergeant,' Samson said to Rogers' lifeless form, 'but you gave me no choice.'

Picking up the corpse, Samson stuffed it into a wooden crate at the back of the storeroom and clipped the lid back on to conceal the grizzly sight inside. Scooping up a nail gun he found nearby, Samson secured the crate further, knowing such a move would extend the time it took for Rogers' body to be found by days, if not weeks. Moving fast now, he returned to the vehicle and the waiting professor.

'You planning on starting a war, Colonel?' the professor asked as he drove out and away from the ordnance warehouse.

'The war never stopped,' Samson plucked a few pills from his pouch and swallowed them with a practised ease, 'and it never will.'

CHAPTER TWENTY-EIGHT

PROFESSOR STEINER THOUGHT the colonel seemed more morose than normal as they left the city of St. George behind them. The truck given to them by Norroso was now laden with a veritable arsenal. Steiner could only guess at what Samson had in mind for it all; whatever it was it couldn't be good, unless, of course, he planned to use it to help those in Steadfast. Somehow, however, Steiner doubted that was the case. The SFSD commander had been as good as his word, though; Steiner looked round at the aging communication devices bumping about on the back seats as the pick-up bounced over the uneven road surface. He believed they might be capable of breaking the GMRC's encrypted feeds, gaining him access to the system that could prove crucial in reinstating himself on the council's Directorate. Whether the kit was sophisticated enough to prevent Joiner from hunting him down first was another matter entirely.

'So, where are we headed next?' he asked, not expecting a meaningful answer.

'Vegas.'

'I didn't take you for a gambler, Colonel.'

'I need to see a man.'

'About a dog?' Steiner said, unable to resist the quip.

'I need some more equipment.'

Steiner, pleasantly surprised his questions seemed to be reaping some results, pressed ahead, knowing he might not find the colonel in such a receptive mood again. 'Communication equipment?' he asked in hope.

'Computer hardware and software, I'm going to need you to hack a secure database.'

At last, we're getting somewhere, Steiner thought, *about time, too.* 'What sort of database did you have in mind?'

'The FBI.'

'Right,' Steiner said, unsure if he was capable of such a feat.

'Will that be a problem?' Samson asked in concern. 'I thought you were some kind of computer genius.'

'Hardly.'

Samson shot him a look of anger.

'But,' Steiner continued, regretting his first response, 'I am pretty good.'

'Stop shovelling that false modesty crap, can you do it or not?'

'Yes, with the right tools, I should be able to.' *What the hell,* Steiner thought to himself, *I already need to break into the GMRC system, why not the FBI too? In for a penny, as they say*. 'May I ask what I will be doing inside their database?'

'No!'

Samson's expression and body language warned Steiner to leave well enough alone. With the conversation as dead as a nail in its door, Steiner got comfortable as they followed the back roads once more, this time their destination the so-called entertainment capital of the world. Steiner had never been to the desert locked city before; he'd always seen it as a crass, vulgar place, full of debauchery and feeding off, and promoting, the baser, uglier traits of the human race. Greed, excess, gambling, lust, it certainly lived up to its self-proclaimed billing of *Sin City*. Steiner planned on keeping his head down when it came to Samson's mysterious and ill-timed quest, he just prayed his disappointment in this regard wasn't going to be assured.

♦

Enormous hoardings pulsed with vibrant, three dimensional displays, advertising events and shows throughout the Las Vegas Strip and beyond. The cornucopia of hotels, casinos, arcades, theme parks and resorts dazzled and amazed, the fantastical architectural splendours weaving their web of beauty and creativity through a skyline built to shine, tempt and titillate on an unprecedented scale. Giant domes and enclosed avenues stretched out in all directions, overlooked by neon signs and sculptured landmarks, bringing with them an endless array of glitz and glamour.

Professor Steiner stared out of his window at the streets, throbbing with revellers and traffic, the noise of thousands upon thousands of people and vehicles only outdone by the pounding music pouring out from almost every other building they passed. Samson stopped the car at a red light and pedestrians streamed across in front of them, coming in from all directions. Ahead, a hotel of immense proportions dominated the horizon. Spinning into the dark sky from its rooftop was a spectacular display of searchlights and lasers, their rays arcing up like the contrails of angels and sprites.

A troop of performing artists cut a swathe along the sidewalk, catching Steiner's eye. Their outlandish garb accentuated the rhythmic beat of their percussion instruments, which they played with a flamboyant vigour to the delight of the onlookers swept up in their wake. It seemed everyone here was trying to escape the dark, dull and often terrifying existence of the outside world. The sheer volume of people was staggering. *Yet another symptom of the dust cloud*, Steiner assumed. It was strange, though; getting into the city had been surprisingly easy, checkpoints lax and almost non-existent in places. It was as if the GMRC protocols had been universally ignored by general consent. Las Vegas had always courted the impression of having laws unto itself and the arrival of AG5 had apparently done little to alter the tradition laid down in decades past.

Samson turned a corner, the bright lights reflecting in the highly polished, lustrous red paintwork of the Dodge Ram pick-up truck. They drove down the side street, the exhaust burbling a deep growl. Steiner noticed some admiring glances aimed their way. He felt a spark of annoyance that he wasn't driving, then suppressed the feeling. *I have far more important things to think about than showing off*, Steiner chided himself, sending his suitably chastened ego to sulk in the deeper recesses of his mind.

'Are we there yet?' Steiner asked, his role of tormentor a pleasing distraction from the immense stresses he was under.

Samson didn't reply, most likely as he didn't have to. Pulling the car into an underground car park, the colonel found a suitable spot and turned the engine off, the keys rattling as he did so. Opening the door, he climbed out and Steiner did likewise.

Samson glared at Steiner and slammed his door shut, the noise echoing through the low ceilinged concrete structure. 'I didn't say you could come.'

Steiner shut his own door. 'I'm not some child, Colonel, whom you can boss around. I go where I please.'

Samson muttered an obscenity and picked a large, army issue overcoat out of the rear seat – something he must have sourced back at the depot – and stalked away, pulling it on over his armour as he went. Steiner trotted to catch up. He'd decided he needed to stretch his legs; hours stuck in the vehicle had made them begin to cramp up. Secretly, something he didn't want to admit even to himself, he'd also been seduced by the sights and sounds on their journey into the city, his previously held beliefs conveniently forgotten.

Samson pressed a button to call an elevator. 'Just keep your mouth shut. The man I'm meeting does not suffer fools.'

Steiner followed Samson into the lift. 'And yet he will suffer you,' he said as the shiny gold doors closed behind him.

Samson ignored him and Steiner, not for the first time, questioned his own sanity at goading such a man. He couldn't help himself, it seemed, he was hard-wired to mock and poke fun at the mean and the wicked. He abhorred bullies and Samson was a bully like no other. Perhaps it had something to do with being on the GMRC Directorate for so many years and the power that came with it, an invulnerability he'd grown accustomed to, perhaps? Whatever the reason, it was frightfully enjoyable, almost addictively so.

The music in the lift, a jaunty little number, seemed quite ridiculous with Samson standing there looking larger than life and as wicked as the skies were dark. A smile crept onto Steiner's lips as he imagined Samson dancing to the tune.

'Having fun?' Samson asked querulously, looking down at him.

'I am actually.' Steiner's smile broadened. 'It's been quite some time since I've had some R&R.'

At those words the doors opened and the two men walked from the lift, a wave of noise sweeping over them from the huge casino floor now in full view. Suspended over row upon row of gambling machines, magnificent gold chandeliers sparkled and shone, shining down their bright light on everything and everyone beneath. Further away, various games of chance played out on tables of various shapes, colours and forms.

They paced down an aisle of luscious red carpet and people pressed in around them on all sides. Samson, who found it hard to keep his temper in check at the best of times, barged people out of his way like an ogre with a toothache.

Steiner slowed while Samson pressed ahead. 'Why don't I wait here?'

'Fine,' Samson said, barely looking back before being swallowed up by the human sea.

Steiner peeled away from the thoroughfare towards a row of slot machines. All were taken except one and Steiner positioned himself in front of it to watch those alongside play their respective games. Coin after coin disappeared from a plastic bucket held by a grey haired woman, ten years his senior, sitting on a stool to his right. As she fed in her money, pressing the transparent brightly lit plastic buttons with an unerring frequency, she glanced over to see him watching her.

'Run out of money, honey?' she asked in a Texan drawl.

'Never had any to start with.'

The woman, dressed in a gaudy cardigan and a pair of mustard yellow corduroy trousers, dug into her stash and placed a handful of coins into Steiner's hurriedly outstretched palms. He looked at her in surprise, her generosity unexpected.

The woman laughed happily. 'Don't worry, sweetie, I've got plenty more where this came from. Knock yourself out.'

Steiner gave her a nod of his head, his smile wide. 'Much obliged.'

'You're welcome, honey,' she said, already continuing her game.

Turning his attention to the machine Steiner inserted a coin and watched the small, different coloured fruits spin round and round until the four adjacent wheels each came to a stop in turn, accompanied by a small bleep. Steiner assessed the games functions and the various buttons that went with it. Feeding in some more coins one at a time, his money rapidly disappearing, it became apparent that he wasn't about to win anytime soon. He now had two coins left and felt cheated and depressed at having lost it all, despite the fact it was not hard-earned, merely a kindly donation. 'It's the principle of the thing,' he said to himself. The machines were clearly rigged to rinse a person of every dollar they possessed. He glanced back along the lines at the people playing, their static stare zombie-like in its addiction.

Looking at the machine, Steiner had an idea. He recalled a news story he'd heard when he'd been lecturing at the California Institute of Technology, thirty years earlier. *Was it that long?* he thought, never ceasing to be astounded by the ephemeral nature of time. The tale, if he remembered it correctly, told of a man hacking into the NSA database using an antiquated dial-up modem. The simplicity of the idea had amazed Steiner at the time, such a wonderfully constructed theory utilising outdated techniques to crack a high-tech and supposedly ultra-secure network – pure genius.

The machine at which he stood had dual controls, button or voice activated. Switching to voice control, Steiner withdrew his small pocket computer and brought up an audio application. After some moments of trial and error he'd accessed the machine's internal system, the hold and nudge buttons lighting up on his command, the simple tones omitted from his computer acting like keys on a keyboard. Figuring out the code to induce a jackpot was now a formality, with a final tap of his index finger the wheels spun round once more. Round and round, until, one by one, they displayed the same image of a bunch of red cherries. Sirens blared and flashing lights erupted from the top of the machine, which flashed and shook itself as coins spewed forth.

'Oh my God, you did it!' His female benefactor looked overjoyed at his success. 'You won!'

Steiner grinned at her and slid his computer back into his pocket, the enemy vanquished. His pleasure at defeating the house was shorted-lived, however, when two pairs of hands clamped down on his arms to escort him away from the confused onlookers as the coins, still ejecting from the machine, now cascaded onto the floor itself.

Steiner soon found himself descending in an elevator. 'Have I done something wrong, gentlemen?' he asked, knowing all too well his own guilt.

The two bald-headed burly men, dressed in matching black suits, remained silent, their grip on him undiminished. On the breast pocket of each, the word 'security' had been embroidered in bold white lettering. Steiner was led down a cold, white-walled, basement corridor and into an area filled with a huge wallscreen, divided into scores of separate streams, all showing various parts of the casino, inside and out.

A man in a shirt and tie approached and addressed the two gorillas either side of Steiner, 'Put him in holding room five.'

'Yes, sir,' one of the apes said, his cruel beady eyes looking at Steiner like a crocodile eyeing up its next gazelle at the watering hole.

Steiner was shoved into a grey, empty room, but rather than being left alone, ape one, the no-necked wonder that seemed to have some capacity for speech, remained with him.

Steiner raised an eyebrow. 'Any chance of a drink?'

The man didn't respond.

'That's a no, then.' He sighed and removed his spectacles to clean the lenses.

Steiner didn't have long to wait before a commotion outside the room lured the security guard away, the door opening and closing behind him. He heard people yelling, followed by loud thuds and crashes. Then silence. The door to the room opened again and Samson stood there glowering, before moving out of sight of the now vacant doorway. Steiner emerged from the small cell, his brief stay over, and looked around the room. The orderly office he'd glimpsed on his way in now looked like a raging bull had swept through it. The main screen was shattered and desks had been upended. The two security guards lay comatose on the floor, while three of their colleagues, equally prone, moved weakly, the occasional moan escaping their lips. Samson, meanwhile, ripped a piece of hardware from a server in the corner of the room and then stalked out, with Steiner following close behind.

'I take it that's the security footage from the casino?' Steiner said as they made their way back down to the car park.

Samson stopped walking and held the hard drive up to Steiner's face, his pent up fury making the device shake in his hand. 'Are you trying to get us caught?'

It was Steiner's turn to keep his thoughts to himself, much to Samson's further disgust. Steiner knew he'd made a mistake; he needed to keep out of the limelight, not jump into it. Unfortunately he was used to having a team of people surrounding him, guiding his hand almost every step of the way. This was the first time in thirty years he'd been effectively working alone, the conductor of his own music, so to speak. His enthusiasm, usually carefully directed, had been unleashed. He'd always known he possessed what bordered on a split personality; deadly serious, calm and in control while at work, and almost juvenile when at play. Now that Samson had put saving those in Steadfast on hiatus, Steiner found himself adrift; that was until the colonel had completed whatever business he felt compelled to undertake.

The two men got back into the pick-up and Samson drove them

out onto the neon splashed streets. Steiner rubbed his tired eyes, the urgency to free those in Steadfast reasserting itself in the forefront of his mind. He knew it was easy to blame Samson for his own shortcomings; while the SFSD commander had derailed Steiner's plan, he knew he couldn't afford to let the gravitas of the situation escape him again, no matter how much he wished to temporarily unburden himself of his responsibilities.

Steiner, unwilling to even bother striking up a conversation with his unwanted companion, took it upon himself to inspect the communications equipment Samson had retrieved from the military outpost. Engrossed in the task, he suddenly became aware that they'd stopped moving and the truck was now parked just down from a nightclub where revellers queued up outside, waiting to gain entry. The large building bore a huge sign, the letters lit up in deep shades of purple and blue, proclaiming it to be *The Asteroid Club*.

Steiner glanced at Samson. 'I take it your man at the casino didn't have what you were looking for?'

The colonel slipped the vehicle out of gear and switched off the engine. 'He did – information. The owner of this club has what I need.' Samson made to get out of the car, but paused when Steiner stayed in his seat. 'I need you with me this time.' Samson's words were spoken as if they'd been dragged out of him by means of torture.

'No, I think I've caused us enough trouble for one day. I'll stay here.'

Samson made a strangled noise, exhaled and looked down at the floor, fighting hard to keep control of his temper. 'You come when you're not wanted and stay when you are. You're testing my limits, old man. Now get out of the damn truck!'

Steiner shook his head but did as requested. This time he put on a plain green baseball cap that had been poking out of one of the sacks on the back seat. Pulling it down low to hide his face, Steiner followed the tails of Samson's overcoat as he took the lead, walking past the line of young folks looking to dance their troubles away.

The entrance to the club boasted four huge searchlights, their intense ice blue light tracing great circular patches of illumination on the dark clouds above. A deep thumping beat pounded from inside the building, the energy of the sound waves palpable through the pavement – even outside. Eight enormous bouncers stood guard on the door, herding people in and out two at a time. Samson approached one of the men, leaning forwards and speaking into the man's ear to be heard over the noise of the music. The bouncer shook his head. Undeterred, Samson continued his verbal barrage, his stance becoming aggressive, which only served to bring four of the bouncer's colleagues to his aid. The five doormen arranged themselves in a formidable semi-circle around the marginally smaller figure of the colonel, the breadth of whose shoulders were accentuated by the armour cladding he wore under his coat, making him appear even more powerfully built than he was. The fact that the bouncers thought they needed five of them to quell one man showed how seriously they took Samson's physical threat.

Steiner hung back and watched, wondering what Samson would do as he held his ground against the overwhelming odds.

The sound of a high-powered sports car tore Steiner's attention away to the road outside the venue. He recognised that sound; a V8 engine. A dual tone MKII Ford GT40, one of Steiner's all-time favourite sports cars, came roaring into view. Iconic and timeless, the stunning black and chrome machine came to a stop adjacent to the entrance. Enclosed by super wide tyres, each sidewall displaying an immaculate white *Goodyear* logo, lavish, deep-dish alloys sparkled in the light. The front doors opened and out stepped two tall and incredibly beautiful brunettes, long, silky legs accentuated by revealing clothing which made Steiner feel chilly just to look at; and look he did, as did others in the queue. Cameras flashed from all directions as previously unseen photographers gathered around the two women, who glided up the steps and on into the club. Celebrities, Steiner assumed, his eyes drawn back to the car, which was now being attended to by a lucky valet.

Steiner felt a hand grab his arm. It was Samson, directing him back to the pick-up. Steiner looked back; two of the bouncers watched as they walked away. Inside the Dodge once more, Samson punched the dashboard, leaving a large dent.

'Perhaps there's a back way in?' Steiner said, never thinking he'd ever be trying to give Samson any words resembling support.

Samson didn't reply. Instead he delved once more into his supply of red pills, throwing a small handful into his mouth and chewing down with speed. Sticking the truck into gear, he reversed against the flow of traffic, sending other cars dodging out of his way and honking their horns in protest.

♦

Lucy Marshall had worked in the exclusive Asteroid nightclub for two years. She enjoyed her work. Free drinks were a perk, plus she got to know the DJs and the bouncers, which gave her a certain status amongst her peers as being part of the in-crowd. From time to time she even managed to get into the VIP area where all the top stars came to party on a regular basis. The Asteroid Club had been Vegas' top nightlife venue for years now, attracting only the best clientele. It was the place to be, the only place to be if you were someone of note. People who were somebody went to the Asteroid, and people who wanted to be somebody went to the Asteroid. That's all you had to know.

Lucy worked in the VIP section on the front desk and cloakroom, and she'd just that moment received a pair of delicate and extremely expensive jackets from two of the world's top models, Asilina Salerno and Atalanta Varushkin. The two women now waited for their special gift bags, provided to all such guests by the Asteroid's owners. Chewing her gum in time to the thumping uplifting dance music, Lucy picked out two of the bags from underneath the counter and gave them to the picture-perfect brunettes.

A loud noise and shouting made the two models look round towards the entrance, and Lucy also peered with interest through the haze of the smoke that seeped down from the main part of the club, an effect laid on once a week for the *Impact Night* promotion. She heard screaming, and ten doormen came steaming out of the main building to rush outside. The noise seemed to go on for ages. Through the huge windows that made up the front of the foyer, Lucy saw the great floodlights blink out as if someone had turned the power off. A small crowd had gathered around the cloakroom and one of the models, Asilina, walked elegantly to the doors to see what was happening, at which point she screamed. Out of the haze a shadowy figure emerged, its glowing green eyes quite frightening to behold.

The man, if that's what it was, shimmered and shifted as it moved, the smoke and light distorting around it in an abnormal way, making it appear to slip into the background from whence it walked. Heavy metallic footfalls clanked on the marble flooring as it passed by, the people parting like the sea before the prow of a mighty ship. Hushed cries and whimpers could be heard over the music. People shrank from its passing and Lucy stood transfixed when the ghostly eyes turned in her direction, before it was gone, only the disturbed smoke testament to its existence.

Lucy, suddenly wondering why the doormen had not returned, rushed from behind her desk. Outside the front entrance the sight that greeted her was disturbing. Around twenty bouncers lay on the ground, some struggling to rise while others lay still, barely moving. The press of people that had been waiting to enter the club had moved back some fifty feet, as if giving whatever event had transpired room to unfold.

Lucy bent down to one of the injured, a brick wall of a man called Delmar whom she knew well, and one she'd never seen beaten and bruised like he was now. 'What happened?' she asked him, momentarily distracted when a small old man with a beard, wearing a baseball cap, walked up the steps and into the building.

Cradling his left arm, Delmar groaned. 'Something, came out of nowhere. Didn't get a good look at it. Whatever it was, it was strong, really strong.'

Lucy soothed him as he let out another cry of pain, the sound echoing the mournful and emotive police sirens responding in the distance.

♦

Professor Steiner picked his way past the sprawling forms of the nightclub's doormen and made his way inside. The display put on by Samson had been both terrifying and awe inspiring, as he cut his way through the men like a razor-edged scythe through grass. Granted, the colonel had the advantage of being armoured and camouflaged, but still one couldn't help but be impressed by the speed and skill on display as he took down twenty men built like blocks of granite. Part of him had been hoping the colonel would fail, while the rest knew he had to succeed, for the sake of those in Steadfast.

The fracas outside appeared to have had no effect on the people at the bars and on the dance floor, the partying continuing unabated. The interior of the club was so loud Steiner was finding it difficult not to put his hands over his ears for protection. Samson was nowhere to be seen and Steiner pushed his way through intoxicated men and women in an attempt to head upstairs for a better view of the vast dance floor and surrounding areas. Finally, reaching the first floor, Steiner entered a section marked *VIP Lounge*. He assumed large men normally prevented general riff-raff like himself from entering such sections, but seeing as Samson had taken out what had to have been the majority of such guards, he was able to swan in like he belonged.

This area, like the rest, heaved with people. Steiner felt dizzy and disorientated as the music thumped, the lights pulsed and the strobes flashed. Finding a chair amongst the press of hot bodies he sat down, attempting to get his bearings and regain his faculties. Before he could settle, a breath of air on his neck made him shiver and he turned to come face-to-face with a beautiful woman on a stage, bending down towards him, her face and movements sensual in the pulsating strobe. Standing up, Steiner realised to his intense embarrassment the young lady was stark naked and gyrating provocatively towards him as he watched, mouth agape. Someone caressed his arm and he looked to his left where another woman had appeared, similarly dressed – or not, as was the case in this instance. Eyes wide, like a rabbit in the headlights, Steiner felt heady, intoxicated even; it was a long time since his pulse rate had been increased thus. With the rapidly rhythmic lights hypnotising him, Steiner felt a large hand clamp down on his shoulder from behind, breaking the spell. Looking round and then up, he saw two green glowing eyes and the sporadic image of Samson's armoured body, appearing then disappearing, on and off, on and off, in the flashing white lights surrounding them.

Samson pressed a button on the side of his helmet to reveal his grim face. 'No time for sightseeing, Professor. I need you to see something.'

I've seen enough already, Steiner thought to himself as one of the naked dancers blew him a kiss goodbye. The two men, now in the middle of the dance floor, found themselves in bright, constant lighting as the thumping percussion ceased, to be replaced by an uplifting vocal section of the song. Everyone in the area put their hands in the air and cheered. The lights dimmed and a single pulse of strobe lighting flashed out, accompanied by a booming beat. The baseline gradually kicked back in, the music rising to a crescendo as the lasers and strobes in combination drove the people into a frenzy. Steiner thought, *if I was forty years younger, I might be tempted to join in*, as it is was, however, he just wanted to get away from the relentless noise.

After Samson and Steiner had broken free of the crush, another obstacle arose in front of them in the form of eight doormen pushing through a pair of double doors. Samson moved Steiner behind him, reactivated his armour and then launched himself at the nearest man. Steiner watched while Samson's indistinct form, transformed into some kind of ethereal demon, dispatched the men arrayed against him in quick and brutal succession until only he remained standing. Ignoring a crowd of shocked spectators, the colonel beckoned Steiner onwards, and the two men disappeared into the rear of the building where the offices were located.

Samson opened and closed doors until he found the one he desired. Steiner, following him into a brightly lit area chock full of crates and boxes of all shapes and sizes, was relieved to hear the music fade when the heavy door swung shut behind him. To the left, fifty feet away, a man – most likely the nightclub's owner – stood behind a desk, the gun in his hand pointed at the colonel.

'The police are outside!' The man exuded fear like dark smoke from an oily fire. 'There's no escape!'

Samson walked towards him and the man's weapon discharged, sending a bullet ricocheting from Samson's armour and off into the room. Steiner ducked for cover. The armour clad figure of the colonel bore down on his hapless victim and three more shots rang out before Samson knocked the weapon away with the back of his hand. Grabbing the man by the hair, his other hand clasping his jaw, Samson lifted him off his feet with pure, brute strength.

'I was told you have some computer equipment, some *special* computer equipment,' Samson said to his struggling prisoner as Steiner approached warily. 'You will show me where it is immediately. Do you understand me?'

The man nodded as best he could with the colonel's fingers clamped around his face.

'Good.' Samson let the man go. 'Where?'

The Asteroid's owner rubbed his sore face with one hand and pointed with the other to the corner of the room, where a door lurked in the shadows. Samson grabbed the man and kicked him forwards with a steel shod boot.

'Are you out of your mind?!' Steiner said after they'd passed through the doorway to descend some stairs. 'You complain I nearly get us caught and then you pull a stunt like this, probably bringing half the Las Vegas police department down on us!'

Samson looked at him. 'Relax.'

'Relax! How can I relax?!'

An unresponsive Samson moved into the basement and through into another room, hastily unlocked by their prisoner, leaving Steiner to simmer in a melting pot of his own fury.

'There.' The owner of the club indicated a metal cabinet against the far wall. Samson stormed over to it and ripped the doors open with such force that one came off in his hand; he threw it aside with disdain, the thin metal panel crashing to the floor.

Steiner walked to the shelving and began sorting through the hardware on display. 'I'll need a box.'

Samson, anticipating his request, dumped an orange plastic crate at his feet. One by one, Steiner selected the pieces of equipment he would need to access the FBI's computer network. Regardless of Samson's methods, he'd sourced the right kit for the job. Everything here was cutting edge, the latest quantum processors, data miners and artificial intelligence. In fact, it was so advanced he wasn't convinced anyone outside of the military or GMRC should have access to it. A small stamp on the side of one of the cases, read *Property of the GMRC*. He picked up the other items in his box; everything had the same marking on it, confirming his fears. 'Where did you get this?' Steiner asked the nightclub owner, brandishing a device at him. 'You were selling this on the black market? Do you know the punishment for such a crime?'

The man stared at him tight-lipped and then returned his attention to the colonel, clearly more focused on Samson's physical threat than anything Steiner had to say.

Samson snatched the item from Steiner's hand and all but chucked it into the box. 'Time to go, Professor.'

Steiner was about to retort, but realised the illegal activities of one man were hardly high on his agenda right now. He picked up the box, struggling under its weight.

Samson withdrew his sidearm and pointed it at the man's chest. 'Where's your escape route?'

'I don't know what you're talking about.'

Samson cocked the hammer. 'Last chance.' He raised the gun to the man's head.

Not surprisingly the nightclub owner relented. 'Behind the cabinet.' He flicked a hand to his right.

Samson lowered his weapon and leaned his weight against the piece of furniture; with a screech of metal, the cabinet slid to one side, revealing an unlit opening behind. Samson let go and the hidden exit began to close. Pushing it back once more, he held it open so Steiner could move past and into the dark. With one hand on the cabinet, he raised his pistol and shot the man in the head, the body falling to the ground without a sound.

Steiner gasped in shock, the man's murder carried out by Samson with an indifference akin to an arbitrary task, like putting on your glasses or turning out a light.

Steiner gave Samson a savage look. 'You really care nothing for the life of others, do you?'

'Why should I?' Samson illuminated their escape route with his helmet's inbuilt torches. 'According to you everyone's living on borrowed time as it is. Come 2045, no one on the surface will be left alive; tell me if I'm wrong?'

Steiner didn't – couldn't. The colonel was right.

'As far as I see it,' Samson said, 'they're all six foot under, they just don't know it yet.'

CHAPTER TWENTY-NINE

STEINER STARED out of the window at the endless blackness, the low whir of the Dodge Ram's electric engine lulling him to sleep, its soporific embrace hard to resist. Occasionally a car sped past in the opposite direction, its headlights dazzling him back to full alertness before the process started again, eyelids drooping, mind slowing.

Vegas lay far behind them now. Apparently the colonel's source at the casino had been very forthcoming about the nightclub owner's secrets. Steiner wondered if the man still lived; he doubted it given Samson's track record, the thought a sobering one.

They had exited the nightclub without hindrance via the secret passage, emerging into a street conveniently close to where Samson had parked the pick-up truck. The police, who had indeed descended on the *Asteroid Club* en masse, were none the wiser when Steiner and Samson drove past and on, out of town. *And why would they have been?* Steiner thought. They were looking for someone presumed to be still in the building, not two men cruising by in a classic car.

Once Samson had deemed enough distance lay between them and the city, they had driven a little way out into the desert to catch a few hours' sleep. Steiner had dozed fitfully, one eye on the road, searching for any sign of pursuit. The colonel, however, went out like a light, his training helping him to grab rest when he could; in spite of the precarious nature of their circumstances.

Back on the road again after their stop, Samson had continued their drive west across the southern states. After two more hours had passed, they arrived at, and then successfully navigated entry into, the *City of Angels*. Once again Steiner had been issued with a temporary pass, this one allowing him four hours inside the Los Angeles County checkpoint boundaries. Samson, as he had back at St. George, bypassed the roadblock, moving in on foot to be picked up by Steiner a mile further down the highway. Now back in the driving seat, literally and metaphorically, the colonel brought them to a darkened office block on the outskirts of Culver City, in the western district of the county.

'Wake up, old man,' Samson said, rousing Steiner from his slumber.

Steiner opened his eyes, unaware that he'd drifted off yet again. Instantly alert, he followed his armoured companion out of the car and onto the street. Breaking into the deserted building, Samson guided Steiner inside and prompted him to set up the equipment they'd taken from the now deceased nightclub owner. Patching into the internal connections within the office, located on the first floor, Steiner's doubts about Samson's intentions manifested themselves as the time neared for his skills to be utilised. Engineering a code sequence, Steiner brought up the login screen for the FBI's internal computer network, the holographic wall monitor in the office displaying the agency's well known seal as a rotating three-dimensional graphic.

'So, Colonel,' Steiner said, spinning his seat around to look at Samson, his hands clasped before him in pensive anticipation, 'what is it you require me to do inside the FBI's network – exactly?'

'I need you to locate an agent in the L.A. field office.'

'Who?'

'Brett Taylor.'

'Why?'

'You don't need to know why, just do it.'

'If you think I'm going to break into the secure network of a government agency without knowing why first, then you don't know me very well.'

Samson glared at him. 'Don't push me, Professor.'

Steiner folded his arms across his chest, his face hardening. 'Or you'll do what, Colonel? You obviously need me as much as I sadly need you and if you resort to your default setting of violence first and talk after, then you'll find my services are no longer available to you.'

Samson's jaw tightened as his rage, never far from the surface, battled to unleash itself at the obstacle before it.

Steiner watched while Samson struggled in his own internal, private tug of war. 'The ball's in your court, Colonel, and it's your call.'

Samson held Steiner's gaze, perhaps seeking to melt his resolve by sheer force of will. Unfortunately for the colonel, he only bowed to such pressure when he had absolutely no alternative. Steiner raised a questioning eyebrow.

Samson released Steiner's gaze and moved to look out of the window. In the distance the high-rises of central L.A.'s financial district thrust up into the dark skies, their windows lit up like sparkling jewels in a physical embodiment of the power and influence enjoyed by those that occupied the offices within.

A minute's silence passed before Samson spoke. 'I have a child – a daughter.'

Steiner waited for the colonel to continue; when he'd failed to do so after another minute dragged by, Steiner took it on himself to coax forth further information.

'And in light of what you now know about the Earth's future,' Steiner said, keeping his tone as neutral as he could, 'you seek to relocate her to USSB Sanctuary?'

Steiner took the colonel's continued silence as an affirmation of his insight. *But why the FBI?* Steiner asked himself. *Had the girl and her mother been placed in protective custody to escape the violent and unstable colonel?* This seemed the most likely explanation, which also meant the colonel sought to relocate the girl against her will.

'What about your daughter's mother?' Steiner asked. 'Do you plan on kidnapping her too?'

Samson continued to stare out at the distant skyline, but when he spoke his voice was bitter. 'Her mother is dead.'

Steiner was tempted to ask Samson if he'd had anything to do with the untimely death, but common sense prevailed. 'And this FBI agent will know where your daughter is?' Steiner said instead, finally grasping the full picture that had eluded him since Samson had forced him into this macabre sideshow.

Samson turned to face Steiner again, his face set. 'Help me or not, I will find her; but with your help, I can get in and out without being detected.'

'In and out of where?' Steiner was confused.

'The field office,' Samson said in anger, as if Steiner was being purposefully obtuse, 'it's a few miles from here.'

'You want to break into the FBI's L.A. field office? The second largest FBI stronghold in the country; are you insane?'

'I'm not fucking MAD!' Samson's eyes bulged and spittle shot from his mouth.

Steiner stared at the man in disbelief. *I must have hit a nerve,* he thought, *and a raw one at that.* What with his little red pills, his wanton murder and this, Steiner could well believe the colonel would qualify as a candidate for committal. *If I ever get reinstated at the GMRC,* Steiner promised himself, *I'll make a point of having the colonel's record checked.* How the military could let someone like him continue as a serving officer in a highly sensitive black project, God only knew.

'If you'd told me about your daughter before, Colonel,' Steiner said, staying calm, 'I could have saved us all this trouble. I implore you, forget this—' Steiner paused, having been about to use the word madness. 'Idea,' he said instead. 'Help me resume my position within the GMRC and I promise you I will have your daughter moved to a USSB of your choosing.'

'It's too late for that,' Samson told him, his composure regained. 'Besides, your chances of returning to the GMRC are slim at best,

Malcolm Joiner has seen to that. My daughter comes first, Steadfast second.'

'Have you considered staking out the offices and then speaking to this agent elsewhere?' Steiner asked. 'It would be a lot easier, don't you think?'

'It would, but seeing as surveilling any government office is now a virtual impossibility due to twenty-four hour drone cover, we'd be picked up in a matter of hours. A tactical incursion into the offices will not be expected and will be incisive and quick, in and out, minimising exposure.'

Steiner's faint hopes of diverting Samson from his crazy plan were in tatters; it seemed his only option now was to try and ensure its success. 'So, when I locate this Brett Taylor,' Steiner said cautiously, 'you'll then need me to stay in the system, help you gain access to the building and guide you around any obstacles you encounter inside. You'll extract the information you need from the agent about your daughter and then I'll guide you back out again, correct?'

Samson nodded.

'Fine, I'll do it, on one condition; you do not kill any agents, including Taylor. Tie him up and then hide him, but under no circumstances kill him. If you renege on this, I'll pull the plug and you'll be on your own. Agreed?'

Samson studied him for a moment. 'Agreed, now get to it.'

Steiner, not caring for Samson's tone one iota, turned back to the screen and the stacked computer equipment on the desk. He flicked the switches on each deck and the machines whirred to life one by one, the hum of their sophisticated cooling systems creating a pleasant background harmonic. Steiner interlaced his fingers and splayed them out in front of him, cracking the synovial fluid in his joints and stretching out the tendons and muscles, generating a pleasant sense of relaxation in preparation for the work ahead.

Accessing the artificial intelligence system, Steiner activated its start-up code, effectively bringing the machine to life.

'Wake up now,' Steiner said to it as the A.I.'s human interface window popped up on the wall display. In its centre an amenable metallic depiction of a human face rotated on its axis. After a few seconds the face snapped to the front, its eyes opened and it peered out of the screen in curiosity.

'Hello, my name is A.I. 152, please state your designation and the task schedules you wish me to undertake today.'

Steiner detached a microphone from the A.I.'s console and attached it to his collar. 'Hello, 152, my designation is – Professor – and I need your help in bypassing multiple encrypted access ports on a multi-string system.'

'Thank you, Professor,' the A.I. said, its eloquent and musical lilt pleasing to the ear. 'I have assessed the processing power you have linked to my console and deduced the chances of your tasks being completed at a probability of thirty-eight per cent. Do you wish to proceed?'

'I do, thank you, 152. I will control your work by command code. Please keep me updated on counter measures instigated against our tasks in real-time.'

'Certainly, Professor.' 152 fell silent, its simulated features feigning an expression of concentration as it carried out its duties.

Steiner entered his first line of code, his finger hovering over the Return key. He looked to Samson. 'Right, I'm about to go in, final chance to back out is now.'

Samson came to stand by Steiner's chair. 'Do it.'

Steiner nodded and depressed the key, sending lines of code flashing onto the screen.

'Bypassing in progress, Professor,' 152's voice intoned as the procedure of breaking into the FBI's system was instigated. 'Counter measures encountered – processing.'

Steiner analysed the system overview streams at the side of the screen. His fingers moved across the keyboard, slowly at first, then picked up speed as the security programmes within the FBI system attempted to counteract his commands. Line upon line of code spewed forth from his fingertips, his hands a blur as his mind worked furiously to keep up with the information relayed to him by the artificial intelligence.

Steiner swore. The system he was trying to access was quite alien to him; he was beginning to wonder if he could breach it after all.

'What is it?' Samson's eyes searched the screen for signs of a problem he couldn't possibly comprehend.

'Hang on,' Steiner said, distracted, 'having – a problem here.' He spun up another system, funnelling various data streams from one machine to another, trying to keep up the charade to the FBI mainframe that everything was as it should be.

Samson stepped closer. 'Can you do this or not? If you can't, then—'

'Quiet, man! Just let me work.'

Gradually, protocol by protocol, Steiner turned the tide; he'd lost some battles but he was winning the war. After what seemed like hours, but was in actuality only thirty-five minutes, the FBI login screen, ensconced in its own window, flashed once and then displayed the message *ACCESS GRANTED*, in bold green lettering.

'We're in!' Steiner navigated to the FBI's internal menu system and scanned down the page. 'It seems personnel files are held elsewhere.'

'Most likely in D.C., on a stand-alone system.' Samson indicated a heading entitled *Field Offices*. 'What about that?'

Steiner entered the section Samson had suggested and scrolled down a list until he reached Los Angeles. Hitting the Enter key, Steiner assimilated the page, drilling down into the information within, flashing up page after page until he found something of real use. 'This should help, I think.' Steiner expanded a holographic map out of the screen and into the room.

Samson walked around the image of the L.A. office block, his face and body turned a mixture of blue and green by the projected graphic that now floated in front of him.

Steiner tapped a few more keys and added real-time locations for all staff within the building, a function designed to aid emergency services in the event of a fire or terrorist attack.

'There!' Samson jutted a finger at a small red figure seated at a desk on the fourteenth floor.

Steiner enlarged that section; the small floating tag above the virtual image of the person was now clearly visible as *Special Agent Taylor, B.* 'Looks like your luck is in, Colonel.'

'We'll see.'

Steiner swivelled in his chair. 'I'll need your helmet's communication frequency so I can establish a secure uplink to it.'

Samson handed it to him so he could swipe it over the computer's induction port.

'Automated failsafe tracing in progress, Professor,' the A.I.'s voice interrupted through the office speaker system.

Steiner returned his attention to the screen. '152, can we stop the trace?'

'Negative, Professor,'

'How long until the system locates us?' Steiner asked.

'Sixty-three minutes, sixteen seconds and counting.'

A small box displaying the minutes and seconds as a countdown timer appeared in the top left hand corner of the wallscreen.

'You'd better get—' Steiner looked round to see the office door swinging shut and the colonel gone, 'going.'

Turning back to his computer, Steiner set-up a coms link to the colonel's combat system and fitted a small device to his right ear. 'Colonel, if you can hear me, you have sixty-three – no – sixty-one minutes to get to, in and then back out of the field office.'

'Roger, that,' Samson's voice replied.

'I'm connecting to the live video feed from your helmet's camera,' Steiner continued, tapping away at his keyboard, 'and I've already taken control of the building's internal and external surveillance streams. I should be able to guide you inside and to your target, hopefully without them knowing you're there.'

Samson confirmed he'd received the extra information, leaving Steiner to contemplate the possible ramifications of his actions. *Everything will be fine*, he told himself. They won't even know he's there. *He has camouflage on his armour and an inside track on his surroundings; this is what he's trained to do. What could go wrong?* A lot – was the answer that sprung to mind.

With the seconds and minutes ticking by on-screen, Steiner's tension grew. His neck became tight as he leant forwards, bunching up his shoulders to watch real-time video footage of Samson driving to the FBI building. Thankfully the field office was only a short drive from where he now sat, a convenience no doubt premeditated by the colonel long before they'd even arrived in The Golden State.

Steiner watched everything from Samson's perspective on his wallscreen as he approached the imposing seventeen storey building that was the Federal Bureau of Investigation's L.A. field office. The camera angle panned up, the colonel surveying the fourteenth floor using his visor's spectral scanners. Steiner looked to the window displaying the multiple camera feeds from the FBI's own internal security system. Carefully, he manipulated the field of view on the cameras and created a clear path to an emergency exit on the far right of the structure, enabling Samson to enter unnoticed. Now deep within the FBI network, Steiner also set about unlocking a route through the building to Special Agent Taylor, by disabling the digitally activated bolts that were used to prevent access to various areas of the office complex.

'You're good to go, Colonel,' Steiner told Samson over the radio, 'I've just sent the real time 3D render of the building to your visor. Follow the path I've laid out for you and your presence will go unnoticed by the security guards, you should also be able to dodge any agents by utilising the same image.'

'Copy, that,' Samson replied, arcing his path round to intercept Steiner's route.

'Professor,' the A.I. said, its expression on the screen mirroring the concern in its voice, 'I have encountered an unforeseen issue, line sixteen hundred and twenty-seven in your command code is invalid, please advise.'

Steiner's attention flew back to his command window. Frantic, he searched for the problem raised by 152. There it was; an innocuous segment of text, a search string and value which he'd entered in error. As he rushed to correct the issue, retyping a few commands, the A.I.

spoke again. 'System spike, information interrupt. Connection lost, Professor.'

Steiner looked to Samson's video window and saw a metal-clad hand pushing open an emergency exit door. 'Colonel, stop, go back! The FBI has regained control of the system. We're blind! Abort!!'

'Are you fucking kidding me?!' Samson's voice crackled over the speakers.

Steiner saw Samson hesitate in the doorway.

'System breach detected, Professor,' the voice of 152 told him. 'Trace protocol prioritised, time until completion, twelve minutes, eight seconds and counting.'

'Oh my God.' Steiner watched in horror as the timer on the screen rapidly descend until it read the new time. A flashing red light brought his attention back to the image relayed from Samson's helmet. A beacon pulsed on and off in the corridor and a siren echoed through Samson's two-way com system as Steiner spoke to him. 'Colonel, get out of there!'

But Samson didn't reply, instead he started into the building at a jog.

'What are you doing?!' Steiner yelled as he tried to slow the trace instigated by the FBI.

Samson continued his advance, without deviation.

'Colonel!' Steiner said, watching in disbelief as Samson walked boldly through an automatic door and into the building's main lobby, a large depiction of the FBI emblem visible on the immaculate tiled floor before him.

Steiner saw Samson's left arm move over his shoulder, drawing down a strange looking weapon which he then fired into the security scanners in front of him. A pulse of energy shot forwards, sending a devastating explosion ripping through the atrium. Debris flew in all directions. Security guards who had been heading towards Samson, their guns raised, were blown backwards, while other people dived for cover.

'Dear God,' Steiner whispered in shock, the realisation of the colonel's actions sinking in, 'what have I done?'

CHAPTER THIRTY

Richard Goodwin waited with trepidation for the arrival of Commander Hilt. An emergency meeting had been called by the Darklight leader, its purpose as yet unknown. Whatever had transpired, it had to be important as other officers from the black-clad security force filtered into the large command tent. Lost in abstract thought, Goodwin paced around the back of the enclosure away from the gathering soldiers, his mind inexorably returning to recent events like a honey bee drawn to nectar.

A few weeks had passed since Goodwin and Kara had experienced the incident with the light in the abandoned Anakim city and Goodwin had, understandably, been on edge throughout that period. He'd never felt comfortable in the endless darkness of Sanctuary, his depression only held at bay by Kara's company. Now, however, the black pit they were forced to endure had evolved into something far more sinister. Areas of the camp he'd once sauntered through, he now avoided. Basically, anything that wasn't touched by light, whether directly or by reflection, he gave a wide berth, fearful of what might be lurking within.

His anxiety, Goodwin knew, had been well founded, but the fact of the matter was no further contact or sightings of the wraithlike glow had since been reported. Commander Hilt's recon teams, sent to investigate the disturbing phenomenon, had returned with nothing. Goodwin, ignoring an inner voice that shrieked in ardent opposition, seemingly throughout every fibre of his being, had even ventured back to the city with them to make sure they'd searched the correct building; they had and many others in the immediate vicinity besides, all turning up no trace, except for the odd half print from one of Goodwin or Kara's own shoes.

Ever since security had been stepped up around the camp, word had spread like wildfire amongst civilians and Darklight contractors alike about Goodwin and Kara's encounter with the entity. Initially the tale had taken on a life of its own, but Goodwin and Hilt had been quick to play it down in order to keep a semblance of calm amongst the people. Even though Goodwin's, and to a similar extent Kara's, nerves remained suitably frayed, everyone else around them, as the days and weeks drifted by, appeared to forget the event had even occurred. Goodwin was pleased, of course, that panic had not ensued; although peoples' indifference to what could only be described as a threat only served to add to his continued unease.

'Ten-hut!' one of the Darklight officers said, and every soldier snapped to attention in response.

Commander Hilt strode into the tent, his XO, Major Offiah, at his side.

'At ease, Darklight.' Hilt moved to stand near Goodwin, his men forming up to look in his direction. 'Sir,' Hilt said in his deep voice, acknowledging Goodwin.

'Commander,' Goodwin replied, with a nod of his head.

Soon after a few civilians arrived and filed into the room, Kara among them. She gave Goodwin a questioning look, as if asking what the meeting was about. Goodwin returned the expression with one of his own and an almost indiscernible shrug of his shoulders. He had no idea either. Behind Kara were a few people from Goodwin's old Steadfast management team and, bringing up the rear, Sergeant Alvarez, the commanding officer from USSB Sanctuary's captured U.S. Army Decontamination Team.

'That's everyone, Commander,' the dark skinned African, Major Offiah, told Hilt.

'Thank you, Major.' Hilt cleared his throat. 'You've all been called here, because of a discovery made by one of our patrols a few hours ago. Such is its nature and implications I believe it's imperative we act both immediately and unanimously.' Hilt glanced to his right hand man. 'Major, if you will.'

Major Offiah placed a small screen onto one of the flimsy tables in the middle of the room and powered it up; everyone else, including Goodwin, shuffled forwards in an attempt to get an unobstructed view of the display.

A black and white pixelated image started playing and resolved itself into a clear colour picture.

'This footage,' Hilt said, 'was recorded by a helmet-cam during a routine sweep on the west coast of the lake.'

Goodwin watched the footage unfold. The small Darklight team, seven or eight people strong, roamed the area around the western shoreline, the controlled sweeping movements of their light beams intersecting one another as they utilised a set formation for the patrol.

'What's that?' a voice could be heard saying, close to the head-cam operator.

The direction of the camera angle shifted when the wearer moved their head in the direction of the speaker's voice. 'What's what?' another voice said, a woman's, loud enough, Goodwin assumed, to be the owner of the helmet that had recorded the video they now watched.

'A light, in the distance,' the other soldier said, excited, 'there, can't you see it?'

The woman swore before getting on her radio as those around her, weapons now raised, fanned out into a defensive configuration and slipped into a purposeful jog towards the distant light, now visible on screen.

'Command, this is Lieutenant Manaus.' Her voice shook as she ran to keep pace with her colleagues. 'Contact sighted, at our location, in pursuit, over.'

'Roger that, Lieutenant,' the communication came back. 'We'll reroute another team to your coordinates. Keep us posted.'

'Copy that, Command, Manaus out.'

Goodwin watched with bated breath as the Darklight team converged on the light, which shimmered and distorted strangely before blinking out of existence.

'Fuck, where did it go?' Manaus slowed to a walk near the water's edge. 'We were right on top of it.'

A Darklight man appeared in front of the camera from out of the darkness. 'Into the water, that's the only place it could go, we had it penned in.'

'Lieutenant!' another voice said, drawing Manaus even closer to the shoreline and a muddy strip of land separating the lake from the hard earth of the chamber's floor. 'You need to see this.'

The head-cam moved over to a man who had dropped to his haunches and was peering down at the patch of earth before him, the ground illuminated by a torch on the side of his rifle. When Manaus approached, he looked round, his face etched with concern. 'Take a look,' he said.

'What is it?' Manaus placed a hand on his shoulder and looked to where he pointed. Tracks in the mud led into the dark liquid of the lake. 'They look like boot prints,' she said.

Goodwin and everyone around him looked at the image with the same focused intrigue as the lieutenant had, hours past.

'And that's what they are,' Hilt's voice said.

Major Offiah paused the recording, bringing Goodwin's attention back from the scene at the lakeside.

'Boot prints?' Goodwin was confused. He'd been expecting something; he didn't know what he'd been expecting, but not that, not footprints.

Hilt looked to Goodwin. 'Yes, made by U.S. military issue boots, to be precise.'

'What does that mean?' Kara said, her voice mimicking Goodwin's previous tone.

'It means,' Hilt replied, now addressing everyone present, 'that the USSB have located our position.'

'What?!' Goodwin's eyes widened. 'How can that be? Are you sure?'

Hilt nodded as others began muttering to one another at the news. 'As sure as we can be; Sergeant Alvarez and his men have all been accounted for during the time of the incursion and their footwear inspected.'

'And my men put under guard,' Alvarez said, his tone bitter.

'A necessary precaution, Sergeant,' Hilt replied.

'According to you.' Alvarez pushed his way past two Darklight men to bring himself to the fore. 'How do you know it wasn't Goodwin's ghost?'

'That's Director Goodwin, to you,' Major Offiah told Alvarez, clearly annoyed at the sergeant's disrespectful tone.

'That light wasn't like the one I saw—' Goodwin looked at Kara. 'That we saw. And it was no ghost.'

'The mind can play tricks on us all – *Director*,' Alvarez said, the barbed inflection for the benefit of Major Offiah. 'I'm beginning to wonder if you saw anything at all.'

'Whatever the director and Dr Vandervoort witnessed,' Hilt said to the belligerent sergeant, his tone leaving no doubt that he was dismissing Alvarez's assertions, 'did not leave size ten boot marks behind it. We must assume the two are separate in origin, unless proven otherwise.'

'If troops from the USSB have found us, then there's a way into this chamber,' Goodwin said, 'which means there's also a way out.'

Hilt's expression remained impassive. 'Indeed, we always suspected some of the submerged waterways might lead to the USSB. The fact that they can reach us, however, does not mean that we can reach them. As I've said before, we don't have the capability to negotiate these underwater channels.'

'Surely this is a good thing, sir,' one of Hilt's lieutenants said. 'If we can capture one of those interlopers, or a team of them, we can then use their gear to navigate the water.'

Major Offiah picked up a map. 'We need to find out how many of them have made it through to this chamber, and on how many occasions.'

Goodwin looked around at those present. 'Shouldn't we be asking another question? What is the U.S. Army doing here in the first place? What are their intentions towards us? We know we entered Sanctuary without authorisation; they could be planning on just leaving us down here to rot, in which case they won't return and our chance of escape has already gone.'

'Perhaps Sergeant Alvarez can fill us in on some of the details,' Major Offiah said, staring at the U.S. Army man with a hostile eye.

Alvarez, never one to shy away from conflict, met the Major's gaze with a challenge of his own. 'Fill you in on what?' His tone was mocking. 'I don't know anything; I've been down in this accursed hole for as long as you all have, brought here against my will, as were my men.'

'But you've lived in the USSB for years, haven't you Sergeant?' Goodwin said. 'Surely you must know something that can help us further?'

Alvarez chuckled, the sound harsh and without humour. 'You lot never stop, do you? I've told you before; do I have to say it again? I don't know shit. I'm a sergeant leading a small decontamination team, an NCO, not a general, colonel or even a lieutenant. I've given you what information I have on this part of Sanctuary—'

'Which is very little,' Major Offiah said.

'—what more can I do?' Alvarez continued, ignoring the interruption.

Goodwin considered the sergeant; his appearance had altered drastically since his capture, his hair growing long and his face unshaven. Despite having the facilities available to wash and clean his clothes, Alvarez remained grubby and dishevelled, a far cry from the clean cut image displayed by his Darklight counterparts, who still maintained their strict standards of dress and appearance at all times. Goodwin knew Hilt neither liked nor trusted the man, and he could understand why; the more he got to know Alvarez the more he disliked him, too.

'Whatever their purpose here,' Hilt told them, 'it makes no difference. We can't afford to divert our resources any longer. I'm sorry, sir,' Hilt said to Goodwin, 'but we need to cull our patrols and stake out the lake shore. Whatever you saw in the city hasn't returned and this new development could prove pivotal to our escape from this chamber.'

Goodwin was aware that all eyes were on him. 'Very well, Commander, do what you feel is necessary.'

'Thank you, sir. In the meantime,' Hilt continued, addressing his officers, 'I want all personnel combat-ready immediately. Full armour at all times. No exceptions. If the U.S. military comes in force, we'll be ready for them. Do we understand each other?'

'Sir, yes sir!' the Darklight officers said as one, making Goodwin shift in discomfort at the sudden loud and unified response.

'I'll issue detailed orders to your combat systems shortly,' Hilt told the assembled ranks, 'dismissed!'

The majority of the Darklight officers began filing from the tent to go about their duties.

Hilt turned to his second in command. 'Major, can you take Sergeant Alvarez back to his men? I'll inform you when they can be released back into gen-pop.'

'Yes, sir,' Major Offiah said, 'with pleasure, sir.'

'Gen-pop.' Alvarez sneered at Hilt, as Offiah fronted up to the army sergeant. 'We're not in a prison, Commander.'

'Just because there are no guards or bars, Sergeant,' Hilt said, his tone severe, 'does not mean we're not all prisoners down here. Take him away, Major.'

'You'll regret this, Commander!' Alvarez said as the major manoeuvred him out of the tent. 'I'll make sure of it!'

'I think you might have made an enemy of him,' Goodwin said after the sergeant was out of earshot.

Hilt remained unmoved. 'The man's a duplicitous fool.'

'Even so—'

Hilt looked at Goodwin, his expression mild. 'He'll calm down,' he said, his concern about angering the sergeant apparently non-existent. 'We can't afford to take any chances.'

With Hilt's military orders out of the way Goodwin, with the Darklight leader's assistance, went on to discuss with the remaining civilians various contingencies in case a military assault did occur in the future; specifically evacuation plans from the lake's surface and beaches. After decisions had been made, people dispersed and Goodwin was left alone with just Kara and Hilt in the ramshackle command centre.

Kara surveyed some of the maps strewn out on the desks, depicting areas of the cavern already scoured by the tireless reconnaissance teams. 'How go the searches, Commander?'

'You're aware the southern expeditions came back empty handed?' Hilt asked her, looking to Goodwin for confirmation.

'Yes,' Kara said, 'Richard told me the bad news.'

'The tunnels beneath the city are still to yield their secrets,' Hilt continued. 'If there are exits from this chamber down there, we haven't found them yet. We're still to hear from the north, but we should be getting a sitrep within the week.'

'Do you think we should be looking for the USSB at all?' Kara said to Hilt.

'What else can we do?' Goodwin answered her, Hilt seemingly perplexed by the question.

Kara shrugged. 'Perhaps we should be looking for routes to the surface, tunnels headed up, not down.'

Goodwin shot Hilt a quick look, but the Darklight man failed to notice. Goodwin hadn't told Kara about the other meteors destined for Earth, but he couldn't help but worry in case he disclosed the secret by accident. He hated keeping things from her, even more so when he had to lie to keep up the pretence. Now, thankfully, wasn't such an occasion as there were no tunnels going upwards whatsoever. In the future, the idea of the surface being a safe haven would no longer be relevant, but for now anything would be better than where they were; *except perhaps Steadfast*, he thought sadly.

'We've looked for any and all exits, Doctor,' Hilt replied, 'up, down and sideways. I agree the USSB doesn't have to be our only goal, but it is by far the nearest and most attainable destination available to us at this—'

A small bleeping noise caught their attention and Hilt moved to one of the tables, picked up a small device and placed it in his ear.

'This is Hilt,' he said, his hand held to his ear while he received the communication. 'What?! How?' A few more seconds passed as whoever spoke to him relayed their answer. 'What's his condition?' He moved to the tent's exit, the question making Kara and Goodwin exchange looks of concern. 'Very well, just find him.'

'Problem, Commander?' Goodwin asked.

Hilt removed the earpiece. 'Alvarez got the drop on Major Offiah and fled into the city.'

Kara gasped. 'Is the Major okay?'

'Concussion, and a bruised ego to go with it, I imagine.' Hilt's face was grim. 'He took the Major's torch and sidearm too.'

'What's the man thinking?' Goodwin said. 'He's got nowhere to go.'

Hilt snorted. 'As I said before, the man's a fool. He won't get far, though, two teams are out searching for him already.'

'I hope they find him,' Kara said, her face showing her disquiet.

'I wouldn't worry about him too much,' Hilt told her, 'we've got movement sensors all around the camp, he'll trip them before he can cause any harm.'

'You don't understand, I'm not worried *about* him,' Kara said, 'I'm worried *for* him, out there alone in that city; it's not somewhere I'd want to be on my own.'

Goodwin thought back to the huge empty towers, the unending darkness and – inexorably, inescapably – back to the blood-curdling shriek that had accompanied the shimmering unexplained light. 'No,' Goodwin murmured in agreement, looking out of the tent at the deep, pervasive gloom beyond, 'neither would I.'

CHAPTER THIRTY-ONE

SERGEANT ALVAREZ SAT in the black void with his back against a building, its smooth, curved surface cradling his body like the arms of some giant maternal stone mother. He'd so far managed to evade the Darklight teams sent to recapture him, and more by judgement than luck, he believed. He knew this place played havoc with telecommunications and other pieces of tracking kit, so he'd headed deep into the Anakim city, a sure-fire way of preserving his newly won freedom.

The look on Major Offiah's face was priceless when I wrested the pistol from his holster, Alvarez remembered with pleasure, even now holding the heavy weapon comfortingly in his hands. *The black bastard had thought I was going to shoot him where he stood; I would have, too, if I hadn't known Hill would have me mercilessly hunted down in retribution. But smashing the gun around the back of Offiah's head was almost as much fun. I'd have given him the boot, too, if that civilian hadn't disturbed me,* Alvarez thought, the memory a bitter one.

Alvarez sighed in relaxation, almost enjoying the solitude of the blackness he'd grown accustomed to. The first night he'd spent alone in the dark had been traumatic. As soon as he'd switched off his small torch to preserve its battery life, the complete lack of discernable light had instantly driven him to turn it back on again. Slowly, he'd trained himself to leave the torch off for longer and longer periods until he'd been able to drift off to sleep, only to wake with a start some time later, his fingers scrabbling to switch the light back on once more.

Fortunately his timepiece, a gift from his mother, had proved an invaluable resource in more ways than one. First, it possessed its own surprisingly powerful, light; and secondly it ensured he knew what time of day it was – critical in the dark when all sense of chronology went out of the window. It was now his third day on the run and he'd worked his way first north and then back east, in the direction he knew the lake to be located. His plan was simple; pilfer food from the fishermen at the lake and roam the western shoreline for sign of his USSB comrades. He'd always known much more about Sanctuary than he'd let on. Darklight and Goodwin had him and his men taken by force. They were the enemy and had to be resisted. If that meant gaining their trust and then sabotaging them from within, then so be it; that's exactly what he'd sworn to do. Every member of his decontamination team had also been willing to withhold certain types of information. Unfortunately, they didn't really know anything about the chamber they were in; nothing concrete anyway, and nothing to aid their escape in any case. He, after all, wanted to reach the USSB as much as Goodwin and his ragtag Steadfast crew.

Alvarez's number two, Corporal Walker, had been a great help during their time under the watchful gaze of Darklight. Walker had also aided Alvarez in his attempts to acquire their weapons, so much so that Alvarez, had – on occasion – needed to calm the man down. Alvarez's thoughts strayed to Corporal Walker and the rest of his decontamination team, currently being held against their will back at the camp; it made his blood boil to think Offiah still lorded it over them. A sudden noise made Alvarez snatch up his torch and turn it on. He aimed the beam of light around the curious structure he now frequented. It was one of the smaller towers in the city, in terms of its footprint anyway; Alvarez didn't know how high the thing went, nor did he care. It was situated on the outskirts of the city, providing excellent access to the lake, while also being close to the area where the Darklight recon team had come into contact with his USSB brethren. Its strange design, inside and out, now illuminated by his torch revealed nothing out of the ordinary, so he flicked the light off once more and looked at his watch; it was nearing one in the morning; time for him to sneak out to the lake and nab some much needed food.

Standing up, he froze in mid-stretch as a small light in the distance caught his eye. A single luminous glow, much like he'd seen on the footage at Hilt's meeting, recorded by Lieutenant Manaus on her head-cam.

'Fuck a duck,' Alvarez said out loud to himself, 'it must be my lucky day.'

Switching his torch back on, he ran in the light's direction, following it as it made its way from the lake and into the city. *There's no way it's a Darklight team*, he thought, *they never operate with just a single light source.*

'Hey!' Alvarez shouted, now only a couple of hundred yards away. 'Sergeant Alvarez, USSB Sanctuary, slow down, fellas!'

Rather than decrease in speed, the light kept moving and then blinked out of existence, most likely going behind one of the buildings. Alvarez picked up the pace and was soon rounding what must have been the tower in question, but there was no sign of the light.

'Shit!' Alvarez stamped his foot in frustration at his missed opportunity; he knew all too well he could ill afford to miss out on such fortuitous breaks. Turning back, he caught a glimmer of movement out of the corner of his eye. Snapping his head round in its direction he caught the tail end of an afterglow, heading deeper into the city. 'Sweet glory,' Alvarez said, his hopes soaring once more as he set off in pursuit.

Alvarez ran further and further into the Anakim metropolis, but the men from the USSB always seemed to be that much quicker than him; just staying the same distance ahead, almost as if they were deliberately matching his speed. Realising he couldn't keep up with them for much longer, he redoubled his efforts, running flat out in a last ditch attempt to catch them. As he pounded along, the light from his elusive army colleagues finally getting closer, his torchlight threw up a disturbing sight – a huge chasm directly in his path! In a split second decision Alvarez threw himself to the ground in a desperate bid to halt his headlong dash into oblivion. His arms and legs spread wide, his body hit the floor, the torch flying from his grasp. Letting out a cry of terror as he slithered across the dusty, gravel surface, he felt his legs drop over the abyss, his torso following suit. Alvarez forced his fingers into the loose sediment, his nails biting into the harder substrate beneath, grinding him to a stop on the brink of the cliff edge. His eyes wide in fright, he watched the beam of light from his torch spiral, end over end into the air below, until it bounced once against the rock wall and went out, the distant echo of the impact its final declaration of existence. Thrust into darkness, Alvarez heaved himself back up, rolling away from the chasm and to safety, his breath coming in deep, rapid gasps.

He lay there for some time, gathering his thoughts while he recovered from the fright of his life. *I don't think I've ever come that close to dying before*, he thought, his heart rate gradually dropping back to normality. Another thought, a worrying one, worked its way to the forefront of his mind: how had the soldiers he'd been following cross over the chasm so quickly? He'd watched the light carry on without deviation before he himself had encountered the large fissure, its expanse far too wide to leap over. Pushing the disturbing question away, he pressed the button on his watch, its light seeming less powerful than he remembered it. A strange clicking noise made him swing round, his watch extended in front of him as he sought to shine its faint glow at whatever had made the sound.

'This is Sergeant Alvarez,' he said, a tremble to his voice, 'Decontamination Team, USSB Sanctuary. Who's there?'

A light appeared fifty yards away; it glinted and glistened in the darkness, its green and blue tinge fluctuating strangely as it did so, almost mesmeric in its fundamental effervescence. Alvarez took a step back from it, the weird clicking noise restarting, getting louder and more insistent before developing into a guttural growl. Alvarez, shaking uncontrollably, felt a trickle of water run down the inside of his leg. A high pitched screech shattered his last shred of sanity as the light surged towards him. Stumbling backwards, the last sensation Alvarez had was of falling into a deep, black void, his own screams ringing in his ears as his eyes locked on to the light which followed him down into the bowels of the earth.

CHAPTER THIRTY-TWO

'WHAT THE HELL IS IT?'

'No idea, but it looks pretty.'

'Pretty?'

'Don't you think so?'

'Hmm, I'd say more like disturbing, or ungodly.'

'It's been going on for some minutes now,' a deep voice said from behind, making the two of them jump at the interruption.

Goodwin looked back at Hilt. 'Commander, what do you think it is?'

'An electrical discharge of some kind.' Hilt looked up in the same direction as everyone else who had gathered at the edge of the camp. 'I have to agree with the doctor on this one, sir, it is pretty.'

Goodwin looked at Hilt in amazement, the word *pretty*, not something he'd ever imagined the hardened mercenary ever saying.

Hilt glanced at Goodwin and gave him an odd expression, the downturn of his mouth and raised brows conveying his willingness to stand by his comment despite the shock it had invoked.

'See, I told you,' Kara said, 'how can you not call that pretty?'

Goodwin looked back up at the spectacle, giving Hilt a final look of confounded disappointment before he did so. *I can see their point, I suppose*, he thought to himself, watching the pinnacle of the distant Anakim tower throb as a wave of purple energy pulsed up its length to discharge towards the ceiling of the chamber, over a mile above.

'One of my lieutenants tells me it's one of the tallest structures in the city, if not *the* tallest structure,' Hilt told them, as another ripple of purple light flowed up from within the dark of the metropolis to erupt from behind the other surrounding towers and swirl around the building's pointed spire.

'Why do you think it's started now?' Goodwin asked.

Kara pondered the question. 'Perhaps it always happens at this time of year.'

'Or it's a once in a lifetime event,' Hilt said.

A man in front of them, earwigging on their conversation, glanced back. 'Or our presence has sparked off a chain of events that has activated some ancient mechanism.'

'An electrostatic build-up through the city, maybe,' Kara said, 'discharged when a certain mass has been reached?'

They were all plausible theories, but none sated Goodwin's curiosity.

A Darklight soldier approached from behind and handed his commander a pair of VSE goggles. Hilt held them up to his eyes for some moments and watched the energy spike discharge once more, up into the rocky roof of the ceiling. 'Interesting.' He handed the device to Goodwin for him to try.

Goodwin looked through the lenses, their enhancement of the visual spectrum displaying the phenomenon in a grey, crystal clear image. With the scene magnified, Goodwin could see the branches of electrical lightning dispersing into the air at the building's summit and flashing to the ceiling, sending out tiny trails of white light in all directions. Goodwin watched a few more of the pulses before passing the goggles to Kara.

'I've sent a team to investigate,' Hilt told Goodwin. 'It'll take them half a day to get there, but it's worth a look, I think.'

'Most definitely, Commander,' Goodwin said before, as quickly as it had begun, the repetitive cycle of purple light stopped. A groan of discontent swept through the onlookers. Everyone waited for some time before, one by one, and then in groups, they broke away, going back to their normal routines, the fascinating display accepted as being over.

Goodwin, with Kara at his side and the Darklight commander just behind, walked back into camp, their conversation about what they'd just witnessed immersive in its detail and scope. As they approached the command tent, a heart wrenching scream of despair split the quiet, sending all three of them running to locate the source.

Coming in from the other direction a Darklight soldier held a sobbing woman in his arms, trying to pull her back to her feet from where she'd collapsed to the floor. Kara, the first to react, took over, offering soothing words of comfort to the near hysterical woman.

'Rebecca?' Goodwin said, realising who it was as others in the vicinity rushed to the scene, drawn by Rebecca's terrible cries of pain and torment. 'Rebecca, what's wrong? What's happened?' he asked, anguished at her suffering.

'I'll take her inside.' Hilt bent down, scooped Rebecca up and carried her into the camp's central tent, Goodwin and Kara close on his heels.

Hilt placed Rebecca down on a pile of discarded clothing, quickly assembled by Kara to act as a place of comfort in an area otherwise free of any kind of soft furnishings. Goodwin got a glass of water, which he managed to get Rebecca to sip as she calmed while Kara continued to whisper to her soothingly.

Rebecca tried to speak, but her shallow breathing made the words stick in her throat as she fought to get them out.

'Deep breaths, Rebecca,' Kara said, 'slow, deep breaths.'

Rebecca shook her head. 'I can't – I couldn't – find her.'

Goodwin crouched down before her. 'Find who?'

'Susan.' Rebecca's face crumbled again as the tears came. 'Susan's gone!'

'Gone? Gone where?'

Rebecca sobbed harder.

'Come on, Rebecca, sweetheart,' Kara said, 'you need to tell us what's happened.'

Another soldier appeared in the tent, with Joseph in tow. The young handicapped man rushed to Rebecca's side, embracing her and holding her tightly, trembling himself.

'I came – I came back to our tent and somehow Susan and Joseph had sneaked out,' Rebecca told them, stroking Joseph's hair. 'Julie and Arianna were beside themselves. I ran out to look for them, expecting them to be close by—' Rebecca paused again, wiping away her tears as her voice strengthened. 'I saw Joseph in the distance, at the edge of the camp. I called out to him, but he didn't seem to hear me. I ran over to where he'd been, but by then he'd moved out beyond one of the floodlights, beyond the boundary. I had my torch with me so I turned it on and ran after him, heading straight out into the dark. I heard a noise in the distance, followed by Susan's screams, I called out, shouting her name and Joseph's. Neither of them responded. I kept shouting until I was hoarse, and eventually I found Joseph, on his knees. He was shaking uncontrollably, he'd wet himself too. There was no sign of Susan. I tried to search for her, but Joseph wouldn't move forwards and I couldn't leave him in the dark again. I managed to drag him back towards the camp and I can't really remember the rest. A soldier started taking me back here, but I knew Susan was still out there, on her own, alone. I tried to tell him, but I couldn't get the words out. I couldn't—' Her voice broke again.

'Joseph.' Goodwin touched the boy's shoulder; he whimpered and flinched from the contact. 'Joseph,' Goodwin said again, moving round to try and look into his face, 'it's me, it's Winnie.'

Joseph's eyes opened a fraction and he stared into Goodwin's face. Goodwin gave him a comforting smile, noticing the handicapped man's limbs still shook and spasmed as his body attempted to rid itself of the massive amounts of pent up energy created by his trauma.

'Joseph, what did you see?' Goodwin asked.

Joseph closed his eyes, his body shaking in response to the question.

Goodwin cupped the poor boy's cheek. 'Joseph, where is Susan?'

Joseph opened his eyes again. 'Noise,' he whispered across Rebecca's shoulder, his grip on his carer unrelinquishing.

'Noise?' Goodwin said. 'What noise?'

Joseph let out another whimper and shut his eyes.

Goodwin was about to stand back up, but before he could Joseph started making a strange sound that got louder and louder until he was shrieking in one extended scream, his eyes wide, his face a mask of terror.

Goodwin stumbled backwards in shock and fear, the hairs all over his body standing up on end. He stared at Joseph in horror as the boy quietened and hid his face in Rebecca's shoulder once more, his shaking unabated, and whimpering increased.

'What is it?' Hilt asked, seeing Goodwin's expression. 'Sir, what's wrong?'

'That sound—'

'That was exactly the same sound that we heard in the city,' Kara said, her voice as distressed as Goodwin felt.

Hilt looked from Kara to Goodwin. 'How can that be?'

'The boy can mimic sounds.' Goodwin tried to dispel the awful noise produced by Joseph from his mind. 'He's seen what we saw in the city. Susan isn't lost, she's been taken, by whatever, or whoever, that light is.'

Hilt contemplated them both, perhaps judging the conviction of their claims. Apparently satisfied the information was sound, he turned to one of his men. 'Lieutenant, get me my armour.'

'Sir!' The man sped from the room.

Hilt strode to his command desk and flicked some switches on the main console before picking up a communication device and holding it to one ear. 'This is Command. Code Red alert. All units receiving this message return to base immediately. I repeat, Code Red.'

'Sir,' Major Offiah said, 'what about the men at the lake; shouldn't we leave at least a token force in case the U.S. military return?'

Hilt muttered something unintelligible but maintained his calm. 'Very well, make it happen.'

Offiah got on his radio.

Another Darklight soldier approached the commander. 'Sir, the sensors didn't activate in the quadrant where we found the woman and the boy. We have no data on movements in that sector for the past hour.'

'You're telling me we had a malfunction at the exact time one of our number goes missing, in the same location?'

'Yes, sir – well – no, sir – I mean, the equipment is sound. We've tested it. It just didn't work when it was supposed to.'

Hilt's face darkened. 'Then it's no coincidence.'

'You think this thing, this light, manipulated your systems by design?' Goodwin said.

Hilt's mouth tightened before he nodded in confirmation. 'Whatever this thing is, it's turned out to be more of a threat than expected. I won't underestimate it again. It's come into this camp, disabled a high-tech piece of hardware and made off with an unarmed and vulnerable woman; but it's shown its hand now and I aim to ensure that will be the first – and *last* – mistake it makes.'

The lieutenant returned with the commander's armour. Hilt inspected the black hardened panels before, piece by piece, clipping them to his body with clinical precision.

'Major,' Hilt said, attaching his formidable chest-plate.

'Sir?'

'I want every available man and woman with a torch assembled in this camp a-sap. Recall all the reconnaissance teams from the tunnels. I want this girl found and I want her found now.'

'Yes, sir.' The Major scurried from the enclosure, his superior's words motivating him like no other.

The Darklight leader secured the final section of his armour, completing the process of encasing himself in the impenetrable black shell, the white Darklight insignia and his name and rank on the chest and shoulders. He then placed the substantial helmet down on the central table, ready to be worn at a moment's notice. Next to this he laid his large assault rifle. Finally, the knife he'd been using as a paperweight was returned to its home; a sheath built into the armour on one side of his chest-plate.

'Sir,' Hilt said to Goodwin, 'when everyone is ready I'll need you to coordinate our civilian response with my men. No one goes out alone and no one goes without an armed escort.'

Goodwin nodded, his thoughts racing, the turn of events taking on a life of their own. 'Commander,' Goodwin said, bringing Hilt's attention back to him. 'If you think the sensors going down aren't a coincidence, what about the light on the tower? The two events coincided just as closely, don't you think?'

The Darklight leader gestured for Goodwin to follow him out of the tent and they stopped once they were out of earshot. 'The thought had crossed my mind.' Hilt's brows furrowed in an uncommon display of emotion.

'There's something else, isn't there?' Goodwin said, perceiving the Commander's continued unease.

Hilt nodded, moving yet further away from the command tent. 'This – *incident* – has also occurred in close proximity to the light at the lake and the relocation of my patrols from around this camp. If that hadn't happened, there would have been no way anything could have taken Susan the way it, or they, did.'

Goodwin didn't like the implications of what Hilt was saying and it must have shown as Hilt's expression grew graver still.

'You think the U.S. Army footprints were simulated somehow?' Goodwin said.

'We can't rule out anything at this point. As crazy as it sounds, we could be dealing with something beyond our comprehension. From what I've gleaned from Alvarez and his men, they class Sanctuary Proper – as they call it – as a highly dangerous environment, full of ancient technology and materials that can prove extremely hazardous to human health.'

'I thought Alvarez wasn't so forthcoming with his information?' Goodwin said.

'No, you're right. He only released his knowledge sparingly, but when he did it was with a care that seemed rehearsed. That's why I had his tent bugged as soon as they were released from custody.'

Goodwin whistled in appreciation. 'The sergeant would've gone berserk if he'd known.'

'He was paranoid enough to keep talk within the camp to a minimum,' Hilt said. 'On the odd occasion he, or one of his men, slipped up, we were listening. We never got much, just titbits here and there.'

'If the footprints were a diversion—' Goodwin left his sentence hanging.

'Then,' Hilt continued, 'it would mean whatever we're dealing with is capable of differentiating between two military units to the finest detail. It also knows exactly how to manipulate us into an appropriate response. Which is unsettling, to say the least.'

Goodwin thought for a moment. 'Another possibility is that the light at the lake is an untimely, unconnected event. Alvarez is still out there somewhere; he might have had a hand to play with the light on the tower and even the footprints at the lake.'

'Whatever is the case, our hand has been forced.' Hilt paused before continuing. 'I'm sorry, sir, it appears I've failed you. It won't happen again.'

'Nonsense, Commander. You've failed no one. Under the circumstances you've been exemplary in every department. If anyone is to blame, it's me.'

'Thank you, sir, but on this, we'll have to agree to disagree.'

A soldier ducked his head outside the tent. 'Sir, you're needed.'

'Go to work, Commander,' Goodwin said. 'Find her, find Susan.'

Hilt nodded once, his expression set as hard as stone. His director had commanded and he obeyed.

CHAPTER THIRTY-THREE

FORTY-EIGHT HOURS HAD PASSED since the mentally handicapped woman, Susan, had gone missing. Neither Hilt nor Goodwin had slept much during that time, tirelessly working round the clock to make use of their resources as best they could. The twenty-five thousand strong civilian contingent had been separated into five hundred groups, each fifty people strong. These civilian teams were each assigned five Darklight soldiers, and even now they combed the vast area around the camp and beyond, searching for any sign of Susan. Floodlights near the centre of camp were moved further out into the darkness, acting as points of reference for the team leaders as they guided their people to the zones allotted by those back at base.

Further afield, the remaining available Darklight reconnaissance units delved deeper into the city and surrounding areas, scouring every inch of land, their specialised equipment making steady work of what would otherwise be a near impossible task.

'This is pointless!' Goodwin threw a map to the ground and stalked away to the entrance of the command tent. Standing there, staring out into the dark, his thoughts as ever dwelling on Susan, Goodwin felt a small hand slip around his waist.

'We'll find her.' Kara moved in front of him to take his chin in her other hand. 'We just have to keep going, keep searching.'

'This place is too big,' Goodwin said, her words, while appreciated, not helping to relieve his growing despair at their lack of progress. 'We've been here for months on end, every day we've found new structures, new tunnels, new cave systems. How can we expect to find one small woman in a place this big, this dark? It's a damn labyrinth!'

Kara didn't reply, perhaps fearing – as he did – that the longer Susan was missing the more likely it was, if they did find her, they would be recovering a body.

Goodwin sighed; he unhooked himself from Kara's embrace and returned to pick up the discarded map, dusting it off before replacing it back on the table. Smoothing it out with both hands, he looked up at the three lieutenants tasked with helping him coordinate the search. 'So Hilt's team has already covered this quadrant?' Goodwin pointed at an area within the city.

'Yes, sir, but—'

The soldier was cut off as the main radio crackled to life, announcing an incoming communication from one of the search teams.

'Civilian team, Lambda Eight, reporting,' the voice said, sounding excited, 'we've found something; we think it's part of a bracelet!'

Goodwin, his hopes lifting, snatched up the handset. 'What does it look like?'

'It's broken.' The reply came back after a short pause, testing Goodwin's patience to the limit. 'But it has a few stones and shells left on it, the stones glow bright blue in the dark.'

'That's it!' Goodwin smacked the table. 'That's Susan's bracelet!'

'Where are Lambda Eight on the map?' Kara asked one of the soldiers.

'There ma'am.' The woman placed her finger in a sector to the south-west of the city.

Goodwin's attention homed in on the area in question. 'We don't want to pull everyone into the area.' He rubbed the back of his neck, deep in concentration. 'She may no longer be there, or it could be a trick of some kind.'

Kara gave him a look. 'A trick, you think whatever took her is that intelligent?'

Goodwin scanned the map, deliberating as to which teams to move. 'Yes,' he said absently, 'possibly.'

Just then another incoming transmission interrupted his thought process. 'This is Hil—' a voice said, before breaking up.

One of the soldiers adjusted the system's frequency and Goodwin picked up the radio. 'Say again, is that you, Commander?'

'This is Hilt.' The message was repeated, much clearer this time. 'Do you copy?'

'Five by five, Commander,' Goodwin said. 'Go ahead.'

'I heard the previous transmission. I'm repositioning to their location.'

'Copy that, Commander, keep me updated.'

'Will do, sir. Hilt, out.'

♦

Another day of searching came and went and the Darklight leader returned to camp, bringing with him the remains of Susan's bracelet but no further news. Goodwin glanced over at the piece of handmade jewellery on the side of the desk at which he worked and couldn't help but remember the sweet, vulnerable and unassuming woman that had made it. The other in the matching pair, even now, encircled his wrist, a constant reminder of the loss and guilt that he felt over her disturbing abduction.

Despite the initial breakthrough there seemed to be no accompanying trail which they could follow. A large proportion of the search parties had been reassigned to the area surrounding where the bracelet had been found but, as yet, nothing even resembling a lead had surfaced.

It was mid-afternoon when an unexpected visitor, Corporal Walker from the decontamination team, was escorted to the command tent, requesting an audience with Hilt and Goodwin.

'You wanted to speak to us, Corporal?' Hilt said.

'Yes, Commander.' Walker looked from Hilt to Goodwin and back. 'It's a matter of some importance.'

Walker, Sergeant Alvarez's second in command, was now in temporary charge of the small unit of U.S. Army troops still held under guard in the camp. The corporal was slim and of average height, with cropped dark hair and a goatee beard. He wore the baggy green uniform worn by U.S. soldiers the world over and had developed a slight facial tic since Goodwin had last seen him; he wondered if it was perhaps precipitated by the stress of detainment.

'Well, Corporal?' Goodwin said, when Walker failed to speak.

Walker eyed the other people in the room; a few civilians, but mostly Darklight troops, populated the desk where the search for Susan was being co-ordinated. 'May we talk in private?'

'Negative,' Hilt said, in no mood for having his time wasted, a stance Goodwin himself held to.

'Out with it, man,' Goodwin said, as Walker continued to procrastinate.

'Right.' Walker's cheek and eye twitched in tandem. 'Since Sergeant Alvarez left—'

'Absconded,' Goodwin corrected him, noticing as he did so that Major Offiah watched Walker from across the room.

'Yes,' Walker continued, 'since the sergeant *absconded* and the disabled woman went missing, I feel it's time to come clean on a few things.'

Goodwin gestured to him. 'Go on.'

'Alvarez – the sergeant,' Walker said, 'he'd always been on the decontamination teams in Sanctuary, as have the rest of the unit you have under guard. I've been at the USSB longer than everyone else, though – three years longer, to be precise – and I wasn't on a decon team during that time, but a different regiment that worked in and around the military laboratories along with a civilian outfit called the SED.'

'SED?' Hilt repeated, unimpressed by what he'd heard so far.

'Sanctuary Exploration Division,' Walker told him. 'They go out into Sanctuary Proper, where we are now, and photograph and dig up ancient sites built by the Anakim. It's a highly secretive outfit as they get to go where others don't, far outside the USSB.'

'And you keep this information to yourself?' Goodwin wasn't sure where this was leading.

'It's more than my job's worth to blab about it,' Walker said. 'But the fact is when I worked there, while I never got to see anything very interesting, I did hear things.'

Goodwin frowned. 'Such as?'

'Such as, years back, the elite Deep Reach survey teams from the SED used to explore to the east of the USSB; that was, until a whole unit, along with Terra Force support, went missing and the eastern programme was shelved – permanently.'

'We're east of the USSB, aren't we?' Goodwin said.

Walker gave a solemn nod.

'What happened to this *Deep Reach* team?' Hilt asked him.

'Officially? They were deemed the victims of an earthquake, and the whole region was declared unsafe for human habitation or exploration.'

'Unofficially?' Goodwin said.

'Word has it they encountered something, something that left more of a trace than the official documents let on.'

Realisation suddenly dawned on Goodwin. 'Something, you mean the light, don't you? You knew and you didn't tell us?' Goodwin was enraged by the man's deceit. 'Do you know what you've done?!'

Hilt held him back as Walker quailed at his fury.

'How many men were in this Deep Reach team?' Hilt said, his tone urgent.

Walker stared at Goodwin, who still seethed with anger.

'I said!' Hilt roared, grabbing Walker around the throat, lifting him off his feet and slamming him into the rock wall, 'how many men?!'

'For—' Walker gasped, unable to speak as Hilt's giant hand throttled him.

'Sir!' Major Offiah tried to pull Hilt away from a rapidly reddening Walker.

'How many, Corporal?' Hilt repeated, shooting a look at his Major that made Goodwin fear for the man's life.

Offiah held his hands up and backed away, Hilt's wrath seemingly indiscriminate.

'Forty,' Walker croaked, as he tried in vain to free Hilt's mighty grip.

Hilt released his hand sending the corporal falling to the floor. 'Call back all civilian search teams,' Hilt said to one of the coms operators, who looked as frightened of Hilt as Corporal Walker did. 'NOW!'

The soldier got onto the radio, his training kicking into gear.

Walker looked to Goodwin as he stood back up. 'I swear we didn't create those boot prints at the lake. I've never heard of any USSB units going through water-filled tunnels, either.'

Goodwin's contempt for the man vied with the anger he felt towards him. 'You admit you don't know everything, though.'

'No, I don't. But I think when we came to Sanctuary, humans I mean, we disturbed something down here, something that was better left alone. Not Anakim, but something, something else—'

'That's why you kept pestering me for your weapons for all those months, isn't it?' Hilt's voice was full of fettered rage. 'Isn't it?!' he bellowed.

Walker nodded in confirmation.

'Sir,' Major Offiah said to Hilt, his tone attracting Goodwin's attention, 'we've lost touch with three of our men in one of the western reaches of the city.'

'How long have they been out of contact?' Hilt turned from Corporal Walker to give Offiah his undivided attention.

'Five hours. They were scheduled to report in two hours ago.'

'Two hours,' Goodwin said, 'and you've only thought to tell us now?'

'Normal protocol, sir,' Offiah told him, 'we give our recon teams more leeway as they travel further, often underground where communication is difficult or impossible. It was flagged up when they failed to submit their report, but many of our teams get caught out similarly on a daily basis; this one is the first to breach the two hour window, however.'

'Sir, an emergency flare has been sighted two miles west of the city,' a Darklight communications operative told Hilt.

'That's our missing team,' Hilt said, 'they must be out of coms range. Major, secure the camp; reinstate all Darklight personnel returning with the civilian search teams to form a secure perimeter. I want weapons hot, visors down, combat systems activated.'

'Yes, sir!' Offiah got to work on his orders.

Hilt looked to another soldier. 'Lieutenant, tell all recon teams in the vicinity of the flare to converge on its location.' Hilt, shrouded in his matte black suit of armour, picked up his helmet and slid it over his head, the visor up, his face visible inside it. 'Sir,' he said to Goodwin, 'I'm heading out to my men; emergency flares are only to be utilised as a last resort, so they're either in difficulty or they've found something, maybe both. I'm bringing this situation back under our control, you have my word. If I fail, I recommend you replace me with another officer of your choosing.'

Goodwin looked at Hilt, lost for words. He nodded his head as Hilt waited for his response.

'Thank you, sir. You men,' Hilt gestured to three Darklight soldiers who'd been poring over some maps, 'with me.'

And with that, the Darklight leader and his men left the tent, vanishing into the subterranean night.

CHAPTER THIRTY-FOUR

Goodwin paced the edge of the camp's exterior, waiting for the imminent arrival of the Darklight leader. Hilt had only been gone six hours, but the unexpected speed of his return had set Goodwin's nerves jangling. For some reason only discernable to the Commander, he'd declined to comment on his findings during his brief communiqué, just saying, 'You need to see it for yourself.'

He didn't have to wait much longer before the hulking figure of Hilt emerged out of the gloom, accompanied by a large unit of soldiers, all similarly garbed in black armour, an array of formidable weapons on show.

Goodwin fell into step beside Hilt. 'What news, Commander?'

'I'm sorry to keep you waiting, sir,' Hilt said, his mood grave. 'The flare drew us to an area where we found a previously undiscovered tunnel system. We wouldn't have found it at all except the entrance, concealed beneath the ruins of an ancient monument, had a curious symbol embedded into its rock surround.'

'Anakim symbols are two a penny down here,' Goodwin said, as they made their way into camp and towards their hub of operations, 'why was that one so special?'

'It glowed, bright blue.'

Goodwin looked sharply at the Darklight man. 'Bright blue?' He pulled up his sleeve to reveal his bracelet, which emanated its faint radiance in the half-light. 'Like this?'

Hilt peered at it. 'Exactly like that. I recommend you take that off. If that's what drew the creature to Susan, it might return for you.'

'Creature?'

Hilt glanced at him. 'Sir?'

'You said, *drew the creature to Susan*; what have you found, Commander?'

Hilt looked at him once more, his expression unfathomable. 'A turn of phrase, but one that may yet prove accurate.'

'Tell me.' Goodwin led the way as they cut left and onto the main thoroughfare of the campsite.

'I had a few hundred men at the scene when I arrived,' Hilt said, resuming his narrative. 'Once we'd found these new tunnels we entered, seeking the three man recon unit we suspected had preceded us. It wasn't long before we found a locator beacon, no doubt left by one of the team for us to find. A little further in, we found another and then a ... trail.'

'Trail of what?' Goodwin asked, the command tent now in sight ahead.

'Blood.'

The evocative word flooded Goodwin's mind with all manner of images, many of them distinctly unpleasant.

'Following this,' Hilt continued, 'we arrived at a cylindrical structure with a high vaulted roof, where we found this.' He held aloft a helmet Goodwin recognised as one worn by Darklight's reconnaissance personnel, the shape narrower and more streamlined than the bulkier, combat orientated headgear sported by Hilt and the rest of his

mercenaries.

'It looks in bad shape.' Goodwin noticed one side of the helmet had been crushed. 'But, there's more that you're not telling me, isn't there?'

'There's no point telling you any more,' Hilt said, as they walked inside the tent. 'It's better if you watch.'

'Watch what?'

'You may remember, all Darklight helmets have an array of tech integrated into a comprehensive combat system.' Hilt placed the battered helmet down next to a portable computer on one of the desks. 'Which includes solid state memory chips, cameras and perhaps most advantageous in this instance, *automated* recording protocols.'

Hilt connected the helmet to a port on the computer, positioned the screen so Goodwin could see it and then streamed the video file. 'Take a look,' he said, moving back to stand alongside Goodwin, 'but be prepared, it's hard to watch.'

Goodwin swapped glances with Major Offiah, who'd been by Goodwin's side during Hilt's excursion.

'Captain,' a man's voice said, the sound coming out of the screen's speakers. 'I think I just saw something, two towers down.'

'You think, or you did?' another man's voice replied.

'Did!'

The pale blue image on screen showed a bright light gliding quickly across the ground some way away, between an avenue of Anakim structures.

'I see it too, Captain,' a woman's voice said, her armoured shape creeping into view on the right side of the screen, rifle in hand.

Another person strode into frame, the slits in the helmet glowing like demonic eyes as the man looked at the camera's owner. 'Don't just stand there, Dixon, you idiot,' the captain said, sprinting off, 'after it!'

The woman followed her CO, and Dixon, the director of this production, swore and started running as well, the image on screen moving up and down in response, rhythmically attuned to his gait.

The crew of three sprinted through the ghostly city at speed, their agility impressive considering the armour they all wore. Further ahead, the ethereal light Goodwin was all too familiar with flew onwards, the Darklight recon team in hot pursuit, the gap between them increasing.

Rounding a corner, Dixon all but knocked over his female colleague who'd pulled up behind the captain, standing a few yards ahead, his weapon raised as he scanned the area, now devoid of any movement or light.

Dixon was breathing hard. 'Fucking hell – that thing's quick.'

'Quiet,' the captain said, and then walked forwards, rifle still at eye level. 'Activate visor-radar, echelon formation on my six.'

The two Darklight soldiers moved out in front of Dixon; he brought up the rear, completing the short, diagonal column. Goodwin watched the image as it rotated this way and that, Dixon's rifle scope in shot as the man surveyed the terrain around them.

'Command, this is Recon Delta Two Six, over,' Dixon, said in a hushed voice. 'Still no signal, sir.'

'Copy that,' the captain replied. 'Keep calm, we knew this section might be a dead spot.'

The recon team moved as one towards the crumbling structure of a huge plinth, on which stood a colossal statue that looked like it had once resembled an animal. Across the ground, to one side, another large section had collapsed, its shape no longer easily determined; the ravages of time masking what might have been the figure of an Anakim warrior. An object, twenty foot in diameter and resembling a head, had detached from the rest of the fallen stone monument and lay at the furthest reaches of the debris, as though it had been severed from its body by the powerful swing of an equally immense sword.

The scene changed as Dixon's attention was drawn towards a dark hole at the base of one the walls. The display on the screen darkened as he scrolled to a different type of spectral image; now visible within the pit was a dim glow. 'Captain, look at this.'

The Darklight officer came to a halt. 'Henderson, cover us.'

'Yes, sir.' The woman dropped to one knee, her rifle at the ready.

The captain moved back to Dixon's side. 'I don't see anything.'

'Try T.I.I.,' Dixon said.

'T.I.I.?' Goodwin looked to Hilt for an explanation.

'Thermal Image Intensifier.' Hilt's eyes were fixed on the screen.

'Good job, Dix.' The captain held out a hand. 'Drop me down.'

Dixon grasped the captain's hand and lowered him down into the hole.

'I see an entrance,' the captain said, almost disappearing from view. 'Henderson, stay topside; Dixon, get your ass down here.'

Dixon switched back to the pale blue visual image and the picture on the display lurched as he turned and dropped down into the hole, aided by his colleague beneath. Now below ground level, Dixon and the captain walked a few paces along a tunnel, the floor littered with rubble and the walls wreathed in cracks. A wide archway, ten feet high and the same in width, came into focus. Around the arch an inscription had been carved into the stone, its meaning lost long ago to time's unyielding embrace. In the centre of this text a large symbol glowed with a brilliance Goodwin knew to be as blue as the stones on Susan's bracelets.

A faint noise, seemingly far away, could be heard through the speakers.

'Jesus wept.' The captain traced the symbol of the cross on his chest. 'Did you hear that?'

Dixon's camera moved up and down. 'Yeah, it sounded like a girl's scream.'

The captain hung his head for a moment as if in deep thought. 'We have to go in.'

'But we're off the grid.' Dixon sounded worried. 'We're almost at the two hour cut-off.'

'Fuck that!' the captain said. 'We may never get another chance at this; if that poor girl's down there, we have no choice. Henderson, do you read me?'

'Yes, sir,' came the response.

'Send up an e-flare and follow us down; Dixon, lend a hand.'

Dixon walked back to where he'd entered the hole and looked up to see Henderson firing a projectile high into the firmament above. A trail of smoke streaked out behind it until, seconds later, a small detonation was followed by a piercing bright light that filled the screen. Stowing her weapon, Henderson climbed down into the hole, helped by Dixon, and the pair rejoined their leader, who waited at the gateway into the newly discovered tunnel complex.

'Okay, movement sensors on.' The captain checked his weapon and ammo clips. 'Switch to your combat spectrum array. For God's sake don't shoot at anything that moves; there's a civilian down here and I don't want her killed by friendly fire, understand?'

'Copy that, Cap,' Henderson said. 'Lock and load.'

'That's an affirmative, Captain.' Dixon cocked his own rifle and the image on the screen changed to a multi-layered, multi-coloured feed.

'Right,' the captain said, 'I'll take point; Henderson, the rear.' The captain blew out a whoosh of air, psyching himself up, then put his assault rifle to his shoulder and ghosted through the arch. 'Let's go.'

Goodwin watched as the small unit made their way through the tunnels, which branched off in all directions. After a while, the captain ordered Dixon to place a small locator beacon on the ground; the device had a small lamp on the top and pulsed out a bright light once every few seconds. Pressing on further, the team located a central passage that all other paths converged on. A second beacon was laid down and then another; fifty feet on, the captain stumbled upon the first drops of blood.

'Is that what I think it is?' Dixon said.

The captain, squatting on his haunches, dipped a gloved finger into a droplet that was part of a distinct trail leading off into the darkness ahead of them. Opening the visor on his helmet, he looked at the smear before rubbing the substance between his thumb and forefinger. 'Yes, it's blood alright.' The captain stood back up, lowered his visor and advanced more warily. 'Stay sharp, people.'

A strange high-pitched sound reverberated through the tunnels, making Dixon freeze in place. 'What the fuck was that!'

'Dixon, man-up and move your ass,' Henderson's voice told him as the captain moved ahead.

Dixon, scurrying forwards, soon halted again as the captain put the flat of his palm in the air, signalling for them to stop. In front, the tunnel turned a sharp left.

'Henderson, get up here.' The captain waved her forwards.

The form of the Darklight woman passed by Dixon, who shot a look back at the emptiness before shifting sideways against the wall, ensuring nothing could creep up on him from behind.

'Moving,' the captain said, as he and Henderson, covering each other in tactical formation, edged around the kink in the passage.

Dixon, rounding the bend behind them, could see they were now in a weird, cylindrical shaft. Instead of rock, the walls glinted like dark metal. The surfaces had been deeply engraved and sculpted, creating miniature labyrinths beneath, almost as if the abnormal construct consisted of multiple layers, one inside the other. These fantastically intricate and abstract carvings glowed from within with a curious wavering light. In the centre sprawled the body of a man.

Henderson turned it over with the tip of her rifle, an arm flopping loose as she did so. 'It's Sergeant Alvarez, Captain. From the looks of his heat signature, he's stone cold; must have been dead for a while.'

The captain joined her and looked down at the lifeless form. 'He's got extensive injuries, all his limbs are broken and there're some big wounds here, on his torso; he would've bled out quickly.'

A loud noise ahead made them jerk their guns in its direction; they all held that pose for some moments, but nothing else stirred.

'Let's keep moving.' The captain stepped over the body of the dead soldier.

As they moved through the metallic tube Dixon kept glancing at the strange walls, even putting his hand out to touch them as he passed by. Forty feet on the tunnel opened out into a large, square room, hewn out of the rock; in the corner the shape of a small person could be seen huddled against the wall.

The captain motioned for Henderson to approach, while he and Dixon entered behind, covering her and each other. As Henderson got within ten feet, the person turned to face her. It was Susan!

Henderson held out a hand 'It's okay, sweetie, you're safe now.'

Susan, her clothing, arms and face streaked with dirt and blood, didn't move. As she sat there without making a sound, staring without seeing, her body trembled, the movement morphing into a continuous and violent shake. Her eyes swivelled to focus on something behind the Darklight unit, before they widened in terror and her mouth opened in a silent scream.

The image from Dixon's helmet camera flickered and then a terrible noise filled the room. Susan put her hands to her ears and buried her head in her lap. Gunshots cracked out and Dixon spun round. The captain fired at a light that surged towards Dixon, who didn't even let off a single shot as the image on the screen distorted and went black. Horrific screams and gunfire still emanated from the speakers for a while, until everything fell silent, only the faint sobs of Susan in the background an indicator that Dixon's helmet microphone was still active.

'Oh my God,' Goodwin said, the whole episode disturbing him to his core. A faint noise in the room, echoing Susan's own cries, made Goodwin turn; he saw Rebecca standing in the entrance to the tent, her hand over her mouth in shock, tears streaming down her cheeks and her eyes filled with despair.

'Commander—' Goodwin said, but Hilt had already paused the recording on the computer, albeit far too late to protect Rebecca from the horrors they'd all just seen.

Kara, standing just behind Rebecca, gave Goodwin an anxious look, before dragging Rebecca from the tent. Goodwin went to follow them out, the compulsion to attempt to relieve Rebecca's distress a strong one.

'Wait,' Hilt told him, 'there's more.'

Goodwin paused, torn between a dichotomy of duties. Knowing Kara would have things in hand, he relented, motioning for Hilt to continue; he needed to see it all, he *must* see it all.

The commander resumed the recording, the black screen a welcome relief from what had gone before. They continued listening for another minute, the occasional whimper from Susan making Goodwin feel helpless and sickened by her plight. Finally, the movement of something large in the room could be heard, a scraping of what sounded like metal on stone.

'What is that?' Major Offiah said.

Hilt held up his hand for quiet as a strange clicking noise grew louder, before becoming a deep penetrating growl, followed by the hissing of white noise as the audio stream failed.

'That's it.' Hilt turned off the computer.

Goodwin rubbed his face with both hands, trying to get his mind round what he'd just observed.

'We found nothing else at the scene,' Hilt said to Goodwin and Offiah, 'except for Dixon's helmet and a lot of blood.'

'No bodies?' Offiah looked perplexed. 'What about Alvarez?'

Hilt shook his head. 'Nothing, nor any weapons or equipment.'

'So whatever this thing is, it clears up after itself,' Offiah said.

'But leaves behind a helmet,' Hilt added.

'You think it left it there on purpose for us to find?' the major asked.

Hilt shrugged his shoulders. 'Perhaps.'

'Why is Susan still alive?' Goodwin looked from Offiah to Hilt. 'Why hasn't it killed her too? It doesn't make sense.'

'I have a theory,' Hilt said, 'but you're not going to like it.'

'Go on,' Goodwin told him.

'It could be keeping the bodies—' Hilt hesitated, 'to feed on.'

Goodwin stared at him in horror. 'And Susan?'

'Fresh meat,' Offiah said.

'Jesus Christ.' Goodwin walked away from the two soldiers. He felt like he was going to be sick. Leaning over, he took a slow, deep breath.

'It's only a theory,' Hilt said, when Goodwin had recovered somewhat.

'What are you doing here, Commander?' Goodwin asked, his voice weary as Hilt began moving around the tent, gathering up pieces of kit and stuffing it into a large backpack. 'Why aren't you out there, looking for Susan?'

'I needed to show you what we're up against. My men are still at the scene, some documenting the site for analysis, the rest fanning out into the tunnels. It's a new system, massive, interspersed with its own sub-chambers. I think it may even lead us out of this chamber, but we won't know until we follow it to its conclusion.'

'You're leaving us?' Goodwin said in realisation.

Hilt zipped up his bag. 'As I said before, it's time to bring events back under our control, don't you agree?'

Goodwin nodded.

'I have every faith in you, sir,' Hilt told him. 'Major Offiah will handle operations here while I'm gone, he'll serve you well.'

Goodwin looked to the Major, who gave him a brief nod. Hilt spoke to his command team for a few minutes before heading out of the camp, accompanied by Goodwin and Offiah. At the boundary between the lights of the small city of tents and the dark void beyond, Hilt rejoined the men who'd been with him when he'd returned to camp with Dixon's helmet. There was a flurry of activity as other Darklight personnel brought various bits of gear from the rest of the camp. Huge backpacks crammed full of supplies were heaved onto broad, armoured shoulders.

A female Darklight operative approached her commander, handing him a substantial and exotic looking beam weapon.

'Extra ammo has been put in your backpack, sir,' she told him.

'Thank you, Lieutenant.' Hilt checked the weapon's systems and mechanisms with practised ease; he then secured his thermal sword onto his back, the grip sticking out to one side over his shoulder. 'Sir, we did find one other thing at the site.' Hilt took something out of one of his pouches and held it out in his hand.

Goodwin looked at the other half of Susan's bracelet, only a few stones and shells remaining attached.

'Have you still got the other half?' Hilt asked.

Goodwin nodded and withdrew it from his pocket.

'I need to take it with me, and the one on your wrist, too.'

Goodwin gave him a quizzical look.

'If it was the stones that drew this thing to Susan,' Hilt said, 'then it could save us precious time in locating it.'

Goodwin couldn't quite believe the commander wanted to use himself as bait, but it was comforting to know the man seemed willing to go to any lengths to ensure Susan's safe return. Goodwin slid the bracelet off his wrist and placed it, and the fragments of the other one, in Hilt's hand.

'Thank you, sir.' Hilt tucked the objects away.

'Your team are ready, Commander,' the lieutenant told him.

Hilt nodded in confirmation and turned back to Goodwin. 'As you can see,' he stood aside to let Goodwin get a good look at the troops behind him, 'I'm taking with me seventy-five of our best men and women. We're fully loaded, but you'll still have ample supplies here, if required.'

Goodwin surveyed Hilt's unit, their matching black armour and formidable array of weaponry an intimidating sight. He also noted that ten of them carried black, sheathed, thermal swords, like their leader.

'Bring her back to us, Commander.' Goodwin held out his hand, which Hilt shook.

'I'll find her, sir.' Hilt placed his helmet over his head, the visor raised, enabling Goodwin to still see his face.

'And stay safe,' Goodwin added, all too aware of what the Darklight leader was going up against.

Hilt surprised Goodwin with a small half-smile. 'This thing likes to hide in the dark,' Hilt told him, pressing a button on the side of his helmet; the visor and face plate slid together to form a solid, unyielding shield and the internal combat system within powered up, a deep blue glow emanating from its slanted eye-like sculpturing. 'Two can play that game.' He pressed another button on his wrist, sending a shimmering light dancing over the panels on his armour, until his whole body faded into the darkness behind it, only the top of his sword and glowing eyes visible; like a shadowy knight possessed by a malevolent and powerful spirit.

The ghostly figure of the commander saluted Goodwin and then turned to stride towards, and through, the ranks waiting for him.

'Darklight, move out!' Hilt said, his powerful voice ringing with authority.

As one, the Darklight unit activated their camouflage systems, each one melding into the blackness around them, their glowing eyes disappearing into the dark as they turned and followed their leader into the void.

'Good hunting, Commander,' Goodwin said, watching Hilt fade from view, 'and good luck.'

CHAPTER THIRTY-FIVE

AN EAR SHATTERING blast tore through the foyer of the FBI field office in Los Angeles. Government agents and security personnel alike were blown from their feet while others dived for safety. Debris, which flew in all directions, seemed to cascade down in slow motion before Samson's eyes, the devastation an immutable, incontrovertible declaration of intent.

'Colonel!' Steiner's voice rang out within his helmet. 'We agreed no killing, what are you doing?! If you—'

Samson severed the connection between them, cutting Steiner off mid-flow. He had no time for such redundant protestations. Firing off another bolt of energy from his futuristic beam rifle, the recoil forcing him backwards, he obliterated another swathe of the reception area before tossing a couple of grenades into the mix, one towards the elevators and the other at front entrance.

Using the schematic of the building retained within his combat system, Samson ducked down a stairwell leading to the basement, two successive and deafening explosions booming out and a bullet zinging past his head as the door closed behind him. His armour's cloak might help him blend into the scenery, but his form was still very much observable, especially under bright office lights. Taking the stairs three at a time, Samson ran to his first objective, the generator room.

Flying down a central hallway, smashing open any doors that barred his way, he soon reached his destination. Warning signs plastered the locked, metal door that faced him. Taking a small magnetic grenade from his belt, he snapped the device onto the door and retreated ten feet before detonating it. Blown from its hinges, the door disappeared in a loud bang and a cloud of smoke. Ghosting through the dust that hung in the air, Samson analysed the setup within. Walking to a set of thick cables which came out of the wall and down into a large, multi-point junction box, Samson grasped the first two with his shielded, composite gloves and ripped them out. Sparks flew and crackling electricity coiled around his wrists. He repeated the process twice more and the lights in the room failed, to be replaced by emergency backups, their low-powered red light dull compared to those he'd just rendered useless throughout the office block.

Samson moved back into the darkened hallway, the slits in his helmet aglow with the green light from his combat system. Running further down the hall, he saw two FBI agents approaching. They hadn't seen him. He stopped and pressed himself flat to the wall in a small alcove. The two men were almost on him now, the red lighting casting deep shadows as they hunted him down, pistols drawn, covering each other as they moved in textbook tactical fashion. Sadly for them, Samson had no time for such naivety. The first man came within reach and Samson seized his gun, clamping his hand around the end of the muzzle. The agent fired on instinct, the resulting back blast engulfing the man's head, making him scream out in pain. In the same motion, Samson fired his own sidearm into the second agent's chest, the exploding round ending the man's life and splattering the walls with his flesh.

Leaving his two victims behind, Samson continued to the end of the hallway. Ignoring the elevators, now disabled by his own hand, he dodged into a stairwell and stormed up the steps. Samson moved swiftly upwards, floor by floor. Shouts from below and above told him his pursuers sought to hem him in. Lashing out with a fist as he went by, he activated a fire alarm to add to the confusion of his enemy. Turning on his helmet's air filters, he deployed two smoke canisters, one up and one down. Stooping low, he placed a thin heptagonal mine in front of a doorway before carefully stepping over it to move out onto the seventh floor.

A hail of bullets greeted him, the projectiles ricocheting off his armour and forcing him to turn his head to protect his visor. Unable to go back the way he'd come, he returned fire with his pistol. A host of small explosions subdued the onslaught, giving him time to dive behind a wide pillar and remove his rifle from his back. Getting his bearings, his visor's HUD informed him six tangos closed on his position. Gunfire tore at the other side of his cover, spraying concrete chunks in all directions. Narrowing his weapon's beam, he rolled from his position and fired three shots in quick succession before standing up behind another pillar. Three tangos remained, their firepower reduced but unrelenting as they tried to keep him pinned down. Unclipping a tiny aerial drone from his belt, Samson threw it into the hallway, directing it through the air with his eyes via his visor. A small strobe light on the miniature machine ignited at his command, flickering wildly, sending shadows cavorting in all directions. Samson made his move. Diving out in one fluid motion, he despatched two men with his rifle before taking out the remaining agent by directing the drone at his neck, the small device embedding into his carotid artery and felling him where he stood.

In that instant the building's low-level illumination switched back to ordinary bright, white office lighting. They'd transferred to another power outlet, a tertiary generator, Samson presumed. A huge blast from down the hall made him stagger back. The booby trap on the stairs had been triggered, the high-yield mine destroying the surrounding fabric of the building and sending the floor sagging down.

Making haste, he thundered down a carpeted corridor, a few administrators screaming in terror at his passing. On the other side of the building he went up another flight of steps, his exertions liberating. He felt calm and relaxed. He lived for moments like this; in the midst of a storm his mind became centred. Tenth, eleventh, twelfth, the levels flashed past. The thirteenth came and went and then he was bursting out onto the fourteenth floor.

Looking this way and that, he saw the area was open-plan and empty of people. Damn it! Where was everyone? More importantly, where was Agent Taylor? Walking between the unending rows of desks, searching, his rifle's scope guiding his vision, Samson re-evaluated his previous thoughts on the professor. He'd been too quick to buy in to Steiner's supposed intelligence, the man failing him when it came to the crunch. *If he's a genius then I'm a fucking saint*, he thought.

A ping sounded at the far end of the room, announcing the arrival of an elevator. He whirled around and ducked to watch the doors slide open. Nobody emerged, the interior void of occupants.

'Drop it,' a steady voice said from behind.

Samson checked his visor, wondering why his movement sensors hadn't detected anything.

'I said, drop it,' the woman said again.

Samson stood and placed his rifle down on the desk in front of him.

'Turn off your cloak.'

Samson reached out to his left wrist.

'Slowly,' she said.

Samson completed the movement with care, unsure what kind of weapon she possessed. At point-blank range, in the right place and with the right ammunition, his armour could be breached. Switching the camouflage system off, Samson's green and brown panelling reappeared.

'Turn around.'

Samson did so, his hands in the air. In front of him stood an FBI agent in a grey suit, a semi-automatic rifle pointed squarely at his visor. *Clever girl*, he thought in admiration; worthy adversaries were hard to find.

'Get on your knees,' she told him.

Samson glanced at the identity badge clipped to her breast pocket before kneeling down.

'Interlock your fingers and place your hands on your head.'

Samson did as he was bade, noticing two separate units of FBI agents, dressed in full combat gear and armed to the teeth, exiting from opposite stairwells at the far end of the room.

With her colleagues bearing down on them, the agent stared into Samson's mask, her eyes full of fire and hatred. 'I don't know who you are,' she said, 'but I'll make sure you fry for this and I'll be there to watch!'

Samson wasn't paying attention. His eyes darted over his visor's internal display, using the visual command system to divert his helmet's internal power supply to his armour's chest panel. With a final flick of his eyes he initialised the process he'd just prepped. A blinding flash of light made the agent blink and Samson surged upwards. She pulled the trigger. The report from the gun echoed out, the bullet missing him by inches. Grasping the agent's shoulder in a bone crushing grip, he threw aside her rifle and placed his pistol to her head before pulling her back against his chest to face the forty agents who rushed to encircle him.

'Back off!' Samson dragged his captive with him while turning in sharp, quick movements to prevent anyone from risking the shot.

'You've got nowhere to go.' The lead agent moved to the fore. 'Put down your weapon and surrender.'

Samson kept moving away, the crescent of rifles in front of him following his every motion.

His captive struggled. 'Shoot him!'

Samson grasped her tighter and pushed his pistol harder against her head. 'Take another step forward and she dies.'

The lead agent put his hand up to halt his team's advance.

This was an unusual position for Samson, face-to-face with an adversary but unable to strike them down. Whenever he'd faced a hostage situation previously, he'd always been on the other side and he'd always taken the shot. To the casual observer it would appear to be a stalemate, but both sides knew the status quo couldn't and wouldn't endure. Soon another FBI team would come up from behind him and the game would be up.

Backing further away, his options dwindling, something caught his eye between the agents' black-clad forms. Without another thought he shifted his hold on his human shield, putting the gun under her chin and pressing it hard up into her windpipe to prevent her from attempting to move. With his free hand he slid a second pistol from a leg holster and fired two quick shots at his abandoned beam rifle, lying on the desk twenty yards away. Both projectiles hit true, exploding on impact with the rifle's unprotected underbelly, the second piercing the beam weapon's unstable fuel cell and unleashing an explosion that ripped through the building.

The violent shockwave threw Samson and his hostage from their feet, propelling them backwards to slam into a wall. The FBI agents, who'd been standing close to the blast, were either incinerated or cut to pieces by flying debris. The ensuing fireball erupted through the empty window frames and into the dark sky of Los Angeles, the glass within having already blown out milliseconds before.

Samson rose unsteadily to his feet and shook his head to clear the high-pitched ringing caused by the blast. He saw the crumpled form of the FBI agent lying a few feet away and checked for a pulse; she was alive.

Samson surveyed his surroundings. The entire fourteenth floor had been devastated. A wide gash had been ripped through the floors above and below. Debris hung down from the edges, cabling and pipework exposed, the occasional spark of electricity flashing in the darkness. Samson picked up the unconscious government agent and slung her over his shoulder. He strode to the building's edge and looked down. People milled about outside in confusion; lights flashed and sirens blared as the LAPD streamed in from outlying areas of the city to heed the distress call from their besieged FBI comrades.

Samson's visor highlighted the distant approach of a cluster of drones and helicopters. He had to move. Retrieving one of his pistols from the floor, the other nowhere to be seen, he activated his camouflage panels once more and then shot out the floodlights below, plunging the exterior into darkness. Turning round, he adjusted the woman's body on his back, making sure she wouldn't fall, and then held out his wrist and fired a small metal bolt into the exposed concrete floor above. Attached to this bolt, now firmly embedded and secure, was a strand of high-tensile cable, capable of carrying great loads over greater distances. Samson might be above ground, but his Terra Force training and equipment were versatile in nature; they had to be, by definition.

Samson abseiled down from the fourteenth floor, increasing his velocity all the way. At the last moment he impeded his rate of descent before touching down on the ground and detaching himself from the cable with the flip of a small lever. Unseen in the darkness, he carried his prize through a gap in those gathered, all of them unaware that the one responsible for their displacement slipped past unhindered.

Samson soon reached the pick-up truck, which sat just off the main road, shrouded in shadow, the floodlights from the beleaguered FBI stronghold now only operable on one side. Police patrol cars screeched to a stop in front of the building, blaring sirens whooping to silence, doors opening and slamming as armed officers rushed to the scene. With more squad cars being drawn in like a swarm of flies to a steaming, noxious landfill site, Samson hurried to offload the FBI agent in the passenger seat before tearing round to the other side and jumping in, yanking the door shut with a bang.

One by one, searchlights from air and ground response teams lit up the area, their discs of light blinking into existence to dance over the area like a disco on an epic scale, its reach immense and intensity bright. Depressing the clutch pedal and sticking the Dodge Ram into gear, Samson put his hand on the key, preparing to turn on the ignition. Before he could, however, a bright white light encompassed the vehicle from above. If he believed in alien abduction he'd be expecting a visit from E.T. very soon. As it was, the blades from a helicopter in the skies overhead beat down their steady rhythm, a giveaway to the illumination's terrestrial source.

Samson hesitated as the aircraft circled the pick-up, hoping they'd lose interest in a dark immobile vehicle. Tense moments dragged past before the chopper and its searchlight drifted away.

The truck's interior light blinked on and Samson snapped his head right. The agent had come to and was trying to get out! Leaning over, he tore her hand from the door, shut it, and pushed her down into the foot-well. She was still groggy from the blast and moaned feebly in response. Her attempt at escape had drawn the attention of the helicopter straight back to them. The light was now fixed on their position and Samson sighed as the aircraft sank lower to the ground to project its beam inside the cabin.

'Fuck,' he said and turned the key.

CHAPTER THIRTY-SIX

PROFESSOR STEINER STARED in shocked disbelief at the wallscreen opposite, the continuous whir of computer equipment on the desk around him white noise in an otherwise silent room. After Samson had taken it upon himself to launch a full scale assault on the Bureau's L.A. field office, Steiner had been blind to his activities, the colonel having seen fit to disengage their audio-visual link after Steiner began his protestations.

While Samson committed who knew what atrocities inside, Steiner, housed a few miles away, battled against the trace instigated by the FBI mainframe which endeavoured to reveal his location, the ultimate culmination of such an eventuality being his untimely apprehension. He wasn't sure what would happen if a top GMRC official like himself, albeit a deposed one, should be arrested on charges of terrorism. He was under no illusions, however, that Intelligence Director Malcolm Joiner would use it to his advantage and the hundreds of thousands of people Steiner strived to rescue from Steadfast would be forever lost. That was an outcome Steiner simply couldn't allow, under any circumstances.

'Professor,' the voice of the artificial intelligence programme said, stirring Steiner from his myriad of thoughts, 'trace protocol has determined our city of origin. Time until completion, twenty seconds.'

Steiner waited; he'd prepared his countermeasures as best as he could. Watching the seconds on the digital clock on screen tick away to zero, his finger hovered over the Return key. He had to time this right. Ten – nine – eight – seven. The timer flashed red. Four – three – two, Steiner hit the key. The black command code window displayed the following white text:

```
Trace Diversion: Executed_

Target: GMRC Mainframe;
    exuString = "server=NewYork_Hub"
    extensionAccess = "NYH_AG896FGae%002"
    systemPort = "id=159v;override=directorate"
    systemSpike = "id=bypass;password=bypass"
    linkStringCrack = "filename=152"
```

Steiner waited in anxious turmoil as the timer remained frozen on two seconds.

'Trace diversion completed, Professor,' A.I. 152 told him. 'Time until completion—'

Steiner watched the digital numbers on the clock rapidly increase.

'Thirty-five minutes and thirty-eight seconds, and counting. Well done, Professor.'

'Thanks,' Steiner replied drolly to his computerised companion, his mouth dry and his fingers moist with tension-induced sweat. His ploy had worked, redirecting the FBI trace into the monster server array of the GMRC's North American disaster recovery network.

While it had delayed the FBI lifting the veil on his whereabouts, it was only a temporary reprieve; he wouldn't be able to prevent the trace from completion a second time. He just hoped his infringement into the GMRC computer system wasn't detected. *If only accessing the GMRC's highly encrypted communication lines were as easy to manipulate,* he thought.

Having bought himself more time, Steiner's attention returned to the colonel; he needed to speak to the man, inform him of the finite timeframe available. He also needed to aid their escape from the authorities. Steiner's threat of abandoning Samson if he killed any agents had been a bluff to prevent unnecessary bloodshed; in actuality he was in no position to enforce any such obligation. As much as he loathed being complicit in the death of any person, in this instance he took comfort from his childhood Sunday school teachings, specifically those of the ancient Greek philosopher, Aristotle, *'The securing of one individual's good is cause for rejoicing, but to secure the good of a nation or of a city-state is nobler and more divine.'* Or, as one of Steiner's favourite science fiction characters later famously paraphrased, '*the needs of the many outweigh the needs of the few*'.

No longer able to traverse the FBI computer system, their cameras unavailable to him, Steiner needed to find another way to see what was happening on the ground around the large office block situated on Wilshire Boulevard. Using a quantum processor, now standing idle, Steiner harnessed its power to break into the Los Angeles Police Department's transmission relay. Coursing through their frequencies like a shot of morphine in the blood, Steiner soon found what he was looking for. With a few purposeful key strokes, four windows popped up on the large wall monitor. Spacing out the windows, Steiner patched in the relevant live streams from his chosen sources. The two on the right were images from separate LAPD aerial drones, while the images on the left were from two police helicopters. He reasoned that if Samson had launched an attack on the FBI, then at least one of the units would be directed to the scene, or so he hoped.

Peering at the screens over the tops of his glasses, Steiner was dismayed to see all four streams were circling the one building.

'What have you done, Colonel?' Steiner said to himself, noticing the searchlights that swept the FBI offices and the surrounding area weren't just emanating from the drones and helicopters he'd hacked into, but from many other sources too. Police cars were everywhere, their lights flashing in almost every camera angle, and more poured in, seemingly every second. One particular image suddenly commanded his full attention. A helicopter hovered in front of a bright red, Dodge Ram pick-up, its powerful light shining into the vehicle. Was that Samson sitting in the driver's seat? It was hard to tell as the headlights of the vehicle blazed to life, the front of the pick-up rearing up as the driver – surely the colonel – floored the accelerator. Steiner tapped in a few more commands and switched on the police radio, combining the real-time shots from the helicopter with the audio of those that manned it.

'Control, possible suspect sighted,' the helicopter co-pilot said, 'corner of Wilshire Boulevard and Veteran Avenue. Red vintage Dodge Ram pick-up. No visible plates – in pursuit east on Wilshire.'

'Copy, Twenty-Four Bravo One,' the police dispatcher replied, 'proceed with extreme caution, support units en route.'

Steiner watched the helicopter gain altitude and turn to follow the speeding red truck, its taillights blending in with the light traffic that still flowed towards the centre of the city. The aircraft, unrestricted by land bound obstacles, soon caught Samson up, the searchlight tracking the truck's every move as it powered through red light after red light. Creeping into view on the ground the flashing lights of police cars could be seen, some of them power sliding in from interconnecting roads to join the chase.

Two black helicopters shot past the LAPD aircraft, making it sway wildly in their wake.

'Jesus Christ,' another voice said, Steiner assuming it to be the pilot. 'Are they trying to knock us out of the air?!'

'Control,' the co-pilot said, 'FBI air responders have compromised our position. Please advise?'

'Copy, Twenty-Four Bravo One, the FBI are taking the lead on this one, hang back and provide direction for ground units.'

Steiner could see the FBI helicopters taking a more aggressive stance over the fleeing truck.

'All units, shots fired,' the co-pilot said.

Steiner watched in horror as a stream of muzzle flashes burst from the Ram's driver side window. Small explosions flashed over the tail rudder on one of the black FBI choppers. Smoke billowed from its disabled rear rotor as it fell from the sky to explode in a great fireball, taking a couple of cars on the opposite carriageway out with it.

'Control, paramedics and fire-fighters required at intersection of Wilshire and Santa Monica Boulevard. Aircraft down, multiple casualties. Suspect utilising a high-powered automatic weapon.'

'Received, Twenty-Four Bravo One,' the dispatcher said after a momentary pause, 'emergency services have been notified and are en route. Keep your distance; our UAVs will take the lead.'

The police helicopter dropped further back and Steiner saw the FBI aircraft follow suit. A few multi-bladed drones flew in to drop down above the red pick-up as it continued to weave through the traffic at speed, their searchlights taking over where their human counterparts had left off.

Sirens sounded outside Steiner's building and his eyes flicked to the trace timer, twenty-nine minutes and five seconds remained. He rushed to the first floor window to see three police cars speed by, followed by two fire trucks and an ambulance. He was safe, for now.

Returning to his seat, Steiner saw Samson was now shooting at the drones, flames bursting from the muzzle of his gun while he drove like the madman he was, careering into, and smashing aside, any driver stupid enough to remain in his way.

'Twenty-Four Bravo One,' the police dispatcher said, 'be advised, drone footage suggests possible hostage in pick-up's passenger seat; all units advised to hold fire unless they have a clear shot at suspect. Shoot to kill has been authorised. I repeat, you are authorised to shoot suspect on sight.'

'Roger that, Control. We have unlocked our gun turret and are weapons hot.'

'Correction,' the dispatcher said, 'hostage is confirmed, identity unknown but appears to be a female FBI agent.'

The co-pilot indicated they'd received the updated information while his colleague continued to track Samson through the city, along with seemingly the whole of the LA police force and every available FBI agent. Surely Samson couldn't remain at large for much longer?

An abrupt series of explosions behind the Dodge Ram answered Steiner's question. Two police cars were blown high into the air, along with a civilian SUV, their mangled frames dropping back to earth, their interiors aflame.

'Control, we have multiple detonations,' the co-pilot said as another police car was blown clean in two, 'looks like the suspect is distributing land mines onto the freeway.'

Another flash lit up the scene, making Steiner flinch, the loss of life mounting as the colonel's rampage escalated. He had to do something, but what? What could he do?

The helicopter flew higher as it encountered a cluster of skyscrapers. 'All units,' the co-pilot said, 'suspect entering New Downtown financial district, taking Route 110 off-ramp onto West 6th Street.'

The footage now showed the red pick-up travelling at high speed through a built-up area, pedestrians and cars trying to get out of its way. Jumping a set of lights, the rear of Samson's truck was T-boned by a police car, sending it spiralling out of control to come to rest in the centre of the junction.

'Suspect stopped at corner of 6th and South Hill Street,' the co-pilot said. 'We have movement inside the vehicle, suspect exiting—'

Steiner, transfixed, saw the indistinct figure of Samson getting out of the driver's side and then opening fire with two black rifles, one held in either hand. The officers from the ten police cars in immediate attendance were either gunned down or could be seen ducking behind their vehicles for protection, returning fire as best they could.

'Officers down, require immediate assistance!' the co-pilot said. 'Suspect heavily armed and appears to be wearing some kind of armour, or shield. I can't make him out; he's blending into his surroundings. What is that?' the man added, perhaps to the pilot next to him.

Steiner saw the FBI helicopter reappear, hovering low behind Samson. A black-clad agent manning a small canon mounted on the aircraft's side fired shell after shell at Samson's shimmering outline. Throwing one of his guns aside, Samson rolled away from the bombardment, which chewed up the tarmac around him. He returned fire on the run, launching a small rocket from his weapon which took the FBI chopper broadside, a crippling blast sending it into a spin and crashing into the street. Its blades bit into the ground before snapping off, and the machine and its occupants were consumed by a huge fireball.

'Engage, engage!' the co-pilot said as they bore down on Samson from the other side, their own mini-gun tearing into the street, its tracer rounds providing the pilot with a guide as he tried to rip Samson to pieces.

'RPG!' the co-pilot screamed as Samson fired another rocket.

The picture from the police helicopter veered to the right, but the missile homed in on them with deadly accuracy. The camera image fizzed and went black and the final screams of the crew cut off to silence.

Steiner, blind and deaf once more, strove to find another source from which to watch. The other images on screen were of little use since they still depicted the crippled FBI field office. Rather than keep trolling through the police transmissions, which were now clogged to bursting, Steiner had a better idea. Taking another quick glance at the tracer timer, which read twenty-four minutes and forty-two seconds, he brought the local news channels up on his wallscreen. He wasn't to be disappointed, every one had the story as breaking news and followed the incident blow by blow. Steiner couldn't believe what he was seeing as he brought up three more channels on screen. CNN and Fox News were already covering the incident and the BBC's worldwide service was just switching to it. It was official; Samson's actions had just gone global.

Patching into the audio from CNN, Steiner listened as the male news anchor described to their viewers what was happening.

'—horrific scenes unfolding on the streets of Los Angeles tonight, as police pursue a suspect they're describing as, "*the most violent and dangerous individual they have ever encountered*". Events started to unfold around a quarter past four this afternoon when an armoured man entered the FBI field office on Wilshire Boulevard and proceeded to wage a one man war inside. Accounts are varied, but many agents within the building are said to have already lost their lives, current estimates standing at around fifty fatalities, while many more incidents carried out by the same individual across town are expected to make this appalling death toll rise even higher over the coming hours. Reports are arriving all the time, indicating that many police officers and civilians alike, have also lost their lives as the deadly game of cat and mouse continues to play out across a city under siege.

'The police are advising all Angelenos to remain indoors or to seek shelter until the individual has been subdued. For their own safety, and under no circumstances, should any citizen attempt to confront, or make contact with, the suspect, who is known to be heavily armed and exceptionally dangerous.

'An emergency helpline has been set up for those finding themselves caught up, directly or indirectly, in this terrorist attack. You'll find the number at the bottom of the screen. We're now going back live to our reporter in the sky, Marianne Gobrinsky. Marianne, over to you.'

The image switched to a picture coming from an aircraft hovering over the city centre; there was a still photograph of the reporter in the top left hand corner of the screen, her name written underneath and a small black graphic representation of a helicopter beside it.

'Thanks, Bill,' Marianne said. 'We've just arrived at the latest scene of carnage and, as you can see below, the streets of the financial district are like a war zone. The burning shells of two helicopters, which were moments ago blown from the skies, are testament to the scale of this attack. Wait ... we've just received information that the fugitive may have an FBI agent as a hostage and has just driven into the newly developed Spring Street Super Mall. Not far from where we are now—'

Steiner watched the image from the helicopter roll sideways as it repositioned to the new location.

In an unconscious effort to rid himself of his stress and angst, Steiner rubbed his hands over his bearded face and worked his fingers beneath his glasses to massage his eyes. *A shopping mall*, he thought in despair, *there'll be children there, mothers*. Groaning, Steiner slammed the desk in frustration.

Malls have cameras and digital wall displays! The thought sprang unbidden to his mind. He snapped upright, his fingers attacking the keyboard with a renewed vigour. This was his chance to intervene and he must seize it. Locating the security network of the mall, Steiner easily bypassed its firewalls and transferred the video streams to his own wallscreen while preventing anyone else from accessing them, including those in the Mall itself. Expanding the window so he could get a good view of the one hundred available images, Steiner turned his attention to the Mall's internal information system, blocking out the human interfaces of those who usually operated it. He entered his message and transferred it to every screen in the building, hoping that he'd get lucky. He wasn't to be disappointed. A minute later, as the trace from the FBI reached eighteen minutes, the speakers in the room crackled before a recognisably abrasive voice spoke. 'You surprise me, old man; I'd have thought you'd have washed your hands of me by now.'

'What you've done is beyond sickening,' Steiner said to Samson, 'but I still need you and if I can't control you, I might as well try and prevent you killing any more people. Now, do you want my help or not?'

'What have you got in mind?'

'Where are you?'

'Southern car park, level four. Orange sector B.'

Steiner looked to his screen, scanning the images. Finding one that looked promising, he enlarged it. 'That area's crawling with police cars,' Steiner told him, watching a patrol car roll slowly past, its light bar pulsing and a searchlight combing the rows of parked vehicles.

'I'd noticed.' Samson's voice dripped with scorn.

'You need to help me a little here. Where *exactly* are you?'

Samson didn't respond.

'Hurry up, damn it.' Steiner flicked his eyes at the countdown clock. 'The FBI trace is down to seventeen minutes.'

'I hid the pick-up in the back of a semi-truck on the basement level,' Samson said, realising Steiner wasn't about to rat him out to the cops – although the thought had crossed Steiner's mind more than once in the previous half hour. 'I'm going to draw them away, double back, offload my gear to another vehicle and then head back to you.'

'Gear! She's an FBI agent, who you've abducted!'

'I had no choice,' Samson told him. 'Get out before the trace ends. I'll meet you on the corner of Slauson Avenue and Port Road; according to my visor that's three blocks from you.'

The line crackled again. 'Colonel? Colonel, are you still there?!'

Silence.

Steiner uttered more than a few choice words.

'My protocols dictate such language is not permitted under current parameters,' the voice of the artificial intelligence said.

'Oh, shut up.' Steiner pressed the mute button on the A.I.'s window. Turning the volume back up on the CNN broadcast Steiner, once again a bystander in proceedings, felt a deep dread at what he might see next.

'—we can only hope.' Marianne Gobrinsky, the helicopter reporter, was still speaking, the image showing the massed ranks of the LA police department descending on the area. 'Some new information fresh in,' she said, 'as the police try to evacuate the building, which will take some time considering its size, a message was seen on the information boards within the mall itself, It read: *red pick-up contact one five two*. The authorities have been tight-lipped about what this message might mean, but it seems clear that the fugitive is receiving outside help.'

Steiner sneered in distaste at his own success, aiding and abetting added to his growing list of crimes.

'This theory,' the reporter continued, 'is reinforced by other reports indicating the security cameras inside the shopping precinct have also been overridden by a source, as yet, unknown.'

CHAPTER THIRTY-SEVEN

NOW INSIDE THE SHOPPING MALL, Samson slid the magazine out from his remaining MX4 assault rifle as he strode along. *Half full, only twenty more rounds*, he thought before shoving it back in with a click. He placed the rifle onto his back-plate, withdrew his pistol and ejected the exhausted clip, replacing it with his final one, containing thirty sub-sonic hollow points. *Not the best ammunition for fighting your way out of a sticky situation*, he mused as terrified shoppers moved out of his way, a woman with a pushchair screaming at the sight of his shimmering form and the array of weaponry on display.

Breaking into a run as panic erupted around him, Samson headed north, aiming to draw his pursuers away from the Dodge Ram.

With his metal-clad boots clanking along the rapidly emptying hallways, he spotted a couple of police officers. They hadn't seen him, the deserted food court he now observed quiet except for the sporadic shouts and screams of the departing shoppers. Pistol in hand, Samson slid the silencer mechanism along the barrel, its composite frame snapping securely into place. A bullet already in the chamber, he selected his first target with his visor and fired, and the female officer dropped without a sound as he switched to her partner; firing again, he rendered the man dead with a similar headshot.

As he advanced, a strange sound made him whirl round, the barrel of his gun pointing straight at the source of the noise. Two big wide eyes peered at him and the baby made a gurgling sound and reached out to grab the gun. Movement in the distance made Samson look up and magnify his visor's image; it seemed an FBI swat team had hunted him down. One of their number, a sniper, was aiming straight at him. Samson saw the man rock back as he fired and instinctively stuck out an arm, deflecting the bullet away from the infant. Another bullet pinged off his helmet, momentarily disrupting his visor display and snapping his head back. Diving to his left, the camouflage system failing, he rolled to his feet. Beginning to enjoy himself, his breathing increased and heart pumping harder, Samson ran for his life.

♦

Professor Steiner looked nervously over at the trace timer in the wallscreen's top left hand corner. Several minutes had passed since he'd last spoken with Samson and the clock showed he had fewer than twelve minutes left. During this time, he'd glimpsed what he thought was the colonel disappearing up a flight of stairs in the northernmost quadrant of the building, but he couldn't be sure.

'Breaking scenes,' said Bill Brightman, the larger than life CNN news anchor, recapturing Steiner's attention, 'we're returning live to Marianne Gobrinsky, our eye in the sky. Marianne what do you have for us?'

Footage from the helicopter appeared next to the image from the news studio. 'Bill, it seems we have activity on one of the rooftops.'

The camera zoomed in on a team of black-clad men shooting at what could only be Samson, his green and brown body armour appearing and disappearing in the dark as a number of LAPD and FBI drones followed his flight with their searchlights.

'The suit he's wearing looks military,' Bill said. 'Can you zoom in any further?'

'I'll patch you into our mini-cam drone.' Marianne altered the aspect to a view directly above the roof itself.

Steiner could clearly see Samson as he returned fire to the swat team behind.

'Yes, it's definitely military of some kind,' Marianne said, Steiner thinking she sounded too excited at the prospect. *The media are lapping this up*, he realised, the idea repulsing him; *don't they know people are dying down there?*

'Are those markings on his shoulder?' Bill Brightman said.

'I'll drop the drone in for a better look.' Marianne changed the angle on screen once more.

Samson looked up when the UAV got too close, the green glow from his helmet visible as he evaded the lights attempting to pin him down, his breath visible as it gusted from his helmet into the cold air around him. As Steiner watched, Samson raised his rifle and fired, sending the screen fuzzing into a mass of black and white pixels.

'Oh my.' Marianne sounded disturbed by what she'd just seen. 'Did you get that? Those glowing eyes?'

Bill Brightman nodded. 'We did – whoa! He just jumped to the next building!'

The camera had switched back to the helicopter's video stream and replayed in slow motion footage of Samson jumping clean across a wide gap, bullets bouncing from his back as he flew through the air. Now returning to real-time, Samson looked to be nearing the end of the road, the rooftop he was on running out ahead. Out of nowhere a helicopter rose above the building, mini-guns firing on either side, spraying Samson with a barrage of deadly hail. Samson faltered and fell before a huge explosion lit up the dark skies, the flames giving way to a pall of thick black smoke.

Steiner didn't really take in what the CNN team said next, he felt stunned and disorientated, not because he mourned the colonel's abrupt demise, but because with his death Steiner's chances of helping those in Steadfast to get to safety had just taken a significant backward step, perhaps irreversibly so. He was on his own now. His eyes darted to the trace timer; eight minutes remained until the FBI acquired his exact location – he had to move.

A few more minutes passed while Steiner finished hiding his digital signature. Hurriedly, aware of his ever-dwindling window of opportunity, he began shutting down the computer hardware. He flicked the switches off one by one, leaving one quantum processor running to ensure the trace continued to be fended off for the longest possible period. Closing the programmes still open on the wallscreen, Steiner's finger paused over the CNN footage. He watched, gobsmacked, as their cameras caught the image of a bright red Dodge pick-up bursting out of the shopping mall's first floor façade. With huge shards of glass flying in all directions, the wheels of the truck slammed down onto the ground, its suspension buckling to breaking point.

'Dear Lord,' Bill Brightman said, grandstanding for all he was worth, 'guess who's back.'

CHAPTER THIRTY-EIGHT

STEINER COULDN'T QUITE BELIEVE what he was seeing. Samson was alive, although by the looks of what faced him, he wouldn't be for much longer. The CNN helicopter footage showed that the car park Samson now found himself in was completely surrounded, not only by the LAPD and FBI, but also by the National Guard, called in to lend a hand to their law enforcement colleagues. Drones and helicopters filled the dark skies above, including those from the world's media tasked with covering the story, their combined lights shedding a bright blanket over the single red vehicle.

'There doesn't appear to be anyone inside the car,' Marianne Gobrinsky reported.

She wasn't wrong. The TV footage showed the interior of the battered pick-up pretty well and Steiner couldn't make out anyone sitting in either of the front seats. Was it really Samson at work? Unconsciously he'd started twisting his wedding band around his finger, the countdown timer for the FBI trace temporarily forgotten, its digits dropping below the two minute mark unseen.

♦

Bent double in the driver's seat of the Dodge Ram, Samson didn't need to use his visor's spectral scanners to know what confronted him outside. Even as he sat there, rifles were being trained on every inch of the vehicle. If he so much as popped his head up, he'd have it taken off in an instant by multiple, high-velocity, armour-piercing rounds.

The only reason he wasn't already dead was because of the person he had crammed into the adjacent foot-well; his hostage. The FBI agent, now conscious, gagged and secured with her own set of handcuffs, stared at him with baleful eyes.

Samson knew he'd been fortunate back on the roof. The helicopter had provided him with the perfect foil against which to stage his own death. Utilising his last two grenades, he'd blown a hole in the roof while at the same time reactivating his camouflage, which he'd managed to repair on the move. After the shockwave passed, Samson had thrown himself down into the thick smoke, landing heavily on the floor below. Still having to act quickly, he'd then hotfooted it back through the mall, avoiding the police, to finally reach the truck. Unfortunately his plan of switching vehicles hadn't accounted for the cops that had decided to set up shop in the same car park where he'd stashed the pick-up. Deciding action was preferable to waiting to be discovered, Samson had driven the vehicle into the shopping area to avoid the squad cars below, before launching it out through the first floor window of the complex's main entrance.

Turning away from the penetrating and unsettling gaze of his companion, Samson tried restarting the engine, which had cut out during its collision with the ground. He kept the key turned and the engine spluttered to life, aided by a push of the accelerator with his hand. Reversing as best he could with his contorted posture, Samson stuck the car in first gear and released the clutch. With the pick-up now rolling forward at a sedate and steady pace, he flipped the switch that the previous owner, the Apache Indian, Norroso, had custom-fitted to the flatbed. A whirring of gears raised the rear tray higher and higher, acting like a tip-up truck. At the critical angle of tilt, where the gravitational pull on the load became greater than the frictional resistance, a long wooden crate slid out past the open tailgate, hitting the tarmac and splintering open. Samson, his hand wrapped around a small transceiver he'd removed from his utility belt, thumb poised over the small button on top, floored the accelerator and then depressed the button.

On the ground behind him, the black, cylindrical, stainless steel prototype device rested on the tarmac, its broken case lying shattered around it. On one side a power bar pulsed green confirming one hundred per cent capacity. Beneath this, in illuminated red lettering, two words:

SYSTEM ARMED

On receipt of the signal to activate, small charges propelled four separate spikes into the ground, a fifth charge jettisoning the top section of the weapon five hundred feet into the air.

A flash of light and a pulse of energy swept through the pick-up and beyond as the tri-phase, electromagnetic pulse-bomb detonated. The dashboard lights flickered and died, the engine cutting out, its electronics failing. Samson twisted the ignition key once more, praying that its tough, antiquated circuitry had survived the EMP. The engine coughed and spluttered before purring back to life, the truck's momentum jump-starting it. Sitting upright, he pulled the steering wheel hard to the right as complete darkness descended within a half-mile radius, the lights of buildings in the distance blinking out to join those already disabled at the epicentre of the silent blast. His visor already set for night-vision, Samson refrained from putting the headlights on as the sky rained aircrafts and drones from above.

With every police car being electric and unshielded against

EMPs, the entire LAPD police force had been immobilised. Only the National Guard operated with gasoline and their transport was static and would be unable to start; at least that was Samson's theory.

A helicopter smashed into the ground ahead and erupted into flame, its frame buckled and broken. Yanking up the handbrake, Samson slid the back end out to miss the carnage by inches. Gunning the accelerator, the Dodge Ram's bored-out, seven litre engine roared in response. With everyone thrown into the pitch-black, Samson drove unimpeded at the weakest link in the ring of parked vehicles. The Dodge's bull bars broke through the line, smashing aside two squad cars and catapulting him out into the street beyond, and freedom.

CHAPTER THIRTY-NINE

A BEEPING SOUND made Steiner tear his gaze away from the final TV shots of what had looked like Samson setting off some sort of energy weapon. His eyes widened as the trace timer slipped past ten seconds.

'Holy—' Steiner's heart rate skyrocketed as knee trembling, palpitation inducing panic set in.

'Trace complete, Professor,' the A.I. said, 'the game is up. The chicken is cooked, the broth is boiled, the bread is buttered, the—'

Steiner tore 152's console from its socket and stuffed it into a satchel, along with anything else he could grab, before fleeing out of the door and rattling down the stairs as fast as his legs could carry him. Bursting out into the low-lit street, he paused to calm his mind, taking long, deep, slow breaths, despite the sound of approaching police sirens in the distance. Suppressing his emotions, he recalled the location the colonel had suggested for their rendezvous, the corner of Slauson Avenue and Port Road, three blocks away. But in what direction was that? In the heat of the moment he'd failed to consult a map and going the wrong way could prove disastrous.

He could see the red and blue flashing lights now, a mile away, but he hadn't made director general by being easily distracted. Sifting through his mental imagery of the final stages of his arrival into LA with Samson, he slowed his breathing further.

There, he had it! The vestiges of a visual memory, a vision of a lamppost, attached to it a green sign with white letters reading *—son Ave*. It was the best he was going to get, a partial name, and he'd already started running to his left, happily in the opposite direction to those that hunted him down. Pulling out his baseball cap as he ran, Steiner pulled it onto his head before rounding a corner and disappearing into the endless night.

♦

The cold air and brisk wind gnawed at Steiner's hands and face while he waited in the shadows on Slauson Avenue. He'd been relieved to find his memory recall had been accurate and that the only Avenue in the area ending in the letters *s, o* and *n* had been the one he'd required; or at least that was how luck would have it, bringing him to his current location. A few blocks away a black helicopter hovered over the building he'd vacated only a few minutes before, like an immense raven delivering a ubiquitous portent of his ruination.

Where is Samson? he asked himself. *Did he escape or is he even now being questioned about my whereabouts?* Perhaps he'd been killed, and was lying in a pool of his own blood inside the red pick-up, or he'd turn up being chased by all and sundry. Whatever the case, if the colonel hadn't arrived in ten minutes Steiner would have to relocate and then start planning how he'd escape the city. Being on the run and alone, without any military support, would test him to his limits; just to remain free would be an immense challenge. Helping Steadfast would have to take a back seat until he could manoeuvre himself into a better position, preferably outside of the United States.

Five more minutes passed before a set of headlights approached along Port Road, the rays of light growing stronger every second and the shadows from the surrounding foliage increasing in sharpness and density. Steiner moved back into the trees, dropped to his belly and wriggled under a bush. The vehicle stopped at the intersection, its electric engine inaudible. Steiner peeked out from beneath a low branch, his face pressed down against some damp leaves. From what he could tell the vehicle was a dark blue sedan, unmarked, with the potential of having an FBI agent at the wheel. He could ill afford to make the first move. If Samson was within, he'd need to instigate contact.

The car door opened and the suspension lifted as someone got out. Steiner held his breath, trying to hide any hot vapour that could alert someone to his presence.

'Stop hiding in the bushes,' a curt voice said from out of the dark, 'and get in.'

Steiner scrambled out from his seemingly inadequate hiding place and ran over to the car as the colonel, still fully encased in his green and brown protective shell, returned to his seat. Clambering in, Steiner deposited his bag behind him and put on his seatbelt.

'The streets are running alive with cops,' Samson said to him, turning down a dark side street, 'the FBI and National Guard, too; we need to hole-up until things calm down.'

Steiner's anger surfaced. 'You planned this all along, didn't you? The weapons you amassed on our way here were in preparation for this – this—'

'I didn't plan it. I planned *for* it, there's a difference.'

'Semantics from you, Colonel, is like asking a dying dog to explain Einstein's theory of relativity, a distasteful lesson in absurdity.'

Samson said nothing for a moment, perhaps trying to figure out if Steiner had insulted him or not. 'I prepare for all eventualities,' he said, driving them into a rundown industrial district of the city.

'And fighting your way out of the FBI field office was one of them.' Steiner's tone was accusatory.

Samson didn't respond at all this time and Steiner wondered why he was even bothering to get the man to admit to his guilt; he was a remorseless shell, a stone cold killer.

A couple more minutes passed with Steiner twitching in anxiety every time he saw a light in the sky. The police and FBI would be sending out every available asset they had in their hunt for Samson, his hostage and anyone connected to him – *namely me*, he thought – which meant the deployment of all available UAVs and any remaining helicopters. With this in mind, Steiner was more than happy when Samson drove them into a three storey derelict warehouse and stopped the car.

'Get out,' Samson said, leaving the car running and stepping out of the vehicle to stride around to the boot.

Steiner, collecting his bag, followed him out into the dilapidated interior of an old twentieth century brick building, its roof hanging down in places, water dripping down into shallow pools beneath.

With the boot lid up Steiner could hear a muffled voice emanating from within. Samson bent down and dragged out the FBI agent, lifting the hooded, trussed and squirming body up onto one of his shoulders. Leaving the boot open, the colonel carried his hostage through a maze of long unused offices, finally kicking open a rotting wooden door and heading down into a damp and uninviting pit of a cellar. With the lights on the colonel's helmet ablaze, Steiner followed him down the worn steps. Dumping his captive on the floor, Samson disappeared back up the stairs, leaving Steiner in darkness until he switched on his computer phone. The colonel soon returned with a large satchel and some weapons, which he placed down before opening the bag up and withdrawing a lantern, its light shining out to illuminate the dank low-ceilinged room they now found themselves inhabiting.

Steiner eyed the forlorn form of the government agent with pity. The woman's smart blue suit was stained, torn and singed in numerous places.

'So what's the plan now?' Steiner asked. 'Are you planning on adding torture to your litany of crimes?'

Samson didn't respond, choosing instead to remove his helmet before picking the woman up like a sack of potatoes and dumping her down at the rear of the room, away from the light. If Steiner had felt guilty before, his shame intensified even further now. It wasn't that he felt a woman's life was worth more than a man's, but he was old school and always felt more protective toward the fairer sex, even though, nowadays, this idea might be construed as politically incorrect by some, and even misogynistic by others.

Delving back in his sack, Samson withdrew a power pack and plonked it down at Steiner's feet.

'Patch into the local police channels,' Samson told him, 'we need to know what they're up to.'

'Just like that,' Steiner said. 'I'm not a miracle worker.'

'What's the problem? You have power, you have your computers.'

'I haven't got any hard lines and that tiddly little battery isn't going to power 152's console or anything bigger than my computer phone.' Steiner rummaged in his own rucksack to see what he'd managed to salvage in his rush to get out of the office. He had the A.I. console, a single quantum processor unit, a bundle of cables and some peripherals, and that was pretty much it. Nothing that could run off the battery Samson had provided, at least not in the capacity he would need to break into the encrypted transmissions while remaining undetected.

Samson's brow furrowed, his pale blue eyes fixing Steiner with an unreadable expression. Steiner wasn't going to cave in to pressure and returned the man's gaze with a steady one of his own.

'Just do what you can,' Samson said, breaking the impasse. Retrieving his helmet, he returned to the stairs.

'Where are you going now?'

'To move the car; if it's found, I don't want it anywhere near us.'

With Samson departed, a noise from the back of the room made Steiner glance apprehensively in its direction, the shape of the agent moving as she struggled against her restraints.

Muttering to himself, Steiner tried his best to ignore her, concentrating instead on setting up a basic computer system with his computer phone's fold out screen at its heart. Running an aerial lead up the stairs, he had an improvised workstation set up in six minutes, an old plastic crate he'd found nearby functioning nicely as a seat. While cracking the law enforcement networks was out, he was able to patch into local and national television broadcasts and soon had a couple of channels streaming side by side on his phone's display. Having watched them for a few minutes, trawling through the various programmes on offer, his disquiet had increased exponentially, transforming into outright fear and desolation.

Standing up, Steiner took off his glasses and stared into space, one hand on a hip, his thoughts dark and his emotions bleak. After what he'd just seen he was under no illusions as to the severity of the challenge they now faced and the veritable shit storm Samson had thrust them into. An unprecedented manhunt was underway. GMRC curfews had been brought forward by three hours; all serving police officers on leave had been recalled and the Governor of California had declared a state of emergency. One local channel reported that the assistant director in charge of the Bureau's LA field office had been one of the casualties in Samson's initial assault and that the FBI Director himself was flying in from Washington D.C. to assume command, accompanied by every available resource he had at his disposal. Samson had started a damn war and Steiner's choice to stick by his side had backfired spectacularly. He realised, with the bitter irony of hindsight, that he would have been better off on his own trying to save those left behind in Steadfast.

'Oh, Nathan,' Steiner murmured, wishing his friend were there to console him, 'I've made a terrible mistake.'

♦

Samson had returned some time later, having hidden the vehicle to his satisfaction, and then left once more citing as his reason the fact that they would need food and clean water for the indeterminable duration of their stay. Steiner, his mood mirroring his oppressive and lacklustre surroundings, hardly acknowledged the colonel during his flying visit, opting to stay sunken in the mire of his mind.

As time ticked by, Steiner switched off the computer to conserve energy and then glanced over to the area of the cellar, deep in shadow. In an effort to ease his psychological burdens, he picked up the lantern and walked across to the FBI agent. The noise of his approach made her face, covered by a rough linen sack, move almost comically as she strained to hear, or see, whoever – or whatever – drew near.

Crouching down in front of her, the fluid in his ankles popping, Steiner reached out and pulled off the hood. The woman, in her mid to late twenties, blinked against the bright light before settling her eyes on Steiner's own, their fear plain to see, their plea for mercy, heartbreaking. A large cut on her forehead had dried to a congealed mass, strands of her hair caught within it; Steiner extended his hand to move a cluster of the light brown locks away from her face. Shrinking from his touch, she protested pitifully, her voice still muffled by the crude cloth gag tied around her head.

Steiner held up his hands. 'It's okay, I won't hurt you. Here—' he made a small gesture with his right hand before moving it to her mouth, 'let me get that for you.'

Pulling at the knot, Steiner worked it free until the strip of cloth fell away to her lap. 'Better?' he asked.

The agent, her features broad and strong, her lips thin, spat out some remaining fibres and moistened her lips with her tongue. 'Yes.' She coughed, trying to clear her throat. 'Thank you.' Her anxious eyes darted around the room. 'Where's your friend?'

Steiner noticed the tremor in her voice and gave her a comforting smile. 'He's not here. Don't worry, I won't let him hurt you.'

She looked at him with scepticism. 'No offence, but I don't think you could prevent him doing anything.'

'I have my ways,' Steiner said. 'In some aspects I'm as much a prisoner as you, of circumstance maybe, but a prisoner nonetheless.'

The FBI agent considered him anew. 'I don't suppose you fancy just letting me go?'

Steiner would have dearly loved to do so, but if he did, he risked compromising his position even further. *If that is even possible*, he thought, while considering his current state of disarray. *I just can't afford for anything else to go wrong*, he decided, *too many lives are at risk*.

'I'm sorry,' he said, 'as much I want to wash my hands of this – whatever this is – I can't.'

The resulting expression of defeat on her face was almost too much to bear. 'I can loosen these for you, though,' he said, by way of recompense, indicating the handcuffs, her hands appearing red and puffy from the pressure on her wrists.

'Please.' She held out her arms to him.

Loosening each loop in turn, he adjusted the small levers that protruded from each side of the stainless steel device, noticing they'd left dark red marks where Samson had tightened them almost to the point of cutting off her circulation. When she rested her hands back into her lap, Steiner glimpsed her identity badge, still clipped to her breast pocket. Beneath the famous logo and her photo were the words *Special Agent*, and next to this her name, written in her own hand.

'You're Brett Taylor?' he said, thrown off guard.

Amazingly, she managed to muster a small smile. 'I prefer Taylor. Were you expecting someone else?'

'Sorry, I just assumed you were a man.'

'Assumptions are the mother of all fuck ups, at least that's what I'm told.'

'You're new to the job?' he asked, picking up on the inference.

Her meek eyes welled up. 'Sort of, I was a beat cop, been with the Bureau coming up eight months now.'

Steiner gave her hand a squeeze before a sound upstairs made him come to his senses. 'I'm sorry, my dear.' He stuffed the gag back in her resisting mouth and tugged the hood back over head. 'Shh, I'll get you out of this mess, just give me some time.'

Snatching up the lamp, Steiner hurried back to his computer, switching it back on just as Samson clanked down the steps.

'Food,' the colonel said, dumping down a bulging sack, 'and water.' He placed a large orange cylindrical canister on the floor.

Steiner read the writing on the side of the odd looking container. 'Sanitation waste filtration, you want me to drink something used to filter out public toilets?'

'It's clean,' Samson said unimpressed by Steiner's complaint, 'and it's from a private trailer.'

The thought of it made Steiner queasy. 'A trailer that still uses it for toilet water.'

'Take it or leave it, I don't care.' Samson removed his helmet once more and sat down on the floor to rest his back against a supporting pillar in the middle of the room, his eyes closing in preparation for sleep.

'You don't care about anything, that's the problem,' Steiner said, his hackles rising. 'You murder innocent people like slaughtering cattle and disobey my direct orders, effectively condemning hundreds of thousands of civilians to a premature death!'

One of Samson's eyes crept open. 'Says the man who nominated himself to go for help, the great man who preaches courage, but is the first out of the sinking ship, saving his own hide ahead of those he supposedly holds so dear. You make me sick; you understand nothing of loyalty, of family.'

'Loyalty!' Steiner couldn't believe what he was hearing. 'Like the loyalty you showed your men when you left them for dead before executing them yourself? You sick, twisted bastard!'

Samson surged to his feet and seized the front of Steiner's red coveralls. 'What did you say?!' Samson yanked Steiner in towards him, his eyes wide and manic.

Steiner felt something metallic press against his temple. His eyes flicked left to see Samson's pistol there, its polished frame glinting in his hand.

'Say it again!' the colonel bellowed, almost frothing at the mouth. 'Say it!'

Something swung through the air and cracked against Samson's head, snapping it to one side. The pistol fell from his hand, his iron grip dropping from Steiner's clothing. Eyes glazed, his heavy, armour-clad frame clattered to the floor in a heap.

Steiner looked up in shock at the dishevelled form of the FBI agent, her breathing heavy, her hands wrapped around a rusty piece of pipe. Before he had time to comment, she'd snatched up Samson's gun, tucked it in the front of her trousers and then turned the colonel over to bind his hands with some thick cable. Moving quickly to his legs, she repeated the process, pulling with all her weight and strength to bind him as tightly as she was able.

Steiner watched her in silence, unsure what to do at this unexpected turn of events.

Hauling Samson's considerable frame over to the central pillar, agent Taylor sourced some rope from the colonel's satchel and went about securing him in place, weaving together his arms, legs, hands and feet in an inescapable fibrous web.

She placed a foot on the colonel's chest and heaved back, the rope cinching tighter and tighter, its individual strands creaking under the strain. 'Thanks for loosening my cuffs by the way,' she said to Steiner as she worked. 'It's lucky you're so gullible otherwise he might have killed you.'

Steiner looked at the woman in confusion. Her whole demeanour had altered and not just because she was free. No, this was an extreme transformation from an unassuming, tearful, fledgling agent to one of strength and a self-confidence verging on arrogance. Her tone even sounded deeper and less feminine than before. She was a special agent and was definitely in charge.

'You tricked me,' Steiner said, 'playing the fragile woman in distress.'

She glanced at him. 'I wouldn't take it too personally. I did what I had to do. Those cuffs weren't as tight as they looked, I'd been pulling at them for some time trying to get them loose, the extra bit of slack gave me the room I needed.'

'How long have you been an agent?'

She finished her task and stood up. 'Nearly six years, but I was a beat cop before, that bit was true.' Walking towards him she peered at the TV stream and then removed the gun from her belt and pointed it at Steiner's chest. 'Now,' she said, 'who the fuck are you?'

Steiner looked at her, his expression dubious.

Her eyes narrowed. 'You doubt me?' She stepped closer. 'I could easily say I shot you in self-defence. There's no one around to say otherwise and you're just as culpable for the deaths of all my colleagues as that fucker behind me. Give me one good reason I shouldn't shoot you where you stand?'

Steiner watched the gun in her hand and swallowed, his judgement of character apparently failing him for a second time in quick succession. 'I'm nobody.'

'Pah,' she said, 'you're insulting me now. Going by the way you carry yourself, the way you stood up to him and by the sound of your little altercation, you're also his superior. Remember who you're talking to, profiling people is what I do. So, I'll ask you again – who are you?'

Steiner didn't reply.

'Who are these hundreds of thousands of civilians that are condemned to death?' she said, trying a different tack and quoting the words he'd said to Samson.

Steiner stared at her, unwilling to speak.

Her eyes flashed and a snarl escaped her lips. Pushing Steiner back against the wall, she switched the gun to his forehead. 'What does that piece of shit I've just tied up want with me?'

Steiner stared into her eyes, no longer doubting her resolve. 'He needs you to help him find his daughter.'

'Is that what he told you?' Her laugh verged on the hysterical. 'You might want to get your facts straight next time you lend him a hand. Do you want to know the truth, you piece of shit?' She cocked the hammer. 'Do you?!'

A bead of sweat ran down the side of Steiner's face, he closed his eyes fearing the worst.

'Then I'll tell you,' she whispered, her face inches from his, her breath warm on his cheek, 'I *am* his daughter.'

Steiner's eyes flared open, his pupils contracting as Taylor stared at him intently. 'Your father?' he said, 'Samson is your father?' *No wonder he'd refused to abort when the alarm had tripped*, Steiner thought, *his daughter had been within his grasp. It all makes sense, in a perverse, insane kind of way*.

'You think this makes us buddies?' She pushed the gun harder against his head, her finger still on the trigger. 'That man is a monster. He may have contributed to half my DNA but he's as much my parent as you are.'

Steiner's mouth went dry, induced by the arousal of fear. The madness in her eyes and her recent disclosure about her parentage sowed more seeds of doubt in his mind as to her willingness to end his life.

'Still refusing to talk?' she asked.

'I'm sorry, I can't tell you any more, there're things going on here far greater than you could possibly imagine.'

'You think so?' She yanked him away from the wall and shoved him forwards. The gun to his back, she manoeuvred him round to look at the TV, still streaming on his computer. 'You think you're in a position to bargain with me?' she said. 'Take a look. Either I kill you, or you tell me what you know; you decide.'

Steiner barely heard her; he was too busy looking at the images on screen. One was a picture of the colonel bedecked in his armour. Alongside this was another photo, taken at a checkpoint, of Steiner himself. Underneath both were the following words, in big bold letters:

FBI MOST WANTED
TERRORISTS

$50,000,000
FIFTY MILLION DOLLAR
REWARD

'You're up shit creek, old man,' Taylor said in his ear, the gun against his neck, her manner, inflection and words frighteningly similar to those of the colonel. 'It's do or die.'

CHAPTER FORTY

THE LORRY BOUNCED and rolled as it travelled along an uneven section of road. The thin metal panels that made up the box-like container behind the driver's cab flexed and wobbled, the noise echoing inside the empty space like some giant distorted instrument. The vehicle lurched again and its chassis impacted the surface beneath with a loud BANG, awaking its occupant with a start.

Jessica Klein's eyes flew open, her gaze darting around in alarm. *Where the hell am I?* she wondered, the small, dull light above doing a poor job of illuminating her surroundings. She deduced by the sound and motion that she was inside a moving truck of some kind.

Her sense of time shot to pieces, Jessica tried to recall how she'd ended up where she now found herself, but her befuddled mind refused to give up its secrets. Why can't I remember anything? she thought, trying to quell the rising panic within her. Concentrating hard, she willed her memory to work. Books, an image of rows of books drifted out of the ether. A library – I was in a library – yes, that's right. But why was I there? Answers – I went there to find answers about the GMRC and what they were covering up. To find out why so many of my colleagues at the BBC disappeared and died in unusual circumstances. Yes, and Eric – I met Eric in the library. No – wait – that's not right.

A searing pain lanced through her head as if an electrified, white-hot needle was slowly being inserted into her eye. In agony, she put a hand to her forehead and then pushed her palms hard against her eye sockets to try and relieve the pain. She stayed thus for some moments, curious red and orange shapes on black flashing before her subdued vision. The migraine-like sensation gradually subsided and Jessica opened her eyes once more.

No, she said to herself again, resuming her internal monologue, *I met Eric outside, in his van*. She remembered hearing the blades of a helicopter in the dark, the sensation of running through thick snow. A GMRC team had been sent to the Berlin library to track them down. And then there was Bic, the international hacker, the cyber terrorist. He'd been the one who'd warned that her life was in danger. He was the reason she'd left her London home. Why she'd left her family behind in England – Evan, the girls.

A groan from nearby made her tense. Someone else was in there with her. 'Who's there?'

A faint voice came from behind some large cardboard boxes, 'Jessica, is that you?'

'Eric?'

'*Ja*, it's me.' Eric's German accent sounded slurred.

Jessica leaned forward from what felt like an uncomfortable pile of metal chains; looking back, she saw that's exactly what she'd been resting against. *No wonder my back hurts*. She rubbed the protruding ridges of her spine through her jumper and the T-shirt beneath. *I'm sure I was wearing a jacket*, she thought, suddenly feeling the icy chill in the air and glancing around before spying her coat close by. Picking it up, she shrugged into it and then stood up. Her head, still feeling battered and bruised like a boxer had been using it as a speed-ball, protested at the sudden movement and she almost vomited. The swaying motion of the vehicle didn't help things and she was forced to grab onto a cargo net that hung down from some crates opposite. Stumbling forward, she navigated some obstacles before rounding the boxes and looking down at the slim form of Eric. The youthful

German computer hacker, aka *das Gespenst*, the self proclaimed Ghost, held his head in his hands.

She dropped to her knees next to him. 'Eric, are you okay?'

'Apart from the mother of all headaches, yes. *Scheiße*, what did they do to us?'

'I can't remember, weren't we in a monastery?'

'*Ja, aua, scheiße*, my hard hurts.'

'You mean head,' Jessica said, unable to stop herself from correcting his English.

'*Ja*.'

'I think they injected us with something.' Her memory was solidifying from its esoteric stupor. The sensation of lying on the floor and her hands being tied behind her back sprang to the forefront of her mind. 'Yes, I remember now, they tied us up with cable ties, interrogated us, and then kept us under house arrest.'

Eric looked confused. 'Weren't we there for a few weeks?'

'I think so.' She tried to will the fog of her mind into chronological coherence. 'Yes, or at least it seemed that long. So much for your *Da Muss Ich*, or Bic, or whatever he's called.'

'Nein,' he said, lapsing into German, 'ich kann nicht glauben, er würde uns verraten.'

'You may not be able to believe it,' Jessica sat down next to him and made herself comfortable as her mind cleared, 'but betray us he did. If being held against our will for days on end with only weak gruel and stale water to sustain us hasn't convinced you otherwise, I don't know what will.'

Eric didn't say anything for a while, most likely coming to terms with being let down by his idol. What did they say? To avoid disappointment, never meet your heroes, or something along those lines. It was sad but quite often true; people who could appear perfect from a distance would invariably turn out to possess the same myriad of flaws as everyone else, just in a different order and perhaps not as obviously apparent. No one was perfect, least of all those that courted fame and notoriety. *I should know*, Jessica reflected in a rare instance of critical introspection, *I'm supposedly famous; well, more notorious now, I suppose, and I've got flaws galore.*

'I think they stuck a needle in my bum,' Eric said.

Jessica couldn't help but chortle at the remark, but she had to stop as it made her head pound. Now that he mentioned it, her left-hand buttock was a little sore. Reaching back she touched the area with tentative fingers. 'Ouch – yep, me too.'

The movement of the truck, which had settled back down into a smooth unimpeded ride, once more became uncomfortable as it audibly slowed and jolted over rough terrain, making them and everything around them shift and slide sideways. When the sensation of motion ceased, low voices could be heard conversing before the sound of the vehicle's doors opening and closing reverberated through the rigid steel shell that enclosed them. More talking could be discerned, louder now, but still unintelligible to Jessica's ears; whatever language they spoke it wasn't German or English.

Behind them, on the other side of the double doors, clasps were unlatched and a metal bolt slid back. Jessica and Eric struggled upright as they prepared to confront their captors. One of the doors swung outward and the light of a torch aimed inside made them shield their eyes.

'*Anhem mesteyqeza*,' someone said in a guttural tongue, '*lekm athenyen, alekherwej*!'

Jessica and Eric looked at one another, mystified.

'*Aussteigen*,' the man repeated in German. 'Get out!'

Jessica walked forward, Eric at her heels, both with hands raised against the bright light. Reaching the opening, she climbed down from the rear of the truck and onto frozen, ice strewn soil. Eric dropped down beside her, his shoes, like hers, crunching and cracking the crystalline water underfoot. Looking around it was clear they were no longer in an urban area. Snow laden pine trees all around stood tall and silent in the darkness, illuminated by the lorry's red taillights. Breathing in the fresh, freezing air, small puffs of breath expelling from her mouth, Jessica focused on the two men in front of them. Both were similarly dressed in thick, heavy fleece overcoats, military style steel toe-capped boots, and combat trousers, and each wore a thick black belt around his waist, attached to which was a holstered pistol. They were dark-skinned with swarthy faces and black hair, their beards short and wiry. One eyed Jessica and Eric with hostility as he puffed on a fat cigar, the end glowing orange as he took another drag.

'*Yenbeghey an tekwen hena*,' the non-smoker said to his friend, taking out his pistol, '*ayen hem*?'

The other man shrugged and expelled a large smoke ring from his mouth, its undulating shape floating away before disintegrating into nothing.

Jessica had given enough broadcasts and interviews in her day to realise the men were speaking in Arabic, although her understanding was limited and her ear untrained to distinguish one dialect from another, so they could have been saying anything for all she knew. She just hoped it wasn't something like: *shall we kill them both now or later?* At the sight of the weapon Eric had grabbed Jessica's arm, possibly fearing the worst.

The two men turned as another vehicle approached along the narrow dirt road, the man with the gun giving a wave of his hand in recognition. The compact truck came to a stop, the green and brown camouflage paintwork, high ground clearance and green canvas rear cover pulled tightly over a square sub-frame, a dead giveaway as to its military origins. The petrol engine continued to idle despite the vehicle now being stationary, its exhaust propelling out hot pollutants in a continuous, steady stream. The driver's door opened revealing a depiction of the German national flag on the side. A man emerged, his feet impacting the ground in tandem as he dropped down from his lofty position. He had a rifle slung over one shoulder and wore similar attire to those greeting him.

'*As-salam alaykum*,' the man said, sauntering over.

'*Wa alaykumu s-salam*.' The cigar smoker put his hand to his heart and shook the newcomer's hand.

After exchanging a greeting with the pistol-wielding third man, the new arrival appraised Eric and then Jessica in turn; the two of them now brightly lit under his transport's blazing white headlamps. He said something to his friends, who laughed in response, the joke no doubt, Jessica assumed, at her expense.

'I'm glad you all find this so amusing.' Her tone and manner wiped the smiles from their faces.

'Shush,' Eric said in fear.

The man with the rifle walked up to her, looking her up and down with disdain. He lashed out with the back of his hand, catching Jessica hard across her cheek.

'Hey!' Eric moved forward.

'*Ead eleyh*!' The man grabbed his rifle and pointed it at Eric, who put his hands up and stepped back again.

'Don't worry, Eric.' Jessica stood up straighter and pushed her long dark locks back behind one ear, the short red wig having been discarded back at the Stuttgart monastery. Her face stinging, Jessica stared defiantly back at her assailant, her psychological constitution preventing her from kowtowing to his intimidation. The man held her gaze and then muttered something and spat at the ground at her feet before stalking off to the rear of his truck. *Prick*, Jessica thought to herself, rubbing her face; the blow had brought back her headache.

Just when she thought things couldn't get any worse, the rear flap of the truck clanked down and five white-clad soldiers got out, all wearing balaclavas and sporting assault rifles. The apparent leader of this team shouted some commands in German to those around him, before marching straight up to Jessica to speak in a heavy German accent. 'Jessica Klein?'

She looked up at him. 'Yes.'

'*Gut, bekommen in der Rückseite des LKW*.' He indicated the military truck he'd just vacated. 'Get in.'

Jessica hesitated, unsure where this was leading.

'*Ach, kommen*,' the man said impatiently, pulling her forwards by the arm.

Eric made to follow, but another soldier pushed him back. 'Jessica!' Eric cried out.

'Eric!' She pulled back. 'What about him? *Was ist mit ihm*?!'

The soldier, in no mood for games, kept her moving. '*Er bleibt hier*, he stays.' He yanked her round to the rear of the vehicle and pushed her up into it.

Jessica felt bereft and exposed without Eric, whom she'd grown to like during their time together. She also felt a maternal instinct towards him, and a bond born of their shared experiences. She prayed he'd be okay without her, any optimism about his safety, and hers, deriving from the fact that they'd kept them alive this long; why would they change things now? Not wanting to think up any reasons to fracture her brittle confidence she pushed the thoughts from her mind.

Inside the truck an identical bench ran down either side. Jessica stayed standing, reluctant to get comfortable. Heavy black boots clattered up onto the metal floor-pan, the soldier's bulky frames forcing Jessica to take a seat as they crammed in around her. The leader, who'd manhandled her, sat nearest the cab and banged a gloved fist on the metal panel, signalling to the driver they were ready to leave.

The vehicle rolled back and then executed a tight six-point turn while Jessica looked out of the small rectangular opening between the tailgate and canvas roof. She felt a wash of emotions when Eric came into view, still standing in the same position, with the cigar smoker and his friend for company. He looked as forlorn as Jessica felt. Seeing her, he raised his hand in farewell and Jessica waved back as the truck moved off into the dark snowy forest. She watched until a bend in the road obstructed her view. With her young German friend no longer visible, she was left with only the grim, silent masked men around her for company in a new – and wholly unwanted – reality.

♦

The journey into the depths of the snowbound forest went on and on, the endless bouncing and jolting almost hypnotic as Jessica rocked around inside the vehicle. Four hours must have passed and the truck now crept up an ever-increasing incline, the rocky road turning treacherous. Jessica guessed they were still inside Germany, although she couldn't be sure. The duration of her enforced sedation could have lasted for hours or even days; for all she knew she could even be on another continent.

The soldiers around her spoke little during the drive and to her, not at all. Up and up they climbed and Jessica's clothing, which she'd stolen from the house back in the small town of Aalen, did little to keep out the freezing temperatures. With her teeth chattering, her sporadic shivering had become uncontrollable, the now continuous movement bringing the attention of one of the men upon her.

'*Sie hat den Tod einfrieren*,' the man said to his superior; Jessica barely heard him.

'*Ach*.' The leader stood up, took off his coat and pulled it around Jessica's small shoulders. Crouching down in front of her, he did up the zipper and then vigorously rubbed her frost nipped fingers before breathing onto them, his own hands cupped around them, trying to increase the warmth and blood flow. After a while of this treatment, the tips of her fingers regained some feeling, sharp pains and tingling sensations confirming they hadn't become frostbitten. He then switched his attention to her arms and legs.

'*Danke schön*,' Jessica said; her teeth still chattered a little, but her shivering had subsided.

The man nodded to her before sitting back down, leaving Jessica wrapped in his thick, warm coat.

Not much more time passed before the truck ground to a halt, the steep topography finally becoming too great for the vehicle to go any further. The men around her clambered out and hopped down to the ground; one of them held out a hand, which Jessica refused, opting to get out under her own steam.

Torches were switched on one by one, until five beams of light radiated out into the mountainous landscape around them. The great trunks of many conifers, their bark coated with ice and snow, could be seen disappearing into the darkness like many immobile giants standing to attention and awaiting orders from an otherworldly omnipotent source.

As one, the men moved away from the truck and on up into the forest. Jessica, encouraged to move into their midst, glanced back to see the relative security of the truck vanishing from sight.

'Where are you taking me?' she asked, not relishing trekking through the uninviting wilderness. '*Wo bringen Sie mich*?'

No one answered her, but she didn't have to wait long before they came across a small yellow tent hidden amongst the trees and boulder-strewn forest floor. From within this tiny haven emanated a bright warm glow. In the centre and at its peak a chimney poked out, puffs and wisps of smoke swirling up into the starless heavens.

All but one of the men bypassed this oasis, the leader of the troop stopping to hold Jessica back and reclaim his coat. '*Warten im Inneren*.' He pointed to the tent, let go of her arm and turned to leave.

'Stop,' she said in German, 'where are you going?'

'We're continuing on, you need to wait in the tent, someone will meet you inside.'

'What's this all about?' she asked, but he was already walking away, following his men up into the mountains.

Confused, Jessica unfastened the tent flap and ducked inside, quickly closing the opening behind her to preserve the hot air within. The tent was larger than it had appeared from the outside. A small chimney had been erected in the middle, powered by a wood burning stove; cunningly constructed to prevent any flames or sparks igniting the padded floor under and around it. It was the wavering light from this fire that had glowed so invitingly from without. At the back lay an unfurled sleeping bag, its crumpled creases and central indentation indicating it had recently been used by its owner.

As minutes turned to hours, Jessica made herself comfortable, enjoying the warmth that eroded the chill that had pervaded every fibre of her clothing and body. Feeling filthy and unwashed in her ill-fitting clothes, she tried her best to clean herself up, combing her tresses with her nails and wiping her face with hastily collected snow melt.

A while later, the tent flap rustled before flopping open to reveal a man in a thick, bright orange jumpsuit. He had a pale, yet jovial, windburned face framed by a tight fitting fur lined hood. 'Ah, hallo,' the man said upon seeing her. 'You've come a long way,' he continued in German. 'I hope they didn't treat you too badly.'

Jessica sat up straighter as he entered the tent. 'Who are you?'

'What? Didn't they explain? No, why would they – any of them.' Looking annoyed, he took off his thick orange mittens and put his hands out to the stove, rubbing them together for extra warmth. 'My name is Franz, and you are Jessica Klein, no?'

Jessica nodded. 'But I don't understand any of this; I was imprisoned, drugged and then driven out here, wherever here is—'

'Imprisoned, drugged, oh dear. That is not good, not good at all. Those people are thieves and criminals, not to be trusted; the whole lot of them. Some, I think, are linked with a terrorist group out of the Middle East, the People's Arabian Militia; perhaps you've heard of them?'

Jessica shook her head.

'No? You surprise me, a woman of the news such as yourself. But then these are dark times, full of censorship and oppression; things are not like they were, they are kept hidden, secret. That is why the likes of me end up rubbing shoulders with the likes of them, dark days indeed.'

'So where are we? And who were those soldiers? They weren't terrorists.'

'We are in the northern reaches of the Alps, in Austria,' Franz said, 'and those soldiers were most definitely not terrorists, but troops from the German army, moonlighting, if you will, across borders.'

'So why am I here? What's all this about?'

Franz gave her an odd look. 'You don't know? But you must know, he told me you knew.'

'Who told you I knew what?'

'The man who set up this meeting, of course, DMI, *Da Muss Ich.*'

CHAPTER FORTY-ONE

Jessica stared at Franz in disbelief. '*Da Muss Ich* set up this meeting, Bic – the cyber terrorist?'

'Yes, it has been arranged for some time. He didn't tell you?'

Jessica thought back to her brief conversations with Bic via the computer, some of her memories still jumbled from whatever powerful drug the kidnappers had pumped into her. 'He did mention something about meeting a GMRC insider,' she said, 'but that was before he betrayed us, before we were taken captive.'

'There is someone else with you?' Franz asked in concern. 'I can only get access for one person, no more, two would be an impossibility.'

Frowning and disregarding his question, Jessica rubbed her temples trying to piece together the disjointed puzzle in her mind. 'You're the man who works on the classified programme, aren't you?' A section snapped into place. 'The insider who can tell me the truth about the GMRC and what they're hiding?'

Franz smiled at her. 'Do you want to see?' he said, a twinkle in his eye.

♦

Jessica traipsed through the freezing Austrian alpine forest dressed in bright orange clothing, provided for her by Franz who, a few steps ahead with a torch in his hand, guided her to a destination that would finally reveal the GMRC's most secret of truths. What that would be she could only guess at, but the anticipation was palpable and increased with every step she took.

They'd been walking for a couple of hours and Jessica's tired limbs vied with a thirst for water to see which could exact on her the most discomfort. After cresting a ridge and dropping down into a valley, Jessica thought she glimpsed lights in the distance through the trees, lots and lots of lights.

A deep rumbling noise built in the skies overhead, getting louder and louder until a deafening roar shot past, disturbing the snow-clad treetops. Another high-speed Sabre fighter followed in its wake, both heading down the valley at frightening speed.

'Air patrols,' Franz said over his shoulder, dislodged snow falling around them in the torchlight, 'regular as clockwork, nothing moves down here without them knowing about it.'

'What about us?' Jessica asked, 'they know we're here?'

'Of course, I should know, it's part of my job; I work in the security centre.'

'Security centre for what?'

'You'll see.'

Jessica stifled an angry retort. Franz, while amiable, was certainly not forthcoming about what he was taking her to see, putting her off with ambiguities which seemed to amuse his penchant for the dramatic.

With the trees thinning, the slope bottomed out to a gravel and slate laden basin. Encircling this massive clearing stood a chain of mighty floodlights, higher than the trees that encircled them. At the far end of the valley a monstrous wall stretched across like an enormous uncoiled snake that had been turned to glistening, grey stone, its petrified carcass serving others in its death.

A resonating hum made Jessica turn to see five tandem coaxial rotor helicopters skimming in low over the trees before crossing the large open expanse and moving on towards the distant monolithic wall. Each of these black aircraft bore the gleaming white logo of her nemesis, the power hungry and out of control behemoth, the GMRC.

Further along, after walking around a tiny portion of the basin's edge, which resembled the shallow pit of an open mine, they reached a small white building. Next to this stood an open-top vehicle, a kind of dune buggy with massive oversized wheels and a transparent shell. They climbed into the front seats, the edges of the low profile tyres now higher than their heads, and a bright blue head-up-display blazed to life on the front windscreen. Pressing a touch button, Franz started the electric engine and drove them towards the activity around the wall.

He passed her a red, hard hat. 'Put this on,' he said, still speaking in German.

She put on the helmet and he followed suit, his own helmet white.

'And you'll need this.' He dangled a metallic badge on a chain before her, the cold wind whipping at it through the open vehicle.

Accepting the proffered lanyard, Jessica inspected the curious design of the accompanying card. The GMRC logo was engraved in the top right-hand corner and on the left was her facial image and her pseudonym, Eliza Sterling, the name her deceased friend and colleague, Martin, had given her prior to her leaving England. Putting the chain around her neck, Jessica felt a certain amount of trepidation as the wall grew nearer. The astounding structure must have been over a hundred foot high and bristled with lights all along its formidable length. She could see now that it wasn't a barrier, but an enclosure, the sides at each end curving round and out of sight.

Bouncing along in the buggy, they skimmed along next to the wall; armed soldiers could be seen patrolling high above, on top. The sentries wore white balaclavas and identical clothing to the men who had escorted her to the meeting with Franz.

An entrance through the wall came into view and Franz turned to her. 'When we get inside, let me do all the talking; you're a security inspector from another facility and are there to observe only.'

'What facility?' she said, alarmed by the lack of detail to her cover story.

'They won't ask.' He slowed the vehicle. 'They're not allowed to know.'

'Convenient,' she said.

He flashed her a smile that looked more like a grimace. 'That card is all you need. *Da Muss Ich* and I have ensured your entry will go unnoticed; as long as we keep to the plan nothing will go wrong.'

'I've heard that before,' Jessica muttered under her breath.

'Act natural,' he said, the vehicle stopping on a flat piece of concrete, 'here we go.'

Here we go where? Jessica thought. The imposing gates in front of them still stood tightly closed with no sign of opening. The futuristic buggy rocked as the ground beneath them shifted. Slabs of concrete reared up all around and they sank into the earth, their descent giving the impression that the wall rose higher above them.

The platform shuddered to a halt, revealing a road ahead blocked off by a substantial metal barrier that protruded from its tarmac surface. On either side, a team of grey garbed men and women emerged from glass partitioned offices built into the super-sophisticated underground security checkpoint. Some scanned the exterior and interior of the vehicle, while others ran Franz's and Jessica's identity badges through a handheld computer, even stopping to take DNA and hair samples from each of them. Jessica hoped Franz and Bic had done a good job at gaining her access; she could see herself locked up permanently if her deception was exposed. The security personnel were apparently satisfied with their checks and Franz rolled the car forwards and onto another platform. A large rectangular scanner rose out of the floor, its metal frame zipping up and down and around them at a frenetic pace, a plethora of crystal blue laser-like lights covering every inch of the buggy and its passengers with their pervasive fan-shaped beams.

'Put this on.' Franz handed her a small face mask, the two small discs on the front marking it as a piece of breathing apparatus. Jessica did so just before a white light above shone down on them and jets of warm mist blasted over every inch of the vehicle like some out of control, ultra high-tech car wash. Once this process had subsided, the buggy and their bright orange outfits glistened with a fine film of residue. A loud buzzer blared out and the metal barrier sank into the floor, allowing Franz to drive over it and down a long, brightly lit tunnel.

When they emerged from below ground onto a raised, single-lane road Jessica caught her breath; the panorama before her was awe-inspiring to behold. Above, a transparent covering stretched away in all directions. Travelling further in, Jessica could tell that this massive see-through dish, if viewed outside from the air, would resemble a funnel; similar to the end of a wind instrument like a tuba, but with the hole in the middle being much smaller and the curve shallower.

Below the elevated highway, Jessica could see that this gargantuan, shielded, indoor area, a few miles across, had indeed been built over an open mine. The huge pit descended in great steps of rock hewn from the earth's crust; down and down they went, each level supporting a whole host of pipework and cabling ranging in diameter from the size of a person's arm to the width of a large house. All around, a web of interconnecting turbines powered the facility, their giant, bulging shells arranged in a series of systems so complex it boggled the mind just to look at.

Throughout this structure, people could be seen carrying out their duties, all wearing the appropriate hard hats and various coloured coveralls, perhaps denoting their specific department or team. At the epicentre of this mass of activity a towering structure thrust up from deep underground, creating the supporting hub for the vast, translucent, inverted funnel-dome around it. The top of this central tower also extended above the dome itself, cutting a path to the air outside. From her vantage point inside the buggy, Jessica saw that numerous circular platforms sprouted from the sides of the building, many of them occupied by the large black helicopters she'd seen only a short while before.

'Is it safe to speak in here?' Jessica asked as the road spiralled in towards the centre.

Franz glanced at her. 'Yes, while we are in the car, anyway.'

'What is this place for? It's huge, all these people, equipment, machines.'

'This is not huge, just wait, you'll see. Look, we are almost there.'

Jessica looked to her right as they neared the tower. During their drive inside they had gradually been descending. The surface now lay hundreds of feet above them, the wall that stretched around the outside so far away it looked small when viewed through the transparent funnel overhead.

Franz slowed the vehicle, directing it inside one of many small external carports built onto the side of the structure. Powering down the car, they both got out onto a smooth metal floor and walked into the building through a wide open arch.

'Good morning, Franz Veber, Eliza Sterling,' an automated female voice said as they passed inside, a red laser scanning them both while on the move. 'Welcome.'

Ensuring she kept her thoughts to herself now they were inside, Jessica looked around the interior. Wide, oval-shaped corridors fanned out in every direction, comprising frosted glass floors and thick, durable gloss-white, composite wall-mouldings; it was a pleasing fusion of aesthetic design and functional austerity.

Continuing down one of these passageways, Franz and Jessica, still wearing their respective hard hats, found themselves engulfed in a hive of activity as they cut through a bustling control room. Controlling what, Jessica wasn't quite sure, but wallscreens and complicated projections adorned every surface. Franz stopped soon after to converse at length with a man holding a clipboard, his grey uniform embroidered with a black version of the GMRC's logo. Nearby, Jessica stood trying to look inconspicuous. Apparently satisfied with whatever Franz had told him, the official walked away, giving Jessica a nod in passing, which she returned, along with a smile that felt more like a rictus grin than a friendly gesture.

Setting off again, Franz led her through a series of turns culminating in a breath-taking circular atrium, the centre dominated by a huge open shaft as wide as a football pitch and containing a single, equally monstrous, multi-floored platform surrounded by an abundance of complex machinery.

'Is that what I think it is?' Jessica said, keeping her voice low.

'It is okay to speak freely again,' Franz told her, 'but if you're thinking it's a subterranean lift shaft and accompanying elevation transport module, then yes, that is exactly what it is.'

'But it's so—'

'Big?'

'Yes.'

'It's a matter of logistics.' Franz ushered her to a far smaller human sized lift at the atrium's edge. Entering it, he pressed a button. 'If you have a lot of material to move, you need something big to move it with.'

A high-pitched whine indicated the elevator moved down at speed, Jessica spying on an interior panel the words, *vacuum lift*. The sound stopped and the doors opened to reveal an astounding sight.

'Now that is big,' Franz said, moving out into by far the largest indoor area Jessica had ever seen.

They stood on a metal gangway, suspended high up on the side of an outer wall. The huge lift shaft they had seen above cut through this section and continued its way down unhindered, destination unknown What so amazed her, however, was that it wasn't the only shaft in sight. Miles apart, separated by the mother of all loading bays, other lift shafts could be seen in the far distance. On this great floor, huge vehicles, themselves dwarfed by the warehouse in which they operated, loaded and unloaded all manner of containers.

'This is incredible.' Jessica was awestruck.

Franz nodded. 'The structure you saw on the surface is one of many; they all meet here underground and then continue on down to the main complex below.'

Jessica stood there for some moments, taking it all in. 'I'm sorry, what?' she said, realising what he'd just said. 'This isn't the main complex?'

Franz grinned at her. 'This?' He gestured with a hand at the immense area before them. 'No. This is just a staging area. It's small in comparison to what lies beneath.'

'Small?' Jessica said.

'Yes. Look here.' He guided her to a schematic attached to a nearby wall. 'This is one of the surface structures, where we entered.' He pointed at a small disc shape near the top of the diagram. 'Here,' he said, indicating a larger area below, 'is where we are now, and this,' he continued, his finger drawing her eyes further down to the bulk of the diagram, 'is the main facility.'

Jessica looked at it, finding it hard to comprehend the sheer scale of it. 'But what is it? What's it for?'

'That,' Franz said, looking proud, 'is EUSB Deutschland.'

CHAPTER FORTY-TWO

'EUSB?' Jessica noticed a curious emblem in the bottom right hand corner of the wall diagram:

'European Union Subterranean Base,' Franz said, before a beeping alarm alerted him to his computer phone. 'Time's up, we need to go.'

'But I need to see more.' Reluctant, Jessica followed him back to the vacuum lift.

'That's all I can show you. I don't have clearance to go down into the main structure. Not yet anyway.'

'But you will?'

'Yes, in less than twelve months now, I get to go.'

Having had to stay quiet while they journeyed back through the tower complex, Jessica was full of questions when they returned to the buggy; questions that Franz, frustratingly, didn't seem to be able to answer. As they exited the base by a different route, thankfully without hindrance, Jessica pressed him further for information.

'But you must know why it was built,' she said, as they bounced along over rough terrain in the transparent vehicle.

Franz scratched his chin. 'Well, for protection against the fallout from AG5, for sure.'

'The GMRC told us that AG5 wasn't that great a threat,' Jessica said.

'And it wasn't,' Franz replied, 'we're still here aren't we?'

Jessica thought for a moment. 'True, unless the fallout is going to be worse than predicted, or worse than we were led to believe? I think that must be it. That's why they're siphoning off all the water and food. This is where it's going, to this base.' She paused. 'But no, even a place as large as that couldn't take all the world's resources, there's no way—'

'This isn't the only base,' Franz said. 'As I told you before, you're supposed to be from another facility, and by that I mean another EUSB.'

Jessica was dumbfounded. 'How many of those things are there?'

'That I know of? At least six in Europe. I guess the Americans and Chinese have similar projects underway.'

'Then that must be it. AG5 has caused more problems than they expected and these bases are to provide shelter for those lucky enough to be inside, leaving everyone else to fend for themselves on the surface as civilisation collapses in on itself.'

Franz didn't respond to her theories. Jessica continued to deliberate as they dropped off the buggy and made their way back to the tent, once more plunged into darkness with only torches to guide their way. Another hard slog through the freezing conditions ensued, until at last they reached the welcome shelter of the tent. Back in relative warmth, Jessica realised while she may have found out the disturbing truth hidden by the GMRC, she had failed to document it as Bic had required. She said as much to Franz who allayed her fears.

'That's been taken care of,' he said, 'I've already recorded footage over a number of months and have passed this to *Da Muss Ich*. He needed you to see it for yourself, to give credence to your findings.'

'How long have you known Bic – *Da Muss Ich*?' she asked, as she changed back into her other clothing.

'Many years now.' He turned his back so as to afford her some privacy. 'He came to me when I had reached my lowest ebb, my darkest hour. He gained my confidence and over time I came to trust him like a brother. We worked together so I could infiltrate this facility and that was ten years ago now. He has great foresight and a sense of purpose I have rarely seen.'

'Have you ever met him? In person, I mean?'

'No – not once in all that time. He says it would be too dangerous for both of us to know his real identity.'

Jessica could understand that; such a disclosure would also destroy the anonymity he had worked hard for so long to maintain. Pondering on what she'd learnt, she devoured some food and water left by the soldiers during one of their security sweeps, which left her feeling sufficiently refreshed to start the final leg back to the road with Franz, once again, acting as her escort.

Reaching the stony, dirt track, Jessica was pleased to see the same military vehicle that had dropped her off was standing waiting, ensuring she didn't have to wait around in the arctic conditions. Thanking Franz for his help and giving him a brief hug in parting, Jessica climbed into the front of the truck at the driver's instigation.

The journey back through the forest was considerably more pleasant than the previous trip as she now enjoyed the luxury of a heated compartment. She even managed to drift off to sleep, before being nudged awake by the soldier next to her.

'They are ready for you,' he said.

Jessica looked with weary eyes to see a group of people in the road ahead, the light from the truck highlighting them against the white van behind.

Thanking the driver, she got out and, with apprehension, walked to meet the three Middle Eastern terrorists Franz had told her belonged to the People's Arabian Militia.

The leader, whom she'd had the unpleasant privilege of meeting before, opened the rear of the vehicle and she got in without a word. The door closed behind her, the noise of the bolt sliding into place and catches clipping down announcing she'd been sealed inside.

'Eric?' She searched the rear of the truck, but he wasn't in there. Worrying about his safety, she settled down as the truck moved off over the uneven terrain.

♦

The journey back to the terrorists' headquarters lasted about an hour, then the truck stopped and Jessica was led back into the monastery she'd grown all too accustomed to during her time in confinement. Corralled into a back room on the first floor, she felt overjoyed to see Eric.

'Jessica, am I glad to see you.' He gave her a warm embrace. 'I wondered if I'd see you again.'

'Tell me about it. How's the memory?' she asked.

'Better, but I'm not sure why they drugged me in the first place, to be honest. If I wasn't going with you to wherever you went, they might as well have left me here.'

Jessica took a seat at a rickety wooden table. 'I guess they didn't want to leave you on your own, or they didn't realise only one of us could go.'

Eric shrugged, his face noncommittal. 'So where *did* you go?' he asked, intrigued. 'When those goons brought me back, they finally let slip that *Da Muss Ich* had arranged a meeting for you. Turns out he didn't betray us after all, hey?'

'Looks that way. I don't go much on his choice of partners, though. The guy I met told me they're connected to a Middle Eastern terrorist cell.'

'That explains a lot.' He sat down opposite her.

'As to where I went, you won't believe it.'

Eric looked at her expectantly, but before she could regale him with tales of the amazing things she'd seen, they heard people coming up the stairs.

A group of men stormed into the room, at their head the terrorist leader.

'*Sewf tesjeyl alefyedyew balensebh lena alan*!' He waved a small video camera in her face.

Jessica didn't understand.

'You record video for us now,' another man translated, Jessica recognising him as the cigar smoker from her trip.

'Video?' She looked from him to the irate leader and back again.

The leader shoved the camera into the hands of another of his cohorts then grabbed Eric's arm, pulled him out of the chair and pushed the designated cameraman down in his place, gesturing at him expansively while spouting a stream of instructions to him in Arabic.

The man with the camera pointed it in Jessica's direction and then a little red light appeared on one side of it, indicating he'd started it working. The leader then thrust a sheet of paper under Jessica's nose and pointed at it, demanding something from her in his unfathomable language.

'You want me to read this?' She ran her eyes over the paper.

'Yes, read to camera,' the translator said.

Having read through it, she pushed it away. 'I'm not reading that.'

'*Ma*?' the leader asked his translator.

The cigar smoker relayed what she'd said, which didn't seem to go down well.

'*Teqra alan*!!' Wild eyed, he pushed the paper back towards her.

'No.' Jessica shoved the paper away again and looked at the cigar smoker. 'I'm not reading out a list of his demands, nor will I condemn my country's actions on his say so. Besides, I'm a disgraced newsreader; no one will want to listen to what I've got to say.'

The leader received the translation and became, if anything, even more incensed.

'You do what you promised. We kept our side of the bargain,' the English speaking terrorist relayed to her. 'That was the deal—'

His leader rattled off another barrage of angry words, pointing at Eric, and the man continued the translation. 'And *Da Muss Ich* tells us people *will* listen to you. You read or we kill your friend.'

'What?!' Jessica and Eric said in unison.

'I agreed no such thing!' Jessica half stood in protest and was immediately forced back down by a man behind her. 'Tell him, I didn't agree to this; tell him!'

The man told his boss what she'd said, but he threw a hand in the air dismissively before rattling off his retort.

'You didn't agree, but *Da Muss Ich* did; he said you would read. That is why we agreed to help you. You read, or your friend dies.'

Jessica looked to Eric in despair as the leader held out a hand and was given a pistol by one of his men. 'Wait,' she said, 'let me speak to Bic, *Da Muss Ich*, let me speak to him.'

The terrorists had a heated discussion and then one of the men left the room. He returned shortly after with Eric's touchscreen device, which she had used to speak with Bic during their escape from Berlin. The man placed it on the desk in front of her. She looked at it, before typing in a question:

Bic, you promised I would read out their statement?

. . .

YES _ came the immediate response.

I can't read it out.

Pass the device to their leader _

Jessica handed the screen to the leader, who snatched it from her grasp. Jessica looked at Eric, who was justifiably worried. Not much time passed before the terrorist threw the touchscreen back onto the table, pointed his gun at Eric and fired.

'No!' Jessica screamed.

Eric slumped to the floor, blood smeared on the wall above him.

'Read,' the leader said to her in English, cocking the hammer as he did so.

She hesitated and the gun fired again.

CHAPTER FORTY-THREE

JESSICA LOOKED in shock at the smoke rising from the end of the terrorist's handgun. She looked down at her chest. No blood spot appeared and she felt no pain – anywhere. He'd missed on purpose. A warning shot. Before anything else happened, the touchscreen bleeped and Jessica instinctively picked it up to see what Bic had said. It was in Arabic, but as she watched another message appeared in English, a single word.

DUCK _

Duck? she thought, her mind in turmoil. A bright light and a deep hum from outside the first floor window caught everyone's attention. More guns were drawn and Jessica threw herself to the floor. The windows shattered and thunderous gunfire tore into the room. Jessica covered her head with her arms as the onslaught continued, glass and shell casings raining down around her. And almost as soon as it had begun the noise ceased, only the light and hum remained, and the occasional tinkle of glass dropping to the floor.

Jessica raised her head to see that all the terrorists were dead and the room riddled with holes. Getting up, she couldn't help but notice a large black drone hovering at the window, on its front a stark white GMRC logo. Unthinking, she rushed to Eric's side. Putting two fingers to his neck she was relieved to feel a strong, steady pulse.

He opened his eyes. 'Jessica?'

'Yes, I'm here.' She checked for the wound and saw blood on his right thigh. Probing with her fingers she located the hole and tore open his trouser leg to reveal the damage. 'It doesn't look too bad.' Her experience as a roving war reporter in her younger days stood her in good stead to make such judgement calls. Moving his leg, making him groan in pain, she confirmed her first thought. 'It's a through and through,' she said, more to herself than him.

Moving away, she took a belt from one of the terrorists' bodies. Returning to Eric, she wrapped it tight, extracting an agonised cry from her young patient. With difficulty, due to her small stature and his height, she helped Eric over to the table and the one remaining intact chair. The drone that had come to their rescue still hovered outside the room, lights ablaze. A beep from the touchscreen, which had somehow survived the brief firefight, made Jessica turn it over.

Jessica Klein, bring Eric to the drone. You don't have much time _

Much time for what?

The GMRC will be with you shortly _

How did they know we were here!? Why did they help us?

She was fearful of getting assistance from anything branded with a GMRC logo.

. . .

They aren't helping you. I am. I hijacked their drone. They know you are there as I told them _

What?! Why?

Because I didn't know if I could save you. The terrorists are unpredictable and I needed to ensure yours and Eric's survival. Redundancy. Now hurry, get onto the drone _

Pocketing the screen, she helped Eric get back up and over to the window. The hovering black drone moved closer to the building, the backdraft from its enclosed twin rotors whisking up her hair in the process. Trying not to look down, she stepped onto the window ledge, Eric managing to get up alongside.

'I'm not sure I can do this!' Jessica said to Eric over the noise.

In no fit state to contribute, Eric gave her a weak smile of support.

As she looked out of the first floor window, the sound of approaching vehicles drew her eyes to the left and then to the right. Two convoys converged on the building, and in the distance a helicopter approached. The GMRC had arrived. Grabbing Eric firmly around the waist, she braced herself.

'On three,' she said.

Eric nodded.

'One, two – three!'

They leapt out into the air and dropped down onto the drone, which fell a few feet as it compensated for the extra weight. Gripping onto the central body of the machine for dear life, her other arm holding Eric in a death grip, Jessica repositioned them both into a more secure position. With their enemy closing in, the drone's blades angled them away from the monastery and propelled them, with gathering speed, out over the surrounding rooftops and off into the night.

♦

With Eric by her side, Jessica skimmed across the Stuttgart skyline on board the GMRC drone controlled by the hacker, Bic. In the moonless sky, the snow laden streets and buildings seemed picture perfect, the lights in and around them shining clear and bright. As far as the eye could see powdery white ice crystals created beautiful, smooth, mushroom-topped sculptures from otherwise mundane, lifeless drudgery. In the air, however, this idyllic setting was brutal, the bitter wind stealing away the breath of those travelling through it unprotected.

The craft banked left to avoid a tall tower block, making Jessica grimace when Eric's weight threatened to break her hold on him. With her hands and face going numb, relief washed over her when the drone decreased its forward trajectory and flew down to hover over a single storey structure draped in a white cocoon of innumerable snowflakes. The turbine-esque rotor blades, channelling their concentrated vortices downwards, cleared a convenient path for Jessica to jump down onto. Eric, looking pale and weak, slid off the drone, barely keeping his feet as he settled next to her on the flat rooftop. No sooner had they disembarked than the drone's blades spun up faster, launching it up and away, to disappear into the night.

Jessica, half-carrying Eric, guided them towards a rectangular structure which contained a door. Pulling her coat over her exposed hand, she pulled the metal handle down, a digital lock that had been showing a red light clicked to green and the door opened. They entered and closed the door behind them, then made their way down some stairs and into a cosy apartment. Heaters had pre-warmed the rooms to a degree over toasty. Jessica's first responsibility was to dress Eric's injury. A few hours later she'd managed to stitch his leg with supplies she'd found in a medical cabinet, before putting him to bed to rest. Whose home this was she had no clue, but it was currently unclaimed and right now she felt too tired to care. Sitting down on a comfortable sofa, she plopped the touchscreen onto her lap and closed her eyes.

♦

Jessica woke to a persistent vibration, unaware of how much time had passed. The portable computer had slipped from her lap as she slept and now lay next to her leg, the display flashing in time to its alert. Picking it up, she read a message from Bic.

We need to talk _

I wondered when you'd get back in touch she wrote, before remembering she could speak into the screen. Selecting the button Eric had shown her previously, her expression turned angry. 'I don't appreciate being thrown to the wolves; those terrorists could have killed us both!'

I am sorry Jessica Klein. Truly. They were the only people willing and capable of taking you to Franz Veber _

'I'm beginning to wonder whose side you're really on.'

I am against the GMRC _

. . .

'You called the GMRC!'

I had no choice _

On seeing those words she had an epiphany. 'You alerted the GMRC to our presence at the library, didn't you? There was no hidden programme on Eric's system, it was you all along.' Jessica waited for the response, her anger increasing with each passing moment.

Please don't tell Eric. He will never forgive me _

And there it was; an instant confession. Jessica ground her teeth and looked heavenward. She'd been played this whole time. Returning her gaze to the screen, she spoke again. 'I won't tell him, but not for your sake. Has anything you've said been true? Was Martin really murdered? Was I really classed as a suicide risk? Are you even who you say you are?'

I am who I am. But you are right to question me, you were not deemed a suicide risk; but your old producer was killed _

'Why? Why did you manipulate me?'

I need you Jessica Klein. You are my eyes and ears. You are my conduit to the people. I had to get you to go to Berlin and I then had to make sure you went to Stuttgart. You would not have listened otherwise _

. . .

'I might have done and if you need me so badly you're going the wrong way about earning my trust.'

The hacker didn't reply and Jessica wondered if he'd logged off the system. His silence served to add fuel to the fire of her simmering fury at having been deceived. A minute later the screen pinged and a new message appeared.

Did you enjoy your visit to EUSB Deutschland?

'Unbelievable,' she muttered to herself, 'Where? Oh, you mean the place you got me to visit under false pretences?

Your tone suggests you are still angry with me _

'No shit, Sherlock.'

I have something which may cheer you up _

No sooner had she read Bic's message than a picture materialised onto the screen, instantly altering her mood. Framed at the doorstep of a house she vaguely recognised was her husband, Evan, and peering out from behind him, the beautiful faces of her daughters, Victoria and Daniela. The photo fluctuated, the scene rewinding before beginning to move – it was footage from a TV camera, along with an audio track.

'—and you don't know where your wife is?' someone was saying, a microphone thrust forwards under Evan's nose, Victoria and Daniela no longer in the shot.

'Not at this time,' he said, 'but she has reassured me she is completely innocent of the crimes attributed to her. My wife is the most honest, law abiding and hard working woman I know; the sheer notion of her taking money to slander the GMRC is preposterous. The video evidence has clearly been falsified in attempt to discredit her claims—'

Jessica watched, her heart soaring in pride and love for her husband as he defended her honour. *He must have decided to speak to the press to clear my name*, she realised.

'I see,' the reporter said, 'but what do you say to the majority of people, and I class myself as one, who say that your wife's claims about some kind of conspiracy are, quite frankly, absurd and her disappearance an affirmation of guilt?'

Jessica's heart sank as Evan floundered on air against the biased interviewer. Near the end of the recording, her daughters came into view and Evan was quick to shepherd them back inside what she now saw was her in-laws' house. The footage ended and Jessica received another message from Bic.

Your loved ones are safe and well _

His motives may be questionable, but a brief glimpse of her family had indeed tempered her mood, regardless of the continuing difficulties they faced.

'Thank you,' she said grudgingly. 'As to EUSB Deutschland, it was an enlightening experience. I now know the truth.'

Tell me _

'The world's stockpiles of food and water are being transferred to colossal subterranean facilities all around the globe,' she told him. 'Franz says there are six in Europe alone and I find it hard to believe the Americans and Chinese haven't done likewise. Everyone on the surface will be left to fight it out in a survival of the fittest, while below the lucky few will continue to live in relative safety until the dust cloud dissipates and the planet's ecosystems return to normal.'

But do you know why? _

'Because the fallout from the asteroid AG5 was worse than forecast or greater than they would have us believe.'

Good. You have done well _

'So what happens now? You do a global hack and release your Playground software thingamajig and then I tell the world what's really happening?'

It's not as simple as that _

'Why not?'

There is something missing. My computations don't add up. This is not the whole truth _

'What other truth could there be?'

. . .

I'm unsure. That is what is concerning me _

'I thought you knew the whole truth?' she said, infuriated.

I know one truth. Not all truths _

'Oh, for f – heaven's sake. This truth is enough; we need to tell people now, before it's too late!'

No. We wait. The GMRC are gearing up for something, something soon, something big. I am close to finding out what. Since AG5 impacted even the GMRC are finding it difficult to keep information contained _

'Can you at least help me contact my family? I need to speak to my husband.'

You seek to warn him. I understand, but it is too risky, dangerous even. The GMRC will be watching them; even for me it would be impossible to instigate contact without them knowing _

Jessica's thoughts were bitter. 'So you say.'

I know you no longer trust me, but what I say is true _

. . .

'So what's with you and the GMRC anyway? When did you first realise something wasn't quite right?' she asked, changing the subject for her own sanity. 'Franz said you've been working with him for ten years, he said you are extremely motivated and dedicated. That kind of commitment comes from somewhere.'

Bic didn't reply at first, the cursor on the small screen blinking on and off as she waited for an answer; the screen bleeped and another message appeared.

I have always known something – as you put it – wasn't quite right. As to my motivations, they are many but my goals are few _

As ever, Bic revealed no more than he wanted to, the hacker's enigmatic persona remaining firmly intact.

'So what do we do next? If you want to wait, how long for? I'm not hanging around indefinitely on your say so. I know enough to at least help my family.'

No. What you now know puts your family in far greater peril. The information you hold is something the GMRC will kill for to keep hidden. If they don't already know of your involvement in Germany, it will only be a matter of time before they do. You have never been in as much danger as you are now _

'Great, so I've got to stay here until you say otherwise? If you think that's going to happen, you don't know me at all.'

I know you better than you think Jessica Klein. Get some sleep. I have something for you to see in the morning _

. . .

'Like what?' she said, but the screen had gone dark, the power turned off remotely by Bic. 'Wonderful.' She slumped back in her chair in defeat. 'Just wonderful.'

CHAPTER FORTY-FOUR

FBI Special Agent Brett Taylor held a cocked and loaded gun to her abductor's head. Behind them, unconscious and tied up on the floor, lay his partner in crime; a man directly responsible for the murder of over fifty of Taylor's colleagues and countless more police officers and civilians, a man she also knew as – father.

The aging man before her, sweat glistening on his bespectacled and bearded face, appeared to be in some kind of catatonic shock, having seen his picture and learned of a fifty million dollar reward for his capture on the news. Becoming the FBI's most wanted could dampen anyone's day.

'Final chance,' she told him between clenched teeth, pressing the gun harder against his head, 'tell me what you know – now!'

The man focused on her, a look of defeat stealing across his features. 'I cannot.' He closed his eyes. 'Do as you will.'

The hand holding the gun trembled and then shook as an internal battle raged within Taylor. The thirst for vengeance for her dead friends screamed at her to pull the trigger. *Pull it!* While her duty and training begged, pleaded with her not to.

'Fuck!!' She pointed the gun at the wooden ceiling and fired off three shots in sheer frustrated anger; the deafening noise in the enclosed quarters of the cellar made her ears ring. Unleashing a stream of curses, Taylor kicked the computer displaying the TV feed to the floor and walked away to lean against a wall. Hanging her head, her chest heaving, she sucked in great gulps of air to reduce the pent up tension and masses of adrenaline that now coursed through her veins.

Regaining some semblance of composure, she looked back to see the man she'd nearly killed watching her, his expression unfathomable. She knew with distressing certainty she'd been a hair's breadth away from ending his life; far too close to a line she'd promised herself never to cross, the reason for such a promise lying only a few feet away, bound and still comatose .

Knowing the old-timer didn't represent any physical threat, Taylor moved to the other side of the room to retrieve her handcuffs. Returning with them, she grabbed the man's wrists and secured his hands behind his back, ratcheting the mechanism up nice and tight.

'Brett,' said a groggy voice, its familiarity freezing Taylor on the spot, 'release me.'

Turning slowly in trepidation, her gaze inexorably came to rest upon those unforgiving, penetrating and disturbing ice-cold, blue eyes. Eyes she hadn't seen since she was twelve years of age. Eyes that she'd hoped never to see again.

'Release me,' her father repeated, the ropes that held him creaking and groaning as he fought against them. Taylor's hand went to the gun tucked in her belt, the security of cold steel comforting in its dense solidity as her fingers wrapped around the grip. Aiming the weapon at Samson, she felt an overwhelming compulsion to shoot.

'Don't do something you'll regret,' the old man said from behind her, 'he's still your father.'

'Shut your mouth,' she told him, but she lowered the pistol all the same. 'You don't deserve a quick death,' she said to Samson. 'Like your friend, you'll be tried and then, God willing, your final days will be spent waiting for a lethal injection.'

Samson glared at her, one eye bleary and bloodshot from the

blow she'd dealt to his head. 'You're making a mistake,' he slurred, still clearly concussed, 'your life – in danger.'

'Not anymore it's not.' Taylor smiled in grim satisfaction and turned away to rummage in a large sack close by. Quickly tiring of searching through it, she upended it, sending its contents tumbling to the floor. Prodding at items with her foot she soon spied what she was looking for – her computer phone, FBI badge and service pistol. Scooping them up, she returned her sidearm to its holster and clipped her badge back onto her belt. Her phone had been smashed, she assumed to prevent any signal from being traced. Looking around she saw another phone on the floor next to the computer she'd all but destroyed earlier. Picking it up, she dialled her office. As she waited for an answer, the call redirecting to Washington, Samson mustered another word.

'Wait—'

'The time for waiting, *father*,' she said, loading the last word with sneering contempt, 'has gone.'

◆

Like a horde of angry hornets, the lights and sirens of emergency vehicles, helicopters and drones descended on a little-used industrial park located in south west Los Angeles. The area, once deserted, now throbbed with activity. LAPD, FBI, the National Guard, everyone was there, responding to a distress call they had all prayed for, but had never believed in a million years they'd receive.

In the back of an ambulance, Brett Taylor received treatment from a paramedic for her minor injuries. In the surrounding area, police officers set up a cordon to halt the huge contingent of media crews that had also caught wind of the latest development in what had turned into an international incident.

Despite her miraculous escape, Taylor still stewed over the words she'd heard spoken between her father and his companion. What secrets did they hold? Who were these hundreds of thousands of civilians in mortal danger and why was the old coot willing to die rather than tell her? It made no sense, no sense at all. There was something about that old man ... she didn't know what it was, but he had a way about him that spoke of power, a rare strength. He'd unnerved her, truth be told, and she wasn't one to be easily spooked.

Knowing the riddle of this man wasn't about to be solved anytime soon, her thoughts invariably switched to her father, or Major Samson as she'd once known him. Going by what she'd witnessed so far, the man hadn't changed one iota in the fourteen years since she'd last had the displeasure of his company, that last time being her mother's funeral. Why he'd tracked her down now, she had no clue, but if there was any reason, any reason at all why he'd taken it upon himself to tear apart her city, she was going to find out about it. That was before he paid for his crimes with his life.

'You're all done here,' the medic told her, 'try and rest that left arm if you can, it'll speed up the recovery.'

Thanking him, Taylor got down from the ambulance, the sling on her arm instantly hindering her ability to function. *I can't be doing with this*, she thought. Slipping her arm out, she attempted to remove the blue padded support that had been secured over her shoulder with Velcro pads.

'Agent Taylor?' a man said while she struggled to rid herself of the sling.

'Not now,' she said without looking round.

'Do you need some help?'

'Get lost, will you.' Finally freeing herself, she turned. 'I've just had a very bad ... day. Sir, I—' She gawked at the sight of the director of the FBI, Patrick Flynn, and behind him a collective of D.C. agents.

The balding FBI Director shook her hand. 'Agent, it's good to meet you. If I'm honest, I didn't expect we'd find you alive, let alone apprehending the men who'd taken you hostage. Outstanding work.'

Taylor felt a rush of pride. 'Thank you, sir.'

'How did you do it? The report I've been given was a little sketchy on detail.'

'Luck and cunning, sir – luck and cunning.'

The director smiled. 'A healthy combination in any situation. What can you tell me about the terrorists?'

'Err—' She was unsure how to proceed. The last thing she wanted was her boss, or anyone else, finding out the mass murderer was her father.

The director looked at her expectantly while she fumbled for the words to put behind a lie. Fortunately for Taylor a timely distraction got her off the hook. Two huge, black, tandem-rotored helicopters descended from the heavens, extracting themselves from the multitude of aircraft, manned and otherwise, that populated the dark skies above. The dust and debris kicked up by the massive downdrafts obliged people to cover their faces with hastily raised arms and hands.

The manmade vortex subsided as the two craft touched down, their thunderous turbine engines cutting out on a command from their respective pilots. Taylor had been expecting to see *FBI* written in big, white letters on the side of the aerial beasts; instead she was surprised to see the familiar GMRC logo emblazoned in similar fashion. *What are they doing here?* she wondered.

The doors on the side of each craft slid back and men in black suits and the green dress uniform of serving officers in the U.S. Army jumped out.

Taylor watched with interest as they momentarily congregated and conferred before heading directly for her, the FBI director and his agents. At their head strode a tall, thin man, with greying hair and a pinched, angular face. Strangely, despite the darkness that continued day and night, the man still saw fit to wear a pair of dark sunglasses, as did some of those around him. *This ought to be good*, she thought, as they approached.

'Ah, FBI Director Flynn,' the man said, drawing to a halt in front of them, 'it's been a while, hasn't it?'

Flynn's demeanour had transformed to one of guarded hostility.

'Intelligence Director Joiner. This is not a national security matter. I'm afraid you've had a wasted journey.'

'I may be director of National Intelligence,' Joiner said, his nasal voice and superior tone already getting under Taylor's skin, 'but I'm also, as I'm sure you're aware, a member of the GMRC Directorate. It's in that capacity that I'm here. I believe you have two of our personnel in your custody and we're going to need you to hand them over – immediately.'

'You've got a snowball's chance in hell of getting your hands on those two men,' Flynn replied vehemently, 'and if they're GMRC, as you say, then it's the GMRC we'll look to when laying the blame for the deaths of nearly a hundred people, half of whom were my agents!'

'I'm sorry,' Joiner said, looking anything but, 'I don't think you comprehend the serious nature of the matter at hand. Those two men are in possession of valuable information, information way above your pay grade. Now if you don't hand them over—'

'Above my pay grade,' Flynn scoffed, cutting Joiner off. 'Who the hell do you think you are waltzing in here like King Canute? You do know the meteorite's hit, or hadn't you noticed? The GMRC's job has been done; your purported power will be vanishing anytime soon. So why don't you toddle off and deal with dust clouds and rotting vegetables and leave the important stuff to the big boys.'

Joiner stiffened at the belittling insult; raising a gloved hand, he flipped up his shades to reveal clear lenses beneath and a pair of dark gimlet-like eyes. 'You forget yourself, Director,' he said, his voice ice cool but laced with venom, 'you can only dream of the power I wield. Nations bend to my will. I can have you replaced within the day; in fact I *will* have you replaced within the day – that is, unless you accept your error of judgement, which was no doubt induced by your limited intellect, and hand over our people.'

Taylor couldn't quite believe what she was hearing, gripped by every word and movement as two of the most powerful men in the country squared up to one another. Such conversations went down in the annals of folklore; this one might top the tree and she had a ringside seat. Looking from one man to the other, she waited to see what would happen next.

The FBI director, momentarily stunned by the retort, rallied and moved forwards to meet the challenge delivered by Joiner like a slap to the face, his expression fierce. 'Delusions of grandeur have always been your problem,' Flynn said, 'and if you think you can bulldoze your way through me with ill-conceived threats then it's your intelligence that's lacking. The GMRC doesn't have the unilateral support it once had; word is on The Hill your precious council is losing political backing hand over fist and while you're off playing God I'm in Washington. By the way, have you seen the President lately?'

Joiner sneered. 'I'm well aware of your weekly tête-à-têtes with the commander-in-chief. If you think he can protect you, you're sorely mistaken.'

'I wonder what would happen,' Flynn said, 'if word got out that two mass murderers escaped justice due to an intervention by the GMRC, an intervention that was beyond their jurisdiction?' The FBI director looked pointedly at the assembled media in the distance before turning back to Joiner. 'Even worse, if it became known those two terrorists were actually in the employ of the GMRC itself? I imagine the civil unrest resulting from such a disclosure would pretty much destroy the tenuous hold the GMRC's precious protocols have on this country's citizens; an event that could even spark off revolts around the world. I wonder how long it would be after the story hit the headlines until the rest of the GMRC Directorate had you voted off the council? Twenty-four hours, maybe, that's a day isn't it? Even with your control of the media, the story would spread like wildfire. In fact,' Flynn looked exultant, 'I could guarantee it.'

Disconcertingly, instead of turning a livid shade of purple at having been outmanoeuvred, Joiner smiled in return, the effect sickly and, Taylor thought, quite repugnant. 'GMRC Population Control Protocol, three nine five,' Joiner said, 'any person inciting civil unrest, or the threat thereof, will incur a fixed penalty of immediate incarceration.' He turned to a black-suited man on his right. 'Myers, arrest FBI Director Flynn, if you will.'

The man nodded, took a pair of handcuffs out of his pocket and advanced on Flynn.

Taylor found herself, as did the other FBI agents around her, automatically drawing her weapon and pointing it at the man who attempted to arrest the director. Joiner's entourage responded, their own guns sliding out of their holsters with a whisper of metal on leather, and the click and clink of steel slides and triggers being brought to bear.

'Gentlemen, please.' One of the military officers stepped between the two factions, his hands raised. 'Director,' he continued, addressing Flynn, 'you may know me, my name's General Donovan, Chief of the National Guard Bureau. One of the men you have in custody is a Special Forces Colonel. I can assure you he will be court-martialled for his actions and sentenced appropriately for his crimes. However, he is a serving officer in our armed forces and as such needs to be disciplined under due process outside of civilian courts.'

Flynn tore his eyes away from Joiner. 'General, I appreciate your position, but I will be pushing for a full civilian trial through the Attorney General's office. Although since double jeopardy isn't an issue between civilian and military courts, you're more than welcome to conduct your own trial once civilian proceedings have been completed.'

General Donovan's expression quickly altered as it dawned on him the FBI director wasn't about to listen to reason.

'Don't concern yourself, General.' Joiner gestured for his men to stand down. 'There's more than one way to skin a cat, isn't that so, Director Flynn?'

The FBI director didn't reply to the ominous comment, opting to just glare at his adversary with poorly disguised hatred.

A disturbance off to one side caught Taylor's attention. Turning, she saw a team of FBI agents and LAPD officers emerging from the abandoned warehouse she'd been in less than half an hour before; accompanying them was Colonel Samson – her father.

♦

Professor Steiner twisted his left shoulder in discomfort as he was led up the steps from the dingy warehouse cellar. The restraints bit into his wrists painfully, pinning his arms behind his back. Tripping, he stumbled and fell. Unable to break his fall, he cracked his head against a wall, fracturing a lens in his glasses in the process.

'Get up, you fuck.' An LAPD officer dragged him back to his feet and shoved him forwards.

Reaching the top of the staircase, Steiner could see the large form of Colonel Samson a little way ahead of him, shackled in chains and a straitjacket, and guarded by a whole team of FBI agents. Blood trickled into the corner of Steiner's eye as he waddled on, the chains around his own ankles making walking difficult. *I must have cut my head*, he thought in distraction as he made his way out into the open air.

When the strange procession appeared, lights shone down on it from every conceivable source, the cacophony of noise from those assembled predictably rambunctious. The onslaught of sound engulfed Steiner like a wave. Helicopters and drones hovered above while police cars and FBI vehicles seemed to occupy every square foot of tarmac in the immediate vicinity. The group walked into an open area where two familiar black GMRC helicopters sat perched on the tarmac, their long static rotor blades splayed down like finger thin petals weighed down at one end by invisible dewdrops.

Steiner looked around, wondering if anyone he knew might somehow be able to rescue him from this ongoing nightmare. His eye twitching slightly, the steady stream of blood pooling in one corner, he stopped dead in his tracks and stared into the face of the man who had created all his woes, Malcolm Joiner. Bold as brass and large as life, the intelligence director locked eyes with him from fifty yards away. Steiner's blood boiled with a ferocity he'd never experienced before, his nemesis viewed through a veil of unadulterated rage and loathing.

'Keep moving.' A policeman prodded him in the back.

Steiner shuffled forwards, refusing to break eye contact with Joiner, as if he could will the man's death just by looking at him.

Eventually he had to concede defeat, and he turned away while his handcuffs were removed before being bundled into the back of a secure prisoner transport. Now standing in the back of an armoured truck, the reinforced metal doors slammed shut in Steiner's face, the locks outside secured with a sickening finality. Looking out through the tiny slit that served as a window, he could see the intelligence director walking back to his helicopters, their great engines powering up in a reverberating roar. The truck shuddered and then moved off. Instead of taking a seat, Steiner remained standing, putting his forehead to the door and watching as Joiner disappeared into his flying limousine. Behind Steiner, police car after police car, sirens whooping and lights flashing, followed him out of the industrial park in a long, victorious motorcade. But Steiner didn't have eyes for such things; his attention was focused on the first black helicopter to lift off from the ground, its great bulk rose into the sky, the GMRC logo on its side pronouncing its invincibility, like the man that rode within it. Higher and higher the craft flew and Steiner watched it all the way until, finally, it disappeared from sight.

Professor Steiner slumped down on a metal bench, his subconscious mind directing his right hand to the small band of gold encircling his wedding ring finger. Twisting the small circle of metal around and around in an endless loop, his considerable mind fixated on two things and two things only: escape and retribution. *I'll make you pay for your sins*, Steiner thought to himself over and over like a mantra. 'I'll make you pay for your sins, Malcolm Joiner,' he whispered, before looking at his glinting gold wedding ring in despair. 'Amelia,' he said, closing his eyes, 'I need you.'

CHAPTER FORTY-FIVE

JESSICA KLEIN AWOKE LATE MORNING, her small frame wrapped in a thick woollen blanket and curled up into a ball on the sofa where she'd fallen asleep the previous night. Yawning, she extended her arms above her head and sat up. Deciding to make use of the facilities available to her, she left the sofa and headed straight for the delightful bathroom she knew to be crammed full of luxury toiletries.

A couple of hours later, after a sumptuous hot bath and the application of an inordinate amount of cream and moisturiser, Jessica raided the owner's ample supplies of beauty products to regain a sense of self she'd almost forgotten existed. She'd also managed to swap the stolen clothing of a teenage boy for the apparel of a woman of adequate taste and similar size, who apparently owned this small bungalow on the outskirts of Stuttgart. If Bic had somehow selected this place with this in mind, he had at least earned himself one brownie point back from the hundreds he'd lost by admitting to his duplicity the day before.

Having checked on Eric a couple of times in the night, Jessica decided to look in on him again. She opened the door to his bedroom and saw that he was awake.

'How are you feeling?'

He grimaced. 'I was shot in the leg, how do you think I feel?'

'Still painful, then?'

'*Ja*.' He dropped his head back to the pillow.

'Would you like a drink or anything?'

'Okay and then you can tell me where they took you; you were just about to tell me yesterday before we were – interrupted.'

'That's one way of putting it,' Jessica said before going back out to attend to his drink. Returning in short order, she found him propped up on two pillows and, after passing him the drink, she sat down at the foot of his bed to begin her tale.

A while later and after many questions from an inquisitive and increasingly excited Eric, Jessica completed the detailed account of her meeting with Franz Veber and the astounding facility in which he worked.

'EUSB Deutschland,' Eric said in awe, 'it's like a forbidden city, a Shangri-La, it's amazing, it's, it's—'

'Extremely disturbing is what it is,' she told him, trying to readjust his mindset to the gravity of the situation that not only faced them, but apparently the whole world, too.

His face dropped a little. 'Yes – I suppose. Although it answers the question of where all the world's resources are disappearing to. I wonder how many of these underground bases there are?'

'Who knows?' she said. 'Ten, fifteen, twenty, even? The problem is what to do with this information now we've got it. Bic doesn't want to let the cat out of the bag just yet as he thinks there's more to uncover. To be honest, I just want to make sure my family is safe. I have to get them into one of these secret facilities or they'll end up living and most likely dying in a dystopian nightmare.'

Eric sipped his drink. 'That might be harder to accomplish if you tell the world about them. Once the word is out everyone will want in.'

Jessica hadn't thought about it like that, but now that she had, Pandora's Box had been well and truly opened and the clash of opposing motivations she now faced couldn't be avoided. Did she tell the world the truth, a truth she knew they must be told, or instead try to save those she loved and held dear? Even if she could miraculously magic Evan and the girls into one of these EUSBs, if she released the information of their existence afterwards she could jeopardise the integrity and safety of the base she'd just installed her family within. Feeling a headache coming on; she gripped the bridge of her nose and squeezed.

Eric looked concerned. 'Are you okay?'

'Yes, fine.' She released her grip.

'So, what do we do now? You say *Da Muss Ich* doesn't want to tell anyone about what we've – he's – discovered yet?'

'That's what he said. I'm actually going to contact him now,' she told him, making the decision. 'He said he's got something to show us this morning. Do you want me to bring the screen in here so you can see?'

'*Ja*, what could it be, do you think?'

Jessica shrugged before ducking back out. Collecting the touch-screen and a packet of crisps she returned to sit down on the bed next to the injured nineteen year old. Handing him the food, she fired up the device.

'Thank you,' Eric said, 'for taking care of me.'

Jessica looked at him; he seemed a little tearful, which made her feel uncomfortable. She usually only did emotions with her family. She gave him a smile and patted his leg. 'Don't mention it. Now, shall we see what your friend has to say for himself?'

'Or herself,' he said.

'You think Bic could be a woman?'

'*Nein*, but I've been wrong before.'

'He's definitely a man, only a man could annoy me as much as he does.'

'Oi, that's sexist.'

'But true.' She grinned and turned on the speech function. 'Bic are you there?'

The cursor flashed in the communication window.

. . .

I am _

'So, what is it you've got to show me – us?'

There is something I haven't told you Jessica Klein _

'That figures.'

'Don't anger him,' Eric said, 'he's helped us this far.'

'Hmm.' Jessica knew full well what Bic had and hadn't done, and that not all of it was as selfless as Eric believed.

A recent series of events has come to my attention. Observe _

The screen dissolved into news footage with accompanying audio from the United States. Jessica watched as a red pick-up truck careered down a multi-lane motorway. Her eyes widened when the occupant proceeded to shoot down what looked like an FBI helicopter and then exploded a number of police cars. The horrific carnage continued for some time, at points, turning into a pitched battle between a man wearing a type of translucent armour and the police and FBI that pursued him.

Eric's eyes grew wider as the destruction went on and on. '*Ach mein Gott. Dieser Mann ist verrückt.*'

'Insane isn't the word,' Jessica said, the film finally petering out after the one man army activated a strange energy weapon, knocking out the camera that filmed him. Bic's message window reappeared.

What do you think? _

. . .

Jessica shifted on the bed. 'I'm not sure. It's big news, of course, a terrible act of terrorism by some maniac wielding an arsenal of high-tech weapons—'

What about you Eric? Did you notice anything? _

Eric beamed, still clearly enthralled by speaking to his idol. 'Hallo, *Da Muss Ich*. The reporter suggested the armoured man was getting help; someone overrode cameras and screens in the shopping mall to send him a message. A hacker, yes?'

Very good, Eric, I will come to that; but there is something else which attracted my attention. When the news channel switched to shooting the event from a drone they were able to get a closer look at the terrorist. There was a symbol on his upper arm which you may have missed _

A static snapshot materialised on the touchscreen device, an image from the TV broadcast they'd just seen. One of the panels making up the man's green and brown armour bore a black emblem on a white background. The image distorted as Bic manipulated and enhanced it with software to produce a flat, front-on composition.

What do you think now? _

Jessica leaned forward. 'Oh, wow, that's just like an emblem I saw back in the German facility.'

'Only this one is a USSB not an EUSB,' Eric said, in excitement.

'USSB Steadfast,' she said. 'Well, that confirms the Americans have the same sort of subterranean bases, doesn't it?'

'United States Subterranean Base, *das ist cool*!'

Jessica frowned at her young friend's continued exuberance. She knew this was far from cool; it just confirmed what they'd already guessed; the threat from the asteroid AG5's fallout was far worse than the general populace had been led to believe. If the Americans had bases, too, the issue was confirmed as a global threat, something she'd been hoping beyond hope might not be the case. Another message from Bic appeared with an accompanying bleep.

I attained this footage and more during its live release, fearing the GMRC would quickly suppress it. Amazingly, such was the scale of the incident that some of the footage is still circulating in the national press of the United States; although this particular shot has since disappeared without trace. It is another chink in the previously invincible media blackout created and maintained by the Global Meteor Response Council.

This information in itself is revealing but it remains in dispute if the man inside the armour is from this USSB Steadfast. He may have come into possession of it by means entirely less clandestine than is first apparent. What makes this event far more valuable to our cause is what Eric alluded to before, the person pulling strings behind the scenes; the hacker who tapped into the shopping mall's security grid.

During the time of the terrorist attack I was already aware of a different type of assault simultaneously being perpetrated against the FBI mainframe; a hack of daring and skill I myself would have been proud to initiate. This individual, from the information I was able to glean from surrounding data streams, while extremely talented, did utilise a GMRC computer system during their digital incursion. To make use of a GMRC server in such a way indicates the hacker was very familiar with GMRC coding and password practices _

'Couldn't he have just hacked the GMRC at the same time?' Jessica asked, the comment making Eric nearly choke on his drink.

No. To break into the FBI system was a tremendous feat but to hack the GMRC at the same time would be an impossibility, such are the security measures they have installed.

Since this hacker was of great interest to me I was pleasantly surprised when I saw the following broadcast _

Jessica and Eric continued looking at the screen as another picture appeared. A photo of the armoured terrorist was situated on the left and to the right of this, an image of a man in his sixties. This unassuming person, looking more like a doctor or teacher than a terrorist, had a brown beard shot through with grey, a pair of glasses and a set of red coveralls. Beneath these photographs a caption read:

FBI MOST WANTED
TERRORISTS

$50,000,000
FIFTY MILLION DOLLAR
REWARD

Eric looked dubious. 'That's the hacker?'

Yes. Do you recognise him Jessica Klein? _

Jessica looked at the picture again, seeing if she could place the face. 'No, should I?'

It was unlikely you would remember seeing him. But you will have done, as will most of the world's older population albeit from a distance and hidden amongst a crowd. Here is another photo, taken twenty years ago at one of the earliest declared GMRC summit meetings _

Bic spooled up a new image showing a large group of assorted men and women in suits, all standing in rows and facing front as their collective photo was taken; on the wall behind these people was the GMRC logo. The image zoomed in to the right of the back row and a man with dark brown hair and a pair of glasses. He was, without doubt, the person displayed in the FBI's most wanted poster, just younger and less careworn.

'Who is he?' Jessica said.

Bic didn't reply, instead switching to yet another official GMRC photo of a similar configuration, rows of men and women, and at the back, this time on the left, the same man.

This scene repeats itself over and over in many other images throughout the years. Some of these photographs I acquired when I managed to break into one of the GMRC's systems a few years back. They prove, beyond doubt, this man is a member of the elite and highly influential GMRC Directorate _

'What—? You can't be serious!' Jessica reeled at the implication. 'Why would someone in such rarefied air become involved in a terrorist attack in L.A.? It makes no sense.'

Why indeed _

'Maybe he's rebelling,' Eric said, 'there must be some people inside the council who think some of the things they're doing are wrong.'

'Perhaps,' Jessica replied, 'but to go out and aid someone in mass murder? I don't think so.'

Whoever he is and whatever his reasons this man and his companion are extremely important to the GMRC. From what I've been able to glean from LAPD radio chatter a GMRC delegation was sent to take custody of them only to be rebuffed by the FBI.

. . .

Jessica was surprised. 'I didn't think anyone could rebuff the GMRC.'

Not many can. There are only a handful of organisations on the planet with enough clout and backbone to defy them and the FBI is one of them _

'How long do you think the Bureau can hold out?' Jessica asked. 'If the GMRC want them, surely it's only a matter of time until they get their way?'

I'm unsure. That is why we must move quickly _

'Move quickly?'

Yes. This is an unprecedented opportunity to get access to a man from the very highest echelons of power. He is the one weak link in a very strong chain. A man who has the secrets I need _

'We need,' Jessica said.

Yes _

'One question,' she said, 'how do you propose we get *access* to a man most likely guarded by more agents and police than we could shake a stick at?'

. . .

I have a plan _

Jessica's eyes narrowed in suspicion. 'That involves what exactly?'

The message window disappeared to be replaced by the live image of a dark-haired man; Jessica jerked back in surprise and Eric swore.

'Trust me, Jessica Klein,' Bic said with a sly wink, 'trust me.'

CHAPTER FORTY-SIX

DEEP below the surface of the earth, thousands of feet beneath the Sierra Madre Oriental mountain range in Mexico, lay USSB Sanctuary; the jewel in the crown of the USA's highly classified subterranean programme. Within this mighty man made marvel was a facility within a facility; the SED, Sanctuary's Exploration Division, a civilian-run outfit overseen and utilised at will by the U.S. military.

At night the SED Command Centre became quiet, inactive, standing by to continue its duties at morning light. Tonight, however, events were already unfolding to ensure this fragile serenity would be ripped asunder.

Riley Orton, leader of the elite Deep Reach Team, Alpha Six, lay on his stomach secretly watching those in the shuttle bay below. He'd been tasked by his commanding officer, Dresden Locke, to keep tabs on the military, who had seen fit to stage an off-the-books retrieval from Sanctuary Proper outside the USSB. Behind this dubious undertaking was one General Stevens, a man known to consider the safety of others to be an inconvenience compared to acquiring newly discovered Anakim technology. Whatever the General was bringing into the SED, Locke wanted to make sure it wasn't anything that would put his civilian teams at risk and Riley was there to make sure everything was documented.

With the cameras from his Deep Reach helmet recording everything he saw, Riley zoomed in on the massive stone monument in which General Stevens and his men had invested a lot of time, effort and resources to transport back to base. Comparing it to the modified air-shuttle they'd used to move it, the ancient Anakim monolith must have been touching fifty feet high, twenty feet wide and the same in depth. He thought back to his unauthorised excursion with Sarah into the nine hundred thousand year old structure, where he'd seen a team of scientists working on something in the ground that emitted a strange energy reading. He knew for certain this giant object was what they'd been analysing that day, before it had been extracted from the ground and hoisted through a hole cut into the building's roof. *I never would have guessed it would have been so big though*, he thought.

Riley bunched his right hand into a fist, frustrated at the injustice of such an important discovery being kept hidden from those that would most appreciate its value. He knew the military would take it apart piece by piece in order to find out its secrets, the total opposite approach that the SED's renowned archaeologists would employ.

A crane lowered the mysterious artefact onto an articulated lorry, the soldiers and military scientists working in unison like worker ants to ensure its transition was smooth and without incident. Riley took some detailed stills of a curious glass enclosure embedded into one side of the multi-sided object. It looked to contain some type of fluid, the truck, as it moved off, disturbing the contents within. As he pondered what this curious monstrosity might be, a bright flash of white light from the shuttle bay's control centre caught his attention. Riley scanned the large glass windows with his visor. Someone crouched beneath one of the operator desks. *What on earth?* he thought. *Has Locke sent someone else to spy for him? Surely not.* Standing, still hidden on his lofty perch – a little used elevated crosswalk – Riley adjusted his visor further before his eyes widened in recognition. 'Sarah? What the—?'

Movement below told him he wasn't the only one interested in this most unexpected of intruders, a Special Forces commando also looked up in her direction.

Riley swore and started running.

♦

Sarah Morgan burst through the doors of the control centre, flying through the air to collide with the soldier on the other side. As she struggled to rise a hand grabbed her ankle, pulling her back. Grappling with the man on the floor, Sarah realised she stood little chance of overpowering him. In seconds she was being hauled to her feet; the other soldier, who'd been chasing from behind, bursting through the doors to lend a hand to his colleague.

'Nice work,' the soldier said, before being knocked out cold by a sucker punch from—

Riley?! she thought. *What is he doing here and why does he have his helmet on?* With no time to care, Sarah made use of the diversion by thrusting herself backwards, slamming her other would-be captor against a wall. The man grunted before Riley waded in with another crunching blow, the soldier's grip on her falling away.

Breathing heavily, Sarah stared at Riley, stunned by his sudden appearance. 'What are you doing here?'

He raised his visor. 'I could ask you the same question.'

'Man down,' a voice said, 'third floor—'

Sarah looked down to see one of the soldiers on his radio. She kicked out, sending the communication device skidding across the floor. Riley bent down and delivered a short sharp blow to the soldier's chin, sending him back to sleep.

'Let's move!' Riley grabbed her hand and dragged her down the hallway.

Running flat out, interconnecting passageways flashed past. An occasional shout from their pursuers made them dart in the opposite direction, hurtling through the maze of the SED complex as though their lives depended on it. Nearing the edges of the building, the transparent walls revealed to them that more soldiers cut off their escape ahead. Riley reacted by guiding them up flight after flight of noisy metallic stairs. Higher and higher they rose through the building, their superior fitness levels helping to keep their adversaries at bay.

They burst out onto the vast roof of the building. Above and surrounding them was the large domed atrium in which the SED was housed. As stunning as it was, draped in shadow and low level night-time illumination, there was no way out; they were trapped.

'We're bolloxed.' Sarah looked around in despair. 'They'll have the whole place surrounded by now. Fuck! They'll lock me up and chuck away the key this time. Three strikes – I'm out.'

'Not yet, you're not.' Riley pulled her onwards towards the roof's edge.

Sarah nearly had a heart attack when he walked straight off the top. Rushing forwards, she saw him on a small platform below, looking up at her.

'Come on,' he said, before moving off down the side of the building along a narrow gangway.

Following him down, she hurried to catch up. Used to climbing, heights didn't overly bother her, but without any gear and in partial darkness she was well aware of the long drop to her right and the disturbing lack of any kind of handrail between her and oblivion. Far below, she could just make out the forms of soldiers ringing the periphery of the ground floor.

Due to the curving nature of the SED's exterior architecture, Sarah soon found herself walking around a bend and almost knocking Riley from the edge.

'Careful,' he said, giving her some more room.

Sarah looked around. 'What do we do now, just hide here and hope they don't find us? If they don't know who we are already.'

Riley grimaced. 'If only it was that easy. You saw what I saw down in the shuttle bay and General Stevens will search every square inch of this building until he has us. He takes the word *privacy* very seriously. Thankfully those soldiers didn't have time to get a good look at us and the internal cameras are down to preserve their clandestine operation, which means we got lucky.' He peered over her shoulder. 'I don't suppose you have anything useful in that backpack?'

Sarah's thoughts went to the bag on her back and the ill-gotten gains contained within; the shaped charges, three waypoint beacons, two sets of Deep Reach uniforms and an air-shuttle manual. She shook her head.

'Pity.'

'So,' she asked, 'what's the plan?'

'That's the plan.' He pointed out into the shadows.

Sarah followed the direction of his finger, out and away from the building. 'Are you kidding me?! You're insane.'

'It's either that or we'll both be spending the rest of our lives in a military prison.'

Sarah looked out across the expanse between them and the atrium wall. Built into the surface were tiny handholds, leading down on a diagonal. At the very top of the advanced climbing course a platform could be discerned, lit by a huddle of dim lights.

'It's too far,' she said. 'We'll never make it from a standing jump. And we'll be climbing without any gear – in the dark.'

'It's not totally dark and you know as well as me climbing is based on touch and feel more than vision. Trust me, I've climbed this course a dozen times, it's not the hardest by any means.'

She gazed down. 'But it's the highest.'

'One of them,' he agreed, 'but if it wasn't doable I wouldn't suggest it. And besides, we only need to make it to the next platform down, not all the way to the ground. We can take a ladder the rest of the way and sneak out without anyone being any the wiser.'

Sarah looked at him and then back out to the wall opposite. Below, she could just see the second platform. 'What about the standing start?'

He moved back a step and gestured for her to look past him.

Beyond, the walkway cut back in towards the centre of the building, a perfect runway to the launch pad on which they now stood.

Just the thought of leaping from the building, hundreds of feet up with no safety net, made her feel sick to her stomach. 'I can't do it.' She stared at the platform across the void. 'No way, it's too far.'

'Sarah, look at me.' Riley placed his hands on her shoulders and then moved them to either side of her head, his eyes looking deep into hers. 'You can do this. I know you can. This jump has been done before, I've seen Cora do it with room to spare and you're faster than she is, you can jump further.'

'Cora's done it? Not in the dark, I'll bet, and not without a safety net.'

'No, not in the dark, but it's not that dark, look again. And believe it or not, she did do it without a net, someone dared her to do it and she did.'

'And I suppose you're the idiot that dared her?'

He gave a wry smile. 'I didn't think she'd go through with it, I admit. She is a crazy one.'

Sarah still wasn't convinced.

'Right,' he said, backing up, 'you can wait here if you like. I'm not sticking around to get banged up.'

Sarah stared at him; her heart was racing and it wasn't even her making the jump. At his insistence she moved back a few steps so he could get a clear run up. Without another word, he sprang forwards, his speed rapidly increasing before he planted his right foot and launched himself into mid-air. Sarah watched with a sense of detached horror as Riley vaulted out into the atrium. He seemed to hang for an age before crashing down onto the platform with a dull thud, rolling to hit the wall to which it was attached. Getting to his feet she could just make out his broad grin as he waved her over.

Adjusting the rucksack on her back, she considered her options. With the choice of life in prison and a near suicidal jump Sarah found herself walking down the short runway, her palms sweaty and her mind in chaos. Not wanting to look at the challenge that awaited her she stood facing in the opposite direction, building up the courage to attempt the ridiculous.

She tightened the bag's shoulder straps. Closing her eyes she whispered a silent prayer before opening them again. She took a deep breath in and then let it out with a whoosh. Unable to put off the inevitable any further she flicked a mental switch.

'Oh fuck, oh fuck.' Spinning round, her mind screamed at her *Go go go!* Her long limbs accelerated her towards the abyss. Slamming her foot down she thrust out into the air, arms flailing, eyes wide, mouth agape. Air whipped around her as she flew through it to come thumping down on the platform moments later. A millisecond after that the wall nullified her forward momentum with a shoulder-numbing impact.

Sitting up, she rubbed her bruised body. Riley held out a hand and she scrambled to her feet.

'You okay?' he asked.

She nodded, an exhilarating mix of relief, accomplishment and joy at having made the leap flooding her body and mind. She'd never felt more alive. A broad grin spread across her face, mirrored on Riley's own.

He grew serious. 'Keep focused, that was the easy bit, we still have the climb to do.'

On the platform, a couple of hundred feet above the ground, they helped one another limber up for the next stage. Riley then pressed a button on his helmet, sending his visor down over his eyes. 'I'll go first; I can enhance my vision to help guide us.' He edged off the platform and onto the first series of ledges and handholds.

Sarah followed suit and the two of them crept down the face of the atrium wall. Halfway down to the next platform Sarah's confidence rose, she felt strong and in control, her training at the SED making the descent easier than she could have hoped.

'We need to pick up the pace,' Riley said from just below.

Stopping, the fingers of both hands wedged into one large vertical crack, she steadied herself. 'What's the problem?'

'Look down – at the building.'

Sarah angled her head to see that bright light streamed out of the bottom five floors of the SED; even as she watched, lights to the sixth blinked on. General Stevens was searching each floor one by one; methodically hunting them down. Soon the search would reach the higher levels and they'd stick out like sore thumbs in a toe factory.

They picked up their rate of climb to reach the lower platform just as illumination blazed forth from the storey next to them. With no time to spare they used the steel ladder to carry on down, hoping they wouldn't be seen by a cursory glance from a soldier searching for them on the inside. Curiously the final rungs before the ground proved to be the part of the climb most fraught with danger. The ring of soldiers preventing anyone escaping from the SED stood barely thirty feet away, guns at the ready and fully alert for what they assumed was every eventuality. Corroborating the well-known expression that fortune favours the brave, the area they stepped down into benefitted from a shadowy cast and while the General's personnel gazed in towards the building, Riley and Sarah were actually behind them in the opposite direction.

Sneaking amongst the various crates, boxes and other non-specific detritus that marred the clean-cut lines of the atrium's outer rim, Sarah and Riley cut a path to the nearest exit. With a final look at the SED's steel and glass exterior, they departed, vanishing like thieves in the night, leaving only the transient aftermath of their actions behind them.

CHAPTER FORTY-SEVEN

A FEW HOURS had passed since Sarah and Riley had encountered one another outside the shuttle bay's control centre and first light within the USSB had broken; replicating the cosmic dance of Earth's planetary body and the life-giving star at the centre of our blessed solar system.

Not wanting to attract attention by returning to their respective apartments, housed close to the SED, they'd decided to retreat to Riley's second home, a place he owned ten miles away on the other side of the base. It was a large diversion, but a necessary one if they were to maintain an inconspicuous distance from the scene of the crime. Travelling separately, in order to avoid any undue attention by the authorities, Sarah rendezvoused with Riley at the proposed monotube station before walking the rest of the way to his home.

The door to his apartment slammed shut with a resounding bang, allowing Sarah to breathe a welcome sigh of relief. They'd made it, escaping General Stevens' clutches hopefully with him being none the wiser as to who'd disrupted his nocturnal activities.

Sarah followed Riley through the open-plan interior of his quintessential bachelor pad, taking in the plush surroundings. 'Phew, that was a mission and a half,' she said.

Riley flashed her one of his infectious grins. 'You could say that.' He opened his fridge, removed two bottles of water and chucked one to her before opening his and taking a long drink.

Slipping her rucksack to the floor, Sarah unsnapped the cap on her bottle and gulped down the cool, thirst-quenching fluid.

'So,' Riley said, his dark brown eyes fixing on her as she drank, 'why were you spying on the military in the middle of the night?'

She lowered her bottle. 'I could ask you the same question.'

'How do you know I was spying?

'Weren't you?'

'Yes, but I was there under orders, I'm pretty sure you can't say the same.'

Sarah felt under pressure as she attempted to execute the lie she'd been concocting ever since they'd made their escape. She'd known the question would come and now that it had, she had to deliver. 'A woman I met yesterday at the SED, Anne-Marie her name was, told me the army were bringing in something else later that evening. I wanted to see what it was.'

Riley considered her for a moment, the silent interlude making her feel increasingly nervous. She covered up her fears by taking some more sips of her water.

Riley chuckled. 'Scrub what I said about Cora being crazy, you take the biscuit. No, make that the whole biscuit barrel!'

Sarah laughed with him, hoping he wouldn't notice the anxiety it masked. 'What can I say? I just can't stand secrets.'

'In all seriousness though, Sarah,' he said, his smile fading, 'you can't afford to take these risks. We only got away by the skin of our teeth. As fun as it was, your luck will run out. Curiosity killed the cat 'n' all that.'

'I know, you're right,' she said, knowing full well she had to take many more such risks in order to get back to the surface. 'I'll behave from now on.'

Riley made a dismissive gesture. 'There's no need to become Mother Teresa, just make sensible decisions; reconnoitring General Stevens and his band of merry men isn't sensible by anyone's book.'

'You were doing it.'

'Under Locke's orders, and besides, I know the SED inside out and upside down. Plus, to my shame, I have my father to back me up if I do cross the army's fine line. You, on the other hand—'

'Hmm.' Sarah decided to change the subject. 'I take it you saw what they brought back?'

'I did, you couldn't miss the damn thing. I'm almost certain it's what we saw those scientists analysing in the ground of that Anakim structure. It had the same energy reading, too.'

Sarah nodded. 'That was my first thought and if the energy reading's the same as you say – did you see the liquid inside it?'

'Yeah, held in some kind of transparent container.'

'Any idea what it could be?'

He shook his head. 'Not a clue. I just hope it's nothing dangerous.'

'They went to a hell of an effort getting it back to base,' she said. 'They must have some plan for it.'

'The power source will be what they're after,' he replied. 'Figuring out how to get the Anakim's technology to work is the holy grail of the moment. Although others would argue deciphering their texts takes precedence.'

'I'm surprised they haven't already cracked it,' Sarah said, 'their writings, I mean, the amount of people they have working on it.'

He sat down on a stool. 'I think they would have, if the Anakim's civilisation hadn't gone on for hundreds of thousands of years. Their scripts differ throughout the ages. We may have a lot of sources now on display in the Smithsonian's Museum of Sanctuary, but very few are from the same time period and they're next to useless as tools for cross-referencing.'

Sarah, taking his cue to sit, hopped up onto the kitchen counter, letting her legs dangle down. Finishing her drink she began fiddling with the lid.

'Were you shouting something just before I arrived?' Riley said. 'Before I saved the day?'

'I might have been.'

He grinned. 'I'm sure I heard you saying *sod you* at the top of your voice.'

'It just came out.' She felt her neck and face flush in embarrassment.

Riley laughed, teasing her. 'I'll have to remember that one when I'm being chased by armed guards – *sod you*!'

Sarah chucked her empty bottle at him. He ducked and it bounced harmlessly off the countertop behind.

'So,' she said, 'will you be telling Cora we matched her feat of jumping from the SED's roof to the climbing platform?'

'Probably not, I don't want word getting out; someone might put two and two together and figure out it was us in the SED tonight. Let's not give the army any more help in finding out it's us they're after.'

'Cora wouldn't blab about it, though,' Sarah said, 'she hates the military more than anyone. I'm sure it won't hurt if I just tell her on the quiet. I want to see her face when she finds out she's been bettered by a puny *girl* like myself.'

'It'd be best to leave it.'

His tone made Sarah think twice about his motives for keeping shtum and she frowned in realisation. 'Cora didn't make the jump at all, did she? You lied to me.'

Riley made a face and got up, his body language appeasing. 'Hear me out before you judge me too harshly. I thought if you believed Cora had done it, it would spur you on. Everyone had agreed it could be achieved, it's just no one had the motivation to risk their life in proving it. Well, that's not true; a few people would have attempted it had Locke not forbidden it and placed cameras there to stop anyone stupid enough to go against his orders.'

Sarah glared at him, her trust in him weakened.

'I needed to give you the confidence to do it,' he continued, battling to win her back round. 'You were facing life imprisonment and I knew Locke and my father would see to it I'd get away with a hefty rap on the knuckles. I didn't do it to save my own skin.'

'So,' she said, 'you risked your life for me?'

Riley still looked worried. 'Err, you could look at it like that, I suppose.'

'Why would you do that?'

He walked up to her. 'You're part of my team, all for one and one for all.'

'And you say I'm crazy?'

'In a good way.' He put his hands on her knees.

Sarah glanced at the over familiar gesture and then back to his face, searching for something more, something she'd seen before back when they'd kissed during the Deep Reach mission.

He moved away from her, the moment passing. 'I better take my helmet back.' He stooped to pick up her rucksack where she'd stashed his headgear for him.

'No!' She jumped down and rushed over to snatch the bag from his hand and put it behind her back.

Riley looked at her in surprise, before grinning. 'What have you got hidden in there?' He tried to lean round and grab the bag from her.

'Nothing.' She struggled to pull out the high-tech helmet behind her back while fending him off from the front.

He backed her up to his front door. 'Come on, what secrets have you got in there? Some cake stolen from Locke's personal stash? Some of Cora's kit? Or a saucy costume, perhaps?'

Sarah laughed, trying to appear innocent. 'No, nothing like that.' Freeing the helmet she pushed it into his hands. 'There you go, all done.'

Riley, still smiling, put the headgear to one side. 'There's something in there you don't want me to see, isn't there?' He made a grab for the bag again.

You're damn right there is, she said to herself, knowing she might be able to explain away the air-shuttle manual, Deep Reach uniforms and waypoint beacons, but never the shaped charges. Realising he wasn't giving up, she dumped the bag behind her back and planted a big kiss full on his lips. Pulling away he looked at her in shock, an expression probably mirrored on her own face.

Before she knew it they were kissing again, their mouths opening as he pressed her up against the door, his body against hers. His hands were unbuttoning her uniform and she found herself losing control.

'Wait.' She pushed him away. 'I can't do this.'

He looked at her, smiling, before leaning in to kiss her again. Despite her protestation this lingering kiss increased her arousal further and she had to make a superhuman effort to push him away a second time.

'No,' she said, grabbing the rucksack, 'I can't.'

Opening the door and walking through, she slammed it shut behind her. Leaning against the closed door, her head falling back onto it, she breathed deep while her heart beat loudly and her body ached for the release she'd just denied it. *I have to go*, she told herself, realising the longer she stayed, the greater the temptation to return built within her. Cursing herself, she strode away from Riley's apartment, her mission at acquiring supplies for her, Trish and Jason's escape plan complete, but her carnal desires for Riley frustratingly unfulfilled.

CHAPTER FORTY-EIGHT

THAT SAME DAY, after fleeing Riley's embrace, Sarah met back up with Trish and Jason to report on the success of her first supply run. Once again they chose to bask in the New Park district beneath the bright yellow rays of the USSB's monstrous weather simulating dome. Rather than discuss matters in a restaurant, as before, this time they decided to take a picnic amongst one of the well-tended meadows that bordered an outlying park.

Beautiful butterflies danced and swooped amongst the wild flowers and grasses. Birds sang in nearby trees and there were even signs that rabbits frequented the area, their droppings prevalent on a grassier section a little way away. Sarah never ceased to be amazed by the ecosystem the GMRC had managed to create within the subterranean base. If she hadn't known any better, if the sky didn't look a tad unreal, she could easily have believed they were on the surface, not thousands of feet below the ground.

With nature's sweet aromas surrounding them, the three friends chatted for a while before Trish asked to see the air-shuttle manual. She listened as Sarah told Jason about her brush with General Stevens' men and Riley's rescue.

'I can't believe he tricked you into jumping,' Jason said, around a mouthful of sandwich, 'I'd have told him where to go.'

'If he hadn't,' Sarah said, regretting ever mentioning it, 'you'd probably have never seen me again. I'd be locked away in a military cell for the rest of my days.'

Jason's expression turned serious. 'Hmm, that doesn't sound too bad.'

'What?' Trish appeared nonplussed. 'Not too bad? How do you figure that?'

'We wouldn't have had to look at her ugly mug again, that's gotta be a win in anyone's book.'

Trish sighed and Sarah shook her head.

Jason beamed foolishly. 'In fact,' he said, 'all things considered, it'd do my eyes a favour if you both ended up in prison.'

'Funny,' Trish said, 'not. I think you're losing your touch, Jas. Don't you think so, Sarah?'

'Yeah, although I did hear ugly people do suffer from bouts of stupidity.'

'In Jason's case, make that a lifetime.'

'I suppose he quantifies the theory that the uglier you are, the longer the duration of denseness.'

Trish laughed. 'That would explain a lot.'

'Unusual features are a sign of a varied gene pool,' Jason said, 'I can't help it if I'm a product of superior beings.'

Sarah sniggered. 'Superior beings; I suppose that'd be an amoeba in your case?'

Trish chuckled while Jason did a good impression of a bemused cuttlefish.

'What's this, pick on Jason day?'

'You started it, fugly,' Trish said, unsympathetic.

'So where are we on the plan now?' he asked, changing the subject and devouring another sandwich like he hadn't eaten for weeks.

Doing her best to ignore his open-mouthed mastication, Sarah considered the question. 'Well, you two can sift through the air-shuttle manual I printed out and find out if it's even possible to steal a shuttle. The shaped charges are done and dusted for when we get to the surface; supposing we need to blast our way out of a sealed cave, that is. And we have three waypoint beacons to help us find out where an Anakim transportation device will take us; plus some Deep Reach uniforms to help you blend in.'

'That's a pretty good haul,' Jason said in appreciation.

Trish looked up from the thick wodge of paper she was reading. 'From what I've read so far,' she flicked through the air-shuttle manual, 'it seems most of the system is automatic. I'll have to go through it all, but it looks optimistic.'

'Where does that leave us, then?' Jason asked. 'Less on a wing and more on a prayer, by the sound of it.'

'I've also got the Deep Reach maps for the temple you found containing the Anakim transportation devices,' Sarah told him. 'They'll tell us which air-shuttle track we need to take out of the SED and the exact route to the temple once we're in Sanctuary Proper.'

Trish put down the manual. 'So all that leaves is the most crucial part of the plan.'

Sarah nodded. 'My pendant.'

'And that's going to be down to your boyfriend to sort, I take it?' Jason said.

Sarah's eyes narrowed while Jason looked back at her innocently. 'Riley said he'd take me on a tour of the Smithsonian's vaults,' she said, refraining from rising to the bait. 'If the pendant's anywhere it'll be there. I'll ask the question about our possessions while we're inside. We'll have to hope he can find them for us, otherwise the whole plan goes up in flames.'

'When will you ask to go?' Trish asked her.

'Considering the military could still slap another tracking bracelet on me at any minute, I was thinking tonight.'

Jason brightened. 'Excellent. I'm beginning to get bored with this place. My job's crap, I can't go into Sanctuary Proper, there're too many rules and regulations down here and way too many army bods enforcing them. Bring on the surface, that's what I say.'

Trish raised her glass. 'I second that.'

Sarah didn't respond, her own view on Sanctuary seemingly vastly different to that of her friends. She loved her new job and enjoyed the company of most of her new colleagues, and then, of course, there was Riley.

'Sarah?' Trish said.

'Yes,' Sarah raised her own glass in salute, 'to the surface.'

CHAPTER FORTY-NINE

After ironing out further wrinkles in their Sanctuary escape plan, Sarah regaled Trish and Jason with tales of the mysterious treasures she'd witnessed being brought back to the SED.

Jason sighed. 'I never get to see the good stuff.'

Sarah suddenly remembered the picture she'd taken that had sparked her flight from General Steven's troops. 'Actually you can,' she said. Taking out her phone, she opened up the large display and brought up the single image, before passing it to Trish.

Jason shuffled closer to get a better look. 'It's huge. Perhaps it's the Anakim's version of a nuclear reactor?'

'How old did you say it was?' Trish asked her.

'Riley said nearly as old as Sanctuary itself.'

Trish's eyes widened. 'Nine hundred thousand years old, that's incredible. And there's still power running through it?'

'According to Riley, yes.'

'Amazing,' Trish said.

'And those three circles , sunk into the metal casing around the glass chamber,' Jason said to Sarah, 'like you said before, they must be how it's activated. If you had your pendant, we could power it up.'

Trish gave him a withering look. 'And that's something only an idiot would say.'

'What?' Jason frowned at her. 'Why?'

'Because it could be a bomb for all we know, you could blow us all up. It could blow up the whole sodding planet. We have no idea what we'd be dealing with.'

'And the military do?'

'They've got scientists,' Trish said, 'lots of highly trained professionals versed in the appropriate fields.'

'That's worse.'

Trish looked at him in exasperation. 'What, how can that possibly be worse?'

Jason looked to Sarah and rolled his eyes. 'Trish, Trish, Trish,' he said sadly, shaking his head from side to side, 'don't you listen to anything I say? Actually,' he said when Trish began to respond, 'don't answer that. But yes, it's much worse. These physicists and what have you are like trained monkeys with an array of wooden sticks. The monkey takes a stick from the pile and puts it in a plug socket, it repeats this process systematically until it comes to the single metal stick that electrocutes and kills it.'

Trish looked unimpressed by Jason's rhetoric, but Sarah thought she could see what he was getting at. 'Are you talking about that weird theory? That we'll keep pushing the limits of science until we do something spectacularly stupid?'

'It's not weird,' he said, 'and yes. Basically the concept is that the reason mankind has never made contact with sentient beings from another world is because as soon as a race reaches a certain technological boundary, they invariably blow themselves to pieces. In fact, there are areas in space that may indicate where these advanced civilisations once existed.'

'Like where?' Trish scoffed.

'Like black holes, or unexplained voids within other star systems.'

'So basically,' Trish said, 'you're saying we shouldn't do any more science at all in case we destroy everything?'

'It's one option, or alternatively, until we have a proper worldwide voting system on which science projects we allow to go ahead and which ones we deem too risky to be worthwhile.'

'He's got a point,' Sarah said, 'it's almost inevitable that someone will devise something in the future that will turn out to be uncontrollable, the law of averages means it'll only take one madman to end us all; which actually might be the reason why the Anakim died out, wiped out by their own scientific advances.'

Jason waggled a finger at her. 'Exactly.'

'That's all very well,' Trish said, 'but it's still a load of old bollocks, as I'd rather have a raft of trained monkeys dealing with something than one untrained one, like you.'

Jason nodded sagely. 'Also a valid point.'

The conversation continued until Sarah decided she couldn't put off calling Riley any longer. After their earlier steamy encounter she was reluctant to add fuel to the fire, but she needed her pendant and she needed it now, so she was left with little choice.

The phone rang for some time before Riley answered. 'Hey, what's up?' He sounded no different from usual.

'I need a favour.'

'I'm listening.'

'Do you remember promising me a tour of the Smithsonian's vaults?'

'I do.'

'How about tonight?'

'So soon after what we just went through? I'm beginning to think you're an adrenaline junkie.'

Sarah chuckled. 'So am I.' She suddenly realised Jason and Trish had stopped talking and were listening with great interest. Jason grinned at her and raised his eyebrows, making her frown and look away. 'How about it then? Fancy showing me this Boneyard?'

Jason burst out laughing and Sarah got up and walked away.

'Someone sounds like they're enjoying themselves?' Riley said.

'It's just Jason being an idiot as usual, so are you up for it or not?'

'Sure, the vaults are totally separate from the SED and over the other side of the Smithsonian's Museum complex. The heat we generated last night shouldn't have any impact there whatsoever.'

'Excellent.' She turned round and looked back at Trish and Jason, now twenty feet away. 'Where shall we meet, in the museum?'

'Yep, down in the basement by the back entrance to the SED.'

She looked at her phone. 'What time?'

'Midnight should do it. You'll have to make sure you get in before closing unless you plan on entering by the SED, but I think only one of us should go by that route to divert any suspicion. I'm sure General Stevens will still have a strong presence down there after our escape. I wouldn't want to be in Locke's shoes today.'

'Won't Locke know it was you, though?' Sarah said. 'He did send you there.'

'Oh, he'll know it was me alright, and he'll tear me off a strip when he gets the chance. You're the one that should be worrying in case he guesses you were the one with me.'

'You won't tell him, will you?'

'Of course not; I'll just say someone else was down there and that I didn't get a good look at who it was. If I say they were short with dark hair it should counter any theories he has on the issue. Besides, the lights were low, that'll be my excuse anyway.'

She was encouraged by his optimism. 'Right, I'll see you tonight, then?'

'Yep, don't be late,' he said and hung up.

Sarah returned to Trish and Jason, who looked at her expectantly. 'It's a go,' she told them, retaking her seat on the rug.

'Don't forget to film it,' Jason said, 'I really want to see what they've got stored away in there.'

'Me too.' Trish picked up the air-shuttle manual. 'And we can use it to add to our growing pile of evidence to show people back in the real world this place actually exists.'

'Good idea,' Sarah said, distracted, her thoughts about exposing Sanctuary mixed. *Why does life have to be so damn complicated?* she wondered.

♦

Later that night Sarah found herself waiting in the dingy lower floors of Sanctuary's museum. Last entry was seven o'clock and after she'd looked around some of the exhibits, which were very interesting, she had to while away one hundred and eighty tedious minutes before the witching hour was upon her.

Sarah checked her computer phone again; quarter past twelve, he was late. Standing up, she paced around the barren corridor on the museum's lowest floor, her footfalls echoing eerily against the oppressive silence like the manifestation of a disturbed apparition. In the wall behind her was the secure entrance to the offices where Dresden Locke had beefed-up security after her first incursion into the SED many weeks before.

Finally, another twenty minutes into her enforced wait, the door leading to the SED opened and Riley emerged.

'About time,' she said.

'Sorry, I've been getting grief all day. We really stirred up a hornets' nest last night. To say General Stevens is furious is an understatement. He's ordered Locke to interrogate every employee in the division to find the people responsible for assaulting his men. Personally, I think he's far more pissed off his late night activities were compromised than he cares about the welfare of his troops. Still, Locke was not impressed and gave me a severe dressing down.'

'Shit, perhaps it's me who should be sorry then,' she said, feeling bad for getting him into trouble.

Riley screwed up his face. 'Nah, water off a duck's back. Besides, Locke was quite pleased in some respects, it gave him ammunition against the General's covert operations. He even told him that if he hadn't turned off all the cameras they'd have been able to catch the people involved.'

'I bet that went down well,' Sarah said.

'Not really, I could hear the slanging match two rooms away.'

'I take it my name didn't come up in the conversations?'

'Not yet,' he said, 'but give it time. With your history it won't be long until you're hauled over the coals.'

'Great, I can't wait.'

'Don't worry, just plead total innocence. There's nothing they can do, short of drugging you with a truth serum.'

'What, they'd do that?' Sarah said, alarmed.

Riley laughed. 'No, don't be silly. They're the army not the CIA. Come on,' he said, walking off, 'let's go take a look at these vaults you're so keen on seeing.'

Sarah followed Riley down the corridor before they worked their way through various types of doors, some sealed by sturdy locking mechanisms, the large wheels adorning them akin to those seen on the hatches of submarines. After passing through yet another one of those gateways, Riley unlocking each one with his multifunction card, Sarah let out a yelp of surprise when a woman appeared, standing waiting on the other side.

She held out a well-manicured hand. 'Hi, you must be Sarah, yes?'

Sarah looked to Riley who followed behind. 'Err, yes.' She shook the outstretched hand.

'Sarah, this is Petra,' Riley told her, introducing the inordinately good-looking, full-figured woman. 'She's going to get us into the vaults tonight.'

'I thought it was just going to be the two of us?' Sarah whispered to him.

'If you'd chosen another night,' Petra said, overhearing, 'you wouldn't need me. But the army have been up to their old tricks recently and we've had to lift up the bridge.'

'Bridge?' Sarah followed their new companion as she led them down a large, brightly lit corridor.

Petra looked back over her shoulder as she walked. 'The Smithsonian's vaults are highly secure, civilians can only gain access via a bridge. But the general has been bringing some large objects in to the military's vaults, which are adjacent to ours, and we had to lift it up.'

'General Stevens?' Sarah shot Riley a look.

'The same,' Petra replied.

'We won't run into him down here, will we?'

Petra laughed prettily. 'Oh Riley, where did you find her? She's a darling! Where are you from, Sarah? Your English sounds strange.'

Sarah clenched her jaw at the woman's words, resisting the urge to slap her round the face. 'England, you may have heard of it, that little place English comes from?'

'She's on my Deep Reach team,' Riley told Petra, apparently oblivious to the belittling comment aimed Sarah's way.

'Oh, I see.' Petra winked at her. 'I thought you were one of Riley's girls. He gives them all the tour, don't you, Ri?'

Riley rolled his eyes and shook his head at Sarah, but Sarah wasn't buying it. 'And you were one of them, I suppose?' Sarah asked Petra.

'We dated for a while, didn't we, Ri? Had some fun—' Petra paused to usher them through a secure door after Riley unlocked it with his key card. 'A lot of fun.' She gave Sarah a sly nudge as she walked past.

Sarah made a face at Petra behind her back as she moved through. *What a cow*, she thought, praying the woman tripped over on her ludicrous high heels and broke something during the fall, preferably her neck. Sadly, however, the conditions weren't sufficiently propitious to induce such a happening and Sarah was forced to endure the vision of Petra's perfect hips swaying from side to side ahead of her along yet another corridor.

After a couple more minutes, her attention was diverted towards something far less galling as they emerged into a cavernous and brightly lit chamber. Square in design, the large expanse, a few hundred feet across, contained within it twenty-two large, round, modular buildings that took up half the available space. Immediately in front of these grey, circular structures and cutting off access to the left cluster of eleven, a similarly coloured walkway had been hoisted into a vertical position. No footbridge led to the other eleven vaults on the right, which were arranged in a similar crescent formation to those on the left, yet in a mirror image and separated from their brethren by an imposing wall; the only way to access them was via a tarmac service road that ran beneath Sarah's elevated position.

Petra approached the bridge's control console and inserted a card. A digital screen powered up, allowing her to enter various commands via a holographic image. The narrow bridge creaked and began lowering on cue. A minute later the walkway had spanned the gap to the Smithsonian's vaults.

'Have fun.' Petra stood aside to allow Sarah through.

Riley thanked her and Petra held onto his arm as he passed. Looking at Sarah she gave him a lingering peck on the cheek. 'You owe me, Ri, call me.'

Sarah stepped onto the bridge and stomped along the ramp, eager to get into the vaults and unconcerned whether Riley kept up. Reaching the end of the walkway, she descended a wide spiral staircase. At the bottom, the entrances to the massive circular vaults stood arrayed in front of her in a sweeping arc, their towering doors creating a formidable barrier to those seeking the secrets within. The wall, which Sarah had seen from her previous vantage point, carved its way through the centre of the chamber behind her, preventing access to the military's vaults beyond.

Riley stopped next to her. 'Which one do you want to see first?'

'What do your *girls* normally choose?'

'I wouldn't take any notice of Petra, she has a tendency to stir things up.'

'So, how many conquests *have* you brought here?'

'I'd hardly call them conquests, but if you're asking, the answer's two, and that includes Petra. I actually got her the job here.'

'Hence she owes you.'

He nodded. 'I worked in this place for a while when I was in the army, ferrying things into the vaults down the service road. I never really got to see anything much, just things going in and out, covered up or in crates. But one time I was asked to help carry some boxes into one of the vaults and I was hooked. The mystery and magnificence of the artefacts I saw inside blew my mind. I wanted to know everything about them, where they came from, who made them and why. All those questions and more fuelled my desire to join the SED. I wanted to be the one to find those ancient relics, to unearth them, to be the first to glimpse their wondrous forms emerging from amongst the rock and soil. To hold them, touch their tactile surfaces and discover the civilisations that gave birth to them. The touch paper to my imagination had been lit and it was never going out.'

Sarah looked at Riley anew as he surveyed the vaults in front of them, his thirst for knowledge, and the need to satiate the addictive thrill that only archaeological discovery could deliver, a familiar tale of obsession; indeed, his words could have been her own. 'I never knew you felt so strongly.'

Riley smiled at her. 'Don't bandy it about, I've got a reputation to uphold.'

'You're secret's safe, Ace.' She took a step forward. 'So, which vault do you recommend first?'

'Well, five of them contain items fresh from site. There won't be much to see in those. The Boneyard,' he pointed to the vault at the far end, 'should be left till last, so we'll start at six.'

Walking to the vault with a large white number six painted on its grey façade, Riley pulled out his multifunction card and swiped it across a pad attached on one side. He entered a code and in response a mechanism inside the door shifted, the clank of metal and the hiss of hydraulics resonating through the structure. The gap between the thick steel portal and its housing edged wider and wider. Instead of being greeted by a gaping opening, inside stood a concave, frosted glass panel surrounding a smaller, transparent door. Next to this smaller entry point various warning signs and instructions had been posted.

'There's a decontamination procedure before you get right inside,' Riley told her, 'you'll need to close your eyes and hold your breath for ten seconds on entering.' He bowed. 'Ladies first.'

Sarah smirked and walked inside and onto a metal grid where an orange light blinked on. Closing her eyes she breathed in. A buzzer sounded and a blast of fine mist engulfed her, blowing out her hair and ruffling her clothes with its intensity. Almost as soon as it had begun, the process was completed, the buzzer sounding again prompting Sarah to open another door and pass into a low-lit interior. Ahead, a wide hallway stretched back into the vault with an even number of rooms on either side consisting of more frosted glass. Above her head, only darkness could be seen. Behind, Riley went through the same procedure before joining her.

'We won't be able to go into any of the rooms,' he said, 'they're hermetically sealed, automatically regulated and require a full body suit and extra decontamination. Trust me, we don't want to be getting into that rigmarole.'

She looked at him in concern. 'You think someone might catch us in here?'

'No, we should be fine at this time of night, but it's best not to tempt fate. Besides, if we went into every room we'd be here for days.'

Moving past the air and gas-tight units, Sarah saw a flaw in his plan. 'If we can't go inside, how are we going to see anything?'

He stopped next to a room. 'Aha,' he said theatrically, 'watch and be amazed.'

Next to the entrance and attached to the non-transparent pane sat a small control pad. He pressed a button and the frosted panel shifted, its opacity evaporating to leave behind crystal-clear glass in its place.

'Impressive.' Sarah gazed inside with interest, her eyes becoming transfixed with the object now on display. To protect any artefacts from being exposed to bright light the room was only dimly lit; however, the illumination was strong enough to expose the treasure within. On a table secured between two posts rested a single sword of dazzling beauty. The blade itself appeared to be an abstract weave of two separate blades, flowing into one halfway along its length. It glittered in the dark, an array of colours reflecting from its unblemished surface. The hilt and pommel, wrought of gold, melded into leaf-like structures that acted as a guard, their tendrils flowing up into the blade itself. The craftsmanship was sublime.

'Oh wow,' she said, savouring the sight, 'how long would you say it is?'

'Longer than I am tall, maybe eight feet?'

'I wonder if they used it with one or two hands?'

'Depends on the owner.' He tapped at a computer screen built into the glass. 'According to this, it's seven hundred and fifty-five thousand years old, which puts it in the Permunioteric era. If I remember rightly the peoples of that age were averaging nine feet tall, so they could have been wielding this thing single-handed.'

She shook her head in wonder. 'Nine feet, that's crazy.'

He grinned. 'You ain't seen nothing yet.' He pressed another button to make the sword disappear from view. 'Come on.' He headed off to the next room.

After seeing a variety of artefacts Riley surprised her again when he activated another system, sending the floor they walked on up to the next level in the vault. The lights above them powered up as the whole floor moved upwards, stopping at the next row of rooms.

'How many floors are there?' she asked.

'Five per vault. A few of the military ones have ten, five in this chamber and another five below.'

'I can never get used to this place,' Sarah said, 'the USSB, I mean. It's like the surface, but with an extra dimension; there's always something above or below you.'

He smiled. 'It does take a little getting used to; still, you've got the rest of your life to adjust. Once a Sancturian, always a Sancturian, as they say.'

'Right,' she said, the reason for her being there reasserting itself in the forefront of her mind.

After visiting a few more vaults and being wowed many times over by their contents, Sarah decided to enquire about her pendant, initially in a roundabout manner.

'I was thinking,' she said, 'about the artefacts I had with me when I arrived at Sanctuary.'

Riley looked at her questioningly.

'I don't suppose you'd know where they'd be stored, do you? I'd really like to see them again.' Mentally she cursed the obvious nature of her request while waiting apprehensively for a response.

'Hmm, good question.' He didn't display any kind of emotion other than mild interest; *and why would he do otherwise*, she thought, *he has no idea what the pendant can do*. 'I can check for you on the archive database, if you like?' he added.

'You can do that?'

'Team leader privileges.' He breathed on his closed hand and rubbed it against his chest in a show of self-praise.

'Excellent,' she said, watching as he accessed a computer in the vault they were currently touring.

He glanced at her. 'Right, description of items please.'

'The first one is a small pendant.'

'Composition?'

'Metal, with markings on. There are actually two of them, both pentagonal.'

'Ah, like the symbol on your Deep Reach helmet.'

'Yes,' she said, impressed but also concerned he recalled her idiotic decision to put such a shape on her helmet in the first place.

More moments passed as the system searched for the set of parameters. 'Hmm,' he said.

'What?'

'Do you want the good news or the bad news?'

'Good.'

'Well, they're on the system, along with the other objects confiscated from you. Parchments and a Mayan tablet, yes?'

She nodded. 'And the bad news?'

'They're not in the museum, but in a vault.'

'That's great, we're in the vaults,' she said, trying to pretend she hadn't planned for such a scenario.

'It would be if they were in the Smithsonian's vaults, but they're not; they're in the military vaults, number three to be precise.'

Sarah's face dropped and with it her hopes of ever seeing the surface again. Part of her was happy, but another, a far greater part, was mortified.

'Let's take a look at the Boneyard,' he said, unaware of the significance of the information he'd just divulged, 'that'll cheer you up.'

Sarah agreed half-heartedly and he led her out to the final vault, number eleven. Entering and undergoing the same decontamination procedure as before, Sarah found herself distracted. *No pendant*, she thought, barely noticing the strange pungent smell of the vault tugging at her senses. *Trish and Jason will be devastated when I tell them.*

By now Riley had switched off the frosted panel on the first room, which was larger than those in the other vaults.

'What do you think?' he said.

Sarah's eyes focused and then widened at the sight that greeted her. As with every other room she'd already seen, the lighting had been set to a low level, casting deep shadows over the most magnificent mummy she'd ever seen. Dressed in a fantastically ornate gown of slate-like material, inlaid with a wealth of silver designs of a complex simplicity, the amazingly well-preserved remains of an Anakim man sat upon a chair, facing her.

Despite his undoubted age and the black desiccated skin pulled tight over solid flesh, his features were still well defined; eerily so, in fact. The strange features of his species, Homo gigantis as she knew it, were more than prevalent, announcing to any observer that what they looked upon was not human. Although, if the abnormal construct of the individual's facial bones didn't give away his ancient origins, his intimidating size had to have done. Even though he sat, Sarah found herself gazing up into his face, a face that lived countless lifetimes back in the depths of a distant past consumed by time.

'So beautiful,' she murmured.

'Magnificent, isn't he?' Riley said reverently.

'How old is he?'

'He's pretty young in the scale of things. Only two hundred and thirty thousand years. He's been nicknamed the Ageless King.'

'King?'

Riley pointed a finger. 'Look at what he's sitting on.'

Sarah's eyes moved to the object beneath the mummified

remains. She could only see the edges of dark cracked earth behind the decaying garments. 'I can't make it out.'

'Hang on.' He pressed some buttons on the control pad.

The mummy slowly rotated on its platform and, coming into view from out of the darkness, a slim yet majestic throne, half caked in the sediment of aeons and half shining with a reddish golden hue.

'They're still in the process of restoring it,' he said, as the mummy's face reappeared, only to stop before them once more. 'Perhaps the most astounding aspect is the age they estimate he lived to before he died.'

'Which was?'

'Three hundred years, give or take a decade or two.'

'Three hundred, how's that possible? Nowhere in the museum do they say Homo gigantis lived any longer than we do.'

'It's not common knowledge. I only know through a contact in the SED and they haven't published their findings yet. Obviously if their work is corroborated by a separate team things could get *very* interesting.'

Before she could take everything in, Riley was guiding her to the next room. This one contained a stone sarcophagus that stood fully forty feet in length. Its design was reminiscent of the Egyptian pharaohs, except the stylisation on the lid looked to have been far more detailed, from the few sections that remained intact.

'I take it the occupant doesn't take up the whole length of that thing?' Sarah said.

Riley chuckled. 'No, they extracted a mass of the deceased's burial possessions, some of which you saw in the other vaults. The owner had succumbed to the ravages of time, even the bones had disintegrated. He, or she, was a little smaller than the Ageless King, about eight and half feet.'

Riley showed her a few more incredible mummies and unearthed burial caskets before taking her to the top floor. This level consisted of just two long rooms, one either side of the one hundred foot walkway in the middle.

Riley paused before revealing their contents. 'You're probably wondering by now why this place is called the Boneyard.'

'Not really, seems pretty self-explanatory, it's where all the Anakim remains are kept.'

'But you haven't seen any bones per se.'

'No, I suppose not.'

'Brace yourself.' He pressed a button to reveal not just one room, but both. The frosted panes she'd grown accustomed to dissolved into clear glass along the whole length of the walkway. Lights inside both areas bloomed to life, caressing their steady yellow light over a sight that literally made her jaw drop.

'Jesus Christ,' she whispered.

CHAPTER FIFTY

THE TOP LEVEL in the final Smithsonian vault had relinquished its final secrets and they stunned Sarah beyond imagination. Skeleton upon skeleton, each complete, stood next to one another, lining the sides of each of the two rooms. Attached to some of these long-dead individuals clung the remnants of clothing as weird and wonderful as that displayed on the Ageless King himself. This astounding array of remains stretched the full length of the rooms on either side; around twenty-five individuals stood shoulder to shoulder in the front row; but arranged behind these was another row, and behind those, yet another.

'How many are in here?' she asked.

'Around a hundred and fifty – come and look down here!' Excited, Riley walked to the far end with Sarah following.

'These two are the biggest we've found,' he said, 'I know the guy on the Deep Reach team that unearthed them.'

Steadying herself against the glass, Sarah gazed up at the stark white bones of two long dead Anakai. 'They must be over ten feet tall.'

'Ten and half,' he said, staring at them.

'Their bone structure looks different to the smaller ones.' she said, comparing the skeletons around them.

'Yes, I think they might be an offshoot. Like these.' He turned round to indicate a set of skeletons in the opposite area.

Sarah felt a jolt of recognition. These bones were much slimmer, their height seven to eight feet. They reminded her of the skeletal remains she'd found in the South African cave she'd uncovered with Jason and Trish. Unlike hers, however, these specimens came replete with skulls.

She noted the differences in the facial structure. There was also a distinct variation in their clavicle and the formation of the humeral head. 'They're a whole different species.'

'Well, definitely a sub species,' he said.

Sarah and Riley spent another hour in the Boneyard discussing the ancient specimens and the various stories and theories surrounding them before finally leaving. Riley slid his card across the entry system to the vault after the door had swung ponderously shut, securing it in place once more.

'Can I access these with my card?' Sarah held up her multifunction card.

He shook his head. 'No, you wouldn't even get into the surrounding corridors. You need level eight clearance or above and you're only a measly seven. Plus, as Deep Reach team leader I get access to places other level eights don't. And this is one of them.'

She looked over at the wall barring her view of the military installation beyond. 'And there's no way you can get into the other vaults?'

He hesitated and then shook his head once more.

'Wait; there is, isn't there?' Her posture straightened at the possibility glimpsed in his Freudian slip.

Riley looked up at a camera array above the vault, before motioning for Sarah to walk with him back to the bridge.

'There is a way,' he told her, 'but I'm not prepared to risk my job over it.'

'Tell me.'

He sighed. 'Don't tell anyone about this.'

'I won't.'

'I mean it, Sarah. Promise me, not a word to anyone.'

'Cross my heart.' She made the movement across her chest.

'In the Boneyard, there's a disused service elevator beneath the room containing the Ageless King. I think it's there in case they want to expand the vault's capacity at a later date. It also happens to back onto a small passageway which runs out to the military vaults on the other side.'

'How do you know it's there?' she asked.

'Because when I worked on the military side I found a way through.'

'You just found a way through? Surely they'd make it more secure than that?'

'Well, perhaps forced a way through is more accurate,' he said, noticing her raised eyebrow. 'What can I say? I used to get bored over there, standing around for hours on end waiting to drop off and pick up loads. I used to spend half my day wandering around and when they were refurbishing two of the vaults they used to be left open and one thing led to another—'

To be fair Sarah didn't really care about the how or the why, the fact that it existed was good enough for her.

'There are actually routes through from each of the military vaults, but I only unblocked one.'

'Does it take long, to get through?' she asked, as they walked back across the bridge.

He laughed. 'Why? Are you thinking about breaking into them?'

She mustered a hearty chuckle in response. 'Yeah, good one,' she said, her duplicitous behaviour coming worryingly easily, 'and while I'm at it I'll storm General Stevens' barracks and give him a wedgie.'

Riley grinned. 'Now that I'd pay to see. But no, it doesn't take long, twenty minutes, give or take. It's a shame they're so uptight over their secrets. I'd give my right arm to know what they've got in there these days, and in the laboratory complex below.'

'Wouldn't your father know? He's a general, isn't he?'

He shook his head. 'Not a chance, it's highly restricted, special access personnel only, or so I'm told.'

Her enquiries complete, talk returned to the collection of artefacts and remains they'd just seen as they worked their way back through the vault chamber's exterior tunnels. They re-entered the museum on one of its upper levels and sauntered through the deserted exhibits in good humour.

'Oi, what are you two doing in here?!' a voice said.

Sarah looked round to see an aging security guard a little way away, shining a torch in their direction.

'Run!' Riley said to her before bounding away.

Sarah stood frozen for a moment as the security guard ran towards her, brandishing his torch.

'Crap,' she said and legged it after Riley.

The two of them soon left the man behind and Riley was laughing when he slowed.

'What are you doing?' she said, catching her breath, 'Why don't we tell him we work for the SED?'

'Where would be the fun in that?'

Before she could answer, two more guards appeared from the other direction and the chase was on again. With Riley leading the way, the two of them led the guards a merry dance before exiting the museum and fleeing back to their SED apartments. The night-time hours had given way to early morning as the rush hour commute got underway, the nearby transport channel filling with vehicles and people, much like any other major metropolis in the world.

Having kept on running until they reached Sarah's apartment, they were out of breath as they entered, broad grins on their faces as their evening's sightseeing ended on a high. Sarah poured Riley a drink in the kitchen before being surprised when his hands slipped onto her waist from behind. He turned her round, his face now mere inches from her own. Her heart beat faster as he leant forwards to kiss her, his lips brushing hers. He stood back, giving her the option to pull away. She didn't, taking his hand she led him into the bedroom. Reaching up she stroked his face, smiling, before kissing him. Her passion increasing, the ferocity of their embrace peaked. They tore at one another's clothing, each craving the touch of the other's flesh.

Naked, Riley hoisted her on up onto his hips as she sank down upon him, wrapping her legs around his waist. Her skin against his, Sarah rose up as she lost herself in the heat of desire. Falling back on to the bed he thrust down upon her, his powerful strokes making her arch her back and grab the bedcovers as she rode the bliss of their sex. As time lost meaning she drew closer and closer to the edge. Letting out a cry of ecstasy, her other hand reached out to grab the headboard, knocking a switch in the process. A mechanical whirring brought her back from the brink and, clasping his body with her arms, she saw the blind to her window rolling up, revealing the walkway beyond and the passers-by as they made their way to work.

Sarah's eyes widened. 'Riley,' she said as he moved rhythmically against her, 'the blinds – people – are watching.'

Riley didn't even glance at the window, choosing to regain her attention by kissing her deeply on the mouth and then down her unresisting neck. 'Let them watch.' He ran his hands over her breasts as he continued to pleasure her.

Sarah neared the edge once more, her face turned to the window as people looked and pointed at the naked lovers that would be the talk of their day.

Sarah shut her eyes, the thrill of being watched adding to the intensity as she climaxed, her body arching higher, her toes curling as her body released an explosive orgasm. As she rode more waves of pleasure Riley didn't stop, bringing her to the edge again, only stopping sometime later when he eventually released himself. Flushed and sweating, Sarah, flicked the switch and the blind rolled back down, ending the spectacle for those partaking in their morning journey to work. Sinking down onto the bed, she rolled over to rest her head on his chest, her right thigh over his. The slow rise and fall of his breathing lulling her eyes closed as her troubles drifted away like never before.

♦

Cloying smoke filled Sarah's lungs, a whimper escaping her lips as she struggled to beat back the flames that sought to consume the ancient Anakim maps cradled in her arms. Fire engulfed the timber house around her, the flickering tongues of the inferno setting her hair alight, the pain unbearable. Letting out a stifled scream, she sat up in bed, her brow and palms damp with perspiration. Calming herself down, she swept the strands of blonde hair that had stuck to her face back over one ear. Next to her, Riley's naked form remained undisturbed, his deep sleep continuing unabated. Leaving him behind, Sarah got out of bed, pulled on a white T-shirt, and went into the bathroom to splash water on her face.

She looked at herself in the mirror, the same blue eyes she'd known all her life looking back at her. Except she knew inside she'd changed and that night had proved it beyond doubt. Having sex in front of strangers would have at one time appalled her, to share such an intimate moment in the full view of others doing nothing to excite her. Now, though, even thinking back to it brought back powerful feelings of arousal she hadn't known existed within her. *If I didn't know better*, she thought, *I'd blame it on a side effect of using the Anakim transportation device*; but she knew her tendency to take risks had been growing steadily for some time. Back in South Africa she'd been willing to risk all to uncover further evidence of Homo gigantis, entering the impact zone of the asteroid AG5 only days before it touched down off the South African coastline. And long before that, even though she'd refused to admit it until now, she'd taken risks beyond the norm. Many years ago, climbing in the Zagros Mountains in Iran, she almost paid the price with her life when she'd misjudged an ill-considered jump. Cave diving in Turkey, again searching for signs of gigantis, she'd risked all to reach an unexplored section of the subterranean system. Numerous other telltale incidents she'd reasoned away also returned from the depths of her memory, unbidden, unwanted, and yet speaking a truth she'd long sought to ignore. Curiously it had taken a moment of pleasure rather than pain to make her confront it. Her mother's death had hit her hard and fast, rending a hole in her life she hadn't been capable of repairing, and it was that single, terrible event that had irrevocably altered her.

'Am I still sane, mother?' she whispered into the mirror. 'Has your death made me seek my own?'

She took off her top to look at herself naked, noting the dark bruises on her shoulders and sides and the pale white scars collected during her numerous misadventures criss-crossing the skin of her arms and legs. Sarah leaned down on the sink to stare deeper into her own eyes, the black pupils failing to relieve her torment. *Perhaps mother's death just exposed a personality flaw I've always possessed?* she thought. A flaw born of the complex fundamentals that go into creating and moulding every person's, every animal's, base desires and needs.

'Do I secretly welcome death?' she asked herself, wondering if that question might yet become a self-fulfilling prophecy summoned from the dark recesses of her mind, remaining unanswered until she resolved her deepest, darkest fears; fears so repressed and integral to her psychosomatic being she might never unravel their self-destructive curse.

'Sarah?' Riley's voice came from the bedroom.

Sarah barely heard him.

'Sarah,' he said again, coming into the bathroom as brazenly undressed as she herself, 'are you okay? I thought I heard you talking.'

Sarah straightened up and brushed past him.

'Is something wrong?' he asked as she picked up her underwear.

Avoiding looking at his toned body, she slipped on her knickers. 'I'm fine.'

'Why don't you come back to bed?' He moved towards her and caressed her hand.

She snatched it away, lifting her arm up for him to keep his distance.

'Have I done something wrong?'

She pulled on her remaining garments. 'No, nothing like that.'

'Then what?'

'I need to clear my mind.' She walked out into the lounge.

He watched her put on her shoes. 'Do you want me here when you get back?'

'I don't know.' She opened the door and looked back at him. 'I'm sorry.'

Closing the door, Sarah moved out into the street, her emotions conflicted, her direction unclear. She needed to get some clarity. Her walk turned into a jog and gradually she increased her speed until she was running flat out, the physical exertion a welcome distraction from her internal turmoil. Eventually she tired and came to stop atop a bridge over a transport channel, looking out as cars whizzed by underneath and the monotube flew past above. She'd never felt as alone as she had in that moment and she was unable to keep a tear from rolling down her face, the salty droplet of water settling between her lips. Refusing to break down, she stood staring out into space, gritting her teeth against a building flood of tears.

'I don't have a death wish.' She gazed down at the black road far below, the welcoming void between her and it beckoning to her with insidious hands. 'I don't,' she said again, another tear streaking down her cheek.

CHAPTER FIFTY-ONE

THE DOOR to Sarah's apartment closed behind her, the latch clicking into place. 'Riley?' she said, moving through the rooms.

No answer was forthcoming; he'd left. Heaving a sigh she decided to contact Trish via her wallscreen and arranged to meet her and Jason back in the New Park district. She then took a much needed shower, the hot water helping to dissolve a melancholy that seemed to cling to her aura like a malignant parasite; its suffocating and pervasive embrace temporarily held at bay. After drying her hair with a towel she pulled on her grey USSB uniform before heading out to meet her two friends.

Returning to their previous meeting place, a sun-drenched meadow under the great dome, Sarah saw Jason and Trish had beaten her to the destination. The two archaeologists lay side by side on a rug looking up at the stunning technological masterpiece that was the artificial sky. Jason pointed something out to Trish, who leaned in to follow the direction of his extended arm and finger, seeking out his intended target.

'Hey, Saz,' Trish said as Sarah plonked herself down next to them.

'Sazza.' Jason acknowledged her. 'How'd it go?' He propped himself up on an elbow.

'Pretty good, I've found where they've stashed our artefacts.'

'Including the pendant?'

She nodded.

Trish sat up. 'You don't look very pleased about it.'

'With good reason, they're locked up in one of the military's vaults.'

Jason swore. 'That's it then, the whole sodding plan, out the window.'

'Not quite,' she told him, 'there might be a way inside. It's risky, but since we haven't any other options—'

'Don't leave us hanging,' Trish said in exasperation, 'spill.'

'According to Riley there's a way through from the Smithsonian's vaults to the military's.'

'That's brilliant,' Jason said, his hopes of getting back to the surface reignited, 'isn't it?' he added, when Trish didn't match his enthusiasm.

'What do you think?' Trish's voice dripped with sarcasm.

Jason looked at her blankly.

Trish groaned. 'Sometimes I worry about you.'

'What, why?!'

'Never mind. I take it there's a lot of security around these vaults?' she asked Sarah.

'Like you wouldn't believe, cameras and security doors all over the shop. You need a special level eight activation on your multifunction card just to get to the Smithsonian vaults. Plus you need a code to enter the vaults themselves, although that won't be a problem as long as it's not changed frequently.'

Trish's eyebrows rose. 'How so?'

'I made sure to memorise the code Riley used to access them, just in case.'

'Nice,' Jason said.

'It would be, except the only way I figure I can get in there is to steal a card capable of opening all the doors.'

'Like Riley's?' Trish said.

Sarah puffed out her cheeks. 'There's no other we know of that would work.'

'And even then you'd have to break into the military vault,' Trish said, 'and God knows what kind of security systems they use inside them.'

'Getting in might be possible,' Sarah said, 'but stealing the pendant and getting out again would be an entirely different ball game. Even if I did manage to make it back out they'd hunt me down, and fast. There'd be nowhere to go where they couldn't find me.'

Jason looked thoughtful. 'That's not strictly true.'

'Here we go,' Trish said.

Ignoring her he looked to Sarah. 'What if we were outside the base, outside the USSB? They couldn't find you then, could they?'

'Don't be an idiot,' Trish told him.

Sarah perked up. 'No, I think he might be onto something, go on, Jas.'

'Err,' Jason said, put on the spot, 'well, I was thinking, if you could make it out with the pendant then the best way to escape anyone chasing you would be to get out of the base.'

Trish made a noise. 'You already said that.'

'*And*,' he said emphasising the word, his face a picture of concentration, 'the only way to do that would be—'

'To steal an air-shuttle!' Sarah said in excitement.

'Yes.' Jason pointed at her. 'Yes! So the plan would be you steal the pendant and then we make our escape straight after on the same night.'

Sarah's eyes lit up. 'That's genius!'

'Ha ha, in your face!' He shoved an open palm towards Trish and rubbed it into her nose.

'Argh, gerroff!' She fought him off; he continued to plague her until she kicked him in the shin.

'Ow!'

'So that's it then,' Sarah said, 'we take the pendant and escape the base all in one go, in and out, literally.'

'Smash and grab, baby.' Jason grinned.

Trish looked at them both as if they were mad. 'I don't like it, too much could go wrong.'

'You just don't like it because it's my idea,' Jason said.

'That's not it at all.'

'It's not a case of any of us liking it,' Sarah said, 'if we want to see the surface again it's all we've got.'

The three of them sat in silence for a while as they each digested the idea of a permanent existence in the subterranean base. Despite the dust cloud currently wreaking havoc on the surface, they all knew the sun would return and life would continue as before. To leave that behind was almost inconceivable, although for Sarah the alternative was far from lacking in appeal.

'Tell Sarah what we found out about the air-shuttle,' Jason said to Trish, breaking the spell.

'Well, we've read through the manual you gave us a few times and I have to say it looks quite promising.'

'It's more than promising,' Jason said.

Sarah sat up straighter. 'It's possible to steal one, then?'

'In theory,' Trish said, 'more so after what you've just told us, but I'll get to that in a minute. The first thing we'd need to do is to select an air-shuttle that's already prepped for launch. This is critical. As far as we can tell, as the launch manual doesn't go into much detail on it, the process of preparing a shuttle is beyond what we'd be capable of doing; the task normally requires a team of people working for a whole day to complete.'

'Prepped shuttles shouldn't be an issue,' Sarah said, 'they normally have at least two ready to go at a moment's notice in case of emergencies out in the field.'

Trish looked pleased. 'Good. From what we understand, the launch procedure for a shuttle is pretty much automatic. We'd just need to prime the appropriate mechanisms using a series of procedures which are reasonably complicated to follow, but not impossibly so. The three of us should be able to sort it.'

'Doesn't it require codes to activate it?' Sarah asked.

Jason nodded. 'Yep, but they're all in the manual.'

'Seriously?' Sarah was taken aback.

'It's not that surprising really,' Jason told her, 'think about it, the SED is a secure facility inside a secure base. It's probably never even occurred to them someone might want to steal a shuttle. Even if someone did they'd know they wouldn't be able to get to the surface as their elevators are locked down.'

'But they didn't reckon on anyone using an Anakim transportation device,' Sarah said.

He gave a wink. 'Exactly.'

'A shuttle launch also requires the use of two multifunction cards with SED level seven clearance or above,' Trish continued, 'which means if we do get the pendant and shuttle, one after the other, if you have Riley's card that particular problem is solved as we can use it in conjunction with yours.'

'Okay,' Sarah said, 'what about controlling the shuttle after the launch?'

'Once the shuttle is underway,' Trish told her, 'the onboard computer regulates its speed and rocket burns.'

'We can just sit back and enjoy the ride,' Jason said.

Sarah looked dubious. 'You won't be saying that after you've ridden one.'

He grinned. 'Wanna bet?'

Sarah couldn't help but let a small smile creep onto her face. If anyone could lighten someone's mood it was Jason. 'Is that it?' she asked Trish.

'There is one thing we don't really know about, the shuttle will come to a stop by itself, but we'll have no clue who'll be waiting at the other end.'

'We should expect a number of ground crew to greet us,' Sarah said, 'but we'll all be wearing Deep Reach gear so I can blag us past, say we're on an emergency recon or something. With an unscheduled arrival it's possible we won't see anyone.'

Trish crossed her fingers. 'With any luck.'

'Something we'll need a lot of,' Jason said.

Sarah murmured her agreement.

'How do you feel about using Riley's multifunction card?' Trish asked her.

Sarah stiffened. 'Fine.'

'Are you sure? You've obviously become quite close since you joined the SED and stealing his card to use in our plan will cause him a lot of problems.'

'Big problems,' Jason added.

'I know,' Sarah said, 'but it won't be too bad for him. He's got the support of Dresden Locke and his father, General Ellwood. Sure, he'll get a firm reprimand, but it won't be like he helped us or anything.'

Trish and Jason seemed to accept her reasoning, which was sound. However, the prospect of betraying Riley did make her feel physically sick; especially now they'd consummated their feelings for each other, feelings which, for her anyway, were very strong indeed. If she'd met Riley at any other time in her life, who knew what could have happened? But as it was her loyalties were firmly divided and it was a subject, quite frankly, she could do without dwelling on.

As their discussion continued, talk turned to what had been contained in the vaults; Sarah wowing Trish and Jason with the things she'd witnessed during her tour. Almost inevitably, though, their thoughts returned to the escape plan, the finer points being argued over and worked out detail by detail.

'So, according to your Deep Reach maps,' Jason said, 'how long will it take us to get to my Anakim temple containing the transportation devices?'

'I've already done a quick check on the route to the temple and it should be a two week trip,' Sarah told him, 'give or take a day or two. The route's already been laid and waypoint markers deployed so what would have taken the first team months to find will take us a lot less. I've given them to Trish so she can work out what air-shuttle track we need to take out of the SED.'

'You didn't tell me she'd given you the maps,' Jason said to Trish, aggrieved.

'You were in the toilet, I forgot, deal with it. What about food, water and other supplies?' she asked Sarah.

'The air-shuttle will be loaded with everything we need and more.'

'Two weeks,' Jason said, 'that's a lot of water.'

'There'll be a remote controlled supply vehicle and an aerial drone, which can carry most of the load,' Sarah told him. 'It'll be challenging but trust me, we can handle it.'

'If you say so.'

'We can collect our Deep Reach gear on the night of our escape,' Sarah continued, 'along with anything else we think we'll need.'

'So that's it then,' Trish said, 'we're almost set to go.'

Sarah gave a shake of her head. 'No, we *are* set to go.'

Jason looked at Sarah and then Trish. 'So we're actually going to do this?'

'Err, hello,' Trish said, 'what have we just been planning, a tea party?'

'When do we go, then?' He sounded anxious.

Sarah made a decision. 'Tonight.'

'What?!' Trish and Jason said in unison.

'The longer we leave it the more likely it is we'll never get out of here,' Sarah told them. 'General Stevens will want to interview me after the incident at the SED and when he finds out my tracking bracelet has gone I'll be screwed. Secondly, Riley's code for the vaults is more likely to change the longer we leave it. Lastly, and perhaps most importantly, I want to get on with it before my bottle goes.'

Jason rubbed his hands together. 'Fucking hell, this is going to be epic.'

Trish looked worried. 'Or a total disaster.'

'It'll be fine,' Sarah said, 'it has to be.'

CHAPTER FIFTY-TWO

A PERFECTLY CHOREOGRAPHED dusk crept over the upper level of USSB Sanctuary; the dimming synthetic sunlight shrouding the subterranean city below in a ruddy hue, long shadows casting phantom nets over the final vestiges of the day. Replicating this eternal ballet of perceived time, in perfect synchronisation, were the other many levels and chambers throughout the base, allowing all Sancturians to indulge in this most fundamental of solar events.

Traffic within Sanctuary's transport system ferried passengers through its vast network, the high-tech and high-speed vehicles an enviable collaboration of man and machine delivering the former safely to its intended destination. As day turned to night human activity slowed, the corridors of the SED emptying much like the museum located on the levels above. Further out, in the Exploration Division's residential apartments, people returned home from a hard day's work. Amongst these predominantly civilian individuals, three unassuming renegades stood on the very edge of rebellion, but only two were fully committed to the road ahead.

'Sarah!' Trish called out to her friend. 'You need to go!'

Sarah sat on her bed fiddling with her multifunction card,

turning the dense metallic rectangle over and over in her hands as she stared off into space.

Jason poked his head around her bedroom door. 'Saz, you need to get a wriggle on.'

Sarah looked up, her fingers stopping to caress the emblem of USSB Sanctuary embossed into one side of the card. 'Huh?'

'You need to get going,' he said, 'the clock's ticking.'

Sarah checked her phone. It was late evening and the plan was a go. She stood up, feeling detached and unreal, almost like she didn't exist. 'Right,' she said, walking out into the lounge area where Trish and Jason had laid out their kit for their journey.

'Are you okay?' Trish asked.

Sarah focused on her friend. 'I'm fine.'

'Are you sure? You've seemed down all day, distracted too.'

'I'm fine!'

Her ferocity took her friends by surprise, the two of them exchanging a meaningful look in response.

'I'm fine,' she said again in a calmer tone, 'don't worry about me. Just meet me where we agreed, okay?'

'Okay,' Trish said, 'but if there's anything wrong you need to say now as it's all our necks on the line, not just yours.'

Sarah ground her teeth. 'I know. Look, I'm just nervous. I've got a lot on my mind, a lot to remember and I don't need you winding me up.'

'She's not winding you up,' Jason said, 'she's just concerned.'

Sarah looked from Jason to Trish, their faces looking anything but confident before the off. 'I'm sorry.' She picked up her rucksack to check everything she needed was inside. Her manner became businesslike. 'Is everything ready?'

'I think so.' Trish looked around at the bags, equipment and clothing laid out around them.

'Shaped charges?' Sarah asked.

Jason scooped one up. 'Check.'

'Air-shuttle manual?'

Trish pointed to it.

'Waypoint beacons?'

'Yes, check,' Jason said.

'Deep Reach maps?'

Trish nodded.

'Deep Reach uniforms?'

Jason picked up one of the red and blue jackets and waggled it about.

'Excellent.' Sarah looked to Trish. 'Have you got the pill?'

Trish handed her a small mauve capsule.

'And you're positive this won't hurt him?' Sarah rolled the small oblong object around in her palm.

'One hundred per cent,' Trish said, 'it's a perfectly legal sedative. It'll knock him out for twelve hours and he'll wake feeling like he had the best sleep ever.'

'Until he realises you stole his card and fled the base,' Jason added.

'Shut up, Jason,' Trish said, furious.

Sarah placed the pill in the pocket of her grey uniform before looking around the apartment one last time, making sure she hadn't left anything behind. Satisfied, she made to leave. 'I'll see you both at one a.m. then.'

'One a.m.' Trish gave her a brief hug.

'Don't be late,' Jason told her.

Sarah mustered a smile, turned and walked out of the door.

◆

It didn't take Sarah long to reach Riley's home as it was located in the same chamber as hers, which was just as well as she was already getting cold feet; any longer and she may have wimped out before she'd even started.

She rang the doorbell and waited for him to answer. The door soon opened and her fear – or was it hope? – of him being out shrank to nothing.

'Hi,' Riley said, 'didn't expect to see you tonight.'

'No, guess not.'

'You're lucky you weren't in work this afternoon, Locke was asking after you; you'd better make sure you go in tomorrow or he'll be out looking for you.'

'Can I come in?' she asked, finding it difficult to maintain eye contact with him.

'Sure.' He stood aside to let her through.

Sarah moved past him and into his lounge where she was pulled up short by the sight of two of her Deep Reach teammates standing in the kitchen, drinking beer.

Jefferson, the broad black-bearded archaeologist and Cora, Riley's second in command, both turned as she entered.

'Sorry, I didn't realise you had company.'

'Not a problem, do you want a drink?'

Sarah shook her head, eyeing his multifunction card which hung, as ever, on a chain around his neck.

Jefferson ambled up to them. 'Ri, we're going to go; see you in the morning, yeah?'

'You don't have to.'

'Yeah we do.' He gave Sarah a small nod and a smile before leaving.

Cora downed her bottle, handed it to Riley and then gave Sarah a look that could kill before following Jefferson out of the door.

'Sorry,' Sarah said after they'd gone, 'I didn't mean to disturb your plans.'

'No biggie.' He cracked open another bottle of beer and took a swig.

'About this morning, I didn't mean to leave you like that, I just—'

'Don't worry about it, water under the bridge.'

They stood staring at each other, the silence between them growing uncomfortable.

'I think I will have that drink,' she said, breaking the awkward moment.

Riley put his drink down to get her a beer and Sarah, her fingers already clasping the sedative inside her pocket, slipped the pill into his drink, the capsule fizzing as it dissolved on its downwards spiral to the bottom. To hide these extra bubbles she picked up the bottle and handed it to him on his return. Accepting a bottle of her own, she watched as he raised her concoction to his lips.

'Wait!' She seized the drink from him before he could take a sip and placed it to one side.

He looked at her in surprise. 'What's wrong?'

'Nothing.' She was lost at how to explain away her actions. 'I—'

He cut her off by leaning in to kiss her. With a rush of passion clouding her mind, Sarah's thoughts and fears drifted away as she kissed him back, the plan she'd worked so hard over falling broken and discarded by the wayside; the laced bottle of beer continuing to effervesce unseen on the kitchen worktop.

CHAPTER FIFTY-THREE

SARAH OPENED her eyes to darkness. Getting out of bed, she ran her hands through her long tresses and picked up her phone to check the time. It was half past two in the morning. Using the dim light of her phone to guide her, Sarah collected her clothes from the floor and retreated to the bathroom to put them on. Returning to the bedroom she tiptoed around to Riley's side, stopping to watch him sleep, his breathing steady and slow. She drank in his form as she contemplated her options. Stay in Sanctuary for the rest of her life with a man and a job that made her happy, or return to the surface and expose Sanctuary and the Anakim, and seek justice for her mother. There was no in-between here; one way or the other it had to be all-in.

Riley moved in his sleep and Sarah looked to his bedside table where his multifunction card lay, unguarded and exposed. *As soon as I take his card my time at Sanctuary is at an end*, she thought. *No more Riley, no more Sanctuary, no more Deep Reach. The end – finito – no going back.* Her thoughts strayed to the surface, the freedom she experienced journeying to many lands, savouring different cultures, exploring new realms. Why should she give that all up? Sanctuary shouldn't be kept secret; it should be for all peoples to visit as they pleased, not for the select few. The existence of Homo gigantis, perhaps the greatest discovery mankind had ever made alongside Sanctuary itself, should be part of human history, not covered up by the GMRC, the U.S. Government or the Roman Catholic Church. She stretched out her hand to pick up the card, but hesitated, her memories of the Deep Reach mission flooding back to her; her times with Riley and her new friends, the wonders she'd seen in the vaults and at the SED. She pulled her hand back before another memory exerted itself, a powerful memory of smoke, fire and pain. Anger swelled within her as she reached down again and grasped Riley's card, her fingers curling around it. Taking a deep breath she picked it up and placed it in her pocket.

Her decision made, she bent down and very lightly kissed Riley on his upturned cheek. Leaving the room she walked towards the front door, noticing on the way the unfinished bottle of beer on the side containing the pill she'd placed within it. Changing course, she picked it up and poured its contents down the sink. Without a backward glance she left the apartment, shutting the front door behind her as quietly as possible. With a lump in her throat and regret like a millstone around her neck, Sarah headed for the SED.

♦

Darkness and silence hung over the area surrounding the Smithsonian's Museum of Sanctuary. The building, bordered by beautifully tended gardens, shone beneath the dull orange glow of the lights encircling its extensive circumference. Now directly below the USSB's mighty dome, wrapped inside its warm atmosphere, Sarah glanced up at the simulated night sky. *Someone went to a lot of effort to make the stars flicker and shine like the real thing*, she thought, her mind suddenly picking up on every detail of the base; she noticed they even appeared to match the correct pattern of the constellations.

Completing the effect was a near perfect representation of the moon; the strength of its light even managing to cast its own shadows as she threaded her way through the greenery, which in the half-light appeared as a darker shade of grey.

Sarah spied the figures of Trish and Jason sitting under a tree, close to where they'd arranged to meet.

'Where the hell have you been?' Trish said in a forced whisper as Sarah approached.

'Sorry, I got waylaid.'

Jason stood up. 'What were you doing all that time, or shouldn't we ask?'

'Let's get on with this, shall we?' Sarah told them, smoothly avoiding the inference.

'Did you get it?' Trish asked.

Sarah plucked Riley's card from her pocket and dangled it on its chain in front of them. 'Come on,' she said, shouldering her rucksack, 'I've been waiting ages for you two.'

'Funny,' Trish said as they collected their own bags and followed after her.

At a small side entrance to the museum Sarah swiped her multifunction card over a security pad, the little used door swinging open to reveal its quiet, dark interior. The three friends scurried through the exhibits, their footfalls echoing in the silent halls. As they descended a wide staircase they were momentarily blinded as a light was shone in their faces.

'Hey, what are you doing in here?' a man's voice said out of the darkness.

Sarah, regaining her vision, saw that it was the same aging security guard she'd met on her way back from the vaults with Riley the night before.

'What's going on, Geoff?' Another guard approached from behind them.

Geoff shone his torch into each of their faces. 'Got three trespassers.'

Sarah curbed her desire to run. 'We work for the SED, we're just passing through.'

'SED, eh?' Geoff tugged at a large wrinkled ear. 'Let's see your passes, then.'

Sarah withdrew her card and held it up for him to see.

'Hmm, seems to be in order, what about you two?'

'They're with me.'

'Sorry, miss, can't let people through if they ain't got a card, dem's the rules. It's more than my job's worth.'

Sarah groaned inwardly. They hadn't even got to the SED yet and they were having problems; so much for plain sailing.

'You've got my card,' Jason said to Sarah, giving her a funny look.

'Oh yes, I forgot.' She pulled out Riley's card and made sure to put her finger over the image when presenting it to the security guard.

He leaned forward, peering at it. 'I can't see the photo, give it here.' Geoff whipped the card out of her hand before she could react. Sarah watched as he looked at the card and then at Jason and then back to the card again. *Shit, we're screwed.*

'That's fine.' He handed the card to Jason.

Jason tried to stop himself from grinning as he made a face at Sarah to indicate his surprise. *The old guy must be partly blind*, Sarah thought, *perhaps their luck was in after all.*

'I forgot my card,' Trish told him, 'sorry.'

'Forgot your card?' the other guard said. 'No one forgets their card, that's crazy.'

'Perhaps you can let it slide this once,' Jason suggested, trying to sound in charge of the situation, 'as you saw I have level eight clearance. If you want I'll give you both a tour of the SED next time I'm back through, how about that?'

'But we don't even know what's down there,' the man said, 'how do we know it's worth it?'

'Oh, it's worth it.' Jason put an arm around Geoff's shoulders. 'It'll blow your minds.'

'Sounds good to me,' Geoff said, after giving it some thought.

The other guard nodded; apparently Jason's offer was too good an opportunity to pass up.

'Excellent!' Jason slapped Geoff on the back. 'Catch you later.'

The companions set off once more leaving the bemused guards behind them.

'Nice blag,' Sarah said to Jason once they were out of earshot.

Jason grinned. 'I thought we were bolloxed when he took Riley's card, silly old sod is blind as a bat.'

'Luckily for us,' Trish said as they worked their way down to the lower floors.

Reaching the first security door without further incident, the three friends changed into their Deep Reach coveralls and matching jackets, Trish's and Jason's having been obtained by Sarah two days before during her supply run at the SED. Ready to continue, Sarah swiped her card through the security mechanism. A buzzer beeped negatively and a red light appeared on the card reader. Sarah swiped it again, with the same result. She swore and tried it a third time; the buzzer sounded again accompanied by the red light.

'Perhaps I can be of assistance.' Jason flourished Riley's card. 'Abracadabra!' He swiped the card through the slot. The door beeped and a green light appeared. 'After you little lady,' he said in a deep voice.

Sarah gave him a droll smile. 'Thanks.'

Moving along they had to pass through another three card readers on their way to the lift, each one only accessible using Riley's card; an item that had turned out to be more critical to proceedings than they'd predicted. Knowing these new security measures must have been installed as a result of her and Riley's recent late night run-in with General Stevens' men, real doubt crept into Sarah's mind about their chances of success. Despite such thoughts tormenting her, Sarah continued to lead the way and, after taking a couple of wrong turns, the three friends arrived at their intended destination.

Much like the new high-clearance level locking mechanisms they'd already encountered, security surrounding the final obstacle into the SED's little used auxiliary entrance had been substantially increased. On Sarah's first impromptu foray into the Exploration Division the safeguards were virtually non-existent, but now another card reader and a glass door prevented access to the platform inside and, beyond this, a biometric scanner had been added, prohibiting access to the lift's controls.

Trish eyed the obstructions. 'I take it this lot isn't normally here?'

Sarah's face was grim. 'No, they're new.'

'Looks like you really pissed them off this time,' Jason said.

'They ain't seen nothin' yet.' Sarah motioned for him to use Riley's card once more.

Jason swiped and the lock bleeped, the transparent barrier swishing aside with a pneumatic hiss. Moving inside, Sarah sent a silent prayer heavenward before placing her forehead against the retinal scanner. A green laser shone across her eye. A palm reader then flipped down. She placed her hand on it and a blue grid lit up beneath. Two perpendicular bright blue lines moved in from the edges, bisecting one another in the centre to form a grid which spiralled out to fill the translucent panel.

'Thank you,' a computer generated voice said. 'Please speak your name and clearance level into the microphone.'

Sarah looked at Jason and Trish before leaning forwards. 'Sarah Morgan, clearance level, seven delta.'

'Thank you, Sarah Morgan. Biometrics identified. Your log-in has been confirmed and recorded. SED access – granted.'

'Sweet,' Jason said, as Sarah breathed a sigh of relief.

The controls to the platform now unlocked, Sarah sent them downwards with the press of a button. The lift rapidly descended and they soon reached the bottom, stepping out into the old brick tunnel. The strip lighting running along the passageway's ceiling disappeared around a shallow bend some distance ahead. Sarah pressed on until they reached the same old rusty, iron door she'd encountered on her first incursion beneath Sanctuary's museum. Inching it open, she peered through. Nothing stirred. The Exploration Division's hallways and rooms, visible from her position, were devoid of any activity.

'Right,' Sarah said, 'we walk like we belong, but we move quickly, okay?'

Trish and Jason nodded, their expressions tense.

Opening the door wide, Sarah moved through into the giant circular atrium that encompassed the massive steel and glass building. Striding forwards, Trish and Jason at her side, a movement off to the right alerted her to the presence of a couple of armed soldiers. She watched out of the corner of her eye as the two men wandered off in the opposite direction. They hadn't been seen. Stepping into the SED. Sarah reminded herself to breathe again now that the danger had passed. Their luck was holding, *but for how long?* she wondered.

Striding along the darkened halls, in the small hours of the morning, Sarah decided to show Trish and Jason the shuttle bay first.

'Wow.' Jason peered down into the two hundred foot wide, oval shaft; the dark pit, like the gaping maw of a titanic slumbering beast, seeming to consume the eight air-shuttle tracks that descended into it. 'How far down does it go?'

'A long way,' she said, before showing them the air-shuttle garages positioned further back around the edge, one of which housed the vehicle they planned to take.

'There's a track connecting all of them together.' Trish pointed out the shiny rails running around the ceiling of the bottom level of the shuttle bay. 'The manual indicates that any shuttle can be moved around this and mounted onto one of the eight outgoing rail-sets.'

'I'll take your word for it,' Sarah said and then led them back up the stairs and through a series of corridors, bringing them to the Deep Reach Alpha Six kit room. Knowing speed was of the essence, Sarah selected the climbing equipment they would need and flung it, piece by piece, onto a growing pile in the centre of the room.

Jason massaged a shoulder. 'That's a lot of gear.'

'We can sort it all out later.' Sarah checked the time on the phone attached to her wrist. 'Just stuff it in those backpacks, we need to hurry we're behind schedule.'

'And whose fault is that?' Trish said, as they each rammed the kit into the three bags.

'Sarah's.' Jason nudged into her.

'Yes, mine.' Sarah shoved him back.

Jason grinned at her, the look easing her anxiety levels a little.

After they'd finished that task Sarah helped each of them into their multipurpose harness. Putting on her own, Trish and Jason helping to do up the rear clasps, Sarah then led them to the so-called *departure lounge* to collect their helmets. Most of the racks were full, intimating that only a few teams still roamed outside of the USSB.

Sarah collected her own helmet, hanging it on her backpack while Trish and Jason started selecting helmets at random to test their fit. After a few minutes they'd both acquired suitable headwear and Sarah took them to the Command Centre which overlooked the shuttle bay.

'We need to keep really quiet now,' she said, before entering the tiered Control Station within the Command Centre, 'don't forget there's a nightshift sleeping in the back room.'

Jason looked horrified. 'What?! You never mentioned that before.'

'She did,' Trish said, 'you just weren't listening, as usual.'

'What if an emergency shuttle comes in?' Jason asked.

Trish jabbed him in the arm. 'We leg it, you Muppet.'

Jason made a face at her and Sarah opened the door and went inside. Putting her bulging backpack down, she motioned for Trish and Jason to stay where they were. Sarah approached the door at the back of the room, locking it as she'd seen the soldiers do only two nights previously. Returning to her friends she noticed Trish looking at the control console with apprehension, the bewildering array of dials, screens and switches enough to daunt anyone.

Trish shot her a look of deep scepticism. 'This looks more complicated than I thought it would.'

'You'll be able to figure it out though, yeah?' Sarah asked, keeping her voice low.

'Sure she will,' Jason said, 'she's the cleverest one here, she'll sort it.'

'You can do this,' Sarah told her, 'I know you can.'

Trish nodded uncertainly. 'I'll give it my best shot.'

'She'll do fine,' Jason said.

Sarah glanced through the window at the oval metal floor below, the giant retractable cover currently sheltering the equally large shaft beneath. 'Will we need to open the shuttle bay floor? If we do you'll need to disable the sirens and flashing lights or we'll have the whole damn army down on us in a matter of minutes.'

'According to the manual,' Trish said, 'and from what I saw downstairs, it seems the shuttles can be launched from the top or bottom floor, as the tracks can be moved as required. I'm not sure why they need both options, but when it comes to launching a shuttle from the lower floor, where you said you were launched from on your Deep Reach mission, retracting the metal floor is still essential otherwise the shuttles are unable to clear it as they rotate on the track prior to the drop.'

'Shouldn't you know this?' Jason asked Sarah.

'You'd think, but I only rode it once. Anyway, just make sure you keep the sirens off, okay?'

Trish gave a thumbs up. 'Will do.'

'When you've chosen the air-shuttle, you'll need to stow our bags in the rear compartment,' Sarah told them, 'but keep your helmets up here. When I get back from the vaults we need to be ready to go.'

'I can't believe we're going through with this,' Trish said.

'Just stick to what we planned and we'll be fine.' Sarah slid her own Deep Reach helmet over her head.

'How long do you think you'll be?' Jason asked as she adjusted the headgear.

'Hard to tell, hopefully, no longer than a couple of hours.'

'It can't be much longer than that,' he said, 'otherwise we'll have the early starters coming into work.'

Sarah nodded.

'Good luck.' Trish gave her a hug.

'You too.' She embraced Jason in turn, before moving away.

'Wait!' Jason said in a hushed voice.

Sarah looked back to see him holding out Riley's card. She smiled in self-mockery and accepted the card from him. 'Be safe,' she whispered and with a farewell wave she was gone.

CHAPTER FIFTY-FOUR

WITH THE URGENCY of their situation driving her on, Sarah ran back through the SED, slowing as she neared the atrium. Keeping the noise of her passage to a minimum, she surveyed the area looking for signs of any military patrols. All was quiet. Quelling an inner voice that screamed at her to run, Sarah strode across the empty expanse towards the old iron door and the brick tunnel beyond. Expecting a soldier to call out to her at any moment, Sarah felt the pressure of paranoia release as she left the atrium behind, the threat of vigilant eyes temporarily averted.

Running once more she soon reached the lift, which she activated to return to the lower levels of the Smithsonian above. After a single wrong turn, Sarah found herself back in the public area of the museum. She looked at her phone; fourteen minutes had already passed since she'd left Trish and Jason. She needed to move more quickly. Recalling the route Riley had led her along the previous night, she located the entrance and went through. Utilising Riley's multifunction card, Sarah unlocked door after door, struggling with the cumbersome hatch-like wheel mechanisms as she passed through; making sure to leave the ponderous obstacles ajar in anticipation of a quick return. She just hoped Riley's ex-girlfriend, perfect

Petra, who looked after the vaults, wasn't pulling a late shift. Even the thought of the woman made Sarah's blood boil.

Building up a sweat, Sarah arrived at the chamber containing the vaults, her progress so far going unnoticed; at least that's what she hoped, anyway. Unlike her previous visit the whole area stood shrouded in darkness, the only source of illumination coming from a limited number of small lights periodically positioned along the surrounding walkways. Thankful she'd decided to wear her Deep Reach helmet, she lowered the visor with a push of a button. The digital head-up-display powered up, casting a faint glow over her face. Switching to a spectral field suitable for the conditions, her surroundings became crystal clear.

The bridge spanning the gap to the Smithsonian's vaults remained in its horizontal position. Relieved to see it so, Sarah padded across it before descending the staircase at the end. She was now faced with the imposing round grey vaults, their doors presenting a united front in silent tribute. As she moved towards vault number eleven lights blinked on, making her freeze in place. Raising her visor, eyes wide, she looked around. *It's just a light triggered by movement*, she told herself, *get a grip!*

After swiping Riley's card over the security pad, Sarah dialled in the code she'd committed to memory, paused, and then hit the Enter button. A series of mechanical noises, sounding much louder than she'd remembered, echoed out into the chamber, the massive vault door opening on command. As before, Sarah submitted herself to the decontamination procedure and then entered the interior of the vault. Once inside, Sarah felt a rush of excitement at being alone in such a secure and restricted place. Suppressing the unsolicited feeling she moved to the room immediately to her right and pulled, and then pushed, at the door. It was locked. She switched her attention to the control device attached to the room's frosted panel exterior. Struggling with the system she turned the glass transparent by mistake, and the Ageless King of the Anakim appeared on his throne. Partially distracted by the mummy's splendour, she stumbled upon the menu sequence to override the door's locking mechanism.

Grasping the chrome handle, she pushed the door open, a resulting expulsion of air and a suction induced hiss indicating she'd broken some kind of gaseous seal. Stepping inside, an overpowering smell of chemicals swamped her senses. Coughing and covering her mouth and nose with a hand, Sarah retreated. Taking a deep breath of fresh air, she pressed a few buttons on the side of her helmet and deployed her visor and breathing apparatus, the two coming together to seal her face inside, her Deep Reach headwear once again serving her well.

She went back in and walked past the form of the giant king. His scale made her feel small – inconsequential – and the dark cavities where his eyes had been seemed to watch her from beyond the veil.

Aching to take a closer look, Sarah had to force herself to focus on the task at hand and ignore the incredibly ancient and fantastical relic sitting close enough to touch.

Knowing the clock was ticking, an intense urgency reasserted itself as she hunted for a way down into the disused service elevator; the place Riley had let slip lurked below. Her vision accentuated by her visor, she allowed her eyes to scan over the scene, but saw nothing useful. Apart from the enthroned mummy, the only other objects in the room were a functional set of cupboards, drawers and worktops. On and around these, placed in groups in trays and on trolleys, were various containers and a variety of implements and bottles Sarah knew well; the tools of a restorer's and archaeologist's trade. But where was the entrance she sought? The floor and walls appeared seamless. With nowhere else to look, she switched the image on her visor to another spectrum and then another, scanning for signs of a hidden entrance. Nothing. She looked at her wrist, her phone telling her she had no more time to waste. Getting desperate, her attention returned to the Ageless King.

'Any bright ideas?' she asked, glancing at the Anakim warrior.

He stared back at her in mute disinterest.

And then something struck her. Perhaps the entrance wasn't just beneath the room with the Ageless King in, but beneath the Ageless King himself! Crouching down, she peered under the platform on which the throne rested. She could see a distinct line in the floor. Without further thought she grasped the edge of the raised dais and heaved. The treads on her shoes gripped the floor well and the mummy, throne and platform moved aside.

Breathing hard inside her mask, Sarah stood up to see that a single square panel sat inset into the floor. She ran to the worktop, plucked out a trowel from amongst its fellows and hurried back to the centre of the room. Planting the blade into the seam, she prised the panel up, lifted it free and threw it to one side. A similar cover lay underneath, a handle in its centre. Sarah lifted it up and out, its density far greater than the floor covering she'd just removed, and dropped it down with a dull metallic clang. A deep hole presented itself, a ladder on one side. Without hesitating, she adjusted her visor's settings, powered up her helmet's twin torches and climbed down into the pit.

Looking around, Sarah could see the abandoned lift shaft widening out below. She continued down some way before a small rectangular opening came into view to her right. This had to be the passageway Riley had told her about, as it headed off as straight as a die towards the military vaults. Stepping off the ladder, Sarah manoeuvred herself into the tiny concrete tunnel. Marvelling at how Riley had squeezed into such a small space, Sarah half crawled, half pulled herself forwards.

A few minutes passed and her slow progress was beginning to really concern her. I have to tackle this all again on the way back, she realised, but if I'm pursued after attaining the pendant they'll soon have me pinned down; this place definitely doesn't lend itself to a quick getaway. Opening her mask to suck air more freely into her lungs, she picked up the pace.

With her knuckles bruised and raw, Sarah found the way ahead splitting off into eleven separate tunnels. Secured over each of these foreboding entrances squatted a sturdy metal grating which prevented anything from passing through; all except one. This must be the route Riley had forced open, she presumed, noticing the cover hanging off the front and the number one painted on one of its interior walls.

Logically, she reasoned that if the open passage, which was located on the far left of the eleven went to military vault one, then it stood to reason the tunnel two places along from it went to vault three and, subsequently, her pendant. Positioning herself in front of the third entrance, Sarah pulled at the metal grate. The metal groaned in protest but failed to give way. She tried again from a different angle. The frame bowed out as she used her legs and a straight back to exert the maximum possible force upon it. Sweat trickled down her neck as she continued to prise the cover loose. While working around the rim, one of the four retaining pins snapped and the metal sagged away from the wall. Spurred on by this advance, she kept up her efforts and the second pin broke soon after. Wrenching the grate out of the way, noticing the number three painted on the wall as she passed inside, she worked her way along this new tunnel.

With yet more valuable time ebbing away, Sarah came out into another shaft. Unlike the one back in the Smithsonian vault, this area was fully functional. In front of her rested the top of an elevator car suspended by a cabling system. *This is it*, she thought, *I'm inside the military vault*. Stepping onto the roof of the lift, she unbolted a hatch and then dropped down into the area below. Now inside a lift much like any other, Sarah turned off her helmet's lights and pressed the 'G' button for the ground floor. Seconds later she walked out into the vault's interior.

Perhaps unsurprisingly the inside of the military vault mirrored the Smithsonian ones in layout and design. A dimly lit walkway ran down the centre of the structure and on either side stood rooms with frosted panels, the only main difference being the area she'd just entered, where instead of a room there was a foyer outside the elevator.

Sarah checked the time on her phone. She'd left the SED just over an hour ago. Reasoning that going back would be far quicker, she estimated she had a maximum of twenty-five minutes before having to return. An image of Trish and Jason popped into her mind making her speculate as to how they were faring, thoughts of the numerous ways the plan could go wrong distracting her.

Snapping back to reality and remembering how Riley had located the whereabouts of her confiscated possessions, Sarah looked around for a computer system. There didn't appear to be a matching console here, but there was a large wallscreen in the foyer. *I hope using this won't alert anyone to my presence*, she mused, pressing a button to bring the display to life. Illuminated by the screen's powerful glow, she was pleasantly surprised to see the system didn't require any username or password to access. *And why would it?* she thought, it was inside a highly secure military vault and anyone using it would presumably have clearance.

Using the touchscreen menu system, which also confirmed she was indeed in vault three, Sarah navigated to a database archive. Selecting the search function she entered a description of her pendant and almost instantaneously a result displayed. Riley had been correct, all her possessions were there and on the vault's fourth level! Keen to be reunited with her artefacts, Sarah took note of a code next to the results, *D88*, and moved onto the walkway. Using a simple control panel attached to a handrail she sent the platform upwards. Lights above her stuttered to life as she came to a stop on the fourth floor.

Sarah looked around in surprise at the dimly lit open planned area on either side of the walkway. No rooms or frosted panels here, just one large circular room lined with row upon row of shelving.

'D eighty-eight,' she said to herself, moving through the orderly corridors with purpose.

The number in the code, she deduced, indicated the row number and the letter, the shelving unit within it. Jogging across to the other side she found row eighty-eight and came to a stop in front of a cabinet labelled with a *D*. Seven shelves rested within this depository, each enclosed behind a tinted shutter. Sarah yanked up the middle one. Inside, lined up side by side, small black plastic trays held various and disappointingly innocuous objects; none of which were her pendant.

She opened the remaining shutters two at time, the second from last revealing a sight that made her catch her breath. Her pendant! Reaching in, she withdrew the metallic pentagonal disc, still on the chain she'd had round her neck on first entering the USSB. With no time to savour the moment Sarah welcomed it home with a kiss before eagerly extracting her other items, which all rested on the same shelf, the first being the smaller, yet similarly shaped, pendant, the next, three Anakim parchments and lastly, the chunky metal Mayan tablet.

Noting each object had been tagged with a plastic label, Sarah slid the small pendant onto the chain alongside its fellow before securing them both around her neck. Tucking them inside her Deep Reach coveralls the two metallic discs rested against the skin of her chest, the sensation familiar and deeply satisfying. The parchments, contained within a plastic wallet, folded neatly into her breast pocket while the tablet slid into a large Velcro pouch on her thigh, weighing her down on one side.

Reunited with her artefacts, Sarah checked the time again. She had fifteen minutes before she absolutely had to return. A thought worked its way to the forefront of her mind; she had an opportunity here, the possibility of getting her hands on more Anakim wonders, to steal from the military like they'd stolen from the rest of humanity. It was an appealing idea and such poetic justice, by her reckoning, was a rarity not to be passed up.

Getting back on the walkway, she descended to the first floor. Now surrounded by rooms, she moved to one and turned the frosted panel transparent. Inside, arranged on a large single bench, lay an array of large and intriguing objects. She recognised one as being the shield she'd seen brought to the SED back by the archaeology team, before the military had swooped in and expelled them all from the shuttle bay. The massive object glittered in the dim lighting, its dark blue and purple hue setting off the gems set into its surface.

Knowing she had no hope of stealing anything so big, she moved to the next room, again turning the glass see-through. At first there appeared to be nothing in this room, but as she moved away a shimmering effect in the air drew her back. Something was in there, but it could only be glimpsed if you moved and even then only an indistinct outline could be seen. It looked like a large oblong box with a statue on top. A little perturbed by this veiled spectre, she moved to the next room. Inside this she saw a veritable library of what must be Anakim parchments, stacked in furled rolls on a twenty foot high rack which spanned the whole side of the room. In the rest of the space stood columns of tall, flat, free-standing cabinets, their black monolithic frames reaching up towards the ceiling. Within each of these, on both sides, were more parchments, their ancient texts splayed out for analysis.

Unlocking the room via the control pad Sarah entered, a vacuum sucking at the door as it opened. Snatching some scrolls from the rack, their super fine and durable material folding with ease, she placed them in her pocket alongside her others. Drawn to some red coloured parchments further along, Sarah saw they were some sort of animal hide, not the high-tech type like hers or the ones she'd just filched. Deciding to leave these alone, something else grabbed her attention like a slap to the face.

Almost in a daze, Sarah walked between the upright displays to stand looking up at a parchment on show just above her eye level. 'No,' she said out loud, shaking her head, 'it can't be.'

But it was. There was no mistaking the design. The image had been a part of her nightmares for months now, permanently seared into her mind for all eternity. Sarah outstretched a hand to caress the parchment before her, the desire for physical contact thwarted by a protective Perspex sheet. It had been many years since she'd last lain eyes on it. The detail was exquisite and the depiction of the Antarctic land mass, perfection.

The precarious nature of her mission forgotten, Sarah stared at one of the maps she'd previously believed to have been lost in the fire that had taken her mother's life. There was no doubt in her mind that it had been one of her discoveries, she'd spent enough hours poring over it – she knew every inch. The fact that she was looking at it now, however, shattered her theory as to who was responsible for murdering her mother.

And to think I'd been happy here at the SED with Riley. The thought now tasted acrid and vile in her mouth. *I even considered staying in Sanctuary and surrendering my freedom to these people!* The sickening betrayal and her pathetic naivety broke something within her. Gritting her teeth, she fought to release the map from its locked case. As she failed to make any impact her frustration skyrocketed and with an incandescent scream of rage Sarah launched herself into the cabinets around her, heaving them over. The heavy display cases slammed into one another, creating a domino effect and causing the entire vertical collection to fall crashing to the floor; the thunderous noise ending when the final ones to topple smashed into the special glass frontage, shattering it into a thousand tiny shards.

Her fury at the deception of those she'd trusted – of Riley – eviscerated any restraint left in her. Returning to the first room she'd approached, Sarah unlocked the door and barged in. Moving to the monstrous shield suffused with priceless jewels, Sarah grasped its edges and hauled it upright. Turning it round she placed her hands on the thick handle, attempting to lift it. A foot taller than her, the artefact was incredibly light for its size and she managed to hold it off the floor for a number of seconds before it dropped back down with a clunk. Seeing the futility of her efforts, her anger subsiding, Sarah made to rest the shield back down, but before she could do so she felt a sensation of heat spread over her hands. The pendant on her neck grew hot and a curious oscillating vibration pulsed through the handle and up her arms. A wave of purple energy rippled across the shield's surface and burst out into the room in a sphere of blinding light. Streams of blue lightning flowed across the floor and walls and out into the vault. Sparks flew from the walkway's control panel and spotlights as they shorted out, the surge of electricity destroying every circuit in its path.

Letting the shield drop, its surface still glowing brightly, Sarah rushed from the room in time to see the last remnants of the expulsion of power flickering up the inside of the entire vault, hot metal embers showering down around her. Plunged into total darkness, the shield's light ebbing away behind, Sarah activated her helmet's systems which had somehow avoided ruin. Her torches ablaze, visor down and senses recovered, the reality of her situation came flooding back. *I have to get out of here!* she thought, desperation upon her. Running to the lift she pressed the call button which failed to light up. Realising the mechanism was fried, she tried to open the doors to get back into the shaft. They held fast. She was trapped!

CHAPTER FIFTY-FIVE

IMPRISONED IN THE MILITARY VAULT, Sarah looked around in despair, imagining the hordes of soldiers that even now must be homing in on her location. *Wait*, she thought. Something she remembered seeing in the Smithsonian vaults sent her running back down the walkway; at the end, as she'd hoped, hung an emergency exit sign. Opening the door beneath, she ducked inside to descend the staircase within. Guided by the lights of her Deep Reach helmet, Sarah emerged into a small corridor running around the vault's curved exterior wall. Passing through a heavy fireproof door, she arrived at another exit. This new metallic barrier had been plastered in warning signs and bristled with complicated security systems, all of which appeared inactive, wisps of smoke rising from some of the circuitry. *Did the power surge from the Anukim shield reach this far?* she wondered.

Above this formidable steel door, in red lettering on a white background, a military sign read:

U.S.S.B. SANCTUARY
United States Military
Scientific Laboratory Complex

Under this, another sign read:

WARNING!
Restricted Area
Level 9 Special Access Personnel Only

Sarah pushed at the door, which swung silently inwards. Wary, but knowing she had no other option, she moved through it and out of the vault. Switching her torches to infrared, to avoid detection, she altered her visor's spectral field allowing her to see in the dark. Now in the laboratory complex, she flicked some switches on a wall next to her. The lights in here were also out. Amazed the shield's energy had extended so far, apparently through solid walls, she proceeded down an empty corridor searching for a way out.

Arriving at an intersection, Sarah surveyed some signs stuck on the walls, the department names and arrowed symbols working much like those found in large hospitals. Sticking to basics, she followed the placard with *Way Out* on it. Jogging along, she heard voices ahead. *Guards*, she thought, *who else would be here this late?* Dodging right down another hall, she went down a flight of stairs and pushed through a set of sturdy double doors, the card reader outside sparking sporadically as she passed. The whole damn security system was fried. Whatever that Anakim shield had done, it was on a massive scale; she just prayed it hadn't reached Jason and Trish back at the SED's shuttle bay.

Moving ahead, she now found herself in a deserted, yet extremely sophisticated, laboratory. Computer equipment abounded, surrounding individual curiosities undergoing various procedures and tests within their own sealed rooms. One such area contained a huge Anakim body lying face up on a slab. While clearly decayed, the form was frighteningly intact, its dark, sunken flesh the only give-away to its incredible age. Finding it hard to ignore the macabre scene, she carried on, the time ticking away and her fear of capture rising.

Making it to the other side of the lab, a buzz of electricity passed over her head and the lights that remained undamaged blinked on. Her helmet's internal computer adjusted automatically, shutting down the torches and returning the visor to its default transparent state. Opening another door, she entered another bland, white-walled corridor. The lights out here had also resumed functioning, the building's systems beginning to reboot after the blackout. Sadly for Sarah it made her escape that much more unlikely.

More voices echoed down the hall; she went to return to the lab but as she cracked open the door she glimpsed two armed Terra Force soldiers entering from the opposite side. Panicking, she sped down another passageway, past a large antechamber and on into another corridor, before sliding to a stop as yet another SFSD patrol approached from that direction, their armoured shadows looming on the wall ahead. Rushing back the way she'd come, she stopped outside an imposing entrance protected by a security checkpoint consisting of turnstiles, full body scanners and large thick panels of glass. The area looked to be even more restricted than the complex she'd already inadvertently infiltrated. Reluctant to enter somewhere so secure in case the locking systems resumed operation, she froze, unsure of what to do next.

Footfalls echoed from either direction. Her eyes widened in fear and her head spun this way and that as she sought a place to hide. She had nowhere else to go. Her hand forced, Sarah opened a toughened glass door, compromising its vacuum seal, and passed into the restricted zone. Behind her, the heavy security door swung closed; adorning its exterior surface were an array of warnings and restrictions. Two of these read:

U.S.S.B. SANCTUARY in partnership with GMRC R&D DIVISION
and
The National Aeronautics and Space Administration (NASA)

WARNING!
RESTRICTED AREA
Level 10 Alpha
Special Access Personnel Only

Below, sandwiched in the very fabric of the glass, were the emblems and insignias of USSB Sanctuary, the GMRC and NASA, and underneath these, an elegant silver logo:

PROJECT
ARES

CHAPTER FIFTY-SIX

DEEP in the bowels of USSB Sanctuary, Sarah moved cautiously forwards, each step drawing her further into the military's highly restricted laboratory complex. With every sense heightened and every muscle tense, her eyes darted in all directions seeking out any danger ahead. The way seemed clear, the many security measures on show appearing dormant, knocked out by the power surge she'd created with the Anakim shield. Aware that she was still visible to the soldiers approaching from outside the glass façade, Sarah vaulted over a turnstile and ducked through a black tunnel-shaped scanner before emerging into a cold, steel-clad room.

On the walls around her numerous white lab coats hung on hooks. In front, there was another door plastered with warning signs and hazard symbols. A noise behind her made her jump. Had someone followed her inside? With no time to think, she grabbed one of the coats and pushed open the door, the steel handle cold to the touch. Cooled gases vented into the air around her as she entered, their mist clinging to her body. After quietly closing the door behind her, she found herself in a long white walled corridor. Running to the end, she came out into a small area surrounded by glass enclosures, each seven foot high and three wide. Inside these were white, full-body hazmat suits with inbuilt breathing apparatus. On the far wall a heavy metal hatch barred her way. Peering through its small letter-box-shaped window, Sarah gazed out at a massive, brightly lit chamber, the size of a warehouse. Within this she could see ten self-contained laboratories, their grey sides full of oblong shaped windows, stacked two storeys high.

With no time to spare, she shrugged into the white coat and deployed her Deep Reach helmet's breathing system, the mask generating an air-tight seal in combination with her visor. Turning the wheel on the hatch through three hundred and sixty degrees, she hauled it open and went through. Closing it behind her, she locked it again by spinning back the adjoining wheel on the other side. As soon as the lock bit a buzzer sounded, then a powerful blast of freezing vapour engulfed her from above and below.

Moving away from the decontamination zone, she searched for a way out. With no obvious exits in sight, she glanced back through the door, inside she could see a man removing one of the hazmat suits from its cabinet. He looked like a scientist rather than a soldier and it didn't look like he'd seen her, but if he did, it wouldn't take long for the Special Forces to arrive. Feeling like a cornered animal, she ran to the right along a metal walkway and descended some stairs, before heading for an archway which took her into another smaller chamber beyond. Out of sight of the entrance, she leaned back against a wall to catch her breath while inwardly cursing her stupidity for touching the shield. *Don't worry about that now*, she berated herself, *you need to get out of here!*

Taking in her new surroundings, she saw, sixty feet away, a familiar sight resting within a semi-circle of tall lighting rigs. It was the mysterious object she'd seen being retrieved from Sanctuary Proper by General Stevens and his men, back in the SED's shuttle bay. Peeking back into the main chamber, she could see the scientist, who'd followed her in, walking away in the other direction. Counting her blessings that she hadn't been spotted, and unable to help herself, Sarah approached the pool of light which encompassed the fifty foot high monolithic structure. The dark, rough, coral-like surface, interspersed with lighter seams of sediment, glinted and glistened under the powerful illumination. Up close, the ancient pentagonal prism soared above her head. Around this bizarre artefact, arranged on either side, were rows of tables blessed with a cornucopia of state-of-the-art scientific equipment and holographic computer screens, all of which appeared to be operating normally, untouched by the shield's power surge. Sprouting from this mass of technological hardware and onto the surrounding floor, reams of cabling snaked out like many long, black giant worms, to terminate on the artefact's rocky substrate.

In front of this most primeval of edifices, a wide set of portable stairs had been positioned. These aluminium steps led up to the rectangular transparent enclosure that lay sunken into the stone, some ten feet off the ground. Sarah glanced back in trepidation. Making a decision, she swiftly ascended the steps to stand in front of the glass-like casing, its edges framed by a heavily corroded metal surround. Inside, the thick, pale, viscous liquid she'd glimpsed before, remained static and lifeless. She looked down at the three indented discs set into a ceramic panel and tentatively reached out a hand. Her pendant and the circular depression grew warm. The colour of the liquid darkened and a small blue glow blossomed into being in its centre; the light intensifying to sparkle like a distant star, beautiful and mesmeric.

'Hey, what are you doing up there?' a muffled voice said.

Snatching her hand away, the light died and the liquid reverted to its pale state. Sarah turned around to see the scientist in the biohazard suit looking up at her from the bottom of the steps, an expression of concern on his face.

Lost for words, Sarah stared back at him through her visor.

'Where's your hazmat suit?' the man said, his tone querulous, 'why are you wearing that helmet, who are you?'

Sarah descended the steps towards him. 'I was sent here to clear up this mess.'

He looked around. 'What mess?!'

'The power failure of course,' she said, improvising for all she was worth.

'Where's your security pass?'

Sarah noticed the official looking rectangular badge attached to the outside of his suit. 'I got special dispensation.' She walked away to one of the monitoring stations.

'Under whose authority?' he said, following her.

'General Stevens. It's a digital certificate. Here,' she picked up a computer tablet and pointed at the graphs, 'look at this.'

The man snatched the device from her. He peered at it for a moment and then looked back to Sarah. 'I don't—' he began before a glazed expression spread over his face and he dropped to the floor unconscious.

Sarah chucked the heavy piece of computer hardware back on the desk she'd taken it from and bent down to see if the man was okay. Looking into his protective headwear she saw his breath appearing as a fine mist on his transparent facemask. Relieved she hadn't killed him, she ripped out some leads from a nearby computer and tied his arms and legs up. With some effort she dragged him out of sight before plucking the security tag from his chest and attaching it to the breast pocket of her white coat. Running back to the main chamber, she was pleased to see no one else appeared to be around; probably due to it being in the middle of the night. Jogging around the rest of the area, she searched for a way out. Out of breath again surprisingly quickly, she slowed to a walk, her limbs feeling heavy and ponderous. There were no emergency exits, she realised. It was as she'd feared, the only way out was the way she'd come in.

Why am I so tired? she asked herself, moving over to lean against the side of one of the grey standalone laboratories, her breathing still laboured. A recollection of feeling similarly drained drifted up from her memory banks. I felt like this after I'd used the Anakim transportation device, she thought. The shield and the thing I just activated must have sapped my energy reserves somehow. It makes sense, she hypothesised, if the pendant taps into my body's bioelectricity to power the ancient technology then it stands to reason such reserves are finite; which means my original theory about the pendant utilising a battery that never runs out is erroneous. Although, while it's an obvious flaw in the Anakim's design, their bodies would have been much larger than mine, thus having a much bigger power source to draw upon.

Pleased with the breakthrough, but distressed by its current debilitating effects and feeling too tired to move, let alone run, Sarah used the enforced break to peer into the laboratory next to her. Nothing significant caught her attention until she focused on the rear interior wall, where a large screen relayed multiple data feeds along with an intriguing image of what looked like live footage from some kind of space station, the large circular structure drifting through what could only be the blackness of space. Moving closer to the window she could make out, in the bottom right hand corner of the screen, the words U.S.S.S. Archimedes, the NASA insignia and, next to that, a silver, winged emblem containing two distinct words.

'Project Ares,' she read out loud, captivated by the scene, which couldn't have been more removed from her current location. Wondering what the American civilian space agency could possibly have in common with Sanctuary and the Anakim, Sarah moved to the next window, where she recognised another artefact she'd seen before, also in the SED's shuttle bay. Inside, resting on the floor, lay the bulky form of a jet-black hexagonal, onyx-type container; one of three fifteen foot long and ten foot high vessels discovered by an archaeological team in the hidden catacombs of Sanctuary Proper, and part of the hoard of artefacts that had included the Anakim shield she'd recently held. The last time she'd seen it the lid had been open, displaying within three rows of small round spheres. Now, the top lay shut, the perfect lines and unblemished reflective surface showed off the fine silver script and symbols that flowed around it.

Her strength was slowly returning, but she was still in no shape to mount any kind of escape. Her curiosity once more getting the better of her, Sarah decided to take a closer look. Rounding the corner, she stepped through the airtight door, its glass frontage adorned with the same Project Ares logo she'd seen moments before, and was subsequently doused in another jet of sanitising vapour. Moving inside, she ran her fingers along the length of the object, relishing its smooth surface and magnificent workmanship. How it had survived so long in such pristine condition God only knew. She'd be fascinated to know where it had been found, such context vital to determining the history of any artefact.

Ignoring a warning sign on the door and passing into another room, Sarah pushed through into a transparent tent which had been erected inside. Within this, on a square aluminium table, sat ten of the multi-sided orbs that could only have originated from the coffin-like creation she'd just visited. Each of these orbs, or more accurately regular dodecahedrons, consisted of twelve pentagonal sides. They were each made of different materials; some had rough, brightly coloured surfaces while others were dull and smooth. All, however, had fine silver symbols inlaid into every one of their sides. They also seemed to be producing some kind of strange high-pitched oscillating noise that made the roots of her teeth tingle.

Trying to dispel this unusual sensation, she leaned in for a closer look. Like the other much larger artefact she'd seen, the scientists had attached to each of these geometric orbs a number of wires, which led off to a host of monitoring equipment bolted to a nearby wall. Opposite, a digital screen displayed various charts and graphs, the data collected plotting across them as she watched.

Deciding these palm sized orbs were perfect for stealing and knowing they would prove difficult to explain away by the scientific community on the surface, Sarah selected the one closest to her. Detaching the small cords around it, she picked it up, noticing as she did so the corrugated surface and extreme weight for something of its size. It felt like a lump of solid lead. Believing two of the orbs would weigh her down too much, she cut her losses and exited the lab, just the one orb cradled in her hands.

Suddenly feeling a lot stronger, her energy levels climbing, Sarah looked at her watch; she had to get back, and soon. As she went to secure the orb in her pocket, a strange tingling sensation ran down her spine, making the hairs on the back of her neck stand on end. The orb grew lighter, its metallic green and yellow flecked surface vibrating and turning smooth. Her hands shook as an intense pain lanced through her head. Crying out in agony she stumbled, the orb falling to the floor and she to her knees. Looking down at her hands, she saw silver symbols on her flesh disappearing as her fingers curled inwards involuntarily. A tortuous seizure tore through her body and she crumpled to the floor, her limbs in spasm. Fitting uncontrollably, Sarah's eyes rolled up into her head before darkness consumed her and time lost all meaning.

CHAPTER FIFTY-SEVEN

SARAH GROANED and opened her eyes. A few feet away, resting on the smooth concrete floor, her eyes focused on the small orb that had rendered her unconscious. Rolling to her knees, she removed her helmet, shook her head and rubbed her face before checking the time. Thankfully she'd only been out for a few minutes and apparently no one else had been alerted to her presence, as all was quiet in the highly restricted chamber. The ten grey twin-tiered labs stood silently around her, unmoved by recent events and – mercifully – still unoccupied.

She got to her feet and took a few unsteady steps before her head cleared and the familiar sensation of clarity returned. Unwilling to let this potent object defeat her, Sarah tore a strip of cloth off her lab coat, folded it over so it was nice and thick, and picked up the orb. She waited to see if the same reaction occurred, ready to drop it to the floor the instant it did. After some time passed she deemed it safe enough to tuck away into her Deep Reach coveralls. Feeling light headed but refocused, she glanced at the phone on her wrist, she was overdue; she had to get back to Trish and Jason or it was game over.

Jamming her helmet back on, a jog turned into a run as Sarah headed back to the hatch she'd entered on her way into the secure area.

'Hey!' a voice said, making her heart skip a beat.

Looking left she saw the scientist she'd knocked out had also returned to consciousness, untied himself and was now running towards the same exit. She sped up, the distance to the door rapidly decreasing as the man also closed the gap, the two of them converging on the single point. Reaching the hatch first, Sarah spun the wheel as the scientist bore down on her. Hauling it open, she dived inside and yanked it shut just as the man arrived outside, his hands slamming against the tiny window.

They stared at one another through the small window; Sarah turned the wheel before meeting strong resistance as he tried to pull it back the other way. Despite his slim build he was deceptively strong and Sarah knew she couldn't keep him out for much longer. Searching for something to jam in the mechanism, something else caught her eye. Reaching out a hand while holding the door closed with her body, her fingers brushed against a red button. Unable to activate it, she let go of the wheel, sending the hatch swinging open.

The scientist appeared in the doorway, a look of shock and horror on his face as he saw Sarah slam her palm against the button.

'No!' he shouted.

A thick metal plate shot down from above, sealing off the entrance and stranding the man inside. The white lights around her turned red and sirens blasted out a continuous warning in response to Sarah activating an emergency contamination lockdown and facility wide alert. If she hadn't realised it before, this time she knew the shit really had hit the fan.

♦

Captain Williams of USSB Sanctuary's Special Forces Subterranean

Detachment had worked in the army's scientific laboratory complex for many years. Originally he'd worked out in Sanctuary Proper alongside the elite teams of the SED, but after suffering a broken leg during a climb he'd been re-tasked with babysitting duties. At the time he'd bemoaned the fact that he'd effectively become a glorified security guard for a bunch of prissy self-involved geeks, and after six years not much had changed. He hated his job and the idiots he was sworn to protect, but apart from demoting himself and taking a hefty pay cut by becoming a regular he was pretty much screwed every which way.

Currently Williams was pulling a nightshift with his colleague, Sergeant Shaw, who had just received a transmission via his radio.

'Roger that, Control,' Shaw said and then looked at his Captain. 'Power's been fully restored.'

Williams shifted the grip on his rifle. ''Bout time.'

'I wonder what caused it?'

Williams huffed. 'Probably some fool messing with something he shouldn't.'

Just as he uttered those words the lights around him turned red and a siren echoed out into the corridors.

'Fuck, what now?' He turned and looked through the glass into the zone he protected.

'You better get in there,' Shaw told him, 'it's protocol.'

'Screw protocol, the last time they tripped this alarm ten people ended up dead; they don't pay me enough to have my face melted off.'

'Melted?'

'I saw the bodies,' Williams said, determined not to set a foot in there unless he was ordered to do so, 'but by all means, if you want to follow protocol, you're more than welcome to take the lead.'

The sergeant considered him for a moment. 'Let's wait; someone will be down in a minute.'

'Good call.' Williams eyed the area as a scientist came running through the security scanners in a white hazmat suit.

Shaw backed away and cocked his rifle. 'How did they get out?'

Captain Williams held his hand up at the scientist as they pulled open the thick glass door. 'Stay inside,' he said, walking backwards away from her.

'I'm okay.' The woman held her own hands up in the air in supplication. 'I'm the one who triggered the system.'

Williams kept his weapon at the ready in case she got too close. 'What's going on in there?'

'A big leak.' Now out in the hallway she moved away from him. 'I'd start running if I was you, the whole place could go up!'

'What?!'

'Run!' She sprinted off.

Williams looked round to see his colleague disappearing down the corridor in the other direction. 'Crap,' he said and pelted after him.

♦

Sarah sped around a corner, pulling off the top of the biohazard suit as she went and throwing it aside. With her shoes squeaking on the tiled floor she left the soldiers far behind her as she ran as fast as she could.

I can't believe I got away with that, she thought, the adrenaline coursing through her system as sirens continued to wail around her. *You're lucky they didn't shoot you*, her internal voice admonished.

Trying to get her bearings, she skidded to a halt as she spied some signs. Discarding the bottom half of the hazmat ensemble, Sarah scanned through the directions for a way out.

'That'll do,' she said, seeing a sign reading *Smithsonian Vaults* and darting away to follow the arrow as if the hounds of hell themselves were nipping at her heels.

She flew up some stairs and soon crashed through an exit to emerge inside the compound containing the museum's vaults. Back on recognisable ground, Sarah went up the spiral staircase and across the bridge, noticing the area was now brightly lit and military trucks roared up the access road beneath her. *If they aren't after me yet they soon will be*, she thought, keeping up her pace as she smashed open a door to carry on towards the museum and the SED beyond.

Hurdling a barrier, Sarah banged open the first of the hatch doors she'd left unlocked on her way in. With their heavy metal frames crashing into the walls at her passing, the sound echoing down the halls, Sarah saw a familiar figure ahead.

'Sarah?' Petra frowned and moved to bar her way '*You're* the security breach?'

Without breaking stride Sarah swung a fist at Petra's smug face; knocking her out cold.

'Yep!' she said, glancing back and feeling a disturbing abundance of satisfaction as she continued on her way.

Before she knew it she'd traversed the museum and the lift back down to the SED. Now running through the brick tunnel, Sarah prised open the rusting iron door, half expecting to see a line of soldiers standing there with their guns trained at her chest. Instead there was only emptiness, the dimly lit atrium as yet undisturbed by her deeds back in the vaults and laboratories. Rushing forwards into the building, Sarah worked her way inside and back up to the SED's Command Centre.

Opening the door to the Control Station, she moved through to find the area empty. *Where the hell are Trish and Jason?* she thought, looking down into the partially lit shuttle bay below.

'Looking for your friends?' a familiar voice said.

Sarah turned around to see Cora standing behind the door.

'Strangest thing,' Cora turned on the lights and walked towards her, 'Riley rang me up in the middle of the night asking if I'd seen his multifunction card. Of course I hadn't, but then that's because you have it, don't you?'

'Where are my friends?' Sarah backed away from her, noticing she held a wicked looking climbing axe in one hand.

'Why? Are you planning on going somewhere?' Cora moved

towards her, axe raised. 'According to the military chatter you've been a very naughty girl.'

'Where are they?!'

Cora smiled and tapped her nose. 'Now, now, impatience is not a virtue. Besides, you should be more worried about yourself than them.'

Sarah realised Cora wanted her to run. Her eyes narrowed and she halted her retreat.

'You're a brave girl.' Cora's face hardened. 'Let's see if I can cut that out of you.'

She swung the axe and Sarah leaned back, the blade nicking her cheek as it slashed past. Diving to the side, she rolled back to her feet before having to evade another strike as Cora slammed the axe down into the desk she'd just been in front of. The woman wasn't trying to stop or maim her – she intended to kill!

Sarah ducked again as another strike came in, but this time Cora had overreached and Sarah was able to counter-attack with a punch to her chin. Unlike the fragile Petra, however, Cora walked through the blow to deliver a head-butt to Sarah's nose. Pain exploded in her face as she felt the bone break. A knee took her in the stomach, knocking the wind out of her, before a fist connected with her temple. Sarah staggered back and Cora advanced, looking to finish her. Sarah yanked the heavy Mayan tablet from her pocket just as the axe swung down at her head. The point connected with the metal plate, the impact throwing Cora off balance and allowing Sarah to scramble clear.

Cora advanced again. Sarah hurled the Mayan plaque at her, but she ducked out of the way. Feeling in another pocket Sarah withdrew the orb and launched the leaden weight at Cora's head. With cat-like reflexes Cora caught the artefact in her hand, grinning as she backed Sarah into a corner.

'I've been waiting to get rid of you ever since you arrived,' Cora said, 'and your duplicity has granted me that opportunity. Riley will find it hard to take when he hears of your death, but he'll get over it. Besides,' she held up her weapon, 'you left me no choice; I had to defend myself when you came at me with this axe. They'll probably even give me a reward for preventing your escape, call me a hero.'

Sarah wiped a trickle of blood from her nose. 'A twisted bitch is what you are.'

'So they tell me.' Cora prepared to strike before her eyes widened and the axe slid from her grasp. 'What—' She looked down at the orb still clutched in her other hand.

Sarah saw the artefact's surface change texture and she put her hands over her ears as a high pitched noise sang out into the room.

Cora clutched at her stomach, the orb rolling from her hand as she convulsed. Dropping to her knees, froth seeped from the corner of her mouth and her eyes rolled up into her head. Toppling over, her body contorted before her back arched up once, twice and a third time to crack sickeningly, leaving her lifeless form twitching on the floor.

Sarah stared in shock at the scene, delighted to be alive but horrified by what she'd just witnessed. Reluctantly, but feeling compelled to do so, she picked up the orb in its cloth covering and stowed it back in her pocket.

A thumping sound accompanied by muffled voices drew her attention to the rear of the room where the nightshift had been locked in. The fight with Cora had awoken them. *Could anything else go wrong?* she wondered.

The door to the Control Centre opened and Trish and Jason entered wearing their stolen Deep Reach helmets.

'Did you get it – the pendant?' Trish said, before gasping at the gruesome sight of Cora's dead body.

Sarah scooped up the Mayan tablet. 'Yes, but we have to go – now!'

Jason tore his eyes away from the corpse. 'What's that noise?'

'The nightshift is awake.' Sarah joined Trish at the main console. 'Is everything ready?'

Trish nodded. 'Put the cards in the slots.'

Sarah withdrew the two multifunction cards and slid them into the apertures. Trish tapped away at the control panel, directing Jason to press some buttons on another computer.

'Erm, guys,' Sarah said, looking at a camera feed showing footage of the SED's atrium, 'you might need to hurry up.' She watched as soldiers streamed in from all directions. The game was up.

Trish glanced at the image. 'Hurry up Jason!' Her fingers clicked faster on the keys.

'I'm going as fast as I can, for Christ's sake!'

Sarah saw an air-shuttle appear from beneath the ground at the far side of the shuttle bay below.

Trish stopped typing. 'We're ready.'

'But the shuttle bay floor is still closed,' Sarah said in dismay.

'We didn't know how to turn off the sirens, but don't worry, it'll open.' Trish's finger hovered over a red button. 'But as soon as I press this we only have ninety seconds—'

A loud booming on the rear door interrupted her – the nightshift were trying to break free!

'Ninety seconds,' she continued, 'to get down to the air-shuttle and secure ourselves in before it launches.'

'What!' Sarah's face blanched.

Jason saw the live camera footage of soldiers rushing into the SED. 'Press the damn button!'

'Ready?!' Trish asked.

'Yes!' Sarah and Jason said in unison.

The nightshift burst out of the backroom.

'Go!' Trish depressed the button.

'Stop!' someone shouted from behind, but Sarah, Trish and Jason were already out of the door, the seconds ticking away as the sirens and beacons in the shuttle bay came to life, the great star-shaped metal floor grinding back.

♦

Sarah's heart felt like it was beating out of her chest as she followed Trish and Jason, who tore down the corridor ahead of her. Shouts from behind made her glance back. Twenty feet away two Control Station workers chased them down. Bursting through a door, Trish and Jason flew down some stairs, but Sarah halted at the top.

'What are you doing?!' Trish screamed at her, slowing down.

'Keep going!' Sarah stepped back behind the door.

Moments later the two men came steaming through and Sarah stuck out a leg, sending both of them tumbling down the stairs. Jumping down after them, Sarah bypassed the groaning bodies by vaulting over the handrail, and rushed to catch up to her friends who were now out of sight.

Corridors and doors flashed past as she counted down the seconds in her mind. She was in the shuttle bay. The platform was ahead. She could see Jason and Trish clambering into the air-shuttle.

Sarah reached the steps, climbed up them and ran along to the front of the vehicle to jump into a seat next to Trish. The back of her helmet clicked onto the headrest just as the safety frame rose up out of the floor to secure her in place. Her helmet's visor lowered, its internal ice blue digital displays blazing to life.

'Abort this launch immediately,' a voice said through the shuttle bay's speaker system. 'You are in violation of SED procedures, stand down!'

'Why can't they abort the launch?' Sarah noticed the shuttle bay floor had only reached half way.

Trish held up a circuit board. 'Because I disabled it.'

Sarah smiled, but the joy was short-lived as she could see through the Command Centre's windows that the soldiers had arrived. The air-shuttle shuddered and rose up into the air. Sirens continued to wail and beacons flashed as the track rose up from below, scraping against the floor as it continued to retract. Sparks showered down as the two mechanisms screeched against one another. With Sarah praying that the system wouldn't fail, the shuttle moved to intercept the rails, making her realise Trish must have set the shuttle to launch from the top tier. The shuttle dropped down so it connected to the track beneath, which had now cleared the floor, its passengers in an upright position.

'Sarah, this is Dresden Locke,' a voice said through her helmet. 'Stop this launch at once!'

Sarah looked up to see Locke standing in the Control Station and by his side, Riley.

The windshield of the air-shuttle glided into place as a countdown timer appeared on her visor. *T minus fifteen seconds,* she told herself.

'Sarah,' Riley's voice said, 'listen to me, the soldiers have just been authorised to shoot, please don't do this, abort while you still can!'

Sarah didn't respond as gunfire tore into the Control Station's toughened windows. The transparent surfaces blurred into opacity as the bullets destroyed their integrity.

'Ten seconds,' Jason said.

The shuttle moved forwards to suspend them over the abyss.

The soldiers were now kicking and breaking the fractured glass with the butts of their rifles.

'Five seconds!' Jason said.

Sarah watched as the windows fell outwards into the shuttle bay and the countdown timer sank to three – two – bullets rained down around them – one.

'Launch!' Jason shouted and the air-shuttle plummeted into the Earth.

CHAPTER FIFTY-EIGHT

A MASSIVE EXPLOSION detonated above them as they fell, a fireball hunting them down the shaft like the flaming claws of a demonic beast. Sarah heard Trish scream while the air-shuttle spiralled downwards, the flames licking at its sides before they outran its Promethean grasp. Wondering what had caused such a catastrophic eruption, Sarah watched the vehicle's main beams powering up to light the tunnel ahead.

Her head rattled against the headrest as their speed increased, before their track diverged from those around it. Rock walls flashed past, the track twisting and turning at dizzying angles, and Sarah's visor displayed a message indicating rocket propulsion was imminent. She braced herself as the burn initiated, thrusting her back into the seat. Ten seconds passed followed by another rocket burn of the same duration. Roaring wind tore at the three friends as yet another rocket fired, propelling them forwards over four hundred miles an hour in the blink of an eye and sending the G-force dial lurching up. The track dipped and weaved, making Sarah close her eyes before a final explosion increased their velocity even further.

Hitting a straight piece of track the air-shuttle, currently inverted, angled upwards at twenty degrees, their acceleration still climbing. An alarm sounded inside Sarah's helmet.

'Warning!' a computerised voice said. 'Unrecognised launch protocols detected. Maximum track velocity exceeded. Deploying emergency brakes.'

Sarah cracked open an eye to see the same message flashing on her visor while the skin on her face rippled backwards under the increasing speed. A jolt ran through the vehicle as the brakes engaged. A high pitch screech slowed them for a few seconds before a loud bang followed by something large and heavy flying past their heads caused the shuttle to surge forwards again.

'Malfunction! Emergency braking system failure. SED Control Station offline. Failsafe protocols unavailable. Manual activation required.'

At the end of Sarah's armrest a panel opened and a joystick emerged. Sarah reached for it but a twist in the track, bringing them upright, forced her hand back down before another rocket fired powering them beyond six – and then seven – hundred miles an hour. A strange air pocket formed on the front of the shuttle's nosecone before a sonic boom shattered the air around them, announcing they'd just broken the sound barrier.

Sarah's vision faded to grey and narrowed. Her body felt like she'd gained a thousand pounds. The G-force dial on her visor crept up still further. The track dipped down and Sarah's vision blacked out, her consciousness slipping. The rockets finally depleted, the shuttle slowed. Sarah's vision returned and she managed to inch her fingers onto the joystick as they shot through the interior of Sanctuary Proper faster than a speeding bullet. Using all the effort she could muster, she pulled the stick back. Small rockets fired on the front of the shuttle impeding them further before the track entered another spiral. Gradually their speed dropped below three hundred miles an hour and a message appeared warning them of imminent track transition.

A transparent sheath shrouded the air-shuttle before the vehicle detached from its rails to continue its journey on a cushion of air through a translucent tunnel. With the journey far from over, Sarah realised this track went much further than the one she'd previously ridden.

They fell once more like a stone out of the sky, dropping towards the centre of the Earth. More twists and turns followed, jarring her to the core until their trajectory levelled out. With the near death experience leaving her shaken, Sarah concentrated on their surroundings, lit up by the shuttle's inexorable advance. Ancient buildings loomed at the edges of perception, some merely large, others monumentally colossal, their ghostly forms cutting stark and unusual shapes as the shuttle passed them by, dressing them in moving shadows with its lights. These lost treasures had lain hidden for untold millennia, unbeknownst to humanity's ancestors evolving on the surface's shores. They were all untouched by man, their secrets held close and their tales lost to time's distant and fickle past.

They slowed further before the tube in which they travelled sank beneath a torrent of water, a great river. Amazed by this transition, Sarah's eyes were drawn to fantastical architecture and long submerged statues, their obscure and often disintegrating beauty exposed as they drifted past, an underwater world briefly glimpsed but one forever remembered.

Their travel slowed yet further, the tunnel emerging from calmer waters. An opening folded back on the shuttle's outer skin and their speed dropped off to bring them cruising into a deserted manmade structure, an SED outpost and their journey's end. Running alongside a platform, much like those in a train station, the air-shuttle glided to a stop.

A small click from near the back of Sarah's head announced her helmet had released from the headrest and the frame securing her in place retracted into the vehicle's floor. Sarah sat for a moment in an attempt to regain her composure and to keep down the contents of her stomach, a plan which, so far, seemed to be working. A nearby retching noise made her turn to see that Jason wasn't adhering to such a strategy. He leaned over the side of the shuttle, ridding himself of his last meal. Trish sat silently next to her, slumped forwards in her seat.

'Trish, you okay?' Sarah nudged her friend with a hand.

She didn't respond.

'Trish?' Sarah pulled her friend upright, sending her helmet clonking back against the headrest.

'Huh?' Trish's eyes popped open. 'Is it over?'

'Yeah.'

'I think I passed out. I thought we were going to come off the track.'

Sarah stood up, feeling giddy. 'We nearly did, something went badly wrong.'

'That's a bloody understatement.' Jason wiped the back of his sleeve across his mouth. 'I nearly crapped my damn pants. In fact—' He looked down at himself.

Trish and Sarah looked at him in dismayed disgust while he wriggled his hips about.

'Nope, false alarm, I'm all clear.'

'Perhaps we entered the wrong parameters,' Trish said, to Sarah as they exited the shuttle.

'But what was that explosion at the start?' Sarah replied. 'That definitely wasn't normal.'

'Err, yeah, about that,' Jason said, 'that was probably my fault.'

Sarah looked at him, puzzled.

'What did you do?' Trish asked in resignation.

'Well, you know you told me you'd disabled the console so they couldn't follow us?'

Trish looked wary. 'Yes.'

'Well I kinda – didn't believe you.'

Trish's eyes narrowed. 'I see.'

'So you did what?' Sarah said.

'So I attached a shaped charge to the launch platform and activated it as we fell.'

'You did what!' Trish said. 'You nearly blew us all up!'

'Yeah, I might have detonated it too soon.' He grinned. 'But that's hindsight for you.'

'You idiot! You fucking idiot!' Trish whacked him round the head.

'Ow! I'm sorry, okay!'

Sarah shook her head and went to retrieve their gear from the rear of the shuttle while Trish continued to rail at him.

Jason, trying to escape Trish's wrath, soon came to join Sarah and the verbal tirade came with him.

'Of all the crazy things you've done, this takes the prize. My sister's dog has more sense than you and it's dead!'

Jason looked thoughtful. 'Wasn't that dog really clever, though, butt ugly, but clever, it won prizes for playing the piano didn't it?'

Trish glared at him 'That was my niece. And no the dog wasn't clever; it liked to chase cars and got run over. The dog was dumb, perhaps the dumbest dog ever, but compared to you it's friggin' Einstein!'

'If you say so, but come on, you must admit, just disabling their console wouldn't have kept them at bay for long; they'd have repaired that quick-time. At least with my way we'll have a good head start. By the time they rebuild the track we'll be long gone.'

'He does have a point,' Sarah said.

Trish gave her a hot stare.

'Well he does,' she said in answer to her friend's expression.

'You could have told me,' Trish said to Jason.

'I didn't think you'd go along with it, you'd have started panicking.'

'With good reason,' Trish said, 'you nearly killed us!'

'True, but I didn't, did I?'

'That's not the point.'

'Pretty much is,' he told her. 'And besides, you nearly killed us by entering the wrong parameters for the launch, so that makes us even and you a hypocrite.'

'Piss off, Jason,' Trish said, the argument taking a serious turn.

'Perhaps it's the dog that has more sense than you.' Jason's tone was scathing. 'One thing's for sure, being a squashed dead dog, it's gotta be better looking.'

Enraged, Trish fronted up to him. 'Are all Welsh men ugly, cowardly pricks, or is it just you?'

'Are all London women cold-hearted vicious cows that look like they've got a cork stuck up their arse? Oh no – wait, that *is* just you!'

Sarah banged the side of the shuttle. 'Shut up! You're acting like children. Stop bickering and grow up! We need to get going; we have a finite amount of supplies. We've got out of the USSB and we have the pendant, but the hard part's still to come; we need to concentrate and get serious. What's done is done. We need to pull together and press on.'

Trish folded her arms. 'As soon as we get to the surface I'm getting as far away from him as possible.'

'Likewise,' Jason said, earning himself an evil stare from Trish.

'I don't know what's with you two,' Sarah said, 'but now is definitely not the time. When we get to the surface you both do what you have to do, but right now, right here, we're in a dangerous, unknown environment with no back-up and no idea of what lies ahead. If we don't work together as a team we're as good as dead.'

'And if help did come,' Jason said, 'it'd be to throw us in prison.'

Sarah held out an upturned hand between them. 'Correct. So right now we're a team, a unit, working and thinking as one, we need to put away our petty differences, okay?'

Jason put his hand on hers and clasped it. 'Okay.'

Sarah looked to her friend. 'Trish?'

'Okay,' she said reluctantly, placing her hand on Jason's.

'Good.' Sarah bound them together with her remaining hand and then stared at them with stern eyes, her face grim. 'Now let's get the fuck out of here.'

CHAPTER FIFTY-NINE

UNSEEN DROPLETS CASCADED down into shallow stagnant pools of inky blackness, their steady plip-plopping mournful trill of solitude echoing through the cracked and decaying chamber system of Sanctuary Proper. A bitter taste of acidic minerals cajoled the senses of those travelling along the paths of a long forgotten civilisation, prehistoric and even – prehuman.

Such was the age of the area in which they trod, Sarah found it hard to comprehend the sheer enormity of the time that had passed since these places had last been inhabited. Even Sanctuary's latterly constructed architectural creations were tens of thousands of years older than humanity's first attempts at a centralised existence. To try to piece together a history of this place would take a hundred, a thousand, lifetimes, maybe more. The prospect of such an undertaking excited Sarah, as did the work being done by the SED. Everything down here was a marvel, but where before it had been a ray of light stimulating her with an elixir of intoxicating energy, it now elicited anger; a simmering fury reignited ten-fold since seeing her map on display in the military's secret vault.

If she'd been determined to reveal the existence of Homo gigantis – the Anakim – to the world before entering Sanctuary, it was nothing to how she felt as she tried to exit it. This single-minded goal had been the sole reason she'd decided to retrieve the orb. Despite its power to immobilise and in Cora's case, kill, the Anakim device was proof positive of the lost race. On its own it was powerful, but alongside the other evidence they'd managed to collect, including her recently acquired artefacts, it was undeniable, unequivocal and definitely one hundred per cent box office. If she wanted to court worldwide attention and maintain it, then she had everything she needed and more.

'Watch it!' Trish's voice sang out into the chamber, bringing Sarah back from her reverie.

'Then don't stand in the bloody way then!' Jason reversed the bright yellow, remote-operated, all-terrain supply vehicle so he could manoeuvre it around Trish, who stood in its path. 'This thing isn't as easy to control as it looks,' he added.

'I'm still getting used to seeing through this helmet's visor,' Trish said, aggrieved.

Sarah stopped and turned. 'Just stick to the second setting on the third spectrum combination, it's the best for seeing in the dark. We need to conserve battery life, so no torches unless absolutely necessary.'

'Can I at least turn the lights on this thing on while I get used to controlling it?' he asked.

'They call it the Centipede,' she told him. The nickname was apt for the sizeable twenty-wheeled machine which moved over rough terrain much like a multi-legged insect, hugging the surface but able to bend its spine at ninety degree angles.

'It can be called bloody Humphrey sodding Bogart for all I care, if I can't tell where the damn thing's headed it's gonna end up at the bottom of a crevasse, along with all our food and water.'

'Okay, switch them on,' she said, 'but be frugal.'

'I'll give you frugal,' Sarah heard him mumble as she walked off.

Declining to comment, Sarah saw the twin lights on the Centipede blaze forth, altering the colour of the terrain ahead through her visor's enhanced display. Pressing a button on the side of her helmet, she loaded the next section of the Deep Reach map on her visor. A graphical representation of their current position appeared, the image incorporating a plotted course to the next waypoint beacon previously laid down by the team that had first found the Anakim temple complex to which they headed.

Now an hour out from the SED outpost, their progress was slow, but when Trish and Jason had properly acclimatised to the new equipment Sarah expected them to be able to pick up the pace. Looking at the maps, she deduced they should be able to utilise the Centipede for almost half the journey before they needed to unload the aerial drone, the UAV the perfect companion when attempting to ferry supplies over the deep fissures that occurred throughout Sanctuary Proper.

It was late afternoon when Sarah called a break to proceedings, all of them in agreement to make camp for the night due to the fact that they'd all been up for over thirty-six hours. With weary limbs resting on uncomfortable ground, Sarah was left to her own thoughts while Trish and Jason sat in stony silence nearby. Usually such an uncomfortable atmosphere would have bothered Sarah, but her current dark mood meant she paid it no heed. Also, her face throbbed painfully from the brutal impact dealt by Cora back at the USSB. No longer wearing her Deep Reach headgear, Sarah reached up and gingerly touched the end of her nose. According to Trish it hadn't been knocked out of shape, but that didn't make it hurt any less. She withdrew her fingers, the area still far too sensitive to accept any further investigation.

With her thoughts returning to process recent events, the ancient dark wood they'd retrieved from close by sparked and crackled within the small campfire, its dense, sweet-smelling smoke drifting on a silken breeze. The occasional pop and sizzle punctuated the quiet as the burning fuel ran low, the embers mimicking volcanic lava by glowing a deep, bright orange.

'It's strange how no one was waiting for us,' Jason said quietly, breaking the silence, 'at the SED outpost I mean.'

Sarah looked over at him. 'They couldn't have been expecting any shuttles to come in and must have returned to the SED.'

'We were lucky,' Trish said.

Jason nodded while Sarah murmured her agreement.

The light of the fire grew lower still, the shadows it cast long and still, no longer moved by flickering flames. No one said anything for another minute until Jason spoke again.

'What happened to that woman, Sarah? The one in the Control Station.'

Sarah saw Trish looking at her too, waiting for an answer.

'That was Cora,' she said after a lengthy pause.

'Riley's second in command?' He sounded surprised.

Sarah nodded, recalling the events from the previous night. 'I found something in the military vaults. At first I couldn't believe or accept what I saw—'

'Which was?' Trish said, when Sarah failed to continue.

'One of the maps that I last saw in my mother's house.' She stared into the fire.

Jason and Trish swapped looks. 'Are you sure?' he asked.

'After seeing it, I lost the plot,' she continued, ignoring his question. 'I tried to take an Anakim shield, but my pendant activated it and some kind of energy wave blew out all the circuitry in the area, cutting off my escape route.'

Trish looked shocked. 'How did you get out?'

'Blind luck. I found an emergency exit and managed to get into the military's laboratory complex as all the security systems were also fried. I wandered around looking for a way out, but ended up in some top secret area and inside I found this—'

She opened a side pocket on her trouser leg and withdrew a chunk of white cloth, which she opened out to reveal the orb within.

Trish and Jason leaned forward to look at it.

'What is it?' Jason asked.

'I have no idea, but when I held it I had a seizure and blacked out. And when Cora held it – well – you saw the results.'

'You should have left it behind.' Trish eyed the twelve-sided object with fear, its metal sheen glinting darkly in the subdued light.

'Shouldn't you put it in something a bit more secure?' Jason said.

Sarah gazed at it. 'It's fine as it is. It saved my life.'

'After almost killing you,' Trish said.

Sarah didn't reply, her mind returning to Riley. How could she have been so wrong about him? He'd seemed so – perfect. He'd made her happy, but he was just like everyone else in the USSB, devious, manipulative or skilled at turning a blind eye. He was part of the very fabric of the SED and the military operation that oversaw it. Everything about that place reeked of hypocrisy. They weren't there to secure knowledge for the rest of mankind; they were there to make sure it never reached the light of day. *And to think I considered staying there with him*, she thought. Staying and living amongst those who were willing to murder innocents on the surface in order to protect their secret and expand their knowledge of the Anakim. The whole place stank to high heaven and the guilt she'd felt about taking his card and going behind his back now seemed ludicrous to her, obscene in its naivety. Of course part of her still ached for Riley's embrace, a part of her bereft at his passing from her life, but she knew such feelings would pass – they always did.

The evening drifted on and Trish and Jason chatted to one another in hushed tones, perhaps reconciling whatever problems existed between them. Eventually they grew silent, falling asleep to leave Sarah alone with her thoughts, the small orb placed before her. She reached out a hand to caress its surface, her touch lingering for a moment before she withdrew it.

Her eyes drooped closed, her breathing becoming steady and relaxed as sleep took her. In her dreams images of the map returned to haunt her and the smell of the nearby campfire induced the nightmare that still lurked in the recesses of her mind. Deeper and deeper she fell, down into a darkness that refused to relinquish her from its eternal embrace. Fire blossomed into being, the torment once again taking hold, her mother's dying cries searing pain into her soul.

EPILOGUE

'WHERE ARE WE AGAIN,' Jason asked, 'west or north of the USSB?'

'South,' Sarah said, surveying the scene ahead with her Deep Reach helmet's visor, Trish and Jason by her side.

'This place is friggin' awesome,' he said, marvelling at the ancient crumbling ruins that surrounded them, the immense vestiges of the Anakim's long hidden legacy undeniable in their timeless majesty.

Sarah pressed another button on her helmet. 'You're not wrong.'

Trish was similarly awestruck. 'I can't believe what I'm seeing.'

'Believe it, and this is only the beginning, a tiny fraction of what's still to be explored.'

Jason shook his head. 'Fantastic.'

'We should get moving,' Sarah told them, 'otherwise we'll never get to those Anakim transportation devices.'

'Two days in,' Trish said, 'two weeks to go.'

'It's like death by chocolate,' Jason said, 'but this is death by archaeological architecture.'

'Come on.' Sarah moved off into the vast chamber ahead, its every surface bristling with weird and wonderful structures of millennia past.

Trish, now in control of the Centipede, followed behind, the yellow multi-wheeled supply vehicle by her side, its wheels kicking up dust and soil as its lights blazed a trail ahead.

Jason looked behind them, something catching his eye. He pressed a button on his helmet to activate the communication system. 'Hey guys, did any of you just see that?'

'See what?' Sarah's voice came back through his helmet's speakers.

'I thought I saw something back here.'

'Like what?' Trish's voice broke up slightly as she moved further away from him.

'I'm not sure; like a light?'

'Stop sodding about,' Sarah said, you're getting left behind.'

'Your eyes will play tricks on you down here,' Trish told him, 'it's a bit spooky.'

Jason searched into the black void with his visor and flicked through its various spectral fields. 'Hmm, I guess so.' He turned round to see Trish and Sarah were now a few hundred feet away. 'Hey! Wait for me!'

The two women slowed and then stopped to wait for him to catch up.

'Come on, lard arse, we haven't got all day.' Sarah cuffed him round the head as he rejoined them.

'Hey, did I show you these cool blue stones I found yesterday?' Jason said, as the three of them started off once more.

Sarah shook her head. 'Nope.'

'They're really cool.' Jason held them out for them to see. 'Check it out, they glow really bright in the dark.'

Trish peered at the luminous objects cradled in the palm of his hand. 'They look radioactive.'

'Nah, don't be silly,' he said, 'they're beautiful, harmless, probably worth a fortune on the surface.'

'Really.' Trish appeared unconvinced.

'Definitely, you could be walking along with a millionaire.'

'Or an idiot,' Sarah said.

'Yes, that's also a possibility,' Jason conceded, laughing, the infectious sound lightening the mood that had hung over them since they'd left the USSB.

The three friends continued to talk and joke as their small forms disappeared into the immensity of Sanctuary, their voices and laughter floating off and fading away into the darkness.

♦

Sometime later, after the companions had vanished from view, the area where Jason had been standing gradually lit up with a bright, shimmering, blue-green light that appeared to hang suspended just off the ground. A noise, like metal scraping on rock, accompanied this ethereal phenomenon and on the edge of perception a curious clicking sound could be heard, growing steadily louder with each passing moment.

A large, viscous lump of inky, black mucus slipped to the floor and a deep snarling growl transformed into a terrifying, bloodcurdling screech, its reverberations echoing out into the pitch-black of the ancient Anakim structure that would be forever known as ... Sanctuary.

Ancient Origins: Dark Descent is continued in ...

Ancient Origins: Let There Be Light
(Book Three of *Ancient Origins*)

available at
amazon

https://geni.us/lettherebelight

It is extremely helpful to have honest reviews, you can be taken to your relevant Amazon site by using this link:

https://geni.us/darkdescentreview

ALSO BY ROBERT STOREY

Ancient Origins: Revelations

(Book One of *Ancient Origins*)

Ancient Origins: Dark Descent

(Book Two of *Ancient Origins*)

Ancient Origins: Let There Be Light

(Book Three of *Ancient Origins*)

Ancient Origins: Genesis

(Book Four of *Ancient Origins*)

Ancient Origins: The Tenth Protocol

(Book Five of *Ancient Origins*)

Ancient Origins: The Lost Prophet

(Book Six of *Ancient Origins*)

https://geni.us/robertstorey

ABOUT THE AUTHOR

Robert Storey's first published novel is *2040: Revelations* This became book one in his Ancient Origins series and was renamed Ancient Origins: Revelations in September 2016. He went on to complete the six books series in 2018.

A year later Robert died at the age of 43.

For more information about Robert and his work, please visit:

fuse-books.com/robertstorey

APPENDIX A

GMRC CIVILIAN PERSONNEL

Professor George Steiner

Director General of GMRC Subterranean Programme
Nationality: American
GMRC Clearance – Level 10 Alpha
Designation – Civilian
Deployment: GMRC Directorate (Oversight) / Transient
GMRC Division: Subterranean Programme
Skill set:
Subterranean structural engineering
Management and leadership
Planning, design and development
Mathematical modelling and forecasting
Computer programming and software development

Malcolm Joiner

Director of U.S. and GMRC Intelligence
Nationality: American
GMRC Clearance – Level 10 Alpha
Designation – Civilian
Deployment: GMRC Directorate / Transient
GMRC Division: Intelligence Division
Skill set:
Espionage and covert intervention
Intelligence gathering, restriction and dissemination
Information pathways / Management and leadership
Psychological warfare

Richard Goodwin

GMRC Subterranean Base Director
Nationality: American

GMRC Clearance – Level 9 Alpha
Designation – Civilian
Deployment: U.S.S.B. Steadfast [U.S.S.B. Sanctuary – unofficial]
GMRC Division: Subterranean Programme
Skill set:
Management and leadership / Planning, design and development

Dr. Kara Vandervoort
Ecosystem Director
Nationality: South African
GMRC Clearance – Level 8 Alpha
Designation – Civilian
Deployment: U.S.S.B. Steadfast
GMRC Division: Subterranean Programme
Skill set:
Biomechanical engineering / Management / Data analysis

Special Agent Myers
CIA Agent and GMRC Intelligence Operative
CIA Special Operations Group (SOG)
Nationality: American
GMRC Clearance – Level 9 Delta
Designation – Civilian
Deployment: Transient
GMRC Division: Intelligence Division
Skill set:
Covert military intervention / Leadership / Strategic planning
Close quarters and unarmed combat

Nathan Bryant
GMRC Subterranean Facility Coordinator
Nationality: American
Global Acquisitions and Intelligence Liaison
GMRC Clearance – Level 10 Beta
Designation – Civilian

Deployment: GMRC Oversight / Transient
GMRC Division: Subterranean Programme
Skill set:
Logistics / Management / Negotiation, arbitration and presentation
Linguistics, communication and translation

Sophie Merchant
Primary Aide to Professor Steiner
Nationality: American
GMRC Clearance – Level 7 beta
Designation – Civilian
Deployment: GMRC Oversight / Transient
GMRC Division: Subterranean Programme
Skill set:
Organisation and presentation
Linguistics, communication and translation

Franz Veber
GMRC Subterranean Base Director
Nationality: German
GMRC Clearance – Level 2 delta
Designation – Civilian
Deployment: E.U.S.B. Deutschland
GMRC Division: Subterranean Programme
Skill set:
Security and overt surveillance

Grant Debden
Primary Aide to Malcolm Joiner
Nationality: American
GMRC Clearance – Level 8 delta
Designation – Civilian
Deployment: Transient
GMRC Division: Intelligence Division

Skill set:
Organisation and presentation / Information pathways
Linguistics, communication and translation
Intelligence gathering, restriction and dissemination

Duncan Sanderfield

Population Control Manager
Nationality: American
GMRC Clearance – Level 8 alpha
Designation – Civilian
Deployment: GMRC HQ, New York
GMRC Division: Population Control
Skill set:
Organisation and presentation / Social engineering
Trend analysis and information pathways

Petra Villalobos

Smithsonian Museum of Sanctuary Vaults Officer
Nationality: American
GMRC Clearance – Level 7 alpha
Designation – Civilian
Deployment: U.S.S.B. Sanctuary
GMRC Division: Subterranean Programme
Skill set:
Administration and logistics / Security and overt surveillance

Dagmar Sørensen

Director of GMRC Research & Development
Nationality: Norwegian
GMRC Clearance – Level 10 Alpha
Designation – Civilian
Deployment: GMRC Directorate / Transient
GMRC Division: Research and Development
Skill set:
Scientific exploration and advance

Black project development and integration
(Special access programmes: acknowledged and unacknowledged)
Information pathways / Management and leadership

Shen Zhǔ Rèn

Acting Director General of GMRC Subterranean Programme & Subterranean Base Director
Nationality: Chinese
GMRC Clearance – Level 10 Delta
Designation – Civilian
Deployment: GMRC Directorate / P.R.C.S.B. Oversight / Transient
GMRC Division: Subterranean Programme
Skill set:
Management and leadership / Structural engineering
Planning, design and development

APPENDIX B

S.E.D. PERSONNEL

Deployment: U.S.S.B. Sanctuary
Designation: GMRC Civilian

Riley Orton
Deep Reach Team Leader
Team: Alpha Six
Nationality: American
Profession: Explorer

Dresden Locke
S.E.D. Facility Commander
Nationality: American
Profession: Explorer

Cora Islanovich
Deep Reach Deputy Team Leader
Team: Alpha Six
Nationality: American
Profession: Explorer

Jefferson Church
Deep Reach Team Member
Team: Alpha Six
Nationality: American
Profession: Explorer & Lead Archaeologist

Anne-Marie Wingmore-Bates
S.E.D. Administrator
Nationality: American
Profession: Administrator

APPENDIX C

U.S. MILITARY PERSONNEL

Colonel Samson

United States Army SFSD Brigade Commander
Special Forces Subterranean Detachment
(Codename: Terra Force)
Nationality: American
GMRC Clearance – Level 8 Alpha
Designation: Military – Special Forces
Deployment: U.S.S.B. Steadfast
(Pseudonym: Colonel Hemmingway)
Skill set:
Overt military action / Sniper tactics and marksmanship
Covert military intervention and counter-insurgency
Close quarters and unarmed combat
Leadership and strategic planning
Subterranean warfare / Subterranean transit

Sergeant Alvarez

United States Army Decontamination Team Staff Sergeant
Nationality: American
GMRC Clearance – Level 5 Alpha
Designation – Military
Deployment: U.S.S.B. Sanctuary
Skill set:
Overt military action / Unarmed combat

Corporal Walker

United States Army Decontamination Team
Nationality: American
GMRC Clearance – Level 5 Beta
Designation: Military

Deployment: U.S.S.B. Sanctuary
Skill set:
Overt military action / Unarmed combat

Sergeant Rogers
United States Army Ordnance Corps
Nationality: American
Deployment: U.S. Army Barracks, St. George, Utah
Skill set:
Overt military action / Unarmed combat / Logistics

Captain Williams
United States Army SFSD
Special Forces Subterranean Detachment
(Codename: Terra Force)
Nationality: American
GMRC Clearance – Level 9 delta (Special Access Personnel)
Designation: Military – Special Forces
Deployment: U.S.S.B. Sanctuary (Scientific Laboratory Complex)
Skill set:
Overt military action / Multi terrain warfare
Covert military intervention and counter-insurgency
Close quarters and unarmed combat
Subterranean warfare

Colonel Weybridge
United States Army Brigade Commander
Nationality: American
GMRC Clearance – Level 8 Beta
Designation: Military
Deployment: U.S.S.B. Steadfast
Skill set:
Overt military action
Counter-insurgency and unarmed combat
Leadership, logistics and strategic planning

Brigadier General Ellwood

United States Army Commanding General
(Division Commander)
Nationality: American
GMRC Clearance – Level 10 Delta
Designation – Military
Deployment: U.S.S.B. Sanctuary
Skill set:
Overt military action / Subterranean warfare
Covert military action and unarmed combat
Leadership, logistics and strategic planning

General Donovan

Chief of the National Guard Bureau (CNGB)
Designation – Military / Department of Defense
Deployment: Member of the Joint Chiefs of Staff
Nationality: American
Skill set:
Overt military action and unarmed combat
Leadership, logistics and strategic planning
Communication, diplomacy and advisory guidance

APPENDIX D

ARCHAEOLOGISTS

Sarah Elizabeth Morgan

Nationality: English

Profession: Archaeologist, Anthropologist

Current location: USSB Sanctuary

Trish Brook

Nationality: English

Profession: Archaeologist

Current location: USSB Sanctuary

Jason Reece

Nationality: Welsh

Profession: Archaeologist

Current location: USSB Sanctuary

APPENDIX E

ALBUQUERQUE RESIDENTS

Rebecca

Nationality: American
Profession: Developmental disability/social worker
Current location: Sanctuary Proper

Joseph

Nationality: American
Mentally handicapped man
Current location: Sanctuary Proper

Susan

Nationality: American
Mentally handicapped woman
Current location: Sanctuary Proper

Julie

Nationality: American
Profession: Developmental disability/social worker
Current location: Sanctuary Proper

Arianna

Nationality: American
Profession: Developmental disability/social worker
Current location: Sanctuary Proper

APPENDIX F

NASA ASTRONAUTS

Tyler Magnusson

Pilot Commander
Nationality: American
Rank: Commander
NASA Clearance Level: AMBER 1 (Segregated Personnel)
Deployment: U.S.S.S. Orbiter One

Ivan Sikorsky

Payload Commander
Nationality: American
Rank: Lieutenant Commander
NASA Clearance Level: AMBER 1 (Segregated Personnel)
Deployment: U.S.S.S. Orbiter One

Bo Heidfield

Space Station Commander
Nationality: American
Rank: Captain
NASA Clearance Level: AMBER 1 (Segregated Personnel)
Deployment: U.S.S.S. Archimedes

APPENDIX G

DARKLIGHT PERSONNEL

Commander Hilt

Darklight Officer

Nationality: American

GMRC Clearance – Level 8 Delta

Designation – Civilian / Private Contractor

Deployment: Classified

Current location: Sanctuary Proper

Skill set:

Overt military action / Multi terrain warfare

Covert military intervention / Sniper tactics and marksmanship

Hostage retrieval and counter terrorism

Close quarters and unarmed combat

Leadership and management / Strategic planning / Reconnaissance

Major Offiah

Darklight Officer

Nationality: Nigerian

GMRC Clearance – Level 7 Alpha

Designation – Civilian / Private Contractor

Deployment: Classified

Current location: Sanctuary Proper

Skill set:

Overt military action / Multi terrain warfare / Leadership

Covert military intervention / Close quarters and unarmed combat

Hostage retrieval and counter terrorism / Strategic planning

Lieutenant Manaus

Darklight Officer

Nationality: Brazilian
GMRC Clearance – Level 7 Gamma
Designation – Civilian / Private Contractor
Deployment: Classified
Current location: Sanctuary Proper
Skill set:
Overt military action / Multi terrain warfare / Reconnaissance
Covert military intervention / Close quarters and unarmed combat

Corporal Dixon

Darklight Soldier
Nationality: American
GMRC Clearance – Level 7 Delta
Designation – Civilian / Private Contractor
Deployment: Classified
Current location: Sanctuary Proper
Skill set:
Overt military action / Multi terrain warfare
Covert military intervention / Reconnaissance

Sergeant Henderson

Darklight Soldier
Nationality: American
GMRC Clearance – Level 7 Delta
Designation – Civilian / Private Contractor
Deployment: Classified
Current location: Sanctuary Proper
Skill set:
Overt military action / Multi terrain warfare
Covert military intervention / Reconnaissance

Captain Iwamoto

Darklight Officer
Nationality: Japanese

GMRC Clearance – Level 7 Beta

Designation – Civilian / Private Contractor

Deployment: Classified

Current location: USSB Steadfast

Skill set:

Overt military action / Multi terrain warfare / Reconnaissance

Covert military intervention / Close quarters and unarmed combat

Leadership and strategic planning

APPENDIX H

OTHER PERSONS

Jessica Klein

BBC Newsreader and TV Presenter
Nationality: English
Profession: Journalist
Relatives: Daniela & Victoria (daughters) / Evan (husband)
(Pseudonym: Eliza Sterling)

Martin West

Television Producer for BBC's Worldwide News Service
Nationality: English
Profession: Producer / Broadcaster

Eric Wolf

Computer Hacker
Nationality: German
(Pseudonym: *Das Gespenst*, the self-proclaimed Ghost)

Bic / Da Muss Ich

Computer Hacker / Cyber Terrorist
Nationality: Unknown
(Pseudonyms: DMI / *Da Muss Ich* / Because I Can /
Deforcement Insidious / D'Force / Elusive D / Oyakata / B.I.C.)

Kuruk

Native American Child
Nationality: American / Jicarilla Apache
Relative: Norroso (father)

Norroso

Native American

Nationality: American / Jicarilla Apache
Relative: Kuruk (son)
Profession: Rancher

Brett Taylor

FBI Special Agent
Nationality: American
Profession: Federal Agent

Patrick Flynn

FBI Director
Nationality: American
Profession: Federal Agent

Evan

Jessica Klein's Husband
Nationality: English
Relatives: Daniela & Victoria (daughters)

James Ashford

BBC News Cameraman
Nationality: English
Profession: Audio Visual Engineer

Keira Jones

BBC News correspondent
Nationality: English
Profession: Journalist

Marianne Gobrinsky

CNN Reporter (Helicopter)
Nationality: American
Profession: Journalist

Bill Brightman

CNN News Anchor
Nationality: American
Profession: Journalist / TV presenter

Lucy Marshall
Nightclub VIP Cloakroom Clerk
Nationality: American
Place of work: The Asteroid Club

Asilina Salerno
Supermodel
Nationality: Italian
Profession: Model / Actress / Singer

Atalanta Varushkin
Supermodel
Nationality: Ukrainian
Profession: Model / Entrepreneur

APPENDIX I

ORGANISATIONS

BBC (British Broadcasting Corporation) – Television, radio and multimedia network broadcaster operating in the United Kingdom and globally / www.bbc.co.uk

CNN (Cable News Network) – American television news channel / www.cnn.com

Fox News Channel (FNC) – American television news channel / www.foxnews.com

CTV News – Division of CTV Television Network, Canadian television news channel / www.ctvnews.ca

United Nations (UN) – International organisation for law, security, human & civil rights, political freedom and world peace / www.un.org

NASA – The National Aeronautics and Space Administration (civilian space agency of the United States government) / www.nasa.gov

CNSA – The China National Space Administration (civilian space agency of the People's Republic of China) / www.cnsa.gov.cn

GMRC (Global Meteor Response Council) – International organisation set up by the world's nations for the protection and preservation of humanity, civilisation and all life on Earth. Consisting of twenty-five divisions, the majority of the GMRC's policies and actions are carried out by a core of twelve divisions (see table below). Each of these divisions operates under one or two of the following three criteria:

PUBLIC: Activities disclosed to society
COVERT: Activities not disclosed to society
CLASSIFIED: Existence not disclosed to society

OPERATIONAL CRITERIA

GMRC DIVISON	*Public*	*Covert*	*Classified*
Subterranean Programme		•	•
Space Programme	•	•	
Research & Development		•	•
Intelligence		•	
Population Education	•	•	
Population Control		•	•
Economic Control	•	•	
Conservation	•	•	
Resource Control	•	•	
Operations & Military	•	•	
U.N. Integration	•		
Oversight	•	•	

Smithsonian Institution – World renowned collective of research centres and museums in the United States of America / www.si.edu

[Author note: I always thought the Institution was called the Smithsonian Institute, but apparently this is a common misnomer.]

Smithsonian Museum of Sanctuary (SMS) – Located in USSB Sanctuary and administered by the Smithsonian Institution, the Museum of Sanctuary is a vast resource on the extinct species, Homo giganthropsis (commonly referred to as the Anakim).

People's Arabian Militia – Middle Eastern terrorist group.

The Apocryphon – A shadowy organisation with links to the Roman Catholic Church. According to texts held within the Museum of Sanctuary, the Apocryphon may be aware the Anakim once existed.

Humanity 1 – British right-wing, extremist group with an anti GMRC agenda and affiliation to terrorist factions in the Middle East and beyond.

APPENDIX J

FACILITIES, UNITS & DESIGNATIONS

U.S.S.B. – United States Subterranean Base

U.S.S.B. Steadfast – A Class subterranean base
Footprint: circa 20 sq. miles (52 sq. km)
Height: 7,500 ft (2.3 km)
Depth from surface: 3,000 ft (0.91 km)
Deepest point from surface: 10,500 ft (2 miles / 3.21 km)
Cubic capacity: 28.7 cubic miles (119.6 km^3)
Year of build: 1996 – 2035
Population: circa 500,000

U.S.S.B. Sanctuary – A Class subterranean base
Footprint: > 314 sq. miles (813 sq. km)
Height: 21,120 ft (6.4 km)
Depth from surface: circa 10,000 ft (1.9 miles / 3.1 km)
Deepest point from surface: 31,120 ft (5.9 miles / 9.5 km)
Cubic capacity: 1,256 cubic miles (5,203 km^3)
Year of build: 2016 – ongoing
Population: circa 20 million
Motto: '*Protegere Et Conservare, Civilitatem, Humanitas Et Omnes Vitam In Terra*' ('To protect and preserve civilization, humanity and all life on earth').

Sanctuary Proper – Ancient subterranean structure
Footprint: > 20,000 sq. miles (51,800 sq. km)
Height: circa 20 to 30 miles (32km to 48km)
Depth from surface: circa 10,000 ft (1.9 miles / 3.1 km)
Deepest point from surface: circa 22 to 32 miles
Cubic capacity: 400,000 to 600,000 cubic miles
Year of build: circa 900,000 yrs B.C.

E.U.S.B. – European Union Subterranean Base

E.U.S.B. Deutschland – A Class subterranean base
Footprint: circa 40 sq. miles (104 sq. km)
Height: 8,500 ft (2.6 km)
Depth from surface: 2,500 ft (0.76 km)
Deepest point from surface: 11,000 ft (2.1 miles / 3.36 km)
Cubic capacity: 28.7 cubic miles (270.4 km^3)
Year of build: 2015 – ongoing
Population: circa 2,250,000

Darklight – Private security firm operating around the world and utilised by various organisations, corporations and governments. Primary client: Global Meteor Response Council.

SOG – CIA's Special Operations Group

Fort Bliss – U.S. Army post, New Mexico / Texas

United States Army Ordnance Corps – Supplies ammunition and weapons to combat troops and units.
SFSD – Special Forces Subterranean Detachment
Division of the United States Army
Member of Subterranean Command
Codename: 'Terra Force'
Active: 2013 – present
Type: Infantry / Special Forces Commandos
Motto: 'No Depth Too Difficult, No Height Too Great – Honor and Country!'
Battle cry / affirmation: 'Ooyah!'
Deployment: United States Subterranean Bases

S.E.D. (Sanctuary Exploration Division) – Founded in 1826 by the sixth President of the United States, John Quincy Adams, the SED has a unique position within USSB Sanctuary in that it has a certain amount of autonomy despite its military oversight. The reason for this independence is mainly due to two factors. Fact one, the SED was operational long before the USSB was built or the GMRC ever conceived. Fact two, the SED was also instrumental in helping the United States government and GMRC create USSB Sanctuary, their knowledge of Sanctuary Proper an invaluable resource to the subterranean engineers during the planning, design and development of the enormous multilevel, underground structure / city.

Types of Team: Mapping, Structural, Archaeological, Scientific and Deep Reach.

Motto: 'Into the dark, into the light, pioneers for life.'

Sancturian – name given to residents of USSB Sanctuary.

Project ARES – Unacknowledged Special Access Programme, or black project, utilising ancient Anakim technology. A collaborative venture between the GMRC's R&D Division, United States military and NASA.

NCO – Non-commissioned officer.

XO – Executive officer.

GMRC Directorate – Executive body ruling over the GMRC. Comprising Directors from the twelve major divisions within the GMRC, the Directorate helps to shape the council's policies and actions around the world.

Motto: '*In Veritate Scientia*' (In Truth, Knowledge).

Deep Reach – Special unit working within Sanctuary's Exploration Division (S.E.D.).

Team Alpha Six – S.E.D. Deep Reach unit.

U.S.S.S. Orbiter One – United States Space Ship. Co-funded and managed by NASA and the U.S. military. Small, modular craft designed for orbital observation and scientific research.

U.S.S.S. Archimedes – United States Space Station. Co-funded and managed by NASA and the U.S. military. Large, modular craft designed for orbital observation, scientific research and classified military applications.

APPENDIX K

WORDS, TERMS & PHRASES

Anakim – Ancient and extinct race of Hominids living on Earth circa 1.2 million to 20,000 years before present-day. Scientific name: Homo giganthropsis (unofficial: Homo gigantis). Alternative plural: Anakai.

Fubar – Fucked up beyond all recognition. Verb: to fubar, fubared.

Janfu – Joint Army-Navy fuck up (alternative: foul up), similar form of acronym to Fubar (see above).

Big Green Dick – The U.S. Army's administration, a phrase coined by disaffected soldiers when it doesn't work in their favour.

Fugly – Very ugly / unattractive, derivative of 'fucking ugly'.

SWAT – Acronym for 'Special Weapons And Tactics'.

Bum Fuck Nowhere (BFN) – A phrase used by U.S. military personnel when they're in the middle of nowhere, usually when lost or deployed to an isolated locale. Alternatives: Bum Fuck Egypt (BFE) or Big Fucking Empty.

Clusterfuck – Colourful military colloquialism describing a disastrous situation born of an accumulation of errors created by individuals or groups (politely referred to as Charlie Foxtrot).

Permunioteric era – derived from the Latin *permunio*, to fortify strongly. Permunioteric is the descriptive term for a time period in Anakim history, between seven hundred and eight hundred thousand years before present-day and when Homo giganthropsis averaged nine feet in height. Anakim remains during this time period have been found amongst heavily fortified structures, hence the name.

Ooyah – SFSD commandos' affirmation / battle cry.

Hounds – Term given to GMRC operators and intelligent computer programmes which scour the World Wide Web and the Under Web for content not deemed fit for public consumption.

The Deep Web – Term for the part of the World Wide Web not appearing on regular search engines. Unindexed content not seen by regular Internet users who frequent the Surface Web. This content can take many forms; some is benign while other content can be more sinister in origin and use, resulting from illegal activity by individuals, criminal gangs, corrupt organisations, companies and sovereign nations, although the latter may argue this is just offensive national defence conducted in their country's best interests. Also known as: Deep Net, Dark Net, Dark Web, Invisible Web, Under Web, Under Net, Hidden Web etc.

The Playground – Part of the Deep Web that is segregated from all other digital content. Able to appear and disappear on command in almost any server, anywhere, The Playground is thought to be impossible to hack, track or intercept. Many hackers believe The Playground to be an urban myth or an impossibility, while others hold it as the holy grail of the hacking world.

Circuit training Intense, gruelling exercise programme designed to increase muscle strength and endurance.

Humphrey Bogart – Iconic American actor (1899 – 1957).

Scheiße – Vulgar German word for shit, faeces or something rubbish / worthless (alternative: *Scheisse*).

Coriolis effect – A term used in physics. Definition: An effect whereby a mass moving in a rotating system experiences a force (the Coriolis force) acting perpendicular to the direction of motion and to the axis of rotation. On the earth, the effect tends to deflect moving objects to the right in the northern hemisphere and to the left in the southern and is important in the formation of cyclonic weather systems. (www.oxforddictionaries.com)

Days of Blood and Dust – Chaotic time period after the asteroid, 2011 AG5, impacted Earth in 2040. The phrase is a reflection of the dust ejected into the upper atmosphere by the meteorite's impact and the blood of the thousands of civilians around the world shed at the hands of their governments in the ensuing social unrest.

' ... *from whence it came.*' – Using '*from*' in front of '*whence*' is grammatically incorrect as '*whence*' means '*from what place, source etc.*', so using '*from*' in front of it is redundant; however, the expression is a standard and well established idiom which has been used in various distinguished texts, including the King James Bible and plays by Shakespeare. [Author note: who knew? ... put your hand down Jason.]

APPENDIX L

LOCATIONS & BUILDINGS

Sanctuary Proper – Ancient underground structure built by an extinct species of Hominid, Homo giganthropsis. Located beneath the deserts and mountains of central and northern Mexico.

Dulce – Small town located in Rio Arriba County, New Mexico, United States.

Ruins of Copán – ancient Mayan city located in the Copán Department of western Honduras.

City of Tancama – Ancient city built by the Huastecs circa 700 AD. Located near Jalpan de Serra, a small town in the state of Querétaro, Mexico.

Sierra Madre Oriental – Mountain range located in the north east of Mexico. Spans one thousand kilometres.

Teotihuacan – Pre-Columbian Mesoamerican city located near Mexico City, Mexico.

Pyramid of the Sun – Biggest structure in Teotihuacan, Mexico.

Novosibirsk, Russia – 3rd largest Russian city located in Siberia.

Tolmachevo Airport – Russian international airport for the city of Novosibirsk.

Sterkfontein Caves – Also known as the Cradle of Humanity. Located near Johannesburg, South Africa.

The Asteroid Club – Nightclub in Las Vegas, USA.

FBI Field Office, Los Angeles, California, USA – Located on Wilshire Boulevard.

Birmingham, United Kingdom – England's 2nd largest city.

Heathrow Airport, London – The main international airport for England's capital city.

City of New York, State of New York, USA – Most populous and arguably the most iconic city in the United States.

BBC Broadcasting House – Building that houses the BBC, the British Broadcasting Corporation (see Organisations Appendix).

St. George – U.S. city in the state of Utah. Bordering Arizona, St. George is located approximately eighty miles north east of Las Vegas.

Berlin – Germany's capital city.

Berlin Hauptbahnhof – Berlin's main railway station.

City of Angels – Nickname for the city of Los Angeles, California, USA.

The Golden State – Nickname for the U.S. state of California.

Smithsonian Vaults – Secure facilities used to store ancient Anakim artefacts and remains. The vaults are located inside USSB Sanctuary and beneath the Smithsonian Institution's sprawling Museum of Sanctuary.

Military Vaults – As above but with extra security and limited access.

U.S.S.B. SANCTUARY United States Military Scientific Laboratory Complex – High security facility run by the U.S. Army. Utilised by NASA and the GMRC'S R&D Division, the complex contains projects and research based on artefacts of Anakim origin.

Shuttle bay – Area inside the S.E.D. from where air-shuttles are launched.

Departure lounge – Nickname given to the staging area in the S.E.D. used by teams prior to launch.

S.E.D. Control Station – Area inside the S.E.D. Command Centre that controls the launch and return of air-shuttles into Sanctuary Proper.

S.E.D. Command Centre – Area inside the S.E.D. complex that houses the Control Station (see above), shuttle bay and the offices for high ranking S.E.D. personnel.

APPENDIX M

TECHNOLOGY, ARTEFACTS & OBJECTS

Thermal Density Reduction (T.D.R.) – Excavation technology utilised in the creation of large scale subterranean chambers.

P.S.S.B.O. – Partial self-sustaining biological organism.

Thermal sword – Darklight personal weapon.

SABRE – Synergetic Air-Breathing Rocket Engine, an engine that operates in both air-breathing and rocket modes. Developed by Reaction Engines / www.reactionengines.co.uk.

SPVU – Sediment Pulse Vibration Unit, excavation device.

VSEs – Visual Spectrum Enhancement goggles.

DPD – Digital Parchment Paper.

Computer control circlet – Digital, infrared human interface device, similar to a mouse, worn on the finger.

Stelae – Carved stone monuments, singular *stela*.

Smith and Wesson (S&W) – Firearm manufacturer in the United States / www.smith-wesson.com.

Air-shuttle – A specially designed vehicle which travels on rails and through a large transparent tunnel / tube. An air-shuttle is the fastest way out of the USSB and into Sanctuary Proper (and vice versa). Propulsion is in the form of gravitational pull, staged rocket burns and strategically placed air-jets (assisted by a low-resistance cushion of air).

Computer phone – Advanced mobile phone with the processing power to run advanced software packages. Acts as a personal computer as well as a smart phone. Computer phones are able to connect to wallscreens and monitors via induction ports.

United States Credits (USC) – Currency used in United States subterranean bases. One USC is equivalent to one U.S. dollar.

Stun gun – High-voltage electrical device used to temporarily incapacitate an attacker by restricting muscle control. Close quarters weapon which requires its two prongs to be placed directly on an assailant's body to function.

Taser – Short and medium range weapon that uses an electroshock to impede muscle control. Fires two probes into an assailant and can also be used as a stun gun (see above) / www.taser.com.

The Centipede – Remote operated all-terrain supply vehicle. Multiple wheels, low ground clearance and an articulated chassis enable the machine to scale near vertical climbs and all manner of obstacles.

A.I. 152, console – Highly advanced artificial intelligence programme installed onto a user-friendly console.

Quantum processor – Super powerful computer processor based on a qubits (quantum bits) rather than bits. These processors can carry out a far greater number of computations than computer architecture utilised in the first two decades of the twenty-first century.

UAV – Unmanned aerial vehicle, also known as a drone.

RV – Acronym used by the military for a rendezvous point.

Dodge – American car manufacturer / www.dodge.com.

Dodge Ram – now Ram Trucks separated from Dodge in 2011.

Ram Trucks – American pick-up brand, previously Dodge Ram until 2011 (see above). Part of the Chrysler Group LLC / www.ramtrucks.com.

Chrysler Group LLC – American international car manufacturer / www.chrysler.com.

AEV – American Expedition Vehicles, 4WD specialist / www.aev-conversions.com.

Wallscreen – Large, interactive monitor attached to a wall, usually taking up the entire surface.

Eurostar – European railway service serving London, Paris and Brussels, connecting England to France via the Channel Tunnel / www.eurostar.com.

Channel Tunnel – Manmade structure beneath the English Channel, located between the southern coast of England and the northern coast of France.

HUD – Head-up display, or heads-up display. Data projection onto a transparent screen / visor / window allowing a user to continue looking in the desired direction while being kept apprised of real-time information.

Deep Space Detection Array (D.S.D.A.) – NASA and U.S. military satellite in high Earth orbit. Categorised as an unacknowledged

Special Access Programme / black project. Capabilities: satellite disruption technology and deep space surveillance imager.

OLED – Organic light-emitting diode. Utilised in monitors, televisions and other visual displays.

Monotube – Public metro transportation system in USSB Sanctuary. Utilising a high-speed mono-rail configuration, the train navigates the subterranean base via a network of transport channels and tunnels.

MX4 assault rifle – Advanced projectile weapon used by the U.S. military and Darklight security firm.

Beam rifle – Sophisticated non-projectile weapon capable of unleashing high-powered energy in the form of a beam.

T.I.I. – Thermal Image Intensifier.

Vacuum Lift – Super fast mechanism used to transport people up or down within a structure / facility.

Deep Reach helmet – High-tech headwear worn by S.E.D. Deep Reach personnel.

Multifunction card (M.F. card) – Given to permanent USSB residents, the MF card acts as a door key, sector pass, credit / debit card, data storage device and identity badge.

Mayan map – Dated at over a thousand years old, the dense metallic tablet was unearthed by Sarah Morgan in 2040 at the Ruins of Copán in Honduras. Consisting of Mayan hieroglyphs around a single line, the simple inscriptions portray a map linking together the ancient Mayan cities.

Anakim parchments – Collected by Sarah, Trish and Jason from a number of sources, these ancient scrolls are made from an unknown material which fails to degrade over time. They also have the capability to store large amounts of data and act like a digital display when activated using Sarah's pentagonal pendant.

Anakim orbs – Ancient relics unearthed in Sanctuary Proper by an S.E.D. archaeology team.

Anakim pendants – two metallic pentagonal pendants found by Sarah Morgan during previous archaeological digs. The larger of the two enables the wearer to activate Anakim technology, although its use is limited by the operator's physical size.

Pentagon – Five-sided polygon.

Anakim monolith / prism – Massive fifty foot high artefact removed from a 900,000 year old building. Unearthed and recovered by SFSD soldiers under the command of General Stevens. The monolith contains a single chamber full of a viscous liquid which is protected by a transparent material.

Anakim shield – Another ancient relic unearthed in Sanctuary Proper by S.E.D. personnel. Found in the same hoard as the orb (see above) and stored in the military vaults beneath the Museum of Sanctuary.

TERMINOLOGY / MAP

USSB – United States Subterranean Base
GMRC – Global Meteor Response Council
Darklight – World's largest private security contractor
SFSD – Special Forces Subterranean Detachment (*Terra Force*)
SED – Sanctuary Exploration Division

Ancient Origins: Dark Descent is dedicated with love to my parents Maureen and Terry, whose continued support proves to be as invaluable as it is inspirational.

ACKNOWLEDGMENTS

As ever, a big thank you to my parents for reading and editing my work, with their help the whole process is a joy instead of a chore. Also my sincere gratitude goes out to my copy editor, Julie Lewthwaite, who helps make everything shine.

Robert Storey, 2016

Addendum:

Fuse Books partnered with Terry and Maureen Storey, following the tragic death of their son Robert. It is our privilege to bring his wonderful books to new readers.

As Rob himself noted above, and we can confirm from our time working together, these books would not have made it to publication without the support of Terry and Maureen.

Devoted parents who could not have done more for their son.

James Blatch & Mark Dawson
February 2020

First published in Great Britain in 2014

This edition 2020

All the characters in this book are fictitious, and any resemblance to actual persons, living or dead, is purely coincidental.

Fuse Books
fusebooks.com

Printed in Great Britain
by Amazon

59337986R00411